Everyone's Just So So Special

Robert Shearman

Praise for *Tiny Deaths*

Winner of the World Fantasy Award

Space age Beckett... Robert Shearman is probably best known for having reintroduced the Daleks into the new television series of *Doctor Who*. In *Tiny Deaths*, he shows the same perverse ingenuity that gave us killer robots crying out for love. Blackly humorous and absurd, his stories examine death from a variety of off-kilter perspectives, upending cliché, jumbling together good and evil, encouraging us to side with the villain and the underdog. Shearman shows up reality as a slippery business, liable to come unstuck through the unstitching of our most hackneyed rigmaroles and rituals.
Times Literary Supplement:

Disturbing and caustic, the stories in this entertaining first collection robustly tackle their unusual subject matter – from the authorities who decide that mere knowledge of mortality is insufficient and therefore notify each citizen of the exact cause and time of their demise, to the child victim of a hit-and-run accident who is reincarnated as her parents' ashtray.
The Guardian

Far from morbid, each bizarrely comic tale has a peculiar interior logic and, although the humour is invariably gothic, it's also clever and oddly passionate... Wistful, dream-like... strangly beautiful... Shearman applies an oddball comic whimsy that doesn't deny the darkness of his stories, but transmutes into something that, through its oddity, becomes comprehensible.
The Metro

This is an excellent and highly imaginative first collection of stories by a writer who is not afraid to approach the big subject, mortality, but who does so from interestingly oblique angles and with a light, kittenish gait. Rather profound, ingeniously plotted.
The Independent

Robert Shearman is a gentle writer. That is to say, his style is quite tender, and his touch on the page is light. So light, actually, that it takes you a while to realise that what he's writing about is actually a bit scary and possibly downright awful. By then it's too late – you're hooked and you just can't stop. These stories display their brilliance in ways both sly and shy, as if lifting their skirts to show off their knickers and then acting as though nothing happened.
Australian Specfic In Focus

Praise for *Love Songs for the Shy and Cynical*

Winner of the Shirley Jackson Award,
the Edge Hill Reader's Prize, and the British Fantasy Award

It's all here: every guilty rationalisation, every twinge of doubt, fear or selfishness; the horror of loneliness, the penury and confinement of unwanted or undeserved affection ... laid out like a litany of your personal failings ... then peppered with those bright shining moments when your heart worked like they do in the movies and made you bigger than yourself, bigger than the world, alive, in love. Shearman sure knows love when he feels it, he can make you feel it too, in all its jagged and slippery glory.
Strange Horizons

Shearman has an uncanny knack of springing surprises from the most mundane of situations. His stories ... probe beneath the veneer of normality with startling and often surreal results ... Shearman's stories are hard to categorise, a unique fusion of the literary and the fantastic, perhaps not surprising from a writer whose credits include Doctor Who scripts and mainstream theatre.
The Guardian

Shearman is indeed a unique voice, though one can find certain echoes of Dahl, Ionesco, Barthelme ... as well as a quick satirical wit and a talent for nailing the smarmy insincerities of cruise directors and time-share salesmen ... Shearman is willing to try anything to get the sheer oddness of his tale across, and his mordant views of love, loss, and terror, may lead in still more unexpected, and very rewarding, directions.
Locus

Throughout the book he will have you remembering moments in your life; times of great happiness but most of all the toe-curling, embarrassing moments that result in the pursuit of "love". I cannot recommend Robert Shearman's *Love Songs for the Shy and Cynical* highly enough. Read it and see your life flash before your eyes.
Fantasy Book Review

The unreal and grotesque drop like ink into the clear waters of everyday living, somehow illuminating rather than polluting the mundane. Shearman understands that nagging loose ends are the strong suit of short stories and his tales are big on black comedy and malignant afterglow. The writing's acute and the imagination is rigorous - he's not so much a Stephen King as a Will Self.
The Word

Shearman runs with his ideas to places that are often wonderful, or sometimes awful but impeccably written. There are scenes of hideous embarrassment that would make The Office proud, dazzling conclusions that turn on the last line or word, and a few bits which you read again to check he actually dared to write that.
SFX

Shearman has a uniquely engaging narrative voice and he steers clear of genre cliché, injecting elements of horror and the surreal into a recognisably real world. As impressive as his quirky imagination is his emotional range: most of the stories are darkly humorous, but humour, horror and genuine pathos all make a powerful impact in a very short space.
The Times

First published in June 2011
by Big Finish Productions Ltd, PO Box 1127, Maidenhead, SL6 3LW
www.bigfinish.com

Project Editor: Xanna Eve Chown
Managing Editor: Jason Haigh-Ellery
With thanks to: Matthew Griffiths and William Petty

All of the stories in this book were conceived as part of a greater whole, but a few
of them were let out into the world early for good behaviour.

Coming in to Land appeared in *Riptide Volume 5,* edited by Jane Feaver; *Cold Snap* in *The Lifted Brow* issue 7, edited by Ronnie Scott; *Featherweight* in *Visitants: Stories of Fallen Angels and Heavenly Hosts*, and subsequently in *The Mammoth Book of Best New Horror 22*, both edited by Stephen Jones; *The Runt* in *Voices From the Past*, edited by Lee Harris; *Granny's Grinning* in *The Dead That Walk*, and subsequently in *The Mammoth Book of Best New Horror 21*, both edited by Stephen Jones. *Patches* was first published in *Wild Stacks 1*, edited by Peter Coleborn. *History Becomes You* was nominated for the Sunday Times EPB Private Banking Award, and in consequence was released by the Sunday Times as an ebook.

Limited Editon UK: 978-1-84435-541-9 / Limited Editon US: 1-84435-541-1
Hardback UK: 978-1-84435-570-9 / Hardback US: 1-84435-570-5
Paperback UK: 978-1-84435-571-6 / Paperback US: 1-84435-571-3

A CIP catalogue record for this book is available from the British Library

Cover art 'Girl On Chair' by Rachel Goodyear, 2008. Courtesy of The Robert Devereux Collection.

Cover design by Anthony Lamb

Printed and bound in Great Britain by Biddles Ltd, King's Lynn, Norfolk
www.biddles.co.uk

About the Author

Robert Shearman has worked as writer for television, radio and the stage. He was appointed resident dramatist at the Northcott Theatre in Exeter and has received several international awards for his theatrical work, including the Sunday Times Playwriting Award, the World Drama Trust Award and the Guinness Award for Ingenuity in association with the Royal National Theatre. His plays have been regularly produced by Alan Ayckbourn, and on BBC Radio by Martin Jarvis. A selection of his plays have been collected in book form as *Caustic Comedies*.

However, he is probably best known as a writer for *Doctor Who*, reintroducing the Daleks for its BAFTA winning first series in an episode nominated for a Hugo Award. He has also written many popular audio dramas for the series for Big Finish.

His first collection of short stories, *Tiny Deaths*, was published by Comma Press in 2007. It won the World Fantasy Award for best collection, was shortlisted for the Edge Hill Short Story Prize and nominated for the Frank O'Connor International Short Story Prize. *No Looking Back* was selected by the National Library Board of Singapore as part of the annual Read! Singapore campaign. The two series of *The Chain Gang*, his short story and drama project for BBC7, both won the Sony Award.

His second collection, *Love Songs for the Shy and Cynical*, was published by Big Finish in 2009. It won the British Fantasy Award for best collection, the Edge Hill Short Story Readers Prize and the Shirley Jackson Award, celebrating 'outstanding achievement in the literature of psychological suspense, horror, and the dark fantastic'. *History Becomes You*, from this third collection, was nominated for the Sunday Times EFG Private Bank Award.

www.robertshearman.net

Love Songs for the Shy and Cynical and *Caustic Comedies* are available from www.bigfinish.com

Acknowledgments

This is a big book, and it's full of strange facts I had to research, and strange fictive weirdnesses I had to negotiate. As a result, there's a huge number of people I have to thank, who've supplied me with historical titbits and hysterical enthusiasm.

Justin Ackroyd, Guy Adams, Nina Allan, Jon & Carolyn Arnold, Lois Ava-Matthew, Rosalind Ayres, Ginny Baily, Elizabeth Baines, Emily Barker, Christie Baugher, Mel Beattie, Deb Biancotti, David Bishop, Lyn Boundy, Erykah Brackenbury, Nicholas Briggs, Owen Bywater, Debbie Challis, Xanna Eve Chown, Michael Cisco, Cathy Collings, Jarrod Cooper, Paul Cornell, Sue Cowley, Ailsa Cox, Alison Croggon, Jack Dann, Ellen Datlow, Emma Jane Davies, Karen Davison, Ian Drury, Kate Eltham, Sue Everett, Jane Feaver, Penny Feeny, Jo Fletcher, Amanda Foubister, Nev Fountain, Leah Friedman, Mark Gatiss, Vanessa Gebbie, Vikki Godwin, Laura Goodin, Felicity Gray, Simon Guerrier, Toby Hadoke, Jason Haigh-Ellery, Steven Hall, Jen Hamilton-Emery, Lee Harris, Lisa L Hannett, Talie Helene, Tania Hershman, Robert Hoge, Stevie Hopwood, Martin Jarvis, Stephen Jones, Sandra Kasturi, Sam and Stuart Kelly, Sue Knox, Alisa Krasnostein, Kim and Del Lakin-Smith, John Langan, Tim Lebbon, Tanya Lemke, Alison Macleod, Adam Marek, Helen Marshall, Zoe McAden, Kirstyn McDermott, Dan McGrath, Gary McMahon, Farah Mendlesohn, Sam Moffat, Steven Moffat, Ian Mond, Louise Morgan, Mark Morris, Simon Murgatroyd, Andy Murray, Heather Murray, Liz Myles, Jonathan Oliver, Tara O'Shea, Ra Page, Elizabeth Peloso, Jane Pemble, Sarah Pinborough, Wena Poon, Lynnette Porter, Charles Prepolec, David Richardson, Jody Richardson, Rebecca Riley, Barbara and Chris Roden, Catherine Rogers, Kim Rose, Brett Alexander Savory, Rhonda Scarborough, Jane Scott, Ronnie Scott, Will Shindler, Mandy Slater, Angela Slatter, Jenne Smith, Cat Sparks, Gill Spaul, Paul Spragg, Katharine Straker, Daren Thomas, Lynne Marie Thomas, Lee Thompson, Lucy Toman, Paul Tremblay, Gabrielle Trio, Alice Troughton, Lisa Tuttle, Simon Kurt Unsworth, Catherynne M Valente, Beryl Vertue, Sue Vertue, Stephen Volk, Peter and Jo Ware, Ian Whates, Sean Williams, Paul Wilson, David Wise, Philip Wolff, Rio Youers.

Told you it was a lot.

To Dad and my sister Vicky. To Suzanne Milligan, for tireless patience and support beyond the powers of any ordinary agent. And especially to my wife Janie – I was in a fearsome grump for the majority of this book, I seem to remember, and you stayed married to me regardless. (The next one I write will be that novel you're after. Promise.)

In memory of Joyce Shearman
1935-2011

CONTENTS

1 AD – The BC years end, the AD years begin. History only starts properly when time starts moving forward at last. **8** – The Roman Emperor Augustus Caesar exiles the poet Ovid. The emperor is either offended by his erotica, or annoyed that some poet's been caught shagging his nymphomaniac granddaughter. *Picture it. For thousands of years time has been running backwards. It's as if all the years have been grains of sand falling through an hourglass – and then finally, when the last grain has gone, someone has flipped the hourglass over so the sand can start flowing in the other direction. The people of the world have been racing through all the Before Christs, and at last they've all run out, and the world has hit the Anno Dominis, big and shiny and new – at last mankind can be moving in the right direction. 'We're so nearly there,' the people must have said. 'Give it another 2,000 years, and we'll be modern.'* **9** – The battle of the Teutoburg Forest. The three legions under the command of Varus are ambushed by German tribes. Over the course of three days, under savage guerrilla attacks, some 20,000 Roman soldiers are massacred. Varus himself commits suicide with his own sword. Emperor Augustus' response to the news is to butt his head against the walls of the palace, shouting over and over again, 'Quintilius Varus, give me back my legions!' He never gets the legions back, of course. He does, however, get back Varus – or, at least, his severed head, which is sent to him by the Germans. History doesn't report specifically what he does to the head, but he probably buries it. *Scientists now estimate the creation of the universe as having taken place thirteen point seven billion years ago – or, roughly, in the year 13,700,000,000,000 BC. But that just makes it all the more magical, don't you think? That there were that many BCs to get through? That there was all that time, an incalculable amount of time, before history could hit that pivotal moment when the ADs started. When Christ was born, and the whole universe changed.* **10** – In China, Emperor Wang Mang introduces the world's first income tax. At the same time he also decides to issue twenty-eight types of coin – made not only of gold, silver and copper, but also tortoise and sea shells. There are suddenly so many different coins in circulation that the people can't tell what's currency and what's not, and the economy grinds to a halt. **16** – The death of Varus at Teutoburg Forest is avenged. Brought back to Rome is the pregnant wife of the German leader. She is displayed with her newborn baby boy as prized trophies in a parade. The son is trained as a gladiator, and is killed in performance before adulthood. **23** – Wang Mang is killed in revolt, his imperial palace is ransacked, and his 1,000 courtiers are slaughtered. This isn't directly because of his clever clever income tax ideas, but let's face it, that'd be just cause. *Doesn't it make you stop and think? Because I know, of course, I'm being silly. There was no significant moment when BC turned into AD, no-one suddenly felt a jolt as time began to be calculated in a forward rather than backward motion. Cleopatra didn't know when she was bitten by that asp that she was just thirty-one years shy of dying on a more modern calendar. But isn't that true for all of us? For us all, doesn't time run backwards? There is only one constant, and that is that we're going to die. We aren't going to die at the same time (most likely), but our days are still like those grains falling through the hourglass – we just don't know how many grains we have left.* **31** – The fall of Sejanus, prefect to Emperor Tiberius. His lover Livilla, sister to the future Emperor Claudius, is killed by her own mother, locked in a room and starved to death. **33** – The execution of Jesus Christ, nailed to a cross at Golgotha. What happens afterwards is a matter of some heated debate, and directly influences a tremendous amount of the events we'll be recording over the next 2,000 years. **37** – The death of the Roman Emperor Tiberius. Accounts say that as his successor, Caligula, speaks admiringly of his memory, Tiberius' eyes open and he asks for food. So Caligula smothers him. **37** – And Caligula becomes emperor. 'Caligula' is a nickname that refers to the little soldiers' boots he wore while accompanying his father on campaigns as a child, and a nickname he so hates that he forbids anyone to use it on pain of death. But it's as Caligula, nonetheless, that we remember him – that, and the fact he'll make his horse a consul, declare war on the sea, and sleep with his own sisters. As a living god you can control everything – but not the mocking nickname by which you're referred to for millennia after your death. Tough. **41** – The last words of Caligula, as he's stabbed to death by the Imperial Guard: 'I am still alive!' No, you're not. *What if we did? What if I could know, for sure, as I'm typing this, that it's not just 2011 AD, it's also MY year 38BD (thirty-eight Before Death). 38 BD for me (if I'm lucky), but maybe 47 BD for you (luckier than me), 8 BD for the elderly neighbour, 1 BD for that poor sod over there with the undiagnosed tumour (he doesn't know it yet, but he's only got months.) What if we all got calendars that counted us down precisely through the rest of the little history that we have left? Would it really make us do things all that differently?* **43** – Caligula's successor, Claudius, passes a law that legalises flatulence. *And it's worth noting, of course, that the people who hit 1 AD never realised it. Indeed, it wasn't until the year 525 that the whole BC/AD distinction was determined in the first place. That's over half a millennium of people walking about with not the slightest notion that they would later be recalculated and catalogued. It's a total rewrite of history as far as they would be concerned.* **61** – Boudicca, queen of the Iceni in East Anglia, leads a bloody rebellion against the Romans. She is utterly defeated. And becomes in the nineteenth century a national heroine. The Victorians rename her Boadicea – which sounds more romantic somehow, and so much more feminine. They erect a statue of her at the foot of Westminster Bridge. She becomes a legend. The question is – why? Boudicca is one of history's great failures. In the final battle 400 Romans fell, compared to 80,000 Britons. Not even the wiliest of spin doctors should be able to put a good gloss on that. Could it be, that of all the British leaders who fell before Roman might, she alone was a woman? Was there something in that which particularly struck a chord with the Victorians, whose own queen commanded an empire larger than one the Romans ever had? Against all the odds, Boudicca has been remembered by history and lionised – and trivialised in the process. **64** – A great fire rages through Rome. It lasts for nearly a week, kills countless people, and destroys nearly two thirds of the city. Many contemporary historians blame Emperor Nero himself for starting it, wanting to make room for an entire new city he can build to his design. Whoever is responsible, it probably isn't the Christians, who are made the scapegoats for the whole affair. They are thrown to the dogs, they are crucified in hordes – and, with cruel irony, they are set on fire and hung up to light the streets at night. *But what's most telling about it is that the dating is determined from the birth of Christ. As if Christ's very appearance had suddenly changed the order of history itself. But for a few hundred years Christianity was a rather shadowy cult that invited persecution; to rename one year, say, as 69 AD, and therefore as sixty-nine years since the birth of a man of little significance to virtually anyone who was living in 69 AD, is to misrepresent entirely what that year could have been like.* **69** – Nero has killed himself. The new Roman Emperor is Galba. His friend Otho revolts against him, and has him decapitated. The new emperor is Otho. Vitellius revolts against him, and forces his suicide. The new emperor is Vitellius. Vespasian revolts against him, captures him, pelts him with dung, chops off his head, and drags him into the Tiber with a fish hook. The new emperor is Vespasian. **69** – And here's the flipside to Boudicca, here's Cartimandua, queen of the Brigantes, whose territory covers most of Yorkshire. She is the traitor queen, the one who refuses to support Boudicca, the one who betrays rebel king Caractacus to the Romans. The Romans can't save her from obscurity. History can't remember her infamy. *And it was a mistake anyway. The man who coined the BC/AD distinction was a monk called Dionysius Exiguus. But he got the date wrong. Historians now date the birth of Jesus Christ no later than 4 BC – or, if you prefer, four years before he himself came into being. So right from the start, the dating of all history is an error.* **70** – Vespasian clearly feels secure enough in his still warm imperial throne to place a tax on public lavatories. His son is horrified by such a vulgar measure, but Vespasian holds a handful of coins under his heir's nose, declaring, 'Money does not smell.' **73** – At the fortress of Masada, under siege by the Romans, 1,000 Jews commit mass suicide rather than fall into the hands of the enemy. **79** – Vespasian declares that an emperor should die on his feet. As he totters about, he tells the world, 'I think I'm becoming a god,' and expires during an attack of diarrhoea. *Dionysus actually realised his mistake. He was appalled. He tried to correct it. He explained he'd got his calculations wrong, that in fact we should all be at least four years further on than we thought. But everyone ignored him. There was only so much mathematics the average sixth century man could take. And Dionysus died ultimately a failure. That's where I come in. I collect historical failures.* **79** – Pompeii is destroyed by volcano. The people engulfed in the lava have their lives preserved in every detail – in a way, they survive the great anonymous rush of history, whereas those who escaped the disaster are lost to us. Was it worth it? **84** – Calgacus, the last independent chieftain of the British tribes, is at last defeated at the battle of Mons Graupius in Aberdeenshire. It is recorded that 30,000 Celts die, and that, in an echo of Masada, Celtic warriors set fire to their own homes and slay their own families to prevent them falling into Roman hands. *And people say to me sometimes, at parties, whenever I might go to parties, they ask, what is it that I do? And they mean for a job, but I don't tell them what I do for a job, why should a job define me? I tell them what I care about. I tell them I chronicle history. I chronicle the history of mediocrity, and futility, and human error. They usually don't have much to say to that.* **96** – The despotic Roman Emperor Domitian is alarmed to hear that the famed astrologer Ascletario has predicted his imminent murder. Domitian asks Ascletario whether he can predict his own death; the astrologer tells him it will be very soon, and that his body will be ripped apart by dogs. Domitian promptly has him killed, and gives the order that his corpse be set on fire immediately to give lie to the prophecy. Suddenly a powerful wind arises, and puts out the pyre – just as, wouldn't you know it, a pack of dogs rush on to the scene, take hold of the somewhat charred astrologer and tear him to shreds. Domitian is now convinced that the prediction is right, that he will be murdered. He is. Seven stabs in the stomach do the trick. **100** – The Gospel of John is being written about this date. At the same time, in India, the compilation of the 'Kama Sutra' begins. Is it fair to speculate on which of the authors were facing the stiffest deadlines? *Sometimes they'll say, those people at the parties, that they don't like history. That they never did that well at history at school. That they found it confusing. And I try to explain. There's nothing confusing about it. The history of the world, all of it, its wars, its empires, each and every one of its decline-and-falls, is really terribly simple. It's the story of a bunch of mediocrities who are trying to look special. And it's my duty, it's my pleasure, to expose the lot of them.*

COMING IN TO LAND

Ladies and gentlemen –

We hope that you have taken pleasure in this Air Intercontinental Flight from Los Angeles to Paris, France. That you have enjoyed the in-flight entertainment system, that you have enjoyed our specially prepared meals and snacks. We hope that you've taken the chance to sit back, and relax – and maybe sleep as we've crossed all those time zones.

We now need to inform you that we will soon be beginning our descent into Paris. And we ask you to pay attention to the following information and act upon it accordingly.

We are currently cruising at an altitude of 30,000 feet at an air speed of 400 miles per hour. The time at our destination is 13.25, so do remember to change your watches if you haven't already done so. The weather looks good and with the tailwind on our side we are expecting to land in Paris approximately fifteen minutes ahead of schedule. The weather in Paris is sunny but cloudy, with a high of seventeen degrees in the afternoon, you may need to wrap up warm, there's a chill to the evening. If the weather co-operates we might get a great view of the city as we descend.

We hope that may be possible. The captain says he'll do his best. That would make it easier for everybody. It all depends upon the clouds. We're fighting these damned clouds.

We will soon be locking all toilets prior to our arrival in Paris, so this would be a good time to use the facilities if you have not yet had the occasion to do so. Go now. It's all right. We'll wait.

I'm sorry, that's all the time we have. I'm sorry. If you could all return to your seats. Yes. I'm sorry, madam. I'm sorry. Please return to your seats, and prepare for landing.

We ask that at this time you secure all baggage underneath your seat or in the overhead compartments. Please take care in storing baggage, and know that the contents of the compartments may have shifted during the flight. Please turn off all personal electronic devices, including laptops and cell phones. Smoking, of course, continues to be prohibited for the remainder of the flight, and will not be permitted until after you have cleared customs and left the terminal building. You are welcome to keep drinking alcohol. If you are the sort to find it calming, if you find it an aid rather than a hindrance to concentration.

Please make sure your seat backs and tray tables are in their full upright position. You may fasten your seatbelts or not. It's all the same to us. If you choose to fasten your seatbelt, insert the metal tab into the buckle by your side and pull on the strap until it is comfortable and secure. But many find that the seatbelts don't do any good. For some they are, if anything, a barrier. For some the seatbelts suggest their faith might be lacking.

And, ladies and gentlemen, be advised. It is all a matter of faith.

Air Intercontinental is proud of its safety measures, and our fleet has a survival rating that is one of the highest in the world. Last year an average of eighty-three percent of all our passengers arrived securely and intact, at any one of our destinations all around the globe. Eighty-three percent. That's not something to be sneezed at. But we know too that faith is a personal thing. And that even with all the support and encouragement from our specially trained staff, not all our passengers are able to sustain that last effort of mental strength necessary to ensure their safe arrival. On every flight there will be those that fail. On any flight, those that will vanish from their seats. That'll disappear completely, and fade into thin air, the moment that the wheels hit the runway.

There are certain precautions that should be taken to give you the best chance this will not happen to you.

We are arriving soon in Paris, the capital city of France. You will not land safely unless you absolutely *believe* in Paris. You are required to have faith in the city, in its culture, and in what it represents. In the very concept of Paris, on a philosophical level. If you have no faith that it's really there, then it won't be.

Playing upon your screens now are certain classic images of Paris to help you in your effort. The Eiffel Tower. The Mona Lisa. An old man on a bicycle waving a baguette. It is important that these be used as a focus for your concentration, and not as a replacement for actual faith itself. You need to believe in Paris, not merely the images put before you. The man on the bicycle will not be there to save you.

Some of you will be returning home to Paris. For you the ideal of Paris should be easier to hold. But be warned. Simply knowing something exists is not quite the same as having *faith* in it. We know tales of French couples, perhaps disillusioned with their lives, disillusioned with each other, who have lived in Montmartre for years, perhaps, who have more *evidence* than most of Paris' existence – and who, nonetheless, didn't make it through touchdown with all their body parts in place. Maybe they got complacent. Maybe, at the crucial moment, they took their minds off Paris altogether. But even if you've lived in the destination city of your flight and feel you've no doubts at all, we ask you still to pay attention and focus. Focus upon what your home *means* to you, right deep down in your soul.

Do not fall asleep or doze during the landing. Heaven knows where you might end up.

For those of you who have never even visited Paris before, your task is necessarily harder. But do not be unduly alarmed. Concentrate on what Paris means to you, too, and why you booked the ticket there to begin with. Why you paid so much money. What it was that drove you to so risk your very existence, and give such anxiety to the loved ones you've left at home, just to visit the place. There must be a strong idea of what Paris is in your heads in order for you to have done that. It doesn't matter how idealised or inaccurate, not if you truly *believe* in it. Faith isn't a spelling test. Just hold on to that inner Frenchiness you have, hold on to it tight, and you'll be just fine.

For those of you who have visited Paris, but have never lived or worked there, you may be in the greatest danger. You may only half-remember a city you once visited when you were small. You may be hanging on to happy holiday memories from when you were a kid – that time when your mummy and daddy smiled at you, when they took you to that park, when they let you feed all those pigeons and eat that ice cream – are you really *sure* that was Paris after all? That you're not getting your holidays mixed up? Think. As you ate your choc ice, can you remember whether it was really the Eiffel Tower that was looming above you? Wasn't it just a common or garden electricity pylon? Be sure.

It is estimated that false nostalgia is responsible for most of the deaths and vanishings on transatlantic travel. False nostalgia kills.

For me, when I need to have faith in Paris, I always think of my time there with Jacques. Jacques and I walked along the Seine hand in hand. We drank Beaujolais and we smoked Gitanes, and he was the perfect lover, we made love right there underneath the night sky of Paris. With the sound of Paris in my ears and the smell of Paris up my nose, and yes, all those people watching, and some of them were tourists, but most of the peeping toms were Parisians through and through. And as he drove deep inside me, 'Mon Dieu!' he cried, and I squealed loud and shrill, I squealed loud so the noise would bounce off Notre Dame, ring right round the Arc de Triomphe, all Paris could hear our rutting, and Paris delighted in it, because that's what Paris is, Paris doesn't care, Paris is a whore, I squealed like a little pig, *une cochonette*, that's what Jacques called me, I didn't know what it meant at the time, afterwards I had to look it up, frankly I was a little disappointed, 'Mon Dieu,' cried Jacques, 'cochonette, merci beaucoup!' So, as the plane descends, as we near the ground, I think of Jacques, it's the thought of Jacques I hold on to, and I think of how afterwards he held on to *me*, so tightly, and how his French peasant sweat tasted.

Some of you may prefer to think of the Louvre, or of croissants.

Please do your best to keep your children calm during the landing procedure. You will have seen how we distributed amongst our younger passengers at the beginning of the flight little picture books of Paris, along with simple but convincing explanations of the city's importance in commerce and the arts. Encourage them now to review this literature, and make sure for their own safety that they have not graffitied flying dragons or similar non-Parisian monsters over the illustrations. We invite you too, if you feel any doubts or weakness, to study the safety card in the seat pockets in front of you. The French translation of what to do in the event of a crash can be very reassuring.

Should the cabin experience sudden pressure loss, stay calm and listen for instructions from the cabin crew. Oxygen masks will drop down from above your seat. Place the mask over your mouth and nose. Pull the strap to tighten it. Then breathe normally. If you are travelling with children, make sure that your mask is on first before trying to help them with theirs.

Should this happen, of course, it might distract your concentration. Alongside the oxygen mask will drop a headset. Place the headset over your ears. Wiggle the toggle to adjust volume. The headset will be playing a medley of typical French music, from *La Marseillaise* to Sasha Distel. If you are travelling with children, make sure that your headset is playing first before trying to help them with theirs.

If you are travelling with children, there is no point trying to hold on to them. It doesn't work. It doesn't work. Believe me. I'm sorry. Believe me.

We are now beginning our final descent. We hope that you have taken pleasure in this Air Intercontinental Flight. The cabin crew have certainly taken pleasure in serving you, and we hope to see you again on another flight very soon.

I didn't mind that Jacques lied to me about being married. He kept the ring on, after all, and every time he waved to the barman for another drink he flashed it in front of my face brazenly enough. Every time he reached out to stroke my cheek. No, I just wish he hadn't given me a false address. What did he think I was going to do, stalk him? I'm a girl from Louisiana. I knew what this fling was, just a fling, right? But when I tried to visit his home, my next stopover in Paris, I found that the street he'd given me didn't even exist. That's what hurt. I never pretended it was love, not even as we were having sex, but it wasn't just *sex*, was it, there was something more to it, wasn't there? I thought so. I believed so. Yes, that's what hurt.

I wonder if his name was Jacques at all.

Landing positions.

Good luck, everyone. See you on the other side.

Oh, Jacques.

Air Intercontinental thanks you for flying with us. We always remember you have a choice.

Oh, Jacques, hold on tight, baby. Hold on, *mon brave*.

102 – The martyrdom of Pope Clement I. There are many legends surrounding the early popes – unsurprisingly, really, considering that at this stage of history so much is unreliable and uncorded, and that anything which touches on areas of faith is bound to come with a certain amount of spiritual baggage. Clement is at first banished to the Crimea, and made to work in the arid marble quarries there – but the teachings of Clement are so pure that wherever he goes springs of sweet water bubble to the surface of the ground and make the desert fertile. This makes the Romans very angry – and though presumably they have the option of making use of his curious hydrating skills, they decide to kill him instead. They take him in a boat some two miles from the shore, hang a heavy anchor around his neck and fling him overboard. This really ought to be the end of Clement. But each year, on the anniversary of his death, the seas recede so that pilgrims can walk to the exact spot where he was executed. So much for legends. But seven hundred years later, two missionaries go out on a quest for Clement's drowned body. They not only find it, they also find the anchor that was tied about him, and they bring them both back to Rome for honoured burial. One of these missionaries is called Cyril. And the alphabet he invents to write of his exploits, and with which he translates the Bible, is thereafter known as Cyrillic. From Pope Clement's death then we derive the Russian language, Dostoevsky and Tolstoy, and the menu in the window of the Kentucky Fried Chicken on Nevsky Prospekt. **105** – According to tradition, the Chinese court official T'sai Lun comes up with the invention of paper. Chinese writing however dates back as far as 6600 BC, which means that all T'sai Lun really achieves is to curb nearly 7,000 years of graffiti. **106** – Shangdi reigns in China. He comes to the imperial throne at only three months old, and is dead within the year. He is succeeded by Andi who, at twelve years old, is positively bursting with maturity by comparison. Both are members of the Han Dynasty – and, indeed, all the Han emperors from this point on are children. Emperor Hedi has enlisted the aid of eunuchs to rid himself of an opposing clan – and this makes the eunuchs increasingly more powerful in Chinese court politics. The eunuchs welcome the idea of putting on the throne children they can easily dominate. That they cannot have children themselves, of course, only makes this the more ironic. **106** – The earliest recorded use of the term 'Catholic Church'. **108** – The ninth legion of the Roman army marches out from Eboracum (York) into Scotland – and are never heard of again. **113** – Roman Emperor Trajan is greeted by Parthian envoys with olive branches as a sign of peace. **114** – Trajan defeats the Parthians. **125** – The death of Pope Sixtus I. Not much is known about Sixtus, not even his name necessarily – as he's the sixth pope since St Peter, it's perfectly possible that 'sixtus' is simply used as a placeholder. This is certainly the case he must be the most obscure pope who ever lived. No interesting tales about anchors or human watering cans for him. Some have tried to rescue him from utter anonymity, though, by suggesting that 'sixtus' is a misspelling of the Greek word 'xystus', which means 'shaved'. In which case there's suddenly a back story for the man, as he lives during the reign of Emperor Hadrian, who had brought the full hairy beard back into Roman fashion. Xystus, or Sixtus, would have been quite the radical, flaunting his bare cheeks in public. Go, Sixtus! **130** – Hadrian visits Thebes – and carves graffiti on one of the legs of the Colossi of Memnon. It's almost as if T'sai Lun hadn't bothered. I've been to visit the Colossi; coach parties come from miles around; those legs are gigantic. And they're cordoned off by ropes. You try to graffiti on them now, you'll be arrested. Tourists back in ancient times had it so much easier. *I've taken my wife on holiday to Egypt four times. I've taken her to Rome, to Athens, to Turkey for the ruins of the Byzantine Empire. All the old broken civilisations beneath our feet. She enjoys it. She asks me sometimes whether we could go on a different sort of holiday, maybe visit Disneyland? But there's no history to Disneyland at all, it only started up in 1955.* **132** – Simon bar-Kokhba lead a Jewish rebellion in Jerusalem. The Jews are offended by the Romans building a shrine to Jupiter on the site of the old temple. Simon establishes an independent Jewish state called Israel. **135** – After a two year war, the Romans conquer the state of Israel. Simon is killed, and Hadrian orders the total destruction of Jerusalem so a new city can be built in its place. The legacy of Simon bar-Kokhba is twofold. His defeat means that the Jews are barred from Israel and are scattered across the empire as refugees. But he's also responsible for the game known as Twenty Questions, or what in Hungary is called the bar-Kokhba game, in which a player has to work out the identity of an object only by asking questions that can be answered with 'yes' or 'no'. This charming bit of party fun is inspired by the way bar-Kokhba can only ask simple questions to a mutilated man who had had his tongue ripped out and his hands cut off to find out who his attackers are. **138** – Hadrian is dying, and wants to put an end to it all. He orders a slave to kill him, but the slave is too frightened to do so. He calls for a dagger, or for poison, and everyone refuses. He calls for his huntsman, and tells him to strike him dead, marking with chalk the exact place on his body he wants to be stabbed; the huntsman runs away in panic. Hadrian rails against the power of an emperor that can have anyone he chooses killed, but who cannot end his own life. **142** – The Chinese alchemist Wei Boyang is the first man to describe an early form of gunpowder solution. That'll come in handy later. **155** – To restore peace between the Jews and the Romans, Emperor Antoninus Pius re-legalises circumcision. **160** – Appian writes the work known in English as 'The Roman History', in which he includes the history of each nation conquered only up until the moment of its conquest. **161** – The Romans have built the Antonine Wall. It is 2.75 metres high, and stretches for 60 kilometres. It's a truly inspiring display of construction. However, only some twenty years after it's been completed, the Romans realise it's impossible to defend, and too expensive to supply with fuel and food. So they abandon it. **165** – The Cynic philosopher Peregrinus Proteus burns himself to death at the Olympic games. He does so to benefit mankind, to show them the way they should disregard death. He at least waits until the final night, though, so it doesn't get in the way of all the fun. In China, a lot of scholars are getting fed up with the eunuchs throwing their (slightly reduced) weight around. Those who stand against them are arrested, killed or banished from the capital. This becomes known as the first of the Disasters of Partisan Prohibitions, and eunuch-centred faction struggles will continue for a generation. **172** – The Roman army is encircled by the German Quadi tribe. The heat is intense. Suddenly a violent thunderstorm sweeps away the Quadi in a torrent of mud, and refreshes the parched legionnaires. We know very little about the Quadi. They have been wiped from the history books, we don't even have any of their pots. And we always get pots, the museums are full of the things. **177** – Marcus Aurelius, the wisest of the Roman Emperors, whose book 'Meditations' is still in print today, begins to kill Christians on a systematic scale. **180** – Commodus succeeds his father Marcus Aurelius, and the period now known as the Era of the Five Good Emperors comes to an abrupt end. From this point on the imperial history will become something confused and squalid, a seemingly never-ending series of tyrants and despots, relieved only by weak generals who'll be murdered by their own armies within months of taking the purple. It's a long slow death, but the glory of Rome ends here. **181** – The volcano at Lake Taupo in New Zealand erupts. It's one of the very largest on Earth in 5,000 years. The effects of it are seen as far away as Rome and China. **185** – Commodus confiscates all private property to finance his gladiatorial shows. Oh, how he loves to be a gladiator. He dresses up as Hercules in a lion's skin, and parades around before the crowds. And the audience never dare not applaud, though there's every evidence he was a rotten gladiator; he selects all his opponents himself, never professional fighters, just random people from the audience, giving them only wooden swords. One day Commodus calls down to the arena all the people who have lost a foot. He ties them up, he gives them sponges rather than stones to defend themselves with. And, pretending to be Hercules killing the giants, he beats them all to death with a staff. For this performance he charges the sum of one million sesterces. **189** – 2,000 eunuchs in the imperial Chinese palace are slaughtered in a violent purge at Luoyang. **190** – Tertullian converts to Christianity, and emphasises how persecution has only helped the growth of the religion. **192** – Commodus is murdered. His wife and chamberlain give him poison, but the sot is so drunk he only vomits it up again. So instead they have him strangled in the bath. **193** – Roman Emperor Pertinax is stabbed to death by his own soldiers. Afterwards the imperial throne is put up for auction, and Didius Julianus offers the army the highest price. Two months later he is executed. An officer is sent to Julianus to carry out the deed, and finds only a terrified man, abandoned by all his friends and supporters, even his own bodyguards. Before he's struck down with a sword, the emperor bursts into tears and shouts, 'What evil have I done? Whom have I killed?' **195** – New emperor Septimius Severus sacks Byzantium and reduces it to a village. **197** – Severus has appointed Albinus to be Caesar in Britain. Now he changes his mind, declares war on him, and forces his suicide. **198** – Zephyrinus becomes pope. He is the first to be acknowledged as one who is corrupt, whose spirituality is suspect. Contemporary historians refer to him as 'ignorant and greedy', 'a receiver of bribes', 'a lover of money'. There will be many, many worse to come. **199** – The Colossi of Memnon, as visited by Emperor Hadrian (qv 130), are famous for the fact that they sing. Ever since an earthquake in 27 BC damaged them, the rising humidity of the morning has caused them to give off a peculiar bell-like tone. Ancient tourists come from all over the world to hear the music, because to be granted a song means that the gods are smiling on you. In 199 Septimius Severus too visits the Colossi. Unlike Hadrian, he doesn't graffiti on them. Instead he tries to repair them. And by doing so, inadvertently silences them forever. Septimius Severus destroys everything he touches, even when he's trying to help. Why can't tourists just leave history well alone? **200** – Japanese Emperor Jingu sends a fleet to invade Korea. So impressive are the ships that the Koreans give in without a fight. *My wife jokes that I spend too much time on this time chart. She says that I must love my history books more than I love her! And I tell her to calm down, relax. It's really not a competition. I can keep both her and the history, I don't have to choose between the two. Sometimes that does the trick. Sometimes it really truly doesn't.*

COLD SNAP

There hadn't been a specific moment when Ben had stopped believing in Santa Claus. One Christmas he'd thought that a fat man in red travelling the world in a sleigh was credible – the next, he hadn't. There'd been no trauma that had disillusioned him. Indeed, it had been a good year, that year; his parents were still smiling back then, every day there were so many smiles. 'Listen,' said his daddy, and sitting him on his knee, and holding him there steady, 'listen, it's okay for you not to go believing in Santa, okay? But just don't go spoiling it for anybody else. Let your friends hang on to Santa as long as they can. Once he's gone, he's gone forever.' Ben hadn't thought of it that way before, that he'd never get that innocence back, and it gave him a little pang, and for one awful moment he thought he might even cry – but it was all right, Daddy wasn't cross with him, Daddy was holding him on his knee, Daddy was holding him safe. 'Is it a deal, old chap?' And Ben liked it when Daddy called him 'old chap', and he assured him, cub's honour, he'd keep his scepticism to himself.

Not that the existence or non-existence of Santa Claus was the sort of topic that was often discussed in the school playground. It was all talk about football and techno battle rangers and whether breathing in close to girls would give you spots. Actually, Ben's belief in Santa Claus had outlived his belief in God. He could more easily conceive of a man who'd spend his time giving presents to strangers while flown about by reindeer than he could a being who'd get stuck up on a cross to save those strangers from their sins. The inconvenience to Santa Claus alone must have been immense, and his generosity overwhelming. But Jesus? There had to be limits.

So, yes, I suppose it's true – seeing Jesus Christ there, in his bedroom that Christmas Eve, his body cast into strange shadow by the dazzling white of the snow falling outside the window, holding in his hand not a sack of toys but, I don't know, a cross maybe, a cross on the road to Calvary – yes, I suppose *that* would have been the greater shock. But seeing Santa Claus there was still quite surprising.

'Hello, Ben,' said Santa Claus. 'Did I wake you?'

'Yes,' said Ben.

'Oh, good,' said Santa.

Ben knew it was Santa right away. He was the perfect synthesis of all the Santas he had ever seen, on Christmas cards, on TV cartoons, on Coca Cola bottles. 'Some children sleep very soundly,' Santa went on. 'You wouldn't believe how hard it can be sometimes, to wake up a child who just doesn't *want* to be woken. It's the hardest part of the job.'

'Really?' asked Ben.

Santa thought about it for a moment. 'No, not really,' he said. 'Flying around the world in one night, that's from the North Pole to the South and back, and zigzagging to all the countries in between, it's not a straight line, you know – now, that's hard. To be honest, waking children hardly compares. To be honest, waking children is comparatively a cinch. But, you know.' He smiled at Ben. 'I'm glad you were easy to wake, just the same.'

'Are you real?' said Ben.

'Yes,' said Santa.

'Okay.'

'Do you want to touch me? You can touch me if you want.'

'Okay.'

'I'll come closer,' said Santa, and shifted his bulk towards the bed so that it wobbled in a very real way, and Ben could see that Santa was real perfectly well now, and he didn't need to touch him, actually, he had proof enough. But, 'Go on, touch that,' said Santa, and Ben thought it'd be rude not to, so as Santa offered him his hand, he brushed one of the fingers, just for a second, 'no, harder than that, if you want to know if I'm *real*,' and Ben grasped it, actually grasped it, the finger as fat as a sausage.

'There we go,' said Santa. 'There, you see.' And this close Ben could see that Santa really was very fat, and very red, and very bearded, and his eyes were twinkling.

'Your finger's very cold,' said Ben.

'The snow's coming down thick out there,' said Santa. 'Cold enough to freeze your blood. Do you have anything to eat?'

Ben thought, tried to remember what his daddy and mum used to leave out for Santa back when he'd believed. 'We've got some mince pies downstairs.'

'I mean, anything warm?'

'I could put one in the microwave.'

Santa considered this. 'Okay,' he said.

So they went down to the kitchen, the little boy in blue pyjamas, the fat man in red following politely behind. 'Try and walk where I walk,' said Ben, 'walk to the edge of the stairs, they creak in the middle.' 'Okay,' said Santa, but he was so fat, and his feet were so big, that try as he might he couldn't avoid the creaks altogether. And Ben winced, thinking that at any moment his daddy might be woken up. In the kitchen Ben turned on the lights, and saw that Santa's beard was not all that white, that was just the snow, Santa's beard looked very grey, and very old. 'I'll get you a mince pie,' said Ben, and opened the cupboard, and took out a box of Mr Kipling's own.

'Something warm,' said Santa. 'Can I have a soup?' And he pointed into the cupboard, and at all the tins of soup. 'I'm not allowed to cook things, not with a flame, not without Daddy,' said Ben. 'It's okay,' said Santa, 'I'll do it, I'm old enough.' And he took from the cupboard the first three tins his hand could claw – pea and ham, and minestrone, and chicken noodle, he all but ripped off the lids with the can opener at such ferocious speed, and poured the contents into one saucepan. He put the saucepan on the gas ring, lit it. Santa stood over the meal as it cooked, and Ben could see that Santa was drooling a little, there was spit running out of Santa's mouth and mixing with the melting snow in his beard, 'I'm so hungry,' said Santa, and winked, almost apologetically – and even though the soup couldn't be warm enough yet, he hadn't let it stand for long enough, 'that'll have to do,' he said, and took a large wooden spoon from the shelf just beside the spice rack, the spice rack Daddy never even bothered to use, Mum had used spices but not Daddy, Daddy's cooking was much simpler – and stuck the spoon into the pan, and scooped up the mix of soups, and ate.

'Would you like to sit down?' asked Ben. He'd even put out a place mat. Santa waved the invitation away, stood over the cooker, and shovelled lukewarm soup into his face. He didn't come up for breath for a good five minutes. 'Thanks,' he said, and smiled at Ben, and wiped bits of noodle and green pea from his beard with the back of his hand, 'yeah, I'll have that mince pie now.' And he took one, and popped it into his mouth whole.

Ben wrinkled his nose. 'If you're Santa – and you are,' he added hastily, he really didn't want to go through all that weird finger touching again, 'then why have I never seen you before?'

'I only visit when it snows. London hasn't had a white Christmas in years.'

'Oh,' said Ben. An intelligent boy, he wondered why, whether this was to do with needing the right reindeer conditions, something like that. Instead he said, 'Do I get a present, then?'

'What?'

'A present. I mean, that's why you're here, right?'

'Right,' said Santa. 'It's waiting for you, right now, under the tree. Shall we go and look?' And Santa grinned soup-spattered teeth, and led Ben into the sitting room, as if it were *his* sitting room, as if this had been *his* house all along. Ben recognised the tree that he and his father had bought and decorated together a couple of weeks ago – but it looked a bit taller now, as if it were standing up straight, as if it were a soldier on parade saluting the arrival of its commanding officer. And the fairy lights were on, and they were *flashing*, and what's more they were flashing different colours, and Ben had been quite sure they hadn't done that before. And underneath the tree, in front of all the other presents, in front of all the *ordinary* presents, was the one from Santa. The wrapping paper couldn't disguise what it was.

'How did you know?' breathed Ben.

'It's what you want, isn't it? It's what you most want.'

'Yes,' said Ben.

'I got your letter,' said Santa, and chuckled. 'And you've been a particularly good boy this year.'

'I didn't write a letter,' said Ben. 'I don't believe in you any more.'

Santa frowned at that. 'I certainly got a letter,' he said, a little huffily. 'I don't come to homes where I'm not invited. What do you think I am?'

'Sorry,' said Ben, and Santa smiled, and opened his arms for a hug. And Ben didn't really want to hug Santa, but he thought he better had, he didn't want Santa to be hurt, and the present *was* just what he wanted, the second thing he most wanted in all the world. Ben couldn't get his arms around Santa, they barely stretched around his midriff, and there was a peculiar smell to Santa's coat, something animal, something Ben thought probably was reindeer.

'Can I open my present now?' said Ben.

'Just a formality to get out of the way first,' said Santa. And suddenly in one of his hands was a piece of old parchment, so long it unrolled down to his knees, and in the other a biro. 'Proof of receipt,' he said, 'sign on the dotted line.' And Ben signed, and then went to the present, and now that he got to it he saw that even the wrapping paper was flashing and changing colour, and he looked at Santa in wonder. Santa laughed. 'Boys like you don't care about fancy paper,' he said, 'it's the present underneath that counts. Rip it open, Ben, rip it apart!' And Ben laughed at that, he couldn't help himself, and he tore into the wrapping paper, and found that there was still more wrapping paper beneath, flashing away. Santa laughed too, 'Deeper than that! Come on, Ben, chop chop!' And Ben tore deeper. 'I love this bit,' said Santa, 'really, this is the best bit, seeing all the kids' faces light up when they get their toys. I always make sure I stay for this.' And Ben touched spokes, and chains, and handlebars, and tyres, and soon enough all the wrapping paper lay upon the carpet, flashing more feebly now, like a dying animal, and then it flashed no more, and then it was dead. And Ben marvelled at his shiny new bicycle.

'It's got eight gears,' said Santa, helpfully. 'It's one of the good ones. Brand new, too, I never deal in second-hand goods. And stabilisers, you know, until you get your balance.'

'Keep away from him,' said Daddy, standing in the doorway.

He was holding a knife, and Ben's first thought was that meant Daddy must have been to the kitchen to fetch it, and he'd have seen all the mess caused by the soup, he hadn't had a chance to clean it up yet – he was in so much trouble.

'Well, now,' said Santa.

'Keep away from him,' said Daddy again.

'I'm nowhere near him,' said Santa, perfectly reasonably. 'He's by the tree.'

'Don't sign the contract, Ben, whatever you do.'

'Put the knife down, Davey,' said Santa.

'No.'

'Davey, come on, put the knife down. You're scaring the boy.' And at that Ben realised that yes, he *was* scared, he hadn't had time to think of it till now. His Daddy didn't look like his daddy, so wild-eyed, shaking. And his name was David, although his friends called him Dave, and his mum used to call him Day – not all the time, just when she was really happy, I love you, big Day, she'd say, and kiss him – but not for a while now, not a long while, most of the time she called him Dave. No-one ever called him Davey.

Daddy licked his lips.

'We both know that you're not going to use the knife,' said Santa.

'You have no idea what I can do,' said Daddy.

'I know precisely what you can do,' said Santa. 'I've got you on my list. Remember? I've *got you on my list.*' Santa walked towards Daddy. 'Keep back,' said Daddy. 'No,' said Santa. 'I'm warning you,' said Daddy, but he was the one backing out of the way. 'Go on then,' said Santa, opening his arms out wide, just as he had to Ben earlier, as if he wanted a hug. 'Go on. Stick me with your knife. It's not a very big knife. And I have so much fat to cut through, so much flesh, centuries of it. Go on, see if you can slice deep enough to hurt me.' 'Keep back,' said Daddy, but Santa wasn't. 'Go on,' said Santa, 'if that's what you want Ben to see. If that's what you want him to remember.' Daddy gave a noise that might have been a sob, and Santa took the knife, and it vanished into a big red pocket. 'You silly boy,' Santa said, 'you silly boy.' Ben thought that Santa must be very cross, and thought that Daddy thought so too, because he flinched when

Santa raised his hand to him – but then Santa smiled, and ruffled Daddy's hair affectionately.

'Don't sign the contract,' said Daddy weakly.

'Don't worry about Ben's contract, just you worry about yours,' said Santa. And at that Daddy went pale.

'No,' he said. 'Please.' And Santa just smiled, not without sympathy. 'Can't you...?' and Daddy licked his lips once more. 'Can't you just go next door? Can't you go somewhere else instead?'

'I could,' said Santa. 'But I came here, didn't I?' And Daddy made a little gulp like a hiccup, and Santa said, 'Now, now, none of that. You'll scare Ben. Don't scare Ben.'

'I've got a bike,' said Ben.

'So I see,' said Daddy.

'It's good, isn't it?'

'It's good,' said Daddy.

'It *is* good, actually,' said Santa. 'Eight gears, stabilisers. Not just any old rubbish.'

'Please,' said Daddy softly.

'No,' said Santa, and that was that. 'You'd better get your clothes on,' he added. 'Both of you.'

'Ben doesn't have to come,' said Daddy.

'You're not going to leave him alone in the house, surely? Not on Christmas Eve. Not when anyone could get in.'

'No,' said Daddy, dully. 'You're right.'

'It'll be an adventure for him.'

Ben liked the sound of that. 'Please, Daddy, can I have an adventure?'

'Of course,' Santa said. 'And you can bring your bike.'

'Can I, Daddy? Can I bring my bike?'

'Leave the bicycle here, Ben,' said Daddy. 'You don't want to take the bike.'

'I do,' said Ben.

'He does,' said Santa.

'It's slippery out there.'

'It's got stabilisers,' said Santa.

'Stabilisers,' said Ben.

'Please, Ben,' said Daddy.

'Let him take it,' said Santa. 'Let him get to ride it with you. Share his bike with his daddy. Give him that pleasure at least.'

Daddy said, 'All right.'

Ben said, 'Hurray!'

Daddy said, 'You'd better go and dress up warm, though. Go and put on your warmest clothes.'

'The very warmest,' Santa said to both of them. 'It's so cold out there, it'll freeze your blood.' And he clapped his hands together. 'No time to waste, come on. Chop chop!'

*

ii

The weather reports said there was going to be a cold snap. No-one was prepared. Industry would be affected, said the news, public transport would be at a standstill. Daddy told Ben that for school the next morning he'd have to wear his very warmest clothes. He'd have to put on his thickest sweater and his thickest gloves, and wear the stripy scarf. Ben didn't like the scarf, it made his neck itch, but Daddy didn't care. 'You're not going down with any bug, not on my watch,' he said. 'Your Mum'll kill me.' Ben laughed at the thought, and said Mum wouldn't kill him. 'Yes, she would,' said Daddy.

Ben made it to school and back again through the cold snap quite intact, the scratchy stripy scarf had beaten off all the germs. Daddy was pleased. 'There you go, old chap. You're okay. You're safe.'

And that evening Ben stood with his daddy by the window, watching from the street lamps how the rain seemed to be slowing down, how it had begun to drift lazily in the wind, as if in no particular hurry to hit the ground.

'It's snowing!' said Ben.

'Yes,' said Daddy.

'I love snow,' said Ben.

'Yes,' said Daddy. 'Still. It won't settle.'

But it did settle. The next morning there was a thin blanket of white over everything. Daddy made Ben wear his scarf to school all the more tightly. 'Still. It won't last,' said Daddy. But it did last.

Ben didn't know why the adults didn't like the snow. It was like rain, but *fun* rain. They seemed almost frightened of it – the weather forecaster kept giving updates about snow conditions with due gravity, and Daddy listened with gravity too, unsmiling, tense. Ben didn't get it. Snow was all over Christmas cards, it was in every Christmas song (well, the good ones, not the religious ones) it *was* Christmas. Pictures of Santa Claus everywhere, beaming out at him, standing knee-deep in the white stuff. 'Do you think we'll have a white Christmas?' Ben asked. 'I shouldn't have thought so,' said Daddy, 'it's weeks off, I'm sure it'll have blown over by then. Don't you worry.' Ben wasn't worried. 'I'm dreaming of a white Christmas,' he sung. It was the only line of the song he knew. 'I've got the video somewhere,' said Daddy. '*White Christmas*. Would you like to watch it with me?' 'Okay.' 'This weekend?' 'Okay.' So that Saturday they watched *White Christmas* together; they cuddled up close on the sofa, Ben liked to do that when they watched telly, in case there were scary bits. There were no scary bits in *White Christmas*. 'Daddy, the song wasn't in it,' said Ben, at the end. 'No,' said Daddy. And then, 'I'm sorry,' as if he'd let his son down.

And still the snow fell.

'Can we have a little chat, old chap?' asked Daddy one evening. And he looked serious, even a bit stern, and Ben felt scared. 'Up here on my knee,' said Daddy, and Ben felt better, he knew up on the knee meant it was going to be all right.

'I know Christmas is going to be a little odd this year,' said Daddy. 'Different.'

'I know,' said Ben.

'But I just want you to know. That we'll have a good Christmas. Don't you worry. Don't you worry about that.'

'Okay,' said Ben.

'Do you believe me?'

'Yes,' said Ben.

'The way to look at it,' said Daddy. 'Is that you'll get two Christmases this year. One with me, one with Mum.'

'Yes.'

'Double the fun!'

'We don't have to. We could still have one together.'

'I'm sorry, old chap.'

'We could talk to Mum about it.'

'I'm sorry, old chap, I don't think so.'

'Okay.'

'But whatever you want, goes. Whatever else. This will be the *best* Christmas ever. I promise you. Hey. Hey, look at me. Hey, Ben. Do I ever break my promise?'

'I don't know.'

'Have I ever broken my promise?'

'No.'

'I do my best. I do my best, you know.'

'Can we have Christmas dinner?' asked Ben.

'Of course we'll have Christmas dinner!'

'I mean, properly. With turkey. And gravy. And those little sausages.'

'Absolutely we will.'

'The way Mum makes it.'

'I'll make the very best Christmas dinner I can. You can help me if you want. Turkey and chipolata sausages, roast potatoes. Stuffing, you like stuffing, don't you?'

'And can we have a Christmas tree?'

Daddy gave him a hug. 'There's no way,' he said, 'that a son of mine isn't going to have the best Christmas tree there is.' And he hugged his son tight, so tight. 'Just as soon as the snow eases off, we'll go and get one. You can help me if you want. You can help, would you like that?'

But the snow didn't ease off. Still the snow fell.

'Daddy,' said Ben that weekend, 'are we going to get a Christmas tree soon? Because all my friends have trees.' 'Yes, Ben.' 'And Mum's got one, she's got her tree.' 'I said yes! Yes, Ben. Sorry. Yes. We'll go and get a tree. We'll go this afternoon.' So they drove into the town centre in the car. 'Look at the speed these people are driving,' said Daddy, 'they're maniacs. In these conditions!' Ben could feel the car slide a little on the road. He thought it was fun. 'You're okay, you're safe,' said Daddy, and Ben knew he was. They bought a Christmas tree from a man selling them on the pavement outside that cinema that had closed. 'Not much left,' the man said, 'the best ones are gone.' It's true, there wasn't much to pick from; on one or two the needles had half-fallen off, and yet the man was still charging thirty-five quid. 'That's scandalous,' said Daddy, and the man just shrugged. 'I like this one!' said Ben. 'Can we have this one?' The tree was a bit on the stumpy side, and at the top the stem split into two on either side, it looked as if it had a pair of mutant ears. 'Look at the ears, Daddy!' laughed Ben. 'I'm sure we can find you a better tree than that one, old chap,' said Daddy, 'what would your mother say?'

'No, I want Big Ears!' said Ben. 'Forty-five quid,' said the man, 'you've got yourself a bargain there,' and he even helped Daddy lug it out to the car, he took one ear and Daddy took the other, 'thank you,' he said with a big grin as he pocketed the cash, 'and merry Christmas!'

The tree wouldn't stand up straight in the living room, it lolled to the right like a drunkard. 'What we need to do,' said Daddy thoughtfully, 'is put all the decorations on the left, to weigh it down a bit.' Ben asked whether they could do the decorations today, and Daddy said of course they could, no time like the present! Where were the decorations kept? Where did Mummy put them? And Ben said he thought Mum might keep them in a cupboard under the stairs. So Daddy went and had a look in the cupboard, he pulled all sorts of things out. 'No luck, old chap,' he said, 'any other ideas?' Ben thought maybe the tinsel and the fairy lights and the balls were all in the spare bedroom, then, in one of the cupboards there, and Daddy asked him if he knew which cupboard might be most likely, but Ben didn't. 'Okay,' said Daddy. He emptied the contents of each cupboard on to the bed, putting them all back in again neatly before opening another one – it was quite a good system, but after an hour or so he tired of it, and just stuck back everything into any cupboard any which way. 'She wouldn't have taken the decorations with her, would she?' asked Daddy. Ben didn't know. Daddy went on, 'I mean, what would be the point? She has, though. She bloody has.' Daddy tried phoning her; she was out; he didn't leave a message. Daddy fumed for a bit, 'I can't believe she'd do that,' he said. 'To me, yes, okay. But not to her own *son*.' He phoned her again, and this time left a message that was very terse. 'Let's have some dinner, old chap,' said Daddy to Ben, 'there's nothing for it.' Ben asked whether they were going to decorate the tree, and Daddy looked a bit helpless, and said they'd have to buy some more decorations first – no, they couldn't go out today, they'd already been out the once – no, look, it was snowing, look at all the snow. Ben ate fish fingers and chips; Daddy had pea and ham soup, he always had soup, he said it was the least bother. Mum phoned back. Daddy listened to what she had to say. 'Oh. Right. But we've... Right. No, I'll go and check. Right. Sorry. Thanks for... thanks for calling back.' The decorations were in the cupboard under the stairs after all, Ben had been right first time; they were all kept within a box for an old vacuum cleaner. They decorated the tree, they got out all the tinsel and the fairy lights and the balls. They put a star on the tip of one of the ears, and an angel on the other. Ben loved it. 'Sorry, Ben,' said Daddy.

Still, the snow fell. Ben's school closed a few days early. 'Lucky you!' said Daddy. 'I still have to make it into work!' Ben was disappointed, though. There wasn't much work to be done at school this close to the holidays, and now he'd never find out how that advent calendar would turn out, it had been getting quite exciting.

The Saturday before Christmas Daddy took Ben back out into the snow. 'Christmas shopping!' he said. 'It'll be fun!' The snow was falling thick now; each day, it seemed to Ben, a mass of adults outside the window were doing their best to wreck the snow, driving over it and walking on it and turning it to mush – but each night the snow fell again, and by morning had brought back the blanket, unbroken, pure. Ben knew he was as much to blame, though – he loved crunching his footprints into the snow, crunch, crunch. Knowing that within an hour of his doing so fresh flakes would cover up any trace he had ever been there.

'I want you to get a really nice present for your mother,' Daddy said, and gave to Ben more money than he had ever seen. 'Can you hold on to that?' Ben could. Ben had no idea what to get Mum, so Daddy and Ben looked around the shopping centre together.

'What are *you* going to get Mum?' asked Ben.

'Oh,' said Daddy. 'Well. We've agreed not to buy each other any presents this year.'

'Oh,' said Ben. 'Okay.'

'It's just easier that way.'

'Okay.'

'We agreed,' chuckled Daddy, 'that this way we'd have more money to spend on you, old chap! So you come out of this rather well! It's all for you!' And then, 'Ben, I'm sorry, what is it, what's wrong?' And Ben said he didn't want the extra presents, he didn't want any of this to be his *fault*. And Daddy hugged him right there, he stooped down and hugged him, and assured him that none of this was anything to do with him. It was adult stuff, just silly adult stuff. 'The truth is,' he said, 'the reason Mummy and Daddy aren't buying each other presents... is that we just don't like each other very much at the moment.' And in spite of himself, Ben brightened at that.

Ben bought his Mum a couple of gift baskets of bubble bath from the Body Shop.

On the bottom level of the department store, on the concourse between a Poundstretcher and a British Home Stores, there was a Santa's Grotto. Surrounding the grotto was a little garden, decorated with fake snow, and tinsel.

'Would you like to see Santa, Ben?' There was quite a long queue, and an unsmiling woman in a booth was selling tickets.

'No.'

'Oh. Are you sure?'

'I don't believe in Santa Claus. I didn't believe in him last year either.' Ben put his head to one side, and considered. 'I probably did the year before.'

'What a funny little chap you are.'

'Don't you remember? You told me. You told me not to tell anyone, in case I spoiled the fun.'

'That's true,' said Daddy idly, 'we mustn't spoil anyone's fun. Shall we go home then?'

'Okay.'

'Okay.'

The snow was falling in thick clumps. Ben laughed at the sight of it. 'Come on, Ben,' said Daddy. 'Let's get to the car.'

'No, Daddy,' said Ben. 'Look!'

And he tilted his head back. He opened his mouth, and stuck out his tongue. And the snow rained on him, it rained all over his face – and some of the flakes too, they landed on his tongue. He turned to Daddy. Eyes gleaming. 'You try it!'

Daddy nearly said no, he so nearly did. But he too put back his head, the tongue came out, he pulled a funny face. 'Gurr,' he said. Ben giggled.

'What does it taste like?' said Ben.

'I don't know. Water. It doesn't taste of anything.'

'No,' said Ben. 'You're not trying hard enough.' He caught a few more flakes, and then smacked his lips appreciatively. 'Delicious!'

'Delicious!' said Daddy. 'Apple pie!'

'Chocolate cake!'

'Ice-cream!'

'Um. Peanuts!'

'Old socks!'

Ben laughed aloud at this one. And they stood there in the car park, as the Christmas shoppers fought their way around them, catching snow on their tongues, and Daddy laughed too. They were both laughing. Ben found Daddy's hand, just as Daddy was reaching for his.

'It's going to be a white Christmas, isn't it?' said Ben.

'Yes,' said Daddy. 'Oh God.' He squeezed Ben's hand a little tighter.

The next day was a Sunday, so that meant Ben got to spend it with his mum. Some Sundays Richard was there too, some Sundays he wasn't. This Sunday Richard was there. 'Come on,' said Mum. 'We're going Christmas shopping, it'll be fun!'

Ben had given up asking his mother why she preferred Richard to Daddy. 'It's not as simple as that,' she'd said. 'But why, Mummy?' 'It's not something I want to talk about.' 'Mummy, why?' And then she'd told him that she didn't want to be called Mummy any more, he was too old for Mummy now, surely? He wasn't a baby. She'd rather be called Mum, from now on, Mum. And that had surprised Ben, and he tried to call her Mum ever afterwards. Even if sometimes he forgot.

Richard had a son, but Ben had never met him. He was a few years older. Richard wasn't going to spend Christmas Day with his son either.

'I want you to buy something for your dad,' said Mummy. And she gave Ben some money, and he thought it was at least as much as Daddy had given for her present, and he was pleased.

'What shall I get him?' asked Ben.

'That's up to you, isn't it?'

Ben was dressed in his warm clothes, thick sweater, thick gloves, stripy scarf. Mum wore a faded fake fur coat Daddy had bought her years ago. As they walked in the town centre snow settled on their hair. 'You look like abominable snowmen!' joked Richard. Ben said he was the abominable snowman, but Mum was the abominable snowwoman, and Richard loved that, 'Good one, sport. Lisa's an abominable snowwoman, all right!' Ben didn't like the way Richard called his mum Lisa, so easy, as if he somehow owned the name. He called Lisa an abominable snowwoman on and off throughout the day, and Lisa always laughed, long after the time it had stopped being funny.

They shopped together for another couple of hours or so. Mum said, 'Richard's got a treat for you, Ben!' And Richard laughed, and said it was only a little thing. He'd bought Ben a ticket for Santa's Grotto. Would Ben like to go to Santa's Grotto? He'd queued all this time to buy a ticket from the unsmiling woman at the booth, and now all Ben had to do was join another queue to see Santa. Would Ben like to see Santa? In Santa's Grotto?

'No, thank you,' said Ben.

'Oh,' said Richard. 'I have already bought the ticket, though.'

'Come on,' said Mum. 'You'd like to see Santa, wouldn't you?'

'I don't believe in Santa.'

'Don't believe in Santa? But he's in that grotto over there!' Richard joked.

'You're going to see Santa,' said Mum. 'Richard's spent all that money.'

'It's only a little thing,' said Richard, 'only seven pounds fifty.'

'Seven pounds fifty! And you didn't even say thank you!'

'I did say thank you,' said Ben.

Mum marched Ben out of Richard's earshot – but not so far, Ben thought, that Richard couldn't hear if he really wanted to. 'Now, listen, mister,' she said. 'I've had enough of this. Sulking all day in front of Richard, when he's trying, can't you see how hard he's trying? Okay, you don't like him. Tough. Because I do like him. In fact, I love him. So you'd better bloody well get used to him. Because he's not going anywhere, not if I can help it.' And then she marched him back to where Richard was smiling, still smiling. 'What do you say, sport?' he said, holding out the ticket. 'Want to see Santa after all?'

The queue to see Santa lasted a good forty-five minutes, and Ben suspected his mother regretted making such a fuss because she'd clearly lost patience after waiting only ten. 'What is Santa doing to them in there?' she muttered. Richard joked, 'Well, they're certainly getting their seven pounds fifty's worth!' At last an elf took Ben away; Mum and Richard waved as he went.

Santa Claus was too young, and he wore padded clothes and a stuck-on beard. 'Ho ho ho!' he said.

'Hi,' said Ben.

'Want to sit on my knee?'

Ben shrugged, and did. He perched there a little precariously, and Santa wasn't allowed to hold him fast the way his daddy could.

'What do you want for Christmas?' asked Santa.

'Nothing.'

'Come on. You must want something. What's your favourite toy?'

Ben shrugged again.

'Do you want an action figure?'

'No.'

'A computer game?'

'No.'

'An – I don't know – what do you call them, one of those Lego things? Come on, kid, help me out here.'

Ben couldn't get what he really wanted, and certainly not from a man in a shopping centre. He'd tried asking Jesus for it, and he hadn't believed in Jesus for years, but he'd asked him anyway. 'If you fix this,' he'd said, 'if you can just make them love each other again, I'll believe in you. I'll go right on believing in you.' But Jesus hadn't listened. Not even when he'd offered the deal. 'If you make them love each other,' and Ben had hesitated over this, then just – hell with it – gone straight ahead and said it, 'they don't even have to love me. They don't have to love me. It's okay. I'll be okay.' But Jesus hadn't done a thing, he didn't exist, and nor did Santa Claus, it was all such rubbish, it was shit.

'A bike?' said Santa Claus. Now a little desperate. 'How about a bike?'

And actually, a bike didn't sound so bad. 'Yeah, go on then, a bike.'

'Great,' said Santa. 'Merry Christmas!' And gave him a present from his sack, something small and square and in shiny paper, that very definitely wasn't a bike. When Ben came out of the grotto, his mum and Richard were talking closely, and giggling. 'Oh, there you are,' said Mum. 'That was quick!'

It was agreed that Ben would spend the night at his mum's; now school was finished, he could be simply dropped back to Daddy's later the next day. Christmas Day with his father, Boxing Day with his mother and Richard, then New Year's Eve with his mother and Richard, New Year's Day with his daddy. That was the plan, it was a good plan, everyone was happy with that. 'Let's get home,' said Mum, meaning *her* home, although her house still didn't feel like home to Ben, it had the wrong smell, it had the smell of *visiting* all over it. Richard settled down in front of the television, Mum made herself and Richard a cup of tea. 'What would you like to do?' she asked Ben.

Ben didn't know.

'How about writing a letter to Santa? It's not too late to reach the Pole, not if we get it to the post box quick!'

Ben said he didn't believe in Santa any more.

'I used to help you to write letters to Santa. Do you remember? Every Christmas?' He did remember, actually, but he wasn't going to admit to it. She looked at him, for a moment she looked almost afraid of him – a very adult sort of afraid, the afraid that comes when you simply don't know what to say any more. 'I love you, Ben. You know that, don't you?'

'Yes.'

'I love you very much.'

'Yes.'

'All right then.'

'Okay.'

'I'll fix you some dinner. All right. Something nice and warm. And then we're going to sit down, just the two of us, and write a letter to Santa.'

'Oh, Mum...'

'Just the two of us, no Richard, all right?'

'But, Mum...'

'No buts. What would you like Santa to bring you?'

'A bike,' said Ben.

'All right then,' she said. 'A bike, that's what we'll say.'

They had dinner that evening, all three of them, and Richard made jokes, and then they watched television, like a family. And Ben was pleased his mum forgot all about the letter to Santa Claus, though he supposed he wouldn't have minded writing one with her really, not if it made her happy.

And still – the snow fell.

iii

Only a few months after they were married, David and Lisa Noakes bought themselves a small house in south London. It was ideally situated. It was just a street away from an underground station, they could be in the city within half an hour. There were lots of local shops nearby, even a little supermarket on the corner. And in walking distance there was a school. 'That might be handy,' said David, 'you know, just in case you still want to have any kids.' David was still a little shy of marriage, he still couldn't quite believe Lisa had agreed to become his wife in the first place. 'Of course I still want kids!' laughed Lisa. 'Silly!' And she kissed him, and he hugged her, and they put a down payment on the mortgage, and that was that.

It was a few years, however, before David and Lisa got around to having that kid. And by then the house wasn't as ideally situated as it had been. The little supermarket had closed down, but nothing had come along to replace it. And Lisa didn't like the other local shops, they were either too expensive, or she got funny looks in there, she said, after one funny look she refused to step inside one particular newsagent's for years. However convenient the underground station, it was also very noisy, and it seemed to attract drunken youths at weekends, they gathered around it at all times of night shouting and flinging bottles. Lisa wondered whether they shouldn't move. 'At least there's the school,' said David. Lisa agreed; but it wasn't an especially *good* school. And David said yes, they really ought to give young Ben the best start in life they could. But they didn't move.

Or, at least, David and Ben didn't.

Step outside David and Ben's semi-detached, and you'd see: cars, all piled up high on the kerbs. The offending newsagent's. A unisex hairdressing salon. A skip, placed down the road months ago, now seemed to be a permanent fixture. An off-licence. Houses crammed tight together in both directions, as far as the eye could see.

What you wouldn't normally see would be a forest. Surrounding the house entirely, as if this thing of bricks and glass were some strange alien imposition upon a landscape so wild that all the trees looked animal, somehow: angry and untamed; the branches jutting out at any angles they wanted to, no matter how sharp, no matter how impossible: the very bark bulged. There was no checking these trees, they were the kings here – and yet they seemed to defer to *something*, because they still shied away from a natural path, and flanked it on both sides. A winding path that stretched on into the distance.

Ben, bundled up in his warmest sweater and warmest gloves and stripy scarf, was surprised to see the forest there. But Santa wasn't surprised, this was clearly what he'd been expecting. And the look on Daddy's face wasn't surprise either. He looked tense, a little resigned maybe, but there was nothing there to suggest he hadn't been expecting this as much as Santa. So Ben decided not to be surprised either.

'Come on, Ben,' said Santa. 'Let's get these stabilisers on your bike. Just until you get your balance!' They clipped right on. 'All right, you're set to go!'

'Are you still sure you want to ride the bike, Ben?' asked Daddy.

'Would you push me, Daddy?'

'Of course I will.'

'You don't need to push him,' said Santa. 'He's got stabilisers.'

'I'll push my son's bike if he wants me to.'

'No, it's okay, Daddy. I forgot, the stabilisers will take care of it.'

'Oh. Are you sure?'

'I'm sure. This is fun. Look at me! I'm riding a bike!'

'Are we walking far?' Daddy asked Santa.

Santa shrugged. Maybe he was being unhelpful. Maybe he just didn't know.

And off they set, crunching the snow down the path the trees had left them. The two men, and the little boy on his bike, sometimes racing ahead excitedly, sometimes ringing them. 'Try to walk where I walk,' Santa told Daddy.

'Why, is the ground slippery?'

'No. But let's not leave more footprints than we have to. Let's not spoil the *beauty* of this.' And it was easy for Daddy to do that, Santa's footprints were so big. Daddy looked behind from time to time, and soon he couldn't see the house, only that single pair of footprints, and the thin grooves where Ben's tyres had cut into the snow. And as the snow fell more heavily, he soon couldn't even see those. All around them was the snow, now a blinding white, Daddy and Ben had to shield their eyes from the glare. Santa put on a pair of sunglasses. 'Here,' he said, and handed Daddy and Ben sunglasses too.

Neither Daddy nor Santa spoke for another hour. On they both trudged, faces grim – except once in a while Santa would catch Ben's eye, and give him a friendly wink. As if to say, this is only a game! Don't let on! And Ben would wink back, when he was sure his daddy couldn't see. The snow continued to fall, but there was no wind to disturb the silence. 'Please,' said Daddy at last. He said it so softly, but it broke right through that silence – and Ben and Santa both stopped, turned to look at him.

'Please,' he said again.

'No,' said Santa. Not unkindly. But firm.

'But I'm all he's got.'

'He's got his mother.'

'His mother and I... it's difficult... we might sort things out one day, I don't...' Santa watched Daddy sympathetically. Ben looked away, suddenly embarrassed. 'I've tried so hard to hold on to him,' said Daddy.

'I know,' said Santa.

'How do you know?'

'I can tell.'

'Daddy, it's okay,' said Ben.

'I've tried so hard,' said Daddy.

'I know. Daddy.'

'I know. I can tell. We can both tell, can't we, Ben?'

'I'm not going a step further,' said Daddy.

'Now, come on,' said Santa. 'None of that. Chop chop!'

'Daddy, don't,' said Ben. Don't what? Spoil the fun for the rest of us?

'Why the bloody hell did you write him a letter, Ben?' said Daddy. He wasn't shouting, not really, but it still seemed awfully loud in the still of that forest. 'He wouldn't have come if you hadn't written.'

'I didn't write to him.'

From his pocket Santa took a letter. He handed it to Ben's Daddy. Daddy recognised the handwriting, and it wasn't Ben's. And he slumped, it seemed he suddenly got very tired. He handed the letter back to Santa.

'Okay,' said Daddy.

'We can walk on?' asked Santa.

'Okay,' said Daddy.

And on they walked.

Soon Ben couldn't ride his bike through the ever thickening snow, he had to push it. 'Walk where I walk,' said Daddy. 'Why?' 'You know. What he said. The beauty of it all. Let's keep the beauty of it all.' Ben tilted his head back at one point. 'Look, Daddy!' he said, and caught the snowflakes on his tongue. 'You do it too.'

Daddy stopped. Daddy caught snowflakes on his tongue too. Santa stopped too, but he didn't try to force the pace, he looked indulgent, smiled at them both, he looked like Santa on a Christmas card.

'Delicious!' said Ben.

'What do you taste?'

'Chocolate cake,' said Ben.

'Marzipan,' said Daddy.

'Apple pie!'

'I can fix that for you,' said Santa. And he did, with just one snap of his fingers. 'There,' he said. And the snow that melted in their mouths tasted of pies, of cakes, of hot fudge, all sweet and creamy. 'No,' said Daddy, gently. 'This is our moment. This is *ours*.' And Santa nodded, a little ashamed, and the snow went back to tasting of bland water. Daddy and Ben held hands and drank the snowflakes until they could drink no more. Then, with just a glance shared, they both agreed to walk on – Daddy's feet dwarfed in Santa's footprints, Ben's dwarfed in his daddy's.

'Not much further now,' said Santa, kindly.

The sleigh was a bit rusted. It had seen better days. So too had the reindeer. They huddled together for warmth. On seeing their master return, the fitter of the pack tried to stand to attention. 'No, no, at ease, boys,' and the reindeer relaxed into their harnesses gratefully.

'Well, then,' said Santa to Daddy, awkwardly.

'Well,' said Daddy.

There was quiet for a few seconds. 'You needn't look at me like that,' said Santa. 'I gave you a good toy, didn't I? I only ever give the best toys.'

'I don't remember what it was.'

'It was probably a bike. I give a lot of bikes.'

'No, it wasn't a bike.'

'Let's just say it was a bike,' said Santa.

Daddy thought about that. 'Okay,' he said.

'I remember your little face lighting up when you got it,' said Santa. 'That's always the best bit. Watching the faces light up.' And Ben was surprised to see that Santa was crying.

Daddy gave Ben a hug. 'I tried very hard,' he said. 'I tried my hardest.'

And Ben now knew he should have been pleading for his father. But he'd been too busy riding his bike, spinning about, cutting those grooves into the snow. He'd been too busy for *months*, going to school, eating his fish fingers, pretending it was all okay, that it was all going to be okay. And it was now too late for him to plead. 'Will I see my daddy again?' Ben asked Santa.

Santa looked genuinely surprised that he'd asked. 'Oh,' he said. 'Maybe. But never like this. Never again like this.'

One more hug. 'That's nice,' said Santa Claus. 'Strip.'

Daddy had put on all his warmest clothes – two layers! – so it took him a while. He made a pile on the ground, sweaters, shirt, vest, then shoes, then trousers, underpants. He remembered the sunglasses, actually snorted in amusement he'd done so, put them on the pile, squinting at the bright white. The last clothes he took off were his socks; he could now delay it no longer, and Daddy winced as his bare feet sank deep into the snow.

Ben wasn't sure he'd seen his father naked before. He looked so fragile. Daddy clapped his arms around his sides to keep warm, but soon stopped, there wasn't any point. He stood there, shivering, his balls fluffed up with hairs standing on end, his willy shrunk to a cork. He looked so *young*. Ben had never thought of his daddy being young before.

'It won't take long, I promise,' said Santa.

And sure enough, the feet were already hooves, better protection against the cold, and Ben could see Daddy sigh gratefully for that. The hide stole over his body, thick and strong, not strong enough, maybe, not in this weather, it could freeze your blood – but warmer than his man skin, that was a comfort at any rate. He pitched forwards when his hands became hooves as well; his head bowed down beneath antler weight.

'That's it,' said Santa. 'There you are. You're beautiful. You're beautiful.' He smiled at Ben. 'Isn't he beautiful?' And Ben couldn't deny it.

Santa turned to the other reindeer. 'This is your new brother!' he said. They were too weary to do much more than shrug their heads, non-committal. 'You all try so hard for me,' he said. 'For me, you fly the skies. You're the best.' He stroked their heads, one by one. He reached one near the back. 'And you, you're so very tired, aren't you? Such a long journey. So many long journeys. But you've always tried so hard.' The reindeer turned its human eyes to Santa, and nuzzled his hand. Santa laughed. 'Thank you. Thank you. I love you.' And so tenderly, he caressed its head. And broke its neck.

In that silence the snap of bone sounded louder than it probably was. It had been such a gentle twist, really, and so quick, the reindeer wouldn't have felt a thing. But it couldn't have been *that* gentle – one of the bones had ripped through the skin ('rip it open, rip it apart!') Ben could see it jutting out, sharp and white. The harness kept the reindeer in place, slumped in death as it was; when Santa released it, the body fell to the ground. The snow that caught it was so soft.

Santa harnessed his new reindeer into place.

'I'll give you the bike back,' said Ben.

Santa stopped.

'I want my Daddy,' said Ben.

He hoped he sounded bold and defiant. He hoped he wasn't crying.

Santa stroked his beard.

'So, what's the deal here?' he said. 'You give me the bike back, I give you back your father? And we're quits? Fair exchange, no robbery?'

'Yes,' said Ben.

'And what, I give the bike to some other kid instead?'

'Yes,' said Ben.

'Interesting,' said Santa.

He went to the bicycle. Looked it over thoughtfully. Ran his finger critically over the frame.

'But see, here's the problem,' said Santa. 'It's been *used*. Hasn't it?'

'Yes,' said Ben.

'You've been riding it in the snow. Your choice. Remember, your choice.'

'Yes,' Ben breathed.

'I only give the best toys. Nothing second-hand.'

'I know,' said Ben.

'Well then,' said Santa Claus. And gave him a grin that was meant to be reassuring. Ben saw that the teeth were somehow still stained green with pea and ham soup.

Santa got into his sleigh. 'You'll be all right,' he said. 'Your mother loves you very much. It moved me, how much. And I'll be seeing you again. Whenever there's a white Christmas.' He gave the reins a single flick. 'Yee-hah, git!' he said. 'On, Donner and Blitzen! Come on, chop chop!' And off he flew into the night sky, so fast that Ben's eyes couldn't follow him.

iv

And this is how the story could end. With a little boy lost. By his side a used bicycle, and a dead reindeer whose blood was now staining the white snow red. But things are rarely that simple.

Ben wheeled his bike home. It didn't take long. The forest was gone; there was the underground station, though. There were no youths outside it now, the trains didn't run on Christmas Day. He had to cross the road, and looked left, then right, then left again, just as his daddy had taught him. He took the bicycle indoors. He went to bed.

The next morning Ben went down to the kitchen. His daddy was sitting there, eating a bowl of cornflakes. Ben yelped, gave him a hug. 'Not now, Ben, I'm having breakfast. Pull up a chair, you have your breakfast too.' Ben poured himself some cornflakes. They ate together. 'After breakfast, we can open our presents,' said Daddy. 'Yeah!' said Ben, 'Happy Christmas!' 'Happy Christmas,' said Daddy.

In the hallway Daddy saw Ben's new bike, propped up against the front door. It had dripped melted snow on to the carpet. Daddy looked at Ben, then tutted, just the once. Then without a word he picked up the bicycle and carried it to the back door, put it out into the garden.

Christmas Day was fine. Really, fine. The presents were fine. Ben opened his presents, taking them from beneath the lopsided tree with the ears. He'd got lots of toys, and a book about boats. ('You like boats, don't you?' said Daddy. 'Yes,' said Ben.) Daddy liked his present from Ben, a selection of male toiletries from the Body Shop. 'Thanks.' Ben wanted to tell him that Mum had bought it for him mostly, it was Mum he should thank, but he knew somehow it wouldn't be the right thing to say. 'I'll go and make dinner,' said Daddy at last. 'Can I help?' 'No,' said Daddy, 'play with your toys, read about boats.' The dinner was fine. The gravy was more solid than liquid, and the turkey was too dry. But the stuffing and the chipolata sausages were great. 'They're the best bits anyway,' said Daddy, and Ben readily agreed. After dinner, they watched television, they watched *Doctor Who* and then *EastEnders*. Ben cuddled up to his father. 'Not too close, Ben, you're being too clingy,' said Daddy. So Ben got off the sofa, and played with his toys a bit more, read a bit more of his boat book. 'Time for bed,' said Daddy.

Daddy tucked Ben in to bed. 'I promised you the best Christmas ever,' he said.

'Yes.'

'That wasn't it.'

'No.'

'But it was okay, wasn't it?'

'It was okay.'

On Boxing Day Mum came to pick up Ben bright and early. 'Merry Christmas!' she said when Ben opened the front door to her, and gave him a huge hug. 'Dave, I know we'd agreed I'd bring him back tomorrow morning, but would the afternoon...' 'That's fine,' Daddy interrupted.

Richard didn't come to the front door, he was waiting in the car. He never came to the door. 'Merry Christmas!' he said to Ben. He was wearing a Santa hat, he looked like a cretin.

Ben opened lots of presents, he got lots of toys. Richard had bought him a present too. 'I hope you like this, sport,' he'd said, and looked really rather nervous as Ben unwrapped it. Ben had already decided not to like it, but it was actually pretty good – it wasn't his *best* toy, but it was definitely in the top five, it was good. They all had Christmas dinner, and that was lovely – 'Delicious!' said Ben – and they all pulled crackers – Daddy had forgotten the crackers! – and they all put on paper hats, even Richard put on a paper hat, he put it over the top of his Santa hat, and he looked even more like a cretin than before, but it still made Ben laugh. They all played some board games. Ben won the first two, Richard won one – 'I'm catching up with you now!' he joked, and picked up the dice, 'fancy another?' 'I'm rubbish at games,' said Mum, 'I just don't have the right sort of brain! I never win *anything*!' And Richard kissed her, and Ben didn't mind much.

On New Year's Eve, Richard was wearing the Santa hat again. Ben wondered if he'd ever taken it off. Mum let Ben stay up till midnight, and have a sip of champagne. 'But don't tell your father,' she said, 'your father will kill me,' and Ben promised. They sang *Auld Lang Syne*, and did the arm crossing thing, even though Richard got it wrong, Ben thought he got it wrong deliberately, but it was a bit funny. 'Happy New Year, darling,' said Richard to Lisa. 'Can't be worse than the old one,' Lisa replied.

The snow stopped falling. The snow melted.

*

Ben had bad dreams. And one night in February, as he lay in bed, he suddenly got it into his head that he was all alone in the house. His daddy wasn't there any more. Anybody could come into his bedroom and get him, and Daddy wouldn't be there to stop them. He got up. He listened at his father's door for any reassuring sounds of snoring. He couldn't hear anything. He began to cry, but as quietly as he could – and then he went down the stairs, walking only at the sides to avoid the creaks. All so that he wouldn't wake Daddy, he mustn't wake Daddy, and it was ridiculous, because Daddy wasn't there to be woken, was he? He wanted to scream out his name. But he was terrified to hear his own voice that loud in the dark, he was terrified that his daddy wouldn't answer. The door to Daddy's study was shut. Ben pushed it open.

His Daddy sat by the computer, completely naked. Ben didn't think he'd ever seen his daddy naked before, he wasn't sure.

It took a moment for Daddy to realise his son was standing there, and then his face flushed. 'Ben! Can't you knock?'

'I can't sleep...'

'Go to bed!'

'I can't sleep!'

'Go to bed, I'll be upstairs in a moment! Go to bed this instant!'

And Ben ran back to his room. By the time Daddy joined him, he'd found time to put some trousers on. Daddy was still a bit angry, but he'd calmed down. 'You can't just go opening doors,' he said. 'It's just not on, is it? What's the matter?'

'I can't sleep,' said Ben. 'I'm frightened.'

Daddy sighed. 'Well, think of something happy.'

'I can't.'

'Of course you can. Don't be ridiculous.'

Ben nodded. 'Okay, I'll try.'

'Good boy.'

'Daddy, on Christmas Eve...' And it was hard to tell in the darkened room, but Daddy seemed to stiffen at that. 'I'm sorry,' said Ben. 'I'm sorry about... I'm sorry.'

Daddy didn't say anything for a long while. And Ben wanted to go on. He wanted to say he'd betrayed his father, that was why he'd lost him. And he wanted him back. And he wished Daddy would call him 'old chap' again; he did it once in a while, but only without thinking, and then Daddy would look guilty as if he'd been caught in a lie.

But Ben had said too much as it was, he knew it, far too much. Daddy said at last, 'Go to sleep.' And so Ben did.

It was wholly a coincidence that only two weeks later Daddy told Ben he had something serious to discuss with him. He sat stern behind the kitchen table, and Ben wished he'd invite him on to his knee, he could take anything he said if it were knee-given. 'You like Uncle Richard, don't you?' Daddy and Mummy had been talking, and it seemed only fair that Mummy got to live with Ben for a while. Instead, even. And the schools were better in Mummy's area, it was more practical. So.

Ben was confused, he couldn't work out who'd betrayed whom any more. 'You still love me, don't you?' asked Ben. 'Of course I love you, you're my son,' said Daddy. And he could have left it like that, but he didn't, *he didn't*, he said, 'But I just can't reach you any more.'

Ben still visited his dad most Sundays. One day Daddy said, 'I've found a girlfriend. Her name's Annie.' Ben asked if he had to meet Annie, and Daddy looked a bit awkward, and said not yet, Annie didn't like children very much. And Ben was glad. 'But I've got a picture of her on the computer, would you like to see?' Daddy was posing with his arms around a woman, and they were both smiling, but it seemed to Ben Daddy was smiling too wide, the way he smiled whenever he saw Mum on the doorstep. Annie looked very young. Daddy looked old. Ben had never thought of his daddy being old before.

*

'Let's get those stabilisers off!' laughed Richard. 'You're not a baby any more!' He took Ben to the park, and there they practised balancing on the bike. 'It's all a question of not wobbling,' said Richard. Richard held the back of his saddle for a while, and then it took Ben a few seconds to realise he'd let go, that Ben was riding the bike, he was doing it all by himself. 'Yeah!' said Ben. 'Yeah, you did it!' said Richard. Richard said he'd taught his own son to ride a bike a few years ago; Ben had met him now, but he didn't have anything to say to him, Justin was fourteen, what was there to say to someone so old? 'We did it!' said Richard. 'Didn't we? Give me a hug.' So Ben did. 'You'll be able to ride that bike everywhere now!' said Richard. Ben agreed. But he didn't ride the bike much after that, it'd been more fun with the stabilisers.

Richard and his mum never got around to marrying. Which meant it was much smoother altogether when Richard dumped her for someone else. Ben listened to his mum cry over the phone at his university halls. 'I've tried so hard, Ben,' she said. 'But he just didn't try at all.' 'He just didn't love you enough,' said Ben. He played with the phone wires. He hated these phone calls with his mother, he never knew what to say. 'You'll find someone else,' Ben went on, 'you deserve someone better, Lisa.' 'I don't want anyone else,' said Lisa. 'Okay.' 'I want Richard, don't I?' 'Okay. Well, then.' 'You're a good boy, Ben.' 'Okay. I've got to get off the phone soon, there's a queue.' 'I wish you would call me Mum.'

Ben invited his father to his graduation ceremony, but he wasn't able to make it. Four years later, when he married Sophie, he invited him to the wedding. Daddy did make that one. But Ben didn't put him up on top table with his mother, he put him on table twelve with some of the minor guests. If his father were offended, he didn't show it. After the reception, before Daddy drove home alone, he found Ben. He shook Ben by the hand. 'Well done,' he said. 'Thanks for coming,' said Ben.

Right from the beginning Ben and Sophie had discussed children. 'I don't want any,' said Sophie. 'Nor do I,' said Ben. 'I'm not sure what I'd say to one!' Sophie laughed, and agreed – better to get a cat instead. When Sophie turned forty, she told Ben she was leaving him. She'd found someone else, someone she thought she could mother babies for. 'It's not you,' she said, 'it's my biological clock ticking.' Ben had thought for some time that maybe the cats weren't enough, that maybe cracking out a baby or two wouldn't be such a bad idea after all. But he really hadn't wanted to pressure Sophie with his doubts, he'd kept them to himself. He told her at last how he felt. She looked torn, genuinely torn. 'But I've already found a new boyfriend and everything,' she said, and left.

He and his father sent Christmas cards to each other, and on Christmas Day itself Ben would always phone. One year he forgot to send the card, and apologised for that during the annual call. 'Oh, don't worry,' said Daddy, 'I don't like Christmas cards anyway!' Ben laughed; nor did he; they agreed they were a waste of money.

they never bothered sending any to one another ever again. Pretty soon after that the phone calls dried up as well. 'I love you, Dad,' said Ben, quite unexpectedly that last year. There was a baffled silence on the other end, and then Daddy said, 'And I love you too.' But still, the phone calls dried up.

His mother died first, and Ben thought that was wrong, it should have been his dad, it should have been the other way round. He knew it was a cruel thing to think, but that didn't stop it from being just what he felt.

*

The weather reports said there was going to be a cold snap. But Ben was prepared. The snow began to fall, and the experts said it wouldn't settle, but it did settle; then they said it wouldn't last, and it did. People began to talk about the possibility of a white Christmas. London hadn't had a white Christmas in over forty years. Probably global warming was to blame.

Christmas Eve. When Ben looked out of his window, he saw the usual view, a building site and Budgen's. If he opened the front door, he saw a forest. He went to the kitchen. He took out some mince pies. He took out some soup, too. Then he went to the living room, sat on the sofa, and waited for midnight.

Midnight came, and midnight went. Ben got bored. He turned on his television. *White Christmas* was playing. A part of the TV schedules for a hundred years, and still going strong. Ben couldn't concentrate on it, switched it off. He let himself doze for a bit. He found he could doze quite easily, now he had no-one to talk to.

One in the morning. Then two.

Ben sighed heavily.

He put on all his warmest clothes. Sweater, gloves. Not a scarf, though. Scarves made his neck get scratchy, and he'd long ago realised the joy of being an adult is that no-one can make you wear scarves if you don't want to.

He went out into the cold. He walked through those animal trees, down that winding path, crunching through the snow. Half a mile along he realised he'd forgotten to bring sunglasses, he'd forgotten how bright the white was. He considered going back to fetch them. Then, 'Oh sod it,' he said, out loud, and marched onwards.

Eventually he found Santa Claus. Santa was leaning, winded, against a tree. 'I've been waiting for ages,' said Ben.

'Yes. Sorry. I'm a bit... oof... I'm a bit out of puff.' Santa Claus looked old and cold. 'It's so hard to keep going, Ben,' he said. 'They don't believe any more. They don't believe in *anything*.'

'Come on,' said Ben. 'Rest on me.' And he took Santa by the arm, and gratefully Santa leaned into him. And together they hobbled onwards down the path, back the way Santa had come.

They didn't talk for all those hours. Except for just the once. When Ben asked, 'How much further?' and Santa replied, 'I don't know. I've never known.' And then added, as an afterthought, and it didn't seem connected at all, 'I tried so hard. I tried so hard.'

At last they reached the sleigh and the reindeer.

'Well, then,' said Santa.

'Well.'

And then nothing. 'Oh, for God's sake,' said Ben impatiently. And he began to strip.

He made a pile of clothes on the forest floor. He took off his socks last, and his feet burned against the ice. He liked that. He wanted them to burn.

'And now you,' he said to Santa.

For a moment Santa looked surprised. And then there was the flutter of a smile, gone in an instant; it might have been nothing more than a grimace against the falling snow. Santa took off his big red coat, his great black boots. He took off his beard. The beard was fake, it had always been fake.

And there both men stood shivering in the snow. Ben looked Santa over, and Santa gave an apologetic smile, acknowledging the poor figure he cut. He wasn't fat any more. He looked as if he hadn't been fed in weeks. Ben could see Santa's ribs pushing underneath his skin, and that in the cold the ribs were turning blue.

Ben put on Santa's suit. He put on the beard.

Santa licked his lips. 'Are you going to break my neck?' he asked. But Ben told him to get dressed. Into all the warmest clothes Ben had. Santa was too thin for them, they hung baggy, he looked as if he were drowning in them.

'Go home,' said Ben. 'There's mince pies waiting. And hot soup. Go home, into the warm.' And the man who had been Santa Claus nodded, and without saying another word, turned and went.

Ben inspected his reindeer. One of them nuzzled at his hand, turned to him with those all too human eyes. And Ben didn't know for sure, but he *believed*. That his father had been with Santa all the time. That he'd once betrayed him, but now he'd won him back. That they'd been lost, both of them – but were now found.

And the snow continued to fall.

211 – The last words of realisation for Emperor Septimius Severus: 'I was everything, and it was all for nothing.' *It was my mother who gave me my love of history. One birthday she bought me a book. It was big, and red, and hardback, it was called 'The Wise Old Owl's Book of Famous People', and on the cover there was the Wise Old Owl himself smiling at me, and pointing with a wand. Mother said, 'I know you like to be told stories. Well, now you've got lots of them – and the best part is, they're all absolutely true!' Inside there were drawings: a woman in armour (Joan of Arc), a man with a cigar (Winston Churchill), a man in a ruff (Sir Francis Drake). They were splendid, each and every one of them. They were my new friends. And every night Mother would read to me about them – 'Tell me the one about Marie Curie!' I'd say. 'Tell me the one about Genghis Khan!' I don't remember what my father bought me, a piece of worthless crap probably, it was a long time ago, we aren't talking about my father.* **211** – The cruel Severus is succeeded by the crueller Caracalla. He shares the imperial throne with his brother Geta, but quickly has him murdered, and marks the start of his supremacy by having more than 20,000 Romans massacred. **217** – Caracalla is under no illusions that he has enemies, so surrounds himself with soothsayers and clairvoyants, and under their instructions puts to death anyone they say may be plotting against him. One day Macrinus, the prefect of the imperial guard, intercepts a letter that warns Caracalla he is not to be trusted; he knows his life will be forfeit, so decides that he might as well try to assassinate Caracalla anyway, and fulfil the prophecy. On a journey by horse, Caracalla needs to answer the call of nature, and dismounts. While he stands at the side of the road taking a piss, Macrinus has him stabbed in the heart. Caracalla is only one of several monarchs who will die during toilet activities, and by no means the most painfully (qv 1016, 1437, 1760). *And after my mother had wished me good night, and turned out the lights, and closed the door – I'd get out my torch, I'd take the book down from the high shelf where she'd put it, I'd read more under the covers. Napoleon, Charles Dickens, Henry VIII, Oliver Cromwell, Boadicea, George Washington, Louis XIV 'The Sun King', Sir Thomas a Becket, poor King Harold who got an arrow in his eye at the battle of Hastings. Friends all, all friends – and each of the drawings had two dates underneath – and I understood that the first of these dates was the year in which my friends were born. And so I realised too that the second date... was the year in which they died.* **218** – Macrinus is proclaimed emperor, but true to Roman form, he doesn't last long. The armies soon back the 14-year-old Heliogabalus. Macrinus tries to commit suicide by throwing himself from a chariot. All he succeeds in doing is breaking his shoulder. Which means that when, inevitably, he is put to death, it at least puts him out of the misery of his fracture. **222** – Heliogabalus has no illusions that he will suffer a violent death. It has been prophesied. And he glories in that. He insists that when his end comes, it must be expensive and full of style. He leaves around the palace, for easy access, golden swords he can be stabbed with, satin nooses he can be hanged by, jars of poison that are encrusted with gems. He has a high tower built from which he can hurl himself, and has the ground beneath, upon which his imperial body will be dashed to bits, studded with gold and jewels. In the end his death is not what he had planned for, as is so often the way with death: when the soldiers stab him, the eighteen-year-old god is hiding in the arms of his mother. Both mother and son are thrown into the sewer. *And the faces in the drawings weren't smiling at me, they were smirking. And they had cold hard eyes. Because my book was full of corpses. The Wise Old Owl had trapped them in his book, and that's what history was, a catalogue of what's dead. And I began to imagine there were worms. Crawling out of Napoleon's eye, out of Boadicea's mouth, around Churchill's cigar, wriggling, flexing, getting on my sheets and on to my pillow. And I screamed.* **235** – Roman Emperor Severus Alexander is put to the sword by his own army. His arms, too, wrapped tight around his mother – all he can do in his final moments is repeat over and over again that everything is her fault. **238** – Father and son, Gordian I and Gordian II, rule as Roman Emperors together. Gordian II is killed by the army. Gordian I, on hearing the news, strangles himself with a belt. They have been in power for two weeks. **238** – Maximinius the Thracian succeeds the Gordians. He is stabbed to death by his own soldiers. **238** – Pupienus and Balbinus succeed Maximinius. Soldiers break into their palace, and lynch them. **244** – Emperor Gordian III is killed by Philip the Arab. **248** – Rome celebrates its thousandth anniversary by slaughtering hippopotami and giraffes at the Colosseum. **249** – Emperor Philip the Arab is killed by Decius. **251** – Emperor Decius is killed in battle, after being betrayed by Trebonianus Gallus. **253** – Emperor Gallus is killed by Aemilian. **253** – Emperor Aemilian is killed by his own troops. *My father was angry. He put the book back on the shelf. 'Now go to sleep,' he commanded. But I didn't want it in my room, I didn't want it where its worms could get me. My father told me to stop being so childish. My mother told me it was just a nightmare, told me everything would be all right – but I said, I told her, we're going to end up dead like Marie Curie! I couldn't be safe with the book in the room. I couldn't be safe with the book in the house. My father had to take it outside, put it in the garden bin.* **260** – Emperor Valerian is captured in battle by the Persian king, Shapur I. He suffers the indignity of being used as a human mounting block; wherever Shapur goes, there will be Valerian too, and Shapur will step upon his bowed back every time he wants to get on or off his horse. And Shapur shouts at him that this, finally, is reality, this – not Roman heroism, not the lies depicted on all their frescos and in all their art and in all their poems, not history – because Roman history is over now, all its glory and conquests, the weight of history has betrayed him, and reduced its oh-so-powerful emperor to a mere footstool for a savage. When Valerian protests, Shapur has molten gold poured down his throat, has him flayed, has his skin stuffed with straw, and puts him on display in a temple. And whenever in future Roman emissaries approach the Persians, they are always beckoned into the temple, so they can see Valerian in all his dead imperial grandeur. **262** – The Temple of Artemis, one of the five remaining Seven Wonders of the World, is destroyed by the Goths. **268** – Emperor Gallienus is murdered by his own soldiers. **270** – Emperor Quintillus is murdered by his own soldiers. **272** – In Lutetia (Paris), Saint Denis and his companions are beheaded for preaching on the road leading to the temple of Mercury. Denis is not put off by such a distraction, however – and, so the story goes, picks his head up, and walks another six miles with it, continuing his sermon all the way. When the sermon ends, Denis realises he is actually dead and should fall over, and that spot becomes the future burial place for the kings of France. Denis becomes the country's patron saint – and the hill which he so supernaturally climbed is Montmartre – literally, Martyr's Mount. At least when Denis dies, his death means something. It's not just the latest in a series of pointless coups and stabbings, he gets to show off an entire miracle in the process. A shrine is built and no-one even dreams of hanging his flayed skin within it. *It was my present. My book. I knew then, I knew – I would either conquer history, and make it mine – or I'd be frightened of it forever. I waited until the house was asleep. I went downstairs, so carefully. I went out into the garden. My heart was thumping in my chest. I wasn't sure what I was most frightened of: the still of the night, or the hundreds of deaths waiting for me in the wheelie bin. I fished the book out. It was covered with old teabags. It felt colder, wetter. The Wise Old Owl was pointing his wand, and right at me. And I spoke to him. I dared him. I said, if you can make me dead, make me dead now. The Owl could do nothing. He was all feather and bluster.* **275** – Emperor Aurelian is mobbed, and hacked to death by sword. **276** – Emperor Tacitus is killed by his own soldiers. **276** – Emperor Florianus is killed by his own soldiers. **282** – Emperor Probus is killed by his own soldiers. **283** – Emperor Carus is killed... by a freak bolt of lightning. At this point it might be worth noting, every single Roman Emperor seems to come to a particularly sticky end, stuck, in fact, on the wrong end of something very sharp. Which begs the obvious question. Why would anyone want the job? Were the emperors at this time just exceedingly dim? And I think the answer goes back to what Vespasian said when he died way back in 79 AD, and the mocking words of King Shapur of Persia, too. These poor stooges are in thrall to the charms of history. They hear the name of Caesar, and they think of Julius, of Augustus; they believe, sad fools, that they will follow in their tradition, that in spite of all the blood and chaos around them that when they take that imperial seat that somehow they'll be catapulted back to a time in which they too could have been special. Carus is lucky. Good for Carus. He doesn't reign more than a few months, but still, imagine the relief when the lightning's volts hit him. At least when he dies, frazzled and fricasseed, he can pretend that he's still popular. (It's worth noting – sadly – that after his death, the senate ensures that any reminder of Carus is destroyed, his name is struck from all official lists, and his memory is damned. So he may have not been so popular after all.) *I took the book back to bed. I read it under the covers. I read all the dates of death. And I began to write them out, on a piece of paper, I would make them mine, I wrote them all out, one by one. In strict chronological order.* **284** – Emperor Numerian is killed by his father-in-law. **285** – Emperor Carinus is killed by his own soldiers, etc. etc. Enough, enough! **291** – In China, the War of the Eight Princes. There's a power vacuum in Luoyang; Emperor Hui is nominally in charge, but he's mentally ill, and his stepmother exerts the greatest authority over him. There emerge eight separate princes from the Sima clan to challenge this. Take a deep breath: Hui's wife Jia calls upon Sima Yao and Sima Wei to overthrow the stepmother. This gives power to Sima Liang, Hui's grand-uncle. This isn't what Jia has in mind, so she convinces Sima Wei to kill Sima Liang. Then denounces Sima Wei, and has him executed. Jia then has Sima Yu killed, who is her stepson. With me so far? Sima Lun, the guard commander, rebels against Jia, has her killed, and seizes power. This angers Sima Yao (remember him?) who leads a rebellion of his own, which results in Sima Yao being killed by Sima Lun. In response, Sima Jiong pops up out of nowhere, and leads a coalition with Sima Ying and Sima Yong against Sima Lun. Sima Lun is killed. Sima Jiong then sets himself up as sole powerbroker over Hui, which only antagonises all the surviving Sima princes, and is killed by Sima Ai. Sima Ai is bumped off by Sima Yue. Sima Ying takes charge of Hui, and flees Luoyang with him; he's defeated in battle by Sima Yong, who is defeated in battle by Sima Yue. Sima Yue has Sima Ying and Sima Yong put to death. So at the end of 15 years of (greatly confusing) conflict, Sima Yue is the winner! Emperor Hui certainly isn't; he probably doesn't have a clue what's going on, and Sima Yue does the only really rational thing and poisons him. And the struggle has depopulated the whole of northern China... No, really, enough.

RESTORATION

The Curator said that it was the responsibility of every man, woman and child to find themselves a job; that there was a grace and dignity to doing something constructive with the long days. The purity of a simple life, well led – everyone could see the appeal to that. But the problem was, there really just weren't enough jobs to go around. This made a lot of people quite unhappy. Not so unhappy that they gnashed their teeth or rent their garments, it wasn't unhappiness on a Biblical scale – but you could see them, these poor souls who had nothing to do, there seemed to hang about them an ennui that could actually be smelt.

Some people said that it was patently unfair that there weren't enough jobs. The Curator could create as many jobs as he wished, he could do anything, so this had to be a failing on his part, or something crueller. And other people admonished these doubters, they told them to have more faith. It was clearly a test. But they thought everything was a test, that was their explanation for everything.

Neither group of people liked to voice their opinions too loudly, though. You never knew when the Curator might be listening. The Curator had eyes and ears everywhere.

When the job at the gallery came up Andy applied for it, of course. *Everyone* applied for it, yes, man, woman and child – and though Andy hadn't been there long enough yet to realise the importance of getting work, he still knew the value of joining a good long queue when he saw one. He obviously hadn't expected to get the job. That he might do was clearly absurd. And so when they told him he'd been selected he thought they were joking, that this was another part of the interview, that they were monitoring his response to success, maybe – and he decided that the response they were looking for was probably something enthusiastic, but not *too* enthusiastic – and he managed to pull off a rather cool unsmiling version of enthusiasm that he thought would fit the bill, then sat back in his chair waiting for the next question – only starting from the cool, unsmiling reverie when they made him understand there really *weren't* any more questions, that that was it, the job was his.

Andy didn't know why he'd got the job. But he still had his own hair. Or, at least, most of it – and perhaps that's what made him stand out from the other applicants. Certainly there were others he'd queued alongside who were far better qualified, and more intelligent too, who had even done revision so that they'd give good answers at the interview. When Andy had been quizzed he hadn't known what to say, and he'd just nodded his head a lot, he fluttered at them his brown and quite unremarkable curls, unremarkable in all ways save for the fact he had so many of them; he showed them off for all they were worth, that's what did him well in the end.

Andy hadn't even been to an art gallery since he was a child. He'd been taken on a school trip. He'd been caught chewing gum, and had got into trouble; then he'd lagged behind the main party and got lost somewhere in the Post-Impressionists, the teacher had had to put out an announcement for him, he'd got into trouble for that too. He knew that the gallery here would be much bigger, because everything was bigger here – but he still boggled at the enormity of it as he walked through the revolving doors. There were no small exhibits here. A single work of art would take up an entire room, and the rooms were *vast*, as you walked into one you had to strain your eyes to find the exit at the far end – the picture would run right round all the walls, and extend right up to the ceiling a hundred feet in the air. Andy couldn't stand back far enough from the art to take in the sheer scale of even a single picture; he always seemed to be pressed up close to the figures caught in the paintwork, he could honestly marvel at the extraordinary detail of each and every one of them. But seeing these figures in context, that was much more difficult. He read the plaque on the wall for one picture: '1776', it said. And now he could see, yes, the Americans jubilantly declaring their independence, and the British all looking rather sinister and sulky in the background. He went through into the next room, and presented there was 1916. And 1916 was a terrifying sight – the work took in the one and a half million soldiers dying in the trenches, in Flanders, at the Somme, and it seemed to Andy that every single one of these casualties was up there stuck on to the wall, shot or blown apart or drowning in mud. It was a dark picture, but yet it wasn't all mud and blood – look, there's Charlie Chaplin falling over at a skating rink, there's Al Jolson singing, Fred Astaire dancing, there's the world's first golf tournament, that'd be fun for all.

Andy shuddered at the carnage in spite of himself – because, as he said out loud, it wasn't really there, it wasn't really *real*. And he couldn't help it, he chuckled at Chaplin too, he grinned at all those golfers putting away to their hearts' delight.

There was no-one to be seen at the gallery. The rooms were crowded with so many people living and dying, but on the walls only, only in the art – there was no-one looking at them, marvelling at what they'd stood for, marvelling at the brushwork even. There was a little shop near the main entrance that sold postcards. There was no-one behind the cash register.

'What do you make of it?' asked the woman behind him.

He didn't know where she'd sprung from, and for a moment he thought she must have popped out from one of the pictures, and the idea was so ludicrous that he nearly laughed. He stopped short, though, because she was frowning at him so seriously, he could see laughter wasn't something the woman would appreciate, or even recognise, this was a woman who hadn't heard laughter in a very long time. He presumed she *was* a woman. Surely? The voice was high, and there was a softness to the eyes, and to the lips, and there was some sagging on the torso that might once have been breasts – yes, he thought, definitely woman. Her head was completely smooth and hairless, and a little off green, it looked like a slightly mildewed egg.

Andy tried to think of something clever to say. Failed. 'I don't know.'

'Quite right,' said the woman. 'What *can* you make of it? What can anyone make of anything, when it comes down to it?' She stuck out her hand. Andy took a chance that she wanted him to shake it; he did; he was right. 'You must be my new assistant. I don't want an assistant, I can manage perfectly well on my own, I do not require assisting of any sort. But the Curator says different, and who am I to argue? The best thing we can do is to leave each other alone as much as possible, it's a big place, I'm sure we'll work it out. Do you know anything about art?'

'No.'

'About history?'

'No.'

'About the conservation and restoration of treasures more fragile and precious than mere words can describe?'

'No.'

'Good,' she said. 'There'll be so much less for you to unlearn.' And she gave at last the semblance of a smile. Her egg face relaxed as the smile took hold, the eyes grew big and yolky, the albumen cheeks seemed to ripple and contort as if they were being poached.

'How did you know,' said Andy, 'that I was your new assistant?'

'Why else would you be here?'

She said she'd take him to her studio. She led him out of the First World War, back through the Reformation, through snatches and smatterings of the Dark Ages. She walked briskly, and Andy struggled to keep up – as it was, it was the best part of an hour before they reached the elevator. 'I'll never find my way through all this!' Andy had joked, and his new boss had simply said, 'No, you won't,' and they hadn't talked again for a while.

She pulled the grille door to the elevator shut. 'Going down,' she said, and pushed at the lowest button on the panel. Nothing happened; she kicked at the elevator irritably, at last it began to move – and fast, faster, as if to make up for lost time. Andy was alarmed and tried to find something to hold on to, but all there was was the woman, and that didn't appeal, so he stuck his hands tight into his pockets instead. The woman did not seem remotely perturbed. 'Now, you might think that the gallery upstairs is huge. Well, it *is* huge, I suppose, I've never been able to find an end to it. But only a small fraction of the collection is ever on display. Say, no more than two or three percent. The rest of the art, the overwhelming majority of it, we keep below. We keep in the vaults. And it's in the vaults that we care for this unseen art. We clean it, we protect it. We restore it to what it used to be. What's up top,' she said, and she jerked a finger upwards, to somewhere Andy assumed must now be miles above their heads, 'is not our concern any more.'

Andy was still catching up with what she'd said fifty metres higher, his brain seemed to be falling at a slower rate than hers. 'Just two or three percent? Christ, how many paintings have you got?'

She glared at him. She thinned her once feminine lips, she showed teeth. 'They're not paintings,' she said. 'Never call them paintings.'

'I'm sorry,' said Andy, and she held his gaze for a few seconds longer, then gave a single nod, and turned away, satisfied.

The elevator continued to fall.

'My name's Andy,' said Andy, 'you know, by the way.'

'I can't remember that. I can't be expected to remember all that.'

'Oh.'

'You've got lots of hair. I could call you Hairy. Except that won't last long, the hair won't last, it'll just confuse me. Tell you what. I'll call you "Assistant". That'll be easy for both of us.'

'Fair enough,' said Andy. He'd been about to ask her her name. He now thought he wouldn't bother.

And then he was surprised, because he felt something in his hand, and he looked down, and it was *her* hand – just for a moment, a little squeeze, and then it was gone. And she was doing that macabre poached smile at him. 'Don't worry, Assistant,' she said softly. 'I used to call them paintings. I once thought they were just paintings too.'

*

'All right, Assistant. I'm giving you 1574 to practise on. 1574 is a very minor work. If you damage 1574, who's going to care?' And she unrolled 1574 right in front of him, across the table of his new studio, across *all* the studio – she unrolled it ever onwards until 1574 spread about him and over him in all directions.

'Is this the original?'

'Who'd want to make a copy?'

What surprised Andy was that the archives down below were in such poor condition. The art was stacked everywhere randomly, although he was assured by his new boss there was a system – 'It's *my* system,' she said, 'and that's all you need to know.' Some of the years were in tatters, the months bulging off the frame, entire days lost beneath dirt. 'You might suppose they'd be irreparable,' she told him. '1346 was in a terrible state when I started here, there was a crease in the August, running right through the battle of Crecy. But with diligence, and hard labour, and love, I was able to put it right.'

It was odd to hear her talk of love, that such a word could come out of a bald ovoid face like hers. She seemed to think it was odd too, looked away. 'But diligence and hard labour are probably the most important,' she added.

And although Andy had no affection for these works of art, had no reason to care, when she told him that the collection wasn't complete he felt a pang of regret in his stomach for the loss. 'Ideally,' she agreed, 'the gallery is meant to house a full archive, from prehistory right up to 2038. But there are entire decades that have vanished without trace. Stolen, maybe, who knows? More likely destroyed. Some years were in such a state of disrepair there was nothing I could do with them, some years just decomposed before my eyes. 1971, for example, that was a botched job from the start, the materials were of inferior quality. It crumbled to dust so fast, before the spring of 1972 was over.'

'What does the Curator think of that?'

She sighed heavily through her nose, it came out as a scornful puff. 'The Curator's instructions are that I take responsibility for the entire collection, the whole of recorded history.' She shrugged. 'But I can't work miracles. That's his job.'

And now here was Andy with his own year to take care of. He gave 1574 a good look. And his boss gave *him* a good look as he did so; she just folded her arms, watched him, said nothing. 'It's not too bad,' said Andy finally. 'It's not in as bad a condition of some of the others.'

'It's in an *appalling* condition,' she said. 'Oh, Assistant. You've been looking at all the wrong things, you don't know what's good and what's shit, but never mind, never mind, I suppose you have to start somewhere. Look again. Now. The year is *filthy*, for a start. Look at it, it's so dark. Do you think that 1574 was always this dark? Only if it had been under permanent rain clouds, and in fact, the weather was rather temperate by sixteenth century standards. Now, that's not unusual, you have to expect the original colours to darken. Natural ageing will do that – pigments fade and distort from the moment the events are lived, as soon as they're set down on canvas. Rich greens resinate over time, they become dark browns, even blacks. The shine gets lost.

'But in this instance,' she went on, and prodded at 1574 with her finger, so disdainfully that Andy thought she'd punch a hole right through it, 'it's worse than that, because we can't even begin to *see* how badly the pigments have been discoloured. They're buried behind so much dirt and grease. And soot, actually, that's my fault, I probably shouldn't have stored it next to the Industrial Revolution. Dirt has clung to the year, and that's not the fault of the year itself, but of the varnish painted over it. For centuries all the great works of art were varnished by the galleries, they thought it would better protect them. And some people even preferred the rather cheesy gloss it put on everything. But a lot of the varnishers were hacks, the varnish wasn't compatible with the original oils of the year itself, it'd react with them. And that's when you get smearing, and blurring, and dirt getting trapped within the year as if it's always been there.

'And that's just for starters! Look at the cracks. Dancing through the night sky of March 1574 there, do you see, they stand out so well in the moonlight. Now, I admit I like a bit of craquelure, I think it lends a little aged charm to an old master. But here, yes... these aren't just cracks, they're *fissures*, they're causing the entire panel to split out in all directions. Pretty soon March won't have thirty-one days in it, it'll end up with thirty-two. And that's all because of the oils drying, yes? The oils go on the canvas nice and wet, then they dry, the very months dry, the days within get brittle and flaky, the whole year contracts and moves within its frame.'

'And what can we do to stop that?' asked Andy.

She very nearly laughed. 'Stop it? We can't stop it! Oh, the arrogance of the man! Do you think *any* of the years here are in the same condition as when they were created? They're dying from the moment the paint has dried, all the sheen and brightness fading, the colours becoming ever more dull, the very tinctures starting to blister and pop. These are precious things, these little slices of time we've been given – and from the moment a year's over, from the moment they all start singing to usher in the new, the old one is already beginning to fall apart. The centuries that pass do untold damage to the centuries that have been, there's no greater enemy to history than history itself, running right over it, scraping it hard, then crushing it flat. And some days I think that's it, all I'm doing is kicking against the inevitable, I can do nothing to stop the decay of it all, all I can do is choose the method of decay it'll face. And that's on the good days, the ones where I fool myself I'm making the blindest bit of difference – on the others, and, are you listening, Assistant, there'll be so *many others*, I feel like I'm surrounded by corpses and pretending I can stop the rot, and I can't stop the rot, who are we to stop the rot, we're working in a fucking morgue.'

'Oh,' said Andy. 'That's a shame.'

She blinked at him. Just once. Then pulled herself together.

'Frankly,' she said, '1574 is a dog's breakfast. And that's why I'm setting you on to it. You're hardly likely to make it much worse. Off you go, then, 1574's not getting any younger, is it?'

Andy pointed out he had no idea where to start conserving and cleaning a year.

As far as he knew, he was supposed to run it under a tap! He chuckled at that, she didn't chuckle back. So he asked, very gently, whether he could watch her work for a while, to see how it was done.

She took him to her studio.

'This,' she said, and she tried to keep a nonchalance to her voice, 'is my current project.' But Andy could see how she was smiling, she was just happy to be back in front of her work again – and then she gave up trying to disguise it, she turned round to him and *beamed*, she ushered him forward, invited him to look, invited him to see how well she'd done. She'd mounted a section of the year, the rest was rolled up neatly, and it seemed to Andy that she'd made an altar of that section, that it was a place of worship. '1660,' she said. 'Most famous for the restoration of the Stuarts to the British throne, and I think that's why the Curator will like this year especially, he's very keen on the triumph of authority. But there's so much more to 1660 than dynastic disputes, really – December the eighth, there's Margaret Hughes as Desdemona, the very first actress on the English stage! And that's Samuel Pepys, the diarist, September twenty-fifth, drinking his first ever cup of tea! All the little anecdotes that throw the main events into sharp relief, history can't just be kings and thrones, if you're not careful it becomes nothing but a series of assassins and wars and coups d'etat, and the colour is just a single flat grey. And that's not what we're about, is it? We've got to find the other colours, Andy, we've got to find all the colours that might get forgotten, what we're doing *is* important after all!' And she suddenly looked so young, and so innocent somehow, and Andy realised she'd bothered to remember his name.

He watched her as she worked, and she soon forgot he was there, she was lost in bringing out the light in Pepys' eyes as his first taste of tea hit home, his questing curiosity, his wonder (his wrinkle-nosed disgust!) – and she was happy, and she even began to sing, not words, he didn't hear any words, she seemed at times to be reaching for them but then would shake her head, she'd lost them. And she didn't notice when he sneaked away and closed the door behind him.

*

Over the following weeks Andy began to fall in love with 1574.

It wasn't an especially distinguished year, he'd have admitted. It was most notable for the outbreak of the Fifth War of Religion between the Catholics and the Huguenots – but this was the *fifth* war, after all, and it wasn't as if the first four had done much good, so. It was marked by the death of Charles IX, King of France, and Selim II, Sultan of the Turks, and try as he might, Andy couldn't find much sympathy for either of them. The Spanish defeated the Dutch at the battle of Mookerheyde – when Andy picked off the surface dirt he could see all the surviving Spaniards cheering. And explorer Juan Fernández discovered a series of volcanic islands off the coast of Chile, and he named them the Juan Fernández Islands, and it was a measure perhaps of how little anyone wanted these islands discovered in the first place that the name stayed unchallenged.

But none of that mattered.

For research Andy had looked at 1573 and 1575, the sister years either side, and they were really very similar at heart, with a lot of the same crises brewing, and a lot of the same people causing those crises. But Andy didn't like them. In fact, he despised them. It was almost as if they were both faux 1574s, they were trying so hard to be 1574 and just falling short, it was pathetic, really. He'd dab away with his cotton swabs, removing the muck that 1574 had accumulated, and he poured his soul into it, all his effort and care, he gave it the very best of him, 1574 *was* the very best of him. And he loved it because he knew no-one else ever would, this grisly year from a pretty grisly century all told, twelve unremarkable little months that had passed unmourned so many centuries before.

He would dream of 1574 too. Of living in 1574, he could have been happy there, he knew it. It wasn't that he needed to sleep; no-one needed sleep any more, sleeping acted as a restorative to the body and it wasn't as if his body could possibly be restored. But he went to sleep anyway, as useless as sleeping was. He slept so he could dream. 1574 would have been perfect for him, so long as he'd kept away from all those Catholics and Huguenots, they were a liability.

One day his boss came to see him. He was so enjoying the work, he was rather irritated that he had to put a pause to it and give her attention.

'You've completely smudged that night sky in October,' she said.

'I was a bit too free with the solvent,' Andy admitted.

'And God knows what you've done to the craquelure in Spain, it's worse than when you started.'

Andy shrugged.

'You're really very good,' she said. 'I'm impressed.'

'Thank you.'

'You don't need to thank me.'

Her new-found respect for his work meant that that she began to visit more often. Every other day or so she'd come to peer at his 1574, clucking her tongue occasionally (in approval or not, Andy couldn't tell) tilting her head this way and that as she took it in from different angles, sometimes brushing key areas of political change and social unrest with her fingertips. Andy minded. And then Andy found he'd stopped minding, somehow – he even rather looked forward to seeing her, it gave him the excuse to put down the sponge and give his arms a rest.

'What was your name again?' she asked one day.

Andy thought for a moment. 'Andy,' Andy said.

'I like you, Andy. So I'm going to give you a piece of advice.'

'All right,' said Andy.

'There's only so much room in a head,' she said. And she smiled at him sympathetically.

'... Is that it?'

'That's it.'

'Fair enough,' said Andy. And she left.

She came back again a day or two later. 'It occurs to me,' she said, 'that the advice I offered may not have been very clear.'

'No.'

'You remember that I came by, offered advice...?'

'Yes, I remember.'

'Good,' she said. 'Good, that's a start. I like you, sorry, what was your name again?'

Andy sighed. He lay down his cotton swab. He turned to face her. He opened his mouth to answer. He answered. 'Andy,' he said.

'It's an absorbing job, this,' she told him. 'It kind of takes over. You fill your head with all sorts of old things, facts and figures. And memories can be pushed out. Personal memories, of what you did when you were alive, even what your name was. There's only so much room in a head.'

'I'm not going to forget my own name,' Andy assured her.

'I did,' said his boss simply, and smiled.

'I'm sorry,' said Andy.

'Oh, pish,' she said, and waved his sympathy aside. 'Names don't matter. Names aren't us, they're just labels. Names go, and good riddance, I don't want a name. But who we *were*, Andy, that's what you need to hang on to. You need to write it down. I did. For me, I did. Look.' And from her pocket she took out a piece of paper.

'1782,' the message read. 'Tall gentleman, wearing top hat. Deep blue eyes, the bluest I've ever seen. And the way the corners of his mouth seem to be just breaking into a smile. Special. So special, you make him stand out from the crowd, you give him definition. Make him count.'

'I carry it with me everywhere,' she said. 'And if I ever lose myself. If I ever doubt who I am. I take it out, and I read it, and I remember. That once I was in love. That once, back in 1782, there was a man, and out of all the countless billions of men who have lived through history, against all those odds, we found each other.'

And she was smiling so wide now, and her eyes were brimming with tears.

'You don't know his name?' asked Andy.

'I'm sure he had one at the time. That's enough.'

She put the paper away. 'Write it all down, Andy,' she said. 'Don't waste your efforts on all the unimportant stuff, your job, your house, whether you had a pet or not. That's all gone now. But your wife, describe your wife, remind yourself that you too once loved and were capable of inspiring love back.'

'Oh, I didn't have a wife,' said Andy.

The woman's mouth opened to a perfect little 'o'. She stared at him.

'I never quite found the right girl,' Andy went on cheerfully.

The mouth closed, she gulped. Still staring.

'You know how it is. I was quite picky.'

By now she was ashen. 'Oh, my poor man,' she said. 'My poor man. You must have already forgotten.'

'No, no,' Andy assured her. 'I remember quite well! I had the odd girlfriend, some of them were very odd, ha! But never the right one. Actually, I think they were quite picky too, ha!, maybe more picky than me, ha ha! Look, no, look, it's all right, it doesn't matter...'

Because he'd never seen her egg-white face quite so white before, and her eyes were welling with tears again, but this time she wasn't smiling through them. 'You must have forgotten,' she insisted. 'You must have been loved, a man like you. Life wouldn't be so cruel. Oh, Andy.' And impulsively, she kissed him on top of the head.

'You're beginning to lose your hair,' she then said.

'Am I?' asked Andy.
'You should watch out for that.'

*

She didn't visit for a while afterwards, and it wasn't surprising at first, he knew how easy it was just to get lost in the work, but after a bit he began to wonder whether he might have offended her in some way – he couldn't remember what way that might have been – and he supposed it didn't matter if he had, he didn't like her very much (or did he? – he didn't *recall* liking her, that had never been a part of it, but) but, but then he realised he missed her, that her absence was a sad and slightly painful thing, that he should put a stop to that absence, he should set off to find her. So he did. He left 1574 behind and went looking for 1660, and he couldn't work out how to get there, he walked up and down corridors of the twelfth century, and then the tenth, it was all a bit confusing, there were Vikings every which way he looked. And it began to bother him that he couldn't decide where 1660 came in history, was it after 1574, was it before? And he thought, sod it, I'll turn back, and he walked in the direction he had come, but somehow that brought him to the fifth century, and there were no Vikings now, just bloody Picts. He didn't think he could find 1574 let alone 1660, and he started to panic, and he was just about to resign himself to the idea of settling down with the Anglo-Saxons, maybe it wouldn't be so bad – when he turned the corner, and there, suddenly, was Charles II restored to the throne, there was Samuel Pepys, there was *she*, there she was, sitting at her desk, paintbrush in hand, and all but dwarfed by the Restoration in full glory.

'Hello,' he said.

But she didn't reply, and he thought that maybe she was concentrating, she didn't want to be disturbed, and he could respect that, he'd have wanted the same thing – so he waited, he bided his time, so much time to bide in all around him and he bided it. Until he could bide no more – 'Hello, are you all right?' he asked, and he went right up to her, and she still didn't acknowledge him, he went right up to her face. And her eyes were so wide and so scared, and her cheeks were blotched with tears, and her lips, her bottom lip was trembling as if caught in mid-stutter, 'No,' she said, or at least that's what he thought it was, but it might not have been a word, it might just have been a noise, 'nonononono.' 'Do you know who I am?' he asked, and she looked directly at him, then recoiled, it was clear she didn't know *anything*, 'nonono,' she sobbed, and it wasn't an answer to his question, it was all she could say, each 'no' popping out every time that bottom lip quivered. 'Do you know who I am?' he asked again, 'I'm...' and for the life of him at that moment he forgot his own name, how ridiculous, 'I'm your assistant, yes? I'm your *friend*.' And he moved to touch her, he wanted to hold her, hug her, something, but she slapped him away, and the tears started, she was so very frightened. 'I'm your friend,' he said, 'and I'll look after you,' and he knocked aside the slaps, he held on to her, and tight too, he held on as close as she'd let him, and he felt her tears on his neck, and they weren't warm like tears were supposed to be, oh, they were so *cool*. 'I'm your friend, and I'm going to look after you, and I'll never stop looking after you,' and he hadn't meant to make a promise, but it was a promise, wasn't it? and 'Just you

51

remember that!', but she didn't remember anything, not a thing – and he held on to her until she *did*, until at last she did.

'Andy?' she said. 'Andy, what's wrong?' Because he was crying too. And she looked so surprised to see him there, and so glad too – and he thought, *Andy*, oh yes, *that* was it.

*

One day, as Andy was sponging down a particularly anonymous Huguenot, she came to him. She looked awkward, even a little bashful.

'I've been thinking,' she said. 'You can give me a name. If you like.'

Andy turned away from 1574. 'I thought you didn't want a name.'

She blushed. 'I don't mind.'

'All right,' he said. 'What about Janet?'

She wrinkled her nose.

'You don't like Janet?'

'I don't,' she agreed, 'like Janet.'

'Okay,' he said. 'Mandy.'

'No.'

'Becky.'

'No.'

'Samantha. Sammy for short.'

'Tell you what,' she said. 'You give it a think, and when you come up with something you like, you come and find me.'

'I'll do that,' said Andy.

He resumed work on his Huguenot. The bloodstain on his dagger-gouged stomach shone a red it hadn't shone in hundreds of years. Andy worked hard on it, he didn't know for how long, but there was a joy to it, to uncover this man's death like it was some long lost buried treasure, and make it stand out bold and lurid and smudge-free.

Next time she came she was wearing a ribbon. He didn't know why, it looked odd wrapped around her shiny bald forehead. Why was the forehead so shiny? Had she done something to it? 'I've been thinking,' she said.

'Oh yes?'

'What about Miriam?'

'Who's Miriam?'

'Me. I could be Miriam.'

'You could be Miriam, yes.'

'Do you like Miriam?'

'Miriam's fine.'

'Do you think Miriam suits me?'

'I think Miriam suits you right down to the ground,' said Andy, and she beamed at him.

'All right,' she said. 'Miriam it is. If you like it. If that works well for you.'

'Hello, Miriam,' he said. 'Nice to meet you.' And they laughed.

'I love you,' she said then.

'You do what, sorry?'

'I think it's so sad, that no-one ever loved you.'

'I don't know that *no-one* ever loved me...'

'And at first I thought this was just pity for you. Inside me, here. But then it grew. And I thought, that's not pity at all, that's love.' She scratched at her ribbon. It slipped down her face a bit. 'I mean, I might have got it wrong, it might just be a deeper form of pity,' she said. 'But, you know.'

'Yes.'

'Probably not.'

'No.'

'Probably love.'

'Yes.'

'I want you to know,' she said, 'what it feels like to inspire love. You inspire love. In me.'

'Well,' he said. 'Thank you. I mean that.'

'Do I inspire love in you?'

'I hadn't really thought about it,' said Andy.

'Would you think about it now?'

'All right,' he said. 'Yes. Go on, then. I think you do.'

'Oh good,' said Miriam.

She left him then. He got back to his dying Huguenot. The Huguenot seemed to be winking at him. Andy didn't like that, and swabbed at the Huguenot's eyes pointedly.

When Miriam returned the ribbon was gone, and Andy thought that was good, it really hadn't looked right. But, if anything, the forehead was shinier still. And there was a new redness to the lips, he thought she must have spilled some paint on to them.

'If it is love. Not just pity on my part, confused politeness on yours. Would you like to *make* love?'

'We could,' Andy agreed.

He hadn't taken off his clothes for years now. But they were removed easily enough, it was just a matter of tugging them away with a bit of no-nonsense force. Miriam's clothes were another matter, they seemed to have been glued down, or worse – Andy wondered as they tried to peel them off whether some of the skin had grown over the clothes, or the clothes had evolved into skin, or vice versa – either way they weren't budging. It took half an hour to get most of the layers off, but there were patches of blouse and stocking that they couldn't prise away even with a chisel.

They stood there – he, naked, she, as naked as they could manage without applying some of the stronger solvents.

'You go first,' she said, and he thought he could take the responsibility of that – but then, as he came towards her, he stopped short, he couldn't recall what on earth he was supposed to do. He looked at her, right at her egg face, and she was smiling bravely, but there were no clues offered in that smile, and he looked downwards, and it seemed to him that both of her breasts were like eggs too, perched side by side on top of a rounded belly that was also like an egg – her whole hairless body was like a whole stack of eggs inexpertly stitched together, God, he was looking at an entire omelette! And though she wasn't beautiful, it was nevertheless naked

53

flesh, and it was vaguely female in shape, and his prick twitched in memory of it, in some memory that it ought to be doing *something.*

'I do love you,' he said. 'I love you too,' she replied. And they approached the other. And they reached out their hands. And their fingers danced gently on each other's fingers. And he stroked his head against her chest. And she bit awkwardly at his nose. And they bounced their stomachs off each other – once, twice, three times! – boing! – and that third bounce was really pretty frenzied. Then they held each other. They both remembered that part.

The next time she came to visit him in his studio they had both completely forgotten they'd once tried sex. And perhaps that was a blessing. Andy was absorbed in an entirely new Huguenot corpse, and she seemed to have grown new clothes. But she remembered her name was Miriam now, and so did he; they clung on to that, together, at least.

*

1574:

In February the so-called Fifth War of Religion breaks out in France between the Catholics and the Huguenots; the Fourth War had only ended six months previously. War Number Four didn't, as you might gather, end very conclusively. The Huguenots were given the freedom to worship – but *only* within three towns in the whole country, and *only* within their own homes, and marriages could be celebrated but *only* by aristocrats before an assembly limited to ten people outside their own family. King Charles IX dies shortly afterwards. He was the man responsible for the slaughter of thousands of Huguenots in the Saint Bartholomew's Day Massacre. Reports say that he actually died sweating blood; he is said to have turned to his nurse in his last moments and said, 'So much blood around me! Is this all the blood I have shed?'

And then

In November, the Spanish sailor Juan Fernández discovers a hitherto unknown archipelago. Sailing between Peru and Valparaiso, and quite by chance deviating from his planned route, Fernández stumbles across a series of islands, no more than seventy square miles in total area. Fernández looks about him. There are bits of greenery on them. They're a bit volcanic. They're not much cop. He names them after himself, and you can only wonder whether that's an act of grandeur or of self-effacing irony. For the next few centuries they serve as a hideout for pirates; then the tables are turned and they make for an especially unattractive new penal colony.

And then

In December, Selim II, sultan of the Ottoman Empire, dies. Named by his loving subjects as Selim the Drunkard, or Selim the Sot, he dies inebriated, clumsily slipping on the wet floor of his harem and falling into the bath. His corpse is kept in ice for twelve days to conceal the fact he's dead and to safeguard the throne until his chosen heir, his son Murad, can reach Istanbul and take power. On arrival Murad is proclaimed the new sultan, and there is much rejoicing, and hope (as ever) for a new age of enlightenment; that night he has all five of his younger brothers strangled in a somewhat overemphatic attempt to dissuade them from challenging his new authority.

And then

Andy's hair fell out. It had been a slow process at first. For weeks he'd had to keep picking out stray strands from the solvent, he kept accidentally rubbing them into the picture – Juan Fernández' beard seemed to grow ever bushier, Charles IX died sweating not just blood but fur. And then, one day, it poured out all at once, in thick heavy clumps that rained down on his shoulders – and Andy was fascinated at the amount of it, it seemed he wasn't just losing the hair he already had but all the potential hair he could *ever* have had, the follicles were squeezing the hair out in triple quick time, as if his skull had contained nothing but a whole big ball of the stuff just waiting to be set free. The hairs would bristle out towards the light, thousands of little worms making for the surface, now covering his scalp and chin, now turning his head into a deep plush furry mat – and then, just as soon as the hairs seemed so full and thick and *alive* they'd die, they'd all die, they'd jump off his head like so many lemmings jumping off cliffs – and Andy couldn't help feel a little hurt that all this hair had been born, had looked about, and had been so unimpressed by the shape and texture of the face that was to be their new home they'd chosen to commit mass suicide instead.

And then

The hair stopped falling, there was simply no hair left to fall. And then – Andy had to sweep it all up; it took him quite a while, there was an awful lot of it, and he resented the time he spent on doing that, this was work time, this was 1574 time. And then and then and then – he forgot he had ever had hair at all, he had no thoughts of hair, his head was an egg and it felt good and proper as an egg, 1574 was all he could think of now, 1574 was all there was, 1574 ran through him and over him and that's what filled his skull now and all that was ever meant to, Huguenots, drunken sultans, the flora and fauna of the Juan Fernández Islands, 1574 for life, 1574 forever.

And then...

*

And then sometimes she would visit him and he'd have forgotten who she was, and sometimes he would visit her and she'd have forgotten who he was. But most times they remembered, and the memory came on them like a welcome rush. And they might even celebrate; they'd put their work aside, they'd get into the clapped-out old elevator, pull the grille doors to, and ascend to the main gallery itself. And they'd walk through the exhibits on display, they'd turn the lights down low so it was more intimate, low enough that to see the art properly they'd have to squint a bit, as if even for just a little while it wasn't the most important thing in the room; they'd walk through the centuries together, but not be overwhelmed by the centuries, they'd walk at such a gentle pace too, they were in no rush, they had all the time in the world; they'd walk hand in hand. And Andy thought they must look such a funny pair, really. Almost identical, really, bald and white and plain – she just a little shorter than him, he a little more flat-chested than her. They must have looked funny, yes, but who was there to see? (Who was there to tell?)

He didn't like it when he forgot her. So he wrote down on a piece of paper a reminder, so that whenever he felt lost or confused he could look at it and find new purpose. 'Miriam,' he wrote. 'She's your boss. Works with you here at the gallery. Very good with the varnish. Works too hard, takes herself too seriously, not much of a sense of humour, but you know how to make her smile, just give it time. Not pretty, she looks like she's been newly laid from a hen's backside, but that doesn't matter, she's your friend. She's the only one that knows you, even when she doesn't know herself.'

One day Miriam came to find Andy, and he remembered who she was clearly, he remembered her at a glance without the aid of the memo. And he smiled and he got up and took her by the hand, and she said, 'No, not today, Andy, this is business.' And she looked sad, and maybe a little frightened, and the bits of her face where she'd once had eyebrows seemed to bristle in spite of themselves.

She'd received a missive from the Curator. It had come in an envelope, bulging fat. She hadn't yet opened it.

'I don't see what's to worry about necessarily,' said Andy. 'Isn't it good that he's taking an interest?'

'This is only the third missive he's ever sent me,' said Miriam. 'The first one was to appoint me to this gallery, the second one was to appoint you to me. He doesn't care what we get up to here.' She handed him the envelope. 'This is bad. You read it.'

But it didn't seem so bad, not at first. The Curator was very charming. He apologised profusely for giving Miriam and Andy so little attention. He'd been up to his eyes, there was so much to do, a whole universe of things under his thumb, and regretfully the arts just weren't one of his main priorities. But he was going to change all that; he was quite certain that Miriam and Andy had been working so very hard, and he was proud of them, and grateful, and he'd be popping into the gallery any time now to inspect what they'd been up to. No need to worry about it, no need for this to be of any *especial* concern – no need for them to know either when his visit might be. Remember, it was all very informal; remember, he'd rather surprise them unawares; remember, remember – he had eyes and ears everywhere.

That he referred to them both as Miriam and Andy was a cause for some concern.

And he finished by adding a request. A very little request, attached as a P.S.

The Curator said there were two ways of looking at history. One, that it was all just random chance, there was no rhyme or reason to any of it. People lived, people died. Stuff happened in between. This seemed to the Curator rather a cynical interpretation of history, and not a little atheistic, didn't Miriam and Andy agree? The second was that there was a destiny to it all, an end resolution that had been determined from the beginning. The story of the world was like the story in a book, all the separate years just chapters building up to an inevitable climax – meaningless if read on their own, and rather unfulfilling too. The entire span of world history only made sense if it was considered within a context offered by that climax – and what a climax it'd been! 2038 really was the Curator's absolute favourite, he had such great memories of it, really, he'd think back on it sometimes and just get lost in the daydream, it was great.

And that's why the Curator wanted to see, in all the years preceding, some hint of the end year to come. He didn't want them to interfere with the art they'd been conserving – no – but, if within that art they saw some little premonition of it, then that'd be good, wouldn't it? Maybe they could *emphasise* his final triumph, they could pick out all the subtle suggestions throughout all time of his ineffable victory and highlight them somehow. The value of art, the Curator said, is that it reflects the world. What value then would any of these years have if they did not reflect their apotheosis? Their preservation would be worthless; no, worse, a lie; no, worse, treason itself. History had to have a pattern. And up to now Miriam and Andy had been working to conceal that pattern – with diligence, he knew, and hard labour, and love, he could see there'd been lots of love. All that had to stop, right now.

And if they couldn't find any premonitions to highlight, maybe they could just draw some in themselves from scratch?

Miriam said softly, 'It goes against everything I've ever done here.'

Andy said nothing for a long while. He took her hand. She let him. He squeezed it. She squeezed it back. 'But,' he then said, and she stopped squeezing, 'but if it's what the Curator wants,' and her hand went limp, 'and since he owns all this art, really...' and she took her hand away altogether.

'It's vandalism,' she said. 'I can't do it, and I don't care if it's treason to refuse. You... you, Aidan, whatever your name is... you do what you like.'

She left him.

He studied 1574. He looked at it all over. He knew it so well, but it was like seeing it with fresh eyes, now he was trying to find a part of it to sacrifice. He took out a pen. An ordinary modern biro, something that future conservationists could tell was wrong at a glance, something that wouldn't stain the patina or bleed into the oils underneath. Andy wasn't much of an artist, and so the demon he drew over the battle of Mookerheyde was little more than a stick figure. It looked stupid hovering there so fake above the soldiers and the bloodshed. He didn't even know what a demon looked like, he'd never seen one, he'd imagined that Hell would have been full of the things but they'd always kept to themselves – and so his drawing of a demon was really just the first thing that came to mind. He gave it a little pitchfork. And fangs. And a smiley face.

He wondered if this would be enough to satisfy the Curator, and thought he better not chance it. He drew a second demon over Juan Fernández discovering his islands. The pitchfork was more pointy, the smile more of a leer.

He went to find Miriam. She was crying. He was crying too. And that's why she forgave him.

'I don't want you taken from me,' he said, and he held her. 'Please.'

'I'm sorry. It's a betrayal. I'm sorry. I'm sorry.'

'Then I'll do it. Let me do all the betraying. I'll betray enough for both of us.'

And they would walk the gallery again, hand in hand through the centuries. But this time, as they reached the end of a picture, Miriam would stop, she'd turn away, she'd close her eyes. And Andy would get out his pen, sometimes just a biro, sometimes a Sharpie if the year was robust enough to take it, and he'd draw in a demon or two. And Andy was surprised at how much easier it got, these acts of desecration; and his demons were bigger and more confident, sometimes they fitted in to the action superbly, sometimes (he thought secretly) they even improved it. He desecrated 1415, he desecrated 1963, he desecrated each and every one of the years representing the First World War. And it seemed to Andy that he was beginning to see the Curator's point; he'd see there was something foreboding about these years, maybe there *was* something in the design of them all that forecast the apocalypse.

But she wouldn't let him touch 1660. 'It's mine,' she said.

One night they reached the 1782 room. The Americans were in the throes of revolution, the French were chuntering on towards theirs. Andy thought 1782 had great potential, there were plenty of places where a demon or two would fit the bill. Miriam stood up close to the year. She reached out. She stroked it. When she pulled her hand away, Andy could see that her fingers had been brushing the image of a man in a top hat. His eyes were the most gorgeous blue, and around his mouth played the hint of a flirtatious smile.

Miriam took out the piece of paper from her pocket. She read it. She dropped it to the floor.

'It's the man you loved, isn't it?' said Andy.

'No.'

And she reached out again, stroked the face again. This time Andy could see it wasn't done with affection, but with professional enquiry. 'I must have worked on this,' she said. 'Look at the man's face. There was a rip here, from the neck, up to the forehead, look, it took out one of his eyes. I worked on this, I recognise my handiwork. I put his face back together.'

And now that he was looking closely, Andy could see she was quite right. The work had been subtle, and so delicately done, but an expert could see the threads that bound the cheek flaps together.

'What I'd written down, it wasn't a memory,' said Miriam. 'It was an instruction for repair. I never knew this man. I never loved him, and he never loved me. All I ever did was to stitch his face up.'

She ran.

By the time Andy caught up with her she was back at her studio. She was painting. Each stroke of her brush was so considered, was so small, you'd have thought that not a single one could have made the slightest difference – but their sum total was extraordinary. On the canvas she had created a demon. And the oils she'd chosen were perfect, they seemed to blend in with the background as if the demon had always been part of 1660; and its eyes bulged, and saliva was dripping from its mouth, its horns were caught in mid-quiver; it looked at the complacent folly of the seventeenth century with naked hunger. And it hung over the shoulders of King Charles II as he celebrated the restoration of the Crown, the spikes of its tail only an inch away from the Merrie Monarch's face, if Charles just turned his head a fraction to the right his eye would get punctured. And the demon's presence seemed artistically *right*, it was an ironic comment upon fame and success and the paucity of Man's achievements – yes, the King was on his throne, but time would move on, and the human race would fall, and nobody could stop it, or nobody *would*, at any rate; and all of this, even this little slice of long past history, all would be swept away.

'It's beautiful,' said Andy. 'At painting, you're. Well. Really good.' It sounded quite inadequate. And had Andy not known better, he'd have thought the demon in the picture rolled its eyes.

'I know,' said Miriam. But she wouldn't look at him.

*

They didn't know when the Curator came to visit. Only that another missive was sent one day, and it said that his inspection had been carried out, and that he was well pleased with his subjects.

They hoped that would be the end of it. It wasn't.

*

The Curator's final missive was simple, and straight to the point. He said that he thought the work of the gallery was important, but that the art on display wasn't; there was only one significant year in world history, the year of his irrevocable triumph over creation, all the bits beforehand he now realised were just a dull protracted preamble before the main event.

He wanted to display 2038. And only 2038. 2038 was big enough, 2038 could fill the entire gallery on its own. All the other years could now be disposed of.

There were jobs going at the gallery, and everyone queued for them, man, woman and child. And this time everyone was a winner, they *all* got jobs – really, there was so much work to do! The chatter and laughter of a billion souls in gainful employment filled the rooms, and it looked so strange to Andy and to Miriam, that at last the art they had preserved had an audience. They squeezed in, the gallery was packed to capacity – and yes, everyone would stare at the pictures on show, and perhaps in wonder, they'd never seen anything so splendid in all their lives – or maybe they had, maybe they'd lived the exact moments they were ogling, but if so it was long forgotten now, everything was forgotten. They'd stare at the pictures, every single one, and they'd allow a beat of appreciation, of awe – and then they'd tear them down from the walls.

And there were demons too, supervising the operation. So that's what they looked like, and, do you know, they looked just like us! Except for the hair, of course, their long lustrous hair.

The people would rip down the years, and take them outside, and throw them on to the fire. They'd burn all they'd ever been, all they'd experienced. And over the cries of excitement of the mob you'd have thought you could have heard the years scream.

And once they'd destroyed all that had been on view in the public gallery, the people made their way down to the vaults. Miriam stood in her studio, guarding 1660 with a sharpened paintbrush. 'You can't have this one.' And a demon came forward from the crowd, just a little chap, really, and so unassuming, and he punched her once in the face, and her nose broke, and he punched her hard on the head, and she fell to the ground. She didn't give them any trouble after that.

Andy found her there. She wasn't unconscious as he first thought; she simply hadn't found a reason to get up yet.

'This is all because of you,' she said. 'You made me fall in love with you, and it drew attention. This is all because of us.'

And in spite of that, or because of it, he gave her a smile. And held out his hand for her. And she found her reason.

They went through the back corridors, past the hidden annexes and cubbyholes, all the way to his studio. 1574 was still draped over it, higgledy-piggeldy, January and December were trailing loose along the ground. Andy had never managed to learn even a fraction of the order Miriam had insisted upon, and for all that her life's work was in ruins, she couldn't help but tut. But seeing 1574 like that, less an old master, more a pet, it was suddenly homely and small, not a proper year, a year in progress – it was a hobby project that Andy liked to tinker on, it had none of the grandeur that the Curator was trying to stamp on and destroy. And for the first time, Miriam surprised herself, she felt a stab of affection for the old thing.

'We can save 1574,' he told her.

And she knew it was worthless. That had the Curator sent his thugs to take 1574 from the beginning, she'd have given it up without a second thought. An unnecessary year – but now she helped Andy without a word, he took one corner and she the other, and together they rolled it up. And because it *was* so unnecessary, it rolled up very small indeed, and Andy was able to put it in his pocket.

No-one stopped them on the way to the elevator. There was nowhere to go but up. And there was nothing up there. Not any more.

Andy pulled the grille doors closed. He pressed the highest button that there was, one so high that it didn't even fit upon the panel with all the other buttons, it had to have a panel all of its own. It hadn't been pressed for such a long time, there wasn't much give in it, and when it finally yielded to Andy's finger it did so with a clunk.

The elevator didn't move for a few seconds.

'Come on,' said Andy, and kicked it.

*

The lift doors opened out on to the Earth. And there was no air, there was no light, there was no dark. There was no *time*, time had been stripped out and taken down to the art galleries long ago, time had been frittered away then burned.

'We can't stay here,' said Miriam. 'I love you. I'd love you anywhere. But this isn't anywhere, I can't be with you here.'

But Andy took 1574 out from his pocket. And holding out one end of the scroll, he *flung* out the other as far as he could. And the year unrolled and flew off into the distance. And when it had unrolled all that it could, after it had sped over the crags that had once been continents and oceans, when the far end of it could be seen flying back at him from the opposite direction, Andy caught hold of it, and tugged it flat, and fixed the end of December to the beginning of January. And it lay across the earth, all the lumps and bumps, and yet it was still a perfect fit.

'This won't last. He'll come and get us in the end,' said Miriam.

'He will. But not for another 450 years.' And then Andy kissed her, straight on to the mouth. He hadn't remembered that's how you were supposed to do it, but suddenly it just seemed so logical. And they kissed like that for a while, one mouth welded to the other, as the Middle Ages settled and stilled around them.

*

They'd bask for a bit in August if they wanted the sun; then, to cool down, they'd pop over to February and dip their toes in the chill. And if they wanted to be alone, away from all the kings and sultans and soldiers and peasants and peoples set upon their paths of religious intolerance, then they'd hide in November – and November on the Juan Fernández Islands, just before Juan Fernández himself arrived on the scene. They spent a lot of time there. Alone was good.

They practised making love. If the mouth on mouth thing had been inspired, it was the tongue in mouth development that was the real breakthrough. They kissed a lot, and each time they did they both felt deep within the stirrings of dormant memories – that if they just kept at it, with diligence and labour, then they'd work out the next step of sex eventually.

'I love you,' Andy would tell her, and 'I love you,' Miriam would reply. And they both wrote these facts down, privately, on pieces of paper, and kept them in their pockets always.

Miriam's nose healed. It didn't quite set straight, but Andy preferred it the new way; the very sight of its off-centre kink as it came up at him would set his heart racing faster. And the bruise where she'd been struck at last faded too. In its place there grew a single, shiny, blonde hair. Miriam felt it pop out of her skull one day and squealed with delight.

'It's all coming back,' she said to Andy. 'Everything's going to be all right again.'

And Andy had seen enough of history to know that one lone random hair didn't necessarily mean much. But he laughed indulgently as she combed it into position, and she laughed at his laughter, and then they both forgot what they'd been laughing at in the first place – but that was all right, that they were happy was all that mattered. And then they started the kissing again, and all they knew and heard and felt was each other, and they ignored the stick figure demon chattering and giggling above their heads.

304 – The martyrdom of St Lucia. According to legend, Lucia is plagued by a suitor who has fallen head over heels in love with her. He besieges her with his attentions. He begs her to become his wife. She simply isn't interested; could he leave her alone now, please, so she can get on with studying the Bible? When he complains that he is haunted by the beauty of her eyes, she cuts them out, and sends them to him with a message suggesting that he can now leave her to her devotions. Rather aptly, St Lucy becomes the patron saint of blindness. *My mother taught Sunday school and, I think, sincerely; Jesus wasn't mentioned much at home, but I never doubted that Mother was on more than a nodding acquaintance with him. I used to watch as she somehow transformed herself in front of all the other children – the way her face would light up as she told us Bible stories, would light up with purpose. Mother liked stories, but only if they had a happy ending or a moral – which I suppose to a person of faith is much the same thing. And so she approved of my new love for history. After all, in history the wars always ended sooner or later, and the right side invariably won; the evil empires were always toppled eventually; everyone died, but the goodies went to heaven.* **313** – Roman history is gobbling up its emperors. Emperor Severus has been made to open his veins; Emperor Maximian is found hanged in the palace; Emperor Diocletian starves himself to death. Emperor Maximinus Daia, too, determines to take his own life. He chooses poison, and decides that the last meal he takes it with will at least be one he enjoys: he throws a huge banquet of rich food and drinks lots of wine. The practical upshot of this is, most unfortunately, that a poison that would normally be very speedy isn't properly absorbed into his now bloated stomach. It takes him four whole days to die, and as he's waiting, he goes completely mad. He eats dirt to try to numb the pain, and eventually slams his head so hard against a wall that his eyes fall out of their sockets. And then – and this is where we can see a sea change in historical attitudes towards Christianity – before he dies, the blind Maximinus reputedly finds God and converts. **315** – Maximinus isn't the first emperor to claim conversion on his deathbed. Galerus, who dies in agony from testicular cancer in 311, and gives off such a stench that his doctors can't bear to get close enough to treat him, suddenly exclaims before his final moments that he believes in Jesus Christ and calls an end to all persecutions. (He does, however, have his doctors beheaded for retching uncontrollably at his stink.) But technically, the first true Christian emperor is Constantine the Great. Historians report that at the battle of Milvian Bridge he dreams he's instructed to put a sign of Christ on his soldiers' shields. With a new religion to power them on, Constantine's army utterly annihilate their enemies, and Constantine is convinced: from this moment, it's Jesus all the way! Constantine becomes an emblem for the Catholic Church from this point on, and chroniclers of the time start writing in unlikely last-gasp conversions for the 'bad' emperors before him. And history undergoes a massive rewrite. And when history changes, even retrospectively, future time changes as a result, as it struggles to live up to a past that never necessarily took place. **316** – St Blaize is martyred by having his skin torn off by iron combs, and is subsequently made the patron saint of woolcombers. You'd have thought that it would have been a rather tactless position to be given, and combs would really be the last thing he wanted to spend eternity considering. At least St Lucia had a chance to become something of an expert on blindness; for Blaize, combs were just something that happened to him, why should the poor sod have to be defined by them? **320** – Forty Roman soldiers are left naked on the middle of a frozen lake in Armenia, and told they can only be allowed to warm up by the fire if they renounce their faith in Christ. The choice is simple – if they believe in this new god, they must become martyrs to him. Only one soldier recants. The remainder stand there and die. And so impressed is one pagan soldier by their constancy, that he strips off and joins them and takes the place of the deserter. **336** – The very first Christmas is celebrated. **337** – On the death of Constantine the Great, the Roman Empire is divided amongst his three sons. Whatever you might say about Constantine – his establishment at the Council of Nicea of the first consensus for Christian belief, the way in which he strengthened and consolidated an empire that had fast been dissolving into chaos – any man who names his children Constans, Constantine and Constantius suffers either from a raging ego or a woeful lack of imagination. *If you're not afraid of death (and my mother never was), then I suppose that all history does have a happy ending. They say that history is guaranteed that, because it's always written by the winning side. But I'm not so sure that's true, actually. I think that at the time history is written no-one has a clue whether they're the winners or not, no-one can get the perspective to tell. If we had to say who the winners are now, really, at the beginning of the twenty-first century, would future generations agree with us? That just because we can see the times we live in, and smell them, and touch them, and maybe even influence them – why should that make us experts over a bunch of academics hundreds of years from now who've got the future equivalent of Wikipedia at their fingertips? When if they don't like the facts, they can change the interpretation of them retrospectively, they can change what we were all thinking or feeling, they can edit our stories to make sure they're consistent with the way the future plays out.* **363** – One Roman Emperor stands against the tide of Christianity. His name is Julian, and the nickname he earns is the Apostate. I find it hard not to feel some sympathy for him; he gives Christianity a go (as I did, with my mother in attendance), and he finds it wanting. Not only does he think the New Testament is of poor literary quality (as stories go, the Greek classics are just that much better written), but for all their religious purity the three brothers in the Constantine gang had murdered his brother. Julian declares himself a pantheist; he believes that there is a divine force present through the whole of nature. And alone amongst the assassinations and suicides of his imperial predecessors, his death has 'hero' written all over it. He rides into battle against the Persians, and is so keen to be at the forefront of the danger that he forgets even to wear his armour. Separated from his bodyguards, from his own army, he fearlessly attacks an enemy who a century ago so deeply humiliated Valerian and what the Roman Empire stood for. You can imagine him out there, fighting to preserve that dignity that the old histories had taught him – even though they're histories for a nation changed beyond recognition, a land that now worships Jesus Christ rather than the traditions that made Rome great. He's struck by a spear – deep, it sticks into his liver; trying to pull it out, he severs the very tendons of his fingers. He is dismounted. He is carried back to camp. There on his deathbed he tries to comfort his grief-stricken friends, he even indulges in a little philosophy about the divine nature of the soul. Christian historians claim that his final words are, 'You've won, Galilean!' And, of course, the Galilean has. Because Julian is the right emperor at the wrong time. He's a failure, brushed away from the history books, because he's tragically out of step with the changing world. But there's a magnificent dignity to this brave forgotten emperor, a man who dares to question the faith that's presented to him. And I only wish he'd been one of those represented by the Wise Old Owl in that specious catalogue he made of the great and the good and the noble. **364** – Julian's successor, Jovian, dies soon after him. Reports differ on the reason for his demise. He is killed by excessive consumption of mushrooms. Or he is killed by inhaling too much smoke from a brazier. Or he is killed by the fumes from the new paint in his bedroom. Either way, in this instance, the Wise Old Owl got it right when he omitted him from his book. *All those historical figures so lionised in my Wise Old Owl book – how would they know they'd be future heroes? Good Queen Bess, Bonnie Prince Charlie, Alexander the Great – how lovely to be called good and bonny and great – but they all just died the same, didn't they? Facing the unknown?* **365** – St Hilary of Poitiers faithfully predicts that this is the year the world will end. He's wrong. *Did Jesus know? That's what I would have liked to have asked my mother. Did Jesus know when he died upon that cross that he was a hero? And that he was changing history forever? Surely he had doubts, there wasn't just the self-satisfied 'forgive them they know not what they do' but a despairing 'why hast thou forsaken me?' Don't you think there was a chance he thought he'd blown it, he was dying for nothing, he was another obscure failure swept along in the wash of time? (And don't you think that would make his legacy somehow all that bit more impressive still? It's hard for me not to find Jesus just a little bit smug – he comes to Earth, sets up a plan to get himself killed, and in the process alters on both grand and personal levels the lives of billions of people. I have a lot more sympathy for him if even at his apotheosis, nailed to a cross, he believed there was another boy from that carpentry school reunion w ho'd done something better with his life.)* **375** – Emperor Valentinian wins a war against the Quadi, who send envoys to offer their surrender and sue for peace. But Valentinian is in a royally bad mood that day, victory or no victory. As he prepares to meet the Quadi, his horse rears up on its hind legs just as he's about to mount it. The disgruntled emperor orders the right hand of the stable boy to be cut off. The Quadi arrive. They beg forgiveness, but Valentinian is already out of sorts, and flies into a rage. He harangues the ambassadors, he tells them they should be grateful to the Romans for defeating them. And then, suddenly, he stops still. The words choke in his throat. His face turns red, he loses breath, he loses consciousness, he loses his life. The fool has enraged himself into a heart attack. **385** – Priscillian, the bishop of Avila, is executed for heresy. He is therefore the first person in the Christian church to be killed for believing in Jesus in a different way to the majority. It's the first legalised instance, after over 300 years of being persecuted by outsiders, of Christians persecuting their own. **389** – Emperor Theodosius I (later canonised as Saint Theodosius) massacres 7,000 rebels in Thessalonica. He then performs a public penance for his actions. So that's all right. **391** – The great library of Alexandria was founded some seven hundred years ago, its mission to gather all the world's knowledge. It is the first clear attempt in history to put aside concerns of nationalism, and reach beyond the petty confines of state borders for the common good of all. Here, scholars from far and wide research new mathematics, astronomy, physics; here, the concept of science itself is first put into practice. In the murk of this long and confused distant past it stands as a bright light, a beacon of hope that mankind might develop, become something better than it could be or even should be. Theodosius, however, has outlawed paganism. And the books contained within the library are not Christian. So the library is destroyed. **395** – On the death of Theodosius, the empire splits into two. It will never again be a single power. At this stage, the area surrounding Rome is a malaria infested swamp. *And my mother bought me an exercise book, so I could start writing a time chart. I had a new devotion. I didn't go to Sunday School again.*

DIRT

After sex Duncan liked to stretch out. He liked to take full possession of the bed, he'd spread out like a starfish, one leg would go to one corner, the other to the other, and he'd open out both his arms and reach for the walls. If it was a moment of selfishness he felt he deserved it, he put in a lot of effort during sex, he tried to be as sensitive and attentive as could be. And it was hard work too, he was nearing forty now and he could get a little winded with all that effort; frankly, the sex was fun but hardly relaxing; frankly, the stretching out afterwards was one of the best bits.

And it wasn't as if he could do it at home, because his wife got in the way. So after he'd had sex with Natasha he was especially pleased that she got up without his even dropping a hint, she didn't need all the reassuring cuddles Annie did, up Natasha bounded and went straight to the sink. Ran the tap and began washing away, scrubbing at her face, her hands, her fanny. He stretched out as far as he could, enjoyed the way his limbs now felt uncoiled and loose, and watched her.

'That was nice,' he said. 'Are you all right?'

'Oh yes,' she said, and turned to him, and smiled. 'I like to be clean.'

It hadn't been the first time they'd had sex. There'd been that time on Thursday, when they'd gone for a walk together in the evening. She said she had something she needed to ask him about, and that it was quite private, she didn't know who else to turn to. And he said that he was there to help, that was his job, she should feel free to say whatever she liked, he was a friend. Think of him as a friend – and it was quite balmy outside, really, for October at least, why not take a stroll with him? She told him that she wasn't enjoying university very much. She was a bit lonely. He asked her whether she'd left a boyfriend at home, and she wrinkled up her nose and said that didn't bother her, that was just sex, she'd had that before, boys would always be up for that. But she didn't have many friends, all the other students thought she was a bit odd. And that was fine, she said, she didn't want their friendship, but once in a while she felt lonely all the same. Everyone around her was so *young*! And she said it so fiercely, this little girl with that little girl's face suddenly pouting, it was all he could do not to laugh. And he told her she wasn't odd, that wasn't the word, she was *special*. And she wasn't young either; okay, technically she was young, if you went by age and years and things, but she was clearly very smart, she had an old soul. And they fucked in his car. Car sex wasn't great, you couldn't stretch afterwards, not without doing yourself a mischief on the gear stick. And she hadn't been particularly good at it, and she hadn't been much better in bed either, when he'd suggested they try somewhere more comfortable three days later. But she was okay. And he liked the way she got up afterwards and let him stretch.

She'd already put on her glasses. She was washing her face around them, which Duncan thought seemed rather odd. She only took them off for the actual fuck, she left them on even for kissing, he kept knocking his nose against the lens.

'I don't suppose we're going to be doing this again?' And, 'It's okay,' she added quickly, and turned from the mirror to flash him another look, another smile, 'it doesn't bother me, I'm not in love with you or anything, and I bet you've got a wife, I bet. I'm sorry, I'm being rude, would you like a cup of tea, I've got some tea.' Duncan asked if she had anything stronger, and she smiled, and said she was afraid not – she didn't drink very often, not really. She didn't smoke, or do drugs, only drank alcohol on special occasions. Vodka only, only on special occasions. No, she didn't have any vodka.

And it was then that Duncan found the little plastic bag under her pillow. 'You've been holding out on me!' he laughed. His arms had done as much stretching as they could, and he'd just tucked his hands under his head, propping it up that bit higher so he could best work out how to answer her tactfully – no, he didn't think they should do this again, he was in love with his wife, of course he was, and this was just a minor lapse, no, okay, two minor lapses if you counted the incident with the gear stick – and it might be best if she didn't tell anybody, because yes, they were both fully mature consenting adults, but as ridiculous as it was in this day and age the university still frowned upon relations between students and faculty members, even though she wasn't *his* student, even though she wasn't in *his* faculty – Christ, he'd only slept with a handful of girls, and after that last one took the break-up so badly he really thought he might be in trouble, she'd very nearly reported him, this was why he'd *vowed* never to do this again, especially not twice, especially not with such an odd girl as this one – and that's when his fingers touched plastic, and teased at it because it felt so strange there, and pulled the little bag out into the open.

She looked at the bag, and blinked. 'It's dirt,' she said.

'I don't care about the quality...'

'No, really dirt. You know. Earth. Um. Soil.' And Duncan gave the bag another look, and he supposed it *did* look like soil, not much like dope at all. That said, he couldn't be sure, he wasn't an expert on dope. He was a tutor, so his only encounters with it came from obliging students as fully prepared spliffs, he never needed to see it in its natural plastic baggy form.

'May I...?' he said, and opened the bag, dipped his fingers into the dirt. And she immediately stiffened, made a move to stop him – saw she was too late, and shrugged as if she didn't care. 'Sorry,' he said, and carefully rubbed his fingers clean, making sure that every single speck fell back into the bag. She shrugged again, but this time she clearly relaxed.

He expected that she might say something in explanation, but instead she now busied herself around the kettle. He wondered whether he should ask the obvious question, but really didn't want to, and really wasn't sure he *cared*, actually – if a girl wanted to stash a bag of dirt under her pillow, really, wasn't that her own business? And there was silence for a while, and just as he thought he'd have to bite the bullet and ask anyway, just to break the tension, Natasha said, 'You're going to think I'm weird.' She said it very seriously.

'No, I'm not,' said Duncan. He suddenly felt very vulnerable, lying there naked on the bed, and pulled the duvet somewhat ineffectually over his privates.

'I always sleep with the soil,' said Natasha. She was still doing something with the kettle – what? surely it could boil by itself? 'It reassures me. You see, it comes from Russia.'

'I see,' said Duncan, at last. 'It's Russian soil.'

'It is.'

'I see,' said Duncan again.

And she came over and sat beside him on the bed. He shifted a little to let her, and hoped it didn't seem as if he were flinching. 'You'll have noticed that I have something of a passion for Russia,' she said.

And he hadn't. And now he looked around her little room, and saw that there were posters covering the breezeblocks – that was Lenin, and that was a sickle and hammer, and that was a map of the whole former Soviet Union marked in black, to Duncan it looked like one great dirty inkblot dwarfing the rest of Europe beside it. If he'd seen the posters at all he'd assumed that they were a typical student flirtation with radical politics, something cool to suggest she was just as distinctive as everybody else. But no, there were books on the shelves too – Dostoevsky, Tolstoy, Chekhov, and other writers he'd not heard of, Pelevin, Lermontov, Brodsky. He turned back to look at Natasha full in the face, and her eyes were gleaming behind those owlish spectacles of hers, and even though she was otherwise naked somehow even they made her look just a bit Russian too.

'Is there anywhere in the world where you just feel you *belong*?' And Natasha's eyes weren't gleaming, they were *blazing*. 'A place where you just, I don't know, make sense. Do you know? Know what I mean?'

'Oh yes,' said Duncan.

Natasha nodded. 'I'm Russian,' she said softly. 'I know that sounds silly, I've only been the once. I wasn't born there. But I have a Russian soul. Do you believe that? I need you to believe that.'

'Is there any part of Russia,' said Duncan slowly, 'how do I say, that you feel you particularly belong to, or...'

'No, no...'

'Or is it the whole...?'

'No, just Russia, the whole thing.'

'The whole thing,' said Duncan. 'Well. That's handy. It's a big country.'

'It is.'

'A lot of places to belong.'

Natasha nodded again, so earnestly, and her spectacles shook down her nose, and her boobs jiggled. 'The Russians *know*,' she said. 'They know what it's all about. We all think we're so important. With our daily lives, you know, our hopes, the lot. But the Russians believe in something greater than they are, that they're *not* just individuals, they're part of Mother Russia, they're part of a force, a movement, a belief, I... I'm not putting it very well.'

'No, go on,' said Duncan.

'They believe in something greater. We're all so selfish, we all think we're so fucking important,' and she swore so gently, and looked so excited like a little girl, it was really quite sweet. 'They believe in their mother country, all through history, the tsars, the Soviets, it doesn't matter what, they have an identity, they know who they are. They know who they are, we're all so fucking important, but we don't know who we are, do we? Do you know who you are?'

Duncan knew so much depended upon the right response, and gave just the slightest shake of his head.

'I'm part of something greater anyone here can understand,' she said, and it was a celebration, oh, those blazing eyes. 'I'm going to live in Russia one day, I know it. I don't speak Russian yet, but I'll learn it, I am already. And I'm going to marry a Russian man, I'm going to be so happy, just you see.' And at that he felt a sudden pang, he didn't want her to marry anyone, he didn't want her to go away – he wished he could make her eyes blaze like that, had he ever made anyone's eyes blaze, ever, really? – and he kissed her on the lips. 'Thanks,' she said, a little surprised. 'Hey, would you like to see my name in Cyrillic?'

'Sure,' he said, and up she leaped to her desk. She wrote carefully on a piece of paper. 'That's my name in Russian,' she said. 'That's me.' And the kettle gave a click as the water at last came to a boil. 'Do you want some tea?'

*

There was an envelope under his door the next morning. Inside was a sheet of card, and on it thick black Russian writing. There was a note with it – 'I thought you might like this. It's your name in the Cyrillic alphabet. I couldn't find an equivalent for Duncan, so I went with Dmitri. It's the closest I could get. Dmitri Brown.'

*

Duncan taught English literature, with particular emphasis upon the modern novel. He quite liked the modern novel, but he did wish that modern novelists would stop churning out quite so many of them, it made it very hard to catch up. He didn't think the other tutors respected him much, with their Miltons and their Chaucers and their Dickenses, and maybe that was why he'd still not been offered full tenure. When the suggestion had been made that for three nights of the week he could be a monitor in a student hall of residence, being on hand to help all the first years settle in and deal with any of their problems, he realised that the extra money would be useful. And Annie hadn't minded at all – not a bit of it. 'The nights you're not here will just mean the nights you are are more precious,' she said. 'You do what you need to do!'

He sometimes pretended she'd given him a knowing wink when she'd said that. That she was turning a blind eye to his little infidelities. That she was in some ways even urging him on. 'You do what you need to do!' she'd laugh at him, and so every Sunday, Tuesday and Friday he'd take an overnight bag on to campus, and sleep in one of the student domiciles. And, with increasing regularity, that domicile would be Natasha's.

He'd assumed that Natasha was studying something to do with Russia. Russian lit, or Russian history, there was probably even something on Russian music these days. But not a bit of it. 'Russia's my life,' she told him. 'I'd betray it if I *studied* it.' So he asked her what she did study, and she said it wasn't important, she was only taking a degree at all to ride out the time until she could be free to do what she wanted. 'No, but what is it?' he asked. 'Psychology,' she said, and wrinkled her nose. 'Yeah, I know.'

One night she asked him whether he'd like to handle her dirt. And he understood from the way she said it, so tentatively, ready to laugh it off if he said no, just what a big deal this was to her, and how close he'd come to blowing everything with his clumsiness before. He cupped his hands, and with due reverence she poured some of Russia out from the bag. He'd expected to feel ridiculous sitting there holding a few clumps of soil, but he didn't – she was awed, and he let himself be awed too. The dirt was grey and so very dry. 'This is Russia?' he asked. 'That's Russia,' she confirmed. 'Wow,' he said, and was rather impressed by how much he meant that. 'My Dad went on a business trip to Moscow,' she said, 'and took me along. I was twelve. I didn't want to leave. I think I screamed a bit on the last day, I think he was a bit ashamed, he smacked me. I wouldn't get on the plane without a piece of Russia, so I grabbed some of the ground, I filled my pockets with as much of the ground as I could, what you're holding there, Duncan, that's a bit of Sheremetyevo Airport.' Duncan looked at it with renewed respect. 'And I put it beneath my pillow, no matter where I stay, and I sleep on it every night, so every night my head is resting on Russia. Until I go back to Russia. Until I move to Russia for good.' 'And when you move to Russia...?' he asked, and she frowned, and said, 'Well, I won't need it then, will I? I mean, Russia will be all around me. It's only dirt, isn't it?'

She didn't like to mention her parents. 'They don't understand me,' she said. 'They think I'm odd.' Duncan said that was a shame, and she said she didn't care. 'When I live in Russia, I'll never see them again. It's as simple as that.' Duncan said that was a shame too, and she just said, 'They have other children.' Duncan said he wanted to understand her, she was such a special girl, he needed to understand – 'If you want to understand me, understand Russia. Read Tolstoy.' He supposed she was a Communist. 'No, Communism failed,' she said. 'Stalin and gulags. But at least Russia gave it a go.' So he supposed she liked the tsars. 'No, no, the tsars were worse than Stalin! You don't understand. If you want to understand, Tolstoy, read Tolstoy.' As a present she gave him a copy of *Anna Karenina*. It was a bulky book, and Duncan didn't have much time to read even the modern novels that were queuing for his attention. But for Natasha he tried; the Penguin classics edition weighed in at 800 pages of small type, so he calculated that if he got through fifty of them a day he'd finish the thing in little more than a fortnight. Natasha was impatient to see what he thought of it, so he quickly had to up his quota to sixty pages, then seventy-five. At first as tedious as homework, the novel grew on him, and although there were a tad too many chapters about ploughing fields for his tastes, he soon learned to skim these bits. When Anna finally killed herself he felt genuinely affected – her death was as much of a release to Duncan as it had evidently been to Anna. He told Natasha this, and she literally clapped her hands with delight. 'Now you understand! Now you understand *me*! Because I am Anna Karenina!' Duncan went a little pale at that, and told her earnestly that she should never throw herself under the wheels of a train – she must promise him that, it'd break his heart – and Natasha laughed as if he'd made the biggest joke, and kissed him.

And it wasn't just Russia; sometimes they'd discuss personal things. She never asked about Annie, she was too considerate for that. Or maybe she simply wasn't interested. But one day she did ask him about children. They'd just had sex, and it was afternoon sex, so they'd both need to get dressed again, they both had lectures to attend – he was stretching out like a starfish on the bed thinking idly about retrieving his trousers from off the floor, and she was scrubbing away all trace of him at the sink. God knows what made her think of children just then, scrub scrub scrub, but out came the question – did he regret not having any? And out came his reply, quick as you'd like – he told her that no, he'd never felt the urge for that, anything but! That as an academic he needed to live inside his head a lot, and he didn't want to live in some child's head as well. That in order to produce any great thoughts about modern novels he needed to be just a teensy bit selfish. Duncan had said such things for years, and even knew where to stick the little laugh to suggest that he didn't think he *was* that selfish, not really – but now as he said it it all just sounded so pat, so glib. He stopped short. He watched her as she dried herself with a towel. And he told her he thought maybe he did want children after all. He wasn't sure. He definitely hadn't in the past, he hadn't been pretending. Or he was fairly definite he hadn't been pretending. But now... Just perhaps. Perhaps he was missing out on a good thing.

'Yes,' Natasha said, a bit smugly, Duncan thought, and lit a roll-up. 'I knew that.'

'What do you mean?'

'You're drawn to me, and deep down it's because I'm fertile. Maybe not consciously, but that's what it's all about.'

He tried to deny that, told her that he wanted to be with her, you know, for her. But she just smiled. He asked her if she was particularly fertile then. 'Oh yes,' she said, and blew out smoke, and lay on the bed, and propped herself up beneath his shoulder, beneath Lenin. 'I'm fucking fertile, actually, darling.' Sometimes Duncan liked it when she called him 'darling', it made her sound so mature, it made her sound like they were equals.

Duncan did think for a moment that this self-revelation was rather important – or, at least, potentially important; it wasn't something he'd ever been able to express before, it wasn't something he'd even known he'd wanted to express. He couldn't have told Annie, it was too late there, it would have devastated her – but here, in the presence of this nineteen-year-old girl, so young and yes, so fertile too... he could tell her anything, he could find out things about himself he'd never have guessed. He could shape himself into someone new entirely. And he tried telling her that, tried telling her how important that made her (and, of course, how honoured). And he wondered whether this new void he'd discovered inside himself, this need for kids, might be something just a little bit ennobling, and a bit selfless, might be something he could even build a little mid-life crisis upon. And she just said, 'Yes, yes,' and laughed, and stubbed out her spliff, and kissed him on the mouth, and snuggled against his body to sleep. They both missed their lectures that day.

She'd taken to smoking dope in a big way, and Duncan rather suspected she'd done so to impress him. Sometimes he thought that was rather sad, but most of the time he simply didn't remember to care. She didn't keep the baggies under her pillow, but everywhere else in the flat, behind the books, beneath the underwear – but not under the pillow, not with Mother Russia, she was keeping her new passion apart from her old. And he didn't know, he supposed that at least was a good thing.

It wasn't just the dope – sometimes when he kissed her on the mouth he could taste beer on her breath, or cider, or flat wine, and he knew she must have been out at the bar again with all those other students she had once professed not to like. 'Oh, they're just friends,' she'd say. Whenever Duncan suggested they meet, Natasha would do her level best to accommodate – but he sometimes could tell that she had to break off with these other friends to do so. She was still an odd girl: she still only wore flat shoes, and no make-up, and long velvet skirts that billowed out and made her look a bit like a tsarina, she still always wore that black Russian hair of hers down and long all over her shoulders and back. But she wasn't *quite* so odd now, she was acceptably odd, she was clearly happier, more relaxed. Her eyes still blazed only when discussing Russia, but they now looked healthily bright when discussing all manner of other things – last night's TV, some band she'd seen at a gig, campus gossip. She was normalising. Duncan supposed he should be proud that he'd helped her to do that, that was supposed to be part of his job after all, to help out students who were having problems. And that one day when she left him (and he knew she would, surely) she'd look back on him with gratitude as a useful stepping stone towards social adequacy. And the thought of that turned his stomach into knots, and made him almost breathless with jealousy. 'We know why I'm with you, it's your fertility,' he joked one day in bed, but there was an edge to his voice that he couldn't hide – she didn't seem to notice it, though, or was just ignoring it if she had – 'but why are you with me? Psychoanalyse yourself. What on earth are you doing with a middle-aged nobody like me?' And she smiled, and kissed him on the cheek, not passionate, but nice, even maternal, and she put her head to one side seriously, so seriously, and considered. And said, 'Do you know, I'm still trying to work that one out.'

She still bought him books. He loved Dostoevsky and Gogol. He liked Turgenev even more than she did, she found him just a bit woolly. And he bought her presents too – he'd type 'Russian' into the search engine on eBay, he'd bid for Russian jewellery, Russian vases, Russian silks. She most liked the Russian dolls he won for her; she lined them up all along the top of her bookshelf, and they became her favourite hiding place for her dope. And they'd lie in bed together, and they'd discuss Russia, and he'd catch himself, and think, I'm only *pretending* to like Russia, surely!   and sometimes he'd think, surely, I'm only pretending to like her. They read to each other bits of Pushkin, and marvelled at his descriptions of Saint Petersburg. 'I so much want to visit Saint Petersburg,' she said. 'But I only want to do it with you, darling.' And they kissed on that, and then he promised her he'd only want to see it with her too – and on that they kissed again, longer and harder, and then they fucked on a sea of impossible holiday plans. 'We can go to the Hermitage!' she squealed, as he bounced around on her. 'We can walk down Nevsky Prospekt, arm in arm!'

And sometimes they wouldn't fuck at all, sometimes all they'd need to do was talk of Russia.

In December Natasha's first term as an undergraduate came to an end. She told Duncan that her parents would be picking her up. 'I don't want you to meet them,' she said. 'Will you promise me you won't try? I'm not ashamed of you. I'm ashamed of them. You do see?' He said he did. The morning before they were due to arrive he arranged it so he'd sleep with her – it wasn't a night he was scheduled to stay on campus, but he told Annie that the end of the semester was playing havoc with the schedules, and Annie didn't seem to mind. He gave Natasha a whole bag full of Christmas presents – more Russian jewellery, more dolls – and she told him she didn't celebrate Christmas, that's what everybody else did, it was the one time of year she wouldn't give presents on principle. He felt a bit crass. She gave him a little parcel, but it wasn't anything festive, she stressed it wasn't a Christmas present – indeed, it wasn't a present at all, this was just for safekeeping until she came back. The next morning Duncan stayed in his own room when Natasha's parents arrived – but he listened out for them behind his door, he hadn't promised he wouldn't do that. He heard them swagger down the corridor as if they owned the place; 'Have you learned anything useful yet?' said a man with a wheezy laugh who just had to be her father, 'Oh, your hair is such a mess,' said a woman, 'Claire, darling, why don't you get it cut?' Duncan watched from the window as they all crossed the car park. He'd half hoped that he'd see a family resemblance, get some clue where this Natasha of his had come from – maybe, with the mother, a clue where Natasha was heading towards too. But mother and father both looked so very English and soft, it really did look for all the world that they were kidnapping some poor foreign skivvy and taking her home to wait on them. Duncan waved at Natasha, but knew that she wouldn't be able to see him, not really – she wasn't wearing those owlish spectacles of hers.

'It's not a present, it's just for safekeeping until we're together again.' And she'd given him a plastic bag of his own, and in it was about half of the Russian dirt she'd taken from Moscow Airport. 'You can put it under your pillow,' she'd said. Duncan didn't put it under the pillow, he thought that Annie might find it. But he kept the little bag inside his jacket pocket, and fingered it every time he thought of Natasha, and every time he felt alone.

Christmas couldn't pass fast enough. In January Natasha returned. Once more Duncan waited in his room while her parents dropped her off. Then he went straight to hers, knocked on her door. Her hair had been cut. She wouldn't discuss that. She wouldn't discuss the Christmas holidays either. He hugged her. They kissed. 'I've missed you so much,' he said. 'I've missed you too,' said Natasha, 'can I have my soil, please?' 'Oh,' said Duncan. 'I'd rather hoped I could hang on to it. I'd rather hoped it could be my soil.' 'No,' said Natasha. So he gave it back.

*

In February Duncan was to turn forty. Natasha knew that, but she never referred to it. And nor did Annie, for the most part – which was why he was so surprised that evening she asked him whether reaching the milestone was going to cause him any concern. 'I know some people fall to pieces when they turn a decade,' she said. He said he was fine, actually; no, he was better than fine, he was pretty happy at the moment. So hitting his forties wouldn't bother him at all. And Annie said she was pleased, and said she'd *thought* he'd been happy recently, he'd certainly given her that impression. She'd turned forty herself a few years before, and it hadn't bothered her either – nothing bothered Annie, not ever. And that's when she told him she'd got a special birthday present prepared. A weekend holiday, just the two of them! To Saint Petersburg, she'd noticed he was taking an interest in Russia these days, there were all those books around the house. Wasn't that lovely? Wasn't that exciting? Didn't she deserve a kiss? And he tried to tell her that he wouldn't get the time off work, he had responsibilities to his students, for Christ's sake, *responsibilities* – and she laughed, and said she'd already called the department, and they thought it was all a great idea. So they'd fly out on the Friday afternoon, and back on the Sunday. That'd give them one full day for all the touristy things, and then a good few hours the next for shopping. She'd checked the guide books (oh, yes, she bought them in secret – and now she had Russian books of her own!) and she'd found out that you could get through all the important sights in a day, so long as you put your back into it.

As soon as he could, he texted Natasha. 'I need to see you,' he said. But it wasn't one of his evenings on campus, and she had other plans. 'cant u wait till sun?' she asked. 'No, it's really vitally important I see you, I'm so sorry, but it's a matter of the utmost urgency,' he wrote back, and an hour or so later she responded with an 'ok'.

'What's the matter?' she said when she opened the door to him, and straight away he put his arms around her and gave her a big hug, and clung on to her, and she said, 'Jesus, what is it?' And he told her that he was so afraid she'd be angry, and she said he should just come right out and say it. She gritted her teeth in readiness. And he explained the whole thing, and her teeth ungritted. 'Oh,' she said, 'well, never mind.' 'We'd promised to do Russia together,' he said, 'I always promised I'd only ever see it with you...' 'Yeah, I know,' said Natasha, 'but if Annie's bought the tickets, it can't be helped.' 'I thought you'd be so upset,' said Duncan, and Natasha thought about this, and said she was upset, a little bit. 'I knew you would be,' said Duncan. 'It's all right,' said Natasha, 'thinking it through. I mean, we'll still go one day, won't we?' 'We will,' said Duncan fervently. 'Well,' said Natasha, 'I was the one who introduced you to Russia in the first place. It's only right that you'll be the one who'll introduce me to Saint Petersburg.' She smiled at the thought. And he told her that she was adorable, she was so selfless, and so good, he thought she'd have been so jealous, he knew *he* would have been – and she said there wouldn't be much point, would there? There was never any point. 'You're so adorable,' he said, 'I adore you, I love you.' He'd never used the L word before. 'I love you too,' she said. 'Do you really?' 'I really do.' And they kissed, and she asked if he wanted to stay the night, and he said he couldn't really, and she said that he'd better not, no, she had a tutorial to prepare for anyway. They kissed again. And she said that this was something to celebrate, they'd both used the L word, she'd doubted they ever would – and she pulled out a bottle of vodka from under the bed, she only drank vodka on special occasions. And so they swigged vodka, and it *was* special, even though Duncan suspected she drank vodka rather a lot anyway. And they shared a spliff. And then Natasha said she'd better get on with her tutorial work, and Duncan said, right, right, and that he was about to suggest he should leave. 'Just don't do *everything* in Saint Petersburg,' said Natasha, 'leave something for us to discover!' And Duncan promised, and returned to Annie, and told her cheerfully she could book the flights, he'd sorted it, it was okay. And Annie reminded him she already *had* booked them. 'Oh yes,' he said.

She'd booked the flights with Aeroflot. After the aeroplane had taken off, and she pronounced that his birthday had now officially started, Annie gave Duncan an extra present. Something he could unwrap. She'd asked in the bookshop for a

Russian novel they'd especially recommend. Duncan thanked her. She asked him whether he already had it, and he assured her that of all the world-famous Russian classics in his now considerable collection, *Anna Karenina* was the very one he hadn't yet bought. He pretended to read it as she studied her guide book. 'I think I've got our itinerary sorted,' she said at last. After they'd landed, they caught a taxi to their hotel, somewhere cheap and central that boasted central heating as its major selling point. The double bed was as hard as a board. 'This is cosy,' said Annie. And they went out for an evening meal, and Duncan thought that they should try something essentially Russian, and so they found a little place that sold borscht. Annie said her borscht was fine, but a bit too beetrooty for her liking.

Next morning in the breakfast room he had Rice Krispies, while she pushed out the boat with her Raisin Bran. Then they set out to explore Russia. They went to the Hermitage. 'That's a lot of art,' said Annie. 'You can see why they had a revolution.' Then they went to the Church on Spilled Blood, built on the very site where Tsar Alexander had been murdered, and Annie found it all a bit morbid. They walked down Nevsky Prospekt, and there they saw the café where Pushkin had eaten his final meal right before being shot in a duel protecting the honour of his wife; it was now next door to a Kentucky Fried Chicken. Colonel Sanders was offering something fast and appetising in unreadable Cyrillic lettering. They popped into Saint Isaac's Cathedral ('lots more art') past the statue of the Bronze Horseman ('you wouldn't want to meet him in a dark alley!') and walked along the River Neva ('pretty'). Annie asked if Duncan would like her to take a photograph of him standing by the River Neva, and he said he would; then she asked if she could have a picture of her standing by the river too; then Annie stopped a passer-by who spoke perfect English to ask whether he'd take a picture of *both* of them, and he did, and that was great, it meant they had three pictures of themselves posing by the River Neva in every possible permutation. They walked further along the Neva, and found themselves back at the Hermitage. 'So that's Saint Petersburg done!' said Annie, and she closed her guide book with satisfaction. She said she was hungry, and agreed to have another traditional Russian dinner – but she couldn't face borscht again, and couldn't decide what she might prefer, so they ended up in Pizza Hut. A Deep Pan Super Supreme cost them fifteen hundred roubles, and Annie thought they'd been had.

The hotel room was very cold. Annie said, 'They've turned the central heating off, why turn the central heating off?' She cuddled up against Duncan for warmth. He turned out the light.

Eventually she said, 'Would you like to make love?'

'Oh,' he said. 'I hadn't been thinking to, actually.'

'We haven't for a while. I thought. Being on holiday... We are on holiday.'

'Yes, we are,' agreed Duncan. 'But the bed's a bit hard.'

'It is a bit hard,' said Annie.

There was silence in the dark. Silence, except for the distant pounding of Britney Spears from a nearby bar. 'I love you,' said Annie.

'Thanks,' said Duncan. And he added, 'I love you too.'

'I want to make love.'

'Yes,' said Duncan. 'Do you mind if we don't, though? It's been a long day, and I'm a bit tired. And not here, actually, do you mind if we wait until we get home? It feels wrong here. In Russia. Let's not make love in Russia. Annie? Do you mind?'

Silence. Britney Spears finished her song, started another. 'Yes,' said Annie. 'Yes, I do.' And she grabbed his penis, and pumped it into life.

The next day, as Annie browsed for blouses in Top Shop, Duncan took refuge in a souvenir shop. He found a postcard rack, just to the left of the shelves of matryoshka dolls as Disney characters. He bought a postcard, rather a nice one of Peterhof Palace framed with fireworks. 'Hello from Russia!' he wrote on it. 'Russia is shit. It's shit without you. I'm walking on Russian soil, and none of it is as good as the stuff you keep under your pillow. I wish you were here. I shouldn't be here without you. I love you. I love you. Lots of love, D.' And he put four 'x's. He stuck a stamp on it, popped it into a letterbox, and went back to Top Shop. 'I quite like this blouse,' Annie told him, 'but I can get the same one back at home. Shall we go?' 'Let's go,' he said.

As soon as they'd cleared baggage reclaim at Heathrow, he texted Natasha. 'I'm back! Russia was nothing without you. When can I see you?' She responded, 'Bet u smell of Russia! lol'. To that he said, 'Nothing without you. When can I see you?' 'Not this week, sorry, essay hell! Soon.' And Natasha put a sad face at the end of the message, which was supposed to make everything better.

He got back home at the end of the weekend. Until Thursday she still responded to his texts. Then she stopped altogether. He'd knock at her door in the halls of residence, but she was never in. 'I must see you,' he wrote to her. He wrote one message by text, the other on a piece of paper he slid under her door. 'Are you all right? Are you ill?'

At last he caught her on the Sunday. He was knocking at the door, ever so softly, if she were ill he didn't want to disturb her – and she opened it. She didn't seem at all surprised to see him. 'What?' she asked. 'Hello, Natasha,' he said casually, 'I was just wondering how you were.' 'Oh, you'd better come in,' she snapped at him, so in he went.

'Is something the matter?' he asked.

'I got your postcard,' she said.

'Oh yes,' he said. 'Sorry about that. You wouldn't believe the day I was having. Was I too forward? I was too forward. Did I say the wrong thing? The L word. I did, didn't I, Natasha?'

She let him suffer for a few seconds longer, and then spoke. 'I don't care what you wrote on the postcard,' she said. 'Don't you see? You wrote it *on a postcard*. You sent me a bloody *postcard*.'

'There wasn't a very good selection,' said Duncan.

'The Russia I love doesn't *have* postcards,' she said. 'It's the Russia of Tolstoy. It's the Russia of the tsars, of white nights, of troikas. Not postcards. Not sell-out bits of tourist shit like postcards.'

'Right,' said Duncan. 'No, I get it. Sort of.'

'You're saying Mother Russia is a whore. You're saying my mother is a whore.'

'I don't think I was saying that,' said Duncan. 'Look. You must know that Russia *does* postcards...'

'Of course I know Russia does postcards! I'm not stupid. But it doesn't mean I ever expected to *receive* one. Not from you. I loved you.'

'Right,' said Duncan. 'And I love...'

'And I loved Russia too. But no. Not any more. It's dead to me. You've killed Russia.'

He saw that she'd taken down all her posters, that the dolls he'd given her had gone.

'Russia made me special,' she said. 'With Russia, I was different. Now I'm nothing. You've made me nothing.' He tried to hold her, tell her she wasn't nothing, she was the very opposite of nothing – she was *something*, that was it – 'Don't touch me,' she hissed, and he backed off. Listen, she was an important something, a something that he loved. He needed her. He needed her so badly. Being in Russia had shown that to him, but it wasn't just Russia, it was always, he knew that he always needed her now. 'I've taken the soil,' she said. 'And I've flushed it! Yeah, I flushed it down the toilet. Now do you see? Now do you understand? Now get out. I never want to see you again.'

She moved out from the halls a couple of days later. He heard that she was sharing with some third-year students in the town. And then he heard that she'd dropped out of university altogether. He made enquiries about it, as delicately as he could, and found out that the psychology department hadn't been surprised. She hadn't attended a single lecture or tutorial all term.

*

One morning he said to Annie, 'I'm not going into work today.'

'Oh,' said Annie. 'Aren't you feeling well?'

'I'm feeling perfectly well. I'm just not going into work today.' In fact, he didn't go into work the next day either. In fact, he didn't go into work ever again. By the end of the first week a concerned faculty phoned to ask whether everything was all right. Annie was terrific. She explained that Duncan needed some time, and arranged a paid sabbatical for him, so that, starting immediately, he could research the more gruelling of the modern novels. Duncan wasn't happy when he heard that she'd done this. He phoned the faculty and told them they could go and fuck themselves. Annie called them again to apologise, and actually managed to make everything all right again. So Duncan called the faculty one last time, told them to go and fuck themselves and no returns.

He sat at home all day, watching television and smoking dope. He got the dope from Natasha's old supplier. He said to Annie, 'I don't love you any more.'

'No, I know,' said Annie.

'I haven't loved you for ages.'

'I know that too,' said Annie.

'Yeah, you just know it all, don't you?' And he threw the television remote control at her.

He would have liked to have moved out, but he had nowhere to go. Annie put him in the spare room. He liked the spare room. He was able to stretch out on the bed, and no-one got in the way.

'This would all have been different,' he told Annie, 'if we'd had children.'

'Yes,' said Annie. 'Maybe.'

One day he told Annie he needed money. He was going to fly to Russia. He had to fly to Russia. 'All right,' said Annie. 'Do you want me to come with you?' No, he didn't. 'And will you be coming back? To me?' Duncan said he supposed so, what else was he supposed to do? She booked the flight for him on expedia.com.

On arrival in Russia he stood in line for over an hour, as stone-faced immigration officials checked each and every passport, visa, reason for entry. 'You know, you make it very hard to get into your country,' Duncan told one of them. 'And it's not an especially great country to begin with.'

He went to the Hermitage.

He went to the Church on Spilled Blood.

He went to the Pushkin café, and then went next door to get himself some Kentucky Fried Chicken. While he was eating there, and watching the kids behind the counter serving with such hatchet faces, he realised that Natasha had been right. That the whole point was that the Russians didn't think of themselves as special, but that Mother Russia was special. That they believed in something greater than they were. And that they despised KFC, and the tourists they were feeding their KFC, and that they despised him, maybe him most of all; they'd only take these trappings of Western decadence so far, they'd only allow so many Pizza Huts and Top Shops and matryoshka dolls of Mickey Mouse and Donald Duck and all their happy friends. That there'd be a reckoning. And soon – Russia would turn on them, and it would bite, it hated them, and it hated him. The kid who'd served him his chicken fillet burger without a smile, he had revolution in his eyes, his eyes *blazed* with it, look at them blaze. Duncan wanted to tell the man sitting next to him the importance of this revelation, but the man moved away.

He went to the Peterhof gardens, because he'd decided that it was there he'd find the best quality dirt. He sealed it in a plastic bag, and hid it at the bottom of his rucksack.

As he attempted to pass through customs, he was removed from the line and taken to an interrogation room. He had to wait half an hour before he was joined by an official. 'Do you realise the penalty for smuggling drugs?' he was asked. Duncan said, 'It's not drugs. It's dirt. It's just dirt.' The official left the room, and then returned a little while later. 'Why are you wanting to smuggle dirt?' 'Because it's Russia,' said Duncan. 'Oh, come on, you can spare a bit of Russia, can't you? It's so big.' The official told him he wasn't going to press charges, since Duncan had only attempted to carry a small quantity of soil on board the plane. He should consider himself very lucky, and should he ever try anything of this nature again, he could be facing incarceration or a hefty fine. 'Can I keep the soil?' asked Duncan. 'No.'

He'd only come to Russia for the dirt, and he'd failed. He wasn't surprised to have failed, not given his track record. And indeed, he saw this new confirmation of it as really rather something to celebrate, and ordered a double vodka in the bar. Why not vodka, he was in Russia, after all. And then he ordered another double vodka. At some point during the succession of double vodkas he realised he was sitting under the leaves of an enormous potted plant. That there were potted plants all over the bar, it seemed that no-one could enjoy a double vodka without being confronted by one. And that all of these plants were buried deep within soil, within good old-fashioned Russian soil.

Natasha may have never mentioned her parents much, but Duncan had learned enough to track down their phone number through directory enquiries. 'Hello,' he said smoothly, and he sounded cool and authoritative, he hadn't for so long, and he remembered that once he'd been a persuasive academic lecturer, and that he'd lied about Martin Amis and Will Self with utter self-confidence. 'I need to find the current address for Claire Finchley.'

From the front door, it was a fairly nondescript house. Nothing special. But it took half an hour of psyching himself up before Duncan could ring the bell.

Natasha answered. She was shocked to see him.

He was shocked to see her too. She'd cut her hair right back. She was wearing make-up, surely? Yes, the face looked a bit redder around the cheeks, and bluer around the eyes, that had to be make-up. And she was pregnant as well, that was new, wasn't it, yes, he supposed it was. But, look! She was still wearing those glasses! Those owlish glasses, the ones he'd long known had only plain glass in them, she only wore them for effect. He could still reach her, convince her. Without those glasses, he'd have lost hope. Without those glasses, he'd have walked away.

'Duncan!' she said.

'Natasha,' he said.

'Claire?' called a male voice from inside the house.

'I'm all right, darling,' she called back. 'Duncan, what is it? What do you want?'

And he wanted to tell her that he loved her, of course. He wanted to tell her that he wanted her back to put everything right, he'd gone off the rails a little but she could help him, she was still wearing the glasses, she hadn't changed that much, and that meant maybe neither had he. He wanted her because she was that special, she could do that, she could save him, she could. He wanted to tell her he wished she'd been *his* daughter, he'd have been so proud of her, he'd have named her whatever she'd liked – it would have been a different relationship between the two of them, of course, particularly regarding all that sex, but it would have worked, he wished she could have been his child.

'I don't want you to hate me,' said Duncan.

'I don't.'

Duncan thought about this. 'I don't want you to hate me,' he said.

'Claire?' came the voice again, and a man appeared – well, a *boy*, really, no more than a boy, so young. He didn't look Russian in the slightest. He put his arms around Claire protectively.

'I have something for you,' said Duncan. 'Look. Look.' And he pulled out his plastic bag of dirt. And he reached inside, took out a handful. And put it in his mouth. 'Look, look,' he said again, and as he did so some of the dirt spilled out, on to his chin, on to his shirt, down on to the doorstep – but that didn't matter, he'd got *so much* dirt, he could afford to waste it! 'Look,' he said, and she was looking, she was aghast but she was definitely looking, and he began to chew another handful, 'look, I've found Russia. I've brought you Russia. It's yours. It's for you, it's yours. Russia's in me. Look. Russia's in me.'

My mother bought me an exercise book, so I could start writing a time chart. She said we could have fun with it, fill it together. The book was a stiff hardback, and had the words 'Young Reporter' embossed upon the cover. And it had 120 pages, and it was wide ruled, with no margins. On each of the wide ruled lines she wrote a date, starting with the current year (that was 1979), then going backwards. There were twenty-three lines to the page, so we passed my birth year very quickly, but Mother was much older, it took nearly two entire pages before we got to a time when she hadn't been in the world. And to each date we assigned one event, just one, the one that we decided was the most historically significant. 1969 – First man walks on the moon, 1956 – The Suez crisis, 1945 – We all beat the Germans, hurrah! I'd look the dates up in the family encyclopaedia, and I'd tell Mother what I deemed most important, and she'd nod, and she'd write it out carefully in that neat round handwriting she had. Such neat handwriting, with a little squiggle for the tail of a 'g', and the dot above the 'i' being a perfect circle. 1929 – The Wall Street crash, 1919 – The Treaty of Versailles, 1912 – The sinking of the Titanic. **406** – As Roman influence begins to wane, a number of their officials are set up as emperors of Britain away from direct imperial control. The least successful of them all has to be Marcus. He is put in power to defend the Britons against the Germanic hordes; he is murdered a few weeks later when the Germans knock them for six. **407** – Although, it has to be said, Marcus' replacement, Gratian, hardly does much better, and he's quickly murdered too. **408** – But everywhere is under threat. The most brilliant military commander of the time is Flavius Stilicho, who alone has repeated success against the Goths and the Vandals as they make designs upon the Roman Empire. There's a campaign against him by his political opponents; there are jealous mutters of ambition and betrayal; he is taken into captivity by Emperor Honorius. Stilicho does not resist, only wanting to safeguard the stability of the teetering empire – and for his loyalty, is decapitated. Without a general of Stilicho's authority there can be little resistance to the German invaders. It's only a matter of time now. Rome is doomed. **410** – The Visigoths sack Rome. It's the first time Rome has been successfully invaded for 800 years. **411** – Gratian's successor is Constantine III. The British nobility write to Honorius in Rome begging for help against the barbarian invasions, but Honorius is up to his eyes with barbarians of his own, and writes back that the British should defend themselves. They see this as a bald statement that Roman rule in their country is over, and that they can now rid themselves of the few stragglers who haven't yet abandoned them. Constantine is executed on 18 September. He is the last Roman to have ruled Britain. *Sometimes it would be easy. It was just obvious what was the most important event, it just sort of stepped up to the plate and announced itself. But the further back in time we went, the more obscure it all became, and some years were so busy. 1666 – The Great Fire of London, or the Second Anglo-Dutch War? We chose the Great Fire because I'd been taken to London by Mother and Father once for a birthday treat, and we'd been to see 'The Jungle Book' in a cinema, and I'd had sweets. And I'd never been anywhere Dutch. After a while, Mother let me do the write-ups in my own handwriting; looking back now, it wasn't as neat, but it got neater and more confident as the centuries went by – as we see the population of the world become more primitive and shuffle back into the Dark Ages so, conversely, my command of the pen becomes increasingly sophisticated. I'd take the time chart into school, in my lunch break I wouldn't be in the playground with the other kids, I'd be in the library finding good strong epochal milestones so I could fill more entries: 1776, 1649, 1588, 1492. Mother had only intended we go back as far as 1066, she said that's when history started – but I disagreed, there were so many years to catalogue before then, at least 1065 of them.* **415** – The death of Hypatia, the first notable woman in mathematics; her contributions to science include the invention of the hydrometer, and her mapping of the celestial bodies. In Egypt, under orders from Bishop Cyril, a Christian mob attacks her chariot in the streets. The monks strip her naked, then drag her to the church, where she's set on fire. In effect, she becomes the first 'witch' murdered under Christian authority. **418** – In an attempt to foster some understanding between the Romans and the Huns, it is agreed that a twelve-year-old German lad is taken to court and shown the way the Roman nobility lives. While he is there, so surreptitiously, the child studies their military manoeuvres, and speculates on how they might be thwarted. His name is Attila. The Romans have welcomed with open arms into the very heart of their society the man who will destroy it. **422** – The walls of the Colosseum in Rome crack during an earthquake. *And my father thought it was silly, and even my mother thought I was getting too old for it, and she stopped helping me, she said she had other things to do now, she was too busy with the cooking and the cleaning and making our home nice. So I continued secretly, I had my tenth birthday, then my eleventh. I made a rule for myself. I couldn't move on to an easy year, like, say, 1066 (the battle of Hastings), before I'd solved 1067 (for which, finally, I plumped for Olav III and Magnus II becoming joint kings of Norway).* **422** – The birth of Casper, who as a teenager goes on to rule the Mayan city of Palenque, which he will do for a rather impressive 52 years. We do not know his real name, only that he existed, and that he had a long reign. He is named Casper because his name glyph in the Mayan alphabet looks like the cartoon character, Casper the Friendly Ghost. A bit. **431** – Nestorius, patriarch of Constantinople, is banished into the Libyan desert by the Council of Ephesus for preaching that Christ had both a human and divine nature. **433** – Attila becomes leader of the Huns. He will be named the 'Scourge of God', and his attacks on both Eastern and Western branches of the Roman Empire will bring them to their knees. **438** – The last known gladiatorial combat in the Colosseum takes place. **438** – Body parts of John Chrysostom are taken to Constantinople as relics. **440** – On Crete a man emerges who claims to be named Moses – and, like his Biblical namesake, has been sent by Heaven to lead his followers to the Promised Land. He orders his people to jump from the cliffs, promising that the seas will part when they do so. The people jump. The seas stay where they are. Moses and his followers get very wet, and then very dead. **445** – From this year dates the foundation of the first Dynasty of the kingdom of Powys, in eastern Wales. Legend states that St Germanus visits in a thunderstorm, and King Benli refuses to give him shelter. Instead he finds shelter with one of Benli's slaves, Cadell, who protects him from the weather and gives him food. Inevitably Benli's castle is struck by lightning, and the old miser burns to death – and the good-spirited servant Cadell is appointed king by Germanus in his place. There's probably a moral somewhere in here to be drawn – either about the wisdom of being nice to saints, or the dangers of holidaying in Wales. **451** – Attila is finally defeated at the battle of Catalaunian Plains by Flavius Aetius. Aetius had spent his childhood at the kingdom of the Goths, on a similar school exchange programme to the one Attila had enjoyed in Rome. **452** – Anko becomes emperor of Japan after a family bloodbath. **452** – The last known usage of the Demotic script, the language of the ancient Egyptians, as a piece of graffiti on the walls of a temple. **453** – Attila the Hun dies. Not on the field of battle, but during his wedding party. After a long drinking bout he contracts a fatal nosebleed. **454** – Emperor Valentinian III invites Aetius to a meeting in his throne room, and jealous of his military successes, kills him (qv 408, really). It's a typically self-defeating thing for the Roman Empire to do to one of its few generals with any genius for actually beating barbarians; an adviser says, 'I am ignorant, sir, of your motives or provocations; I only know that you have acted like a man who has cut off his right hand with his left.' **456** – Anko, emperor of Japan, killed in family bloodbath. **459** – The death of St Simeon Stylites, who ensured the salvation of his soul by the mortification of his body, and spent the final 37 years of his life standing on the top of a narrow pillar in the Syrian desert. *Once I'd made my decision I stuck with it. I only went back and changed one date after it had been selected. For 1970 Mother had suggested I write down my own birth – 'Because,' she'd said, 'you're going to be so important one day, I just know it.' But even then I thought that was a fraud – that, realistically speaking, when future historians looked back upon that year, they would probably judge of even greater significance the Apollo 13 crisis, or Tonga becoming an independent state. I crossed my birth out, wrote Tonga in. The first few pages of the book were all so much neater, written by my mother so carefully, and with that favourite ink pen she kept only for time chart entries and for Christmas cards. I spoiled it, that very first page, with my childish scrawl in biro. But I stand by the desecration, I'd take historical accuracy over good penmanship any day, I'm proud of that. Because Mother was wrong. I didn't become important. I never was special. I'm nobody.* **461** – The murder of Majorian, the last Western Roman Emperor whose authority extends beyond the Italian border. The power vacuum that now dominates allows a Visigoth called Ricimer to become kingmaker, and set up a series of puppet emperors. When Majorian begins to show a trace of backbone, Ricimer has him beaten, kicked, and beheaded. **462** – The Statue of Zeus, one of the four remaining Seven Wonders of the World, is destroyed by fire (qv 262). **463** – Granny died here today. **465** – Ricimer tires of his new emperor, Libius Severus; he dies in mysterious circumstances. **472** – Emperor Anthemius gives Ricimer his daughter in marriage. Ricimer and Anthemius fall out. Anthemius tries to disguise himself as a beggar to hide from Ricimer; the disguise simply isn't good enough. **472** – Ricimer appoints Olybrius his new Roman Emperor. A month later, Ricimer dies of tuberculosis. Olybrius doesn't outlive him for long. **476** – The last Roman Emperor is called, ironically, Romulus Augustulus. The very name seems to be crying out to history, that this man might be taken seriously – the founder of Rome, and the founder of the imperial line, all rolled into one man! This is one emperor who survives his downfall. He abdicates in favour of the Hun Odoacer, and is given a generous annual pension, and allowed to live a carefree life on a country estate. And so it ends with a whimper. **476** – In China, the teenage emperor Cang Wu Wang decides for fun to shoot blunt arrows at a target he has painted on the belly of a sleeping minister. The minister wakes and murders him. **493** – The Vandals' control of the former Roman Empire is shortlived. Odoacer surrenders it to the Ostrogoths, and is murdered for his pains. **493** – St Patrick dies. The Battle for the Body of St Patrick ensues. **494** – Mingdi murders his two young prince nephews in order to take the Chinese throne (qv 1483). **496** – Frankish King Clovis, ancestor of the royal line of France, defeats the Alemanni in battle by invoking the name of Christ. He converts gratefully on the spot. *And Mother never saw the correction I'd made, so she was never hurt by it. She'd lost interest in my time chart long ago. And my wife never showed interest in it either. The only person who ever did was Annie. She showed too much interest; let's face it, in the end, that's probably what killed her.*

ALL THE BUZZ

There's a part of the brain that determines the type of person we find attractive. We can't help it. It could be chemical, it could be genetic, something to do with DNA, I don't know – we didn't choose it, this trigger, we've all got one, and it leaves us weak at the knees. For some what makes them buzz is a simple thing. It's a woman's height, or a man's beard, certain clothing, certain perfume, lipstick, stiletto heels, Scottish accents, perfectly smooth rounded bald heads. I had a boyfriend once who admitted to me that what really turned him on were women with large hands; this was bed talk, and we'd just made love, so I felt naturally self-conscious anyway, and my hands are quite petite. And he said it was just a silly thing, it didn't matter, he loved me whatever – but I noticed from that point on, whenever we were out in company, I could always catch him stealing a look at the end of each and every woman's arm we encountered. After a while I had to stop watching, it upset me too much. And we split up shortly afterwards.

My sister had a thing for Jehovah's Witnesses. She told me she's known it ever since she was a little kid, but she kept quiet about it, she thought it was something weird or dirty. But now in her twenties she'd come out about it, she freely paraded the fetish sites for Jehovah's Witnesses, and talked regularly on online forums. I asked her what the appeal was, but she said it was hard to explain. 'Maybe,' she said, 'it's because they look so earnest, and so convinced, and so naïve.' And she thought for a bit longer, and then said, 'And I like the way they come to your door. It's like pizza delivery.'

One sight of a *Watchtower*, she said, and that so, so sincere smile, was enough to turn her to jelly. It didn't matter whether they were young or old, fat or thin, male or female. My sister had got herself quite a reputation amongst the Jehovah's Witness community, and quite a few gave a wide berth to her otherwise unassuming semi-detached house. And quite a few, it has to be said, didn't.

Some weeks after the final Big Hand Incident left me a singleton, my sister gave me a call. 'When did you last have sex?' she asked. I said I couldn't remember – but I'm pretty sure I could have if I'd put my mind to it, I was just distracted because I was descaling the kettle. And, 'Hello, Amy,' I added. 'Can't remember is too long ago,' said Amy, 'it's high time you got back into the saddle.' She told me that she knew lots of eligible men I could be fixed up with; sometimes the Jehovah's Witnesses came in pairs. I pointed out that Jehovah's Witnesses were her thing, not mine – indeed, I harboured no particular sexual urge for any recognised religious cult – and she pooh-poohed that, said that I shouldn't knock a fetish till I'd tried it. 'What's your fetish again?' she asked me, and I reminded her that I was turned on by attentive kindness and polite conversation, that's what usually did it for me. 'Well, there you are, then,' said Amy, 'these guys have polite conversation coming out their ears!' And she said she wouldn't take no for an answer, and that I was to be at hers on Saturday to double date, seven o'clock sharp. I could bring the wine. Just the one bottle – the Jehovah's Witnesses wouldn't drink much.

All week long I tried to think of excuses to wriggle out of it, but everything I came up with centred around morals and common decency, and I knew from experience such concerns were unlikely to hold much sway with my sister. And so, with heavy heart, and a bottle of Malbec, at seven o'clock, dolled up to the nines, I rang the doorbell to her house. 'Hello, hello!' she said perkily, then gave me an inspection. I hadn't been on a first date in ages, and wasn't really sure how to dress – my ex-boyfriend and I had had a relationship which seemed based upon a series of second dates mostly, we never quite found the intensity to move on to third – but we'd definitely passed first date territory quite some time ago. 'You'll do,' said Amy, 'though you might want to remove a layer of make-up or two, they've got funny ideas about painted harlots.' As I scrubbed at my face in her bathroom, Amy outlined the plan. 'Let me do the talking,' she insisted, 'I can read their signals.' I was relieved to hear this, as I'd been hoping not to say anything at all for the entire evening.

And at length the doorbell rang. 'Hello, hello!' said Amy, as she opened the door. Standing on the porch were two young men in suits, they looked terribly smart and clean. 'Hello,' said one of them, 'can I ask if you'll be prepared to hear our good news?' He smiled politely, and showed ultra-white teeth – and so did his companion, and I looked at them hard to see whether polite toothy smiles were enough to set off the fire in my belly, but they weren't. Amy accepted the *Watchtower*, and showed them both in. 'Do you believe in the coming kingdom of Christ?' asked the other man, and Amy said that she didn't, but that she was very open-minded. 'And so's my sister,' she said, and nudged me, and I said that yes, I was open-minded too, in fact I was quite the most open-minded person I'd ever met. And both young men smiled politely at this, and Amy gave me a frown, perhaps she thought I was trying too hard.

Amy took me into the kitchen on the pretext that she needed to unblock the sink. She ran the tap so that the Jehovah's Witnesses next door couldn't hear. 'Which one do you want?' she said. 'I don't mind,' I said, 'I'll take whichever one you don't. Whichever one is the least Jehovah's Witnessy.' She gave this a bit of thought, and then said, 'They're both *fairly* Jehovah's Witnessy,' and she plumped for the one with the blonding moustache, and that left me with the one with the protruding Adam's apple. She turned off the tap, and we both went into the sitting room. 'Hello, hello!' she said.

It soon turned out that the one with the Adam's apple was, embarrassingly enough, called Adam – and I wanted to swap, I wasn't sure I'd be able to keep a straight face. But Amy seemed oblivious to my hints, and pretty soon she was taking Mr Moustache by the hand and leading him upstairs. 'You two can stay down here. The sofa opens up into a camp bed, by the way.' Adam and I made some small talk, and I asked him whether he had a long shift of Jehovah's Witnessing ahead of him that night, and he said it wasn't too bad. A few minutes later we heard the bedsprings from upstairs pound away in a regular rhythm. 'Do you want to hear about the kingdom of Christ?' he asked, and I told him I didn't really, I'd just as soon get the sex over and done with. He kissed me on the mouth, and he tasted of spearmint, my God, he must have brushed his teeth hard to get them that white; his breath was so fresh I could feel it beating the smell of my own into submission. We then opened up the camp bed, and we struggled a bit with that, we both came very close to laughing, it came very close to being fun – but then Adam pulled himself together, I could tell he wasn't overly comfortable with laughter. We had sex. He asked me if it'd been all right, and I said it was – but I couldn't lie to him, he was a holy man, it wouldn't have been proper, and I said it hadn't done *much* for me; he looked disappointed, and I said it was the whole religious thing, in no way had it been the way that with every grunt his Adam's apple bulged out like a bullfrog that had put me off. We lay back on the sofa and he asked if I was ready to accept his offer of the true gospel, and he looked so eager that I said he should go for it. But I soon had to stop him. It all sounded such nonsense. 'Don't you believe in a power higher than yourself?' he asked, 'something that gives your life shape and purpose?' I said I didn't, I was perfectly happy without all that, and he asked if I were really happy, and I insisted I was, I'm afraid I lied to a holy man after all. 'Knowing you're in God's hands,' he said, 'it's such a buzz. A buzz better than sex, a buzz better than anything you can imagine.' I thought this was a *little* tactless considering we were still wrapped around each other; I told him, somewhat stiffly, I'd had enough of discussing God now, and he, stiffer still, said he quite understood. He got dressed and left. I wasn't sure what to do, whether to go home or not – Amy and the moustache were still at it upstairs, they were on their seconds by this stage – and I thought it might look rude to leave without saying goodbye. When Amy at last came down she was appalled to find me on my own. 'What have you done with the other one?' she asked. I shrugged. She listened to what had happened, and was angry with me. 'For Christ's sake, sis. You have to make some little *show* of converting. Christ, they're not pieces of meat.'

That night I took my *Watchtower* to bed with me. It was a surprisingly bright and cheery read, especially considering that it was so fixated upon impending Armageddon, they seemed awfully excited about it. At the end of the magazine there was a phone number. I dialled it first thing the next morning, right after breakfast. 'Hello,' I said, 'I want to be a Jehovah's Witness.' The voice on the other end sounded a little suspicious at first. 'You want to subscribe to our doctrine, to believe in the Bible as the literal word of God, and to put the Lord Jesus Christ before all others?' 'Whatever you're into, I'm into,' I agreed. I decided it was politic not to say I was looking for the buzz Adam had mentioned, that it seemed attentive kindness and polite conversation just weren't pushing my buttons any more. I went along to a first meeting, and discovered there people just like me – a little bit lost, maybe, just looking for something better. And their beliefs were reassuringly familiar. If I'd gone for Islam or Shinto as my faith, I'd have been right in at the deep end, but this was just like the Christianity I'd learned at school – but less fuddy duddy, with fewer of the boring parts, and perhaps a stronger emphasis upon the evils of blood transfusion. I met Adam there. He looked a little scared to see me at first, but he soon realised I wasn't there to expose the fact he'd had sex with a heathen. On the contrary, he'd managed to convert me. 'Have I really?' he asked me softly, over a plastic cup of orange squash. 'I've never converted anyone before. Bless the Lord!' And do you know, he actually cried.

And the smart clothes! I loved their smart clothes. I went to Marks & Spencer, I bought the smartest clothes I could afford. The power suit made me keep my back straight, I looked so much slimmer, and I pulled my hair back into the tightest bun I could. As I checked myself in the mirror I quite frightened myself, I looked so ferociously evangelical. I was now just perfect to go out to doorsteps and try to spread the word of God; Adam accompanied me those first few months. Adam was always with me, Adam had saved me, after all. He was very good, he let me be the one that rang the doorbell, that never failed to excite me. What I grew to love was seeing that moment on the strangers' faces, when polite enquiry gave way to horror or fear or downright hatred. They'd be embarrassed in their hatred, usually, they wouldn't know what to say – 'I'm not interested, thank you' – but it was hatred all the same. And I soon realised that there was the buzz, the buzz I'd been looking for – it caused a squelch in my gut that was like sex, the first time it happened I was so taken aback I actually stumbled and Adam had to prop me up. Because all these years I'd been despised by men – for not being pretty enough, for not wearing the right clothes, for not listening to the right music, for not being Amy. For talking too much, or talking too little, for all manner of talking inadequacies altogether. And now I could *control* their rejection, it was me making them reject me each time I rang that doorbell, they were my puppets if they only but knew it. And the best of it was, they rejected me for something that wasn't even *true* – I didn't believe in God, not at all. When I got into the Jehovah's Witness kick I did *try* to believe, I really thought it might be better if I could – but it all seemed *so* unlikely, really, that some being would love us all, each and every one of us the same. There's a part of our brain that determines we'll be drawn to some more than others, surely God too would have some sort of fetish? So they'd slam the door in our faces, and Adam would look so crushed, and I'd be secretly delighting in the buzz – if they held in contempt everything I *didn't* stand for, surely, deep down, they might like me after all?

Adam told me that he loved me. I didn't take much notice at first. I assumed this was a religious thing, the word 'love' fairly flew around at some of those Jehovah's Witness meetings, I can tell you. I told him I loved him too, just as I loved the whole miracle of creation. No, he had to explain that he really loved me, the way a man loves a woman, the way Abraham loved Sarah, the way Jacob loved Rachel, the way David loved Abigail and loved Michal and loved Ahinoam and loved Bathsheba. I was his ideal woman, so saintly, so demure – and so brunette too, he had a thing about brunettes, they gave him a buzz. He loved me so much that he was rather afraid it might surpass his love for God, and he'd been very worried about that, he'd had to have a few very serious prayers about the matter, and now God had told him it was all okay, he'd given him the big thumbs up. Adam invited me back to his house for sex. He'd tried too hard to recreate the magic of our first time, he'd even bought a camp bed especially, but our attempts to roll it out from the sofa weren't nearly so amusing the second time around. Again, the sex was all right. But afterwards he was full of plans for marriage and the sanctity of our blessed union and how our love would blaze like a lighted candle for the glory of the entire church – and I had to be straight with him, I told him I didn't like him all that much. There's a part of our brain that determines the type of person we find attractive, we can't help it. It was the second time I'd made him cry. I tried to reassure him; I told him gently that I didn't believe in God at all, I was only pretending. But, strangely enough, that didn't seem to make him feel any better.

After I'd destroyed Adam's faith, and he left the Church, I'd sometimes see him stacking shelves in Sainsbury's. All matted hair and yellowing teeth, he looked so much younger like that. He always gave me a cold shoulder, he was even hostile – and it gave me cause to wonder at the way we can love a thing one day and not the next. That our fetishes can fail us. Amy is a case in point. I hadn't told my sister I'd converted, and one day I thought I'd drop in on her in my converting get-up while brandishing a few copies of the latest *Watchtower*. It takes a lot of effort to surprise my sister, but on this occasion I certainly succeeded. She invited me in for a cup of coffee, and danced around me nervously, not knowing what to do, not knowing whether to touch or keep well away. One moment she'd be pawing and prodding, then she'd be recoiling to the other side of the room and trying to press herself into the wall. A couple of weeks later she gave me a phone call. 'You've ruined everything,' she said. 'Whenever I have a Jehovah's Witness over, whenever I turn off the light, in my mind's eye the only face I can see is yours.' I sympathised, I could quite see how that would be off-putting. 'And it gets worse. I know you're faking it. You don't believe in God. And now, when I'm banging away, the doubt creeps into my head. What if *they're* faking it too? I seize up at the thought. Last night I seized up so hard I couldn't finish right, I had to fake my way through to the end. He was faking, I was faking, love is spoiled if there's that much fakery going on.' She didn't speak to me again for nearly a year. She was that furious. And then one day she called me again. She sounded wiser, at peace. 'I hated you for a while,' she admitted, 'I really did. But now the fetish was gone, I realised I had to look elsewhere. And that means now I've found someone *real*, who loves me for who I am, and I can love him too, for himself, not for some strange quirk he has. It's honest and it's true and I think that it's forever, and I have you to thank, sis, for showing me the way.' She paused, then said, 'But I've got to admit, the sex is *awful*.'

I never wanted to change anyone's lives. Perhaps amongst my Jehovah's Witness friends, I was really the only one who didn't. Most of them have gone now. Some of them moved on to other cults – Mormons, Moonies, we lost a few to the Christian Scientists when they came to town, they did a very impressive recruitment campaign, frankly they left us standing. And Barry and Gary, they dropped out of religion altogether, they discovered love and homosexuality, they gave up knocking on people's doors and took instead to gay pride marches. I've now been one of the longest-standing members of our Church; all the new Jehovah's Witnesses come to me for advice and support, and they're all so fresh-faced and keen and naïve, I can quite understand what Amy used to see in them. If I only weren't old enough to be their mothers – one of our newer converts called me Mummy recently, quite accidentally, and then he blushed bright red – and oh, it almost broke my heart. I still ring strangers' doorbells, and yes, there's still a thrill to that, the anticipation of something new and exciting on the faces of the people that I'm bothering – but I've seen it all, every put down, every type of bored disgust. Try as I might I can no longer raise the squelch inside my tummy that turns me on. I hold out the *Watchtower* in my hands, 'Can I talk to you about the good news?' I say, holding it tight in my hands, showing the hands for all they're worth – and one day I hope to find a gentleman behind some door, one who'll see how petite the hands are. 'I love petite hands,' he'll say, 'they're just my thing.' He won't be able to help it, it might be chemical, it might be genetic, there'll just be a piece of his brain that the very sight of me will send buzzing. And he'll smile, and he'll open the door wide, and I'll drop the *Watchtowers* to the ground. And I'll follow him in.

501 – The brief inglorious reign of Chinese Emperor Hedi. Nicknamed the 'idiot eastern marquis', Hedi hates learning, and has his tutors killed. He also puts to death his six brothers. He is overthrown after a long siege at Nanjing in which no fewer than 80,000 of his subjects die of hunger, and his head is sent, preserved in wax, to his successor. **509** – King Clovis further extends his territories. He persuades Chlodoric to kill his father, Sigebert the Lame, ruler of the Rhineland Franks. In thanks to Clovis, Chlodoric elects to offer him something nice from his father's treasure chest – and as he rifles through it, Clovis has his skull split with an axe. Clovis consolidates Sigebert's kingdom within his own. **517** – Sigismund, king of Burgundy, marries his second wife, and his son insults her. So Sigismund has him strangled. Sigismund is later canonised. **518** – Traditionally, the date given for the battle of Mount Badon, in which the Saxons were defeated in battle by King Arthur. The effect is devastating; the Anglo-Saxon Chronicle falls silent for seventy years. *King Arthur is the most famous of all the English monarchs, and he may not even have existed. Don't you just love the irony? Historians hate it, of course, they sneer at poor old Arthur – well, I say, 'poor Arthur', but he doesn't care, he'll be safe in his fame long after their monographs about the dubious provenance of early Anglo-Saxon myths fall out of print and turn to dust. Arthur may not be real. But he's the best history of all – with Arthur you get knights on quests, and damsels in distress, and armour shining, and honour – it's history, without all the facts getting in the way to spoil everything.* **524** – Boethius writes 'The Consolation of Philosophy', in which he states that love of wisdom and of the Christian God is the highest state of happiness that humanity can aspire towards. He is executed without trial in Pavia. **525** – Dionysus Exiguus introduces a system of dating for the Christian era, and, as we have seen, balls it up from the very start. **526** – An earthquake in Antioch kills 250,000 people. *Wouldn't it be better if all history could be like Arthur? If we could extract the Real Events from it, and replace them with the Legend – how much more enticing would be the English Civil War, say, or the Great Depression, or the electoral campaign fought between Gordon Brown and David Cameron? I'd far rather bin the battle of Mount Badon if it means I get to keep the Round Table, and Excalibur, and Sir Gawain and the Green Knight. Do you think there were any green knights, for real, at Mount Badon? Don't you think that all the knights were just the same bland grey? History – forget that small hysterical 'hi', that syllable of pomposity – what we want is 'story', I want the entire chronicle of civilisation to be a story, an infinite number of interrelated short stories. Like the story of me, and of my wife, and of my baby daughter.* **529** – Byzantine Emperor Justinian I orders the closure of the Academy of Athens, on the grounds that its studies are unchristian. It was founded by Plato in 387 BC. *I wasn't unattractive. I've seen the pictures. But I didn't know many girls, I was too busy during school break working on my time chart. But I got snared in the end. When I hit the teens, when all the girls around me stopped being shy and ran rampant with breasts and hormones. I got snared by my future wife – she wasn't the prettiest, but she was certainly the most persistent. She asked me out on a date. I said yes. She didn't leave me a lot of options. She'd run off with my time chart, she said she wouldn't give it back unless I agreed to go to the cinema with her.* **539** –Mediolanum (Milan) is besieged by the Ostrogoths. The Germans starve the city into submission; they spare the garrisons there, but massacre the civilian population and raze the place to the ground. **542** – The long-forgotten successor to King Arthur, his cousin Constantine, comes to the throne. Straight away he faces an uprising by the sons of Mordred, but, having defeated them, has them both murdered as they seek sanctuary in the church. For this Constantine is struck down by God. No-one says, moreover, what he did with the Round Table. **542** – A plague spread from Constantinople kills 300,000 people. **545** – Justinian I insists that the people of Constantinople adopt the Roman date for Easter. Demonstrations and strikes ensue. **547** – Chinese emperor Liang Wudi is a Buddhist; he is attracted to the idea of compassion, so rare in a sixth century monarch, does all he can not to authorise executions, and bans the sacrifice of animals (insisting upon the substitution of pastry imitations). Three times he resigns the throne to become a monk. This sanctity only puts a gulf between him and his people – and eventually his son Jian Wendi rebels against his father's beliefs, and once more puts Nanjing under siege. By the time Wendi breaks into the palace, only one tenth of his father's garrison has survived. Wudi, sick and starved, but to the last a man of peace, greets his treacherous son with the words, 'You have campaigned long. You must be tired.' **549** – Some historians believe that the legendary King Arthur was, instead, Maelgwyn, the King of Gwynedd, who dies this year. Maelgwyn is pretty much semi-legendary himself, and does give a rather darker slant to the Arthur myth. The historian Gildas records that he was a cruel tyrant, and 'first in evil'; that in his youth he took the throne by killing his uncle. Then he has a pang of conscience, and for a while at least becomes a monk. His monkery doesn't last for ever, however; pretty soon he falls in love with his nephew's wife, abandons the church, and murders both nephew and his own wife so he can marry again. *And I can no longer remember the historical accuracy of that first date with my wife-to-be, but I know the myth. The myth she'd repeat to me over the years, in anecdote form, on anniversaries, whenever the nostalgia took her. How we hadn't liked the movie, how we'd got bored halfway through. How the boys behind us kept kicking our seats. How we'd left, and gone out alone into the night.* **550** – Mark, king of Dumnonia (Cornwall), takes the throne. By prophecy he learns that he will be killed by one of his sons, so executes each and every successive wife as soon as she falls pregnant. One of his wives manages to escape for a while; by the time he finds her, and beheads her, the son has already been born, and will grow to fulfil the prediction. **552** – Totila, king of the Ostrogoths, faces a 20,000 strong Byzantine army at the battle of Taginae. With the prospect of reinforcements due later in the day, Totila delays the fighting by putting on a cabaret show for the enemy. With both armies facing each other in deadly earnest, Totila puts purple plumes in his helmet and spends the morning giving a demonstration of horse tricks and spear handling, whirling the weapon around like a drum majorette. Once he learns the reinforcements have arrived, he attacks – and the bemused Byzantines kill him. **553** – The historian Procopius publishes his 'Anecdota', or 'Secret History'. It's a gossipy and bitchy account of Justinian and leading Byzantine figures – it's full of lust, and titillation, and sequences in which the monstrous emperor can even make his own head vanish. As such, it reads as the earliest ancestor of tabloid journalism. **554** – Chinese Emperor Yuandi has two great passions in his life: his collection of literature, and his cruel suppression of all enemies. He believes his library of magical texts has the power to protect him and make him supreme. He's defeated in battle, and in response decides to punish that very literature: he sets on fire his entire library, wearing a white robe of mourning as he puts to death the 100,000 books that have failed him. *If I prefer myth to fact, then why, you may well ask, do I compile this time chart? Why do I choose to bolt down event after event, rather than let everything drift into the beautiful murk of legend? Why. Because. Because I don't think history deserves it. History is ugly, and, and coarse. I want to punish history. I want to batter at it until it bleeds, until its bloated body breaks apart and bleeds. Here are some more facts. Here they are. Enjoy. Enjoy. Chew them over, bite down hard, bite down so it hurts.* **565** – The first recorded sighting of the Loch Ness Monster. **573** – Nothing but family spats amongst all the Frankish kings. Brunhilde urges her husband Sigebert of Austrasia (king of the Rhineland) to go to war against his brother Chilperic I (king of western France), because Chilperic has strangled his wife Galswintha (who is also Brunhilde's sister) so that he can marry his mistress Fredegund. The mutual hatred between Brunhilde and Fredegund will fuel forty years of war. It's like a soap opera. **575** – Fredegund has Sigebert assassinated. Chilperic's son, Merovech, promptly marries the widowed Brunhilde, his own aunt, to strengthen his chances of becoming king. His stepmother Fredegund is furious, insistent that only her children should have power, and has Chilperic declare war on his son. The defeated Merovech is carted off to a monastery. Brunhilde, in response, tries to seize the regency through her own son Childebert II. Chilperic negates that by adopting Childebert himself, all his other children by now having been murdered by Fredegund. Chilperic regrets this when Fredegund gives him a new son, Clotaire, and he ends up murdered. **575** – St Oran bricks himself up alive in his new church as a sacrifice to God. **580** – The death in battle of King Peredur of York, believed to be the basis for Sir Perceval, Holy-Grail-hunting knight of the Round Table from Arthurian legend. **582** – There are reports of blood raining down all over Paris. **584** – On the death of Chilperic, Fredegund and Brunhilde go to war. Fredegund plots to kill Childebert. When he dies, he leaves two sons Thibert and Thierry to rule in his place. Brunhilde has Thibert killed. Thierry declares war on Clotaire, but dies of dysentery. Fredegund as evil stepmother is traditionally seen as the inspiration for the Cinderella folk tale. See – another myth, another legend. **586 –** Visigoth King Leovigild executes his son Hermenegild when he refuses to renounce his Catholic faith. **587** – Japan's first Buddhist monastery is founded, after the anti-Buddhist clan there is murdered. **597** – St Augustine goes to Kent as missionary to convert the Saxons. (The story that Bede tells us is that he was inspired to do this once struck by the appearance of British slaves he saw at market in Rome – 'These are not Angles, they're angels,' he says wittily, which suggests that the church in England is founded on a very bad pun.) Augustine successfully converts King Athelbert, and becomes the first Archbishop of Canterbury. On Athelbert's death, his son Eadbald takes the throne – he promptly renounces his faith and marries his own stepmother. *She wants some time apart, and of course I agree, time is what I'm all about. She wants to pack her bags and go, taking just the essentials, just until she sorts out what's what, and she asks me to go out for a couple of hours, she doesn't want me to be there when she leaves. She asks me to take Annie with me. She's leaving me with Annie. She's leaving Annie too. So I go and sit in the pub. I shouldn't bring a little girl into a pub, and I get a funny look from the barman, but Annie is nothing if not well-behaved and mature, she sits down quietly with her lemonade and plays stacking all the beer mats. When we return home my wife has gone, she's vanished – and my wife has set the burglar alarm; it beeps away at me to tell me that the house is empty now, that we're all on our own, it prompts me to enter a four-digit code. It's 1709, that's because we got married on 17 September, but I've always thought of it as the battle of Poltava, and the beeping gets urgent now, faster, and I think, what if I just stand here, what if I do nothing at all, and I wait it out, and I close my eyes, and I hold Annie close to me to protect her from the blast as the angry sirens explode all around and wash clean over us.*

FEATHERWEIGHT

He thought at first that she was dead. And that was terrible, of course – but what shocked him most was how dispassionate that made him feel. There was no anguish, no horror, he should be crying but clearly no tears were fighting to get out – and instead all there was was this almost sick fascination. He'd never seen a corpse before. His mother had asked if he'd wanted to see his grandfather, all laid out for the funeral, and he was only twelve, and he really really didn't – and his father said that was okay, it was probably best Harry remembered Grandad the way he had been, funny and full of life, better not to spoil the memory – and Harry had quickly agreed, yes, that was the reason – but it wasn't that at all, it was a *dead body*, wasn't it, and he worried that if he got too close it might wake up and say hello.

And now here there *was* a corpse, and it was less than three feet away, in the passenger seat behind him. And it was his *wife*, for God's sake, someone he knew so well – or, at least, better than anyone else in the world could, he could say that at least. And her head was twisted oddly, he'd never seen her quite at that angle before and she looked like someone he'd never really known at all, he'd never seen her face in a profile where her nose looked quite that enormous. And there was all the blood, of course. He wondered whether the tears were starting to come after all, he could sense a pricking at his eyes, and he thought it'd be such a *relief* if he could feel grief or shock or hysteria or something... when she swivelled that neck a little towards him, and out from a mouth thick with that blood came 'Hello'.

He was so astonished that for a moment he didn't reply, just goggled at her. She frowned.

'There's a funny taste in my mouth,' she said.

'The blood,' he suggested.

'What's that, darling?'

'There's a lot of blood,' he said.

'Oh,' she said. 'Yes, that would make sense. Oh dear. I don't feel I'm in any pain, though. Are you in any pain?'

'No,' he said. 'I don't think so. I haven't tried to... move much, I...' He struggled for words. 'I didn't get round to trying, actually. Actually, I thought you were dead.'

'And I can't see very well either,' she said.

'Oh,' he said.

She blinked. Then blinked again. 'No, won't go away. It's all very red.'

'That'll be the blood,' he said. 'Again.'

'Oh yes,' she said. 'Of course, the blood.' She thought for a moment. 'I'd wipe my eyes, but I can't seem to move my arms at all. I have still got arms, haven't I, darling?'

'I think so. I can see the right one, in any case.'

'That's good. I do wonder, shouldn't I be a little more scared than this?'

'I was trying to work that out too. Why I wasn't more scared. Especially when I thought you were dead.'

'Right...?'

'And I concluded. That it was probably the shock.'

'That could be it.' She nodded, and that enormous nose nodded too, and so did the twisted neck, there they were, all nodding, it looked grotesque – 'Still. All that blood! I must look a sight!'

She did, but he didn't care, Harry was just so relieved she was all right after all, and he didn't want to tell her that her little spate of nodding seemed to have left her head somewhat back to front. She yawned. 'Well,' she said. 'I think I might take a little nap.'

He wasn't sure that was a good idea, he thought that he should probably persuade her to stay awake. But she yawned again, and look! – she was perfectly all right, wasn't she, there was no pain, there was a lot of *blood*, yes, but no pain. 'Just a little nap,' she said. 'I'll be with you again in a bit.' She frowned. 'Could you scratch my back for me, darling? It's itchy.'

'I can't move.'

'Oh, right. Okay. It's itchy, though. I'm allergic to feathers.'

'To what, darling?'

'To feathers,' she said. 'The feathers are tickling me.' And she nodded off.

*

His first plan had been to take her back to Venice. Venice had been where they'd honeymooned. And he thought that would be so romantic, one year on exactly, to return to Venice for their first anniversary. They could do everything they had before – hold hands in Saint Mark's Square, hold hands on board the vaporetti, toast each other with Champagne in one of those restaurants by the Rialto. He was excited by the idea, and he was going to keep it a secret from Esther, surprise her on the day with plane tickets – but he *never* kept secrets from Esther, they told each other everything, it would just have seemed weird. And thank God he had told her, as it turned out. Because she said that although it was a lovely idea, and yes, it *was* very romantic, she didn't want to go back to Venice at all. Truth to tell, she'd found it a bit smelly, and very crowded, and *very* expensive; they'd done it once, why not see somewhere else? He felt a little hurt at first – hadn't she enjoyed the honeymoon then? She'd never said she hadn't at the time – and she reassured him, she'd *adored* the honeymoon. But not because of Venice, because of him, she'd adore any holiday anywhere, so long as he was part of the package. He liked that. She had a knack for saying the right thing, smoothing everything over.

Indeed, in one year of marriage they'd never yet had an argument.

He sometimes wondered whether this were some kind of a record. He wanted to ask all his other married friends, how often do you argue, do you even argue at all? – just to see whether what he'd got with Esther was something really special. But he never did, he didn't want to rub anyone's noses in how happy he was, and besides, he didn't have the sorts of friends he could be that personal with. He didn't need to, he had Esther. Both he and Esther had developed a way in which they'd avoid confrontation – if a conversation was taking a wrong turning, Esther would usually send it on a detour without any apparent effort. Yes, he could find her irritating at times, and he was certain then that she must find him irritating too – and they could both give the odd warning growl if either were tired or stressed

– but they'd never had anything close to a full-blown row. That was something to be proud of. He called her his little diplomat! He said that she should be employed by the UN, she'd soon sort out all these conflicts they heard about on the news! And she'd laugh, and say that he clearly hadn't seen what she was like in the shop, she could really snap at some of those customers sometimes – she was only perfect around *him*. And he'd seen evidence of that, hadn't he? For example – on their wedding morning, when he wanted to see her, and all the bridesmaids were telling him not to go into the bedroom, *don't*, Harry, she's in a filthy temper! – but he went in anyway, and there she was in her dress, she was so beautiful, and she just *beamed* at him, and kissed him, and told him that she loved him, oh, how she loved him. She wasn't angry. She wasn't ever going to be angry with him. And that night they'd flown off to Venice, and they'd had a wonderful time.

So, not Venice then. (Maybe some other year. She nodded at that, said, 'Maybe.') Where else should they spend their anniversary then? Esther suggested Scotland. Harry didn't much like the sound of that, it didn't sound particularly romantic, especially not compared to Venice. But she managed to persuade him. How about a holiday where they properly *explored* somewhere? Just took the car, and *drove* – a different hotel each night, free and easy, and whenever they wanted they could stop off at a little pub, or go for a ramble on the moors, or pop into a stately home? It'd be an adventure. The Watkins family had put their footprints in Italy, she said, and now they could leave them all over the Highlands! That did sound rather fun. He didn't want it to be *too* free and easy, mind you, they might end up with nowhere to stay for the night – but he did a lot of homework, booked them into seven different places in seven different parts of Scotland. The most they'd ever have to drive between them was eighty miles, he was sure they could manage that, and he showed her an itinerary he'd marked out on his atlas. She kissed him and told him how clever he was.

And especially for the holiday he decided to buy a satnav. He'd always rather fancied one, but couldn't justify it before – he knew his drive into work so well he could have done it with his eyes closed. He tried out the gadget, he put in the postcode of his office, and let it direct him there. It wasn't the route he'd have chosen, he was quite certain it was better to avoid the ring road altogether, but he loved that satnav voice, so gentle and yet so authoritative. 'You have reached your destination,' it'd say, and they'd chosen a funny way of getting there, but yes, they certainly had – and all told to him in a voice good enough to be off the telly. The first day of the holiday he set in the postcode to their first Scottish hotel; he packed the car with the suitcases; Esther sat in beside him on the passenger seat, smiled, and said, 'Let's go.' 'The Watkins are going to leave their footprints all over the Highlands!' he announced, and laughed. 'Happy anniversary,' said Esther. 'I love you.'

On the fourth day they stayed at their fourth stately home of the holiday a little too long, maybe; it was in the middle of nowhere, and their next hotel was also in the middle of nowhere, but it was in a completely different middle of nowhere. It was already getting dark, and there weren't many streetlights on those empty roads. Esther got a little drowsy, and said she was going to take a nap. And the satnav man hadn't said anything for a good fifteen minutes, so Harry knew he *must* be going in the right direction, and maybe Esther sleeping was making him a little drowsy too – but suddenly he realised that the smoothness of the road beneath him had gone, this was grass and field and *bushes*, for God's sake, and they were going down, and it was quite steep, and he kept thinking that they had to stop soon surely, he hadn't realised they were so high up in the first place! – and there were now branches whipping past the windows, and actual trees, and the car wasn't slowing down at all, and it only dawned on him then that they might really be in trouble. He had time to say 'Esther,' because stupidly he thought she might want to be awake to see all this, and then the mass of branches got denser still, and then there was sound, and he hadn't thought there'd been sound before, but suddenly there was an awful lot of it. He was flung forward towards the steering wheel, and then the seatbelt flung him right back where he had come from – and that was when he heard a snap, but he wasn't sure if it came from him, or from Esther, or just from the branches outside. And it was dark, but not yet dark enough that he couldn't see Esther still hadn't woken up, and that there was all that blood.

The front of the car had buckled. The satnav said, 'Turn around when possible.' Still clinging on to the crushed dashboard. Just the once, then it gave up the ghost.

He couldn't feel his legs. They were trapped under the dashboard. He hoped that was the reason. He tried to open the door, pushed against it hard, and the pain of the attempt nearly made him pass out. The door had been staved in. It was wrecked. He thought about the seatbelt. The pain that reaching it would cause. Later. He'd do that later. Getting out the mobile phone from his inside jacket pocket – not even the coat pocket, he'd have to bend his arm and get into the coat first and *then* into the jacket... Later, later. Once the pain had stopped. Please, God, then.

Harry wished they'd gone to Venice. He was sure Venice had its own dangers. He supposed tourists were always drowning themselves in gondola-related accidents. But there were no roads to drive off in Venice.

*

He was woken by the sound of tapping at the window.

It wasn't so much the tapping that startled him. He'd assumed they'd be rescued sooner or later – it was true, they hadn't come off a main road, but someone would drive along it sooner or later, wouldn't they? It was on the *satnav route*, for God's sake.

What startled him was the realisation he'd been asleep in the first place. The last thing he remembered was his misgivings about letting Esther nod off. And some valiant decision he'd made that whatever happened *he* wouldn't nod off, he'd watch over her, stand guard over her – *sit* guard over her, he'd protect her as best he could. As best he could when he himself couldn't move, when he hadn't yet dared worry about what might damage might have been done to him. What if he'd broken his legs? (What if he'd broken his spine?) And as soon as these thoughts swam into his head, he batted them out again – or at least buried them beneath the guilt (some valiant effort to protect Esther that had been, falling asleep like that!) and the relief that someone was there and he wouldn't need to feel guilt much longer. Someone was out there, tapping away at the window.

'Hey!' he called out. 'Yes, we're in here! Yes, we're all right!' Though he didn't really know about that last bit.

It was now pitch black. He couldn't see Esther at all. He couldn't see whether she was even breathing. 'It's all right, darling,' he told her. 'They've found us. We're safe now.' Not thinking about that strange twisted neck she'd had, not about spines.

Another tattoo against the glass – tap, tap, tap. And he strained his head in the direction of the window, and it hurt, and he thought he heard something pop. But there was no-one to be seen. Just a mass of branches, and the overwhelming night. Clearly the tapping was at the passenger window behind him.

It then occurred to him, in a flash of warm fear, that it was *so* dark that maybe their rescuer couldn't see in. That for all his tapping he might think the car was empty. That he might just give up tapping altogether, and disappear into the blackness. 'We're in here!' he called out, louder. 'We can't move! Don't go! Don't go!'

He knew immediately that he shouldn't have said don't go, have tempted fate like that. Because that's when the tapping stopped. 'No!' he shouted. 'Come back!' But there was no more; he heard something that might have been a giggle, and that was it.

Maybe there hadn't been tapping at all. Maybe it was just the branches in the wind.

Maybe he was sleeping through the whole thing.

No, he decided forcefully, and he even said it out loud, 'No.' There had been a *rhythm* to the tapping; it had been someone trying to get his attention. And he wasn't asleep, he was in too much pain for that. His neck still screamed at him because of the strain of turning to the window. He chose to disregard the giggling.

The window tapper had gone to get help. He'd found the car, and couldn't do anything by himself. And quite right too, this tapper wasn't a doctor, was he? He could now picture who this tapper was, some sort of farmer probably, a Scottish farmer out walking his dog – and good for him, he wasn't trying to be heroic, he was going to call the *experts* in, if he'd tried to pull them out of the car without knowing what he was about he might have done more harm than good. Especially if there *was* something wrong with the spine (forget about the spine). Good for you, farmer, thought Harry, you very sensible Scotsman, you. Before too long there'd be an ambulance, and stretchers, and safety. If Harry closed his eyes now, and blocked out the pain – he could do it, it was just a matter of not *thinking* about it – if he went back to sleep, he wouldn't have to wait so long for them to arrive.

So he closed his eyes, and drifted away. And dreamed about farmers. And why farmers would giggle so shrilly like that.

*

The next time he opened his eyes there was sunlight. And Esther was awake, and staring straight at him.

He flinched at that. And then winced at his flinching, it sent a tremor of pain right through him. He was glad to see she was alive, of course. And conscious was a bonus. He hadn't just hadn't expected the full ugly reality of it.

93

He could now see her neck properly. And that in its contorted position all the wrinkles had bunched up tight against each other, thick and wormy; it looked a little as if she were wearing an Elizabethan ruff. And there was blood, so much of it. It had dried now. He supposed that was a good sign, that the flow had been staunched somehow, that it wasn't still pumping out all over the Mini Metro. The dried blood cracked around the mouth and chin as she spoke.

'Good morning,' she said.

'Good morning,' he replied, and then automatically, ridiculously, 'did you sleep well?'

She smirked at this, treated it as a deliberate joke. 'Well, I'm sure the hotel would have been nicer.'

'Yes,' he said. And then, still being ridiculous, 'I think we *nearly* got there, though. The satnav said we were about three miles off.'

She didn't smirk this time. 'I'm hungry,' she said.

'We'll get out of this soon,' he said.

'All right.'

'Are you in pain?' he asked.

'No,' she said. 'Just the itching. The itching is horrible. You know.'

'Yes,' he said, although he didn't. 'I'm in a fair amount of pain,' he added, almost as an afterthought. 'I don't think I can move.'

'Not much point bothering with that hotel now,' said Esther. 'I say we move right on to the next, put it down as a bad lot.'

He smiled. 'Yes, all right.'

'And I don't think we'll be doing a stately home today. Not like this. Besides, I think I've had my fill of stately homes. They're just houses, aren't they, with better furniture in? I don't care about any of that. I don't need better furniture, so long as I have you. Our own house, as simple as it might be, does me fine, darling. With you in it, darling.'

'Yes,' he said. 'Darling, you do know we've been in a car crash. Don't you?' (And that you're covered in blood.)

'Of course I do,' she said, and she sounded a bit testy. 'I'm itchy, aren't I? I'm itching all over. The feathers.' And then she smiled at him, a confrontation neatly avoided. Everything smoothed over. 'You couldn't scratch my back, could you, darling? Really, the itching is *terrible.*'

'No,' he reminded her. 'I can't move, can I?'

'Oh yes,' she said.

'And I'm in pain.'

'You said,' she snapped, and she stuck out her bottom lip in something of a sulk. He wished she hadn't, it distorted her face all the more.

'I'm really sorry about all this,' he said. 'Driving us off the road. Getting us into all this. Ruining the holiday.'

'Oh, darling,' she said, and the lip was back in, and the sulk was gone. 'I'm sure it wasn't your fault.'

'I don't know what happened.'

'I'm sure the holiday isn't ruined.'

Harry laughed. 'Well, it's not going too well! The car's a write-off!' He didn't like laughing. He stopped. 'I'll get you out of this. I promise.' He decided he wouldn't tell Esther about the rescue attempt, just in case it wasn't real, he couldn't entirely be sure what had actually happened back there in the pitch black. But he couldn't keep anything from Esther, it'd have been wrong, it'd have felt wrong. 'Help is on its way. I saw a farmer last night. He went to get an ambulance.'

If the Scottish farmer *were* real, then he wouldn't ever need to bend his arm to reach his mobile phone. The thought of his mobile phone suddenly made him sick with fear. His arm would snap. His arm would snap right off.

'A farmer?' she asked.

'A Scottish farmer,' he said. 'With a dog,' he added.

'Oh.'

They didn't say anything for a while. He smiled at her, she smiled at him. He felt a little embarrassed doing this after a minute or two – which was absurd, she was his wife, he shouldn't feel awkward around his wife. After a little while her eyes wandered away, began looking through him, behind him, for something which might be more interesting – and he was stung by that, just a little, as if he'd been dismissed somehow. And he was just about to turn his head away from her anyway, no matter how much it hurt, when he saw her suddenly shudder.

'The itch,' she said. 'Oh God!' And she tried to rub herself against the back of the seat, but she couldn't really do it, she could barely move. The most she could do was spasm a bit. Like a broken puppet trying to jerk itself into life – she looked pathetic, he actually wanted to laugh at the sight of her writhing there, he nearly did, and yet he felt such a pang of sympathy for her, his heart went out to her at that moment like no other. On her face was such childlike despair, *help me*, it said. And then: 'Can't you scratch my fucking back?' she screamed. 'What fucking use are you?'

He didn't think he'd ever heard her swear before. Not serious swears. Not 'fucking'. No. No, he hadn't. 'Frigging' a few times. That was it. Oh dear. Oh dear.

She breathed heavily, glaring at him. 'Sorry,' she said at last. But she didn't seem sorry. And then she closed her eyes.

And at last he could turn from her, without guilt, he *hadn't* looked away, he hadn't given up on her, in spite of everything he was still watching over her. And then he saw what Esther had been looking at behind his shoulder all that time.

Oddly enough, it wasn't the wings that caught his attention at first. Because you'd have thought the wings were the strangest thing. But no, it was the face, just the face. So round, so *perfectly* round, no, like a sphere, the head a complete sphere. You could have cut off that head and played football with it. And there was no blemish to the face, it was like this had come straight from the factory, newly minted, and every other face you had ever seen was like a crude copy of it, some cheap hack knock-off. The eyes were bright and large and very very deep, the nose a cute little pug. The cheeks were full and fat and fleshy, all puffed out.

But then Harry's eyes, of course, *were* drawn to the wings. There was only so long he could deny they were there. Large and white and jutting out of its shoulder blades. They gave occasional little flaps, as the perfect child bobbed about idly outside the car window. Creamy pale skin, a shock of bright yellow hair, and a bright yellow halo hovering above it – there was nothing to keep it there, it tilted independently of the head, sometimes at a rather rakish angle – it looked like someone had hammered a dinner tray into the skull with invisible nails. Little toes. Little fingers. Babies' fingers. And (because, yes, Harry did steal a look) there was nothing between the legs at all, the child's genitals had been smoothed out like it was a naked Action Man toy.

The little child smiled amiably at him. Then raised a knuckle. And tapped three times against the glass.

'What are you?' – which Harry knew was a pointless question, it was pretty bloody obvious what it was – and even the cherub rolled his eyes at that, but then smiled back as if to say, just kidding, no offence, no hard feelings.

The child seemed to imitate Harry's expressions, maybe he was sending him up a little – he'd put his head to one side like he did, he'd frown just the same, blink in astonishment, the whole parade. When Harry put his face close to the window it hurt, but he did it anyway – and the child put its head as close as it could too. There was just a sheet of glass between them. They could have puckered up, they could almost have kissed had they wanted! And at one point it seemed to Harry the child *did* pucker up those lips, but no, it was just taking in a breath, like a sigh, a hiss. 'Can you understand me? Can you hear what I'm saying?' The child blinked in astonishment again, fluttered its wings a bit. 'Can you get help?' And what did he expect, that it'd find a phone box and ring the emergency services, that it'd fly into the nearest police station? 'Are you here to watch over us?'

And then the cherub opened its mouth. And it wasn't a sigh, it *was* a hiss. Hot breath stained the glass; Harry recoiled from it. And the teeth were so sharp, and there were so many, how could so many teeth fit into such a small mouth? And hiding such a dainty tongue too, just a little tongue, a *baby's* tongue. The child attacked the window, it gnawed on the glass with its fangs. Desperately, hungrily, the wings now flapping wild. It couldn't break through. It glared, those bright eyes now blazing with fury, and the hissing became seething, and then it was gone – with a screech it had flown away.

There was a scratch left streaked across the pane.

Harry sat back, hard, his heart thumping. It didn't hurt to do so. There *was* pain, but it was something distant now, his body had other things to worry about. And while it was still confused, before it could catch up – and before he could change his mind – he was lifting his arm, he was bending it, and *twisting it back on itself* (and it didn't snap, not at all) he was going for his coat, pulling at the zip, pulling it down hard, he was reaching inside the coat, reaching inside the jacket inside the coat, reaching inside the pocket inside the jacket inside the – and he had it, his fingers were brushing it, his fingers were gripping it, the phone, the mobile phone.

By the time he pulled it out his body had woken up to what he was trying to do. Oh no, it said, not allowed, and told him off with a flush of hot agony – but he was having none of that, not now. The phone was turned off. Of course it was. He stabbed at the pin number, got it right second time. 'Come on, come on,' he said. The phone gave a merry little tune as it lit up. He just hoped there was enough battery power.

There was enough battery power. What it didn't have was any network coverage. Not this far out in the Highlands! Not in one of the many middles of nowhere that Scotland seemed to offer. The signal bar was down to zero.

'No,' he insisted, 'no.' And the body really didn't want him to do this, it was telling him it was a *very* bad idea, but Harry began to wave the phone about, trying to pick up any signal he could. By the time a bar showed, he was raising the phone above his head, and he was crying.

He stabbed at 999. The phone was too far away for him to hear whether there was any response. 'Hello!' he shouted. 'There's been a car crash! We've crashed the car. Help us! We're in... I don't know where we are. We're in Scotland. Scotland! Find us! Help!' And his arm was shaking with the pain, and he couldn't hold on any longer, and he dropped it, it clattered behind his seat to the floor. And at last he allowed himself a scream as he lowered his arm, and that scream felt good.

The scream didn't wake Esther. That was a good thing. At least she was sleeping soundly.

For a few minutes he let himself believe his message had been heard. That he'd held on to a signal for long enough. That the police had taken notice if he had. That they'd be able to track his position from the few seconds he'd given them. And then he just cried again, because really, why the hell shouldn't he?

He was interrupted by a voice. 'Turn around when possible.' His heart thumped again, and then he realised it was the satnav. It was that nice man from the satnav, the one who spoke well enough for telly. The display had lit up, and there was some attempt at finding a road, but they weren't on a road, were they? And Satnav was confused, poor thing, it couldn't work out what on earth was going on. 'Turn around when possible,' the satnav suggested again.

Harry had to laugh, really. He spoke to the satnav. It made him feel better to speak to someone. 'I thought I'd heard the last of you!'

And then the satnav said, 'Daddy.'

And nothing else. Not for a while.

*

For the rest of the day he didn't see anything else of the child. He didn't see much else of Esther either; once in a while she seemed to surface from a sleep, and he'd ask her if she were all right. And sometimes she'd glare at him, and sometimes she'd smile kindly, and most often she wouldn't seem to know who he was at all. And he'd doze fitfully. At one point he jerked bolt upright in the night when he thought he heard tapping against the window – 'No, go away!' – but he decided this time it really was the wind, because it soon stopped. Yes, the wind. Or the branches. Or a Scottish farmer this time, who could tell? Who could tell?

In the morning he woke to find, once again, Esther was looking straight at him. She was smiling. This was one of her smiling times.

'Good morning!' she said.

'Good morning,' he replied. 'How are you feeling?'

'I feel hungry,' she said.

'I'm sure,' he said. 'We haven't eaten in ages.'

She nodded at that.

Harry said, 'The last time would have been at that stately home. You know, we had the cream tea. You gave me one of your scones.'

She nodded at that.

Harry said, 'I bet you regret that now. Eh? Giving me one of your scones!'

She nodded at that. Grinned.

'The itching's stopped,' she declared. 'Do you know, there was a time back there that I really thought it might drive me *mad*. Really, utterly loop the loop. But it's stopped now. Everything's okay.'

'That's nice,' he said. 'I'm going to get you out of here, I promise.'

'I don't care about that any more,' she said. 'I'm very comfortable, thanks.' She grinned again. He saw how puffed her cheeks were. He supposed her face had been bruised; he supposed there was a lot of dried blood in the mouth, distorting her features like that. 'In fact,' she said, 'I feel as light as a feather.'

'You're feeling all right?'

She nodded at that.

'Can you open the door?' he asked. She looked at him stupidly. 'The door on your side. Can you open it? I can't open mine.'

She shrugged, turned a little to the left, pulled at the handle. The door swung open. The air outside was cold and delicious.

'Can you go and get help?' he asked. She turned back to him, frowned. 'I can't move,' he said. 'I can't get out. Can you get out?'

'Why would I want to do that?' she asked.

He didn't know what to say. She tilted her head to one side, waiting for an answer.

'Because you're hungry,' he said.

She considered this. Then tutted. 'I'm sure I'll find something in here,' she said. 'If I put my mind to it.' And she reached for the door, reached right outside for it, then slammed it shut. And as she did so, Harry saw how his wife's back bulged. That there was a lump underneath her blouse, and it was moving, it *rippled*. And he saw where some of it had pushed a hole through the blouse, and he saw white, he saw feathers.

'Still a bit of growing to do, but the itching has stopped,' she said. 'But don't you worry about me, *I'll* be fine.' She grinned again, and there were lots of teeth, there were too many teeth, weren't there? And then she yawned, and then she went back to sleep.

She didn't stir, not for hours. Not until the child came back. 'Daddy,' said the satnav, and it wasn't a child's voice, it was still the cultured man, calm and collected, as if he were about to navigate Harry over a roundabout. And there was the cherub – all smiles, all teeth, his temper tantrum forgotten, bobbing about the window, even waving at Harry as if greeting an old friend. And, indeed, he'd brought friends with him, a whole party of them! Lots of little cherubs, it was impossible to tell how many, they would keep on bobbing so! A dozen, maybe two dozen, who knows? And each of them had the same perfect face, the same spherical head, the same halos listing off the same gleaming hair. Tapping at the window for play, beating on the roof, beating at the door – laughing, mostly laughing, they wanted to get in but this was a game, they liked a challenge! *Mostly* laughing, though there was the odd shriek of frustration, the odd hiss, lots more scratches on the glass. One little cherub did something very bad-tempered with the radio aerial. Another little cherub punched an identical brother in the face in a dispute over the wing mirror. They scampered all over the car, but there was no way in. It all reminded Harry of monkeys at a safari park. He'd never taken Esther

98

to a safari park. He never would now. 'Daddy Daddy,' said the satnav. 'Daddy Daddy,' it kept on saying, emotionless, even cold – and the little children danced merrily outside.

'Oh, aren't they beautiful!' cooed Esther. She reached for the door. 'Shall we let them in?'

'Please,' said Harry. 'Please. Don't.'

'No. All right.' And she closed her eyes again. 'Just leaves more for me,' she said.

*

For the first few days he was very hungry. Then one day he found he wasn't hungry at all. He doubted that was a good thing.

He understood that the cherubs were hungry too. Most of them had flown away, they'd decided that they weren't going to into this particular sardine tin – but there were always one or two about, tapping away, ever more forlorn. Once in a while a cherub would turn to Harry, and pull its most innocent face, eyes all wide and Disney-dewed, it'd look so *sad*. It'd beg, it'd rub its naked belly with its baby fingers, and it'd cry. 'Daddy,' the satnav would say at such moments. But however winning their performance, the cherubs still looked fat and oily, and their puffy cheeks were glowing.

Harry supposed they probably were starving to death. But not before he would.

One day Harry woke up to find Esther was on top of him. 'Good morning,' she said to him, brightly. It should have been agony she was there, but she was as light as air, as light as a feather.

Her face was so very close to his, it was her hot breath that had roused him. Now unfurled, the wings stretched the breadth of the entire car. Her halo was grazing the roof. The wings twitched a little as she smiled down at him and bared her teeth.

'I love you,' she said.

'I know you do.'

'I want you to know that.'

'I do know it.'

'Do you love me too?'

'Yes,' he said.

And she brought that head towards his – that now spherical head, he could still recognise Esther in the features, but this was probably Esther as a child, as a darling baby girl – she brought down that head, and he couldn't move from it, he could do whatever she wanted. She opened her mouth. She kissed the tip of his nose.

She sighed. 'I'm so sorry, darling,' she said.

'I'm sorry too.'

'All the things we could have done together,' she said. 'All the places we could have been. Where would we have gone, darling?'

'I was thinking of Venice,' said Harry. 'We'd probably have gone back there one day.'

'Yes,' said Esther doubtfully.

'And we never saw Paris. Paris is lovely. We could have gone up the Eiffel Tower. And that's just Europe. We could have gone to America too.'

'I didn't need to go anywhere,' Esther told him. 'You know that, don't you? I'd have been just as happy at home, so long as you were there with me.'

'I know,' he said.

'There's so much I wanted to share with you,' she said. 'My whole life. My whole life. When I was working at the shop, if anything funny happened during the day, I'd store it up to tell you. I'd just think, I can share that now. Share it with my *hubby*. And we've been robbed. We were given one year. Just one year. And I wanted *forever*.'

'Safari parks,' remembered Harry.

'What?'

'We never did a safari park either.'

'I love you,' she said.

'I know,' he said.

Her eyes watered, they were all wide and Disney-dewed. 'I want you to remember me the right way,' she said. 'Not covered with blood. Not mangled in a car crash. Remember me the way I was. Funny, I hope. Full of life. I don't want you to spoil the memory.'

'Yes.'

'I want you to move on. Live your life without me. Have the courage to do that.'

'Yes. You're going to kill me, aren't you?'

She didn't deny it. 'All the things we could have done together. All the children we could have had.' And she gestured towards the single cherub now bobbing weakly against the window. 'All the children.'

'Our children,' said Harry.

'Heaven is *filled* with our unborn children,' said Esther. 'Yours and mine. Yours and mine. Darling. Didn't you know that?' And her wings quivered at the thought.

She bent her head towards him again – but not yet, still not yet, another kiss, that's all, a loving kiss. 'It won't be so bad,' she said. 'I promise. It itches at first, it itches like hell. But it stops. And then you'll be as light as air. As light as feathers.'

She folded her wings with a tight snap. 'I'm still getting used to that,' she smiled. And she climbed off him, and sprawled back in her seat. The neck twisted, the limbs every which way – really, so ungainly. And she went to sleep. She'd taken to sleeping with her eyes open. Harry really wished she wouldn't, it gave him the creeps.

Another set of tappings at the window. Harry looked around in irritation. There was the last cherub. Mewling at him, rubbing his belly. Harry liked to think it was the same cherub that he'd first seen, that it had been loyal to him somehow. But of course, there was really no way to tell. Tapping again, begging. So hungry. 'Daddy,' said the satnav. 'My son,' said Harry. 'Daddy.' 'My son.'

Harry wound down the window a little way. And immediately the little boy got excited, started scrabbling through the gap with his fingers. 'Just a minute,' said Harry, and he laughed even – and he gave the handle another turn, and the effort made him wince with the pain, but what was that, he was used to that. 'Easy does it,' he said to the hungry child. 'Easy does it.' And he stuck his hand out of the car.

The first instinct of his baby son was not to bite, it was to nuzzle. It rubbed its face against Harry's hand, and it even purred, it was something like a purr. It was a good five seconds at least before it sank its fangs into flesh.

And then Harry had his hand around its throat. The cherub gave a little gulp of surprise. 'Daddy?' asked the satnav. It blinked with astonishment, just as it had echoed Harry's own expressions when they'd first met, and Harry thought, I taught him that, *I taught my little boy*. And he squeezed hard. The fat little cheeks bulged even fatter, it looked as if the whole head was now a balloon about to pop. And then he pulled that little child to him as fast as he could – banging his head against the glass, thump, thump, *thump*, and the pain in his arm was appalling, but that was good, he *liked* the pain, he wanted it – thump one more time, and there was a crack, something broke, and the satnav said 'Daddy,' so calm, so matter-of-fact – and then never spoke again.

He wound the window down further. He pulled in his broken baby boy.

He discovered that its entire back was covered with the same feathers that made up the wings. So for the next half hour he had to pluck it.

The first bite was the hardest. Then it all got a lot easier.

'Darling,' he said to Esther, but she wouldn't wake up. 'Darling, I've got dinner for you.' He hated the way she slept with her eyes open, just staring out sightless like that. And it wasn't her face any more, it was the face of a cherub, of their dead son. 'Please, you must eat this,' he said, and put a little of the creamy white meat between her lips; it just fell out on to her chin. 'Please,' he said again, and this time it worked, it stayed in, she didn't wake up, but it stayed in, she was eating, that was the main thing.

He kissed her then, on the lips. And he tasted what would have been. And yes, they would have gone to a safari park, and no, they wouldn't have gone back to Venice, she'd have talked him out of it, but yes, America would have been all right. And yes, they would have had rows, real rows, once in a while, but that would have been okay, the marriage would have survived, it would all have been okay. And yes, children, yes.

When he pulled his lips from hers she'd been given her old face back. He was so relieved he felt like crying. Then he realised he already was.

The meat had revived him. Raw as it was, it was the best he had ever tasted. He could do anything. Nothing could stop him now.

He forced his legs free from under the dashboard, it hurt a lot. And then he undid his seatbelt, and that hurt too. He climbed his way to Esther's door, he had to climb over Esther, 'sorry, darling,' he said, as he accidentally kicked her head. He opened the door. He fell outside. He took in breaths of air.

'I'm not leaving you,' he said to Esther. 'I can see the life we're going to have together.' And yes, the head was on a bit funny, but he could live with that. And she had wings, but he could pluck them. He could pluck them as he had his son's.

He probably had some broken bones, he'd have to find out. So he shouldn't have been able to pick up his wife in his arms. But her wings helped, she was so light.

And it was carrying Esther that he made his way up the embankment, up through the bushes and brambles, up towards the road. And it was easy, it was as if he were floating – he was with the woman he loved, and he always would be, he'd never let her go, and she was so light, she was as light as feathers, she was as light as air.

602 – The rebel Phocas seizes the Byzantine throne. He executes the emperor, after forcing him to watch the murder of his five sons. **604** – Wendi, emperor of China, is killed by his son, Yangdi, who takes power. **610** – A former camel driver called Muhammad begins to preach an entire new religion at Mecca. It's called Islam. It'll catch on. **610** – Heraclius overthrows Phocas; the emperor's own personal guard desert him, and he is captured without resistance. Heraclius has Phocas brought to him. 'Is this how you have ruled, wretch?' he asks. Phocas replies, 'And will you rule any better?' The furious Heraclius lops off Phocas' head on the spot; his corpse is torn apart and burned. *So we left the cinema. And we sat outside it, on a park bench. Nobody took notice of us, we weren't important, just a couple of teenagers with nothing to say. There really was nothing to say for a while, and I said I should get home, and she said – no, wait, not yet. All right, I said. All right, I'll wait. And then she pointed out the stars to me. The Seven Sisters and the Great Bear – she gave them these names, she tried to show me the shapes they formed, but they just looked a random mess to me. I told her this. She laughed, a little shyly. She said that when she thought of history, all those dates, all those battles, she felt the same thing – all just random, no shape to it.* **612** – Catastrophic losses as the Chinese invade Korea. **613** – Fredegunde gets her revenge on her old enemy Brunhilde, from beyond the grave. Her son, Clotaire, has the elderly queen tortured for three days, then stuck on top of a camel and led through his army, before tying her to the feet of wild horses so she's trampled to death. **615** – Jerusalem is sacked by the Persians, who make off with the 'True Cross' on which Christ was crucified as part of their booty. **617** – In China, Yangdi is overthrown. His reign has been marked by extreme profligacy. He has a second capital city built, mobilising two million men to work on the palaces and artificial lakes. His pleasure park alone covers sixty square miles; when he rides there in winter he has the bare branches of its trees hung with silken flowers. Nothing survives today of this city. Yangdi is strangled. *It was a clear night, there were no clouds in the sky, and it was a bit cold, but she didn't want to go home. 'When you look at stars,' she told me, 'you're looking backwards in time. Because the light has taken so long to get here, when it reaches our eyes we're seeing how that star looked millions of years ago. It may not even be there any more, it might have already exploded, the explosion just hasn't got here yet.' I knew what she was trying to do, she wanted to share my history with me. And kiss me, of course, she definitely wanted that, as she whispered to me she kept making little feints at my face with her lips. So I let the lips meet. We kissed. We kissed for a long time, and it was distracting, it was hard to keep my mind on important things. And as she sucked at my tongue I thought how great it would be if she were right – and that when we disengaged we'd look up and all the stars would be gone, they'd all have blown up aeons ago and we'd have missed the whole thing. And once the idea was in my head I couldn't let it go, I couldn't resist a peek, I pulled away from her and looked up at the sky to see. I was very disappointed. So, I think, was she.* **621** – Muhammad is said to have flown to heaven from Mecca and back on a winged unicorn. Being the 666th year since the inauguration of the Julian calendar in 44 BC, with the apocalyptic dread that number inspires, Christians use the importance of this year to Islam to foster anti-Muslim dread for centuries to come. **624** – Muhammad leads a decisive victory against the Quraish in Mecca at the battle of Badr, only sustaining fourteen casualties. In Islamic history this has been attributed to divine intervention, and the conflict is described in detail in the Qu'ran. What Christ accomplished through crucifixion, Muhammad accomplishes with military genius, or God's favour, or luck – and on one single day in March history bends around Islam and changes forever. And into the twenty-first century, the name 'Badr' is frequently used by Muslim armies and paramilitary groups. **629** – Conversely, in Scotland, there emerges a ruler of less military renown. Domnall Brecc (or 'Spotty Donald') comes to the throne of Kintyre; he will fight four major battles against Ulster, and lose every single one. **630** – The eight-year-old emperor of Persia, Ardashir III, is murdered by the general Shahrbaraz. Shahrbaraz reigns a full six weeks before he too is murdered. **630** – Heraclius recovers the True Cross. To make his victory all the grander, he insists on carrying the cross as he enters Jerusalem. He finds that amongst all the pomp it's too heavy – but once he gets down from his horse and removes the crown from his head, the cross miraculously becomes light, and the city gates open to him of their own accord. **638** – Islamic forces capture Jerusalem. They will keep control of it until the Christian church leads a crusade against them 450 years later. **639** – The death of King Dagobert, the strongest king in France for another hundred and fifty years. But he becomes best known for featuring in a nursery rhyme over a millennium later, 'le bon roi Dagobert', in which he's cast as an idiot who needs his chief adviser to extricate him from ridiculous mishaps. In spite of all his achievements, this rhyme becomes especially popular during the French Revolution to poke fun at the monarchy, and the long history that'd being wiped aside. **641** – The fifteen-year-old Byzantine Emperor Heraklonas is suspected of murdering his brother (who, in fact, dies from tuberculosis). Heraklonas becomes the first reigning emperor to be subject to mutilation, and his nose is cut out. **642** – Emperor Taizong issues a decree throughout China that severely punishes men who, in order to avoid his military conscription, deliberately break their own legs. **643** – Crown Prince Li Cheng Qian loses favour at the Chinese court. He is obsessed by Turkey – speaks only Turkish, wears Turkish clothes, lives in a tent, and steals sheep – choosing to cook the sheep, nomad fashion, over a camp fire. **645** – The Isshi Incident. The Empress of Japan is so spiritually polluted by an assassination of a court official in her presence that she renounces the throne. **646** – Alexandria is betrayed to Islam by its gatekeeper. *And I thought of the stars and the planets, and how we couldn't get to them, and how because we couldn't get to them nothing bad ever happened to them, and because nothing bad ever happened they had no history. Try to compile the history for the planet Jupiter, for all its massive size it'd make a very small time chart. The biggest event in Uranus' history was when it was discovered by Herschel in 1781, and the joke is it wouldn't even have known about it. Or, I don't know, maybe I'm wrong. Maybe it was a very big deal for Uranus. Maybe it felt it had finally earned some respect – 'I've been validated!' – maybe it had a party up there, maybe it invited all the other celestial bodies, and they celebrated. And had nibbles. And danced. Uranus would have reassured Neptune it'd have its own discovery soon (1846); hang on in there, little Pluto, they'll get to you eventually (1930). I phoned my girlfriend that night to tell her this (I thought she had to be my girlfriend now, we'd kissed, hadn't we?) It was pretty late, though, and I think I woke her parents, they sounded cross. I told her that the planets had parties, that they just wanted a bit of history too. 'You're weird,' she told me. But she laughed as she said it, and it didn't stop her wanting to see me again.* **653** – After his conversion, Sigebert II of Essex is murdered by an excommunicated kinsman sick to death of the king's desire to forgive everyone in a true Christian spirit. **653** – Pope Martin I is abducted by Byzantine Emperor Constans II, and left to die in the Crimea. **655** – King Cadfael of Gwynedd flees the battle of Winwaed, earning the nickname Cadomedd (Battle Shirker). **656** – Outbreak of the first Islamic civil war, in the battle of the Camel. It destroys the unity of the Muslim ummah, and permanently divides Islam into Shi'a and Sunni sects. **660** – Lady Wu Zetian takes power in China. On her ascent from concubine to empress she has strangled her own baby and framed a rival for the murder; she has poisoned a sister, a niece and a son, and forced another son to hang himself; she has had four grandchildren whipped to death. Now she celebrates her supremacy by taking the former empress and the senior concubine, amputating their limbs, and throwing their remains in a wine vat to die. **663** – Constans II moves his court from Constantinople to Italy, in a last ditch attempt to stop the Arab conquests, and to restore Rome as the seat of the empire. He fails spectacularly. The Roman Empire will continue in name until the fifteenth century, but no future emperor will set foot there. **668** – Constans is murdered in his bath by his chamberlain. *In 2006 they decided Pluto wasn't a planet any more. I bet all the 'proper' planets ostracised it, they didn't invite it to any more parties.* **671** – The Anglo-Saxon Chronicle grimly reports, 'This year happened that great destruction among the fowls.' Even the chickens have it bad in the seventh century. **672** – Emperor Kobun rules in Japan, before being usurped by his uncle in the Jinshin War. **672** – The Picts under the leadership of Drust are so crushed in battle with Northumbria that it's said their bodies block two rivers. **676** – King Athelred of Mercia invades Kent and destroys the church at Rochester. He later becomes a monk. **680** – At the battle of Karbala, the Shiite leader Hussein is killed. His followers declare him a martyr, and the battle site becomes their holy city. **681** – Emperor Constantine IV mutilates his brothers so they are ineligible for rule. **685** – Plague kills everyone in a Northumbrian monastery, save the abbot and a child – who will grow up to be Bede, the father of English history. Oh, those who chronicle history, they always get lucky. *And there's one more historical story about Pluto. On 21 June 2006 Pluto's newly discovered moons were named Hydra and Nix. For a while. Max Mutchler and Andrew Steffl must have felt like giants in the astronomical field; they were the men who had found moons to a bona fide planet. A small planet, and a distant one, but a planet nonetheless – and that glory lasted less than three months, because in September Pluto was relegated to 'dwarf planet'. I'm sure that Mutchler and Steffl were still treated with the same respect at the Hubble Space Telescope staff canteen, I'm sure no-one tried to trip them up or spit in their food. I don't know, though. People can be so cruel.* **686** – Empress Jito takes the throne in Japan, and has her stepson executed on trumped-up charges of treason. **686** – King Caedwalla establishes his brother Mul as sub-king of Kent; a few months later rebels trap Mul in a house near Canterbury and burn him alive. **692** – The Byzantine army under the command of Leontios is crushed by Muslims at the battle of Sebastopolis; Emperor Justinian II is furious, and has the general imprisoned for three years. **693** – The death of Brude III, king of the Picts. When his dying body is prayed over all night, he shows in the morning marked signs of recovery. The monks believe it's a miracle – but also that a miracle sets up expectations far too high for Brude to meet, so they let him die. **694** – Egica, the Visigoth king of Hispania, decides that the Jews are in league with the Muslims, and sentences them all hereafter to slavery. **695** – Leontius is freed. He responds by leading a revolt against Justinian, and mutilating him. The emperor, now called 'the noseless', is banished. **698** – The Muslims capture Carthage from the Byzantine Empire, and utterly destroy it. Leontius is deposed by the army. They cut off his nose. *Don't judge me because I decided to kill my child. I don't judge you, because you decided not to kill yours.*

WITHOUT YOU, I WOULDN'T BE ALIVE

There weren't very many regulars at the shop. It wasn't a very good shop. The turnover of stock was regular enough, but none of the books that were donated were up to much – not since Oxfam had opened up the road, that was what got all the interesting stuff, all the first editions and complete encyclopaedia sets, it was a glamorous name, Oxfam, you couldn't compete with that. So what they got stuck with was all the airport novels, the beach trash, all the school texts, anything that had been water damaged. Nothing with which to lure your discerning charity shop browser.

But there *were* regulars, and Barbara always had a smile for them. There was the woman who popped in two or three times a week looking for Mills and Boons – Barbara didn't know why, the woman was ever so pretty, and young, and looked so sweet; if Barbara had ever looked as sweet as that she wouldn't have wanted to *read* about romance, it was sad, really. And then there was the old man with the stick, he'd come most weekends, asking if they had any Dan Dare annuals. 'Do you have Dan Dare?' he'd ask politely, and of course they never had, and he'd thank Barbara and leave, there'd never be the slightest emotion to it, he'd never show any disappointment or resignation, he'd accept the news of Dan Dare deficiency with absolute calm. Barbara wondered whether he had any better luck at Oxfam. She bet he did.

Then there was the other man. The man who came on Monday afternoons. Barbara didn't like him much, not at first.

He wasn't an old man; he was much younger than Barbara, at any rate. But he moved like an old man, as if he was weary of everything, as if the world's problems had all been placed on *his* shoulders for *him* to deal with exclusively – and Barbara supposed he might indeed have problems, but how many problems could a man have? He was the one visiting the charity shop, not the one working in it.

She'd put him in his mid-fifties; he might even be late forties, at a push. It was hard to tell. It might help if he lost a bit of weight, it might help if he smiled a bit. Because he didn't ever smile, no matter how much Barbara would flash hers at him when he went to the cash register. And he wouldn't say much, he'd only grunt, no matter how cheerily she'd try to make conversation – 'ooh, these'll keep you busy for a while!' if he was buying more than one book, or 'oh, I like her,' if he was getting a Catherine Cookson, or 'ooh, scary!', if it were a Stephen King. The grunt wouldn't be a rude grunt, but it'd be a lazy grunt, and that somehow made it so much worse. And he was *peculiar.* The man who wanted Dan Dare scanned the shelves for Dan Dare; the woman who liked Mills and Boon went straight for the heart-throb section. This man looked at everything. He'd start on the left of the top shelf, work his way along, then having reached the end he'd work his way backwards on the shelf below. Forwards and backwards until every shelf had been covered, and picking up *every* book. Looking inside it, inside the front cover, at where Barbara would have pencilled the price – then swiftly putting it back into its place. Drawing books, cookery books, books about travelling abroad, novels in both hardback and paperback editions: he'd look at them all, he'd give each and every one his inspection.

One Monday Barbara decided to stop smiling at the man altogether. Indeed, she'd even give him a frown. Indeed, she'd bristle with displeasure when he came close – contrary to her charity shop training all those months ago. He didn't even notice. 'What are you getting all these books for?' she asked him curtly.

'I beg your pardon?' he said, and blinked in surprise. And it was a gentler voice than she'd expected. And she supposed she might have pushed the curtness too far after all.

'It's just that there's no rhyme or reason to what you buy,' she said. 'I can make no sense of it.'

'There's rhyme *and* reason,' he said, and gave her a smile, just a little one, the first one he ever gave her. 'Look.' And he picked up a copy of a Delia Smith. Delia was on the cover brandishing an egg. He opened it, pointed inside.

'What am I supposed to be looking at?' asked Barbara.

'The inscription.'

She read it. It was in faded biro. *Without you, I wouldn't be alive.*

'I don't get it,' said Barbara.

'Doesn't it strike you as a bit odd?' asked the man.

She looked at it again, frowned. *Without you, I wouldn't be alive.* 'No, not really,' she said at last.

'What do you suppose it means?' he asked patiently.

Barbara shrugged. 'I suppose the book's a gift to someone,' she said. 'And the person who's giving it is in love. You know, and is saying, "Hello, I can't live without you".'

'Then why not say that? "I can't live without you", that's fairly standard. It's the stuff of pop songs. But this is back to front. "Without you, I wouldn't be alive" – it's emphasising the "you", isn't it? It's putting the stress right on the recipient.'

'I suppose so.'

'It seems a bit aggressive. Don't you think? "I can't live without you", nice and comfy. "Without you, I can't live" – as if there's a *responsibility* here. Don't you think?'

'Hmm,' said Barbara.

'As if there's even *blame*. "I'm alive, I may not necessarily want to be, so what are you going to do about it?"'

'Hmm,' said Barbara. 'Hmmm. I don't know. Don't you think it's just back to front accidentally?'

'No,' said the man. 'I really don't. Look at the comma. What's the comma doing there?'

'It breaks the sentence up a bit.'

'Yes, that's what commas do,' said the man. 'But it's not really necessary here, is it? It makes perfect sense without it. If anything, it's a bit archaic. This is a writer who knows *exactly* what he wants to do. And that's why the comma is there, it's to tell the reader that everything is deliberate. The aggression, everything, that this isn't just your usual bit of love guff gone wrong.'

'Okay,' said Barbara.

'So you've got this single sentence, this single *weighty* sentence, full of passion and, yes, even a threat there. And where does he write it? It's in a *cookery* book.

Something factual, something with, I don't know, lots of *ingredients* in, and pictures of cakes. A cookery book, of all things!'

'Why?' asked Barbara. 'If it's got the importance you're suggesting...'

'Exactly,' said the man, 'exactly. Why? I don't know, I'll never know.' And he closed the book up tight. 'But it's a story, isn't it?'

'This is what you do?' asked Barbara. 'You collect books with messages inside them?'

'They were part of people's lives,' said the man. 'Thousands of these books published, millions sometimes, all sitting there in bookshops, all uniform, exactly the same. And then someone comes along, and writes something in the front, and they become unique. And you get this glimpse of another person, another life. Another story to the one that's actually in *print*.'

'So you don't care what the book itself may be...?'

'Never.'

'And you wouldn't read what the book has to say, the novel, or the recipes, or...?'

'What's the point? Those are the bits they *want* you to read.'

Barbara smiled. 'It's a lovely idea,' she said. 'But I think you're wrong. I think that message, it just got turned backwards, that's all. There's nothing to the comma, it's just a comma. And it was just inside a cookery book because the person happened to like cooking.'

The man shrugged. 'You may be right,' he said. He paid for his books and left.

After he'd gone, Max scurried over. Max didn't like confrontation, and had been hiding at the back of the shop with the used blouses and the used skirts. 'Are you all right?' he asked. 'He seemed a bit cross.'

'He wasn't cross, he was just *intense*,' said Barbara. She quite liked Max, but he wasn't very good with people, and the fact he clearly wasn't able to see the difference between anger and depth didn't surprise her. Max always wore a cardigan, and his eyes watered a lot, it made his face look very tragic and just a bit irritating. Barbara thought he was probably retired, or widowed or gay.

*

You say you want something that'll last longer than flowers or a box of chocolates. So I got you this!

It's over 800 pages, and the writing's very small! (And no pictures – I flicked through, I checked!) So this ought to last a while!!

It'd take me years to get through a book like this. I'd never reach the end!

I love you. I hope our love lasts as long as it would take me to read this book.

*

I asked the man in the shop, and he said this was the best book they had.

You can't be sure with shop assistants. If it isn't the best book, let me know, I've kept the receipt. I think he was the manager, mind. He was the only one wearing a tie.

*

Usually when people brought donations into the shop, Barbara wouldn't take much notice – she'd thank them, of course, profusely, and take the bags from them (often bin liners, actually, which more or less summed up the average quality of the donations) and she'd lug them into the back room. Max could poke through them, or maybe one of the other volunteers.

But now she'd ask, 'Any books?' And if there were, she'd take a look. The majority, as she expected, didn't have inscriptions inside at all. But if there was any writing, she'd put the book to one side. 'Happy Christmas' was quite a common one, and so was 'Happy Christmas!' and Barbara couldn't decide whether the addition of the exclamation mark made it more interesting or less interesting. Of course, it didn't really matter what she thought. It mattered only if it interested *him*. She'd ask on Monday. She'd ask next time he came to see her.

'No,' he said, 'the exclamation mark makes no difference whatsoever.'

'Oh,' said Barbara. 'I thought after that business with the comma...'

'Some people just use exclamation marks, some don't. It's no big deal. It's not a story, is it?' Barbara supposed not. He looked through the stack of books she'd kept aside for him. 'No, these are all useless,' he said.

'Oh dear,' she said.

'Not *everything's* worth having, just because it's got a dedication inside,' he told her. 'Christmas presents are usually not worth the bother. Everyone gives presents at Christmas, they have to, there's so little thought in it.'

'And birthdays?' asked Barbara.

'Birthdays aren't so bad,' said the man, already looking away from her, already bored. 'People get caught on the hop at birthdays, they sometimes come out with all manner of stuff. Look,' he added, and turned back to her, and even glared a little, 'could you stop picking books out for me? I like going through the shelves myself. That's the point.'

'I was just trying to help,' said Barbara.

'I can see that.'

'I could take your name and phone number,' said Barbara, and her heart skipped a little as she said it, and she didn't really know why, 'and I could give you a call if anything comes in.'

'Good God, no,' said the man, and he looked genuinely disgusted by the suggestion. 'I'm sure you mean well. But this is *my* thing, all right? It's what *I* do. And these books,' and he waved a hand at the pile she'd prepared so carefully for him, 'are pathetic. Really.'

'I see,' said Barbara.

'No offence,' said the man.

'None taken.'

He didn't give her a smile that Monday.

Barbara wondered what his name and his phone number might be.

*

Dear Baby Bob,
   Welcome to the world!
   You're far too young to read yet, we know. But one day you'll open this up. And then you must

come to us, whatever we are doing, and we'll sit you on Daddy's lap. And Mummy will read to you. You'll love Tigger, and Eeyore, and silly old Winnie the Pooh. The bit where they hunt the heffalumps!

We'll never let you down. And if we do, you tell us, and we'll try harder.

This is your very first book, and there'll be many many more.

*

Do you remember how we met? I've bought this book for you in honour of that moment.

The room was packed, but for me, suddenly, there was no-one else there but you. Our eyes met across a crowded room. And from that moment I knew, I just knew, that I'd found the love of my life. From then on everything would be different. When you first spoke to me, do you remember what you said? 'You're beautiful,' you said. I blush to think of it. And you have such a great voice. And every time you say it to me now, and you do, every day, I still blush. I'm the luckiest woman in the world. xxxx

*

'What are you doing?' asked Max.

She looked up, a little guiltily. Then decided she'd no reason to feel guilty at all. And explained.

'Oh,' said Max. 'Is that a good idea?'

'It's not as if the books belong to anyone, is it?' asked Barbara. 'They're just going to sit here on the shelves. And if all it takes to shift them will be something nice written inside, then what's the harm? It's all the more money to the starving children in Africa, isn't it?'

'I wasn't worrying about the children in Africa,' Max said. 'I was thinking more – of *him*.'

'Why?'

'Well,' said Max. 'The books you're selling him will be fakes.'

'How can they be fakes? He collects books which have things written inside. These will have things written inside.'

'I don't know,' said Max. 'He might not see it that way.'

'He won't mind,' said Barbara. 'He'll never know.'

Inside the first book she'd gone for something rather romantic – a gift, she imagined, from a loving wife to a loving husband. Maybe it was an anniversary, or maybe it was just an act of impulse! Oh, the ambiguity! And inside a copy of *House at Pooh Corner* she'd written something for a little baby. As she began to write out this second one, she realised she needed to disguise her handwriting a little, so made it a bit shaky. She liked the effect, actually. She liked to imagine this was written by a mother so overcome with adoration for her newborn son that she couldn't hold the pen straight.

When he came into the shop, she deliberately looked down at the counter, studied the cash register. Max retreated unhappily to the second-hand skirts. The man did his usual trick of examining each and every book. On the second shelf he found a copy of *The Da Vinci Code* by Dan Brown; on the bottom, amongst all the oversized children's annuals, he found the Pooh.

He brought them both to the till. 'Find anything interesting?' she asked, as blandly as possible.

'I'm trying to decide which one to get,' he said.

'Why not get both?'

'Because I don't collect multiples,' said the man, 'and these have both been written in by the same person.'

Barbara blushed at this. 'Are you sure?' she said. 'The handwriting doesn't look the same.'

'It is the same.'

'This one's much shakier.'

He said nothing to that.

'I think I'll go for the children's book,' he said. 'It's sadder.'

'It's not sad,' said Barbara. 'You've not read it properly...' Then she picked up the book, 'I bet,' she added, and read her handiwork, and nodded. 'There's nothing sad in that.'

'They're both *pretty* sad,' said the man. 'This Dan Brown, it's *awful*. She's telling this husband of hers how they first met, and in such detail. I mean, wasn't he there? Shouldn't he *know*? Maybe she's making it up.'

'Oh,' said Barbara.

'But if she *is* making it up, why at least not make it more interesting? "Eyes met across a crowded room" indeed, what nonsense. The woman's either living a cliché, or she's only got the imagination to *think* in clichés. I'm not sure what's sadder. Yes, I do.'

'Oh,' said Barbara again. And then, 'But the dedication to the baby. That isn't sad at all.'

'Yes, it is,' said the man. 'Because it's *here*.'

Barbara shook her head. 'I don't understand.'

'This is a special book,' said the man. 'The first present given to an infant. By doting parents. Too doting by half, from the sound of it. This book is *precious*. So why's it been given to a charity shop?'

'I don't know,' said Barbara.

'Because the child's dead,' said the man.

'No,' Barbara breathed.

'Maybe the baby was ill right from the start. Maybe that's what the message is, a message of desperate hope. For a child they *know* isn't going to read it. Maybe that's why the handwriting is so shaky.'

'Oh, please stop,' said Barbara. 'Please.'

'I'll take Winnie the Pooh,' said the man.

Barbara rang it up on the cash register. 'I thought what you were doing was *sweet*,' said Barbara. 'Collecting all these little love stories.'

'I don't believe in love,' said the man flatly. Then he thought about this, and said, 'No, that's not fair. I believe *they* believe in it. The ones who write inside the books. But at the end of the day, they just chuck them all aside. I'm only able to buy their loving inscriptions because someone stops believing in them.'

'You prefer the inscriptions to be sad?' asked Barbara.

'They're all sad.'

'Do you want a bag?'

*

I hope you enjoy this book. It was my favourite book when I was a girl.

I suppose this isn't the sort of book you'd normally read. It is a bit girly. And about horses! But it means a lot to me.

I suppose lately I haven't been feeling myself. That's not because of you, I don't think it's you. But I'm not sure who I am any more. And this book used to make me very happy, horses and all. I think I liked who I was back then. So if you're going to understand me, I think you'd have to like this book. And if you don't, then maybe you're not worth having, and all this isn't good for me any more.

I look forward to your feedback.

*

All the reviews say this is the funniest book of the year.

Do you remember when we used to laugh?

*

She kept a notebook by her bedside.

It wasn't hard coming up with her little stories of love. They were all so close to the surface of her thoughts, she'd had no idea they'd been there bubbling away, and when she picked up her pen, out of her they'd just *stream*, set free at last. So sad, so full of despair, all of them writing their dedications to people who wouldn't notice, or wouldn't care, or wouldn't even bother to read them, fobbing the books off on the nearest charity shop without a second thought.

She felt badly for them, all these wounded little souls. All trying to put such a brave face on things. Some of them doing rather better at it than others.

The hard part wasn't creating the fictions. It was putting them down on paper. She experimented in her notebook, but the best she could come up with was a slight variant on the shaky handwriting she'd used for the Pooh book. That wouldn't fool him for a moment.

'I could write them out for you, if you like,' said Max.

'They need to look different,' said Barbara. 'All of them, very different.'

'I understand. I can do that. I know I can.'

'Why would you want to?'

'Well,' said Max. 'I mean. It's for the starving kids in Africa, isn't it?'

'Yes,' said Barbara. 'We'll be helping those poor starving children.'

'Well then,' said Max. And began to practise.

And on that next Monday, both Barbara and Max waited to see whether the man would fall for it. He frowned a little at one of the books, and Barbara's heart was in her mouth, what would she say if he challenged her? But it turned out that he was only trying to make out the price, it had been obscured by Max's little essay. He bought both books without comment.

'You're really very good,' said Barbara, 'thank you!' And she gave Max a hug. In one book the writing was small and spidery, in another the pen strokes were confident and bold, in a third he was able to affect the scrawl of a dyslexic child.

'You've a real artistry for this,' said Barbara, 'it's real art.' 'Thank you,' said Max, 'give me a hug.' 'Of course you can have another hug!' said Barbara. 'Thanks,' said Max, and as she squeezed him tight his eyes watered.

'Funny sort of hobby,' Barbara said lightly to the man one day. 'What must your wife think!'

'I'm not married,' said the man. 'And it isn't a hobby.'

'Doesn't mean he hasn't got a girlfriend,' said Max, when Barbara told him later.

'Of course he hasn't got a girlfriend!' said Barbara. 'Don't be silly. He'd have said, wouldn't he? It would have been the perfect time for him to have said it.'

'Or he might be gay,' said Max.

'Ha!' said Barbara merrily. 'You wish!'

One Monday she put *Paddington Marches On* on to the shelves too early. A mother came to the till, Paddington in one hand, small child in the other.

'It's not for sale,' said Barbara smoothly.

'It was on the shelf,' said the mother.

'It's been reserved.'

'It was on the shelf,' said the mother again, 'and my son likes Paddington books.'

'He won't like this one,' said Barbara. 'This is the one in which Paddington *dies*.'

'I don't remember that,' said the mother.

'Oh yes. It's very traumatic.'

'Paddington's a bear! Bears can't die!' And the little boy burst into tears.

'Everything dies,' Barbara assured him. 'Bears, most especially of all.'

An hour or so later, as the man bought himself the copy of *Paddington Marches On*, Barbara asked whether he remembered the *House at Pooh Corner* he'd bought from her a month or so before.

'Yes,' he said. 'What about it?'

'The woman who donated it came back to the shop,' said Barbara. 'And I asked her. I asked her whether her baby had died.'

'Oh?'

'You were wrong,' said Barbara. 'The child's fine. The child's fine, he's doing well, he's happy. There's no tragedy. He just didn't like Winnie the Pooh, that was all it was.'

'Well then,' said the man. 'Then there *is* still a tragedy. Because every child ought to like Winnie the Pooh.' And he surprised her with a grin, and it was only the second time he'd ever smiled at her.

That night Barbara went to bed, and wrote half a dozen stories in her notebook, and she had to reject them all because they were too cheerful.

*

Dear Mum,
  Happy Christmas.
  I know this will be a hard Christmas for you, but remember — you're not alone.
  xxx

*

Here's a little something for you to read on your flight.

Thank you for the week we've had together. It was magical. You were magical.

I mean what I said – I'll never take you away from your home, or your wife, or your children. But spare a thought for me once in a while, won't you?

See you next year? xx

*

Max wasn't happy. 'Are you sure you want me to write this?'

'Yes,' said Barbara.

'I don't want to write it,' said Max. 'I'm not going to write it,' he said to her, an hour later.

An hour after that he found her at the cash register, after she'd sold somebody a portable television with a broken remote. His face was puffy, and his eyes were more watery than usual. 'It'll change everything,' he said.

'I know.'

'Are you sure?' he asked again.

'If you can't write it, I will,' said Barbara. 'I've got the book right here.' It was *The Royal Horticultural Society Book of Garden Flowers*, a coffee table tome with a large enough inside front cover to take everything she wanted to say.

'No, I'll do it, I'll do it,' said Max. 'I do it better than you.'

She stood over him as he wrote, round and broad, and all too legible. *Dear Man, who comes into my shop every Monday.*

And, as on every Monday, the man came into her shop.

She watched him as he sifted through the books. She wasn't going to pretend this time she wasn't staring. He didn't see.

When he found the latest inscription, he stood there and read it for a good five minutes. It was quite a long inscription, but not that long.

He walked over to the cash register.

'Is this true?' he said.

'Yes,' said Barbara.

'This is yours?'

'Yes.'

She looked at him boldly. She wasn't going to look away now.

'Do you think that...?' he asked. 'Do you want...?'

'Yes,' she said.

'We could maybe do something.'

'Yes.'

'Have a meal. Tonight, if you want.'

'Is this a date?' Barbara asked.

'There's a nice Italian up the high road.'

'Is this a date?' she insisted.

'Yes, all right,' he said.

'Okay then,' said Barbara.

'Okay.' But he still didn't smile.

'What's your name?'

'Tim.'

It wasn't as good as she'd hoped, but better than she'd feared.

'Half past seven good for you?' she asked.

He nodded. 'I'll see you there.'

'Do you want to buy the book?'

'Oh. Oh. Yes. All right then.'

She put it in a bag for him.

He left.

'You did it,' said Max.

'I did! Oh God,' said Barbara. And she beamed. 'Oh God, I'm so frightened!' She walked down to the used skirts. 'Can I have a hug?'

'I don't want to give you a hug,' said Max.

*

My dear darling hubby bear!

I love you so, so much! You've no idea how much. Sometimes I think my heart is just going to explode! And it gets better day after day, year after year.

You transform me.

The only love I feel that is greater and purer is the pure love I feel for our Lord Jesus Christ. One day you'll see.

x

*

Happy anniversary!

Can you believe it's only been three weeks since we first met, and we fell in love, and you changed my life forever. Happy three week anniversary!

Thank you for being you.

P.S. If you don't love me the way I love you, could you let me know?

*

She ordered a lasagne; he ordered a lasagne too. He asked her if she wanted a starter, and she asked him if he was going to have a starter, and he said he really wasn't sure how long he could stay out tonight so he'd better not, but she could have a starter if she liked. And she said that if he was in such a rush she'd better not have a starter either, and he said he wasn't in a rush, not really, and coerced her into a plate of garlic bread.

He asked for a half bottle of wine.

'So, Tim,' said Barbara. 'What is it that you do?'

'I collect books.'

'Yes, I know.'

'You know that.'

'Yes, I do. But that's a hobby.'

'It's not a hobby.'

'Okay,' said Barbara. 'So. Tim. What hobbies do you have?'

'I don't have any hobbies.'

'You must do,' said Barbara, '*everyone* has hobbies.' And she hoped he wouldn't turn it back on her, ask what hobbies *she* had, because she couldn't actually think of any.

He didn't ask.

The waiter lit their candle. At some point, someone turned the music up.

'Excuse me,' said Barbara, after she'd finished her lasagne, 'I need to powder my nose.' He nodded. She made her way to the back of the restaurant, through the swing doors, to freedom. She sat on the toilet and wondered how long she could politely stay there. She wondered if she really had to go back to the table at all. She supposed she better had.

As she threaded her way back through the other diners, all of whom were chatting to each other quite amiably, she thought up a new conversation topic. 'So, Tim,' she said, masking a sigh, as she plopped back into her chair, 'so, do you have a favourite sport?'

'Excuse me,' he said, rising instantly. 'I need to use the toilet too.'

'Okay,' said Barbara.

He was gone long enough that she wondered whether he was coming back – maybe he'd done a bunk, maybe he had more courage than her. She wouldn't have blamed him. Even if she were stuck with the bill, that would seem a small price to pay that she could now go home and put the evening behind her. In fact, she thought, she might as well ask for the bill now. The lasagne had been eaten, the wine all but drunk, and she was in no mood for the dessert menu. And as she cast around for a waiter, the paper napkin in front of her caught her eye.

There was writing on it. In biro.

I'm sorry, I'm really not very good at this. I'm very shy. Please don't be cross.

She read it back a few times. He'd written it very carefully, making sure the thin paper didn't tear. Now she knew, she thought, what *his* handwriting looked like.

She leaned across the table, took his own napkin. She fiddled in her handbag for a pen. She always carried a pen now, just in case inspiration struck for one of her little love stories.

I'm a bit shy too, she wrote. *It's all right.*

The moment she put the napkin back on his place mat, he returned. He read her message grimly. 'I was waiting for...' Then he tutted, took out his pen, wrote for a while. Then he passed the napkin to her.

I was waiting for you to read my letter. And then to see whether you'd write back. I wasn't sure you were going to. I've been hovering over by the toilets for ages, hoping that you would.

'That's silly,' said Barbara. 'You needn't have done that.'

It's easier when it's written down. I'm sorry. I haven't dated for a long time.

I haven't dated for a long time either. It's all right.

I haven't dated for fifteen years, seven months, three days.

Barbara thought about this.

That is rather a long time, she agreed eventually.

I'm sorry. This is all a little odd.

It is odd, yes. But it's all right. If this makes it better for you.

Thank you. I think it does. Thank you.

And then he took the last message back from her, and hastily jotted underneath:

You look beautiful tonight.

They ordered another half bottle of wine, and a stack of paper napkins.

She wrote to him about working in a charity shop, and all its attendant frustrations. He wrote back sympathetically. No, he'd never wanted to work in a charity shop. No, he didn't think he'd have the patience. No, not even for all the starving children in Africa.

Have you ever been in love? Have you ever been hurt?

This latest message from him came a bit out of the blue. She looked up at him, and he was gazing at her intently, waiting for her reply.

Yes, she wrote. And then, so there'd be no doubt which question she was answering, *And Yes.*

He nodded at this.

She wrote: *I think I'm in love with you.*

He read this slowly, and she scribbled on another napkin, *Sorry.* But before she could pass it to him he'd written back a message of his own, *I think I'm in love with you too*, and she scrunched away her apology.

She wished he could smile while he told her he loved her. That would be nice.

Would you like to come back to mine? he asked.

Yes, I think I would.

I mean, I'm not trying to pick you up or anything, this doesn't have to involve sex. Not if you don't want.

Pity.

Oh. So, it can involve sex?

If you'd like it to.

I think that would be nice.

I think it would be nice too.

You'll be gentle with me, won't you? he wrote with a frown, and such big eyes. *It's been a long while. Fifteen years, eight months, twelve days. I might be a little rusty.*

Shall we get the bill? she asked. And he nodded at that, and she looked around for the waiter, and for a moment she forgot how to communicate with him, where was the napkin? – oh yes, speak, speaking. 'Can we have the bill, please?' They went dutch. They were charged extra for the paper napkins.

Barbara put all the paper napkins they'd used into her handbag. She wanted to keep them. He saw her doing this, and he looked pleased. It was the third time she'd seen him smile.

*

I'm sorry.

I wish she had survived.

My husband will never forgive himself. I will never forgive him either. Whatever the courts say, he wants you to know, he'll never drive again.

This book is by way of some small consolation. It helped us when our dog passed away. I know a dog isn't the same, but I hope you can accept this the way it is intended.

*

You say you want me to forgive you. You say you want me to talk. I don't see why I should have to be the one who talks. But whatever. There are lots of words in this book.

    Maybe you could pick a few out, and rearrange them into whatever it is you want me to say.

*

He put on the kettle, and she didn't know why; she didn't want anything to drink, and nor, quite obviously, did he. As they stood there in the kitchen she opened her arms wide for him, 'Come here,' she said, and he *flinched*, he quite visibly flinched. 'Just a hug,' she said, 'it's okay.' And he looked a little doubtful, but he came closer, and she put her arms around him, she *enveloped* him within her arms. He put his arms around her too, and he held on to her shoulders gently as if he were handling Ming china. 'It's okay,' she said again, and even though he was a lot taller she reached up and began to stroke his hair, as if he were a child, as if he were a *dog*, and the grip on her shoulders relaxed somewhat, and the fingers dug in deeper, and began to feel like the grip of a real man.

'Take me to the bedroom,' she said.

'Okay.'

'If that's what you want.'

'Okay.'

They stripped, and she thought being naked in front of a man again might be a problem, but it wasn't at all, she had him to worry about. 'You can look at me if you want,' she said, and he nodded, and indeed he stole the occasional glance. He wasn't as fat as she'd thought, it was his choice of clothes that didn't do him any favours.

She kissed him on the lips. And he responded, upstairs and downstairs too, actually, and Barbara thought, oh, this won't be as difficult as I thought. A little bit of tongue came into play, and she was surprised to realise it was his. 'Well done,' she said to him.

They made love with the lights off. And it was fine, it was perfectly okay; he may have been a little rusty, yes, but then so may she have been, and if they never quite reached the sort of passion to make the rust fly off, it was all very pleasant and all very tender. She wished he'd say something, though. Just a little something, it was so hard to do it in the silence. He'd grunt once in a while, but she thought that was an involuntary grunt, something let out when his nerve endings got the better of him and gave him a physical sensation he'd just as soon not have acknowledged out loud. 'Are you all right?' she said, and 'Are you happy, darling?' and he grunted an assent, and it was a different sort of grunt altogether to the sexual grunts, so she supposed that was enough.

They dozed together for a while afterwards, and that was nice too.

The unfamiliarity of his bed eventually woke her up. She stirred. 'I'm just going to the toilet, okay?' she whispered, just in case he could hear, just in case he was awake, but he seemed like a dead weight next to her. She couldn't find her clothes in the dark. As she stepped outside the bedroom door, she realised she'd no idea where his toilet was.

She found his library. She'd thought it'd be a lot tidier. She'd supposed that all the books he'd collected would be better cared for. But no, the shelves were stuffed full, and there were books still strewn across the floor, sometimes still in their bags (lots of Oxfam bags, she noted, she'd just *known* Oxfam would have better catered for his tastes than her).

And on a table, apart from all the others, in the middle of the room, there were all *her* books. *House at Pooh Corner. Paddington Marches On.* The selected plays of Molière with the stained cover. All the books she and Max had picked out for him to buy.

And, of course, she knew.

He was standing behind her. He was now wearing pyjamas, and it made her feel very exposed.

'You always thought they were fakes, didn't you?' Barbara asked.

'Oh,' he said. 'Barbara. They were just *too* sad.'

'And you bought them anyway.'

He shrugged.

She picked up a couple of them. The one from the mistress on the aeroplane, she'd liked that one. She shivered. Exposed, she felt so exposed.

'Can I get some clothes on?' she asked.

'They're beautiful, the things you wrote,' he said.

'I feel cold,' she said.

He came closer, and she backed away from him. She didn't know why. Yes, she did. 'I don't want to see you again,' she said. 'You knew all this time. You *lied* to me.'

'I didn't lie to you.'

'Yes, you did. Yes, yes, you did.'

'I'm sorry.'

'Will you call me a taxi, please? I want to go home.'

'Of course.'

He left the room. She went upstairs, got dressed.

'It'll be here in ten minutes,' he said. 'And I'm sorry.' He gave her another smile, his last smile, she thought there was a hint of relief to it.

The taxi took nearer twenty minutes. They sat together in the kitchen and waited for it, and didn't say a word.

*

Dear Man who comes into my shop every Monday,

This isn't your fault. I want you to know that I don't blame you for any of this.

You have the power to make me feel very happy. And feel pretty pathetic. I think that's confusing. I think what's most confusing is that somehow you can make me feel both things at exactly the same time.

I didn't even know you could feel happy and pathetic at the same time. But there you are.

I think what is pathetic is that when you make me happy, you don't even know you're making me happy. You've no idea, have you? Not a clue.

Sometimes I lie in bed at night, and I think that, if I think about you hard enough, that maybe you'll think of me.

Do you ever think of me?

I don't know you. I don't even know your name. I don't know if you like animals. (I like animals. I'm more of a cat person than a dog person. But I'll like dogs if you like dogs.) What do you like to eat? Are you a vegetarian? I gave vegetarianism a go a few years ago, but gave up because it turned out I actually like meat.

We laugh at children when they get crushes. We tell them they're silly, that when they grow up they'll love more wisely. God, what do we put them through? I think that maybe as we get older, we just find it harder to feel. Maybe that's it. Maybe that's what happened to me. It's like my capacity for love scabbed over. And now you've taken off the scab.

We can't help the way we feel. I don't want to think of you all the time. I know I should be sensible. But I can't be. I'm not.

You smiled at me twice. Both different smiles, completely different. Most people only have one smile, I think. I think you've got loads of them. Somewhere.

How dare we laugh at these poor kids with crushes? No wonder they get scabs. No wonder, if we tell them that what they're feeling is silly, and useless. We tell them to grow up. Who's in such a hurry to grow up? I wish I could go backwards. The things I could tell myself. How easily I let things go.

But I'd go forwards with you.

Whatever happens to me, every day, no matter how silly, no matter how small. I keep it in my head so I might be able to tell you about it one day. I store it up. There's so much I want to tell you. Let me speak to you, and I may never stop talking. You have been warned!

You collect all those books, and I can't decide if that makes you deep, the most sensitive man I've ever met, or just a bit weird. Maybe you're not so special after all. Maybe you're not special.

Then, more fool me.

I love you.

I'm sorry.

Without you, I would be nothing. Do you understand? I said I don't blame you. But I do, a little bit. Without you, I wouldn't get out of bed every day. Without you, I wouldn't keep going. Do you understand what I'm saying?

Without you, I wouldn't be alive.

*

Barbara waited to see whether the man would return to the shop the following Monday. He didn't. Oh, Tim, she thought. I didn't mean you should stop buying books here, not if you wanted to! But she was pleased as well.

She didn't tell Max how the date had gone, and he never asked. He did keep on asking if she was all right, though. About the fourth time he asked, she snapped, 'Why shouldn't I be?' and he backed off, and didn't ask again.

She'd spread out the paper napkins on her kitchen table. But for the life of her she couldn't remember which order they'd been written in. She should have numbered them as they'd gone along. She could now tell the story of their evening together in so many different ways, finding different answers to each other's questions. Lots of different love stories.

One day Max came into work with a bouquet of flowers. 'Oh,' said Barbara, 'they're nice.' She thought they must be a donation; she thought they must be fake.

'They're for you,' said Max.

'Oh,' said Barbara.

'I tried to write down the way I feel about you,' said Max. 'But the words just wouldn't come out right. I'm not very good at writing things. I'd sooner just say it to your face.' So he told her.

'You're not gay then?' said Barbara, when he'd finished.

'No.'

'I thought you were gay.'

'Oh,' said Max. 'I'm not,' he added, helpfully.

The bouquet was rather large, and Max was rather small, and she felt sorry for him, it looked as if he was being crushed beneath it. So she rescued him. 'Thanks,' said Max. 'I'll put them in a vase,' said Barbara.

'I was wondering, then,' said Max, 'whether at some point I could take you out for dinner?'

'You don't mean on a date?' said Barbara. 'This isn't a date, is it?'

'No,' said Max. 'Not at all, no, no. No.'

'Okay,' said Barbara. 'Dinner would be nice.'

'Great,' said Max.

'Dinner would be lovely.'

'Great. Thanks. Yes, lovely.' And Max looked so happy his watery eyes leaked out all over his cheeks.

'I can't date just yet. I don't want to date. It's just too soon.'

'I can wait,' said Max.

And Barbara kept her notebook by her bedside all the same. For the while she had no new love stories to tell. Sometimes she'd sense the glimmering of an idea, a hint of a love, just behind her eyes as she went off to sleep – but it was never strong enough to write down, it was always gone by morning. But she thought that sooner or later the stories would pour out of her again, she only needed to scratch a little more beneath the skin, and there they'd be, there they'd be. And this time when she wrote them out they'd be fuller and richer. And longer, too, they wouldn't have to fit inside the front of someone else's book, they might just be good enough to fill her very own.

When people discover my passion for history, they ask me crass questions. 'Don't you get confused by all those dates?' Or, 'Isn't it just a lot of wars and dead people?' (And, yes, I do get confused by the dates, and yes, it is indeed just about a lot of wars and dead people, there's a never-ending rush of them both, and when the two collide that's what sometimes makes the people dead in the first place, isn't history neat like that?) The crassest question of all, though, is the one they ask when they think they're trying to be clever, or trying to get me to admit an emotional investment in my studies: what period of history would I have been happiest to have lived through? 'If you had a time machine,' they say, 'you know, hypothetically. If you could pick anywhere.' And of course they're missing the point. What history shows us is that nothing's ever that different, really, people are still just stuck being people, as greedy and petty in centuries before as in centuries to come, all that changes is what hat they're wearing. The adage says that if we don't take notice of history we'll be doomed to repeat the same mistakes; how arrogant is that, we'll repeat the mistakes anyway, do we honestly believe that we can overcome the predictable defeats and losses of history's onward roll merely by paying attention to them? So I answer. I'd be as happy in any time as I am now (if happy is really so important, if you think that happy was a state that most people even aspired to a thousand years ago). The only real benefit of living through the twenty-first century rather than, say, the eighth, is that here the dentistry is better. **705** – The fall of Empress Wu. She takes two Zhang brothers as lovers, and they rule in her place with full authority; drinking and gambling and behaving like wastrels. At last the scandalised courtiers murder them in the palace. Wu is woken up by the commotion, and watches as they're lynched – and then, wearily, goes back to bed. The next day she abdicates. **708** – The no-nosed Justinian II has taken the Byzantine throne back from the usurpers, with help from the Bulgarian army. In return for which, the emperor has given to Bulgaria tracts of land near the Black Sea. Now, three years later, Justinian fancies himself in a strong enough position to declare war on his former allies and take his gifts back. The Byzantines are crushed at Anchialus, and Justinian is one of the few to escape. Three years later he will face another palace coup, and again plead with the Bulgarians for help; this time, he'll be executed. **710** – Roderick seizes power to become king of the Visigoths. He will be the very last. His entire life is obscure, but his failed reign is nevertheless the subject of two operas. **712** – The Muslims invade India. **713** – Byzantine Emperor Philippicus is overthrown by the army, and blinded in a public bathhouse. He is succeeded by his principal secretary, Anastasius II. **715** – Anastasius II is overthrown by Theodosius II. **715** – After a period of relative calm under Pepin, Duke of the Franks, France is once more thrown into chaos. The battle of Compiegne marks the beginning of an ensuing civil war. **716** – King Osred of Northumbria is so violently murdered by the usurper Cenred that the historians note his very death pollutes the air. **717** – Theodosius II is overthrown. *The only person I ever heard give a satisfying answer to the question was Annie. She was five or six at the time (she was near the end), and she'd been gripped by the history bug, and so other children's parents and teachers and the whole gamut of adulthood at its most patronising would all ask her the same thing. 'When would you have liked to have lived?' And she would wrinkle her nose at that, give it some serious consideration, she was really a very serious girl. 'The eighth century AD,' she'd reply. 'Why?' they'd ask. 'What's so special about the eighth century?' 'Nothing,' she answered. 'Nothing at all. That's the idea.'* **718** – A year long siege of Constantinople by the Muslims is beaten off by the Byzantines with the use of new technology, the so-called 'Greek Fire'. It is said this liquid fire sticks to any surface, even water, where it will burn to devastating effect. There is a secret formula for this new weapon of mass destruction, and it's jealously guarded – and, now, forgotten, because the Byzantines struggle to remember after the siege how they made it in the first place. With their weapon lost, they lose their advantage – and, to this day, no-one has ever been able to work out the chemical constituents to recreate it. **722 – ANNIE. 723** – Thor's Oak is a mighty tree sacred to the pagan Germanic tribes. Saint Boniface destroys it with a single swing of his axe – and, when the retaliatory lightning bolt from Thor is conspicuous by its absence, the Germans are so impressed they agree to be baptised. **726** – The first annual sumo tournament in Japan. **726** – Byzantine Emperor Leo III bans the worship of religious images. The great image of Jesus proudly displayed over the entrance gates to Constantinople is taken down, and replaced with a cross. Those workmen who do the job are murdered by a mob. **729** – The battle of Ravenna is fought, between the Byzantine troops and a force of Italians under instruction from Pope Gregory III, who is furious at Leo for his icon hatred. The battle is especially fierce, and thousands of Byzantines are killed. The waters of the Po River are so tainted with their blood that for six years the local inhabitants refuse to eat the fish. **730** – The battle of Ardabil. The Muslims are defeated by the Khazars. They suffer 20,000 fatalities, including their leader, al-Djarrah al-Hakami. The Khazar leader, Barjik, proudly mounts al-Djarrah's head on the top of his throne. **731** – Particularly irritated by the contempt the Khazars have shown their leader's head, the Muslims kill Barjik and destroy his Khazar army. **732** – Bubonic plague kills 200,000 citizens in Constantinople. **735** – A smallpox epidemic in Japan reduces the population by thirty percent. **738** – Eighteen Rabbit, ruler of the Mayans at Copan, is defeated in battle and then beheaded by Cauac Sky, ruler of the Mayans at Quirigua. **741** – Pepin the Short becomes the king of France. His wife is Bertha of the Big Foot. Just imagine the wedding night. **746** – The Franks invite all the nobles of Alemanni, several thousand in number, to a council meeting. All are executed for high treason, at what is later called 'the blood court at Cannstatt'. **747** – The empire of the Turkish Khaganate, a 200 year rule of Inner Asia by nomadic tribes, collapses in civil war. **749** – Tens of thousands are killed in the Golan earthquake in the Levant. **750** – The last of the Umayyad caliphs is defeated at the battle of the Zab. **752** – Stephen is elected pope; he dies of apoplexy three days later. For over 1,000 years he is deemed to be the shortest reigning pope, until the Vatican decree in 1965 that he is only a 'pope-elect', and demotes him. It's like Pluto all over again. **754** – The caliph al-Mansur executes his uncle Abdullah after a failed rebellion. **755** – Emperor Xuanzong of China is forced to have his consort executed during the An Lushan uprising. Weeping, he has his chief eunuch strangle her with a silk cord. *And I was thrilled that my daughter shared my love of history. But I couldn't help feeling a bit jealous too. I remembered my first brush with it, how I'd screamed at all those corpses in the Wise Old Owl book. I said to her, 'You do realise, don't you, that everybody in the eighth century is now dead?' And she blinked. And smiled. And said, 'Yes, Daddy. They're dead. Dead and rotting.' I felt proud of her. And, yes, jealous. Would that I could have been so wise at her age. So wise, and so emotionless.* **756** – The formation of the papal States; Pepin, the King of France, has been the first monarch to be crowned by a pope, and in return he donates to the papacy the lands that will give them such political importance internationally. **757** – Arab writer Ibn al-Muqaffa, famous for his translations of Persian fables, is tortured to death by al-Mansur. His limbs are severed before he is burned alive in an oven. **757** – King Ethelbald of Mercia is murdered by his bodyguard. **759** – Emperor Constantine V's attempts to invade Bulgaria are thwarted when his army is ambushed in the mountain passes of the Stara Planina; his troops are massacred. **761** – The Japanese monk Dokyo begins to exert political power after he successfully cures the empress mother of an illness. Shortly he'll be receiving divine proclamations telling him to take the throne. **762** – Li Fuguo kills the wife of Emperor Suzong; Suzong dies of a heart attack. Suzong's son Daizong kills Li, and takes the throne. **771** – Carloman, king of the Franks, dies of a nosebleed (qv 453). His brother Charlemagne succeeds him. Carloman's widow, Gerberga, flees to Lombardy – precipitating the last Franco-Lombard war, and the destruction of the Lombard kingdom. **772** – Caliph al-Mansur orders that all Jews and Christians in Jerusalem to have their hands branded with a distinctive mark. **778** – At Roncesvalles, Basque forces crush the rearguard of Charlemagne's army, killing his nephew Roland. The battle passes into legend via epic poetry, in which the Basques become Muslim Moors, and Roland is a tragic hero. *The deeper into the past I got, the harder it was to fill in my time chart. In the eighth century I got stuck. There was one date in particular, 783 AD, what famous event was I to put down? I asked my mother. She was honestly surprised I was still doing the chart. I was seventeen years old now; shouldn't I be spending time with that nice girlfriend I had? She said to me – nothing happened in 783. Don't you see – sometimes nothing happens at all. And I wondered what it would be like to live at the eighth century's fag end, and know that nothing you did would be of any relevance. So I wrote it down: 783 – Nothing happens. And I don't know why, I cried. I cried for all those people who had been forgotten and had never done anything worthwhile.* **783** – Nothing happens. **788** – King Elfwald of Northumbria is murdered. He is venerated as a saint because a light is seen shining over the spot where he is hacked to death. *But, of course, we're living in an age where we routinely expect people to be doing historically important things. And every day too – we schedule TV news programmes in prime time slots each and every evening on that very premise. That wouldn't have been possible in the eighth century, there was an entirely different attitude towards the concept of fame, the idea that any given event might have historical consequences would have been utterly alien to the average man. These were matters for kings and emperors. And that makes mathematical sense too. The population of the world today is around 67 billion – that's a huge number – it's statistically likely that somewhere amongst all that lot there must be someone doing something memorable. But in the eighth century the population was only 300 million. If you were to take a r andom 300 million sampling of our 67 billion, and put them in a (large) room somewhere, and tell them to do something of global consequence, the odds are that you'd pick nothing but duds. So maybe, genuinely, nothing did happen in 783 AD. Nothing was invented, nothing was proclaimed. No great thoughts were thunk. There'd have been deaths, and a few assassinations, but no-one who died was anyone worth remembering, just a bunch of non-entities that even their mothers wouldn't love, why should we waste our time on them?* **790** – The army mutiny against Byzantine Empress Irene, leaving her son Constantine VI as sole ruler. **792** – Constantine VI invites his mother back to share the throne with him. **797** – Irene tires of her son, and has his eyes gouged out. He dies of his wounds. *I suppose Annie might have had the right idea. The eighth century doesn't sound such a bad place for a stopover. At least it would have been quiet.* **800** – Charlemagne is crowned Emperor of the Romans by Pope Leo, on Christmas Day in St Peter's Basilica in Rome. It's an acknowledgement that the Roman legacy in the Byzantine Empire has become forever tainted, and that the office of God's chosen monarch has been transferred. Irene is none too impressed.

ENDANGERED SPECIES

I suppose what I remember about Billy is his smile. The way he'd suddenly beam at you, and you couldn't possibly know why – it was a private joke, he wasn't telling. He'd been crying maybe, getting sleepy or getting grumpy, and then out would spring this *grin*, straight at you, all gums and spit, and his eyes actually creasing up with the fun of it all. As if to say, yeah, I'm a baby *now*, but not for long; I *know* babies are pretty ridiculous, all teary and helpless and daft, but just you wait until I can shake this baby body off! Just you wait until I'm a proper human, and can tell you what I'm smiling about!

That smile, it'd break my heart. I think it did. I think it actually did. And when I'm drifting off to sleep, and I sometimes start with a panic because I can't recall what Billy looked like, I can't remember his face, in my mind's eye all I can see is just another podgy baby face like all the others – it's the smile I think of, it's that smile I use as my anchor. Even though, poor little sod, he really had precious little to smile about in the end.

I don't know what Jenna remembers about Billy. That's one of the things we don't talk about.

The doctor told us we shouldn't blame ourselves, that none of it was our fault.

'Of course it wasn't our fault,' Jenna said to him. 'Why should it be?'

The doctor didn't change his tone, just said she was quite right. And that there must be a lot of guilt nonetheless, a lot of shame. And that was all right, we shouldn't feel ashamed of our shame. But that there was nothing to stop us having another baby. Having something else in our lives to love. And that the two of us must be strong, if not for ourselves, then for each *other* – that we had to be the other's rock, because we'd both be hurting so much now, so much. And if it were too soon for another child, how about we practise on something smaller? All that love we still had to give, he could see we had – why not practise on, say, a cat? He said he'd like to see us again, regularly; and Jenna and I took ten minutes sorting out when we could both be free for a further consultation, she didn't want to miss her Pilates class or *EastEnders*, and me, I've got a life too, you know, and we settled at last on Thursday week at seven pm; and I don't quite know why we went to such trouble, because by then we'd both decided we were never going to come back. 'Thursday week,' said the doctor, the same tone of voice, exactly the same tone. 'Excellent. See you then.'

'We're not really going to get a cat, are we?' asked Jenna.

'Of course not,' I said. 'I don't even like cats.'

'I don't mind cats,' mused Jenna, 'but I don't want a cat. Let's not get a cat.' And we both agreed, then and there, not to buy one. That felt constructive. For a while, that really made us feel so much better.

*

We didn't touch. Or, more accurately, wouldn't touch. Or, more accurately still, she didn't touch me. I'd offer my hand to her as we crossed the road sometimes, the way I'd started doing when she'd been expecting, she'd liked it back then, said she'd found it protective – but now she didn't like it any more, or didn't take the hand at any rate, or didn't seem to notice. She sat on the far edge of the sofa from me as we watched television. We'd wash up together, she rinsing, me drying, both of us with our sleeves rolled up, both of us up to our arms in soap bubbles, flesh exposed – but her bubbles wouldn't touch my bubbles, that wasn't allowed, not for all the times I tried so subtly to manoeuvre my bubbles so they could bounce off hers and pop.

In bed I'd lunge my face at her face, and somehow, even in the pitch dark, she'd see it coming, she'd parry it, make sure that my lips never reached her lips, that the best they could hope for was her cheek or her hair.

'I'm only trying to kiss you,' I said. 'Just a kiss. A kiss can't get you pregnant, can it?'

It came out wrong. She didn't reply.

'I'm sorry,' I said.

'It's all right,' she said softly; just the right softness to suggest it wasn't all right at all, after the exact length of pause to suggest how much she was hurting. It was skilfully done.

'I love you,' I said.

'I love you too,' she replied. But there was an upward inflection to it, as if the next word would be a 'but'. I didn't want to hear that 'but'. The unspoken 'but' sort of hung there in the darkness. I couldn't bear it.

'But?' I said, at last.

'But what?'

'You love me too, but?' I said.

'There is no but. I love you too.'

'It's all right,' I said eventually. Softly. I tried to get the softness right, I tried to get the pause right.

'Really,' she said. 'No but.'

I turned my body away from hers, all my aching self away so she'd know I was facing the opposite direction. 'Right,' I muttered. I slept naked, all of that bare skin I had, and not one bit of it was going to touch her tonight, I'd make sure of it. 'Right,' I muttered again, a bit louder this time, in case she hadn't heard – and I knew I wasn't really hurting, I wasn't really staring into the blackness of our bedroom eyes wide open *because* of anything, I was just play-acting; and I wasn't really hurting Jenna either, it was all just play-acting on both our parts – teasing, that was all; and in the morning we'd get up and our baby son would be next door, he'd be smiling at us, he'd be doing The Smile, he'd been play-acting too, and Mummy and Daddy would be so relieved to see him alive and well they'd make love straight away in front of him.

One night, as I rolled towards Jenna, as Jenna flinched, I said to her, 'You know, the doctor did say we really ought to give sex another go at some point,' and Jenna snapped right back with, 'He also said we should get a cat.'

And so, the very next day, we began looking for one.

*

And we were in luck. The local papers were stuffed full of cats. It seemed as if the world and his wife were churning out cats by the bucketload, just so they could flog them through *Exchange and Mart*. In the end we decided we should visit Cat's Rescue, partly because taking an unwanted cat into care would feel like an act of charity, partly because we suspected they might be a little cheaper.

Cat's Rescue was lined with rows of cages. Some of the cats were pressing against the bars and yowling for attention. Jenna didn't like these cats because they were trying too hard. Other cats lay unhappy and drowsy in their baskets. Jenna thought these weren't trying hard enough. She wanted to find the right cat. I thought this was silly, and told her so. After all, we hadn't been able to choose Billy, had we? When we'd gone to the hospital for that first scan, and we'd seen that little foetus on the monitor, and the nurse had pointed out to us his little heartbeat, his little head – looking less to me like a future son than some strange parasite swimming about inside the woman I loved – we hadn't then said, no, don't fancy that one, no, send it back, we'll get something else, we'll get something better. It was the randomness of it all that was important, or so it seemed to me, and so it should be with the cat, wasn't that right, didn't she think? – I didn't necessarily believe this, but I was tired of hanging around all these cats, they were beginning to make my flesh creep, I wanted Jenna to hurry the hell up – so, 'Fine,' said Jenna, and pointed at the next cage, 'whatever. We'll take that one then.'

The woman took the cat from the cage. Asked us if we'd like to hold it, and we said we did. Jenna held it first. Then I held it. Then I gave it back to Jenna. 'Do you have a name for him?' the woman asked politely. 'Billy,' said Jenna, promptly, 'we're going to call him Billy.' I said I wasn't sure that'd be such a good name for a cat, all things considered, and Jenna asked, 'Why not? Why not? Billy's a perfectly nice name!' And the woman looked a bit embarrassed, and the cat struggled in Jenna's arms, and the woman had to rescue it – and then I thought Jenna was laughing, she was taking big gulps of air, sucking them in deep before she had a chance to blow them out, but it turned out she wasn't laughing at all, and she was clutching on to me hard so that she wouldn't fall over.

We didn't get that cat. Indeed, we didn't go back to Cat's Rescue. They didn't say much, but enough to give us the impression that we were temperamentally unsuited to own cats. I thought Jenna might give up on the whole cat idea altogether, thought that might be just as well. But, no, she insisted, she hadn't looked this determined since she'd decided we had to go to prenatal classes together, and we resorted to the ads in the local paper after all. We found one that wasn't too expensive. We went to the address to collect our new cat. He was just a kitten, no more than eight weeks old, he was smaller than my palm, he was a little larger than Jenna's palm. Mostly black, with white bits. 'Do you want two kittens,' asked the girl who was selling the cat, I thought of her, stupidly, as the cat's mother, 'so he has a little brother or sister to play with?' The doctor had said nothing about two cats, so we said no.

The cat didn't say a word all the way home in the car, and I began to wonder whether we'd bought one that was defective. I drove; Jenna sat in the back seat, cradling on her lap the cardboard box containing this new member of our family. She'd keep poking her head inside, and making coochie noises and reassuring clucks. 'Why isn't it saying anything?' I asked. 'It's probably scared,' said Jenna. And later, 'I think it's asleep.' I didn't like the sound of that, what sort of creature sleeps when it's scared, and I thought this defective cat probably wouldn't survive the night – oh God, if it died on us I may never get touched by Jenna again. We turned into the driveway. Jenna lifted the tiny kitten out of the box, held it gently in her fist, up to the window so it could see. 'This is your new home, baby cat,' she said, 'and I hope you'll be very happy here.' And the cat didn't mew, not as such, it wasn't anything as bold or throaty as that – instead, it sort of 'meeped'. 'Meep,' said the cat, and then we all went indoors.

*

We didn't name the cat Billy. I had a few back-ups already prepared, and Jenna didn't object. I named our cat Fluffy. Because, well, he was.

The first thing Jenna did was to plonk Fluffy safely down on the carpet of the sitting room. 'Here you are,' she said, 'do you want to look around?' Fluffy sniffed at the air for a moment, rather incuriously, then curled up and went to sleep.

An hour later he was still at it. His head poking out of a tight coil, like a furry Cumberland sausage. 'Is sleeping all he's going to do?' I asked, perfectly pertinently. 'He's tired out,' said Jenna, 'poor thing. You leave him alone.' 'If we let him sleep now, he won't sleep tonight.' So I picked him up. He opened his eyes lazily. I set him down in front of the stairs. 'There,' I said, 'what do you make of that?' Fluffy considered the stairs. He made some attempt even to climb one, but he was too small, or maybe too clumsy, and the effort of stretching up to it made him fall over on to his back. He wriggled like that on the floor for a few seconds, all paws swimming in mid-air, trying to get purchase on to something. Then he found the floor beneath him, he righted himself. He regained his dignity, pretended he'd never lost his dignity in the first place. And then, had he had eyebrows, he'd have frowned – and had he had shoulders, he'd have shrugged. And he trotted away, set his back to the stairs in utter disdain, and I never saw him even attempt to climb them again.

We'd bought a plastic bowl. We put some cat food in it for him. He didn't seem to care. I had to hold his little head down into the bowl so he could see it. It wasn't of great interest. We'd bought him a litter tray too. And he had no idea what *that* was. I scratched around in it a bit with my fingers, and tried to make enticing noises, and he looked every bit as embarrassed as I felt. Then he pooped straight on to the floor.

They never tell you, when you have a baby, how exciting the poop is. I loved Billy's poop. It wasn't like anything I'd ever seen before – or could remember, at any rate, as I dare say I'd pooped a fair bit myself when I was his age. It seemed odourless at first, but then if you put your nose right into it you'd find out it had a faint sweetness, and it was the colour of English mustard. It was the cleanest poop you could imagine. This was because, we were informed, there were no toxins in Billy's baby body, he was brand spanking new and nothing had gone wrong yet, there was precious little that was impure about Billy to expel. Safe and friendly poop, and indeed Billy seemed delighted by it, he was always sticking his fingers into it and rubbing it over his cot. And I understood the urge. Before he could walk, before he could talk, Billy would have to move beyond the poop of his infancy and into the shit of adulthood – dark brown and smelly like the rest of us – and I admit, I felt a sense of loss that day Jenna told me that part of Billy's innocence had gone. That's it, I thought, pretty soon he'll be at school, then he'll be getting a job, then he'll be out of the house and having pooping babies all of his own. It didn't happen that way, of course.

Seeing the little hard pellets of turd that Fluffy kept leaving over the carpet, I felt a tremendous yearning for my dead son and his sweetshop-scented shit. 'I don't like the cat,' I said to Jenna. 'You'll get used to him,' she told me, 'I love him already!'

That night in the darkness I kissed Jenna on the lips, and she let me. She pressed her lips hard against mine in response. I opened my mouth, and she did the same, but it was only to whisper, 'Really, can't the lips be enough?' And because it was a whisper I couldn't tell whether she was angry, or whether it was really a polite request for information, and I decided to let it be the latter. 'Of course,' I whispered back, 'it's really nice.' And somewhere next door I thought I heard a baby crying.

*

'Why doesn't it ever grow?' I asked. 'Of course he *grows*,' said Jenna, 'he's growing all the time. But it happens so gradually you can't see it.' I thought there was a certain logic to that, but whenever I picked up the cat to check it still stubbornly stayed smaller than the palm of my hand.

It had been three weeks since we'd bought the thing. I didn't see as much of it as Jenna did, of course; she was still on a maternity leave that had been quietly extended by her office into Something Else. 'Does it do anything while I'm not here?' I asked, because for the life of me all I ever saw the cat do was sleep and shed turds. It didn't even meep any more, it was as if that single attempt at conversation had been found wanting, and the cat had decided never to communicate with us again. 'Not much,' Jenna admitted. She thought for a bit. 'He looks out of the window sometimes.'

All the cat books Jenna had bought suggested that you shouldn't let your new cat out of the house for two weeks, but after that it'd have sufficiently adjusted to the idea of 'home' to know to come back. I'd suggested to Jenna already that Fluffy's introduction to the world beyond was long overdue, but she'd always baulked at that; it wasn't time yet, he was still too small. 'Why does he ever have to *do* anything?' she flared up at me. 'Why can't he just be what he is?'

'We'll wait until it's nice weather,' I said. 'This weekend maybe, if it's nice. And we can all go out into the garden together! He won't be on his own, Jenna.' She looked unconvinced. 'Come on,' I said. 'We can't deny him all of the fun of the garden!' It wasn't as if we had a particularly intimidating garden. Nothing too big. Nice lawn, I'd mow that whenever I found the time. Some flowers at the back door. A shed. The patch at the bottom left bare, for some swings maybe, or a little paddling pool.

On Saturday morning Jenna said the sky was too overcast, there was the possibility of rain. But by two in the afternoon even she had to concede there wasn't a cloud in the sky; no, it wasn't warm, or especially sunny, but it was *nice*, nice was all we had been looking for. She carried Fluffy out into the garden carefully, as if he were made of bone china. 'Don't be scared,' she told him, 'Mummy's here with you.' She sat down on the lawn, and I sat down beside her. 'This is nice!' I said, 'like a picnic. But without the food!' Bless her, she laughed too. 'Don't you think,' I went on, 'you ought to let go of the cat now?' 'All right,' she said, and she set him down on the grass – and slowly, ever so slowly, took her hands away. The cat darted its head about with rare interest, and then up at us, as if to say, 'Really, is this world all for *me*?' And I have to admit, at last I felt a wave of affection for the little chap. He took a few tentative steps forward, not quite trusting the greeney carpet that was so much more yielding than the one he was used to – his tail swished about, and that was good, I'd never seen him swish his tail before, I'd forgotten cat tails were even meant to do that. 'You see,' I said to Jenna, 'he's having fun!' Or, at least, I began to say it, I'm not sure I'd quite finished – because suddenly Fluffy threw us both a look we didn't recognise, there was something quite adult in that look, he wasn't a baby after all – and Jenna instinctively reached for him, but he was already a few feet away, she couldn't get to him in time...

And he was away, running – I'd no idea that lazy cat could move so fast – straight into the bushes at the back. His little body hit the undergrowth with such force that it sent leaves flying.

Jenna looked aghast. I managed to laugh. 'He's off exploring!' I said. 'Don't you worry, he'll be back!'

A few hours later the sun set. A little after that, all those morning clouds blew back into position, and it began to rain.

Jenna stood out on the lawn, calling out for him. 'Fluffy!' she yelled. 'Fluffy, please!' I wasn't entirely sure Fluffy knew his name, so thought there was little point to this. 'It's your fault,' she turned to me, and she was positively seething, '*you* named him, you should have called him something more distinctive!' 'You'll get wet,' I said, 'please come in.' She refused. 'At least let me bring you an umbrella.' She didn't want an umbrella, she wanted me to call the police and report a missing cat. I brought her an umbrella anyway.

At two in the morning she finally came indoors. Her hair soaked with rain, her cheeks with tears. I put my arms around her, and she was too exhausted to resist.

We went to bed. She didn't say a word to me while she undressed. 'He'll be back,' I said. 'Don't you worry!' – 'He's dead, isn't he?' she asked.

I said there was no reason to believe he was dead.

'Then he's lost.'

I said he was probably lost, yes.

'Then we'll never see him again. He might as well be dead.'

I said he probably wasn't lost at all. Maybe he was just sleeping under a hedge somewhere. We both knew how much that cat loved to sleep!

'But why under a hedge? Why in the *rain*?'

I pointed out that our cat was... well, a cat. Who could tell?

She got into bed next to me. 'I feel so guilty,' she said. 'Sleeping under this nice soft duvet. I should be out there. I should be sleeping under a wet hedge.'

'If it would be of any comfort to you, we could, you know. Make love.' Over the past few weeks, with the cat in the house, we had become increasingly intimate. The other night I had been allowed to put my tongue in her mouth, and leave it there for *ages*.

'You pick your moments.'

'Fluffy wouldn't want us to suffer,' I said.

And of course Fluffy was dead, such a little kitten out there unprotected, what chance did it have? And I wondered whether I could suggest buying Jenna a *new* cat. But the doctor would probably suggest we'd have to work our way up to a cat, we'd now have to get a smaller pet to practise on, a goldfish maybe. And when the goldfish died, something smaller yet – we could go backwards through the animal kingdom, killing each in turn, until we found our right level – we could lavish our love upon an amoeba, maybe, or on some microbe or other – and then, at last, *then*, we'd have a son we could call our own. And I realised I was crying, and Jenna said to me, 'You don't have a right to grieve, you didn't even *like* him.' And then she was stroking me, and kissing me, my God, she was kissing me all over – and I didn't have the heart to say I wasn't grieving the cat at all but someone else, now long ago and best forgotten – I thought if I did she might stop the kisses... 'I love you,' she said, and this time there wasn't a but, I couldn't hear the merest hint of buttery, and I was kissing her back, and I was trying to work out whether it was too soon to climb on top – when – suddenly – there was the scream of a baby.

We both froze at this.

We didn't discuss it.

The screaming went on.

We disentangled without a word.

'I can't stand this,' Jenna then said. 'I'm going to look for my little boy.' And she got up, put on her slippers and dressing gown, and went downstairs.

I heard her in the garden, calling for the cat. And I heard the baby next door crying. And one or the other lulled me to sleep.

*

When Billy died, I didn't have any trouble sleeping. In fact, if anything, I slept rather more easily. There was an entire weekend, I think, when I pretty much stayed in bed the whole time. I could tell all my sleeping made Jenna cross, but she didn't ever discuss it, she'd just flap around me noisily in the bedroom and keep pulling open the curtains to let in the sunshine. I had to get up and close them again once she'd gone. She barely seemed to sleep at all. She'd keep herself awake with cups of coffee, and sit downstairs in front of the television all night – but she wouldn't have the television on, no, that was altogether far too frivolous. And I'd get cross with her too, that her grief was so much more noble than mine, that she could suffer while I slept. But we didn't ever discuss it, no, we didn't discuss anything. And no matter how much she resisted, she'd have to come to bed eventually – and I'd wake in the morning and see her there lying next to me, and her face in sleep was at peace, so calm – as if she hadn't a care in the world – and it was as if her grief was all a sham, I was bloody sure that when I slept my face at least looked anguished and remorseful, I couldn't even begin to imagine the horrid contortions my sleeping face must have pulled.

That first night that Fluffy went missing, Jenna reverted to type. She sat in front of the television. And the next morning, yes, there she was, next to me in bed, she'd succumbed at last. And once again her face was calm. It was turned to me;

her body was as far from mine as possible, yes, but the face was turned to *me*. And I lay there for a while, and looked at it, and I loved her. I wanted to hold her, I wanted to kiss her forehead – I wanted to reassure her that everything was going to be all right. In spite of everything. In spite of all that I couldn't do, and could never do, and could only ever get wrong. I leaned in to the forehead all puckered up, I did. But I didn't touch her. I didn't want to wake her. Let her sleep.

I went downstairs. A lot of coffee had been drunk. I first put the milk back in the fridge, she'd left it out. Then I collected her coffee mug from the sitting room and washed it up. I refilled the kettle so I could have a coffee of my own. I'd almost finished my coffee before I even thought to go to the back door and see whether the cat was about.

He was waiting patiently on the mat. When he saw me approach, he straightened up, put his paws to the glass of the door.

I opened it. And though he'd been out there all night, in the dark and the rain, the little cat was in no hurry to come in. 'Meep,' he said. '*Meep.*' He seemed very insistent about that. And then he tossed his head behind him. He had to do it a couple of times before I realised that he was *pointing*. And I saw what he'd left in the middle of the lawn.

'Meep,' he said, with satisfaction. Job done. And he now allowed himself a yawn, a really big one, too big for that little kitten head of his. And at last indoors he trotted.

This time I kissed Jenna's forehead. She was fast asleep, I had to kiss it really hard before she stirred. 'Look,' I whispered, 'I have a surprise for you.' And she opened her eyes, and I held out the cat towards her, and I swear, I've never seen someone's pupils grow so large so quickly. She grabbed the cat, 'My little boy's come back to me!' and wrapped it in her arms, in the folds of her nightie, kissed it on *its* forehead over and over again. I was half afraid she'd accidentally crush the thing, that after all this worry we'd be left with a dead cat after all. But Fluffy didn't seem to mind, he even purred. 'Darling,' she said to me, and she hadn't called me 'darling' for a long time, not like that, not without a sarcastic edge, 'did you go out and look for him? Where did you find him?'

And I could have lied. I could have been her hero. And maybe that would have been better, for all our sakes. 'He was just waiting by the back door,' I said, 'as happy as Larry. I didn't need to do a thing! I told you, he was just having a little explore!'

Fluffy slipped out of Jenna's arms, sat down on the carpet, crapped, and went to sleep.

'And he didn't come alone,' I said.

Jenna followed me into the garden to see.

*

At first I'd thought it was just a duck. A very *large* duck, admittedly, but you can get large ducks, can't you? I don't know, perhaps on farms. Its body was sideways on to us, and it was only as I approached it I realised how far the width of its body extended.

'My God,' said Jenna.

'It's dead,' I said, pointlessly. I tried to turn it over with my shoe, but it was too big for that, and all I did was knock some feathers off. I couldn't see how it had died, there was no sign of damage.

'You mean we let Fluffy out,' said Jenna, and she was angry, 'when something like *that* was out here waiting for him? He might have been pecked to death!'

I pointed out that Fluffy was the one who had survived the encounter.

'Oh, don't be ridiculous,' said Jenna. 'What encounter? It's just a dead bird, that's all. Why should Fluffy have had anything to do with it?'

It was hard to explain that knowing glance the cat had given me. The way it had taken *responsibility* for the body – and without fuss, and without shame.

'Just look at it,' she said. And it's true, the beak alone was bigger than the entire kitten, the bird could have swallowed Fluffy in a single gulp. And I looked at its eyes, still wide open, staring up at me. Frightened? If not, startled at the very least! And I knew then, I knew – there may not have been a mark on its body, but this bird hadn't died easily.

'What shall we do with it?' I asked.

'I'll go and get a carrier bag,' said Jenna.

The bird was too large for an ordinary carrier bag. It would only fit inside one of those reusable ones from Waitrose, the ones that cost 75p. It seemed a waste of money, but it couldn't be helped. Jenna held the bag wide open, and I tipped the bird in. I wore gardening gloves, I didn't want to touch something that was dead. It was a bit of a tight squeeze, I had to really stuff it in, I had to wedge the legs down the sides, and I made sure the bird went in head-first so those eyes couldn't see me.

At one point I looked up, and there was Fluffy, pressed against the glass at the back door, watching. I pointed, but by the time Jenna turned, he was gone.

'Leave it out by the bins,' said Jenna. 'The dustmen will take it in the morning.'

When I came back into the house, Jenna called me over to the computer. 'I've found it,' she said. There, on the screen, was a picture of our bird. It looked a lot livelier on the webpage, but it was unmistakably the same species.

'What's an albatross doing over here?' she asked. 'They live *continents* away.'

'Well,' I said. 'I suppose it flew.'

'Yes,' said Jenna. 'I suppose... Oh! They're endangered.'

'That's a shame,' I said.

'We can't just leave an endangered animal by the bins.'

'Why not?'

'Because we'll get into trouble. I'm pretty sure it's illegal. You'd better go and hide it.'

'It's not our fault,' I said, 'if an endangered albatross dies on our back lawn.' Though I was pretty sure it was.

'Hide it respectfully,' said Jenna.

So I picked up the Waitrose bag, walked down the road, and dropped it into the nearest skip.

When I got back, the cat was still asleep. As if he'd not moved a muscle since morning. And here I was, and I was fairly sure I stank of dead albatross. I glared at him.

131

Later that evening the cat woke and stretched. Jenna spooned some food into his bowl, but he turned his nose up at it disdainfully. He went to the back door. He scratched at it expectantly.

'No, little boy,' Jenna said. 'You've had quite enough excitement for now.' But he continued to scratch. 'Meep,' he said. There was urgency to the meep.

I was trying to watch television. 'Oh, let him out,' I said.

'What if he gets lost again?'

'But he didn't get lost. Did he? He came back. Didn't he?'

'But there are wild birds out there! What if there's another albatross waiting for him?' But she let him out. Even she couldn't stand all that pathetic scratching. 'Please don't stay out all night,' she told the cat as she unlocked the door, 'please don't get into trouble.' But he was gone.

She sat back down with me and *Top Gear*. 'Promise me we'll see him again,' said Jenna. And then she gave me a hug.

'Of course we'll see him again!' I laughed. I liked the hug.

*

We lay next to each other in the darkness.

'I could take my nightie off,' whispered Jenna. 'If you like.'

'Yes,' I said. 'That might be nice.'

'I don't want to do anything,' she added.

'No.'

'But I could take my nightie off. Anyway. If, if you'd like.'

'That'd be nice. Yes.'

She got up. I could see her in silhouette, putting the nightie carefully on to the back of a chair. Then sighing, as if returning to bed would now be something of an effort. She got back under the covers. 'Ooh,' she shivered. 'It's cold.'

'I could. Warm you up.'

'Just by holding...'

'Just holding, yes.'

I held her.

'I'm not really that cold,' she said, at last.

'Oh,' I said. 'Do you want me to...'

'No, no,' she said.

Then she said, 'Do you mean, let go?'

'What?'

'Did you mean that I might want you to let go?'

'Oh. Yes. Yes, that's what I meant.'

'Ah. Good, yes. No. No, I don't want you to let go.'

'Good.'

'Yes. Do you think he's all right out there?'

'He's having an adventure,' I said. And then I said, 'Do you want some ear plugs?'

'Oh. No, no, I'm fine.'

'Okay.'

'He'll shut up soon.'

'Okay.'

The baby next door had started crying a little after midnight. It was now gone half past one.

'Do you find it irritating, or...?'

'It doesn't really bother me.'

'No,' I said. 'You can sort of screen it out. So long as you don't think about it too much. And I don't like sleeping with ear plugs. They make me feel as if I'm underwater. And they make my ears itchy. And they give me weird dreams.'

'Are they in the bathroom?' asked Jenna. 'In the cabinet over the sink?'

'Yes.'

'I'll be back in a minute,' she said.

*

We shared the ear plugs in the end. One hour for her, then one hour for me, in rotation, everything fair. When dawn broke it was in the middle of one of my stints, so it was Jenna this time who got up first, who went downstairs to let in the cat – and who had to wake me so urgently.

'You'd better see this,' she said.

Fluffy was on the doorstep. The door was wide open, but he'd stayed outside. He seemed to brighten when he saw me. As if he'd been waiting for me, as if he required my reaction. 'Meep,' he said, tossed his head meaningfully behind him, and then ambled in. This little cat, still no bigger than the palm of my hand, and behind him...

'That's not good, is it?' I said.

'No, that's not good.'

'That's really very endangered indeed.'

'Yes.'

This time there was blood. We could see it pooling out from underneath the body. And there was a trail of it, in a thick red line, running across the grass, over the little rookery at the back, and, impossibly, straight up vertically over the fence.

I turned the body over, and there was a large red hole in its back, all the more garish against the white fur. It looked as if Fluffy had chewed right through.

'Where did it come from?' I asked. Although I knew this wasn't the most pressing question. 'I mean, did it escape from a zoo?'

'We don't have a zoo,' said Jenna.

'Or a circus, or...?'

Jenna shrugged.

'We could just report it,' I said. 'Phone the police. Or the RSPCA. Somebody. It's not our fault. We could just come forward and confess.' But that word 'confess' didn't help, and Jenna was already shaking her head emphatically.

'They'd take Fluffy away. They'd say he was a bad cat, that he has to be locked up, or put down, or something. And, like it or not, he's ours now. He belongs to us. And we have to stand by him.' She frowned. 'We can't dispose of the body out here. It's far too public. We better get it indoors.'

There was some groundsheeting in the shed, back from the days I'd decided what would really fulfil my life would be a new conservatory. I fetched it. We rolled the carcass on to it. It was very heavy, and we both had to put our backs into it, we couldn't afford to be squeamish about touching dead bodies this time, not when there was so much dead body to touch! I felt the urge to close its eyes, those big gorgeous eyes so dark-ringed it looked as if they'd been bleeding mascara. But I didn't. And then we dragged the giant panda up the steps, through the back door, and into the sitting room.

Fluffy was already fast asleep in the middle of the carpet. He'd crapped out some more pellets. We had to pick him up and move him into the corner to make room for his kill, but he didn't seem to mind.

'I can't do this now,' I said, 'I'll be late for work...'

'We're all in this together,' said Jenna grimly.

I phoned in sick.

I went back to the shed. The handsaw was designed for hacking off overgrown branches, not limbs, so it wasn't ideal. But the electric drill was good on the bones, and once over the body with the lawnmower helped a bit too. We didn't have any of those reusable bags from Waitrose this time, we had to use the ordinary-sized plastic ones instead. But in a way that was a good thing, we needed to make these clumps of panda as small and unrecognisable as possible.

And Jenna set to work in the garden, scrubbing away at all the blood stains. After about an hour or so we'd swap jobs. That way I could get some fresh air, and Jenna could play about with exciting tools. Strictly in rotation, everything fair.

We broke for lunch and took stock. The bright red streak across the grass had all but disappeared, but we now had an entire lawn that was almost uniformly salmon pink instead. We'd filled a lot of the bags, but the body we were picking from on the sitting room carpet was still unmistakably a giant panda – I realised this was because I'd started work lopping off all the extremities leaving the head intact, and when all's said and done the head is pretty much the most giant panda-ish thing about a giant panda. With all its paws gone, indeed with a good third of its whole body disposed of too, the panda seemed to be staring out at us in understandable confusion.

And Jenna read from her book how it was perfectly normal for cats to go out to hunt, and then bring their kills back to the house. That it might be an inconvenience for the owners, but that it was unfair to blame the cat for acting out its wild animal instincts. 'After all,' said the book, quite cheerfully, 'if you don' want a cat to be a cat, why get a cat in the first place?' And it suggested we should take these dead birds and mice as they were intended, as loving gifts and tribute from a pet who respected us.

By about half past four the lawn was as close to green as it was ever again going to get, and the panda was chopped up and ready to go. I'd cheated a bit with the head. I didn't want to cut that up. It just seemed a little callous. The complete head wouldn't fit in a bag, but it was okay, I'd put it into a cardboard box, the one that the microwave oven had come in would do.

And when it was dark, we carried out the bags to the car, and put them in the boot. We put some food down for the cat, but as always he didn't show much interest.

We didn't want to leave the panda parts anywhere too close to home. We' decided nowhere within a five-mile radius. I drove, and Jenna was on navigation duty – 'Oh, stop here, here's good, this street's perfect!' And she looked so pleased with herself, she was right, it really *was* a good street, and in front of each house a wheelie bin was standing to attention. So we parked the car, and took out half a dozen bags each. And then we went up and down strangers' driveways, dropping the bags into the bins, I took one side of the road, Jenna the other, and we *ran*, we didn't want to be caught on private property, we didn't want anyone opening their front doors or shouting out of their windows and asking what the hell we were doing. And when we'd filled as many bins as we could, no more than one panda bag in each, no-one would want too much dead panda in their bins, we didn't want to take the piss, we raced back to the car, I jumped in the driver's seat, Jenna jumped in right beside me. Her eyes were shining, her face was flushed. She was happy. 'Where to next?' she said. 'This is fun!'

We disposed of sixty-three carrier bags in sixty-three different wheelie bins on fourteen different streets in three different towns. The microwave oven box was too big; I should have chopped up the head after all. You live and learn. Next time I was presented with a giant panda head, I vowed, I wouldn't be so sentimental. There were lots of boxes left outside the Oxfam on the high road. I left it with those.

When we got back home Fluffy was at the back door. He was pleading to be let out. We both agreed we should keep him in for the night. 'At least until the blood's dried,' I said. He whimpered, he scratched at the glass with his claws. We went to bed. Jenna got up to use the toilet, and after the flush, I heard her go downstairs. When she came back up, I said to her, 'You let him out, didn't you?'

She nodded. Grinned, and it was the same grin I kept seeing in the car, and my heart skipped at it. I don't think I'd ever loved her so much. 'I can't wait to see what present he brings us tomorrow,' she said.

*

We'd been so busy we hadn't had time to buy any fresh ear plugs. So we wore one each. That worked; we'd have wanted one ear free anyway, so we could hear each other should we want to talk. We talked a lot that night.

'Do you believe in reincarnation?' she asked.

'No,' I said.

'No, nor do I,' she said.

And then she thought for a while, and said, 'But I have been wondering. You know. What the chances were. That Billy. You know. Somehow had been born again. As Fluffy.'

I think it was the first time Jenna had spoken to me directly about Billy. Not without a doctor there. Not without a doctor there, to suggest we *always* talked about Billy, that we were okay with all of that. I didn't want to say the wrong thing. 'It's not very likely,' I said.

'No, I know.'

'For a start. I mean. Fluffy was born before Billy died.'

'Oh yes,' said Jenna.

And then she said, 'I suppose there couldn't have been an overlap? I don't know.

Could that be how reincarnation works?'

She didn't say anything else for a while. We just held hands in the dark. At one point I raised her hand so I could kiss it, and she had no idea what I was doing, she thought I was trying to wriggle free. But I wasn't, and I had to snatch her hand back, and then bring it to my lips, and Jenna understood, and she laughed.

'But just saying,' said Jenna. 'If the overlap thing works. You know. And Billy *is* inside Fluffy.'

'Oh yes?'

'Well,' she said. 'I just think. Maybe it's better this way.'

'I'm not sure what you mean.'

'Well. Fluffy's killing all these animals. He's probably killing some right this moment. But he'll get away with it. Because, well. He's a cat.'

'Yes.'

'But if Billy were doing it. If we'd had a son – you know, and he, and he lived – and our son liked to kill things. If he got out at night, and he was killing animals. Murdering people. Then that'd be much worse.'

'I suppose so.'

'You can never really be sure what you're going to end up with,' said Jenna. 'That's the trouble. Who knows what Billy might have turned out like? And yet we'd have had to take responsibility, don't you think, as parents? You want them to be special, but not *that* special, not special enough they like killing things, and all I'm saying is... If we were going to have someone that liked to kill. On balance. I think it's better off we finished up with a cat.'

'I understand,' I said.

'I think I'm over Billy,' she said. 'I think I've moved on! Isn't that great? I feel great. I love you.'

I told her I loved her too.

There was a sudden new bout of screaming from next door.

'Christ,' sighed Jenna. 'What's wrong with that baby anyway? I hate that fucking baby.'

*

The next day it was a rhinoceros.

I don't want to exaggerate Fluffy's achievement. It wasn't a big rhinoceros. It was a very medium-sized rhinoceros.

There wasn't blood this time, and for that we were grateful. We soon found out why. The rhino hide is very thick, it's the best natural defence it has. But how good a defence can it be, if the rhino's endangered anyway – all of these animals, so endangered, it seems almost every single one, no matter how wild or fierce, for all their horns or tusks or sharp teeth everything dies so very easily. And all you need to kill them is just a little *persistence*. That's what we humans are, we're persistent, you've got to give us that – we got the dodo, that was easy, now we'll move on to the tigers and the polar bears and the elephants and things that require a bit more effort, we'll get them in the end. And Fluffy, he'd been persistent too. On the underside of the rhinoceros we found a hole. Fluffy had bitten his way through the hide, and clawed at it, and scratched it to threadbare ribbons – two full inches of raw hide, but Fluffy had done it, he hadn't given up. And it seemed he'd crawled up and into that hole, he'd crawled right into the rhinoceros itself. And then started to eat – he'd eaten the rhino from the inside out, all of it, every last scrap. All our little kitten had left us with was a rhino husk, standing upright on the lawn, quite hollow.

Fluffy yawned at us. It'd been a long night. 'Meep,' he said – he turned big innocent eyes on to us – meep, there you go, all for you. And he went into the house. He crapped on to the carpet. But not a pellet this time, no. The cat set his face in tight concentration, his fur prickled, the body shook with strain. He *winced* – and out heaved a turd, about the size of a large egg, almost as large as Fluffy, brown, and hard, and sharp, and hide-plated. It seemed to make the cat's eyes water. It certainly did mine.

I phoned my office. 'Hello?' I said. 'I'm still feeling a little sick.'

We dragged the rhino indoors. 'You know what would be fun?' said Jenna. 'Hammers! Let's try hammers!' So I went out into the shed to find some.

On my way back through the garden I heard a man call to me over the fence. 'Excuse me,' he said. 'Can I have a little word?'

We didn't know the neighbours. We'd met them twice before to speak to, I think – once at a firework display, once when we'd signed for a parcel when they were out, we took it round the next day, they seemed grateful. I recognised him, of course. I sometimes saw him when he left for work in the morning, sometimes we coincided. I hadn't even known his wife had been pregnant.

'It's about the noise,' he said.

'Yes,' I said. 'It is a bit unreasonable.'

'It is,' he said. 'It really is. So would you mind keeping a lid on it?' And I realised he wasn't apologising for his sodding bloody baby after all.

'Sorry,' I said.

'Because it's not fair, is it? It's no joke. We all have to live together. You don't choose your neighbours, we all have to make do. And hope they're not selfish.'

'No, sorry,' I said. 'What noise is it you're referring to?'

'Your cat,' he said. 'It is your cat, isn't it? The little black one. Outside in the middle of the night, all hours. Yowling away. Bloodcurdling stuff. Getting into fights, I think, what's it doing, for God's sake, what's the matter with the thing?'

'We don't hear anything,' I said. He scoffed at that.

'It'd be selfish at the best of times. But Moira's just had a baby, she's exhausted. We're all exhausted. We can't sleep for the noise, it's draining her, she cries. For God's sake, you're making my wife cry! And it sets the baby off. The baby is up all night. For the sake of my baby, for the sake of my poor defenceless *child*, please, for God's sake, can't you please just shut the *fuck* up?'

'I think your baby's room backs on to our bedroom. I think we can hear it. Sometimes. Maybe you could move the baby into another room.'

'What?'

'I was just thinking.'

'We spent *weeks* on that nursery,' the man said. 'We've got all the wallpaper up. Fairies. Are you telling me we should move our baby and take down all our fairies for the sake of some sodding cat?'

'I don't know.'

'Our baby's special. She's our special little girl. Nothing's too good for her.'

'We had a baby once,' I said.

'Right...?'

'I had a baby.'

'And?'

'And nothing. We had a baby.'

'Then you should know,' he said. 'If you're good parents. You should bloody well know.'

He went away, leaving me with my hammers.

'I think,' said Jenna, 'I can prise some of the hide off. All I need is some leverage. We can bash it with the hammers to soften it up first.' She looked at me. 'What's the matter?'

'I don't want to do this any more,' I said.

'What's wrong?'

'I don't feel very well.'

'Darling,' she said. 'Do you want to go upstairs? Do you want to lie down?'

'I hate you,' I said. 'And I loved you so much, that day in the hospital, and out came Billy, and you were laughing and crying, and I wasn't even sure I wanted a baby, and then I knew I did, and I was so proud, and I loved you so much. What did you do to him? Why did you ever take your eyes off him? Why did you... why did you let... *me*, take *my* eyes... off... All those prenatal classes, what was the point, if he can go to sleep one night, perfectly alive, perfectly breathing, and then... and the next... and there were no toxins in his body, that was the thing, he even pooped perfect...'

'Please,' she said.

'I'm sorry,' I said.

'Please.' Please, what? Please, but really, please *what?*

She put her arms around me. 'No,' I said. 'Please,' she said. 'No,' I said. She began to cry. Good. She couldn't get the word 'please' out, good, but she kept on trying, good.

She took my hand, and led me upstairs.

*

Jenna pulled the curtains tight, and she got undressed. There was still too much sunlight, the room was only dimmed a little, and so I could see her naked, and I realised I hadn't seen her naked for a long time; the skin seemed to hang off her, it looked so very tired, and yet it wasn't unattractive.

'Please,' she said again, and so I got undressed too, and she got to see me naked. I gave her the chance to call the whole thing off, I let her see the whole thing. But she didn't, so I got into bed beside her. 'Please,' so I let her touch me, and I even touched her as well, although I didn't want to, I tried to make her realise that every merest stroke of her skin should be considered ironic.

And I thought about getting on top of her, I knew it would soon be time to do so, that if it was ever going to happen it should be soon, and so I girded my loins in readiness – and then, no, she was on top of me, that was a turn-up for the books, and I wasn't really sure what my loins would make of that, they were surprised, would they ungird in response? – but no, they were rallying! they were holding firm, no, better, rising to the task...

The baby next door began to scream.

'No!' cried Jenna. 'Please!' But the baby wasn't listening, it had no sympathy for us. And Jenna was clambering off, awkwardly, all those naked bits now knocking against each other, and now she too was screaming, she was thumping on the bedroom wall and shouting. 'Please! Please, why don't you die? Why don't you just shut up and *die*?'

And the baby was screaming, and my wife was screaming – and yes, downstairs I heard another join the chorus; the cat, the cat was screaming too. This was no ordinary 'meep' – this was a 'meep' with electrodes stuck into it, this was at full throttle, a war cry, a call to arms. Jenna didn't even seem to notice, she was too occupied trying to tear down the wall with nothing more than the power of her fists and her lungs, so I got up, put on her pyjama trousers, and went downstairs to see what the matter was.

Fluffy was pressed flat against the back door, as if should he just push hard enough he could squeeze through the glass. And maybe he could do that, maybe he could – his tail was standing up, the fur bushed, trying to make himself look big – it looked silly, like a baby getting dressed for battle, a child pretending to be all grown up. But when I neared him he stopped screaming altogether; he fell silent. And he just looked at me – and there was something so serious in that fuzzy face, something so grim and so determined. I opened the door. He fled without even a backward glance.

I went back upstairs. Jenna had screamed herself out. The baby had won. The baby was still going. Jenna just sat on the bed, as if her breath had been knocked out of her.

I sat down beside her.

I told her what I remembered of Billy. That smile. That smile was my anchor. Jenna shook her head. She didn't remember the smile. She told me what she remembered. Her anchor, what she held on to in the dark.

She told me about Billy's hands. He had had such small hands. And they would reach out for hers. But his hands were so tiny, the most he could get purchase at was a single finger. And so, that's what he'd do; he'd grab hold of Jenna's finger, he'd wrap his little hand right round it. For a while Jenna thought this was because he wanted comfort. But then, the baby grew older. He began to gurgle more, he began to crawl, his poop turned brown. Older, and bigger too, bigger all over, and his hands grew bigger. Yet still Billy would reach only for his mother's finger, just the finger, he'd envelop it completely, he'd bury it deep within his fist. And he'd squeeze it a little, not hard, not to hurt, just to let her know he was there. That (Jenna said) he would always be there. He was comforting *her*. He was protecting *her*. And as he held on, he'd look up at Jenna's face, and his mouth would move, and it'd seem to Jenna as if he were trying to speak. Her finger in his hand, his gaze on her gaze, and one day, like that, he'd say his first word, she knew it; and she knew too what that word would be; it would be 'mummy'.

We cried. And we fucked. It wasn't making love, it was too angry for that. And I didn't know whether there could be any love left for us now, but at some point

I thought I might have found a trace of love in it, I didn't think the love had withered away entirely, we'd have to see.

We didn't let the baby screams put us off. We wouldn't. We fucked right through them. And, soon enough, the baby stopped, and there was silence, and we fucked through that too. There were more screams later – but different, adult ones, and there was crying. Sirens outside, an ambulance, or the police, maybe both. We didn't care. We'd found our rhythm now, and nothing was going to get in our way.

*

No-one ever saw the cat again. No-one saw the baby again either. There was a lot of fuss about the missing baby, there were reports in the newspapers, on the TV. There wasn't so much fuss about the cat.

*

When Jenna had fallen pregnant with Billy we hadn't been trying for a baby. She'd told me the news when I came home from work. Later on she'd reveal how nervous she'd been of my reaction. Because although she'd said that having a baby was something we'd have to decide together, she'd already decided, and she was so frightened I'd decide the wrong way, that I wouldn't want our child, that she'd have to stop loving me. She didn't have to stop loving me; I kept my doubts to myself; I danced her around the room, and she was so relieved.

When Jenna fell pregnant with Chris, it was different. And we really talked seriously about having him aborted. 'I just can't go through another loss,' she told me, 'I can't love something just to lose it again.' I said we should wait and see. We didn't have to decide immediately. We'd wait. And we waited so long, we waited nine months, and out popped our second child, and by then it was far too late to make up our minds.

Chris didn't smile the way Billy had. And he didn't grip his mother's finger, and his first word wasn't 'mummy'. But he had his own thing, he'd pull on his ear lobe when he was thinking, it'd break my heart. I think it did. I think it actually did. And he survived.

The neighbours moved away. I think they may even have divorced. Which was sad.

And Chris was a good kid. He didn't always pay attention at nursery, and he could be a bit moody sometimes, there were times he wouldn't eat his dinner. But he never killed anyone, nothing ever died because this new Chris child was in the world. So, when he asked for a pet, we told him he could have one. He had so much love to give, it would be good for him. We went to the shop, and told him he could have whatever he wanted. He chose a hamster.

No-one mentions Charlemagne much any more, do they? When I was a kid, Charlemagne was all the rage, he was given a full page in 'The Wise Old Owl's Book of Famous People'. He was something of a hero, Charles the Great, King of the Franks, founder of the Holy Roman Empire. He seems to have dropped off the radar now, though. I bet very few children want to grow up to be Charlemagne the way I did. I wonder why, I wonder what he did so long after his death to so quickly fade into historical obscurity. I'll try to find out. I'll get back to you. **803** – Stiftskeller St Peter opens for business in the monastery walls of St Peter's Archabbey in Salzburg. It's the oldest continuing operating restaurant in the world, and for the last 1,200 years of history, through Dark Ages and wars and religious schisms and periods of anarchy, has consistently served wine and food. It's quite an achievement. But just try getting a table there in the summer. **806** – Vikings kill all the inhabitants on the island of Iona, in Scotland. **806** – The Saracens sack Nola, in Italy. **806** – Sixth century historian, Gregory of Tours, calculated that this year is when the world would end. **807** – Al-Hakim massacres all the chief citizens in Toledo, Spain. **810** – A swordsman makes an attempt on the life of Byzantine Emperor Nicephorus. When he fails, he claims insanity as his defence. **810** – The Bulgars, under King Krum, wipe out the Avars. **810** – King Godfred of Denmark is murdered by one of his sons, who he's employing as a bodyguard at the same time. That has to cut twice. **810** – Abul-Abbas, the Asian elephant given to Charlemagne by the caliph of Baghdad, dies. The verdict is he's died of pneumonia, probably contracted after swimming in the Rhine. **810** – The Book of Kells is completed by the Celts. To produce the vellum necessary, some 185 calves have been killed. **811** – The kingdom of Essex is demoted to merely a duchy. Sigered, its last king, rules on in reduced circumstances for another fourteen years. **811** – Krum crushes the Byzantine forces at the battle of Pliska. It's one of the worst defeats the Byzantines ever suffer, and deters them from sending troops north of the Balkans again for more than 150 years. Nicephorus is killed in battle; Krum encases his skull in silver and uses it as a drinking cup. Nicephorus' name translates from the Greek as 'Bringer of Victory'. **811** – Staurakios succeeds Nicephorus. But at the same battle that killed his father, a sword blow on the neck has left him paralysed. Two months into his reign he's deposed, and packed off to a monastery where he can die from his wounds. **814** – Charlemagne dies. His embalmed body is propped up on his throne in honour, and stays there, crown on head, sceptre in hand, for the next 400 years. *I phoned up a dozen schools, really good ones, and a couple of comprehensives too. I got their numbers off the internet. At each I asked to speak to the headmaster – or, failing that, someone who understood history at a senior level. I asked what had happened to Charlemagne, why he was no longer considered part of the curriculum. Most people hung up; one woman told me, with apparently full sincerity, 'I don't know who Charlemagne is.'* **814** – On Charlemagne's death, his son Louis I (known as Louis the Pious, and Louis the Affable) succeeds to the throne. He has his uncle Bernard arrested to prevent him from challenging his authority. But Louis won't kill him – he's no monster. Instead, rather piously, rather affably, he gives orders that his uncle be blinded. The operation is botched, and Bernard dies in prison from the trauma of having his eyes gouged out. **820** – Michael, a soldier from a family of peasants, is arrested by Byzantine Emperor Leo V on Christmas Eve for conspiracy. He postpones his execution until after the holidays. But Michael escapes, and assassinates Leo during the Christmas mass. He takes the throne, still wearing the chains from prison, as Michael II (the Stammerer). **823** – Michael's old friend and comrade in arms, Thomas the Slav, is inspired by Michael's rags to riches success. He declares himself emperor too. Michael has him executed. **827** – Valentine becomes the hundredth pope. He dies a few months later. **829** – The Nile freezes over. **832** – The former Doge of Venice, Obelerio degli Antenori, tries to reclaim power. When he fails, his head is displayed in the marketplace. **833** – Louis the Pious is deposed by his sons. **834** – Louis the Pious is restored to the throne when his sons all fall out. **838** – The Stone of Destiny, a lump of drab sandstone that will become the coronation stone for the kings of Scotland, is placed at Scone Palace. **839** – The Picts lose all of their leaders in a Viking attack. **840** – On Louis' death, civil war breaks out between his sons. **843** – At the Treaty of Verdun, Louis' sons establish the division between France and Germany which exists to this very day, and has prompted so many wars. **845** – Persecution of Buddhists starts in earnest in China. More than 4600 monasteries and 40,000 temples are destroyed, and 260,000 monks and nuns are forced to return to abandon their faith. **845** – Charles the Bald, king of West France, is defeated at the battle of Ballon by the Duke of Burgundy. For the next seven centuries Burgundy will operate as an independent state. **845** – Paris is sacked by Vikings. **846** – The Vatican is sacked by Arab pirates. **847** – Thiota, a Christian prophetess, predicts the end of the world this year. She is no more correct than Gregory of Tours (qv 806) – but he had the sense to name a time long after his own death. Thiota confesses she only made up the apocalypse for financial gain, and she's given a flogging. **853** – Was there ever a Pope Joan? The Vatican deny it and put it down to legend – but then, they would, wouldn't they? And it doesn't explain the chairs subsequant popes sit on at inauguration with holes in the seats, so that the rest of the clergy will be able to see their gender by the underhanging genitals. Because the story goes that for a couple of years there reigned a pope who was a woman disguised as a man – and that it's only when on horseback she accidentally gives birth to a child that anyone finds out otherwise. (Well, presumably the man who had impregnated her must have had an inkling.) While it's far more likely that this is a satirical story written by someone with a grudge against the papacy – and only a passing interest in the practicalities of pregnancy – I still do hope that it's true. It would be just one of those little things that would make history so much the richer. (Though, I suppose, Joan herself might think differently. Her little stunt as pontiff allegedly doesn't go down too well with the crowds, who stone her to death. She really ought to have played the miracle card.) **856** – King Ethelwulf of Wessex marries Judith. She is only thirteen. He is sixty-one. **860** – The Archbishop of Reims writes 'On the Divorce of Lothair', outlining his opposition to the French king Lothair breaking the marriage with his wife. It's a seminal work that sets the very foundation for defining the rights and duties of the monarchy, and from this we can see a clear line drawn to the Magna Carta, to the establishment of Parliament, and to constitutional monarchy itself. **861** – But Lothair divorces her anyway. **865** – Threatened with excommunication, Lothair takes back his wife. But she has other ideas, and demands a divorce of her own. **869** – Lothair appeals to the new pope about his unhappy marriage, and sets off to Italy to get his approval. He gets it. Jubilantly, he sets home. And dies of fever along the way. *Charlemagne is my ancestor! I have proof. The mathematics don't lie. Listen. We each have two parents. Yes? They each have two parents too, which means we have four grandparents. And eight great-grandparents. And sixteen great-great-grandparents. Ten generations back, we've all had over 1,000 ancestors. Twenty generations, the numbers double and then double and then double again, we end up with over a million. Multiplying this back to the time Charlemagne was alive, we would all have had four billion ancestors. But as I've said, the population of the entire world then was no more than 300 million. You can account for some of the discrepancy because there's a lot of intermarrying, but it's still one hell of a discrepancy. It would be tempting to think that everybody on the planet at that point must be our direct ancestors, just to keep the maths right – but, of course, that won't be true, a lot of them would have died without children; but anyone with a direct line of descent through 1,200 years of war and plague and famine and persecution would have been. And there are very few people who could fit those criteria – history is so harsh and has such a habit of destroying all the peasants and tradesmen, that direct line would really have to be a royal one. All the royal families of Europe are descended from Charlemagne, and at some (usually obscure) point we must have branched off from that descent too; the mathematical probability that anyone alive today doesn't share a common ancestry with Charlemagne is incalculably small.* **869** – King Edmund of East Anglia is murdered by the Danes. He's flayed, has an eagle carved into his back, is tied to a tree, shot with arrows, then beheaded. His head is found guarded by a wolf, and from that moment a wolf becomes his symbol. Very, very posthumously. **870** – Nuns at Berwickshire cut off their lips and noses to intimidate their Viking attackers. **872** – When Harold is rejected by a princess, he resolves never to cut his hair again until he makes himself king of Norway, just to show her. He earns the name Harold Shockhead. After the battle of Hafrs Fjord he seizes control of the throne and goes to the barber. He's renamed Harold Fairhair, and gets the girl. **878** – King Alfred burns the cakes. **885** – Byzantine Emperor Basil I is killed in a hunting accident; his belt gets snared in the antlers of a deer, and he's dragged sixteen miles. *We are all Charlemagne's children, each and every one of us. Don't you see what this means? I'd always imagined my ancestors were nobodies, just peasant stock, forgotten forever. But now we have touched history, you and I, history is within us, our distant great-great-great-grandfather was a man whose will shaped the very world. And maybe we can't be Charlemagnes, maybe we won't live up to Granddad, maybe instead we'll live obscure lives and die obscure deaths, but we still have that potential for greatness within us, don't you see? History is not something dry or academic after all, it's a family business. I call back the school. I want to share this with the secretary there. Charlemagne is my father, and he is her father – she's my sister – please, sister, please, put him back on the syllabus this very second. Just to give us all meaning, so we can bask in his meaning. She puts me on hold. Muzak plays in my ear. After half an hour I give up waiting for her, I put the phone down.* **887** Charles the Fat of France subjects himself to trepanning to ease his headaches. **892** – Sigurd, earl of Orkney, executes the leader of an opposing army, and ties his head to his saddle. Cantering about proudly and showing off his prize, its teeth bounce up and scratch him. Sigurd dies of blood poisoning. **897** – The Cadaver Synod. Pope Stephen VI has his predecessor, Formosus summoned to court to answer to charges against canon law – nine months after Formosus' death. The corpse is clothed in papal vestments, sat in a chair, and found guilty of all charges. Formosus gets away lightly; he has the fingers he used for blessing cut off. *I've been trying to hold on to Charlemagne you know, but there's no use, he's gone, by AD 900 he's turned to dust. The world has spun on its axis 30,000 times already – and no-one even knows they're spinning – aren't all our ancestors so stupid – isn't Granddad a fool? Everyone who's alive at the top of this page is dead by the time we reach the bottom – and their children are all dead too.* **900** – The Persian scientist Rhazes writes of time that it has a never-ending flow. Too bloody right.

INKBLOTS

Sam's mother was dying; everybody agreed. The doctors said so, and the nurses said so, and Sam's mother herself said so – 'I don't think I can hold on much longer,' she said. And the ambulance was called for, and Sam's mother was taken straight to the hospital. She'd been there for *weeks*. So, Sam was sad, but not all that surprised, the day his father called him on the telephone. 'I think you'd better come over, son,' he said, 'It's time.'

Sam's mother was in a private ward. Sam's parents had decided that Sam's mother was going to die very discreetly. 'Good morning, Sam,' they both said when Sam came in. Sam was carrying a bunch of flowers for his mother; he wasn't entirely sure there'd be much point in buying any, not seeing how she was on her way out, but he thought she might enjoy them in the little while she had left. Now he was glad that he had. Sam's mother looked a little wan and feeble, and suddenly inexpressibly old, like an apple still waiting in the fruit bowl when you get back home from a two-week holiday. But she was very much alive, and kicking, and still perfectly capable of smelling daffodils. 'Oh, daffodils,' she said, 'how kind. Why not take a seat? Your father and I have a proposal for you.'

Sam sat down, and Sam's mother and Sam's father smiled at Sam.

'We've decided to both get tattoos,' said Sam's father.

'To demonstrate our undying love for each other,' said Sam's mother.

'Before your mother does, in fact, die,' said Sam's father.

Sam's father was to have a tattoo of a heart on his arm, with the word 'Margaret' written in flowing letters underneath. Sam's mother was called Margaret. And she had opted for the same heart tattoo, but with 'Alexander' beneath hers. Alexander being, of course, Sam's father's name – though no-one called him Alexander, they called him Al, or Alex, or even Big A, but Sam's mother had decided on the full name God had given him, she wanted this tattoo to be rather formal. The hospital tattooist, they said, was a genius. He'd already worked out a way of building Sam's father's liver spots quite naturally into the overall design, you'd have thought they were a deliberate part of the pattern. And he could bunch up Sam's mother's wrinkles into a tight concertina at the elbow, so he'd have a good smooth surface on to which to practise his craft.

Sam was privately horrified by his parents' dalliance with body art. 'That sounds all right,' was what he said.

'Good morning,' said the tattooist, as he came into the ward. He wore the same starched white clothes of all the doctors, and he wheeled in a trolley upon which he had dyes of all different colours, and a large frightening needle. He smiled politely at the family. Sam thought the tattooist had a ridiculous number of tattoos; he could see them pouring out from under his shirt collars and up to the cheeks, they spread from his shirt cuffs to the backs of his hands. Sam thought that maybe the tattoos continued under his clothes, under all his clothes, over every inch of his body. He wondered whether maybe a tattooist needed to demonstrate that he had a lot of tattoos, just as a dentist needed to display a set of white gleaming healthy teeth, just as a cardiologist needed to show he had a heart. 'Are you all ready?' he asked.

'We haven't told him yet,' said Sam's mother.

'We were just about to,' said Sam's father.

'Tell me what?' said Sam.

'I'll set up the equipment,' said the tattooist.

Sam's father explained that tattoo surgery wasn't given automatically on Sam's mother's healthcare plan; it was an optional extra, and expensive too. But that because it was March – there was a special March discount – the tattooist was offering a special three for two deal. (The tattooist nodded at this, and shrugged comically at his own generosity.) So if Sam's mother and Sam's father were both getting tattoos, there was a tattoo still going spare, costing nothing. And that tattoo could be Sam's.

Sam didn't want a tattoo.

'But it's *free*,' said Sam's mother.

Sam's father told Sam what they'd picked out for him. A nice big heart for his own arm, with flowing writing underneath. 'Margaret and Alexander'.

'Why do I have to have *two* names?'

'I'm not going to live forever,' said Sam's father. 'I'll be going the way of your mother before too long. Best get me on your skin while it's so cheap.'

'Can't it just say "Mum and Dad"?'

Neither Sam's mother nor Sam's father liked this. It didn't really specify who the mum and dad in question might be. They wouldn't feel suitably remembered. 'And you do want to remember us, don't you, Sam?' asked Sam's father. 'After all the sacrifices we made for you?' asked Sam's mother. 'You do want to demonstrate your devotion to us?' they said.

Sam really didn't. He pointed out it'd be painful. And Sam's father tutted, and said it would only be a little prick – well, hundreds of little pricks, really, but they would only be little. And Sam pointed out that the tattoo would never come off. And Sam's mother tutted in her turn, and said that was rather the point.

Sam's father got angry, and reminded Sam of all those extra hours he'd worked in a job he'd never enjoyed, just so he could feed Sam and clothe Sam and give Sam a good education. And Sam's mother got angry (and she really oughtn't to have, not in her condition) and alluded to the stretch marks she'd got giving birth to Sam; she'd never got her figure back, *never*. Now they were asking for just a little sacrifice from Sam in turn. And it wouldn't even cost him a penny. Think of that!

Sam made hurried apologies, and left the hospital.

*

Out in the cold air, Sam could think more clearly. He cursed his father for phoning him in the first place. He cursed his mother for dying in March, when March was special discount month.

It wasn't the pain, actually, now he thought of it – give him something to bite on, he thought he'd be all right. It was the *permanence* of the tattoo, and what that declared to the world. He loved his mother and father. Of course he did. But it was a love he only felt when he needed it, he only gave it room as an occasional houseguest, at Christmas, on birthdays. It wasn't a love that filled his heart during the day, or kept him awake at night. If the love could fade into the background of his mind, then the tattoo representation of it ought to be able to fade as well. A tattoo of his love wouldn't be a lie, not as such, that would be too strong a description. But it would certainly be an *exaggeration*.

If they'd asked for a piercing, then Sam would have agreed. He might have had to give it a bit of a think, but he'd have come round. If it were somewhere acceptable, like an ear, or somewhere discreet, like a nipple. Because he knew that the hole could grow over if need be. If and when his love for his parents died – years from now, possibly, who knows? – then he could take out the ring, and soon be restored to his normal self, perfectly intact and unperforated.

Sam didn't like permanence. He supposed, now he thought of it, and it was a new thought, that that was why he'd never had a girlfriend for long. And when he *had* thought he could have made a go at a relationship, something that might last, something that might not make him feel trapped, that was why he'd still ruined it. Because Sheila had wanted kids, and he didn't. Kids were really the most permanent things of all.

He supposed having a child was a little like having a tattoo. Except at least with a tattoo you could cover it up under your shirt sleeves. Except at least with a tattoo it wouldn't keep needing more money spent on it, year in, year out, as it grew older and bigger and supplanted your life with its own. Especially *this* tattoo, which had already been paid for. Which was absolutely free.

He supposed that, all said, his parents had already branded themselves with a tattoo for so many years. And the tattoo had never repaid that debt.

He walked back to the hospital. He'd do whatever they asked for. And it wasn't as if he was ever likely to get a girlfriend who might complain.

'You're too late,' said Sam's father, and for a ghastly moment Sam thought his mother had already died, she was lying still on the bed – but no, she opened her eyes and glared at Sam balefully. Both parents had bandages on their arms. Sam began to talk about the three for two deal, and Sam's father told him they'd given their extra tattoo to the nice oriental woman who turned the beds; she'd been thrilled; she'd now got a snake twisting up her thigh. 'There was no waste,' said Sam's father. 'Do you realise,' said Sam's mother suddenly, and it was so cold, so matter of fact, 'that your father and I only stayed together all these years because of you? And there was no point. What a waste. What a waste.' Sam had nothing to say to this. 'Leave me alone,' said Sam's mother. 'I think I want to die now, please.'

*

But Sam's mother doesn't die. Sam's father sits by her bedside all night, pouring into plastic cups a constant supply of water that she never wants to drink, and holding her gently by the hand, and whispering that he loves her, and only dozing when she dozes. Fully expecting every time that he wakes that she'll have passed away in the mean time. The next morning her eyes are sparkling bright. 'I want another tattoo,' she says. 'Let's get another tattoo.' Sam's father placidly suggests that one tattoo each really might be enough. She tells him, 'You're just like your son,' and it's the worst insult she can think of. She turns on her side away from him. 'You can go now,' she says.

Sam's mother first chooses a single red rose for her shoulder. And she soon moves on to a crucifix, and a lion's head, and a whole *garland* of roses flowing over her neck and down her shoulders, and an anchor like the one worn by Popeye the Sailor Man. She doesn't want to die. Not while she still has flesh left untattooed. Not while she has a hobby. The hospital discharges her. And on her last day, as she's packing, the hospital tattooist confesses his love for her. He's never known a woman like her. Not someone who so shares his passion for the needle and the ink. She can be his muse, she can be his canvas. She moves in with him. And he takes to displaying his elderly girlfriend to the tattoo communities. They're all charmed by the May to December relationship, she seventy-four, he only twenty-two. She who looks so old and faded beside his youth, she displaying tattoos which are new and bursting with colour beside his own which are now faded and old.

*

Sam's father is left in something of a quandary. 'I'm lost,' is how he puts it to Sam, during one of those conversations where he's overcome his disappointment in his son enough to give him a telephone call. Logically, he can't see what difference any of it should make. He'd resigned himself already to living as a widower, even secretly rather looked forward to implementing a new daily regime of eating, sleeping and television-watching without having to take into consideration the needs of another. Why does it matter, then, whether his wife really is dead, or just humping some tattoo artist on the other side of town? He is lonely. He hasn't quite adjusted to that – and he thinks he might have been able to, quite easily, if he could have factored in the odd visit to his wife's gravestone at the cemetery. He'd have laid a flower there every now and again, and shed a tear maybe. Now he fears instead the social embarrassment of bumping into her accidentally at the supermarket.

He needs someone new in his life. He starts to scan the personal ads in the daily newspaper. He's seventy-six, he knows he's got slim pickings as it is – it's even harder now that any woman he dates will have to be called Margaret to match the tattoo on his arm. It's not that Margaret is that rare a name, but he can't afford to be so choosy. When he finally finds a Margaret he likes, and who clearly likes him, he is elated. She's a forty-four-year-old divorcée, not pretty enough with her lanky hair and her harsh owlish glasses to be picky either. Over linguini at an expensive Italian they confide in each other, they share the same likings in music, in books, and in the efficacy of local by-laws. He takes her back to his house, his cold and empty house. He strips naked for her. She sees the tattoos. She tells him that she doesn't dislike tattoos per se – though she actually finds them a little vulgar – but she can't be with a man who'll sport an indelible print of her name on his arm after only a first date. It isn't fair, is it? It puts too much pressure on her, surely he can see?

Sam's father is destroyed. He'll never find another Margaret halfway so suitable. The tattoo is useless, it seems to mock him every time he has a bath, and he towels himself off afterwards in the bathroom mirror. No matter how hard he towels, the lettering on his arm won't even smear. Then one day he has an idea. He'll buy a pet. He'll name that pet Margaret. He doesn't much like animals, so he starts with a goldfish. He'll try a goldfish, see how it goes, he knows they don't live long. Margaret the goldfish doesn't, it expires within the week, but Sam's father finds it a successful experiment, Margaret doesn't die in vain. He works his way up from a stick insect through a hamster to a tortoise, each of them called Margaret. The tortoise is an act of faith, he knows this is one creature that's bound to outlive him no matter how much he overfeeds it. 'Good morning, Margaret,' he'll say, and display his tattoo to her, and feed her lettuce leaves, and he loves her so much that sometimes he thinks his heart will burst.

*

And Sam? What of Sam?

Sam has never loved. Sam sometimes wonders whether there's something broken inside. He worries about this. He feels hurt when his father's desperate phone calls – 'I'm lost,' he'll say – so often end with his father telling him he's a cold unfeeling bastard and hanging up on him. He feels hurt when his mother looks so awkward around him, all of her friends and her lovers now so much younger than Sam, he feels hurt when she tactfully suggests he no longer sees her in public because it cramps her style. Yes, he's hurt. He can't help it, no matter how much he tries to push such things to the back of his mind.

He has never loved. He doesn't think he's capable of it.

One day at the office he meets a girl called Annie. She's been moved to a work station next to his. He can see her answering the phone and typing on her computer, just at the same time he's answering the phone and typing on his computer. He begins to think about her a lot during the day, and then he starts thinking of her during the night too. She's kind to him. She makes him tea when she's making herself one, often without even asking him if he wants a cup. She's polite and she's sweet and she's so sensible, she wears flat shoes and no earrings and lipstick that's coloured like lip. He loves her, he loves her, he loves.

He asks her out on a date. She says yes.

After the third date he invites her back to his flat, and she accepts willingly enough. When she undresses she reveals a little tattoo on her ankle – it's a butterfly, she says. He stares at it. She is imagining he is admiring it, and she blushes. She asks shyly whether he'd like to kiss it. He doesn't. He does. When he brushes his mouth against the butterfly, it feels like normal skin. Just smooth, like skin.

They make love that night, and Sam finds he can ignore the very idea of that tattoo in the dark, but afterwards, when she is sleeping, tucked into his side and snoring so peacefully like she's always belonged there, he can't but help think of the butterfly. And wonder whether the blue and the black and the yellow inks are leaking and staining the sheets.

But that's the great lie of history. To make us believe, even if we don't feel we're individually significant, that the times we live in are. Every generation of chronicled time has always asserted that their contemporary crises are important, that the decisions made by our leaders in dealing with those crises are pivotal, that the warmongers in distant lands creating the crises are evil and are threatening all civilisation as we understand it upon an apocalyptic scale. Every century is littered with prophecies of the end times, that this, at last, is the climax. And it's because of the way we digest history, the way we rationalise it as an ongoing plotline with a beginning and a middle, and with an end just around the corner, that we can take the whole chaos of the planet and impose upon it a single story narrative of cause and effect. It's reassuring. Because even if we feel individually that we are useless, that we've failed, that we can't even make our wives happy, or our families happy, that if we died tomorrow no-one would mourn us for long – then at least the bigger story around us has a long lasting impact: our parents can remember where they were when Kennedy was assassinated, we can remember where we were when the Twin Towers fell – and it means that we have become part of that narrative, even if we're standing on the touchlines we were a part of something that mattered. My wife may no longer love me, she may barely speak to me any more, sometimes all I get from her that passes as conversation is a series of grunts – but, do you know what, I watched the World Trade Center live, and she only got to see it as an edited repeat upon the news already made distanced by journalist's commentary. I'm history, and she isn't. **902** – The Chinese kingdom of Nanzhao is overthrown. **904** – In papal history, it's the beginning of the Rule of the Harlots, or the Pornocracy – a dark age of the Vatican in which the popes are at their most corrupt, and dominated by power-hungry prostitutes. Sergius III becomes the pope, described as 'the slave of every vice and the most wicked of men'; indeed, he stands out as the only pope to have both murdered other popes (Leo V and the anti-pope Christopher), but also to have fathered another one (John XI). The real authority, though, is his concubine, Theodora, 'a shameless whore,' who 'exercised power on the Roman citizenry like a man'. Theodora soon makes her teenage daughter Marozia mistress to Sergius too – and it's the struggle between mother and daughter to be supreme and to control their own puppet popes that dominate Vatican politics for the next sixty years. **904** – Saracen pirates attack the city of Thessalonica, and sack it for a full week. **904** – Chang'an, the largest city of the ancient world, is destroyed. **906** – Regino of Prum's collection of canon law forms the basis for centuries of witchcraft persecution. **907** – The last emperor of China's Tang Dynasty is murdered, leading to a time of chaos and civil war that will last for over fifty years. **911** – The sickly teenage king Louis the Child of East France dies after an ineffectual reign of military defeats. **914** – Theodora summons to Rome one of her favourite lovers, and has him declared pope as John X. Marozia is furious, and determines to overthrow her mother's choice, and replace him with another John – her own son, by Pope Sergius III. John X, for his part, ditches Theodora as soon as he sets his eyes on a beautiful Italian princess. **917** – The battle of Achelous, one of the greatest disasters in Byzantine history. The forces led by Leo Phokas the Elder are destroyed by the Bulgarians. **919** – His military defeat notwithstanding, Leo Phokas attempts to seize the Byzantine throne. He fails spectacularly at this as well, is captured and blinded, and then paraded through the streets of Constantinople on a mule. **923** – Civil war breaks out in Leon, following the death of King Ordono II. **923 –** King Robert I of France is killed at the battle of Soissons by former king Charles III (the Simple) in single combat. It doesn't do simple Charles much good, though, and he's promptly captured and imprisoned. **924** – Marozia's attempts to overthrow John X fail. She has married Count Alberic, and incites him to rebel against the Pope. John defeats him at the battle of Orte, and forces Marozia to look upon her husband's mutilated corpse. **924** – King Edward the Elder of Wessex is killed fighting the Welsh. His son Aelfweard becomes his unlikely successor; he is a hermit. Never crowned, he reigns bemusedly for sixteen days before his services are dispensed with terminally. Because of his father's success, though, Aelfweard can claim to be the very first king of a united England. **924** – In forty years of campaigning, Holy Roman Emperor Berengar has never won a single battle. He is at last dethroned and murdered by his own men, leaving no heirs. The title is left vacant for nearly forty years. *Whereas the truth is, surely, that even the great movers and shakers of history must have had the same neuroses we had, they probably worried whether their friends liked them or enjoyed their company or talked about them behind their backs, they worried about how often they had sex with their wives, and how good the sex was when they actually did do it, and whether they were even doing it correctly in the first place (maybe, Napoleon thought Wellington always got it on the target every single time, maybe Oliver Cromwell stewed in bed each night fretting about the sexual rapaciousness of King Charles I), they worried whether anyone cared, whether anyone felt they were making a difference. It was easier for the peasants, they knew they were nobodies, they knew no-one would mark down their names and preserve them for posterity – but if you were a king of England, or a Byzantine Emperor, or a pope, you had all the other famous names to compete with – would you pass muster, or just be another mediocrity? These world figures, these men who stared out at me from the Wise Old Owl's book, did they have a game plan at all? Like the rest of us, weren't they just muddling on day by day hoping that they were doing the right thing? (Better declare another war, better expand the empire, better pass a few more bills, better build a few more churches – better to be seen doing something, better look as good a king as Father. And better make the populace feel they're living through Important Times, through Consequence and Change, with everything at stake – better make them feel that all this means something.)* **928** – Marozia at last has John X captured, and thrown into the prisons of the Castel Sant'Angelo. There he is murdered. She still wants her son John to succeed him, but bides her time until he's twenty-one years old. So instead she sets up a couple of placeholder popes to keep the seat warm while he matures; one of them, Leo VI, lasts only seven months before Marozia has him poisoned. **929** – The Christian Duke Vaclav of Bohemia is invited to attend the baptism of his pagan brother Boleslav's infant son. As Vaclav kneels for the prayers, Boleslav murders him. The irony is that the newly baptised son grows up to become a monk. And as for the murdered Vaclav, he lives on in history and song as Good King Wenceslas. He's not a king, though, but a duke; the Christmas carols lied to us. **930** – Eric Bloodaxe becomes king of Norway, and has four of his brothers killed. **931** – Theinhko, king of Burma, is killed by an angry farmer when he eats vegetables from his field without permission. The farmer takes the throne as King Nyanng-u-Sawrahan, but becomes better known as 'the Cucumber King'. **931** – Alfonso IV of Leon abdicates in favour of his brother, Ramiro II, and joins a monastery. **931** – Marozia, at last, achieves her ambitions for her bastard pope-spawned son, and has him appointed pope John XI. **932** – Marozia is attacked by her *other* son, Alberic, jealous of all the attention she has given John. He has her imprisoned in the deepest vaults of the Castel Sant'Angelo. Alberic imprisons his brother John, too, but then releases him on the condition that Alberic will be in charge. After John dies, he spends the next twenty years of his life appointing and dominating four more puppet Popes of his own. As for Marozia in her cell – she survives there, she survives there against the odds for a very long time. And never sees sunlight again for the remaining fifty-four years of her life. **934** – Alfonso of Leon changes his mind about the whole monastery thing, and decides he'd rather be king again. His brother Ramiro disagrees, and blinds him. Alfonso goes back to his monastery. **943** – King Constantine II of Scotland abdicates his throne, and retires to a monastery. **944** – Byzantine Emperor Romanos I is deposed by his son, and forced to become a monk. Monasteries are the retreats of choice for ousted monarchs of the tenth century. Airy and sacred, that's what they're looking for. **945** – Prince Igor of Kiev is killed while collecting tribute money from the tribe of the Drevliane. According to legend, his widow gets her revenge by sending to them a flight of sparrows carrying burning matches, which wipes the tribe out. **946** – While celebrating with his nobles at a party, King Edmund of England spots an exiled thief amongst the revellers. When he tries to throw him out, he is stabbed to death. He is succeeded by his brother Edred, a man so sickly that he can only eat the juices of already chewed food. **950** – Iago and Ieuaf become joint rulers of Gwynedd. They spend the first two years of the reign fighting in alliance to beat off pretenders to the throne – then the next seventeen fighting each other in a bloody civil war. *If history is one long ongoing novel we want to feel that it's heading towards some great conclusion – and we naturally want to believe that we're living through some of the more exciting chapters of that novel, not just the bits of crappy padding all our reader descendants will want to skip through. That his is a time of great and magnificent men, or great and terrible men, that from this point on all future history will be affected irrevocably by the decisions now taken. In the twenty-first century we declare wars no longer simply on nations, like they did in the olden days – because nations are too small now, we've all got the internet, and we can jump on planes and be anywhere within a day – so instead we now declare wars on concepts, so we get wars on poverty and wars on drugs, wars on fascism and then wars on communism, and now, most emphatically, wars on terror itself. The people who lived through the Dark Ages never would have realised they were especially dark; conversely, those so blessed to pass through the Renaissance and the Age of Enlightenment wouldn't have known the difference – they'd still have got hungry, got poor, frozen in the winter, still have been fighting other men's wars, still shovelling dung, still dying of plague, still dying young, still living the same old shit.* **954** – On his deathbed, Marozia's son Alberic nominates his own bastard Octavian as next pope as John XII. **955** – John XII becomes pope, and is the most thoroughly dissolute and corrupt there has ever been. He runs a brothel at the Vatican. He sleeps with his father's mistresses, and even with his own mother. He spends so many nights on the streets of Rome searching for fresh conquests hat women are warned to stay indoors. Prayers are offered up to God in monasteries wishing the pope a speedy death. **955** – King Edwy of England is late ɔr his own coronation feast because he's cavorting with a noblewoman; the Archbishop of Canterbury drags him back to the dinner by hand shouting at him to give up the strumpet. Relations between the crown and the church are strained from this point on. **960** – The Aksumite Empire in North Africa is estroyed by armies under the command of the Jewish queen Gudit, who burns its churches and its literature. **961** – At the battle of Fitjar, King Haakon he Good of Norway is attacked by his three nephews, the sons of Eric Bloodaxe. He defeats them, but is mortally wounded in the conflict. **962** – In London, St Paul's Cathedral burns to the ground. **963** – Byzantine Emperor Romanos II is poisoned by his wife Theophano. Nikephorus II is named emperor by the troops, marches upon Constantinople, and marries the murderous widow. **963** – In Song Dynasty China, the practice of cremation is outlawed. **964** – John XII is murdered in bed by a jealous husband, who has caught him in the act shagging his wife. As one bishop describes it, the husband 'smashed his skull with a hammer and this liberated his evil soul into the grasp of Satan.' **965** – Marozia has had her son and her grandson as popes. Now it's the turn of her great grandson – who becomes pontiff as John XIII. **968** – The future Ethelred the Unready, King of England, defecates in the font during his own baptism as a baby. Dunstan, the same Archbishop of Canterbury who embarrassed King Edwy's coital celebrations at his coronation, pronounces that it's an omen that the English monarchy will be overthrown. As it turns out, he's not wrong. **969** – In Constantinople, Theophano takes as lover her husband's nephew, John Tzimiskes. She's already murdered one husband emperor, she has no qualms about murdering another. On the night of assassination, Nikephorus is warned that his life is in danger, but John and his friends have entered the palace disguised as women, and evade capture. Nikephorus is decapitated, and his body thrown out of a window. On his tomb it reads: 'You conquered all but a woman.' **969** – John Tzimiskes is crowned Byzantine Emperor – but only after he agrees to punish the murderers of his predecessor. To that end, he has Theophano arrested and sent into exile. **970** – A decade long famine devastates France. **971** – Leo Phokas the Younger, son of rebel Leo Phokas the Elder, tries too to usurp the Byzantine throne from John Tzimiskes. Like his father he is foiled, blinded, and exiled. *Annie changed everything for us. Annie made us feel the times we lived in were significant. That the world about us was more brilliant than the one in centuries before, and simply by dint of her presence. I didn't want Annie at first, I admit it. No, what's the right historical word, I confess, I confess it. My wife came to me with an idea. She looked excited, she'd obviously been planning it all day. She asked me whether we could have a baby. She said that we could build something for the future, just the two of us, we could make ourselves a little piece of future that would live on after us and be all our own. Had she told me we could have made a piece of the past I'd have been more interested; if she could have come up with a way of our depositing a child somewhere in the middle of the tenth century I'd have accepted it like a shot. I told my wife that our child wouldn't make a significant contribution to the future, it'd be one more baby being born into an overpopulated world, the statistical likelihood of it being one that would influence history was staggeringly small. How about we go on holiday instead? We hadn't seen the Colossi of Memnon for a while. She said no. So we didn't go anywhere. And we didn't talk properly for months.* **971** – King Cuilen of Scotland is burned alive by Amdarch, Prince of Strathclyde – in revenge for the king's rape of Amdarch's daughter. **973** – Benedict VI is elected pope, under the protection of Holy Roman Emperor Otto I. But Otto I soon dies – and Benedict is overthrown and imprisoned in the Castel Sant'Angelo. There he is strangled by another of Marozia's family. **976** – In Constantinople, Bulgarian Tsar Boris II and his brother Roman are held as hostages. The Byzantines want the Dynasty to die out, so have Roman castrated. Boris is luckier – he has children, but they're only daughters. So his testicles are allowed to stay intact. Phew. **977** – Boris' luck runs out. He escapes from captivity in Constantinople, and makes it to the Bulgarian border. But he's wearing Byzantine clothes, and is shot dead by a deaf and mute border patrol. The castrated Roman manages to make his identity known, and is made emperor. **978** – King Edward of England is murdered by his stepmother – stabbed in the back, and then dragged by his bolting horse. He becomes known as Edward the Martyr. **981** – Holy Roman Emperor Otto II invites nobles to a banquet – where, one by one, he has them throttled to death at table for treason. **982** – Erik the Red discovers a harsh and barren new land, and names it Greenland to lure gullible settlers. Within a generation they have all starved to death, or been killed by the local Inuits. **984** – Three-year-old Holy Roman Emperor Otto III is abducted by Henry the Quarrelsome. **986** – Pope John XV pays a visit to Marozia, still rotting away in her prison cell at the age of ninety-six. He takes pity on her. He exorcises her of her demonic possession. And then has her smothered with a pillow. **987** – The Carolingian Dynasty in France comes to an abrupt end when King Louis V (the Sluggard) dies in a hunting accident. **991** – At the battle of Maldon, Saxon forces are destroyed by the invading Vikings. King Ethelred the Unready is encouraged to buy off the Vikings from this point on, rather than try to fight them any further. He agrees, and offers them 10,000 pounds of Roman silver. This later becomes known as Danegeld; the Danes begin to realise it's far more profitable to extort the English than to kill them. And they can still, when bored, resort to the odd bit of plundering anyway, just to keep their raping and pillaging muscles active. *It's a basic truism that the children of today are much worse behaved than the children of yesterday. The children of yesterday used to say 'please' and 'thank you', they sat up straight, they respected their elders and had decent haircuts and listened to music that had a proper tune. (And I wouldn't disagree with that. The children in my town are horrifying. I daren't go into the local newsagent's now, there's always a gang of kids outside, smoking and swearing and spitting. In my day we were much better; we hadn't got time for such stuff, we were too busy eating our Spangles and reading our Whizzer and Chips.) My grandparents too complained that the children of my father's day were worse than the children of their day – and you can be sure that their parents looked back with nostalgia at the Tiny Tim-like cherubim of the Victorian age. So there's an obvious conclusion to be drawn from this: the further back in time you go, the nicer and more innocent the children become. And by the time you've reached the tenth century, they must have all been positively angelic. This seems to hold true: the role of children throughout history seems to be as flaxen-haired victims – too weak and hopeless to be good kings (poor old Louis the Child, qv 911, or the Princes in the Tower, qv 1483, or John the Posthumous, qv 1316, or Ivan VI 1741), they only exist to be shining beacons of virtue compromised by a world of war and brutality. There are moments when they try to get their act together and be more assertive (qv 218, 1212), but they are laughably bad at it, and always fall flat on their faces like the ineffectual munchkins they are. Conversely, however, it is a basic truism that adults today are better than our forebears were. We give more easily to charity. We try to be tolerant. We try to be less racist and warmongering, we broadly agree that most women should be given equal rights to men (so long as they don't rub our faces in it and get all 'feminist' on us), and we tut with forgiveness when Grandpa says something ignorant about the darkies because that's just 'what people used to think in his day'. By the same process of logic, then, the further back in time you go, the nastier and more bigoted the mature man must have been – in exaggerated contrast to the children, who by the Dark Ages were so saintly their feet barely touched the ground. How sudden the transition must have been when the kids hit puberty, and in one fell swoop turned from being perfect lambs of God into psychopaths hell bent on rape 'n' pillage sprees. And that's why I didn't want children, really. I explained it all, just like that, to my wife. Children are confusing.* **994** – The Byzantines are defeated by the Turks at the battle of Orontes. **995** – Olaf seizes the throne of Norway; Haakon goes into hiding in a pigsty with his slave Kark. Olaf finds their farm, but cannot find the king – he loudly offers a reward for any man who can bring Haakon to him. Kark cuts off Haakon's head, and brings it out to Olaf. Kark's reward is that he, too, is beheaded. He dies like a king. **995** – Kenneth II of Scotland has ordered the murder of a son of Fenella, daughter of the Earl of Angus. Fenella invites Kenneth to a banquet, at which, in his honour, she presents him with a lifesize statue of the king holding out a real apple. Fenella invites Kenneth to take it – but the statue is booby trapped, and with the fruit removed from position hidden arrows shoot from his own likeness and kill him. **997** – Boleslav II of Bohemia – nicknamed the Pious, and the nephew of Good King Wenceslas, and the one who was baptised as a pretext for his uncle's murder – storms the city of Libice and exterminates the reigning Slavnik Dynasty, killing them even in church. **996** – King Robert I's first action, upon becoming king of France, is to cast off his unloved wife and marry another. It provokes the wrath of the pope, because he's not only committing bigamy, but also incest. **999** – And we reach the end of the first millennium, amidst widespread panic and apocalyptic fervour. There is the rumour Pope Sylvester II has only won the Papacy by playing dice with the Devil, and will give the world to Satan on the stroke of midnight. Those attending mass at St Peter's do so in sackcloth and ashes. Other pilgrims travel to Jerusalem for the end of the world, renouncing their homes and possessions as they leave; thousands die upon the journey, but the lucky ones wind up Mount Zion in droves, awaiting the return of Jesus. *1,000 years later the world's population is again gripped by millennial fear, this time with the threat of the Y2K bug. Overnight, computers will no longer be able to operate, aeroplanes will fall from the sky, riots will break out on the streets. Someone I know actually withdrew all the money he had from his bank account and kept it under his bed; others stockpiled food in case in the chaos there was a rush on all the supermarkets. Within minutes of the new year, after I'd shared a bottle of champagne with my wife, and watched the fireworks displays on television broadcast from a dozen different nations, I went upstairs to my office to check whether my PC was still working. It was. And I knew that this was a good thing, and of course, I was relieved. But – I admit it, I do – by about 5 January, the holidays now over, the turkey eaten, the presents binned, and all the blockbuster movies no longer part of the TV schedules, I found the anticlimax disappointing. I began to wish that the twenty-first century had begun in confusion and bloodshed, I wanted us thrown back in time to a world where we would all have to start again, where history was no longer something that could wash over us but was something to be fought for. And I wasn't the only one. God knows I can't have been the only one. My wife couldn't understand it. She said, 'But, darling, everything's all right, everything's just the same, it's all just the same as it always was.' And I tried to explain it to her, how what I wanted was just a little bit of magic in my life, that in an instant we could have moved from 1999 to 2,000 and genuinely been propelled somewhere new, that just one second might have changed everything, that between the final bong of Big Ben and the first bar of Auld Lang Syne all that we knew might have been swept aside, the magic, the magic – and she looked so hurt, she said, 'But aren't we magic enough? Can't I be magic for you?' And I told her no. I admitted no. I now knew she never could. I now understood that. And I think at that point that she too, yes, she wished that the Y2K bug had bitten us too. And we went into a new millennium, she and I, we stuck together, we didn't break up (though we discussed it, though she mentioned it in bed when the lights were off when she was fighting back the tears), all was the same, and yet it wasn't, it wasn't, in an instant everything had changed. And at last she said to me, she said it very quietly so I had to strain to hear, she said, 'Our baby could be magic. Our baby would change everything.' So I agreed*

TABOO

Your sister's phone call wakes you. You know it must be your sister even before, fumbling, you pick up the receiver. Who else would call at half four in the morning?

'Emma?' you say, and you're right, it's Emma.

'For Christ's sake,' your wife mutters, and sighs loud and heavy, and you think that Emma must have heard.

'What do you think of camels?' Emma asks.

'Emma, is something wrong, it's the middle of the night...'

'No, no. I checked. There's an eight-hour time difference, it's early evening for you now.'

'I don't think so.'

'Are you sure?' she says. And you can picture her narrowing her eyes, giving you that long hard glare, the way she always does when you contradict her – nothing hostile, not as such, not aggressive – just very forthright. Right from childhood you could never hold that glare, you'd always look away. 'Are you sure, because I *checked*.'

'Maybe you're right. Are you in London? Is everything okay?'

'Everything's wonderful,' Emma says. 'I'm in Egypt. It's very hot in Egypt. What's it like in Sydney?'

You don't live in Sydney, you live in Melbourne. 'It's hard to tell, it's dark outside...'

'Yes, yes, it doesn't matter, listen. Listen, I'm getting married.'

'Well,' you say. 'My God. I mean. Well done.'

'Christ,' says your wife, and she sighs again, and this time it's so loud that Emma *must* have caught it, and you cradle the phone away defensively. 'If your sister is going to be rude enough to wake us up in the middle of the night, when we've both got work in the morning, there's no reason why you should have to *compound* that rudeness by carrying on a conversation with her in the bedroom.'

'No, sorry,' you say to your wife, and you get up, you take the phone with you. 'Sorry,' you say to Emma.

You close the bedroom gently, you open the door to the sitting room, you close that too behind you, gently. You sit down on the sofa. 'Right,' you say to Emma. 'So. Start again.'

'I'm getting married,' she says.

'Yes, I got that bit.'

'I decided to go on holiday. I wanted a little bit of me time, I hadn't had any me time in a long time. Barry never gave me any me time, so when Barry and I broke up, I thought this is my chance, I went straight to lastminute.com.'

'And Barry is...?'

'Barry is nothing, Barry is history,' Emma says. 'Keep up. I'm not marrying Barry.'

'No.'

'I *thought* I was marrying Barry, but Barry wasn't the marrying type, or so it turned out. Forget about Barry, I don't want to hear about Barry again.'

151

'Fair enough.'

'Besides, Barry never proposed. I'm marrying Abdul.'

'And Abdul is...?'

'I'm getting to that. I wasn't looking for romance, you know, frankly, that's the *last* thing I was looking for. I'd worked it out. I'm better off without men. Men are just shits. You're a man, you'd know. But Abdul and I connected right away. There was just a bolt of electricity, you know, when we first met? It was the same for both of us, I thought at last, this is the one. And besides, Abdul isn't a man, he's a camel.'

'You did,' you agree, 'say something about camels.'

'What do you think about camels?'

'Erm,' you say. 'I don't think I've ever met one.'

'Not even at a zoo?'

'I might have seen one at a zoo,' you concede. 'I don't think I *met* one at a zoo.'

'I haven't told Mum yet,' Emma says. 'I think Mum will be very angry. I think she's a bit racist. And a bit animalist. In fact, I don't think I'm going to tell her. She'll only try to upset me, and I don't need upset, not in my life, not right now. The only person I'm inviting to the wedding is you.'

'Oh, right,' you say, and you do actually feel flattered, 'thanks.'

'Will you give me away?'

'Yes,' you say, 'yes, of course. Emma. When you say "camel"...'

'Yes?'

'I mean. Are you really happy?'

'I'm very happy,' she assures you. 'I've never been happier.' And you know, you can hear the sincerity in her voice, and it makes you happy too. 'Do you think that you can get here for Thursday? The wedding's not till Saturday, but there's all sorts of things to prepare, and I could do with a hand.'

'Thursday?' you say. 'Hang on. Why so soon?'

'Why wait? I tell you, Abdul and I are in *love*.'

'Right.'

'And anyway, Abdul is nice and heavy at the moment, he's been storing food. Best get it done while the weight is in the zone.'

'Right. Well. I'll get on and book my flights, then.'

'Great. I love you.'

'I love you too.'

'How's your wife...?'

'Kirsten's fine.'

'And your daughter...?'

'Tammy's fine.'

'Good,' she says. 'See you soon, then.' And hangs up.

*

When you go back to bed your wife is very deliberately pretending to be asleep, and when your alarm wakes you in the morning she's doing the same thing, her eyes are squeezed tight and she's refusing to stir. So it's not until you get home in the evening you can tell her your plans. In your lunch hour you went to the bookshop and bought a guide to Egypt, you think the pictures of the Sphinx and the pyramids will excite her as much as they do you.

'That's so typically selfish of your sister,' she says. 'How dare she decide when and where we take our holiday!' She points out that she only gets four weeks' leave a year, and one of those has to be spent visiting her father in Brisbane, and another her mother in Adelaide, and the two remaining weeks are consequently very precious, and it's up to *her* where she spends them, not your bloody sister. 'Going all the way round the world for her wedding, as if. It's not as if she came to our wedding.'

The location of your wedding created the need for much negotiation between your family and your wife's – it began like negotiation, anyway, but soon took on the air of a war summit, with demands flying back and forth across the oceans in ever more hectoring language and with ever less room for compromise. And the Australian contingent eventually won, they dug their teeth in and refused to budge, they won the war not with better ammunition but simply by sheer reserves of manpower, it seemed as though Kirsten had unlimited numbers of cousins her family could produce whenever they needed more muscle. The ceremony finally took place in a chapel in Melbourne with a vast army of in-laws in attendance, and none of your own family at all. The concession made in the treaty was that before the wedding you and Kirsten would take a holiday in England, so that the bride-to-be could be met by *your* family; Kirsten said it was like being inspected under a microscope, like being poked at and prodded by a whole gang of slack-jawed drongos who'd never seen an Aussie before. 'But you like Emma,' you say. 'You don't mind Emma.' And at this Kirsten snorts in derision, she *hates* Emma, didn't you know? – and you didn't, you knew that Kirsten hated your parents, and Uncle Bill and Aunt Val, and your only surviving nanna, and your cousin Tim, and your cousin Tim's kids – but that she hated your sister as well is news to you. And makes you feel just a little sad.

'But we've always talked about going to Egypt some day,' you point out, 'so now seems as good a time as any!' And Kirsten tells you you've *never* talked about going to Egypt, when on Earth have either of you even mentioned Egypt, and on reflection you think maybe she's right, maybe you've never discussed Egypt whatsoever. So.

'If you want to spend your money flying to Egypt, then that's fine,' your wife says. 'But I'm saving *my* money for *my* holiday.' You ask whether you can take Tammy, but Kirsten tells you that taking her out of kindergarten would be disruptive to her emotional wellbeing, she'll take her on holiday herself later in the year. You check the prices to Cairo, and it costs a couple of thousand dollars. When you click on the Buy Now! bar button on the webpage, your heart skips at the expense of it all. You speak to Emma again on the phone; she explains that because of circumstances, circumstances she'll feel more comfortable explaining face to face, she can't offer to put you up – perhaps you could find a hotel? And you do, and that's another thousand dollars gone right there.

Your little girl gets very excited about the idea that you're going to Egypt. She races around the kitchen shouting that Daddy is going away, and drawing little pyramids everywhere. She's never spent a day without you there since she was born. 'You do understand you're not coming with me?' you ask her. 'You do understand I can't disrupt your wellbeing?' 'Yes, yes!' cries Tammy, and she races around all the more, she doesn't seem bothered by that remotely. It's an early flight to Cairo – you have to make your goodbyes to Tammy the night before. 'I'll bring you back a present,' you promise her, 'something nice and Egyptian,' and she says, 'no worries.' You bite your tongue, you do wish she wouldn't say things like that. You don't mind the fact that your daughter is Australian, you just don't want her to end up like one of the crass ones. When you talk to Tammy, you sometimes feel it's just to cram English-accented conversation into her head – Kirsten gets to talk to Tammy lots, she has more time to do so, so you do your very best in the evening to counter that, you sit your little daughter on your knee and speak proper English phrases at her. But just recently it's been hard to find things to say.

'You be good for Mummy,' you say, and Tammy smiles at you, and she promises she will; 'you be good for Mummy too,' she says. And at that moment you've never loved your daughter so much or so fiercely, you want to pick her up and hold her close and never let her go and press down kisses hard upon her head, you want to fold her up and stuff her in your suitcase – you can't wait until she's older, what a perfect little woman she is going to be! But you don't do any of these things. You smile back at her, you give the mobile over her head a little push so that Tammy can see all the animals in the zoo twirling gently above, you close her bedroom door.

*

It's two long flights to Cairo, and by the time you get through customs you're really very jet-lagged, and that's why when your sister greets you you don't recognise her at first. That, and the fact she's wearing a black hood over her face.

'It's called a burqa,' she says helpfully.

'I thought that was a Muslim thing.'

'But I've become a Muslim,' she said. 'In honour of my husband-to-be.'

You hail a taxi. 'It's quite a long way,' Emma says. 'I hope you've got lots of money.' You ask Emma whether you can look at her face, and she tells you she's pretty sure only her husband will be allowed to do that, and you assure her that family members are allowed to as well, though really you've no idea, you'd have looked it up in the Egypt guide book if you'd thought it was going to be an issue. So she sort of shrugs, and checks that the taxi driver isn't peeking in the rear view mirror, and lifts her veil. Her face is a bit fatter than you remember, she looks so happy and she can't stop smiling, it's obvious she's been smiling a lot. She looks beautiful. Being in love suits her. You tell her so. She beams all the more.

'I'm so excited for you,' you say. 'My big sister, getting married! The Muslim thing's a bit weird, though, isn't it?'

She frowns. 'Everyone here's Muslim. Anybody who's anybody, anyway. It's not hard. I've looked in the Qur'an, it's just like being a Christian, it's all about being nice to people, with Eastern bits.'

You realise you're far too tired to talk to your sister. She's always easier to deal with after a solid eight hours' sleep; you knew that even when you were children, there was an exact time to leave her and hide in your bedroom. You've come all this way to see her, and now you suddenly feel shy, and you're annoyed at yourself for that. So you watch the road for a while. You wonder why the taxi driver is going so fast, and how he's able to fit his car into the little gaps in the traffic without crashing, and whether he's ever run anyone down on the pavement. And after only a few minutes' such musing it dawns on you you'd far rather talk to your sister after all – and you manage to wrench your eyes away from the window and the chaos around you and turn back to Emma. But she's finished talking now too. She's back behind the burqa, and it seems to have sealed off her face, there can be no conversation through all that cloth. But she sees you're looking at her. And although her expression is of course unreadable, she takes your hand. She squeezes it.

You're not quite sure what to expect from an Egyptian house. You were half expecting it to be some sort of shed, or a wigwam even. But it looks from the outside just as modern as any normal house might be. Bricks, windows, a large garage. The taxi driver jabbers something. He shows you the fare. You don't know if you're supposed to haggle or not, isn't haggling part of what goes on here? And the fare does seem to have a lot of noughts. So you make a half-hearted attempt to haggle, and the driver scowls angrily, and you give him what he asked for in the first place and add a tip. He takes your suitcases out of the boot and bumps them on to the pavement hard, and then drives away. Your sister asks you for the taxi fare that brought her to the airport to pick you up; she borrowed the money, she'll have to pay it back. So you offer her the same amount. 'No, more than that,' she says.

And you go into her new home. 'We'll have to be quiet,' she says. 'It's family time.' She explains that her fiancé is owned by a man called Ali, who rents out camel rides to tourists. Ali has very kindly allowed Emma to stay in a spare room on condition that she does the housework – cleaning, cooking, general chores. In fact, she'd better get back to work: she was given permission to meet you at the airport, but only if she made up the time when she got back, and now she's running a few hours behind.

You stand in the doorway of the sitting room and peer in. Three teenage children are watching television; one of them is listening to an iPod as he does so, so loud that you can identify the song from where you're standing, it's something by Christina Aguilera. Their mother is watching television too. It looks like a game show – but every so often the children laugh at it uproariously, so maybe it's something entirely different. The mother never laughs, never smiles. 'Hello,' you say. They ignore you. Neither the mother nor the little girl, you notice, are wearing burqas. Your sister pulls her own burqa down smart, and fetches a vacuum cleaner out of the cupboard. She plugs it in, turns it on, and the cleaner isn't new, it coughs and rasps. Without a word the mother levels the remote control at the television, presses a button, and turns the volume up loud over it. The noise of vacuum cleaner and widescreen high-definition TV compete for a moment, but the TV wins – it's very loud, and you wonder whether the neighbours might complain. Your sister cleans the carpet around the sofa, around the coffee table; the little boys lift their feet so she can clean underneath, and the little girl doesn't bother – and every thirty seconds or so they burst into laughter at the antics of the game show host, they laugh and laugh.

'Would you mind doing the dishes?' your sister asks.

So you go into the kitchen, you rinse all the plates and the cutlery, then you stack them all in the dishwasher. You don't turn the dishwasher on. You don't think that should be your job.

And at last the vacuum cleaner is turned off, and your sister comes to join you. 'Thanks for that!' she says. 'Phew!' The television volume stays just as loud, she has to talk quite loudly herself just so you can hear her. The game show ends and segues into something that might be a cop show – whatever it is, there are lots of sirens.

'Emma,' you say, 'this is all very nice, but I'm very tired, I should be getting to my hotel...'

'No, no,' she says, 'no, I need you to meet Abdul. He'll be getting home from work soon, you'll see.'

And sure enough, very soon the door opens. And Emma looks nervous, she adjusts her burqa once more, and she leaves the kitchen to greet the master of the house. This, I take it, must be Ali; his wife and children wear modern clothes, but he has a grey sheet wrapped around his head, he looks like something out of the history books, frankly, he looks like a camel driver, a *peasant*. He pulls his headscarf off, and you see that underneath he looks just as western and civilised as anyone else, the costume was a bit of a fraud. The children turn the TV off at last, and they hug him, all smiles. He hugs them back, but he's too tired for smiling. His wife gives him a single nod, and he nods back.

And Emma steps forward, and offers him the money you gave her earlier. He counts it slowly, carefully. Then gives her too a nod. 'Hello,' you say, and he looks at you for the first time, and then *you* get the nod, nod number three – it's not a friendly nod, and again it's without a smile, but it's at least respectful, and it feels like the first proper acknowledgement you've had since you arrived in the country.

'May I?' asks Emma, and Ali says, 'Yes.' And Emma takes your hand, excited, and Ali frowns at that. And Emma doesn't care, she's already pulling you out of the door, out of the house.

'Where are you taking me?' you say.

'To meet my new husband.'

She pulls up the garage door. Inside there's a family car, nicely polished, new. And to its side, on a bed of straw, a camel.

'This is Abdul,' Emma says, at last lifting her burqa, and you can see how her face is glowing with pride.

Abdul is very definitely a camel. Now you're there, face to face, confronted with the full camel bulk of it, there's really no escaping the fact. It isn't a donkey, or some strange humpy-shaped horse, this is your actual bona fide ship of the desert – and he's big, and he's hairy, and he looks at you with clear disdain.

'So,' says Emma. 'Here we all are!'

'Nice to meet you,' you say to the camel, but your new brother has already turned away.

'Isn't he wonderful?' enthuses Emma. 'Just look at his eyes!' But you can't, Abdul is demonstrating only his arse, it's clear he has eyes only for your sister. 'So deep and, and soulful. Oh, I could drown in them. And these long eyelashes, wouldn't you just *die* for eyelashes like that? And he has, you know, three eyelids.' She kisses the side of his face, and the camel's breathy groan turns into a harrumph. 'Camels are the most beautiful creatures in the world, and Abdul is the most beautiful camel, so.'

'That's great,' you say, and 'How long do camels live for?'

'About forty years.'

'Right.'

'Abdul's only seven now, so the chances are we'll die about the same time. That's what I'm counting on, I don't want to outlive Abdul. Only seven, he's my toyboy, really!' And she laughs.

'Right.'

She nuzzles at his face. He harrumphs again.

'Right. Well, look, I best be getting to bed...'

'You can't go yet,' says Emma. 'Please.'

'I'm really very tired.'

'You don't understand. This is a Muslim wedding. I'm not allowed to see the groom beforehand unless I'm chaperoned. No-one wants to chaperone me. I haven't seen Abdul in *ages*.'

And it occurs to you that your sister barely even *knows* this camel she's getting hitched to. And then something else.

'Wait a moment,' you say. 'Are you telling me you haven't yet... you know...?'

'We can't have sex until we're married. Obviously.'

'But... for God's sake... I mean, how can you tell if...?'

Before you married Kirsten, she insisted she tried you out in all manner of positions. When she found one you were good at, she allowed you to propose.

'The anticipation,' whispers Emma, 'is *wonderful*,' and she licks her lips.

Abdul harrumphs, but it's a very different sort of harrumph this time, it's directed at you.

'Oh, hello,' you say. And you back away a bit.

'Don't worry, he's just wanting to know you better.' Abdul gets to his feet, those spindly legs straighten, you think they'll never carry such a bulky lump, but no, he's upright and tall and without so much as a stagger he's bearing down on you. 'Keep still,' says Emma, so you keep still, and the camel sticks his pointed head right at you, he opens his mouth, out of it pops a red sac that bulges at you querulously. He harrumphs louder, and it's clearly not a happy harrumph, he's agitated now, he's shaking from side to side and that red sac seems to be *pulsating*, 'oh dear,' says Emma, and he hawks a sea of spit into your face.

'Quick!' your sister says. 'Take off your jacket!'

'But it's my best jacket...'

'Take it off!'

And you do, and you hold it out to Abdul, and now he's ripped it from your hand, he's tearing into it, he chews it and spits out patches from it on to the ground, he's jumping on it and destroying that jacket as if it were his mortal enemy.

'I don't think he entirely trusts you,' says Emma. 'But he'll come to understand in time how much you mean to me.'

'I want to go to the hotel now.'

The taxi arrives. You don't think it's the same driver, but really, they all look much the same. 'Thanks for coming all this way,' Emma tells you through the car window as she sees you off.

'You bet.'

And she can't help it, she can't keep in the giggle. 'I'm getting married! Me! Just think!'

*

But it isn't marriage, not really. The technical term for it is civil partnership. And yet that still isn't enough for some people, it'd seem – they say that their relationships are not given proper respect by society, that they demand equal rights. They're always going on some demonstration march or another, they'll be asking that their animal spouses get the vote next! – and when you go to work each morning some creature-hugger with a placard is always soliciting for your signature outside the train station at Flinders Square.

You consider yourself a tolerant and open-minded sort of man, but you do wish they'd stop making a fuss. Because they're bloody lucky, really, haven't they got enough? A hundred years ago they'd have been locked up for what they're now allowed to do in public. They ask that their animal loving be treated as something natural and normal – but it isn't natural, it's not normal, you can't say it is, if God had wanted humans to fall in love with animals then the union would be able to produce children. Not that you're religious, but the religious groups are correct on that, at least, surely – and you're not arguing about the *ethics* of bestial relations here, as you say, you're a tolerant and open-minded person, but there's no arguing that it makes any kind of biological sense. And yet when you try to say this in the office you're shouted down as being bestiophobic. It really makes you sick.

But the law now states that sexual relations are permitted between a human and a consenting animal. For a while it was hard to determine what actually proved the animal was consenting – after all, it wasn't as if they could tell us whether they were up for it or not, and if we simply all waited until they were eighteen years of age the vast majority of them would be dead. At last it was agreed that an animal's suitability should be judged on body mass, and that the four-legged bride or groom in question must weigh at least one and a half times the amount of its human counterpart. The theory being that if you try to make love to a horse or a rhino or an elephant, and it's not too happy about the arrangement, it will have the strength to resist – but try to shag a reluctant gerbil, say, and there's really precious little the gerbil can do about it. One and a half times the body weight guarantees a beast's complicity in any carnal act you might share – and if you try it on with a gerbil, no matter how much she might seem up for it, or how flirtatiously she twitched her whiskers, then it's statutory rape, clear and simple.

You suppose your sister is now one of those people who would go on marches. Which is funny, because you can't picture her being the sort who'd want to march about anything.

You've got nothing against creature-hugging per se (so long as it's within the privacy of their own homes, so long as you haven't got to see it, so long as it's not shoved down your throat) you say live and let live, you say they're not hurting anybody (except themselves) you're not a bigot, you're not a bestiophobe, you're tolerant, and you're open-minded, and. And you're just lucky you're normal, and in a normal relationship, one that is healthy and clean and childbearing. But coming face to face with your sister's fiancé has made you upset, and you don't like that, it's annoying to discover you're just a little bit prejudiced after all. It wouldn't be so bad, you reflect, if she'd found an ordinary animal, something close to home; you can imagine you'd be very accepting if your brother-in-law were a horse of good Anglo-Saxon stock. But no – she had to go and find something exotic, some zoo creature, she had to go and fall for some fucking Arab.

*

In your hotel room you open up your laptop and fire off a quick email home. 'Hello from sunny Egypt! It's very hot! Wish you were here. Miss you loads. Lots of love, give Tammy a hug from Daddy.' And then you go on to Google, and type into the search engine 'camel sex.'

You read about the camel penis, and are shown a diagram that measures its length and breadth. You read how, when aroused, the penis is in a different axis to most mammals', and when erect enters the female from the reverse direction. You find out the camel's right testicle is slightly bigger than the camel's left testicle.

You break into the mini bar.

You read how a camel in heat is referred to in Arabia as the 'hadur', literally, 'the braying one'. You suppose there's a lot of braying in camel sex. You read that, when he's rutting, the camel will secrete behind the ear a sticky smelly residue. That he'll grind his teeth uncontrollably during copulation. That his mouth will froth, he'll gargle, he'll spit. He'll piss, and he'll swing his tail back and forth through the stream of piss to swish the piss about. That all this water loss, this very deliberate waste of precious fluids, is part of a courtship ritual designed to impress the female. That he'll blow out his soft palate (the dula) to turn her on the more; that, for his part, he'll sniff at his partner's genitalia, and the smell of urine from a non-pregnant female will excite him no end.

You drink the mini bar dry.

When at last you sleep you dream of fat hairy hooked cocks impregnating your urine-drenched sister, and though she's wearing her burqa, you can somehow tell throughout the whole thing that she's grinning from ear to ear.

*

Emma phones you in the morning. She's been given permission to take a whole afternoon off work so you can explore Cairo together. The taxi pulls up outside the hotel, she waves at you to get inside. Once again she is wearing her burqa. She hands another burqa to you. 'Put this on,' she says.

'What for?'

'I want to show you where Abdul works. Abdul's marvellous at his job! But Ali doesn't like me being there, he says I'll distract him, bless.' And she gives a very dry and very un-Muslim-like chuckle. 'I don't want us to be recognised, you're going to have to cover your face like me.'

So you put on the burqa. The air conditioning of the taxi makes the cloth ripple across your face, and the sensation is not unpleasant.

And you pay the driver, and you and your sister stand and watch Abdul and his master work. Ali is transformed; the surly and serious man you met last night is now all smiles, he wheedles his way around the tourists, he invites them all to inspect his camel, to see what a fine beast it is, to take a ride to the Great Pyramid in such style – and he's so good at it, no-one seems able to blank him or walk away, no-one, not even the Americans. He's such a good actor. And Abdul is a good actor too, because whenever a foreigner approaches he lowers his head towards them and flutters his eyelashes and even parts his lips into some sort of camel smile, he doesn't seem to mind when the children pull his ears or pick at his coat or dribble ice cream on him, he's the very picture of patience, the very model of Oriental dignity – and amongst all the sphinx snowglobes and mummy paperweights and postcards of the pyramids, amongst all these imitations of history made cheap and plastic, he looks like the genuine article, he looks himself like a piece of antiquity, so old and so very wise. And for the first time you understand why your sister could have fallen in love with him. 'Hoosh hoosh!' says Ali, and Abdul stoops to let tourists on to his back; 'Hoosh!' and he straightens up, and the tourists are raised high in the air, each one of them laughing and crying out in surprise at the sudden speed of it. And you picture your sister up there, mounting her camel husband as much as she wants for the rest of her life.

You watch for a good hour and a half. Emma never gets bored. 'Isn't he wonderful?' she'll say. You begin to get tired, and there's a reservoir of sweat pooling at the top of your thighs. You suggest that maybe there's more to see in Cairo than her husband, what would Emma recommend? And she says she doesn't know, she hasn't done any of the tourist stuff. 'You never do, do you, when you're at home?' And you resist the urge to remind her she's only been here in Egypt for two weeks.

You go to the Cairo museum, you pay for two tickets. You walk around the exhibits, and the collection is vast. Everywhere there are mummies and canopic jars and little stone pots with heads of jackals. But it seems to you that you've seen it all before, in dozens of other museums all around the world, and you really might as well be in London or Paris or Prague; my God, for a civilisation that collapsed thousands of years ago they certainly left an awful lot of stuff behind, didn't they? But Emma is happy. She says to you at one point, 'It's beautiful, I'm so proud that my country could produce all this,' and she talks a little of Mother Egypt. 'I'm so proud you're here,' she whispers too, and she takes you by the arm, and the eyes behind the burqa slit are wet with tears, and you can't tell whether she's crying out of awe and admiration for the pharaohs or out of love for you – and then you realise with a start you've spent all this time looking out of a slit too, you forgot to take the burqa off, you've been walking all around the Cairo museum wearing a bloody burqa, you feel like an idiot.

'Come on,' you say, and take her to the café. The food there costs a fortune. You buy two coffees, and two sandwiches, and a pastry, you pay for it all. Emma gobbles down her sandwich. She looks so hungry suddenly, and you let her eat your sandwich too.

'You're a good person,' she says suddenly. You don't know where that's come from. You then see she's eaten the pastry as well. 'You're a good guy. I think you're kind, and I don't think you've got the easiest life, and you put up with a lot. And me. I think you put up with me.'

'Oh,' you say. 'I don't know about that.'

'I never found good guys. I always ended up with the other sort of guys. The selfish shit sort of guys. If I'd met someone like you, God, I don't suppose I'd now be marrying a camel.'

You blush, and you wish you were still wearing your burqa. She doesn't say anything else for a bit, and you wonder whether she'll do her usual trick, whether now she's let show a little emotion or humanity that she'll sweep it away with some dismissive gesture. But she doesn't. She doesn't.

'I always thought you saw me as a bit of an idiot,' you say.

'No.'

You don't look at her. 'You pulled my hair. You kicked me. I never thought you even liked me very much.'

'I haven't pulled your hair.'

'Not recently. I mean. But when we were kids.'

'Well. You're my little brother.' As if that explains everything.

'Are you sure you want... Are you sure that... Emma?' And you'd like to carry on, but you mustn't ask, and you're still not looking at her, you still don't dare, and even if you did what would be the point, her face would still be veiled, wouldn't it? 'I just want you happy,' you say, and you leave it like that, and maybe that's just as well.

*

That evening at the hotel you check your email and there's nothing from your wife, so you write to her again. 'Hello from sunny Egypt! It's still very hot here! I haven't heard from you, are you all right? Wish you were here. Today I went to the Cairo museum. I think you'd have liked it. I know you like museums, and it was a very big one. Lots of pots everywhere. I wish you'd been here to see them. I miss you. How are you, are you all right? Write soon. Give Tammy a hug from her Daddy.'

Then you decide to take a walk. As you leave the hotel the doorman stands to attention and calls you sir. He looks funny dressed up posh like that, like an English gentleman from a hundred years ago, top hat and spats. (He must be baking.) You walk around the streets for an hour. This is Cairo, the real Cairo, isn't it? Your clothes cling to you, damp and sticky, you wonder why anyone would choose to live here. I mean, you know that historically people just settled where they were born, but nowadays, in these days of international travel, why do all of these Egyptians stay? The roads are noisy. The sand is everywhere, it looks like dirt. You go back to the hotel, and the doorman stands to attention once more, once more calls you sir, so efficient – you bet he doesn't even recognise you from last time – and you wish he wouldn't call you sir, you didn't ask him for that, you didn't ask for anything.

In the room you check your email. Still nothing from your wife, but then, you suppose, she's probably asleep. You consider phoning, but you'd only wake her. You'd only make her cross. You write to her once more.

'Me again! I've been thinking. I may extend my visit here, if that's all right. I don't know how long. But I think my sister needs me.'

You open the mini bar, and it's empty. Not so fucking efficient after all, for all their fancy doormen, for all their top hats, they've let you down. You phone reception, you demand they restock your mini bar at once. A waiter in a red velvet jacket comes up soon after, lines the shelves with little bottles, smiles at you widely, says 'sorry sorry'.

You write another email.

'I don't think it's working out. I don't think I love you any more.'

You drink a whisky. And then think, why not? And send it.

And you think, oh, Tammy. Tammy. You'd have grown into such a beautiful woman. And you try to picture how beautiful, like a model maybe, like a girl on the cover of a glossy magazine, like a pin-up.

You lie on the bed. You turn on the TV. There's some sort of game show on. You can't work out what the rules are, but the host is quite funny, all the audience seem to be laughing at him, what a character.

*

It's now the day before the wedding, and Emma and Abdul have to be weighed. It's a formality, of course. Your sister is a fat woman, but it's obvious that her camel is big enough to resist her sexual advances should he want to. But everyone has to be weighed regardless, that's the law of the thing.

Ali has booked an early morning appointment for the marriage weigher. He wants Abdul out there at the tourist sites as soon as possible, the groom still has a full day's work ahead of him. The marriage weigher arrives promptly, wearing a suit and carrying all the paperwork. He brings with him a couple of assistants who are responsible for lugging the large set of scales.

The weighing takes place within the garage. Your sister goes first, and she's easy; she strips off completely naked, climbs on to the scales. It seems so strange to see her exposed when since you've arrived she's always been smothered in purdah. She stands still for a few seconds, breasts drooping, minge flashing, but nobody is interested in what she looks like, it's the digital reading of her weight that they care about. She comes in at 167 pounds. Even though it's hot and sweaty here, and she doesn't appear to eat much, she's still a big girl.

Abdul is harder work. He simply doesn't want to be weighed. Ali does his best to coax him, he says 'hoosh, hoosh!' he tries smiling, he tugs at the rope running through his nostrils. The weigher's assistants try to push him on to the scales by force, they take one bottom cheek each, but Abdul doesn't like that at all, he harrumphs his misgivings about the matter most insistently. 'Let me try,' says your sister, 'he'll listen to me.' And as she approaches Abdul, he does indeed calm down, he stops jerking his head from side to side, he seems to concentrate on the words she breathes into his ear. 'Please, darling,' she says. 'Because without this, we can't get married. We can't be together, and I love you so much.' Abdul nods his head a bit. He considers what she says. He trots forward to the scales, contemplates them studiously. Then pisses on them.

Ali sighs, he keeps looking at his watch; at last he gives in, he takes out money, he offers the man in the suit a bribe. The man doesn't seem in the least surprised. He takes the cash, he counts it, it looks very dirty to you, why is Egyptian money so dirty? Then he writes something on a form, he tears off a receipt. It's all over. The bride and groom are deemed compatible.

While your sister is getting dressed, Ali comes up to you. You think he is going to offer some appropriate platitudes about the forthcoming marriage, and indeed you get in first – you smile, and you say, 'Don't they make a lovely couple?'

'I do not like your sister,' he says.

You don't know how to respond. You know you should defend her. But he's taken you totally by surprise. 'Oh,' you say. And then, 'Hey. Wait a moment. Hey!'

'I do not like it, all these foreigners, coming over here and marrying our camels. Take her home with you. Take her back to England.'

'Hey,' you say. 'Now then. Now, you wait.' Because that's just *racist*, isn't it? That's just fucking bigotry, and he should feel *lucky* that an Englishwoman is prepared to marry an Egyptian, what the fuck does he think Egypt is? – it was big once, mate, it was powerful, but the civilisation's long gone, the civilisation has crumbled to dust, it's ruins and pots and canopic jars from now on for the likes of you, it's canopic jars forever. And all you do is grovel around in the sand trying to fleece tourists, you're in the shadows of something greater than you can ever be, and they're thousands of years old, they were made by *primitives*, you can't reject us, you can't afford to be picky, you fucking *need* us. But what you say is, 'I don't live in England now, I live in Australia.' And, at this, he shrugs.

Abdul's close by, he's been listening. And you think that even if you can't defend your sister properly, even if you haven't got the guts, he should at least try – she's his *wife*, after all. Well, not yet. But tomorrow. Really bloody imminently, he should be showing her respect already, he should be putting in the practice. But Abdul sort of shrugs too, as if in imitation of his master. And then he's led away to start his day's work.

Your sister has heard nothing of this. She looks so excited. 'It's all over!' she says. 'The forms are signed. I'm getting married tomorrow morning!'

'I know.'

'I mean, I was always getting married tomorrow morning. But now I am, officially!'

'I know.'

'I'm so happy!'

You tell her you'll be there, how much you're looking forward to it, that you'll give her anything she needs.

'The night before a Muslim wedding all the women get together, they celebrate with song and dance. But I don't know any women here. It's not strictly proper, but would you spend my last evening as a singleton with me?'

*

You spend the afternoon in the hotel. You don't check your email.

*

'They call them henna nights,' Emma explains. 'The bride has her hands and feet dyed with henna on the eve of her wedding.'

'Do you have any henna?'

'No.'

You didn't bring any henna. You did, though, bring the contents of your mini bar.

'I'm not allowed to drink,' says Emma. 'I'm a Muslim.'

'You're not a Muslim until tomorrow,' you point out. So she takes a little bottle of Drambuie and downs it in one. You have a Courvoisier. She has another Drambuie. You have a Smirnoff. She has her third Drambuie. You have your first Drambuie.

'If you've got something to say,' Emma pipes up suddenly, 'then I think you should just come right out and say it.'

'I haven't got anything to say.'

'No, come on. Come on. Ever since you got here, no, come on. Look at me. Yes. If you don't like Abdul, I think you should just have the balls to say so.'

'All right,' you say. 'I don't like Abdul.'

'There you go.'

'I don't think he's good enough for you.'

'That wasn't so hard, was it?'

'I don't think you should marry him tomorrow. He stinks and is covered in sand. He stinks of sand.'

She has another Drambuie. She's got a real taste for Drambuie. You think maybe she wants to be rescued. Is that what this is? Is that why she brought you to Egypt? She wants you to rescue her?

'He's a camel,' you say.

'Yes.'

'He's just a camel.'

'Yes.'

'I mean, he's not even a special-looking camel. He's not even some sort of supercamel. He looks just like the other camels. And what's this about you being a fucking *Muslim*?'

'If I'm going to be in Egypt, I want to live my life here properly, and it's a very beautiful thing, actually, and I feel that in my soul...'

'Don't give me that. You don't believe in anything. You've never believed in anything.'

'Just because *you've* never properly assimilated, it doesn't mean I shouldn't.'

'Assimilated?'

'Assim. Oh. Is that right, did I get the word right?'

'I think so.'

'Fuck,' she says, and drinks the last Drambuie. 'Because you don't, do you? You don't commit to anything. I mean, how long have you lived in Australia, and you've still got your English accent, you're still holding on to your accent, what's that about?'

'I like my accent the way it is.'

'You never commit. You never did. This wife of yours, and that kid, I mean, what do they get out of you?'

'I'm leaving Kirsten,' you say. 'And my kid.'

'Well then.'

'You see?'

'I'm sorry to hear that. But don't... don't then start on me about *my* marriage. When you can't even...'

'I wasn't...'

'When you can't even... do it... with marriage. Yourself, yes.'

'I wasn't. I wasn't saying anything of the sort.' You pause. 'I don't think you even have a soul.'

Since there's no more Drambuie, no matter how hard she looks, she settles for a Bell's.

'You couldn't wait to run off to the other side of the world,' she says. 'As far away from mother as you could get. You left me alone with her in London. After what... afterwards. I was the one, I have to be the one to visit, to see her every week. Most weeks. Don't you criticise, I do my best, she's not easy. And you took away the right to have an opinion when you ran away, I think so, I really do.'

'Well,' you say. 'Well. Well, and what are you doing?'

'As far away,' says Emma, and throws the little glass bottle on to the growing pile, 'as far away as I can get.'

You both sit there for a while.

You reach out, you put your hand on her shoulder. It feels awkward. It looks awkward. It was meant to be supportive, you think, somehow, or conciliatory, something nice anyway. You think it would be a mistake to move it away.

'So long as you're going to be happy,' you say at last. 'Because that's all I worry about. Because I do worry, big sis. Because I love you. You know I love you, don't you? I love you.' And you squeeze the shoulder a bit, you think with that you've earned the right to move your hand now. You do.

She says nothing to this. Then, 'I want to see Abdul.'

'I didn't think you were supposed to see the groom before the wedding...'

'I'm not.' And she flashes you a grin, and you're so grateful for that, and you smile back. 'But it's not as if Abdul is going to tell, is he?'

And so you creep out of the room, out of the house. You think you're probably very quiet, all things considered, but you really couldn't swear to it. Out to the garage.

And there is Abdul. And he's shagging another camel, he's riding her doggy-style, he's swinging about from side to side like it's some fucking slow dance, they're both braying away like there's no tomorrow.

'Oh my God,' says Emma, and she runs out.

And Abdul doesn't even bother to look ashamed, he just turns those big soulful eyes on you, and gives a slow and deliberate blink. And you can bet there's a sticky smelly residue even now being secreted behind his ears – and it occurs to you that this lady camel couldn't have ended up here by accident, Abdul didn't just pick her up drunkenly in a bar, she must have been *brought* here – and my God, those Egyptians must *really* hate your sister.

You walk up to Abdul. Abdul doesn't flinch. Abdul doesn't care. Abdul doesn't even slow down his rutting, the shit, no, Abdul is busy. 'Shame on you,' you say. 'Shame on you.' And you spit in his face.

You go outside. She's standing on the pavement. She's shaking. She's wearing the burqa, she's protecting herself. She's smoking a cigarette, though, and every so often she has to raise the burqa to take a puff. You didn't even know she smoked.

'I'm sorry,' you say.

'It's what you wanted, isn't it?'

She's angry, she'll say anything. So you stand with her while she finishes her cigarette. While she fishes for another one, and she can't get the lighter to work, her hands are all over the place, you help her.

'Thanks.'

'Well, I think he's mad,' you say.

'Really?'

'Very mad. He's the maddest camel I've ever met. To choose anyone over you.' And she smiles at this. 'If I were a camel,' you say, 'I would treat you right. If I were a camel,' you say, 'I wouldn't be able to keep my hands off you. Paws. Hooves. Whatever camels have.'

'Hooves,' she agrees.

'Hooves then,' you say. And you give her a little kiss on the cheek. She gives another smile, just a small flash of one, a thank you. She takes your hand. She sighs. So you give her another kiss, again just on the cheek, no grander or bolder than the first.

And somehow then you are kissing her properly, and *hungrily*, and she's kissing you too, it isn't just one way, it really isn't. There are lips everywhere, and tongues and it starts off gently enough, just a little exploratory mission around the gums – and you think, so *this* is what it's like inside my sister's mouth, and it's just like all the other girls' mouths, it's just like Kirsten's mouth. It's nothing special, you know, but nor is it anything *wrong*, it's just a mouth. But it isn't, either, really, is it, and as you kiss something pops into your head about saliva, and that saliva contains your DNA, and that if someone swabbed the inside of Emma's cheek right this second they probably wouldn't be able to tell apart your tongue leavings from hers – and you fight off that thought because it really ought to be putting you off, but it doesn't, strangely, anything but. And you kiss, and you wonder who it was who started the kissing, it must have been Emma, it can't have been you, you'd never have given in to those urges – after all, you never have before.

And you're pulling off your trousers, and you're pulling off her bra, you're right out there on the streets of Cairo and you don't care, out plop breasts, out plops a willy, and there's so much sand on the streets and you hope the sand doesn't get into the cracks, the dirty sand gets everywhere, and you look down at the willy, and it isn't great, but at least it doesn't hook backwards, at least it's *normal* – and the breasts look normal too, so very normal – and the shock appearances of one or other of these really very normal protuberances has an effect – 'No,' says Emma, 'no,' and she pushes you away.

'What is it?'

'No,' she says, and dashes back inside the house.

You follow her. She's in her room, she's breathing hard, she's staring at the mound of little mini bar bottles as if she's never seen them before and wondering how they got there. You want to take her hand and offer her some comfort. Just comfort, but you don't quite dare.

'It's just wrong,' she says.

'For God's sake,' you say, and you try not to sound impatient. 'After what Abdul's been up to behind *your* back? I think you're entitled, don't you?'

'That's not what I'm talking about,' she says.

It takes you a moment. 'Oh. Right. Of course.'

She picks up one of the empty bottles. She tips it into her mouth to see if there's anything inside. She sticks her tongue in the neck to reach a few stray drops.

'It's nonsense,' you say. 'You know full well, give it a few years, having a relationship with your brother will be perfectly acceptable. God, you're allowed to do it with the same sex now, you can do it with animals. Family members are right around the corner. All we are, we're just a bit ahead of our time.'

'Is that what you think?' she says, and the voice is curiously flat. 'That what is between us is just ordinary?'

'Yeah,' you say. 'Sex, it's just a little thing, isn't it? It's not worth all the melodrama. It's such a little thing.'

She nods, and you think she's agreeing with you, and you're pleased. 'I don't want you at the wedding,' she says.

'You mean you're still going ahead with the...?'

'And I don't want you there.'

'But I brought my suit,' you say.

'I'm not sure, actually, if I'm honest,' she adds, and there's no anger in it now, that's what makes it so terrible, 'that I even want to see you again.'

*

Kirsten has emailed. She says that you're stupid and you're selfish. But she's worked too long at this marriage of yours to end it so suddenly. So, spend as long as you want in Egypt. She'll be patient. Let her know when you're coming home, she'll pick you up from the airport. You can start all over again, everything will be all right. And then you'll talk, and if you still don't want to be with her, then fair enough, if you still don't love her, fair enough. But think of Tammy, she knows you love Tammy, you've always been such a good father.

And you lie on the bed, and you do indeed think of Tammy. You strip right down, it's so very hot, and there's nothing cold to drink in the mini bar, you strip right down, you lie on the bed naked, you think of Tammy. And how beautiful a woman she'll grow up to be – she'll be a model, she'll be on the cover of glossy magazines, she'll be *perfect*. She'll look a bit like your sister, but younger, fresher, thinner. You can start all over again. Everything's going to be all right, you can start all over.

*

The next morning you don't know what to do with yourself.

You check your phone, just in case your sister has called. She hasn't. You check your email. There's something new from your wife, dripping with forgiveness probably, but you don't bother to open it yet.

'Take me somewhere touristy,' you say to the taxi driver.

All the camels are lined up, and they're all going to the Great Pyramid of Giza.

It's one of the Seven Wonders of the World. It is, in fact, the only one of the Seven Wonders of the World that still exists. 'This'll do,' you say.

'Hoosh, hoosh!' says the camel driver, all smiles, he's such a happy fellow. And you get on to the camel's back, right behind the hump. 'Hoosh!' Up you rise, and you dig your heels into the camel's side, hard.

'The Great Pyramids of Giza!' the driver calls. And you're off, a whole train of you, pasty-faced westerners all looking pale and weedy, all looking like children as they giggle and gawp and play at being Arabs. The camel paces forward, and you roll with his gait – you feel a bit nauseous, actually, you wonder how long the journey will take, it's like being on a rough sea and you think if there's more than ten minutes of this you might just throw up. But the camel is patient, and calm, and suddenly you feel calm too. And he seems to hold you no grudge for kicking him, maybe under that tough hide he didn't even feel it.

On the top of the camel you feel like you're king of the world, you feel like a pharaoh, he's making you feel so special, he's making you feel like you're the only one he's ever had on his back.

And you ride out into the desert, tourists ahead of you, tourists behind you, but you try to ignore them, you pretend you're on your own, that it's just you and the camel. And he's in no rush, and by God, he's *solid* under there, and strong, and confident, the camel's got a confidence you don't think you'll ever have.

At last you reach the pyramid. It's been there on the horizon for ages, of course, but you refuse to look at it seriously until you get close, you want to get the full impact of it – you'd rather look down at the sand, you'd rather look at the camel. But there it is now, finally, unavoidably, it's not going to get any bigger – 'There!' says our guide, rather unnecessarily. And yes, it's *different*, but the camel harrumphs a bit, he's seen it all before, he's none too impressed. And from now on you're taking your cue from the camel. As pyramids go you're sure it's one of the biggest – but you know, if it's size that's the issue, there are bigger things out there, you've stayed in bigger hotels, shopped in bigger department stores, parked your car in bigger car parks even. And you say out loud, for the camel's benefit, you suppose, so he'll know you're in accord – 'It's just a little thing, isn't it? Really. Just a little thing.'

1002 – Ethelred the Unready tires of the many Scandinavians who have been assimilated into English society, fearing that they may be covertly aiding the activity of the Vikings, and gives orders that they should all be killed on St Brice's Day. (Such a thing, of course, where an entire people will be judged under suspicion, and executed accordingly, because there are racial connections with terrorists, would never happen today.) The massacre is bloody and widespread – but, of course, not quite widespread enough, and that leaves plenty of angry Danes keen to retaliate. Swein Forkbeard, king of Denmark, swiftly returns to England to exact revenge. Ethelred proposes an increase in the tribute he gives the Danes but it's not enough to stop the renewed Viking wrath. **1004** – General Xiao Talin of the Chinese Liao Dynasty is killed at the battle of Shanzhou by a crossbow sniper. **1005** – Le Trung Tong becomes king of Vietnam. He is assassinated only three days later. **1005** – Kenneth III of Scotland and his son are killed at the battle of Monzievard. *Sex doesn't feel the same when you're trying to create the future. It requires a lot more concentration for a start; you can't just whip it in and then whip it out, you can't construct a child lazily – not, at least, if you want it to be historically significant – there should be effort in its invention, there should be earnest and sober deliberation, it shouldn't be conceived in some vague stream of consciousness. My wife got ready in the bathroom. She washed all over, used some of that bubble bath that smelled like pine, she put on her poshest perfume, applied generous quantities of depilatory cream. And I prepared too, I read my favourite passages of history for inspiration. 'Après moi, le deluge,' 'We shall fight them on the beaches,' 'Veni, vidi, vici.' She got into bed, smooth all over and smelling like a Boots' chemist shop, and I climbed on top of her. I tried to impress on her the gravity of what we were doing, I tried to make her understand that this was an awful responsibility – that if this went according to plan, we'd not only be changing our lives forever, but those of everyone else on the planet too: we could be creating another Charlemagne, another Jesus, another Hitler. She kissed me, and I think maybe it was to get me to shut up.* **1006** – The volcanic eruption of Mount Merapi showers all of central Java with hot ash. **1009** – After twenty years of construction, Mainz Cathedral is finally completed. It is extensively damaged by fire on the day of its inauguration. **1010** – Malcolm II of Scotland defeats a Viking army at the battle of Mortlach. To commemorate the victory, Malcolm has a church built there, the walls constructed with enemy skulls. *And at each thrust I tried to keep my concentration. I kept my mind in focus by reciting mentally all the battles of the Wars of the Roses, both major and minor, at first in chronological order, and then organised by first Lancastrian and then Yorkist victory, and then in terms of body count. In, out, in, out, the battle, of St Albans, 14, 55, the battle, of Blore Heath, 14, 59. 'Wait a moment,' my wife said, 'I'm not comfortable, you're squashing me,' and so, as she adjusted, I mused that though the battle of Blore Heath was technically a victory for the Yorkists, the winning army the very next day was captured by an even better army, it was just another failure, it didn't achieve anything, what was the use? And on the battlefield the brook had flowed with blood for days afterwards. 'I'm comfy now,' she said, 'as you were,' and my interpretation of the battle's aftermath had helped fill the caesura created by my wife's wriggling, I hadn't lost my stride.* **1010** – At Malmesbury Abbey in Wiltshire there is an early attempt made by a man to fly. A young monk called Eilmer is so inspired by the birds and stories of Greek mythology that he makes himself a pair of wings and leaps from the abbey tower. He glides for 200 yards or so, before hitting the ground with a bump that breaks both his legs. *And she fell pregnant. Oh yes. Veni vidi and vici. Vici through and through. Thank you, Julius Caesar, and good night.* **1011** – Ibn al-Haytham is a genius Iraqi scientist working in Egypt. He makes contributions to the understanding of optics, anatomy, astronomy, engineering, medicine – he is later referred to in medieval Europe simply as 'The Physicist'. But this year he bites off more than he can chew. He promises the caliph that he can regulate the floods of the Nile, and then realises it's impossible. So to prevent the disappointed caliph from executing him, he pretends to be mad – and spends the next ten years surviving under house arrest in feigned insanity. **1011** – Brothers Gurgen and Sambat III are the last princes of Klarjeti, an independent province of Georgia. They are invited by their cousin Bagrat, who has recently become king of a newly unified Georgia, to negotiations in one of his castles. There they are murdered, and Klarjeti ends up absorbed into the kingdom. **1012** – The Danes lay siege to Canterbury, and capture the archbishop. They try to ransom him, but he refuses to help them – and so, after seven months of imprisonment, he is executed. It is said that killing him with the back of an axe is an act of Christian charity on behalf of a convert known only as Thrum. Alphege is the first Archbishop of Canterbury to meet a violent end. He will not be the last. *Nine months later she gave birth to a daughter. She suggested we call her Annie, after her own mother. I said, sure, why not? I'd had a whole list of boy's names up my sleeve, just in case we'd got lucky: William (the Conqueror), Frederick (the Great), Suleiman (the Magnificent). I'd even been toying with Genghis, not too seriously, just flirting with the idea, maybe Genghis as the first name and Khan as the middle, I'd have liked a boy called Genghis. But a girl's name, well, really, that was my wife's department – and if she wanted to name her after her mother, that was up to her. My wife's mother was not a woman, I thought, who had even an ounce of historical profundity within her – she was wide-hipped and fat-thighed, and somewhat flaccid of face, her mouth always seemed to hang open whenever I looked at it as if she hadn't quite got the wit to pull her lips together, eyes too wide and brow too furrowed, her face was deep set in a mask of permanent bewilderment. She was nervous – always nervous – always nervous of me, at any rate, I don't know what would get into her, I certainly wasn't judging her, I'm not one to judge! She could look as thick and lumpen as she liked. Not everyone has to be historical, and not everyone has to be profound, and we need the bystanders and the peasants if only to witness what's going on, if only to be done to rather than doing, if only to give genius some context. We need the clods. Not like my mother, my mother could have been special, if she hadn't subjugated herself to someone more special still, if she hadn't become an also-ran before the altar of Jesus. 'Let's call her Annie,' said my wife, 'it'd make my Mum so happy,' and I said, sure, why not? Why not, what difference will it make?* **1012** – Prosecutions for heresy are started in Germany. **1013** – Swein Forkbeard invades England. Ethelred flees the country, and on Christmas Day Swein is recognised as king. At last, some 225 years after first raiding Devon, and after countless lives have been lost, the Danes have finally conquered England. Nothing will be the same again. **1014** – Except Swein dies some six weeks into his reign, falling off a horse. Ethelred is recalled from exile, the nobles exacting from him first the promise he'll try harder this time. **1014** – Byzantine Emperor Basil II crushes the Bulgarians at the battle of Kleidon, and takes 15,000 prisoners. He sends them home to King Samuel – but blinds them first, sparing only one eye of each man in a hundred so they can see well enough to guide the others home. When King Samuel is presented with the thousands upon thousands of gaping sockets, and the sheer scale of his defeat, he faints on the spot. Two days later he is dead from a stroke. **1014** – King Brian Boru of Ireland defeats the Vikings at the battle of Clontarf. While retreating, though, a few of the Norsemen happen upon the king's tent, and they rush in and stab him while he's offering prayers of gratitude to the Lord. **1016** – With Ethelred the Unready dead, Edmund Ironside succeeds to the throne. But Swein Forkbeard's son Canute has other ideas – and, once more, the Danes invade England. Edmund is defeated in battle and goes into hiding. And as he sits upon the toilet to relieve himself, an assassin hidden underneath rises up and stabs him in the bowels. **1017** – Kiev burns. **1018** – The last Bulgarian leader is captured, and Bulgaria becomes part of the Byzantine Empire. **1019** – Yaroslav the Wise murders his three brothers and is made Grand Prince of Rus. **1024** – In India, Emperor Mahmud sacks the Hindu centre of Somnath, massacring some 50,000 people and looting the temple treasures. **1026** – King Canute and his brother-in-law Ulf quarrel over chess. When the losing Ulf decides he doesn't want to play any more, Canute calls him a coward. Ulf retorts that Canute is the coward, if his recent showing in naval warfare is anything to go by. Canute broods upon the insult all night – and, the next morning, has Ulf murdered. **1028** – Romanos III marries Zoe, and together they rule the Byzantine Empire. Immediately Zoe is obsessed with the idea of producing an heir; she takes magic potions, wears amulets, incants spells – all to no effect. She becomes increasingly disillusioned with her husband, and begins to plot his death. Zoe is fifty years old. **1030** – King Olaf II of Norway is killed at the battle of Stiklestad fighting rebelling farmers and peasants. A year later, when his tomb is opened, his body is found uncorrupted, and the hair and nails have grown – so the man slain by his own people is made patron saint of the country. **1031** – Bezprym overthrows his brother Mieszko II to become king of Poland. **1032** – Bezprym is murdered, his other brothers appalled by the extreme cruelty of his reign. And the newly castrated Mieszko returns to the throne. **1033** – Unusually harsh spring weather in Europe: all the apocalypse theorists still smarting that the world didn't end on the millennium take this as a sign that it'll end instead 1,000 years after the death of Christ. Panic, bloodshed, and stupidity. **1034** – Malcolm II of Scotland is killed at Glamis Castle. It is said you can still hear his blood bubbling under the floor. **1034** – Zoe of Byzantium openly parades her new lover about, a chamberlain called Michael. When Emperor Romanos protests, he's found suddenly dead in his bath. Zoe marries Michael the same day. **1035** – On the death of King Canute, Alfred Atheling, one of Ethelred the Unready's sons, tries to take back the English crown from the Danes. He is betrayed, blinded, and put in a monastery. Harold Harefoot instead takes the throne. **1040** – Duncan, king of Scotland, is killed by Macbeth. No haunted visions of daggers, of blood that won't wash off no matter how hard it's scrubbed, no guilt is recorded by historians at all. Why would there be guilt? This is the eleventh century. **1040** – On the death of his brother Harold Harefoot, Harthacanute takes the English throne. Harthacanute so hates Harold that he has his body exhumed, beheaded, then thrown into the Thames. **1041** – In Bulgaria, Peter Delyan mounts a successful uprising against Byzantine rule. His second cousin Alusian joins his ranks. One night at dinner Alusian takes advantage of the fact that Peter is drunk; he cuts off his nose and blinds him with a kitchen knife. Alusian is declared emperor in his place, but Alusian has already planned to betray Bulgaria back to the Byzantines. Though blinded, Peter manages to lead his troops into battle against the conquerors – but is captured and executed. **1041** – Michael IV, once Zoe's chamberlain, now her husband and ruler of the Byzantine Empire, dies. He does so refusing the pleas to see his wife, whom he has long had banished from sight and kept confined under guard. Zoe adopts her nephew, who will reign as Michael V, and who promises to respect his beleaguered aunt-mother. On his accession he promptly exiles her to a monastery on charges of regicide. **1042** – Michael V is overthrown (and blinded, naturally, and put in a monastery, of course). The Byzantine senate insist that Zoe cannot take the throne by herself – how about she shares it with her sister Theodora? The arrangement is a disaster; the two sisters hate each other. So Zoe decides to assert her supremacy by marrying for a third time, going back through a list of all her ex-lovers until she finds one that is suitable. Constantine Dalassenos is thrown out of her presence when he is unable to mask his revulsion for the aged queen, and Constantine Atroklines is murdered just a few days before the wedding – probably by his existing wife, who has reasons to baulk at the arrangement. She finally settles on Constantine Monomachos, who comes to the throne on condition that his younger and prettier girlfriend is made empress as well. Zoe agrees, and shares both throne and bed with husband and mistress, dying happily some years later with all her palace rooms redolent with the scents of ointments and perfumes – she has transformed them into secret laboratories designed to invent potions which might stave off her wrinkles. *When a man impregnates a woman, on average some 300 million sperm are shot out into the vagina, all on a mission to fertilise the egg that will then grow into a child. 300 million, that's about the entire size of the world population in the eleventh century. That's a lot of sperm; it's tempting to think that the winner sperm that makes it will be the strongest or most powerful, a supersperm. That means every single person you see is grown out of some champion Olympic level swimmer. But it doesn't work like that, does it? When I look at my postman, for example, I can only wonder at the quality of the two hundred and ninety-nine million nine hundred and ninety-nine thousand nine hundred and ninety-nine sperm that lost. Maybe the supersperm was held back and mobbed by a whole faction of jealous mediocre sperm that resented his talents. History is littered with mediocrities who have got in the way of greater men's potential: what if Edward the Black Prince had become king of England instead of Richard II (1377), what if Oliver Cromwell had passed the Protectorate to someone more deserving than his son (1658), what if the Florida recount had given Gore rather than Bush the presidency of the United States (2000)? And what if, say, at the moment of my child's conception, another sperm, a better sperm, had fertilised another egg, a better egg? Would I have a different child altogether? Was my great son thwarted from being because an ineffectual daughter got in the way?* **1042** – Harthacanute dies drunk at a wedding feast (qv 453). **1045** – Pope Benedict IX abdicates in favour of Sylvester III, taking a large bribe along the way. He soon regrets this decision, and returns to Rome and the office – though not giving back the cash. He then decides to sell the papacy to his godfather instead, who becomes Gregory VI. Benedict then changes his mind again, and returns to be pope. There are now three of them jostling for position in the Vatican – and not one of them has a receipt. *(Because, let's face it – and I don't want to seem controversial here, it's just a fact – historically, women aren't as important as men. It's self-evident. Look at the events listed within this time chart, a good ninety-five percent of them don't even mention the fairer sex. Women simply aren't as effective as men are at provoking wars and fighting wars and losing wars. They're great at many things, don't get me wrong, I'm not being sexist here, give them their due. But their skills lie more in making dinner than in making history. When I saw Annie come out, all bloodied and gunky, and I realised that the doctors had got it right all through the pregnancy, the foetus really was a female, it wasn't that the penis had been tucked away in the shadows during all those scans – I must admit, I lost a certain amount of interest in her. Oh dear. Does that make me a bad father? I hope not.)* **1054** – Cardinal Humbertus, speaking for Pope Leo IX, excommunicates Michael Celarius. As Patriarch of Constantinople, Michael Celarius excommunicates Humbertus right back. So starts the Great Schism between the Roman Catholic Church and the Orthodox Christian Church. It's not until 1965 that both sides agree to rescind these excommunications – but even so, til this day, both churches claim that they and only they are the One Holy Catholic and Apostolic Church. **1057** – Macbeth is killed in battle, and his head brought to Malcolm III on a plate. He is succeeded by his stepson Lulach (the Foolish), a man of such mediocrity that Shakespeare doesn't even bother to remember him. He is assassinated months later. **1059** – Byzantine Emperor Isaac I becomes convinced he has an incurable illness, and resigns from the throne. He is wrong. And lives out the rest of his days in – yes – a monastery. **1063** – King Bela I of Hungary is crushed to death by his own throne collapsing on top of him. **1063** – Gruffydd ap Llewellym, the first man ever to rule the whole of Wales, is murdered by his own men. His head is sent to Harold, Earl of Wessex. And Wales falls into disunity once more. **1065** – King Ferdinand the Great of Leon prepares for his own death by dressing as a monk and lying down on a funeral bier covered with ashes. There he finally expires. **1066** – In spite of his flying attempts more than fifty years ago, Eilmer of Malmesbury is still alive. He is crippled, but alive nonetheless. He sees the return of Halley's Comet, which he last glimpsed in his youth, and prophesies from it the downfall of his country. And so it comes to pass. **1066** – The battle of Stamford Bridge is runner-up in the annual Most Famous Battle Awards. By fighting the Vikings so energetically there, the newly crowned Harold of Wessex exhausts himself when he faces William of Normandy at Hastings. According to the Bayeux Tapestry, Harold gets killed by an arrow in his eye. Dozens of embroiders must have worked on that tapestry, their names lost to us now; imagine how exciting it must have felt if you had been the woman given the job of stitching Harold's death? It must have felt like you were a part of history. **1066** – William is crowned king of England on Christmas Day at Westminster Abbey. Norman guards mistake the cries of celebration for rioting, and kill the crowds. **1066** – A Muslim mob storms the royal palace in Granada to murder the Jewish vizier, and then proceeds to massacre the Jewish population of the city. **1069** – William the Conqueror punishes the Northern parts of his new kingdom that still resist his rule. He rides from York to Durham, setting fire to houses and land, to crops and livestock. 100,000 people die as a result, either from starvation or exposure. **1071** – The Byzantines are defeated by the Turks under Alp Arslan at the battle of Manzikert, and Emperor Romanos IV is captured. When Romanos is brought before Alp Arslan, bleeding and covered in dirt as he is, the Turk at first refuses to believe that such a tattered figure could be the man in charge of the Empire. Then he asks of Romanos what he would have done to the Turkish leader had their positions been reversed. Romanos admits he would have had him executed, or maybe paraded through Constantinople for sport. Alp Arslan considers. Then tells him the punishment he has in mind for Romanos is much heavier. He will forgive him, and set him free. **1071** – The humiliation of the Turks' kindness destroys Romanos. He returns to his own people. They depose him and exile him. He dies as a result of infection that sets in after an especially brutal blinding. **1072** – In Russia, a collection of laws is published under the name 'Pravda'. It means 'truth', and as such is a call to reason and enlightenment. It becomes centuries later the name adopted by the official publication of the oppressive Soviet Communist Party. **1077** – Gregory VII has excommunicated the German Henry IV of the Holy Roman Empire for resisting papal authority. To win back the Pope's favour – and the respect of his countrymen – the penitent Henry walks barefoot in a hairshirt for the whole two month journey from Speyer over the Alps to the fortress at Canossa in which the Pope has barricaded himself. When he reaches Canossa the Pope refuses to have the gates opened to him – he fears that Henry may have brought an army. For three days Henry waits by the gate fasting. He is at last admitted, and forgiven. Later in history the phrase 'going to Canossa' has political connotations for the German people; it is used to demonstrate that no longer should the Germans be obeisant to another power, that they should never back down. Adolf Hitler becomes very fond of it. **1079** – William the Conqueror is defeated by his son Robert in battle in Normandy. **1086** – The passage of a comet kills all the cats in Westphalia. **1087** – In London, St Paul's Cathedral burns to the ground again (qv 962). *And my wife loved my daughter anyway – well, she would, she's a woman too, there's a certain bias there, and besides my wife has always displayed a naivety about historical primacy. (What about Elizabeth I, she'd say? What about Catherine the Great? To which I just wouldn't reply.) And she clung on to that little new baby body, the baby looking so bemused, looking as if it had not the slightest intention of making its mark upon the world, looking as if it really would rather pop back into the stomach, please – and I spotted, I thought, that same vacant facial expression that was on her grandmother's face (and yes, I suppose, on her mother's too), the look of an empty well so deep and ready to be filled with knowledge, but it will never be filled, all the knowledge will just drain away, there's a leak somewhere at the bottom – and I thought to myself, this baby of mine's not going to be a soaring intellect – my wife clung on, and she cried, they both cried, it was like the one was egging the other on, and my wife just said, 'My beautiful girl, my beautiful little girl.'* **1087** – King William falls from his horse and dies. He is too fat for any coffin, and at the funeral the gases that have been building up in his bloated corpse explode and his body bursts. The stench is so bad that the congregation are forced to flee the church. **1091** – London Bridge is falling down after a tornado. **1095** – Pope Urban II makes a speech at the Council of Clermont, urging Christian troops to take back the sacred city of Jerusalem from the Muslim heathens, and to curb the growth of Islam. And so the age of the crusades begins. **1098** – King Magnus III of Norway pays a visit to Scotland, and is so impressed by the fashions he sees there that when he returns to Scandinavia he starts wearing Highland dress, kilt, sporran and all. He is consequently named by his subjects Magnus Barelegs. **1099** – Jerusalem falls to the Christian soldiers, and every inhabitant is slaughtered. Thus ends the First Crusade. (Of the nine Crusades which stain the world over the next 200 years, it's the only one the Christians can claim to have won.) Pope Urban never gets to celebrate the success of the war he started: fourteen days after the capture of Jerusalem he dies, and the news of victory doesn't reach him in time. **1100** – Mary and Elizabeth Chulkhurst are born in Kent. Commonly known as the Biddenden Maids, they are the earliest named set of conjoined twins in the world. They don't get on well, and frequently beat each other. **1100** – William II of England is killed while hunting in the New Forest. Everyone claims it's an accident – but his brother Henry has his coronation already prepared for three days later. And so it goes on.

TIMES TABLE

Mummy and Daddy told the little girl it was going to be *her* day, her big day, her day and no-one else's. 'Happy birthday, kiddo,' said Daddy, and he ruffled her hair (but always so gently), and Mummy said, 'Happy birthday,' and slapped her lips fast down on her cheek (but always so gently, always as if she worried they might leave a mark). Happy birthday, happy birthday. And the little girl pointed out that she was such a special little girl, or so they'd often tell her – they took such care of her, really they never let her out of their sight, really they poured all their affection and deep frowning attention into her and made her their very world – if she was special enough for all that, wasn't every day like a birthday already? She was asking merely for information. And Mummy and Daddy thought about this, and conceded she had a point. Not that it mattered – and the little girl woke up on her seventh birthday, with seven long full happy years already stretched out behind her, and she bathed in the morning light streaming in through her bedroom window, she felt so excited – birthday, her birthday, the day everything (ooh) changed. So excited, in fact, that she'd woken up early; she'd have to wait another hour for her parents to wake up too, and unlock her bedroom door to let her out. And there really was *so* much light from the window, it was sunny outside, it was ideal birthday weather: she remembered all her birthdays so well, of course, and thought that only the sunshine on her second birthday had been any brighter. She told Mummy this when Mummy came to dress her – 'I think this might be my second best birthday ever!' – and Mummy smiled, and Mummy said she hoped it would be the *very* best. But the little girl pointed out the black clouds on the horizon, there'd be a storm coming sooner or later, she'd have to dock the day a few points for that. And she had breakfast, and because it was her birthday she was allowed to have not milk on her cornflakes but whipped cream. 'Time for lessons, kiddo!' said Daddy, and he was smiling so much, and the little girl knew for her birthday they'd be *fun* lessons; Mummy taught her the arts and Daddy the sciences, but only the fun sciences today, only the bits of science that made pretty smoke and funny noises. And the stories that she'd have to read aloud to Mummy from the Big Book to improve her language skills would all have happy endings and the morals wouldn't be too preachy and no-one would die. 'Lessons over, kiddo!' laughed Daddy, 'Lessons over,' said Mummy, and Mummy rang the school bell she had – she'd picked it up from a jumble sale once, she said, and had only meant to use it ironically, but somehow the joke had sort of stuck – lessons over, time for presents! so many presents to open, just too exciting. Daddy had bought her a scientific calculator, something that she could play with when she wanted to do her sums, it did fractions and square roots and *everything*; and Mummy had bought her some books – Mummy said these had been her favourite books when *she* had been a little girl – *Little Women*, and *Black Beauty*, and *Jane Eyre* (with that Mr Rochester in it who kept the madwoman in the attic); and the little girl found it hard to believe that Mummy had ever been a little girl, at least not a little girl like her; and the little girl was very pleased, and said these presents were really very fine, they were the third best birthday presents she had ever received (after the building blocks she'd received on birthday three, and, of course, the meningitis innoculations she'd got on birthday one, so caring, so practical, as presents went they were still pretty much unbeatable) – the above average quality of the presents, and the above average quality of the weather, this was shaping up to be her best birthday ever. And then Mummy gave her another package to open, and inside was a dress – a pink dress – with pink bows – and pink flowers pictured underneath the pink bows. The little girl put it on, and it fitted perfectly, and she wondered whether it would still fit when she properly turned seven years old, that wouldn't happen for another couple of hours yet, and after all she was still wearing the skin and bones of her sixth birthday. But Mummy assured her it wouldn't be a problem. Then there was cake, and there was jelly too, and the little sausage rolls the little girl liked. And it was really all so very good, and the little girl had everything she wanted, Mummy and Daddy hadn't let her down – save, of course, for any *friends*. But she hadn't bothered to ask for any. Mummy hadn't liked it when she'd tried to make friends with the girls next door, she'd only stepped out of doors unsupervised for a few minutes, she'd seen the girls through her bedroom window and they'd seemed to be having so much *fun* and she'd hurried down to find them, they'd been playing with toys the like of which she'd never seen before – and Mummy had shrieked – and Mummy had locked her in her room until Daddy had got back – and Daddy had given her a very stern lecture about how special she was and how it wasn't *safe*; they'd still smiled, of course, and Daddy had still called her kiddo, but the little girl could tell they'd been really very cross. Lucky they really still wanted to look after her and pour into her so much affection and attention. Lucky she was still having a birthday at all. And that's why the bedroom door now had to be locked at all times when she slept. And that was fair. So the little girl knew better than to ask for friends for her birthday, but she still thought that would have been nice; the people in the books had friends, Harry Potter and the Famous Five and even Jesus from the Big Book, he had a gang he could hang out with. And when she slept at night the only people who would be in her dreams would be Mummy and Daddy, they were the only friends she had – and that old woman, of course, the one who was always in that rocking chair, the little girl didn't know where she came from, she made the little girl frightened. But still. Still, never mind. And now it was past six o'clock; the little girl told her parents that she really must be going to bed soon; she'd had a lovely birthday but tomorrow she had to be up bright and early for another day altogether. Wasn't it time for her to get changed? She began to itch. But Mummy said, 'One more surprise, one more surprise!' And Daddy said, 'Don't go just yet, kiddo, don't leave us, one more surprise.' And Daddy beamed. 'Stay in your pink dress,' said Mummy, 'don't change a thing!' And Daddy got up from the table, and said, 'There's someone here to wish you happy birthday,' and he opened the door to the cupboard – and the little girl suddenly thought, it's the old woman, no, don't let her out – and the itching got worse, and she scratched furiously at her arm and she felt some skin slice off. But it wasn't an old woman, not at all, and out of the cupboard filed five other little girls, and all of them were wearing pink dresses too, exactly the same! Exactly the same, except for the fact that the girls were different sizes – the five-year-old girl was bigger than the four-year-old girl, and she was bigger than the three-year-old, and she was bigger than the two-year-old, and she was bigger than no-one, no-one except, of course, the one-year-old baby, she was so cute and wee, nothing could be smaller! So cute and wee in her little pink dress with pink bows and flowers. (The cupboard was quite small, they must have been quite cramped in there all that time.) And of course right away the little girl knew who they were. She recognised them in an instant. She'd known Mummy must have had something up her sleeve; once her bedroom door was locked she had heard Mummy fetch the children down from the attic where they had been stored. 'We've been rehearsing!' said Mummy. 'Go on, girls. Dance for us. Dance for us.' And so the girls did; they looked at their Mummy and Daddy (because they were still their Mummy and Daddy, although Mummy and Daddy had no smiles left for them, not any more) and Mummy and Daddy nodded at them to begin. Happy birthday to you, happy birthday to you, sang the five-year-old version of the little girl – although she didn't sing *really*, she could only mouth the words, but Mummy and Daddy sung them, and if you looked at the five-year-old closely with her jaws working away like that you could almost pretend the music was coming from her. And the four-year-old and the three-year-old and the two-year-old danced around her as she sang, they did charming little pirouettes. And, at the climax of the song, the five-year-old picked up the one-year-old baby, she held her up high – the one-year-old was too small to do anything very much, but oh! she was so cute and wee, of all the bits of little girl on display she was still the best of the bunch. The little girl watched as the bodies of all the years past performed for her, the frills of their pink dresses flapping as they made a pretence of the energetic, and this close she could *feel* their humiliation, just how embarrassed they were, and sense just how much they'd lost, and how much they hated the dark of the attic – and of course she could feel it, they were her, they were all her. She tried to smile at them, to show support, or encouragement, or sympathy, or maybe just to make new friends – but they were too busy to smile back, the song wasn't quite over yet: Happy birthday, they all at last mouthed as one, a dumb chant of celebration – well, not the baby, of course, she just made an adorable little burble. Mummy and Daddy clapped; the puppets all took a bow. Happy birthday, happy birthday. 'And happy birthday to *you*,' the little girl said to her predecessors – because it suddenly occurred to her that it must be their birthdays just as much as it was hers, 'happy birthday to you all, would you like some cake?' And it made her feel quite grown-up to be that generous, she surprised herself, turning into a seven-year-old she would really be quite the adult, mature and responsible and kind. Like Mummy, like Daddy. Better than the six-year-old she'd been. Time to get rid of her, time to shed her, time to bury her away deep in the attic.

14

The teenager liked to watch Mummy put on her make-up. Mummy did it with such concentration, staring so intently in the bedroom mirror. And so unforgivingly too, she inspected her new face of red lips and blue eyes and black eyelashes with such critical disapproval; red, blue, black, so many colours!

Mummy had started wearing so much more make-up since Daddy had left. Mummy had eyes only for herself whenever she applied her make-up; standing in the doorway, the teenager always felt like an intruder, and that was still a new sensation for her. She knew better than to speak, but sometimes she couldn't help it, a question would just pop out. 'How do you put on make-up?' she asked.

'Lipstick goes on the lips, eyeliner on the eyes. Really, it's all pretty self-explanatory.' And the teenager hadn't necessarily expected Mummy to have stopped and sat her down and given her a lesson – the days of lessons now seemed long past – but she had been hoping for something a little more helpful.

So, 'Open wide,' she now said to her thirteen-year-old self, and Thirteen duly obeyed. 'Open wide' was wrong, it was something a dentist would say, not a beautician, but she hadn't yet learned the right magic command. And Twelve opened her mouth too, and Eleven, and Ten, and all of her somewhat sisters – 'No, not you,' she said, 'close up again,' and they did so, one by one, older to younger, their mouths falling shut in a series of increasingly high-pitched clacks.

The teenager had been surprised that Mummy had given her a make-up kit all of her own for her fourteenth birthday. But then, many things that Mummy had done recently surprised her. 'Thank you, Mummy,' she'd said, 'this is my eighth best birthday yet!' And Mummy had made that snort through her nose that she did so often nowadays, and it was odd, because the teenager had an excellent memory, and yet she couldn't remember any such snorting when she'd been a little girl.

'Now, hold still,' said the teenager to her year younger self. She took out a tube of lipstick from her kit. There were so many colours to choose from, she went for the brightest, she went for Sexy Scarlet. She painted Thirteen's lips with a generous coat of the stuff, rolling the stick around the mouth in as wide an arc as she could. The red was creamy and thick, Thirteen's lips were covered completely, and some of it went on to her chin, and a little splodge ended up on her nose. 'Press your lips together,' commanded the teenager, and Thirteen pressed her lips together – 'open up,' and she opened up, 'smile,' she smiled. The teenager assessed her handiwork. 'That's perfect,' said the teenager, though it wasn't.

The teenager had known where the key to the attic had been hidden for a long time. Ever since her seventh birthday, in fact. And she'd kept an eye on it – not because she wanted to use it, but just for information, just for the *facts*. The years went by, and more and more bodies were taken up the stepladder to be shut away in the dark, and the girl never gave her Mummy and Daddy the least reason to suspect she was curious about what had happened to them. The hiding places sometimes changed, but Mummy and Daddy's defences were down, it wasn't hard to work out where the key had been moved to. And since Daddy had left, the hiding place hadn't changed once – the key had stayed in Mummy's jewellery box on her bedside table for nearly three whole years now. And while the teenager was strictly forbidden to look through that box, she guessed it was more because Mummy didn't want her playing with her earrings than because of the key or what the key represented.

But Mummy was out now, and would be out for some time too, if the amount of make-up she'd been wearing was anything to go by. So the teenager had crept into Mummy's bedroom, took the key from the box; she did it so carefully, too, noting just which earrings it was beneath, so she could replace it perfectly later; she'd fetched the flashlight from the kitchen; then she'd pulled down the stepladder to the attic. She'd never wanted to visit her younger selves before. If anything, she tried to forget they even existed, the mere thought of them somehow made her flesh creep. But at last she could put them to some use.

And now, after giving Thirteen's lips a good hard going over, she worked on Twelve's lips too, then Eleven's, then Ten's. 'Open wide,' she'd say, 'open wide,' 'open wide,' and their mouths would flop open ready for her to do her worst. By the time she reached Seven she felt she was getting pretty nifty with the lipstick, most of it was actually staying on the lips. And by the time she reached One, she reckoned herself to be quite the lipstick expert. There wasn't much lip to paint on her baby self, just a quick smear and they were done – 'Open wide,' she said, and the infant grinned as if this were such a funny game, and pouted as best she could, and look! what wonderful lips she now had, bigger and better and more plump, scarlet, a very sexy scarlet.

She had lifted the hatch to the attic. She'd felt unaccountably nervous; 'Hello?' she'd called, and that was stupid, it wasn't as if they were going to reply, was it? She'd played the torch beam around. She supposed she'd expected her predecessors to be stacked up in the corner, really, like flat packs. Instead they were sitting about listlessly, or standing, or caught in what looked like mute conversation. As the light played across their faces, they'd all turned to stare at her as one. She'd wished they hadn't done that.

And there, there sitting apart from all the others, there was Thirteen. Closest in size to her, of course – and she'd not been up here for long, she had fewer cobwebs in her hair than the others. 'Come with me,' she'd said. 'I have a job for you.'

Thirteen had blinked at her stupidly, and then got up and shuffled towards the hatch. Then the other bodies began to lurch forward as well. 'No, no,' said the teenager, 'I only need one of you. The rest of you can stay here.' But they wouldn't listen – it was as if where one went, they all went, in some silent solidarity – no, the teenager thought, as they one by one descended the stepladder into the light, it wasn't an emotional thing at all, it was as if the bodies were bound together by some invisible thread, as if one past self couldn't detach itself from the others.

It had seemed easy enough to sneak just one of her bodies into the bedroom. It was another thing altogether to have thirteen of them, all crowded in. But now that the make-up kit was out, the teenager could see the advantage of it. There were just that many more lips to work on – and nails, and cheeks, and eyes. She could start on Thirteen's first, and she'd slap on the cosmetics any which way, she didn't have to get it right first time.

'Hold still,' she snapped at Thirteen, as she painted all her fingernails Pretty-girl Pink, 'I don't want to have to tell you again.' But Thirteen *was* holding still, that was what was annoying her. It was hard to believe that only a few weeks ago she'd been living inside this body, now so passive and withdrawn. 'I'm going to the school disco tomorrow,' the teenager told her. 'You never went to the disco. You never dared. So hold still, I need to practise, I need to make myself look just right.' Because this is my chance – this is what she didn't say, what she wouldn't dare speak out loud – this is my chance, at last I can be just like the others. And you, she thought, as she held Thirteen's hand and splashed the varnish over her nails, over the knuckles, the pink was splashing everywhere – and you *failed* at that, you did *nothing* to help me fit in. Why did you do nothing? Freak. Freak. And she squeezed Thirteen's hand a bit too tightly, she squeezed hard so that it'd hurt.

Because at school they called her a freak, and she supposed that was right. Freak was just another word for special. The teachers told her it would be a while before she could fit in, but she wasn't sure whether she'd ever fit in, not properly: Mummy and Daddy had tried so hard, but there was so much they had failed to teach her, things that couldn't be automatically provided by pocket calculator or *Little Women*. So she was held down in remedial class, and that meant all the normal kids despised her. And yet she was smart and curious and keen to learn, so that meant all the remedial·kids despised her too. And it hardly helped that because of her condition she wasn't allowed to play sports or games, she wasn't even allowed outside in the playground at break – and the teenager thought the precautions weren't really necessary: yes, the skin was loose and baggy after a birthday, yes, the slightest bump could bring up the most livid of bruises, or knock the skin from the bone altogether – but give it a little time, just a month or three, and the skin would have hardened, it'd have welded itself properly into place. It wouldn't be so *squidgy* to the touch. And the raw angry red of it all would have faded somewhat, it'd merely look as if she'd been stung all over by wasps, nothing to worry about. The teenager had had high hopes when she'd been thirteen that her classmates were getting used to her – they still called her 'freak', but that was losing its venom, it was almost sounding like an affectionate nickname. But then she'd suddenly had to age another year, and she had to adjust to a new skin, and she was right back to square one: blistered flesh hung lumpen off her frame, she kept shedding loose bits of skin and hair, every time she got up from her desk at the end of class she left behind a little anthill of herself – and, worst of all, on her fourteenth birthday she discovered she'd grown ugly metal braces on her teeth. Terrific.

But Mummy had given her a make-up kit for her birthday. That must mean something, that maybe she felt her daughter could be normal after all. The present was left outside the bedroom door, and was unwrapped, and at first the teenager couldn't be sure it *was* a present, maybe Mummy had just dropped it there accidentally, Mummy dropped a lot of things some nights when she came back late – and Mummy wasn't there to ask, she'd obviously stayed out all night with one of her special friends, the girl had to wait until after school to find out whether the make-up belonged to her or not. And Mummy said of course it did, happy birthday; 'All girls like make-up, and you're a girl, aren't you?' And she agreed that indeed she was. Mummy was in a good mood. Now was the time to ask her about the school disco, there was going to be a disco at her school in two weeks' time, could she go, she'd be careful, could she go? 'Sure,' said Mummy. And maybe she could make friends properly now? Maybe she could wear her new make-up? 'Sure,' said Mummy. 'Knock yourself out.'

And Mummy had been home that night, her birthday night, Mummy had been home all night. And so they had a birthday meal together, and there wasn't any cake or jelly or sausage rolls, it was just like an ordinary dinner, but still, that was nice. It was nice to have Mummy there. And then it was time to shed her skin, and she fetched Mummy the special scissors, and Mummy groaned, and said, wasn't she old enough yet to do that by herself? And the teenager supposed she was. She was fourteen years old after all. And she shut herself away in the bathroom, and there was a little pain, and there was a little blood, but all things considered she did better than expected for her first solo effort. And she thought that Mummy would take charge of the thirteen-year-old body and put it up in the attic, but Mummy did nothing, she left the skin lying in the bathroom for *days*; it was there waiting for the teenager when she wanted to brush her teeth, or when she went for a pee. And it made her feel awkward, she didn't know what to say to it, and it just stared at her, she had to close her eyes against it if she washed or had a piss and it made both washing and pissing so much harder somehow. She could have taken it up to the attic herself, of course, but she wasn't supposed to know that the key was in Mummy's jewellery box, getting rid of the body would have given the game away; and yet she thought the skin was beginning to smell; it was all a bit of a quandary, really. When Mummy came home at the weekend the teenager asked her about it, and Mummy said, 'Christ, I'm only human, aren't I? I'm only human.' She got down the stepladder and took the body away, but she made such a fuss about it that the girl didn't think she could ask her any more favours for a while, she didn't think she should ask for make-up lessons for the school disco, she decided she'd be better off teaching herself.

And she'd tried practising on her own face, really she had. But she could never quite get the hang of it. She'd look at herself in the mirror and try to summon up the same critical disapproval she recognised from her Mummy, that seemed the proper adult reaction to have – but disapproval really wasn't enough, she looked like a dog's breakfast, she hated the way she looked, she looked like a child pretending to be a grown-up – no – worse – she looked like a freak pretending to be normal.

She tried to like make-up. But it felt so greasy, and *smelled* so greasy too – and the sensation of it on her face the first time made her want to gag, she felt her skin was suffocating beneath the gloop. And she wondered why all the girls at school wanted to cover themselves up this badly, living like walking talking lies, why they wanted to turn their real faces into hidden secrets? Didn't they have attics they could use instead?

She'd have to learn. She'd have to grit her teeth and learn. If she wanted to fit in.

And to be fair to Mummy, she hadn't stinted on the make-up kit. It was a good make-up kit. It had everything, it was a really good present. There were all the colours of varnish and lipstick and eye shadow, there was a series of eyebrow pencils so thick the teenager thought she could write her homework with them, there was mascara. She tried them all on each of her puppets, they waited patiently and without comment as she decorated their faces. And it seemed to her that as she got better at it, so her younger selves looked increasingly more adult, older than her by far – and the baby at the end was this curious amalgam of innocence and lipsticked eyelash-caked maturity, each new layer of make-up seemed to confer on the one-year-old strange new wisdom. Baby was immaculate – and really, not at all garish, and she looked just a dream in that little pink dress with the little pink bows and flowers – 'I love you,' the teenager said to her, and she honestly did, she couldn't help it. And she turned back to Thirteen, who seemed to be looking on in something like jealousy, Thirteen whose rouged cheeks made her look like a circus clown, whose lashes were so heavy with mascara clumps that she couldn't keep her eyes open properly for the weight. 'Not you,' she said. 'You're a frump. You're a freaky frump.'

She got out the eye pencil. 'Open your eyes,' she told Thirteen. 'No, don't look at me. I don't want you looking at me. Freak. Look upwards. Up. That's it.' And she started to draw a line right under her younger self's eye. It was difficult. She poked her in the eyeball.

When she'd started school, she'd been unprepared for the hostility the other children showed her. The boys weren't such a problem; the boys merely wanted to trip her up, or kick her, or punch her – and, frankly, they didn't want to get that close, they didn't want to touch. But the girls, that was different. They would call her names, they would stare her down with faces so cold and so loathing, they'd *spit*. And the teenager went home from school, some time during that first week, and she was in tears. She went to find her mother. 'Too late for tears now,' Mummy said. 'This is what you wanted, isn't it?' And the girl didn't know what she meant, how could Mummy think she'd wanted *this*? 'You must have realised,' said Mummy. 'That I couldn't take care of you on my own. If you'd been a normal child, then maybe. Maybe. But I'm only human, aren't I? I'm only human.' Mummy said that if she hadn't wanted a big hard dose of the real world then she shouldn't have wanted her Daddy to go away – and the girl said no, she really *hadn't* wanted that, honest – and for a moment she thought this had all been a silly misunderstanding, somehow Daddy had thought his daughter didn't want him any more, and Mummy would clap her hands, and back would Daddy come, and everything would be all right – 'I got the wrong end of the stick, kiddo!' But Mummy didn't clap her hands, Mummy just said, 'If you hadn't wanted him to go, then why didn't you just get better? *Why don't you get better?*' And the girl began to cry again, but this time it was a different sort of crying, no water came out, it made the muscles on her cheeks ache, and Mummy leaned forward, and took her daughter very gently by the chin, and said, so softly, 'Don't be such a cry baby.' And from that moment on the girl hadn't been.

Eye pencils were tricky, weren't they? She jabbed Thirteen in the eye again. A tear of blood ran down Thirteen's cheek. 'Don't be such a cry baby,' the teenager told her, and she jabbed her again. And this close she could feel her pain, but that didn't matter, it still seemed to be coming from so far away, from times past, she jabbed again. Not right in the centre of the eye, that idea made her feel squeamish, though why not, why not? She felt a tear of blood run down her own cheek, she wondered if she blinded her younger self whether she'd be blinded too, and really, if so, why not? 'I'm sorry,' she said to Thirteen. 'I am, but I'm only human, aren't I?' And Thirteen opened her mouth, and the teenager thought at last the girl she had been was going to cry out her pain – but it was opened in shock, and she wasn't looking at her assailant, she was looking over her shoulder. And the teenager turned a little, and saw all of her other selves, they too were agape, their jaws suddenly slack and heavy, they didn't know what to do with their tongues so they lolled every which way – it would have looked funny had they not seemed so afraid. And at last the teenager looked, she wanted to see what had so caught everyone's attention – and saw, standing in the doorway, her mother.

And Mummy didn't say a word, and her face was blank, and she took in the scene, and then she backed away, she left.

The teenager found her Mummy in her bedroom. And she saw that Mummy's dressing tables had been knocked over, and the mirror in which she'd do her make-up had been smashed. The contents of the jewellery box had been flung all over the room. (But she'd taken the key so carefully, hadn't she?)

And Mummy didn't look at her. And when the girl went to her – so tentatively – she realised that Mummy was crying.

'Please,' the girl said, 'please,' and she put her arms around Mummy, and Mummy fought her off at first, but the girl won, the girl was stronger, who'd have thought it? And she held her tight. 'Don't cry,' said the girl, 'I'll be better, I'll be better.' And, lamely, 'I wanted to get my make-up ready for the disco tomorrow night.' And, lying, 'I'll be better, I'll *get* better.' And she was crying as well, and these were real tears this time, there was no blood in them. And Mummy's arms were all around her, and Mummy's tears were warm upon her neck, and now Mummy was *dancing* with her, entwined as though they were dancing their way across the room – and the girl thought, like a disco, Mummy's teaching me for the disco, Mummy's teaching me again! And they danced for nearly a minute, until at last Mummy had manoeuvred her to the doorway. And then Mummy released her, and gave her a look that might have been an apology, but it was so flushed, it was so hard to tell – and then pushed her. Pushed her out on to the landing. Pushed her out of the room. And closed the door, and then there was a key turned, and then the teenager realised from now on it would be her mother who would sleep in a locked bedroom.

28

And as each year passed, and each time she neared her birthday, the young woman would wonder when she came to shed her skin and her bone and her heart and her gut whether she would also shed that little part of her body that housed the love she felt for her husband.

And some years the worry would keep her awake at night. Because she knew it *could* happen, her likes and dislikes did change as she got older and time lurched by. She'd used to like eggs, for years she'd had no problems with eggs at all; on her twenty-second birthday the very sight of them revolted her, they looked like big eyes staring out of the plate at her in judgement. She'd once loved the taste of celery, custard, pilchards; no more. For years her favourite tipple had been sweet cider, she'd look forward to a pint or two of it after a hard day's work. Suddenly, when she turned twenty-five, she found she far preferred the charm of a good house red – and she didn't know whether that was because her taste buds had refined in new maturity, or because her kidneys simply refused to process fermented apple any more. (She had, she supposed, got through rather a lot of it.)

What if one birthday she became a new person, and felt the same about Philip? What if, really, Philip was just another temporary fascination? What if he were just another pilchard?

She'd especially worried about that turning twenty-eight, because she'd spent rather a large part of being twenty-seven feeling rather fed up with Philip. It wasn't that he was doing anything wrong. Philip was as steadfast as ever, he still seemed to love her (God only knew why) he was always there for her. But she began to feel that the presence of his bulk lying next to her in bed was no longer entirely a reassuring one. That there was something in that whinnying snore of his, a snore she'd once found oddly enchanting, that had begun to irritate. That she would look at him over breakfast, before she went to work, or over dinner, once she'd got back, and wasn't certain quite why she was bothering to look at all – it wasn't as if he ever changed, not like she did, he was always exactly the same. 'You all right, baby?' he'd ask when the bother of these thoughts made her frown, 'you all right, baby?' is what he'd ask each and every time, and she'd say that everything was fine, it was fine. And wonder if it really was.

And she didn't want to lose Philip, because who would she be without him?

So, on her twenty-eighth birthday, when she stood there dripping and raw in her new body, it was the first thing that she checked; she thumped at her chest to get her heart going, and she searched that heart for Philip's love, she was prepared to look long and hard if need be – and she didn't *have* to look hard, there was the love, right near the surface. It was as bold and as bright as ever, she loved him as much as she had ever done. And she was so relieved she ran downstairs to find him, right there and then, all her organs flailing and all her nerves jangling, and she gave him the biggest hug, even though the skin was so sensitive it smarted rather a lot.

She also discovered that day she liked doughnuts. Big and squishy, so fat with jam that at first bite they'd squirt out over her chin.

She was enjoying her elevenses doughnut when the woman from personnel came in. 'Hello, dear,' said the woman from personnel. The office was open plan, but the woman from personnel had put her in a room far away from all the others, and the young woman didn't blame her for that; she could quite see that even with all the make-up she now had to wear her pockmarked face might throw her co-workers' concentration. 'Jackie from accounts has died,' said the woman from personnel, 'so, as a mark of respect, this department's taking the afternoon off. You can go home at lunchtime.' The young woman didn't know Jackie from accounts; she didn't know anyone from accounts, actually. 'Don't worry,' added the woman from personnel, 'you'll still get paid for a full day.' The young woman had been a little worried, it was true – she was only a temp, and so was only on an hourly wage. It was all she could manage, really, the temp jobs, and then only when her skin was good and hard. She liked this temp job better than most, the woman from personnel was always very polite, and the office block was just a street away from a bakery that made the very squishiest of doughnuts. She'd been working here for two whole weeks already, that was very nearly a record, and she hoped she'd be here for many weeks more, they seemed to have no end to all the envelopes they wanted her to stuff.

An afternoon off would be just the thing. She decided that she was rather glad that Jackie from accounts was dead, and she felt rather grateful to her, and hoped the demise hadn't been too painful. Now she'd be able to take all the make-up off, wipe away all that thick grease, she could let her skin breathe a bit. Maybe she could even take a bath – a nice, long, cold bath, and the water would be so soothing, it'd lap at all her sores, it'd wash off all the jagged edges and make the scabs feel soft to the touch. She could go home and undress and be herself. Before she got her car from the parking space marked disabled, she stopped off at the bakery, bought herself another doughnut to celebrate.

When she walked up her driveway she could see that Philip's car was parked in the garage. He was having the afternoon off too! And that made her happy – she checked her heart again, and there it was, the love she felt for him beating as fiercely as before.

She didn't call out to him, she would surprise him. She put her keys down on the hall table, but gently, so they wouldn't make a sound. And she went to the kitchen, but he wasn't there, and the sitting room, but he wasn't there either. And it wasn't until she climbed the stairs, and thought she heard him grunting, that she thought anything might be wrong – and even then, only when she was high enough to see over the banisters properly, and there in front of her, crowded around the bedroom, jammed into the very doorway, were so many women. And the women were her, and they all looked so confused.

'No,' she said, but still, not loud enough, not loud enough to stop it, not loud enough to stop the grunting – and she elbowed her way through her selves, and into the room. And there were still more of her, the youngest parts of her, and they looked embarrassed, most were covering their faces with their hands. Except for one, a teenaged one, number fourteen, was it? – her eyes staring out implacably, her mouth wide open too in what seemed like bemusement, you could see the braces on her teeth twinkling through spit. And she was on the bed. And she was naked. And standing close to her, there was Philip, there was her husband, and he was masturbating.

'Oh,' said Philip. Because he'd seen her. And he let his penis go, and it wilted so fast, it had wilted quite a bit even before it slapped wetly against his thigh.

'Oh,' she said.

'This isn't what it looks like,' he said.

*

After the disco, after he'd rescued her, Philip didn't talk to her for a while. She would see him at school, but he'd always duck away, nip into a classroom, nip into the boy's toilet. She supposed he felt ashamed. Maybe he regretted rescuing her at all.

But one day, after art class, and before all the normal children were allowed outside to play, he came up to her. He couldn't look her in the eye, and the girl had felt nervous, she knew he was going to say something terrible. He was trembling with it, what he was going to tell her or accuse her of or insult her with was shaking inside him like lava in a volcano.

'Do you want to go to the cinema some time?'

'Why?'

He shrugged.

That was good enough for her. So she went.

That weekend, they went to see a comedy. He asked her if she wanted popcorn, but she didn't like popcorn, so he didn't buy any – she said he was able to get popcorn for himself if he wanted, but he said he didn't like popcorn either. And he didn't put his arm around her in the dark, and he didn't even try to hold her hand, let alone try to lick at her brain. And even though it was a comedy, he didn't try to laugh at the jokes, she liked him for that most of all. Because the jokes really weren't very good.

'Would you like to go to the cinema again some time?' he asked, when it was all over.

'No.'

'Oh,' he said. 'Okay.'

A couple of weeks later he came up to her. Again, after art class. She supposed there was something about art class that particularly emboldened him.

'I was wondering if you'd changed your mind.'

'I don't want to be your friend,' she said.

'Why not?'

'Because I'm fourteen right now, and that's fine, you like me when I'm fourteen. But one day I'm going to be fifteen, and I'll be different, and you may not like me then.'

'I might,' Philip said.

'No,' she insisted. 'Because I'm a monster.'

So he left her alone after that. For a long while. And eventually she saw that he was going out with Holly Edwards, and she was annoyed to find it made her jealous.

She turned fifteen, and it wasn't a good change. She had no-one there to help her, and there was much more blood than before, and she felt like calling an ambulance, and didn't, she decided she'd tough it out, the worst thing that could happen (after all) is that she'd die. She didn't die. But she wasn't strong enough to go back to school for weeks.

When she finally did, still so raw, still so *ugly*, he was there, waiting.

'Do you want to go to the cinema some time?' he asked.

'What?'

'You're fifteen now, aren't you? It's been a year. Are you fifteen yet?'

'Yes.'

'See? I still like you, now you're fifteen.'

The teenager thought about this. 'You've been seeing Holly Edwards.'

'Only while I was waiting for you.'

'You see Holly Edwards again,' said the teenager, 'and I'll claw her eyes out.'

'Okay.'

'Okay.'

And they went to the cinema once more. It was another comedy this time, but the jokes were better, it was all right to laugh, and so they both did. He asked her if she wanted popcorn, and she had a good look inside her heart, and decided that her fifteen-year-old self loved popcorn. So he smiled and bought them some. 'I love popcorn too.' And he didn't put his arm around her this time either, and he didn't hold her hand, but he did brush it once in a while on the armrest, and a little too often to be accidental. And the teenager didn't mind.

'Would you like to come home for tea?' Philip asked, and she considered, and said yes. 'We can phone your mum and tell her,' he added, and she said that wouldn't be necessary.

Philip had a mother *and* a father, *and* a little sister, he had it all! They were all really nice, though. And after tea, Philip's mother said to her, and it was kind, and it didn't matter, 'You poor thing, whatever happened to you, were you in a fire?' And the teenager said it was a condition. 'Does it hurt?' And the teenager said yes, sometimes. 'I hope you don't mind me asking,' said Philip's mum, and she said she didn't mind one bit.

Upstairs in Philip's bedroom, where he kept all his games and his computer, Philip asked if he could kiss her.

'All right,' said the girl. 'But you mustn't try to lick my brain.' Philip said he wouldn't, and he didn't.

'Would you like to be my girlfriend?' asked Philip.

'I shan't be your wife, though,' said the teenager fiercely. 'I don't ever want to marry you. Promise me you'll never even ask.'

Philip blinked. 'Okay.'

And they kissed again, and his tongue wasn't so well-behaved this time, but it was all right, it still went nowhere near her brain.

*

He said, 'This isn't what it looks like.'

She said, 'What do you think I think it looks like?'

He had nothing to say to that.

*

One day, when taking her out to the cinema, he called her 'baby'. 'Would you like some popcorn, baby?' he asked, something like that.

She laughed. 'Why did you call me "baby"?'

He blushed bright red. 'I don't know. It's what my Dad calls my Mum.'

'I like it,' she said. So he started calling her 'baby' from then on.

They'd only broken up the once. When they were nineteen he'd taken her on holiday to Cornwall. They found a small B&B near Tintagel, nice and quiet, just the way she liked it. On their second night he suggested they go out and have curry together. She didn't much want to, even though it was true that on turning nineteen she'd found in her heart an unexpected passion for chicken tikka masala; she didn't want people looking at her, she was so especially blistered back then. But Philip promised they'd find a restaurant that was empty. Raj Poot wasn't empty, but there was a table near the back, and she could sit facing the wall. 'This is nice, isn't it?' asked Philip over the popadoms, and she agreed, actually, it *was* nice. And then his face had suddenly got all serious and sincere, and she thought maybe he had wind, and then he got down on one knee. Oh God, she thought. And he'd taken out a ring. Oh God, no. And everyone was looking, and some of them were applauding, oh God. And he asked her the inevitable, and there was even more applauding, there was a whole din of clapping and laughter, she hadn't even said *yes* – they all thought she'd say yes, of course she would, the sad ugly girl being rescued by the handsome young man, she was lucky anyone would take her with blisters like that – and she couldn't help it, she got up, she left him there bewildered on his knees, she got up and *fled*.

By the time he got back to the B&B, she'd already finished packing.

'But why?'

'I told you never to propose!' she shouted. 'And you betrayed me!'

'I'd never betray you,' he said.

'Of course you will,' she said. 'One day. You'll leave me. You'll find someone else. You'll go.'

'There'll never be anyone else,' he said. 'I love you.'

'Oh God. Oh God.'

'I love you, baby. I love you so much, baby, baby mine.'

They made love, spreadeagled across the suitcase.

*

He said, 'I'm so sorry.'

She said, 'Fuck.'

He said, 'I didn't touch her.'

She said, 'She's only fourteen.'

He said, 'I didn't lay a finger on her. She got undressed herself. I mean, of course, I asked her to. But I didn't help. She did it all on her own.'

She said, 'Fuck.'

He said, 'I wouldn't do that. You know that.'

She said, 'You told me there'd never be anybody else.'

He said, 'Well. There isn't.'

She conceded him that point.

She said, 'You betrayed me.'

She said, 'How can I ever trust you again?'

She said, 'She's fourteen. Look at her. I'm *fourteen*. Fuck.'

He said, 'I've never done it before. And I'll never do it again. And, I. And I didn't do anything anyway.'

He said, 'It's you. It's only you. I only want you.'

He said, 'I'm so sorry.'

And she said, 'Oh, Philip. Oh, Philip, God, *fuck*.'

And he said. And he reached out to her. And didn't dare touch. 'Let me. Let me. Please. Let me explain.'

*

It was a simple wedding, just Philip's family and friends. Philip's sister was a bridesmaid, and Philip's father agreed to give the young woman away since her own parents weren't available. Philip's mother helped her with her make-up, made sure all the blotches and scabs were covered up for the photographs, and then prised her into her white dress carefully so the skin wouldn't chafe. And she kissed her. 'All these years I've thought of you as a daughter,' she said. 'And now you really are one.'

And she dropped the first of many hints that she'd love to have a grandchild.

'How about it?' Philip said to her one day. 'How about we try for a baby?' And she said no. She didn't tell him, but the fact he'd used the word 'try' put her off, that it was something he clearly thought she may not be physically capable of.

And she knew that actually it *was* possible. She could feel the certainty inside her, a growing broodiness, a desire to produce something that she could love and hold, pour all her attention and affection into – have a little girl in her life that wasn't actually *her*. Mathematically it would work. It would take, what, nine months? She could get through the whole procedure easily between birthdays, between times her bodies needed to be shed – even allowing that after each age change there were a couple of very tender months when her skin wasn't quite solid enough to take sex, when there was a risk that any impregnation might bore a hole clean through her seething insides – yes, even allowing that, there was still a window in which she could conceive and carry a foetus through to delivery. But she was afraid. That she'd go through the whole thing, she'd go through the sex and the pregnancy and the labour and the birth, and she'd fall head over heels in love with the life growing inside her and the baby that popped out. Only to know that as soon as that was over, she'd lose herself to a new body, and that body would be a new mother – and she wouldn't want to let go, she'd hate this future self that would so arrogantly take her child away from her. And only to fear, that in a new body of new likes and dislikes, where you could like pilchards one year and doughnuts the next, where you could be so *fucking fickle*, that she'd no longer care for the child at all. How awful. How evil. To grow up in a world where your mother wouldn't want you.

And Philip pleaded. But he *always* got his way – he got to take her to the cinema, he got to be her boyfriend, he got to be her husband, he even got her to like popcorn. But there was a limit. There had to be a limit. This was it. This was it, here.

'Okay,' Philip had said. And, as far as she'd ever known, he'd never taken an interest in children again.

*

He said, 'Let me explain. I'm so sorry. Baby, I'll never do it again. I'd never hurt you. Please, baby. Please, baby. Baby, let me explain.'

And every time he said the word 'baby', she flicked her eyes to the only baby there, to her one-year-old self. Who was standing beside the bed. Whose eyes were wide, and that innocent face, it looked so frightened.

'I don't want to see you again,' she said. 'Get out.'

And at that he nodded, and he left.

She wanted to put her arms around the fourteen-year-old. She didn't. 'You must be cold,' she said. 'Are you cold? You must be dirty. Come on. Let's get you cleaned up. Come on, let's get rid of all that filth.' And there wasn't any filth to be seen, her naked skin looked so white and so free of blemish, she'd never realised she'd ever been that pretty. She led her to the bathroom – and, of course, all the twenty-six other selves had to come too, she had to shepherd them all into position so she could get Fourteen close enough to the sink. 'Hold still,' she said, and Fourteen held still, that's all she'd ever do, isn't it, just do what she's told, she just stared at her vacantly, 'hold still, no more filth.' And the woman sponged the girl down, she sponged her all over, the hottest water she could stand, she'd burn that filth away, it scalded her hands; she winced, but Fourteen didn't, Fourteen took all she was given. And at last that pretty white skin of hers was red raw. 'He'll never hurt you again,' she promised her, 'no-one will ever hurt you again.'

Once she'd dried her off, the woman looked for the girl's clothes. They were nowhere to be found. 'Where has he put them?' she said out loud, 'what has he done with them?' All her spent bodies turned away, sheepish, as if reluctant to answer. 'Very well,' she said to Fourteen, 'we'll have to make do.' She fetched her some of her own clothes from the wardrobe. They hung baggy on her, the woman was so much fatter than her child self, that must have been because of the doughnuts; drowning in those clothes the teenager looked like a circus clown. 'And time for bed now, it's been a long day,' she called, 'come on!' And she led the girl up the stepladder to the attic, and all the other girls followed, and all the women too. 'That's it, night night!' she said, as she stuffed the last one up there, and down came the hatch, and she locked them in the darkness.

'Fuck,' said the young woman. And she decided to go to the pub. For a moment she hesitated, thought she couldn't leave the children at home alone. Then laughed at herself. She put on make-up, she put on lots of make-up, she inspected the results with critical disapproval, it'd have to do. Then she went to the pub, she drank lots of red wine. She drank cider too.

That night she lay in a bed far too big for her, and cuddled a pillow, and pretended that the pillow had a whinnying snore.

*

The next day she didn't go into work.

She phoned Philip on his mobile. He sounded surprised to hear from her.

'Oh, hello,' he said.

'You wanted to explain,' she said. 'So. Explain.'

'I'm not sure I can.'

'I've checked my heart,' she said. 'And I still love you. It's still there. I can't shed it. No matter how much I want to.'

'Thank you.'

'Don't. Just explain. I want to understand.'

There was silence for a while, and she thought he might have hung up, decided that the marriage wasn't worth fighting for.

'I want you back,' he said.

'So, explain.'

'I am. This is it. I am explaining. I want you back. The way you used to be. When I first loved you.'

'When I was fourteen?'

'It's not about being fourteen,' he said. 'But you were so vulnerable back then. You needed rescuing.'

'I'm still vulnerable.'

'No. Not any more.'

'I'm vulnerable about so many things.'

'No. You're hard. You're so cold and hard, can't you... Don't you know? Don't you know, you didn't fit in before, but now you fit in, you found a way to fit, and left me outside, I...'

'I'm so vulnerable, you have no idea.'

'No.'

Silence. Except for the crying. He was crying down the phone at her, God. She thought that if maybe she could cry, too, she could *prove* how vulnerable she still was. She tried. She failed. So maybe he was right.

'I still love you,' he said, at last.

'Good.'

'But,' he said. 'But.' And he let that hang.

Silence. Real silence now. No crying. It frightened her.

And then, very softly, out of that silence and strange new-found fear: 'Oh, baby, I miss you.'

'I miss you too,' she heard herself say.

'I've missed you for such a long time,' he said. 'Why did you go away?'

'I don't know,' she said.

'And yesterday,' he said. 'It was just. Well. It wasn't sexual. I mean, the wanking. Um. Wasn't sex.'

'No,' she said. 'No, I know.'

'Please, baby,' he said.

'But it can't work now, can it?' And she hated the way she sounded, the way that she was begging him for a solution. 'How can I ever trust you again? I know what you did. I know. I know. How will I ever forget?'

And he said nothing.

Not for a while.

And then, so softly again, and so slyly too. 'Are you sure there's no way you can make yourself forget?'

*

She thought about that all morning. She thought it through.

And then she went up to the attic.

56

The house was old, so of course it made noises. The odd inexplicable creak, even groaning sometimes. But the old woman didn't care. She'd been in the house such a long time, and the noises were just the background hum to her life. She may not have known what it was that caused them, but that was all right, that didn't matter, without them she'd have felt out of place. And that's why the knocking from the attic woke her up. It wasn't that it was especially loud, or urgent – it was new, and new was wrong.

She looked at the alarm clock on her bedside table. A little after five. Too early. Too early to do anything.

Maybe she'd been dreaming.

She lay there in bed, her duvet pulled up close to her chin, her eyes wide open and smarting against the dark. She listened.

It turned six. She could see the faintest hints of dawn through the curtains. There were a few creaks – wait, yes, was that groaning, just a little, she liked the groans? But nothing else. She must have dreamed it after all. She'd dream sometimes, even still. She'd dream of Philip mostly. Or of her mother. And occasionally, that other dream, of the old woman in her rocking chair, her eyes glazed, her teeth blackened. Very probably, the banging had come from one of *those* dreams, that would make sense. And she felt reassured, and she let her eyes close, she could still catch some sleep, and *dreamless* sleep too if she were lucky – when, once again, there it was, she heard it. Soft. But unmistakably there. Knock, knock, *knock*. The final one just a tad more emphatic than the others – not impatient, not yet, just letting the world know it wasn't prepared to wait forever.

She got up. She put on her dressing gown so she wouldn't catch cold.

She went to fetch the key. She went to fetch the flashlight. She realised, as she did so, that her hand was shaking. 'Don't,' she told it.

She stood underneath the attic hatch. Stared up at it, as if just by looking, as if by the mere intensity of her gaze, she could put things right.

She listened out. If there were no more knocks, she might not have to pull down the stepladder. She could leave it alone, and go back to bed. She wouldn't sleep, she knew that now, she wasn't sure she'd ever sleep again, but it'd be warm there, it'd be safer. She stood there for ten minutes. She held her breath, she didn't know she could hold her breath so long. She began to shiver, and she hoped it was from the cold. There was no more knocking. But she pulled down the stepladder anyway.

Very slowly, up she climbed.

It was ridiculous, she thought, for a woman her age to be on a stepladder in the middle of the night – or the early morning, at any rate – and all because of a dream. She could stop right now. She could go back down the steps, put them away, put everything away, put this all behind her. And she wondered, maybe it was the weight of her on the ladder, although she was treading so gently, she didn't want to make a sound – but maybe the ladder creaked, or groaned, or let out a squeal, who knew?, something caught the attention, the knocks began again, more excited than before.

Knock, *knock, knock*! – she nearly fell off the ladder in surprise.

'Hey!' she cried out. 'Hey!'

And she let that be enough for a moment. Because she wasn't really sure where she was prepared to take that line of argument. Certainly there was no response. And then she really thought that having come this far she couldn't just leave it at 'hey'. 'Hey,' she said, 'you up there! Keep it down! Keep it down up there!'

She heard nothing. Not even the sound of her own heart. And that was silly, because she could *feel* it, thumping so hard inside her chest, hey, who turned the volume down? Maybe she'd gone deaf. Maybe she'd finally gone deaf, and she wouldn't hear anything again, and that was something of a relief, it'd ruin her job, but at least there'd be no more knocking, the knocking would be over. She took out the key. She put it in her lock to the trap door – and there was a little click as the tumblers turned and fell, she heard it distinctly, *shit* she thought.

The hatch was still closed. It was unlocked, but still closed. She could lift it any time she wanted to. She could lift it, and climb up into the attic.

And she put her head against the hatch – not touching it, as close as she could get without touching. And she called out, as loud as she dared, and that was louder than she'd expected: 'Hey! You kids! Don't you make me come up there!'

And she turned the key again, and she locked the hatch shut, and she gave it a little push just to make certain it was secure. And she climbed back down to the landing, as fast as she dared, and she pushed the stepladder back into place. And she took the key and the flashlight with her to bed, just in case she needed them again. She knew she wouldn't, of course, she knew she wouldn't go up there again, nothing on earth would possess her ever to go up there again, but just in case, in case. And in spite of herself, and in spite of her still thumping (still silent) heart, the old woman (because she *was* so old now, even at only fifty-six) the old woman went back to sleep.

*

She'd decided to be an old woman the day that Philip died. She'd been with him right to the end, she'd take the bus into town and be at the hospital for all the visiting hours they allowed. 'It's so unfair,' she told Philip, and Philip of course agreed with that; 'What am I going to do without you now?' And the nurse asked her whether she could do anything to help her with her skin, because the stress of it all was making it peel off in thick clumps: 'No,' she said, really rather angrily, 'you just get on with your job, you just make my husband *well*.' But they couldn't make Philip well, not for all their efforts, not for all his wife's tears, and so he died anyway. 'You've never let me down, never, not a single day of your life,' she sobbed. And she decided then and there that that was it, she'd be an old woman now, and she'd never leave her house again.

And that last, at least, was an exaggeration. But she didn't *need* to leave the house. She could order her groceries online, and she made them leave the parcels of food and milk right against the front door so she could pull them in. And she could easily work from home, the company would send her all the information she needed via email, and she could invoice them by email too, simple. And sometimes she'd step out into the back garden, she'd do that, when the fancy took her. But the fancy hadn't taken her for months now, was it even a year? It was always too cold or too hot, or it was raining.

She wasn't proud of her job, but she thought she was at least good at it. She got the names and numbers through each morning first thing, and she could tell even by looking at them on the computer screen which ones would be easy and which ones would be not. Surnames which had three syllables or more were always friendly, surnames beginning with the letters 'M' or 'W'. Avoid women who used diminutives for Christian names, avoid any initial letter like 'I' or 'Q' or 'V' that made the owner sound ostentatiously obscure. It was true that a lot of people put the phone down on her, even the 'M's, but not *most* people, and that in itself was an achievement. 'Hello,' she said, 'may I take a few moments of your time? I'm conducting a survey for market research about health and beauty products, it shouldn't take long, and by participating you'll be eligible for our grand prize!' And she always put the right amount of sincerity in her voice, if people hung up on sincerity like that she knew they'd feel guilty afterwards.

She'd got through twenty-three successful phone calls one day last spring. That had been a record. And she'd never met her bosses, of course, and only rarely spoke to them, but she liked to think they'd been impressed by that.

'What sort of prize?' asked the fourth woman of the day. The fourth woman's surname was Montague, and that was a good sign, but her first name was Trish, which wasn't.

'A year's supply of health and beauty products.'

'Oh. And this won't take long?'

'It won't take long.' If she asked the questions quickly enough, and the answers were given coherently and without hesitation, she could be done in twenty minutes.

'All right,' said Mrs Trish Montague.

'Can I ask whether you buy make-up?'

'Well, yes. Of course I do.'

'And could you tell me which of the following best explains your reasons for buying make-up? a) to look healthy, b) to look young, c) to attract men, d) to look business-like, e) to feel better about yourself, f) not applicable?'

'Hmm. Do I have to say only one?'

'As many as *are* applicable.' The old woman didn't wear make-up any more. It was filthy stuff, it burned the skin. After the funeral, after Philip had finally gone for good – and there were so few people who turned up, and he'd been such a kind man, just a few people from work, and that fat sister he had – and she'd eaten the cake and the jelly and the sausage rolls like a good girl, like a good widow, and then she'd come home, locked the front door behind her, went straight up to the bathroom. And tipped all the cosmetics down the toilet, all the perfumes too, flushed them away. She'd watch them all spiral down the whirlpool, she'd flush and flush again. She'd laughed so much as she'd done so! 'Goodbye, goodbye, good riddance!' she'd said out loud. She'd blocked the drains. She'd had to call a plumber. She'd wished, in retrospect, she'd kept a bit of lipstick back for when she'd answered the door to him, by God she'd looked a sight.

'Could you say the options again?'

The old woman said them again.

'A, b and e.'

'And no others?'

'A little bit of c.'

'I'll put down a very small c.' Knock, knock, knock. 'And how often do you buy lipstick in particular? Once a week, once every two weeks, once a month, more rarely, more often, not applicable?'

'Once every two to three weeks.'

'And which of the following best describe the lipstick you'd choose?' Knock, knock. 'Fashionable, bright, creamy...' Knock knock. 'Which of. Sorry. Which of the following best describe the...' Knock knock *knock*. 'I'm sorry.'

'Are you all right?'

'I'm sorry about the noise. It's been going on all morning.'

'I can't hear anything.'

'You can't hear the knocking?'

'I've got builders in too. We're having a new conservatory.'

'My knocking, you can't hear it?'

'No, I'm all right.'

'It's not all right,' she said. 'I'm sorry.' If a questionnaire was left uncompleted, then there'd be no money, it was all or nothing. But it couldn't be helped, not if...

Knock *knock knock knock knock knock kno…* 'Can I call you back in a minute?'

'But I'm going out…'

'I'll call you back.'

'Do I still get my prize?'

'Yes, yes.' And this time she allowed the rage to drive her through her fear. She snatched up the key and flashlight from her bedroom, she raced up the stepladder, all but punched the hatch door open. She shone the light on to the puppets, and in the sudden blaze they all stopped, looked at her. 'What is it? What do you bloody *want?*'

And she knew there'd be no reply, of course – but then one of them shuffled forward, someone young, younger than her obviously, she couldn't tell which in the attic murk. 'Please, miss,' she said. 'We're cold and hungry.'

The old woman said, 'But you can't talk.'

This was ignored. 'Please, miss. Can you spare some food? Just a bit of bread and cheese. We'd be ever so thankful, miss.'

'No,' said the old woman. 'You don't eat. I have cheese, and bread, and you can't have it, because you don't eat, for God's sake, God, you don't even *talk.*' And she slammed down the hatch, she locked it, she was hurting, she didn't know why.

The knocking continued throughout the afternoon. The old woman didn't phone back Mrs Trish Montague. She didn't phone anyone, how could she explain the knocking? She turned on the television loud, she jammed cotton wool in her ears, and when the cotton wool didn't work she used fingers, she jammed the fingers in as far as they could go, too far, she thought if she weren't careful she'd poke them right through her skull, she thought they'd lick her brain.

'I can't do this,' she gasped. 'I can't.' And she opened the front door. She'd get out, into the world, anywhere away from the attic and the noises of the past coming down from it. And the sunshine streamed in, and she thought it burned her foot, she thought that if she stepped out any further her whole foot would catch alight. 'I can't do this,' she said again, and for a moment even she didn't know what she was referring to, whether it was the staying indoors or the going outside that she couldn't face. And then she closed the door, firmly, resolutely, and she was still in the house with the knocking, and she knew.

And, mercifully, the knocking stopped.

It stopped for hours. She even dared to believe it had stopped forever. She even dared to stand under the hatch, and look up at it, and whisper that it should do its worst.

She lay in bed that night, and she thought she wouldn't be able to sleep, she was still listening. But at last she must have drifted off –

Because she was dreaming. And it was that odd dream, and it was that old woman. But no, not an old woman, because *she* was the old woman, wasn't she? – so what did this make the one in the rocking chair, she was the *ancient* woman, the crone. Rocking all the time, back and forth, didn't she get bored of it? And normally then the dream would fade, but not this time, this time she got *closer* – it was as if the ancient woman was fixed in her mind's eye, she could look upon her more clearly than she'd ever been able to before. Her glassy eyes, her blackened teeth. And it seemed as if the eyes were staring straight at her, as if this weren't her dream at all, as if she were part of the crone's dream – but the eyes weren't curious, they stared at her simply for want of anything better to do. And all the time just rocking, still rocking. And now she could see that the crone was crying — she'd never seen that before — or, no, maybe not crying, maybe the eyes were just so clapped out and broken they simply leaked water — and the tears were lost within the folds of her sagging wrinkles. Rocking in her rocking chair — and this wasn't a *bad* nightmare, this was all there was, there was nothing to be scared of — and then it dawned on her that that was precisely what scared her, that this was *all there was*; the monotony of it, the never-ending rocking...

She forced herself awake.

And saw that she wasn't alone.

*

She turned on the bedside lamp. She was surprised she could do so without screaming. Even in her terror, she felt rather proud of herself for that.

'Please, miss,' said the young woman.

And the young woman hadn't come alone. She'd come with all her sisters, her younger selves, her older selves, they'd somehow squeezed into the bedroom, all fifty-five of them now, and the frightened old woman in the bed was looking upon the whole history of her life as it stared back at her without emotion or warmth.

'Please, miss,' said the young woman again, and her older self recognised her, Twenty-Eight, this was her when she was twenty-eight. One of the late twenties at any rate, back when she was tubby. 'You have to help us, miss.'

'How did you get out of the attic?'

And as earnest as the young woman looked, she still allowed this question a little smile — it wasn't unkind, simply amused. 'But, miss,' she said, 'we've always been able to get out of the attic.'

'And what then? Why now? What? What do you want?'

'Come on, darling,' then the young woman said. For a moment the old woman thought she was talking to her, but then she saw her younger self reach into the crowd, and plucked from it a seven-year-old girl. The little girl blinked at the old woman nervously. And coughed.

'She's not feeling at all well,' said the young woman. 'Hear that?'

And, as if on cue, the little girl coughed again.

'I'm sure it's nothing serious,' said the old woman.

'But it makes her feel so ill. And it makes her throat red raw, miss.'

'It's just a cough.'

'And there are marks on her skin. Come closer, darling, come, show the nice old lady the marks.' The little girl held out her wrists. And they were peppered with spots, red and inflamed, the largest being about the size of a two penny piece.

The old woman shrugged. 'Why are you telling me? I'm not a doctor...'

'Can't we get a doctor, then, miss?'

'No.'

'But what if it's the plague, miss? What if the little girl dies?'

'No-one's going to die,' said the old woman. 'And stop calling me miss. Now, listen. I've got some cough syrup in the bathroom. If I get her some cough syrup, will you all go back to bed?'

'Yes, miss. Thank you, miss.'

'You all stay here,' said the old woman. She pushed her way through her predecessors, went to the bathroom, opened the cabinet above the sink. She found the syrup. The expiry date was over a year before, but she didn't suppose it would matter, it was for someone who'd expired fifty years ago, wasn't it?

She poured out a teaspoon of syrup. 'Now, hold still,' she said to the little girl, 'and open wide.' The little girl gulped the medicine down, and pulled a face. The old woman laughed, and the young woman smiled – 'There, all better now!' 'You'll be better now, darling!' And the little girl coughed.

'Thank you,' said the young woman, sincerely.

'Now, back to bed.'

'We want to stay. We want to stay until she's all better again.'

'That's not the way it works.'

'We want to stay.'

The old woman sighed. 'You can stay up,' she said, 'but just a little bit longer.'

She put on her dressing gown, and led them all downstairs. 'Now, settle down,' she told them. But they wouldn't settle; they walked listlessly around the kitchen, looking in cupboards, opening up jars and pots; in the study they picked books off the shelf, riffled through pages without reading them, then dropped them on to the floor; in the sitting room they turned on the television and kept flicking channels. 'You can have the television on,' said the old woman, 'so long as we all sit quietly and watch it together. Do you hear me? Is that a deal?' And it *was* a deal, apparently; there was some black and white movie on, and it had subtitles, and didn't look very interesting – but nonetheless all the women gathered around the screen, all fifty-six of them, and paid it close attention. All silent, save for the occasional coughing from the seven-year-old, sitting in prime position on the middle of the settee.

During one of the commercial breaks, a welcome splash of colour on the screen, with everyone talking in English about car insurance, the little girl's cough became a long drawn out splutter. She choked, and died.

And it was as if, for a moment, the old woman could feel a year of her life torn out of her head. The memories, gone. The innocence, gone.

'I told you we should have called a doctor, miss,' said the young woman.

'Don't call me miss.'

'What shall we do with the body?'

'We'll put it in the bathroom,' said the old woman, 'out of harm's way. You can help me. Easy now, we don't want to frighten the others.' The others didn't *look* frightened; their attention was fixed on another ad, this time about credit consolidation.

And fighting back tears, because she hadn't cried since Philip had died, she wasn't going to start all that crying again, she took the head, and told the young woman to take the legs. And they lifted up the little girl's corpse, and they carried it upstairs, trying to walk sideways in concert, sashaying a little, as if they were dancing. They laid the body down gently in the bath. 'I'm sorry, baby,' said the old woman, and she stroked the girl's forehead. She now saw that the spots on both wrists had burst, the lumps were like craters, the pus was black.

'Shouldn't we get the doctor, miss?'

'What on Earth for?'

'Well, miss. For all the others.' And the young woman looked her full in the face, and her eyes were so big and trusting. The old woman had to turn away.

When they went back downstairs, there was more coughing. The seventeen-year-old. And the thirty-six-year-old. And the three.

'Shall we get more cough syrup, miss?'

'But there's no point. It didn't do anything.'

'Please, miss. They don't want to miss out on the cough syrup.'

And so the old woman spooned syrup into their mouths, and each of her patients smiled as she did so, and they even whispered thank yous. The three-year-old spilled some down her chin, the old woman wiped it away with her finger, the three-year-old licked at her finger till the syrup was all gone.

And on each of their wrists there, too, were the spots.

The old woman clapped her hands cheerily. 'Who wants bread and cheese?' she asked. 'Bread and cheese for everyone!' So they all had a very little piece of bread, and a very little piece of cheese.

Twenty-Six died before the black and white movie had ended. The next movie was without subtitles, but was no more comprehensible. The three-year-old died within the opening credits, though, and that was a distraction. It wasn't easy to follow the plot either when Seventeen expired with an especially noisy death rattle.

Each time the young woman helped the old woman with the bodies.

The next to fall ill, in order, were the eleven-year-old, the twelve-year-old, the fifty-five-year-old, and the forty-two-year-old. Fifty-Five, in particular, was a shock; she'd only been her a few months previously; it was hard to see someone who looked so very similar turn pale and sickly before her eyes.

'I've got spots of my own,' said the young woman.

'Yes, I can see you have.'

'And I've got a cough. Listen.'

'Yes.'

'Listen.' And the young woman coughed.

'Yes, I know.'

'Am I going to die, miss?'

'Don't call me miss. I'll call the doctor. All right? Would you like me to call the doctor?'

'Oh yes, miss, yes!' said the young woman. 'That would be lovely!' And she clapped her hands at the very thought.

'It's still dark outside. I'll call him as soon as it's light.'

She ran out of cough syrup. But the puppets wanted medicine, so she started to use mouthwash instead. No-one seemed to mind. The mouthwash tasted better than the cough syrup.

By dawn, fifteen of the women had died. There wasn't much space in the bathroom for them any more. The old woman wondered why it was that her younger selves took up so more room dead than alive.

On her left wrist she found a red spot. It didn't hurt. It just itched a little. And she wasn't sure, it might just be because she was tired, she had stayed up all night, but her throat felt a bit croaky.

'Please, miss,' said the young woman. She'd been coughing for hours, but bless her, sickness or no sickness, she'd always done her duty lugging the corpses up the stairs. 'I'm not sure I can hold on for much longer.'

'I'll phone the doctor now. But you must get everyone up to the attic. You'll all have to go up to the attic now.'

'Why?'

'Well, just think,' said the old woman. 'All these women, such a mess! We don't want the doctor to think we live in a mess, do we? We want him to do his best for us.' And the young woman agreed. She led all her fellows upstairs, the ones that were sick and feverish, the ones too that were still well and blissfully unaware there was anything to be worried about.

And the one-year-old baby, she was still healthy. She'd been quite cheerful all night, in fact; sometimes she'd slept a bit, because it really was *very* late for such a little girl to be staying up. But whenever she woke she burbled with delight to see so many potential playfellows about her (even if there were fewer each time). And she'd watch the television screen with only the rapt attention an infant can give – she didn't care that she couldn't understand the plots or the dialogue, she was used to not understanding anything. 'I'll carry her,' said the old woman.

'Thank you, miss,' said the young woman. 'Thank you for helping us, I love you. I love you.' And the old woman felt a lump in her throat, and she hoped it was caused by nothing more serious than guilt. 'It's the crone who's done this, isn't it, miss?'

'What do you mean?'

'The one in the rocking chair. I don't know how she's done it, but she has.' And then the twenty-eight-year-old kissed her on the cheek, and went up the stepladder, and climbed into the attic, and she was never seen again.

And the old woman knew what she had to do. She'd remembered it always, no matter that she'd forgotten the reason she'd done it in the first place. 'I'm sorry, baby,' she said to the one-year-old, 'it'll hurt, I know, and it'll hurt a lot, but after this, I promise, no-one will ever hurt you again.' And then she severed the infant from her other selves, she broke that invisible thread. And upstairs in the attic there was a wailing more terrible than anything mere death or illness could cause. They wailed that they'd been cheated of one of their own, that they realised that they'd never get that little part of their childhood back, they wailed with such despair, and the old woman cried for them. She laid the unconscious body down softly on the floor, then climbed up to the hatch, took out the key, and locked away her sisters forever.

She sponged the blood off the baby's face, and she was relieved, she'd done no lasting damage. And she sponged the blood off the baby's pink dress, and that was lucky too, the blood faded down to a dull pink, it merged easily with the pink bows and the pink flowers. Then she picked her up in her arms, she pressed her close to her, and she could hear the heart beating inside that little chest, at last she could hear her heart. She walked towards the front door. She opened it. She took a breath. She stepped out into the sunshine. It didn't burn her. She didn't catch fire. She walked on.

*

112

They think, because I do not seem to think, I do not think.

They think, that because I keep my face blank, and my eyes hard and set, there is no-one inside.

But I think.

There is no pain. Not now. Not the way they understand pain. My nerve endings are now so ragged and loose, and lost behind so much peeling flesh, they could be blazing, I wouldn't feel it.

But oh, the effort of it all...!

The hammering in my chest. My heart beating against my very bones. I think that sometimes my heart is touching my bones. I think that each time it beats, it's grazed against the side of them.

I think my bones may be chipped.

That's what comes of thinking.

I think. I do nothing but think.

And they force me awake. They surround me on all sides. But, as the years go by, they leave me. They still outnumber me. They will always outnumber me. But soon there won't be enough of them to stop me doing whatever it is I want to do.

I'll hold my breath. I've been practising. Just for a few seconds, they haven't noticed. I'll hold my breath until my cheeks swell and my lungs snap and my eyes pop out on stalks.

I think. I think of nothing else.

They won't keep me breathing forever.

56

And really, very quickly after all that, the old woman forgot everything.

Social services were suspicious. They tried to take her baby away. They would ask her, 'Who is the mother?' – they would have to ask it several times, because the old woman didn't seem to understand the question. 'I don't remember,' she'd at last reply, and she wouldn't seem especially bothered by her ignorance, she'd announce it rather than admit it, as if it were a new revelation to her, and with such an enormous smile. 'Can't I be the mother?'

And of course she couldn't be; she was much too old, and there was no resemblance at all – this strange, malformed, face-twisted woman, patterned with scabs and liver spots, alongside this perfect baby. But someone thought to check their DNA, and discovered that they were definitely family. She clearly loved the baby, and the baby clearly loved her, and they were both very happy. The troubles only started whenever anyone tried to move the baby from the old woman's side – suddenly the baby would scream, and not in infant petulance but obvious *pain* – her skin would erupt into hives, she'd start to itch, she'd scratch furiously at that pretty pink dress she wore, and she'd rip right through it – and no matter how tiny her little fingernails they still gashed deep scars into that smooth baby skin, they drew blood.

Social services would try to take the baby away again, they'd be back. But, for now, they left them alone.

When they'd moved in to the flat, the old woman had taken the one bed, and she'd let the baby sleep in the cupboard. But it wasn't cruel, it was a big cupboard, and she left the door open. And she gave the baby a tea towel for a blanket, and a bag of sugar for a pillow, and the baby seemed perfectly happy in there, she burbled and smiled. But pretty soon the old woman decided it was wrong, even though the cupboard was so big, even though the sugar was so soft. So she took the baby to her bed. She'd lie on her side, and she'd wrap her arms around the baby, tight but not too tight, keeping her nice and secure – and the baby was even happier with that, the smiles were bigger and the burbles more joyful. They'd both sleep like logs.

The flat was very small. But they didn't need space. The neighbours to the left played loud music through the day, the neighbours on the right played louder music through the night. But they didn't need quiet either. All the old woman wanted was to be high, as high up in the air as possible, she didn't even know why – and she had that, she was on the very top floor, she couldn't get any closer to the sky. And sometimes in the evening she'd leave the flat, she'd stand out on the concrete balcony with her baby in her arms, and she'd look out all over the city, so much of it, so very far beneath her, and it'd feel strangely as if it all belonged to her.

The elevator in the tower block was rarely working, and when it did, smelled so badly of piss that no-one wanted to ride in it. Living so high in the air, and with so many stairs to climb, the old woman and the baby didn't get many visitors.

But one day they did.

The three raps at the door were so very confident, and the old woman thought it might be Social Services back for another tussle. Knock knock *knock*.

There on the doorstep was a teenager. Her face was covered in make-up, layers and layers of it, and she wore the reddest lips the woman had ever seen. It was as if she were trying to blast her youth away, as if she were trying to pretend she were an adult true and proper – but it didn't work, she was a kid, she was just a kid. And the woman opened her mouth to ask her what she wanted. But then she remembered. She remembered it all, the memories came back in a sick rush. What she'd done to her, which was terrible. What she'd said, which was worse.

The teenager was still wearing braces. The wire frame still jutted awkwardly out of the mouth from where it had been bent. The teenager still had that missing front tooth.

The old woman thought she was going to throw up. She actually swayed on her feet with the nausea.

'Hello,' she said instead. 'Hello. Won't you come in?'

The teenager did so.

She stood in the flat, looking all around, sizing it up. But not in judgement, not too critically. 'Have you come to hurt me?' the old woman asked, but the teenager said nothing to that.

Instead she found the bedroom. She yawned. She stretched out her arms long and straight, as if she were on a cross, she yawned and there was no sound to that yawn. She smiled at the old woman. Dressed as she was, she got on to the bed. Within moments she was asleep.

The old woman waited for her to wake in the sitting room. She perched herself on the edge of the second-hand settee with the broken springs. She held the baby. The baby slept as well.

At last, some time later, the teenager stirred. She came out of the bedroom. The old woman started as she heard the door open, stood up as if to attention. She stared at the teenager. The teenager stared back. Then the teenager waved, just a little wave, a single flap of the hand. She went into the kitchen. She opened the cupboards. She opened the fridge. There was nothing to be found but bread and cheese, the old woman liked bread and cheese. The old woman shrugged an apology. The teenager raised an eyebrow, almost comically, then grinned.

The teenager toasted the bread and melted the cheese. They ate.

Once in a while the old woman thought she should speak to the teenager. But any words caught in her throat.

The meal over, the teenager grinned again, as if in thanks, as if the old woman had cooked it, as if the old woman had invited her for dinner in the first place. She yawned once more, stretched again, and went back to the bedroom. She closed the door behind her.

The old woman opened the large cupboard. She prepared the little bed for her baby, the baby hadn't slept there for a long time. The baby struggled, she didn't want to go back to the cupboard. 'Ssh,' whispered the old woman, and she gave her the tea towel, she gave her the sugar, 'it's for tonight, kiddo, it's just for tonight.' And at that the baby was comforted. She went to sleep right away. The old woman smiled at that. Then, after a moment's hesitation, closed the cupboard door, she shut the baby away in the darkness. And she locked it. Just to be safe.

She went to the kitchen. She took a knife from the drawer.

She stood over the sleeping teenager. So young, how could she ever have been that young? And pretty too, she didn't need all that make-up, the old woman wished she wouldn't wear it. She stood over her for quite a while. She knew that this time threats wouldn't be enough. This time she'd have to kill her.

The teenager's eyes opened. She sat up.

The old woman sank down on to the bed beside her.

The teenager took the knife from her. 'And this is it,' said the old woman out loud. She thought she should brace herself, but she didn't want to brace herself, suddenly she had no energy for it. The teenager looked at the knife curiously, how odd, a knife in a bedroom! Then put it aside.

She stroked the old woman's hair. The old woman cried. So she stroked the old woman's cheeks too, she stroked the tears away.

'You can stay as long as you need,' the old woman said, and the teenager nodded.

*

The next day the teenager brought to the flat three heavy bags of shopping. The lifts were out, so she'd had to climb all the way up, but she wasn't even out of breath, how strong the young are. And she'd bought eggs and sausages and fresh vegetables and those bits of chicken that had cheese and bacon in, and doughnuts fat with jam. The old woman wondered where she'd got the money. And that night the teenager made her little family a feast.

The baby took to the teenager right away, she reached out her arms for her whenever the girl came near. And the teenager would reach out her arms too, and sweep up the baby within them, close to her flat chest, and the baby would thrill with excitement, and then the teenager would raise the baby high above her head, and the baby would *squeal*. And the old woman would wonder why she'd never thought to do that to the baby, the baby loved it so – but she didn't think she'd better start, it was the teenager's thing. And she supposed she ought to feel jealous, but she wasn't jealous.

And the teenager slept in the bedroom, and the old woman on the settee in the sitting room, and the old woman supposed she ought to mind, but she didn't mind. The old woman slept with the baby in her arms. And one night the teenager came for the baby; without a word she opened her arms for her, and the baby opened hers, and the old woman simply released her to the young girl's care. The girl took the baby into the bedroom with her. And once they were asleep, the old woman went to see. She stood over them, she stood there for quite a while. The teenager holding the baby tight (but not too tight) and both of them were so young, and so fresh, like little sisters cuddling. And she supposed she ought to stop them, she supposed she ought to put a stop to this all right now before it was too late and before she wasn't needed and before she was lost forever, but she didn't.

One night the teenager came for her.

'What is it?' asked the old woman. 'What do you want?' The teenager crooked one finger, and smiled. 'No, I don't know what you want.' The teenager took her by the hand.

In the bedroom the teenager took off her clothes. And the old woman looked at her. The breasts not quite filled out, the child's skin. A little girl pretending to be so grown-up.

'Please,' said the old woman. 'May I?' And she approached her. The teenager didn't flinch. 'Hold still, open wide.' And she wiped away all the make-up, all the lipstick and rouge, all that gunk.

She saw it now, how vulnerable the teenager was underneath, how much she needed rescuing (like Philip had said – oh God, she remembered that too, oh God).

The old woman took off her clothes too. She hadn't bothered to look at her own body for a very long time. She did so now. It wasn't quite as bad as she'd thought.

The teenager lay on the bed. She held the baby in her arms. And the old woman held the teenager. It felt funny to have your arms around yourselves. Spooning yourselves to sleep.

*

It became obvious that the teenager was pregnant. That swelling tummy, the old woman had been trying to ignore it. It couldn't just be down to the doughnuts.

'It's going to be all right,' she told the teenager, and the teenager nodded happily, of course it was. 'We'll look after it.' Yes, of course. And the one-year-old baby smiled, she was going to be an *aunt*.

*

One night in bed the old woman began to cry. She couldn't help it. The sound of it woke the teenager and the baby. She didn't want to wake the teenager, she needed her strength, she didn't want to wake the baby, she needed strength too – everyone needed strength but her. 'I'm sorry,' she said.

The teenager turned the bedside lamp on, and looked at her.

'It'll be my birthday soon,' said the old woman. 'You want me now. You put up with me now, even though I'm so old. But soon, soon, I'll be different, I'll be even older. What will you do with me? What will you do when I shed my skin?'

And the teenager spoke, and she never spoke. She said, 'Ssh now,' and she said, 'Quiet, baby,' and she said, 'I love you, I'll always love you, I love you, baby mine.' And she kissed the old woman on the lips, and the old woman kissed her back. They kissed for hours, and they kissed all over, and the old woman didn't care whether the girl licked her brain, she wanted to be licked everywhere. And then, when they were exhausted at last, they held the one-year-old between them, she lay against the girl's swollen stomach, baby against baby, and the old woman smiled, and the teenager smiled the very same smile. 'It's going to be all right,' they said. And it was.

28

The young woman picked out the teenager with the flashlight. She wasn't difficult to find. Her other selves were huddled away from her. The teenager still looked confused, her mouth frozen into a little 'o', still trying to work out what had happened to her.

'Come here,' said the young woman gently. 'Come to me.' And the teenager staggered forward. She leaned upon a supporting beam. She panted a bit, as if trying to summon up the breath to speak. She licked at her teeth, her braces, in awful hesitation.

'Don't,' said the young woman. 'It's going to be all right.' The teenager shut her mouth gratefully.

'I just want you to know,' said the young woman, 'that I don't blame you for any of this. None of this is your fault. But,' and that 'but' was like a whipcrack, and the teenager couldn't help but look alarmed, 'but I need you to come with me. Right now.'

The teenager moved towards the hatch.

So did all her other selves.

'No,' said the young woman. 'Just her. I only want her.'

But her other selves couldn't, or wouldn't, understand.

'Please help me,' said the young woman to the teen. 'It's only you I need. Help me.' And she added, a little waspishly, 'don't you owe me that at least?'

The teenager thought. Then nodded. Then beat her face hard against the beam.

It caught the young woman quite by surprise, and she hadn't time to flinch from the shared pain.

She shone the flashlight back on the teenager's face. The nose looked out of shape, and there was blood – the young woman had sometimes wondered whether those puppets of hers had blood in them, and now she knew. 'No,' she said, 'what are you...?' But it was too late, the teenager beat her head again.

The wave of pain caused the woman to stumble, she nearly fell through the hatch.

More blood. And the teenager was smiling – smiling at her, in *encouragement*. This is the way, that broken smile said, this is the way it has to be.

So the young woman beat her. And there was no anger to it, not at first, because that wasn't the idea of it – but she thought of her husband wanking over the girl, and the girl not even trying to resist, *accepting* it, *letting it happen* – and that made the punches easier. She hit her around the head, and then kicked at her when she was down. The other selves didn't try to stop her, but they were wailing now, now screaming with pain and with something that seemed a lot worse than pain, more *personal* – and the young woman felt it too, but she had to ignore it, she had to keep kicking.

And the teenager was unconscious, at last – and in a second the wailing stopped, as if a switch had been flicked and the sound put on mute – and the young woman looked at them (she hadn't dared before, not while they were making that terrible noise) and they seemed to have lost interest, they were milling around listlessly as if nothing had happened.

The link between them and the teenager had been severed, and no-one cared as the young woman dragged her body to the open hatch and out on to the stepladder. The woman couldn't carry her – this was a girl before the doughnuts and the cider, before she'd let herself go, before she'd said sod it and accepted the defeat of early middle age – but she was too heavy nonetheless. The woman tried to get the girl's feet on to the ladder, but the limbs wouldn't do what they were supposed to, and she *dropped* her. The teenager dropped like a sack of potatoes down the stepladder and crashed on to the landing below. 'I'm sorry,' the woman called down – but maybe the girl wouldn't have felt it, she was unconscious already.

The young woman sponged the blood off the teenager's face. 'There, there,' she said, as the teenager slept. The girl had lost one of her front teeth. A piece of untethered wire from her braces bent out from the gap quizzically, as if looking for something to hang on to.

The teenager woke up, and managed to blink at her older self through her swollen face. 'You're such a brave girl,' said the woman. 'And no-one's ever going to hurt you again.' She stroked the girl's hair, the girl's cheeks, and the girl closed her eyes at the touch, she nuzzled into the palm like a cat. 'And none of this is your fault. But I need you to listen.'

The teenager gave an impression that she was listening.

'I love Philip. You love him too, don't you, you understand? I'd loved him by your age, hadn't I? And I need him. I need him more than I need you. And I have to believe in him, even though I know he's wrong. I can't let what he did to you come between us. I need to forget. And I can't forget if you're here.'

The young woman opened the front door. She pulled the teenager to her feet. She pushed her outside. 'I never want to see you again,' she said.

The woman had hoped that she might forget quite quickly. But she didn't. Not only could she not forget what Philip had done to her teenaged self, she couldn't forget the beating she'd given herself either. A cup of tea, a little light housework, another cup of tea, no. Nothing could drive those memories from her mind.

When she at last looked out of the window she found out why.

'No, no,' she said to the teenager, as she opened the front door. 'I need you to go. I need you to go far away. You can't just hang about the garden forever. What would the neighbours think?'

The teenager looked at her. Frowned in confusion.

The young woman tutted. 'Oh, for God's sake.' She fetched the car keys. 'Come on, then.'

She let the teenager ride in the front beside her. The teenager wanted the window open; she liked to stick her head out into the wind, and the young woman didn't like her doing that, it made her look like a dog, but she didn't have the heart to refuse. The woman chatted to the girl. She put the radio on, it was good to hear some noise back.

Halfway up the M1, they stopped off at a service station. 'I want a doughnut,' said the woman, 'do you want a doughnut? Let me get you a doughnut.' The doughnuts weren't very good, there wasn't much jam in them at all, the woman was a bit disappointed. But the teenager still managed to get jam all down her face, the woman had to ask her to hold still while she wiped the sticky red gunk away. The woman bought herself a coffee. 'Would you like a cider?' she asked the teenager, she seemed to remember she'd once liked cider. The man at the till wouldn't serve her a cider. 'Can I see your daughter's ID, please?' he asked. The woman told him the teenager wasn't her daughter. The man didn't seem to think that made much difference. 'I'm sorry, madam, I can't serve alcohol to children.' And the young woman tried to explain that the girl wasn't a child, not for all her braces and her youth and such sweet-looking innocence, the things she'd seen, the things she'd done. But the man was adamant. So the young woman bought the teenager an apple juice instead, it was the closest she could get. 'You'll have to pretend,' she told her.

At last she thought they'd driven far enough. 'This looks nice,' she said, as they pulled up to a hotel. And the hotel *was* nice, it had four stars. The room was nice, it had a television and a toilet. The teenager was tired, she lay down upon the bed, spreadeagled across it like a starfish. The woman read to her from the information booklet on the dresser, it came in a nice faux leather folder. 'You can phone down for room service if you're hungry. And there's a pool, and a sauna, and a jacuzzi! There's even a hairdresser's here, you know, for your hair, that's nice.' The teenager didn't argue with her. 'It's all on my mastercard, so you're all right,' the woman assured her. 'You check out next Friday, that's the best I can do.'

She went back home.

But even 250 miles away, even with a complimentary hairdresser, the teenager wouldn't let the woman forget. The memories throbbed in the woman's head like toothache.

The woman had to take another day off work. She drove all the way back to the hotel. She had the receptionist let her into the teenager's room. The teenager was still spreadeagled on the bed like a starfish. 'I don't think you're playing fair,' the woman said.

They checked out of the hotel. They got back into the car. And they drove on together, into the night, and the darkness.

*

She stopped the car on the hard shoulder. 'Get out,' she said.

They climbed up the grassy bank. 'Through there, through the trees,' she ordered. The woman shone the flashlight at her, so she could find her way.

They walked for a while. Far enough that the woman couldn't hear the sound of traffic any more. All she could hear was the girl kicking her way idly through the leaves, and it sounded to her like waves crashing upon a coast – and she had to flash the torch straight down at the ground to check that they really weren't walking upon water.

She felt numb. They could have been on water, they might have been drenched, she wouldn't have known. 'Stop,' she said.

The teenager turned around. Her face was placid, hardly even expectant. The woman shone the light away from that face.

'You just don't take the hint, do you?' she said. 'You just don't get it. I want you gone. You're making me do this.' She took out the knife. She wondered if the teenager could see it. She wondered if she should shine the light on the knife, make it a bit more obvious. She wasn't sure whether this would do more harm than good. 'You've ruined my marriage. You little slapper. You slut, you're to blame for all of this, it's all your fault. Why don't you just fuck off?'

The woman shone the light on the teenager, just to see whether there was any reaction to this. The teenager stared into the light, straight at the woman, straight at where the accusations had come from. The face was the same. The expression was the same. And that was somehow too horrible, that all that venom and despair hadn't made the slightest difference to her, and the woman turned the light back down to the leaves once again and her cheeks were burning with something like embarrassment.

She weighed the knife in her hand. She wished she hadn't brought a knife. She wished she'd brought something else to do the job. But she couldn't put the knife away now, could she? That would look silly. That would look as if she didn't know what to do. But she didn't even think she was holding the knife right, she was gripping it too hard, it was sweaty in her hands, she probably looked so awkward – and she cursed the girl for reducing her to this, stupid fucking girl for making her stand in a forest in the dark holding a knife and getting it all wrong.

She wished the girl would say something. And then, against all hope, she did.

'All right,' said the girl, 'if that's what you want.' She whispered, but the words seemed loud in the still. And, shocked, the woman brought the light up to the girl's face, but she missed the movement of her jaws – all she caught (she thought) was the dying moments of a smile.

And the girl turned around, and she walked away. The woman tried to follow her with the torch, but soon she was lost in the blackness. Soon she couldn't even hear the sound of kicked leaves and ocean spray.

She wondered then what she was doing out there in the cold and the dark. She wondered why she was shaking. She wondered why she was carrying a knife. She didn't like the knife. She threw it away.

It took her an hour to find the motorway again. And another hour to find where she'd parked her car.

*

When she got home, she expected Philip to be there waiting for her. She phoned him on his mobile. 'Where are you?' she said. 'I need you!'

'But do you know?' he said. 'Do you still know?'

'All I know is I love you, and I want you here.' He was back at the house within ten minutes. And he wrapped her tight in his arms. And she told him never to leave her again, not for anything, and he assured her he wasn't going to go anywhere.

And so she forgot.

But not forever.

14

They played ABBA at the school disco, and it was new to the teenager. Even though it wasn't new to the other children, who all groaned and cat-called when it was turned on. She quickly realised that to fit in she'd have to cat-call too, by the time 'Mamma Mia' was booming out she was cat-calling with the best of them.

The dining hall had been cleared, all of the chairs and tables were stacked away. And the wooden floor was covered with a thick rug that bunched up into air bubbles if you dragged your feet along it. There were teachers there, of course, but they were being discreet, they were hiding away so that the children could have their fun. Not that there was much fun on display – most of the kids clung to the sides of the room, not wanting to step one foot on to that ersatz dance floor. But from time to time some might find courage, a song would come on they would recognise and didn't think was too naff – and they'd shuffle into the centre of the hall, and there they'd sashay clumsily back and forth, not looking at anyone, not wanting to meet anyone's eyes. Prefects served orange squash at the entrance; it cost 50p a plastic cup.

It was obvious to the teenager how miserable all her classmates were. She wondered why it wasn't obvious to them.

She was approached by a girl whose name she'd forgotten. 'Do you want to dance?' she asked.

The teenager thought about it. 'Yes, all right.'

The girl laughed. 'You'll be dancing on your own, then, because no-one'll dance with you, freak.'

This seemed like good advice well intended. So the teenager got up, she went right to the centre of the dance floor. There was a song playing that seemed to be about Vienna, but she couldn't make out the lyrics, there was too much distortion from the speakers – she caught the word 'Vienna' every once in a while, but what opinion was being offered about the city she had no idea. She jumped about a bit. She clapped her hands, then waved them above her head. She spun around one way, then another, and that made her dizzy, so she resorted to the jumping again. The song was quite slow, but that was no good, the teenager wanted to dance fast, so she decided to ignore the music altogether and just listen to the sound of all that blood rushing in her head, splashing about as she threw her body around, splashing about more violently the more violently she bopped, and bopping about more violently the more violent the splashing, it was a vicious circle, really.

Then she felt tired, and a bit thirsty, so she bought some orange squash. This time a whole *group* of girls approached her, and she'd forgotten their names too, each and every one. 'You dance like a spastic,' one of them said. And the teenager didn't mind, because her dancing probably had been quite poor, and at least they hadn't criticised her make-up. Her make-up was good, all that practice hadn't been for nothing.

One of the bigger boys spoke to her. 'Do you want to go outside?'

'What's outside?'

He grinned. 'Do you want to snog?'

'Okay.'

She fetched her coat from the cloakroom. When she put it on, she discovered someone had put a letter in her pocket. She read it. 'We don't want you here,' the letter began. She read it, the whole thing, then folded it up carefully, put it away.

She found the boy outside the kitchens, by the big cylinder dustbins the dinner ladies used to chuck away all the leftovers. They smelled of cabbage. 'Do you want a drink?' he asked.

'Okay.'

He took from his duffle bag a plastic bottle. He swigged from it first, wiped the neck dry with his sleeve. She swigged too. It tasted sort of apple-y.

Then he snogged her.

She opened her mouth so wide to let him in that she could feel all the layers of make-up shift and crack like tectonic plates.

And they weren't alone – they were being watched – and she suddenly understood that this was a dare, or maybe a bet. As their mouths closed around each other she heard a few gasps, a few whoops, some admiring applause that seemed almost respectful. And she didn't mind, she decided to put all this down to experience, so what if it wasn't love, the sort of love she'd once seen between Mummy and Daddy long long ago before she got too old and ruined it all? But snogging was odd, definitely *odd* – there was something alive in her mouth, wriggling away like a big fat worm. And she was used to having things alive in her mouth, if she concentrated she could actually feel the individual teeth, the gums, her own tongue, as separate entities altogether, as things growing and breathing somehow independent of her. But this wasn't her tongue, it was an alien, and it was exploring, it was racing around her mouth like a hyperactive toddler. She remembered quite clearly being a hyperactive toddler, and this tongue was just like that, naughty, naughty, it'll knock something over! The enamel of her teeth, the metal of her wire braces – and the strange encounter of fleshy tongue meeting fleshy tongue, so alike and yet so different, what could these foreign tongues ever find to say to each other? And now it was pushing, pushing upwards – and the teenager felt her first stab of real fear –

– Because she doubted suddenly that her mouth was ready yet for this, maybe it hadn't hardened enough. She'd only shed her skin so very recently, and oh, she could feel the tongue now thrusting away, and now bursting through the upper palate, and driving up through the jaw, oh into the skull itself. Dear God, it wasn't going to slow down, it was on a collision course for her *brain*, he wanted to lick her very brain...

She tried to ask him to stop, but it was so hard to speak coherently when there was a tongue the size of the world in her mouth. She tried to push him away, push his shoulders – but he had so many, didn't he, how could he have grown so many shoulders since she'd last looked?

So she bit down.

'Fuck!' he said, as he at last disengaged. There was a spray of blood, and some of it was his, and some of it was probably hers, the hole he must have drilled into her mouth felt coppery and wet. He pushed her to the ground. 'Cunt!' he said, and it was a word he didn't know the meaning of, it was just a word he'd picked up from his dad.

'Leave her alone,' said another boy. He'd been one of those watching, one of those laughing and whooping and urging him on.

'She git my tug,' said the kisser.

'Yeah, but leave her alone.' This boy was half the kisser's size, and he was scared. And the kisser considered whether or not to hit him, you could see the very process of that decision working across his face. He decided not to. He couldn't be bothered. So he spat blood, and maybe it wasn't specifically directed at the teenage girl but it hit her anyway, and he walked off, and the crowd dispersed.

The teenager wondered whether she'd like another orange squash now. It'd take away the taste of copper. But it'd also take away the taste of apple, and she liked that, so she thought she'd leave things the way they were. And she decided to go home.

She was hardly out of the school gates before the shorter boy caught up with her. 'Hey!' he called. 'Wait up!'

'I've had enough dancing now,' she said.

'Let me walk you home. Can I walk you home?'

'Why?'

'To protect you. You know. In case Gordon comes after you.' So that had been what the kisser had been called, yes, Gordon, good at history, bad at maths, she remembered now. And she wanted to tell this boy not to bother, she didn't need protecting from anyone called Gordon, it wasn't a very intimidating name. But instead she said all right.

Most of the time they walked in silence. 'My name's Philip,' he said, 'by the way.'

'I'm not telling you my name.'

'I already know your name. Everyone knows your name. You stand out. You're special.'

She said, 'It's not always very nice to be special.' And she supposed he could have said something reassuring then, something kind. But he didn't. But nor did he say anything rude or hurtful, and that was good enough.

Eventually she said, 'This is where I live.' She stood outside the driveway.

'I'm sorry about tonight,' he said.

'That's okay.'

'I'll see you at school?'

'I suppose.'

'All right.' And she wondered whether he was going to kiss her.

He didn't touch her at all. Instead he just stood there for a while, looking at her. And she wished he'd go, then – and then he smiled, and he said, 'I'm always going to remember you this way. Vulnerable. And sweet. Like this.'

She frowned. 'Why would you remember me?'

He leaned forward – and she thought, this was it, another kiss, and she prepared to bite in readiness. But the lips just brushed her forehead, that was all. 'Well, good night.'

'I don't live here,' she said.

'Oh.'

'This is someone else's house.'

'Okay.'

'I live the other side of town. You can walk me there instead, if you like.'

It took another half hour to get to the right house. And he never asked why she'd tried to deceive him like that. And he didn't kiss her forehead again, but he still seemed friendly enough, and smiled when he said goodbye.

Mummy was there when she got in. 'Oh,' she said, starting from the settee. 'You're back earlier than I expected.'

'Yes.'

'I'll go.'

'No. Please, Mummy. Don't.'

'No, I'll go. I'll go. Well.'

'I had a good time. There was dancing and music. And I made lots of friends. And there was cake, and jelly, and sausage rolls.'

Mummy nodded, unsmiling.

'I love you,' said the teenager.

'Yes, I love you too,' said Mummy, and she went up the stairs, as fast as she could without running, and she locked her bedroom door.

The teenager made herself some tea. She was hungry. The orange squash hadn't been filling at all. She hadn't liked the orange squash. In fact, she hated it. In fact, she'd like to stamp on it, and kick it over, and crush it, and crush all the people who drank it, the fucking cunting thing. And she was so angry thinking about it, how much orange squash there was in the world, and all the people putting it in their mouths, filling their mouths with it, that she wasn't very careful with the knife as she made her sandwich, she cut her finger very deep, there was blood everywhere, she thought the finger might fall off.

She called up to Mummy. She asked her if she wanted a sandwich too. She had made so many, she couldn't eat them all! But her Mummy didn't answer.

She took out the note from her coat pocket.

'We don't want you here. You're not like us. You'll never be like us. And we outnumber you, we always will. We'll get you. You wait, we'll get you. Why won't you just fuck off?'

She opened it out neatly, smoothed over the folds. And left it outside her mother's room.

The mother stayed two more nights, but the teenager never saw her. And she was gone by the weekend.

7

And after all that, after the party was done, and the celebrations were over, after the plates of cake and the bowls of jelly had been cleared away – now, at last, it was time for the little girl to shed her skin. 'Get the scissors, Mummy!' said Daddy, and 'Get the scissors, Daddy!' said Mummy, and the little girl laughed so hard, Mummy and Daddy were both so excited they couldn't work out just *what* they were supposed to do! And she was excited as well. Of course she was. And just a little bit scared, she could feel her new seven-year-old self itching under her six-year-old skin. She didn't want this old skin now, she wanted rid of it. 'Quickly, please!' she said to her parents, 'I don't mind which of you fetches the scissors, but do it quickly!', and she blushed, because she wasn't an impatient girl, but it was ready to come out now, she wanted to grow *up*, couldn't they all just get *on* with it! 'Hold still, kiddo,' said Daddy, and the little girl held still, and he steadied the scissors, and he made a little puncture in the skin, right in the back of the neck where no-one could see it, and the little girl giggled, the scissor blades were so cold and they *tickled* so funnily! And off came the skin and the bones and the organs, and 'Oh God,' said Daddy, 'oh fuck,' and she could see him bite his tongue, because he'd said a bad word, but there was blood, there was so much blood, there hadn't been blood before, they hadn't even needed to put newspaper down on the carpet. And there was pain too, oh yes, but not until Daddy said the bad word, it was almost as if the little girl refused to believe there was anything wrong until she saw the expressions on her Mummy and Daddy's faces, but now she had to admit it, yes, that burning feeling running over her entire body, that wasn't *good*, was it? And the pain was new as well, as new as the blood, and it occurred to the little girl that the two were therefore probably related, pain equals blood, blood equals pain, she'd remember that in future, good, she only wanted information – and it also occurred to her, just seconds afterwards, that the one making all the noise was her, high-pitched and tearful, that was *her*, who would have thought it? Because the very *air* seemed to sting against her coarse skin, the air cut into it and through it and got under it and made it flap. 'Call a doctor!' said Mummy, and Daddy said, 'What would we say, how would we explain *this*?' And Mummy didn't know, so they didn't mention a doctor again, but she did go off and fetch newspaper to cover the carpet, that at least was a help. And then she got down the Big Book, she sat far away and began looking through it, and the little girl wasn't sure why, maybe there were some answers there in the back. Daddy tried to keep her from looking in the mirror but the little girl liked looking in the mirror, and it was her *birthday*, she got what she *wanted*, she looked in the mirror at her seven-year-old body dripping off her rough hewn frame and she didn't like it, quite; all her other bodies had been so pink and shiny and smooth, and this new one was knobbled and bones shards were sticking out and little bubbles kept swelling then popping on the surface. And the bubbles at least were funny, but the little girl didn't like the smell they gave off. And she was so *hot*. 'Oh, kiddo,' said Daddy, 'I'm so sorry,' and he held out his arms for her, he was going to hug her – and then he thought better of it, and the little girl supposed it was good he had, even the thought of Daddy pressing his body all against her (his cool, solid, *normal* body) made her wince – but she was disappointed all the same. Mummy kept reading the Big Book, and she was muttering, was she reading it out loud?, there was nothing to be done with her. 'Am I going to die?' asked the little girl, and it was an entirely new idea, she'd never had an idea like that before – and that was just one other new thing about being seven years old, fancy! – and Daddy said he didn't know

and then

Mummy said they had to get rid of all the other little girls, because there were so many of them now, too many, and they were all staring at her, as if she were to blame, it was putting her off the Big Book, enough was enough, enough was enough! And Daddy said he had his hands full at the moment, he was up to his knees in guts here, couldn't she do something to help rather than just sit there with her Big Book, and Mummy huffed at this, and said, fine, *she'd* get the key to the attic then, where was it? and the little girl did wish her Mummy and Daddy wouldn't argue and would give her some attention instead because she was so scared now and thought she was about to die but Mummy and Daddy weren't looking at her now, they seemed to be *enjoying* having something else to talk about. And Daddy said the key was under the big vase under the kitchen table. And Mummy went to fetch the key. And Mummy brought it back. And Mummy gave it to Daddy. So Daddy led all the puppets up to the attic, and there were six of them now, and the sixth looked so unhappy and afraid, and the little girl wanted to wave at her, tell her it was going to be all right – but then, she wasn't sure it *was* going to be all right, really, was she?, she didn't want to corrupt her brand new body with telling a lie. And the six-year-old had nothing to be unhappy about, not with that clear skin and pale flesh, what was the problem? And she had a lovely new pink dress, with pink bows and pink stuff, so much pink, God, some people didn't know how lucky they were, and besides, she couldn't wave, waving would have hurt so much, waving might cause her hand to fall off

and then

they didn't lock her bedroom door that night, Mummy and Daddy took turns watching over her. 'I'll be here while you sleep, kiddo,' but it was absurd to think she'd get to sleep, even her weight on the bed hurt so bad. But maybe she *did* sleep, and maybe she did dream. Because at length she heard noises from the attic above. Knock knock *knock* – and it was so loud, she thought the puppets were stamping up there, she thought they sounded so desperate, she thought they'd break through the floorboards – but Daddy didn't seem to hear, Daddy was snoring. Daddy's fallen asleep on the job, kiddo. So the little girl got up, and she left her bedroom – and she hadn't done that unsupervised for such a long time, to be free to walk around the house as she chose! – and if it hadn't been quite so very agonising she would have been very happy. But she saw herself in the mirror, and she thought her skin was starting to pink, it was going to be all right, everything was going to be all right! Knock knock *knock* – and she thought it *must* wake Mummy and Daddy, such a racket! – so maybe it was all in her head. So she went downstairs to the kitchen, she fetched the key from underneath the vase. And she went to the attic, she pulled down the stepladder, very carefully, very quietly, though if the knocking hadn't woken up her parents she didn't see why the creak of the ladder would – knock knock *knock*, yes, I'm coming, *knock knock knock knock knock*, yes yes. She opened up the hatch, and climbed into the attic, and only then realised she'd forgotten the flashlight, it'd be dark up there, she'd have to go all the way back to the kitchen again, and it was such a long way, she wasn't sure she could stand it! – but no, no, it *wasn't* dark at all, the attic was bathed in a warm red light. And she realised it was the glow of her own new raw flesh. 'What do you want?' the little girl asked her other selves, and they took her by both hands, they pulled her forward – and it didn't hurt, their touch was cool and comforting. And they took her to the very back of the attic, and there were spiders back there the girl thought, some as big as your head (maybe) but she went anyway. And there was a door. Just a small door, a wooden door, an unassuming door. She hesitated. The little girls nodded. The little girls smiled, they pointed at the door, they nodded, they smiled, they nodded, they seemed so eager, they nodded and smiled, their heads nodding faster and faster now, blurring with the speed, all the little girl could see was their smiles as their other features were lost, open the door, open the door. So she opened the door. And inside was a room – impossible, because it was at the very edge of the house, there was no house left to put a room in – but no-one seemed to have told the room that, it was large, *so* large – and the little girl stepped inside. And it was full of women, she'd never seen so many, there must be a hundred of them! – and little girls too, some of them hardly any bigger than she was – and older women, some of them with pinched faces, and disappointed faces, and flab. And there, in the centre of them all, was a *very* old woman, an *ancient* woman, a crone. And she was in a rocking chair. She rocked back and forth and at each rocking there was a creak, a creak so loud it was almost painful to the ear – and the little girl wondered why she'd not been able to hear it downstairs, it cut through the hush of the room, it cut through everything. Except – no – it wasn't a rocking chair. It was a chair that was being *rocked* – grasping the legs of it, and tipping it backwards and forwards, there were a dozen hands, all from women of different ages, all shaking the old woman. All shaking the old woman awake. And the old woman looked so dead, and her eyes were glassy, and her teeth were black. 'Remember this,' the girl heard, and one of the women was speaking, and she couldn't tell which one – she darted her eyes across them all, but each time she did their mouths had just shut – 'remember, if we keep her awake, we stay alive. We stay alive forever.' The crone looked so frail, just one gust of wind would blow that old skin across the room like ash – 'Remember,' they said, 'remember.' And the little girl promised she would remember, she'd keep her older self alive no matter what it took, no matter the pain and the despair that she'd drag her future bodies through, whatever the cost, she'd stay alive forever, they'd all stay alive forever, even up here in the attic in the dark with no-one there to see – even up here in the attic in the dark with no hope of doing anything or saying anything or making anything worthwhile – because they were special, they were all special, they were so, so special – and she turned back to find her way out, but she couldn't find the door, the exit had got lost amidst all those greedy life-hungry bodies, amidst all that future that she had yet to live.

A few days after the birth my wife came home, and she brought with her that little baby girl of hers. We put the baby in a cot in the spare room; I promised I would paint the walls with something bright or pink, or maybe hang up some nice paper with fairy tale princesses on. Just as soon as the baby would be old enough to appreciate it, I wouldn't waste my time before then. And my wife lay next to me in bed, still with that huge mound of a belly, and it felt strange there was no longer any life in it, it was just a hollow cavern. And she told me how happy she was to be back safe in her own house once more, she'd been having such bad dreams. **1102** – Dobroslav III becomes the king of Duklja (modern day Serbia). He is promptly deposed, castrated and blinded. **1105** – In spite of his barefoot penitent walk to Canossa (qv 1077), Holy Roman Emperor Henry IV has been excommunicated once more – this time, by another pope. His son Henry rebels against him in protest, claiming he owes no allegiance to king or father who has been disowned by the church. At a supposed reconciliation meeting in Koblenz, the emperor is deposed and imprisoned, and Henry V takes the throne. **1106** – Robert, Duke of Normandy, is defeated at the battle of Tinchebrai by his brother, King Henry I of England. He spends the next twenty-eight years of his life imprisoned. **1108** – At the battle of Ucles, the Spanish Christian forces under Alfonso VI are utterly crushed by the Muslim Almoravids. Many of the high nobility of Leon die in the encounter, either killed in battle or beheaded afterwards – and Sancho, the heir apparent, is murdered by villagers while attempting to flee. *She dreamed she'd woken up in the hospital – and she was alone there in the dark, and she reached for her baby, but the baby wasn't there, it had been taken away, and she wanted her baby, she wanted her little girl. So she'd called for a nurse. No-one came. She reached for the light, she said it was such an effort to pull the cord, it seemed now so high above her head, as if someone teasingly had hung it out of reach – she had to strain herself upwards, she felt her newly vacated body baulk at the effort – and her fingers grasped it, she held on tight, she yanked it downwards. No light came on. She pulled at it again, but there was no give in that cord. She had to get out of bed, she had to swing her legs over the side of the bed, she had to find her slippers, it seemed suddenly terribly important to her that she found her slippers – and there they were, by the cabinet, she gasped with relief, for a moment she felt she'd got what she wanted, she could go back to sleep now, all was well. Oh no, not the slippers, the baby, she was looking for the baby, the slippers had simply been a means to finding the baby, they weren't the end result. And she told me she suddenly felt so disgusted at the slippers for letting her down that she didn't put them on after all, and barefoot she stumbled towards the door.* **1109** – Holy Roman Emperor Henry V is routed in battle in Poland. It is said that so many corpses are left behind that the area is overrun with savage dogs intent on feasting upon them. The conflict is thus remembered as the battle of 'Dog's Field', or Hundsfeld. **1109** – In response, Henry attempts to take the city of Glogow, which is sheltering Boleslaw, the king of Poland. He forces the citizens to give up their children as hostages as guarantors of a five day ceasefire, which is the king's ultimatum to surrender. He promises the children will be returned unharmed, whatever Boleslaw's decision. At the end of the five days he lays siege to Glogow, and chains his hostages to the siege engines, in the expectation the Poles will be unable to fire upon their own children. King Henry is defeated, and driven out of Poland. And there stands a monument today in Glogow which proudly lists the names of all the children who perished in the ensuing battle. **1109** – The Principality of Nitra vanishes from the map once the Hungarians depose its final ruler. **1110** – In Italy, the 'Anatomia Porci', a study of pig dissection, is presented at the Salerno medical school. **1111** – Henry V marches on Rome and forces the pontiff to crown him Holy Roman Emperor. Once he's free again, the pope excommunicates him – leaving Henry in the same outcast position from which he was able to sentence and depose his own father. **1112** – In France, the people of Laon declare themselves a commune, and murder their bishop. **1115** – Arnulf of Chocques, the Latin Patriarch of Jerusalem, is deposed from his position for having sexual relations with a Muslim woman. **1117** – In Santiago de Compostela, the people revolt and try to burn their prelate alive in his own palace. *She opened the door, and saw that it was just as dark in the corridor outside – had the hospital had a power cut? Didn't they have back-up generators, what about all those people on life support? (What about her little baby, wouldn't she be screaming in the dark in fear, wouldn't she be screaming for her mother?) She called out for help, she called for a nurse, she called for doctors even, she jumped right up the chain of command. But no-one answered, and her voice seemed somehow to echo in the black, as if that's what black would make it do. And the echo made her voice sound so lost, pathetic. And then she heard it – what was it? – in the distance – high-pitched: scree-scree-scree, that's how my wife described it. And she went down the corridor in search of that sound, her bare feet slapping against the cold of the floor, and the slapping becoming part of the sound, scree-scree-scree-slap, scree-scree-scree, slap. And she hoped the screeing had nothing to do with her little child, but she knew that it must.* **1120** – The White Ship capsizes in the English Channel. It's the Titanic of the Middle Ages, a ship boasting all the latest technology – and all the latest arrogance – felled on its maiden voyage (qv 1628, 1912). Travelling on board is King Henry I of England's only legitimate son, who is drowned. It is said that when the captain fights his way to the surface, he chooses to let himself drown too rather than have to tell the king the bad news. Only one man survives, a butcher from Rouen, whose thick ramskin clothes prevent him from dying of exposure. It is claimed that King Henry never smiles again after the tragedy. Ironically, one man has escaped this fate, by giving up his place on the ship because of a last minute attack of diarrhoea. His name is Stephen of Blois – and, as King Stephen, will subject England to a long and bloody civil war. **1121** – Pierre Abelard, the keenest mind of the twelfth century, the pre-eminent philosopher of his age, has fallen in love with his student Heloise. Heloise's uncle has Abelard castrated. Abelard becomes a monk, and Heloise a nun. The correspondence between the two survives, comprising the most celebrated love-letters in print to this day. **1126** – Edgar Atheling, the last surviving member of 600 years of the House of Wessex, finally dies. The location of his grave is unknown. *And down long corridors, holding on the walls to keep herself steady, and the scree-scree-scree getting louder – and, at last, she saw light. She wanted to run towards it, but she didn't quite dare, and besides she was so very tired, and besides, the slow slapping of her foot against the floor was part of the rhythm to that screeing now, she couldn't break it, it would have been wrong. And even now she said, she knew this was a dream – and it didn't feel fair to be so tired in a dream, didn't that rather defeat the point of sleeping in the first place? She reached the light, and it shone from a room, so dazzling at first she couldn't see anything through the glass – the screeing as loud as it would ever be. And then she could make out what the room was – it was where the newborn babies were kept – there were rows and rows of them, all of them sleeping peacefully. And she could see too what caused the noise – there was a trolley, and each time it was pushed the wheels would scrape over the floor. And on to the trolley were tied a series of balloons, bobbing in the air – but the balloons were made of brown paper. And pushing the trolley was an old man, just a little old man, with a kind grandfatherly face, but he wasn't dressed as a doctor, he wore a cardigan and a flat cap, he looked like a caretaker. My wife saw him stand over a baby. And he'd produce* **1126** – King Louis the Fat of France reaches such a bulk that any horse he attempts to sit on buckles under the weight. *And he'd produce a plastic funnel. And he'd insert it into the sleeping baby's ear. And he'd produce a brown paper bag, and he'd attach it to the end of the funnel – and she could see him murmur something to the baby, and he was smiling gently, he was soothing it – and then the bag would inflate, it'd fill with air (air?), something was pouring out of that baby now at such a speed too, the bag became a balloon. The baby would be still the whole time, utterly unaware that this strange man was filling his bags with the contents of its head – and then, the man would tie this fresh balloon to the trolley, it bobbed about quite innocently. Then, scree-scree, as the trolley was pushed to another baby, and this baby was our baby, it was baby Annie – and, 'No!' shouted my wife, and pounded hard against the glass, but this time her voice didn't echo, it was as if this darkness had chosen to smother it to spite her – but, no, the old man looked up – he saw my wife – he hesitated – he smiled – he went to the door to let my wife in.* **1127** – The provost of the church in Bruges has Charles, Count of Flanders hacked to death while in prayer, because he opposed the profit being made upon the grain sold to the starving. **1128** – The battle of Sao Mamede establishes the nation of Portugal. And is fought by an angry teenager wanting to break free from control by his mother. **1130** – A schism in the Catholic Church erupts when Roger II of Sicily supports Anacletus II as pope rather than Innocent II. **1130** – In Norway, a man named Harald Gillekrist has arrived, claiming to be a long forgotten brother to King Sigurd. Sigurd recognises him once he's proved his legitimacy through trial by fire, but has Harald swear an oath he will not claim the throne while he or his son are still alive. When Sigurd dies, Harald breaks his promise immediately, and he is proclaimed co-ruler with the rightful heir Magnus. **1131** – The Orkney earl Harald I shares power with his half-brother Paul. Harald's mother Helga and aunt Frakok plan to kill Paul with a poisoned shirt. They neglect to tell Harald they're doing this, however, and Harald finds the nice new shirt, gets jealous of the gift, and steals it for himself. He dies in agony. **1132** – Dermot MacMurrough has the abbey of Kilare in Ireland burned to the ground, and the abbess raped. Thereafter he becomes king of Leinster, in Ireland. **1134** – Alfonso the Warrior, king of Aragon, is killed at the battle of Fraga by the Moors. **1135** – The still unsmiling Henry I of England famously dies from eating a 'surfeit of lampreys'. I read about this when I was a child, and vowed I would never eat a single lamprey, just in case a whole one ended up being considered a surfeit. I still have no idea what a lamprey is. I don't want to know. **1135** – Meanwhile, in Norway, Magnus and Harald have reigned peacefully for a while. Now war between the two breaks out. Magnus is blinded, castrated, mutilated and imprisoned in a monastery – and becomes hereafter known as Magnus the Blind. At the same time Sigurd Slembe also arrives on the scene, claiming to be *another* long lost brother to the original King Sigurd – and telling people he's already gone through the whole trial by fire thing, he won't need to do that again, thank you very much. This new Sigurd has Harald murdered in his sleep, and is declared king. **1136** – St Paul's Cathedral burns in a fire (qv 962, 1087). **1137** – Louis the Fat dies of dysentery, which if nothing else, would have solved his weight problems. **1138** – An earthquake in Aleppo, commonly listed as the third deadliest in recorded history, claims some 230,000 lives. **1139** – In Norway, the late King Harald's supporters have not accepted the usurper Sigurd, and have proclaimed that Harald's two sons are King(s) instead. The problem is, they're still infants. Sigurd frees Magnus the Blind from his monastery, and civil war between the two parties breaks out. Magnus is killed at the battle of Hvaler, and Sigurd is tortured to death. But the civil war is not ended; as soon as the infant sons grow up, they start plotting against each other, the chaos aided by *another* pretender arriving from overseas, this time claiming to be one of Harald's sons. It all becomes terribly complicated as still more sons are born, and still more pretenders emerge, and it's not until 1240 that much of Norwegian history really makes any sense. Ibsen later writes a historical play about the period. No-one can understand that either. *'Go on,' I said to my wife.* **1141** – At the battle of Lincoln, Matilda wrests the English throne from King Stephen. **1141** – Matilda is forced to give it back again. **1141** – King Bela II (the Blind), his eyes burned out by his uncle while still a child, dies from a hangover. I will resist the obvious joke about how drunk he must have been. **1144** – A twelve-year-old tanner's boy called William is murdered, and his death blamed upon the Jews, presumably for use in their blood rituals. Though no court can substantiate the accusation, it leads to widespread attacks on the Jewish population, and massacres in London and York. The hapless William is canonised as a saint. **1145** – Pope Lucius II is killed when someone throws a stone at him. **1146** – Zengi, ruler of Syria, is assassinated by a French slave. **1148** – The army of the Second Crusade lay siege to Damascus, but are forced to retreat because their water supplies are cut off. The Second Crusade dribbles to a halt. **1150** – Joscelin II, count of Edessa, is still trying to enlist help to revive the dead crusade; he is captured by the Muslims, publicly blinded, and spends his last nine years of life in the dungeons of the Citadel of Aleppo. **1151** – The first fire insurance policy is issued in Iceland. *'Keep away from my child,' my wife told the old man, and the old man told her to calm down, 'just keep away,' and the old man told her it was all right, take a deep breath, calm down. 'What's in the bags?' she demanded. 'Dreams,' he said. 'The very first dreams of the newly born. I extract them, I make them safe.' 'Dreams can inflate paper bags?' my wife asked, and the old man chuckled amiably. 'The first dream is the dangerous one. All other dreams would be built upon its foundation. And the children who keep this dream intact know who they are, and what they could be, with no doubt, with no fear. They could achieve anything, absolutely anything, they could change history.' My wife asked why he wanted the dreams removed. 'Because we don't want history changed,' he said. 'And it's for the babies' good, the babies will be so much happier this way, it's much better to be an also-ran. Their brains won't expand so fast, they won't press so tightly against the skull, their imagination won't give them so much pain. And they'll still dream, but without that first building block the dreams will have nowhere to grow, they'll falter and die, most will be forgotten by morning, and your child will grow up normal and healthy and bland.' My wife hesitated. 'It's your choice,' said the man. 'Do you want your daughter to be happy, or to be historically significant?' And my wife made her decision. And the man stuck his funnel deep into my daughter's head.* **1152** – King Louis VII returns home to France from the crusades. His wife Eleanor of Aquitaine is distressed to find that he has grown a beard during his time away. She demands he shave it off. He refuses. They quarrel. She divorces him, and marries instead the future King Henry II of England – taking her ancestral lands with her, and igniting a conflict that lasts over 300 years. **1154** – The final entry is made in the Anglo-Saxon Chronicle. **1156** – King Sverker I of Sweden is murdered on his way to church on Christmas Day. **1159** – The death of Adrian IV, the only English pope. He chokes on a fly in his wine. **1159** – Crema, in Italy, is besieged and destroyed by Holy Roman Emperor Frederick Barbarossa. **1160** – King William of Sicily loses all of his father's conquests in North Africa. **1164** – Ragnald III usurps the throne of the Isle of Man, but is killed only four days later. **1167** – The army of the 'Commune of Rome', is assembled, proudly described as the greatest military force seen in Rome for centuries. It outnumbers the forces of Frederick Barbarossa by ten to one – and yet, it's utterly defeated by them at the battle of Ponte Morzio. **1168** – The capital city of Egypt, Fustat, is set on fire by its own vizier, to prevent its riches falling into crusader hands. The city burns for fifty-four days. **1169** – Alfonso the Conqueror, founder of the kingdom of Portugal and so strong that it takes ten soldiers just to carry his sword, traps his leg in a gate. He injures his leg so badly that he can never ride a horse again. **1169** – In a peace treaty between Henry II and Louis VII, the eight-year-old Alys is betrothed to the twelve-year-old future King Richard the Lionheart. It's not the happiest of love matches, even bearing in mind that Louis is sending his daughter to live with his ex-wife Eleanor of Aquitaine. And Alys has not had the happiest of family relationships either, since she killed her own mother during her own birth. As it turns out, Richard doesn't want her – he's a homosexual – and when he *does* later marry a woman, it's not Alys he plumps for, and does so while still technically engaged to her. No-one's quite sure what to do with the little princess, until King Henry eventually takes his son's fiancée as a lover himself – and after his death, she is passed on to Prince John. But Eleanor opposes the match between Alys and John, possibly because she doesn't want her husband's mistress and son's reject and ex-husband's daughter in the family. Who can tell? *I think I hated my wife that night. I stroked her hair for comfort, all the time she told me her story. And I didn't pull it, I could have done, I kept the stroking as light and gentle as I could. But I think I hated her.* **1170** – Archbishop Thomas a Becket is murdered; angry words spoken in haste by King Henry are misinterpreted as orders for his assassination. As he is struck down in Canterbury Cathedral, Thomas prays to Alphege for guidance (qv 1012). **1170** – The Korean court is massacred by the palace guards. **1170** – The earliest recorded date for the making of cheddar cheese. **1171** – Henry II of England invades Ireland, beginning eight centuries of conflict between the two countries. **1171** – Manuel I orders all Venetians in the Byzantine Empire to be arrested, and their property confiscated. **1172** – It's John's turn to be betrothed, to form an alliance between Henry II and Umberto III, Count of Savoy. The five-year-old's bride to be is named Alicia. Before the marriage can take place, Henry's older son, Henry, jealous of the castles given to the couple as a wedding gift, stages a rebellion. It takes two years for the rebellion to be quashed, by which time Alicia has died. **1173** – Construction work begins on a tower in Pisa. But no matter how hard the labourers try to correct the problem, stopping and starting over two centuries, it always leans drunkenly to the right. **1174** – Prince Alexei of Vladimir is attacked in bed by twenty nobles, but he is still strong enough to beat them off. They are in retreat when they hear him moaning with pain – and decide they might as well return and finish the job. **1174** – The last king of the Toltecs commits suicide. **1175** – William de Braose, lord of Abergavenny, summons Welsh nobles to his castle to hear a royal proclamation. And kills the lot of them. The king is irritated that his name has been taken in vain, and punishes William by demoting him. **1176** – Al-Adil I, ruler of Egypt, puts down a Christian revolt, and hangs nearly 3,000 of them from trees around the city of Qift. **1176** – The first recorded eisteddfod, a festival of verse recitations, is held in Cardigan, Wales. Just what the world needs – more Welsh poetry. **1181** – 100,000 die of famine in Japan. **1182** – The Jews are expelled from Paris by order of King Philip II. **1183** – Byzantine Emperor Alexios II is strangled with a bowstring. **1185** – During the Genpei War, the three-year-old Go-Toba is made emperor of Japan when his brother Antoku is overthrown. **1187** – Muslim armies under Saladin defeat the crusaders at the battle of Hattin. On hearing the news, pope Urban III dies of grief. **1188** – The Sultan of Rum dies, and divides his kingdom among his eleven sons. Because that always works. **1188** – Alfonso IX becomes king of Leon; he is nicknamed 'the Slobberer', from his habit of spitting foam from his mouth whenever he is angry. He is angry quite a lot. **1190** – Frederick Barbarossa is thrown from his horse crossing an ice cold river in Anatolia. The water is only waist deep, but he is so weighted down by his armour that he drowns. Legends state that Frederick is not dead, but still only sleeping – and will wake when Germany is to be restored to full glory. *And that night I had a dream too. And I saw the old man. And I realised what my wife hadn't – that he smelled so stale, that his smile was a leer, that his eyes were hard and set. And his fingers – his fingers weren't fingers – they weren't fingers, they were fat worms wriggling and nibbling and gorging upon the stumps of his hand. 'Give my baby back her dream,' I told him. 'It won't make her happy,' he said. 'I don't care.' 'It will give her pain.' 'I don't care.' 'She won't love you for it.' 'I don't care, do you hear, I don't care. Make her special, I don't care.' And I woke up to the sound of my daughter next door crying in her cot. 'I'll check her, you go back to sleep,' I told my wife. 'Thank you, darling,' she said, 'I'm so very tired.'* **1191** – Monks at Glastonbury Abbey proclaim they have discovered the burial site for King Arthur and Queen Guinevere. They lie beneath two stone pyramids which mark the spot – why no-one else thought to look there before is a mystery. The remains are later moved and lost during the Reformation. **1191** – Acre falls to the crusaders, under Richard the Lionheart. He has beheaded the entire Saracen garrison, one by one,all 2600 of them, the execution site awash with blood. The operation takes three days. **1192** – On his way back to England, Richard is captured. A ransom of 150,000 marks is demanded (about three times the annual income of the English crown). Eleanor has her subjects taxed to death, while Prince John secretly offers 80,000 marks if his brother can just be left where he is. **1192** – Conrad I, King of Jerusalem, is assassinated only days after his election to the throne is confirmed. **1193** – On the day of his marriage to Ingeborg, Philip II of France changes his mind, and tries to have his bride sent back to Denmark. He hires men to draw up false family trees to convince the pope that he is already related to Ingeborg. When that is rejected, Philip instead has Ingeborg imprisoned in castles all over France for the next twenty years – for an entire decade she's kept in the castle of Etambes. Still no-one knows precisely what she was supposed to have done wrong. **1196** – Philip then decides to marry Agnes instead. The pope reminds him he already has a wife, but Philip ignores him. The pope declares all children born in France must be deemed illegitimate, that until the king decides to sleep with his real wife, none of his subjects are permitted to sleep with theirs. This ban continues until 1200, so for over three years all French babies are bastards. **1199** – Richard is killed by a crossbow wound, shot by a French boy, Pierre Basile. Richard's last act is to order Basile's life be spared and grant him 100 shillings for his bravery. After Richard's dead, the soldiers flay Basile alive. **1200** – A Byzantine noble, John Komnenos (the Fat) mounts a coup to take the throne. He takes it well enough – but when he sits on it, he is so heavy that it collapses beneath his massive bulk. He is beheaded.

SOAP BUBBLE

Funnily enough, it wasn't his own parents who realised how special George Jones was, but a checkout girl at the local supermarket who was, it must be said, in all other ways wholly unperceptive. She was just scanning the barcode of a tub of baby food with the same indifference she scanned most retail goods when her face broke into a rare delighted smile. 'Is he yours?' she asked Mrs Jones, 'oh, did you see what he just did?' She called across the girl on the till nearest her, and the one next to that. 'It's really obvious when he blows out his cheeks and rolls his eyes,' she said, and sure enough, George did that very thing, and everyone laughed. By now a queue was forming behind Mrs Jones, but the general impatience was soothed when the customers could see just how special George was; at last the store manager came over to see what the problem was and get everything moving again – but not before he, too, had told Mrs Jones how impressed he was by her baby boy. 'He's remarkable,' he told her. 'You could make a wodge of cash out of that,' added the checkout girl helpfully.

Mrs Jones didn't give the matter any further thought that afternoon. She had to put the shopping away and change George's nappy and make sure he took his nap – it was a full-time job. And it wasn't until that evening, eating dinner with Mr Jones around the kitchen table, that she even remembered the incident.

'Apparently he looks like someone off the telly,' she said. 'I don't see it myself.'

Mr Jones shrugged. He didn't watch much television, not these days, not now he had to do overtime to support his growing family.

'It's Kurt Fletcher!' said Annie, with an absolute *squeal*. It was Boxing Day, and the family were visiting the Joneses; the presents had been quickly opened, and Mr and Mrs Jones hadn't got anything, everyone had put their money towards toys that their baby son couldn't possibly want. Annie was Mrs Jones' sister, a dull placid woman whose resting pose rather resembled a cow chewing cud. This squeal was the most excitement Mrs Jones had heard from Annie since they were children. 'My God, that's *incredible*. Mum, Mum! You've got to see this! You like Kurt Fletcher, don't you?'

'Yes, I'd like a bit of Kurt Fletcher,' said George's grandmother, giggling saucily and sucking through her teeth.

'Come over here,' said Annie. 'Watch George. Just watch.'

George watched impassively as the whole family surrounded him on the rug – his parents, of course, Aunt Annie and her rather fey husband Uncle Greg, his eight-year-old cousin Cindy and her younger brother Marc, Granny, and Stepgrandad. 'What are we looking at?' said Marc, pausing briefly from hitting his sister.

'Come on, Georgie, do it again,' said Annie.

And George smiled. He'd not had the slightest reaction all day to these strangers invading his territory and shoving bits of coloured plastic at him, but now he genuinely *smiled*. He staggered to his knees, fixed them all one by one with a stare. Then he blew out his cheeks, rolled his eyes.

'Look at his little hands!' squealed Annie. 'He's even got the hands right!'

And the family laughed, utterly united for once, as George waggled his hands about. The baby burbled, grinned, then did it all again. He did it many times; they just couldn't get enough of it.

'Who's Kurt Fletcher?' asked Mr Jones.

'Oh, you've got to watch him!' said Annie. 'Yes, you've got to, Uncle Tom, he's just the best!' said Cindy. 'He'll be on tonight.'

So, after the family had said their goodbyes and driven away for another year, after they'd put George to bed, the Joneses watched the television together. Kurt Fletcher featured in a soap opera about the everyday lives of people living in the suburbs of South London. Kurt Fletcher himself was a rather unsavoury character, his head a bald bullet; he seemed to be a small-time villain who had at least three girlfriends he'd charm with his wheeler-dealer antics and cocky smile. Whenever he'd be in seduction mode he'd blow out his fat cheeks and roll his eyes, as if to say, come on, I'm not pretty, but you know you can't resist me. When harassed by the local policeman he'd waggle his fingers with an impatient tic – 'Don't go giving me no aggro,' appeared to be his catchphrase, dished out to lovers and the law alike.

'I wish he resembled a better role model,' said Mr Jones flatly.

'I still don't see it,' said Mrs Jones.

A few weeks later Mrs Jones received a letter from her sister. She could almost hear the squeal through the envelope. 'There's a kids' talent contest!' she'd written. 'And you've got to enter George, you've just got to.' And she'd enclosed an entry form cut from the newspaper.

Mr Jones asked her husband what he thought. 'I don't know that looking like a man off the television is a talent, is it?' he said.

'It's not just that. He does that blowing out through his cheeks thing, and waggles his fingers.'

'Do what you like,' said Mr Jones. 'But I don't expect he'll do very well.'

But Mr Jones was wrong. George charmed the first heat judges. 'Oh, look at that smile!' cooed one of them. 'You can tell he's going to be a heartbreaker!' said another. 'You must let me have his phone number when he's older,' she added, only half-joking, as she stamped the form which would guarantee him a place in the National Finals.

For the past two years the contest had been conclusively won by a girl from Chingford who had perfected a spot-on impersonation of Madonna; everyone expected this time would complete her hat-trick. The girl in question was now fourteen years old, and offered routines from the 'Like a Virgin' phase, the 'Vogue' phase, and the commercially less popular but critically well regarded 'American Life' phase. She was already a celebrity of sorts, her teenage face already endorsing both Dr Barnardo's and Burger King; she certainly didn't feel threatened by a little baby, and pranced and gyrated around the stage with total confidence. 'All right, George, it's your turn,' said his mum, 'just do your best.' And George crawled centre stage, in front of a crowd that numbered thousands, a camera trained on him so that his slightest gesture could be shown on a big screen.

And George came alive. He grinned cheekily at the audience, who began to clap. And George *responded* to all that applause – he rolled those eyes and puffed those cheeks and waggled his fingers like he'd never waggled them before. The crowd laughed, and he drank in their laughter, their love; he got up on his knees, managed a few faltering steps.

'Oh God!' said the delighted commentator. 'He's even doing the Kurt Fletcher drunken stagger!' And the crowd as one rose to their feet and gave him a standing ovation.

The Madonna girl had to join George on stage to collect her second place prize. 'The queen is dead,' said the judge, as he set a gold-plated crown on George's head, 'long live the king!' The press interviewed Madonna and she said all the right things, yes, it was good to have competition, yes, George Jones had done very well, no, she didn't think she was past it and she'd be back on the top of her game next year. And when she was sure no-one was looking, she went up to George, now lying victoriously in his pram, and spat in his face.

Straight away George was deluged with offers of representation. The Joneses visited all the prospective agents in their smart, swanky offices; they opted for the one that had the biggest crèche. George would be picked up in people carriers and stretch limos and taken to make personal appearances; at one of them he met the actor Bob Clarke.

'Hey,' said Bob Clarke, grinning the trademark grin that had made Kurt Fletcher so popular, 'he looks just like me! Hey! You going to grow up and be an actor, just like me?'

'Oh yes,' said Mrs Jones.

'We have no idea,' said Mr Jones. 'He's eighteen months old.'

'Yeah, that figures.' The Americanese sounded odd in Bob Clarke's south London accent. 'Well, it's a great job. Look at me, I was brought in to play a heavy for three episodes, but the viewers took me to their hearts, and now I'm the nation's number one loveable rogue!' He did the Kurt Fletcher smile again, and as he bent towards his little lookalike a hundred cameras flashed.

George looked at the actor's arms, reaching to pick him up. Then he looked back at the crowd in a double take, pulled a 'you've got to be kidding me' expression. The audience laughed. Then George blew out his cheeks, rolled his eyes, and spoke his very first words. 'Don't go giving me no aggro,' he burbled, or at least burbled a reasonable approximation of it.

For a second Bob Clarke looked stupefied, but he was a professional, he pulled himself together. 'Hey, you upstaged me!' he said, and very nearly sounded amused. 'Don't go giving me no aggro!' he added, and people dutifully laughed – but the moment had been lost.

Mrs Jones started to watch the soap opera religiously. Not for fun, she'd stress, this was *research*. She'd study the show on first broadcast, then replay the video recording of it three or four times, fast-forwarding and rewinding to the scenes which featured Kurt Fletcher. She'd sit George in front of it all, but more often than not he'd show interest in anything *but* the television screen – Mrs Jones had to keep prodding him to keep him focused. One day he began to grow downy blonde hair; she got out the scissors and snipped every trace of it off, keeping that bald bullet head pure and marketable. Mr Jones watched a little sadly. 'I always thought we'd be able to offer him something better,' he said.

George never disappointed the crowds who came to see him. He'd pose for photographs, he'd grin and finger wag and burble something Kurt-like at appropriate moments. But as soon as his public went home, it was as if George shut off altogether. His face, so expressive before an audience, sagged into utter indifference. His eyes glazed over, they didn't seem to be looking at *anything*. Mrs Jones got a little worried, and the agent introduced them to a celebrity doctor. 'There's nothing the matter,' enthused the doctor, 'it just shows he's at his peak when he's performing! George is a born entertainer! You should be very proud.' And Mrs Jones said that she was.

One night the doorbell rang. Mr Jones got out of bed, opened the front door. Bob Clarke stood there, shivering, smelling a little of whisky.

'Can I come in?' he asked. 'I have to see George.'

'It's two in the morning,' Mr Jones pointed out. 'George is in bed.'

'Please,' said Bob Clarke. 'This affects us both. It's really important.'

So Mr Jones shrugged and let him in. He brought down George, set him on his favourite spot on the rug. 'I'll leave you two alone.'

'Sorry to bother you, George,' said Bob, 'sorry to do this to you. But there's no-one else I could turn to. You and me, we have a connection.' He offered the baby his hip flask, then thought better of it, and took a swig himself. 'The bastards have had enough of me, George,' he went on. 'The producers. They're writing me out of the show. They say my character has played itself out, whatever that means.' And he began to sob silently.

George looked at him sympathetically, and dribbled.

'They say that I'm like this sex symbol,' said Bob. 'But I'm too old to pull that off any more. Too old? I'm only bloody forty-three. Forty-three's still sexy, isn't it, George? It's all such bollocks. So there's this storyline coming up, they promised me it'll be great, I'll leave in a blaze of glory. They're killing me off, in other words. I said, can't I just leave for a while, bang me up in jail or something, keep your options open. I'll be *dead*, George, you can't come back when you're dead, not unless they start doing flashbacks, and this show doesn't do flashbacks.'

Bob smiled bravely at George, and George smiled back, a smile that was Bob's smile, and Bob knew George understood.

'So I'll get a big death scene. But it won't even be me. It'll be a stunt man. It won't even be me.'

At last George fell asleep, the hip flask ran out, and Bob Clarke walked back out into the night and a career in panto. A few weeks later Mr and Mrs Jones watched as Kurt Fletcher's chickens came home to roost – the gangland boss he'd crossed had tracked him down at last. He was shot on the top of Albert Bridge, and he performed a perfectly executed dying fall into the Thames below. 'Well,' said Mr Jones gently, consoling his distraught wife, 'it was all fun while it lasted.'

And everything came to an end, almost overnight. No more photo shoots, no more charity dinners or movie gala premieres with red carpets. That year Madonna won the talent competition, and made a statement as she was crowned. 'If you're going to be a lookalike, pick a star who's got staying power.' It was the last allusion George ever received in the press. Mr and Mrs Jones had another baby, a little girl named Angela, and they both looked carefully to see if there were any popular entertainers she resembled – but there was nothing, her smile was entirely her own, and your heart melted when you saw it. By the time she was twenty years old she had already fallen in love with a man who said she was the dearest and loveliest woman on earth, and he was the lucky one because dozens of others believed it too.

George couldn't remember his brief days of celebrity, but they nonetheless left their mark. When Kurt Fletcher died, it seemed that something within George died as well. He had the same smile, but he no longer knew how to use it – what had been charming when it had belonged to someone else looked vaguely creepy when it was his and his alone. He withdrew into himself even further. He wasn't bullied at school, but only because even the bullies really wanted nothing to do with him – he meandered his way through his schooldays at the back of the class, never raising his hand, and never called upon to answer the teachers' questions. 'Do you want to be an actor?' asked his mother once, and even she, with all her hope, knew he didn't have it in him. 'No,' he replied in that dull whine of a voice, 'I want to work in admin.' And so he did.

Karen worked in Human Resources. Sometimes they'd bump heads, quite literally, over the filing cabinets. At first Karen recoiled from George like everyone else, but after a couple of years of filing cabinet-related half-conversations, she asked him out on a date. It was terrible. He didn't know what to say, or where to look, and spent the evening playing with his fork in the most irritating way. But she persevered. And on the fifth date she saw something directly that she'd only glimpsed before, something that she'd only *thought* was there. And she knew she loved him.

'Are you sure, darling?' asked her mother. 'We'll try to like him, of course,' added her father, 'but, face it, he's *awful*.' 'You just have to catch him at the right moment,' she told him. 'It's a lovely smile, it really is. His timing's just a little off, that's all.'

As for George, he didn't know whether he loved Karen. He wasn't even sure if he *liked* her all that much. But she was very persistent, and all those years at school where he'd not experienced any bullying made him especially vulnerable to it now. They got married, and the service was quite well attended because Karen was very popular, for all her peculiar tastes in men. He made a speech at the reception afterwards which, impossibly, managed to bore and anger the listening guests at the same time.

'You're going to be a daddy,' Karen told him one day. He waited just that fraction too long before saying how happy that made him. 'You see?' she went on. 'I told them you had it in you.'

He tried to be as supportive as possible. He felt for the little kicks when she told him to. He went with her to the birthing classes before the nurse told them, with some embarrassment, that she'd rather he stayed at home; something about the way he looked was scaring the other mothers, and they feared their babies would all come out funny.

The nine months sped by all too quickly. He wondered whether he'd love this child enough. He wondered whether this child could possibly love *him*. The doctors all kept their distance from him as he waited, all scrubbed up for the delivery, and at last he heard from underneath the groans of his wife the surprised screaming of his newborn. And he looked down at it, this red mass of skin and bone, not expecting to feel anything, not yet. And he realised it was a lookalike, this baby was a lookalike. It looked exactly like *him*.

And he reached out his hand to it, this new life, this little scrap, his *son*. And at the same time, his son reached his hand out too. Not in imitation. But as a mirror image. George clasped his son's hand, and it was so small, his fist swallowed it up completely – but he felt inside the fist that little toy hand clasp right back – just as earnestly, with due and solemn deliberation. He stared down at the baby, and the baby stared up at him, those two lookalikes trying to outstare the other, who would blink first? – and George couldn't help it, he began to smile, he began to *grin*, and he couldn't stop, and he got it right this time, the smile wasn't lopsided and it wasn't creepy, it fastened on to his face with correct precision and it was natural and it was free.

1202 – The deadliest earthquake in recorded history kills over a million Syrians. **1202** – The first jesters are appointed in European courts. **1203** – King John of England murders his nephew Prince Arthur with his own hands. He then ties a heavy stone to the body, and chucks it into the River Seine. **1203** – Byzantine Emperor Alexios III flees from the armies of the Fourth Crusade, leaving his wife and daughters to their mercy. **1204** – Alexios IV is pronounced emperor in his stead, ruling alongside his blinded father Isaac. Isaac dislikes his son, and spreads rumours of his sexual perversity. In an ensuing rebellion, Alexios barricades himself within his palace, and entrusts his favourite courtier to take a message of help to the crusaders. Instead the courtier has him strangled, and takes the throne as Alexios V. **1204** – Alexios V is attacked by the crusading army, and after only a few weeks' reign, flees Constantinople. He reaches the base of Alexios III, who welcomes him with open arms, and is given his daughter in marriage. Then Alexios III has Alexios V blinded, and sent back to the city, where he is sentenced to death for the murder of Alexios IV, and thrown from the top of the Column of Theodosius. **1205** – The pope establishes the principle that all Jews are doomed to perpetual servitude for their part in the crucifixion of Jesus Christ. **1205** – King John is so angry with the pope for refusing his choice of Archbishop of Canterbury that he writes to the Saracens, promising to make England an Islamic state if only they will declare war on the Vatican. The pope responds, as ever, by excommunicating him. **1206** – In Japan, the earliest known book about landscape gardening is published. **1206** – An English peasant called Thurkhill attracts the attention of contemporary historians when he claims that he has been taken by Saint Julian on a tour of Purgatory. He is especially lucid when it comes to describing the quality of their torture chambers. **1206** – The Danes invade Saaremaa Island, and force the populace to submit. And find no-one amongst their army is prepared to live there. So they set fire to their own fortress, and leave. **1208** – The Danes are defeated by a far smaller Swedish army at the battle of Lena. **1208** – King Philip of Germany refuses to give his daughter in marriage to Count Otto of Wittelsbach, famed for his bad temper. So, in a fit of that temper, Otto murders him. **1209** – The Albigensian Crusade is launched against the Cathars in France. Simon de Montfort forces the citizens of Carcassonne to surrender. **1211** – Still trying to lift his excommunication, King John sucks up to the Catholic Church by sending to every nunnery in the land a gift of herrings. **1212** – Stephen of Cloyes, a twelve-year-old shepherd from France, leads thousands of children in a crusade against the Saracens. They march 400 miles to Marseilles, where Stephen has been assured by divine inspiration the seas will part for them. They don't. They board ships instead – which take them not to Palestine, as promised, but to Algeria, where the children are sold into slavery. **1212** – The first Great Fire of London – much more destructive, and far less famous, than its seventeenth century namesake. 3,000 people burn to death on London Bridge alone. **1212** – Nicholas, a twelve-year-old boy from Germany, leads thousands of children in a crusade against the Saracens. They march over the Swiss Alps, and make their way to Pisa, where Nicholas has been assured by divine inspiration the seas will part for them. They don't. The pope wearily tells them they should just go home. Most die on the journey back, and Nicholas' father is hanged by angry parents. **1212 – ANNIE.** **1215** – King John signs Magna Carta, establishing new rights for landowning men. A few weeks later both he and the pope reject it and declare it invalid. **1215** – Holy Roman Emperor Otto IV is deposed, and imprisoned in Harzburg Castle – where he is beaten bloodily to death by priests as he confesses his sins. **1215** – Otto's successor, Frederick II, at last takes Charlemagne's embalmed corpse off the throne, where it's been sitting for 400 years (qv 814). The body is reported to be in excellent condition. Considering. **1216** – King John loses his clothes in the Wash. **1216** – John dies, possibly poisoned by a monk. His nine-year-old son Henry is proclaimed king, but the French dauphin Louis sees his opportunity to invade and claim the throne for himself. Louis allies himself with rebellious barons, and soon controls half of England, including London. **1217** – Louis is defeated, and sails back to France again. His brief spell as king of England is barely recorded in the history books, which like to maintain there's been no successful invasion since the Norman Conquest (qv 1688). **1217** – King Henry I of Castile is killed by a falling roof tile. **1219** – The Estonians are on the verge of defeating the Danes at the battle of Lyndanisse, when, according to tradition, a red flag emblazoned with a white cross falls from heaven; the Danish king catches it before it hits the ground, and proudly waving the country's new emblem out before the troops, leads them on to victory. This is heralded in Danish history as a mythical event that asserts Danish supremacy and their adoption by God as a chosen people. **1220** – The first important work of Japanese history is written. It is called, 'The Jottings of a Fool.' *My wife said I should spend some time with our baby daughter. That I should start to share some of her interests. And I suppose I could see the sense of that: get in early, before she had too many interests I'd have to share with. And maybe even, while she was still so young and impressionable, steer her towards a few interests of my own. 'There are the jigsaws she likes, and dolls,' said my wife, as she left the two of us alone, as she took the opportunity to run away for a couple of hours, 'you guys have fun!' I asked my daughter to pick a year. She kept on looking around the room, she kept on looking up at all those dolls my in-laws had bought her, I had to get her attention, I very gently held her by the chin. 'Annie,' I said, 'pick a year, any year you want.' I fetched my time chart down from the cupboard, she traced down the centuries with her finger. 'It's a treat, any year, it's yours.'* **1224** – The last of the Arabs are driven out of Sicily. **1227** – Genghis Khan dies. The location of his burial site is a mystery; to preserve the secret, the slaves who build the tomb are killed by the soldiers watching over them, who are then obliged to kill themselves. The story tells that the only creature that has an idea of its whereabouts is a single female camel. A mother can find its way back to where its offspring has died – and when one young camel is buried with the Khan, it's only its mother's tears that give any indication of the Mongol warrior's final resting place. When, at last, that mother camel dies, the secret is lost forever. **1227** – Polish Prince Leszek I is assassinated. **1227** – The Estonians' long struggle for independence is finally quashed. They will be subject to foreign rule for another seven hundred years. **1227** – Pope Gregory IX begins his pontificate by calling for the Sixth Crusade – and excommunicating Holy Roman Emperor Frederick II in the process, whose departure for the Holy Lands is delayed by an epidemic, as he lies fevered in bed. Frederick appeals to the rest of Europe about the unfairness of this – and, as soon as he is well, takes off to Palestine to honour his crusading vows. But the excommunication is upheld, and pope Gregory takes advantage of his absence by invading his territories. **1229** – Students of the university of Paris get into an argument with a pub landlord over an unpaid bill; this leads to a full riot, with many students killed, and a strike lasting two years in which the university closes its doors. **1231** – Anthony of Padua dies of dropsy. He is canonised less than a year later, the speediest transition to saint in the history of the Catholic Church. He is the patron saint of lost things, and his tongue is still on display for tourists. **1232** – The Roman people drive Gregory IX from the city in a revolt. **1233** – The Inquisition is established. **1234** – In China, Emperor Aizong commits suicide when his capital is under attack by Mongols. Before he does so he passes his throne to Modi. During the coronation the Mongols break in and kill Modi, who becomes the shortest reigning monarch in Chinese history, and who marks the collapse of the Jin Dynasty. **1235** – Elsewhere in China, the Song Dynasty is still thriving. A text of this year records that its capital, Hangzhou, has various social clubs – including the West Lake Poetry Club, the Buddhist Tea Society, the Young Girls' Chorus, the Plants and Fruits Club, the Antique Collectors' Club, and the Refined Music Society. **1236** – Chengdu, a city in Song China, is captured by the Mongols and its one million inhabitants are all slaughtered. **1237** – A fire destroys 30,000 houses in Hangzhou. **1237** – Ryazan, at this time principal city to the Russians, is sacked by the Mongols. **1240** – King Louis IX of France buys the Crown of Thorns, said to be worn by Christ during his crucifixion, for over 13,000 pieces of gold. **1241** – Snorri Sturluson, writer of the great Icelandic epics, is assassinated on the orders of the king of Norway. **1245** – King Sancho II of Portugal is ousted in favour of his brother Alfonso III. **1246** – Twelve-year-old Kaliman I, emperor of Bulgaria, is poisoned; he is succeeded by his still younger brother Michael. **1247** – The last remaining Cathars are massacred at Montsegur. **1247** – Henry Raspe, landgrave of Thuringia, dies without an heir. The War of the Thuringian Succession lasts for seventeen years. **1250** – A plague all but wipes out the population of Naples. **1250** – The last Ayyubid sultan of Egypt is murdered by his Mamluk slave guards. **1250** – The Seventh Crusade stutters to a halt at the battle of Fariskur when Louis IX is captured by the Mamluks in Egypt. He is forced to ransom himself and released on the promise that he will never return to Egypt again. Two days after Louis is captured, his wife gives birth to a son; she names him Jean Tristan (John Sorrow). Even now, on 8 May, the National Day of Damietta Governorate, Egyptians celebrate the anniversary of how they expelled a very important Frenchman from their country. **1251** – News of Louis' capture reaches France (if not, yet, his release). The crusaders have already been feeding propaganda back home saying that Louis has captured Cairo, so his failure is something of a shock. An old peasant claims he has been instructed by the Virgin Mary to lead the shepherds of France on a crusade to Egypt to rescue the king. The mob of 60,000 people, though, never get out of the country, and instead show their patriotic fervour by throwing priests into the Seine, and beating up Jews. **1252** – Pope Innocent IV issues a papal bull authorising the torture of heretics. **1254** – On his return from the Crusades fighting the Muslims, Louis IX orders all Jews expelled from France. **1255** – The nine-year-old Hugh of Lincoln is found dead in a well with marks on his limbs. Under torture, a local Jew admits not only to having killed the child, but also that it is Jewish custom to crucify a child each year. This gives King Henry III the opportunity to make some cash, as he decides that he is entitled to Jewish money if they are convicted as criminals – and, to this end, ninety Jews are arrested and held in the Tower of London accused of ritual murder. As for Hugh, multiple claims soon abound that he was able to perform miracles, and he is canonised. Today his sainthood is abolished. **1257** – Henry III orders the production of a twenty pence coin. It is the first coin to use real gold – too much gold, in fact, as the bullion value of the coins produced is worth more than its face value, and the coins never reach proper circulation as anyone who earns one melts it down for profit. **1258** – Mongols burn Baghdad to the ground, killing as many as a million inhabitants. The Mongols cannot kill the caliph by hand, for fear that the earth will be tainted with royal blood. So instead they roll him up in a carpet and let horses trample him to death. *She picked 1259. I congratulated her. 1259 was a very interesting year. I told her all about the formation of the Oxford Parliament under Simon de Montfort, and the great progress that was towards a democratic style of government. I told her about the Treaty of Paris between France and England, I told her how successful the Byzantines were at the battle of Pelagonia. And she smiled, and she clapped her hands – oh, she was so happy for those Byzantines – more, Daddy, more! – she didn't say that, of course, she still wouldn't speak to me, she only ever spoke to her mother, but I could see how much she wanted to. 'Yes, my darling, I'll give you more, I'll give you as much as you can take!' So I told her too about how the German cities that year formed an alliance against the pirates of the Baltic Sea, wasn't that lovely, and that this is when the Portuguese princess Infanta Branca was born, wasn't that great? Like bedtime stories, but it wasn't bedtime, and they weren't stories either – 'Do you understand, Annie, these people are your ancestors? Simon de Montfort, he's like your granddad, Infanta Branca, your granny! Nod your head if you understand. Nod your head.' I think she understood. She nodded away, in full comprehension of it all. '1259 is a magnificent year,' I told her.* **1259** – It is a terrible year. The Mongols attack Lithuania and Poland, and, at the death of their leader, undergo a bloody succession crisis. King Christopher I of Denmark is murdered at mass with a poisoned wafer. And, in the wake of civil unrest, wandering bands of flagellants spread over Europe, whipping themselves, and singing of the apocalypse. *And I think that's when I fell in love with Annie. Up to that point I'd tried to like her, but it wasn't as if she'd yet achieved a single damn thing. Had she lived, say, in the year 1259, there would not have been the slightest record of her, her entire life span would have been unmarked and unnoticed, she'd have just been one of the many millions living at that time upon the Earth whose very existence might just as well not have taken place. And I think there was a certain honesty to that, don't you? This mania for census reports, for birth certificates, for marriage registers – for God's sake, if we try to remember it all, if everything becomes history, then doesn't the interesting stuff get lost in the swamp? The way that everyone born in the last 200 years is preserved, somewhere, in small print – even though they haven't done anything, even though it's a lie, it's as if they've wormed their way into posterity – 'We'll never be truly forgotten,' they say, 'not so long as there's some mention of us on file in Somerset House!' Better surely to fade into nothingness – like all the sperm with which I filled my wife that just didn't swim fast enough, that didn't make the grade, like all those potential babies that didn't get to the egg in time – that's what Annie was until then, she'd just been some lucky fusion of sperm and egg, but not necessarily the right sperm or the right egg. And then, at the year 1259, she'd gurgled so adorably, and I loved her, and I knew then that she was the best egg sperm cocktail there could ever be. That she was going to be important. That she was going to make a difference.* **1262** – Adam de la Halle writes 'La Jeu de la Feuille' (The Game of the Whip), acknowledged as being the first French farce. There are going to be many, many more of them, usually performed by provincial repertory touring companies, and by boys' schools. **1263** – Mindaugas, the only Christian king of Lithuania, is assassinated by his cousin. **1264** – The Jews are massacred in Canterbury. **1264** – Civil war breaks out in England between the Crown and the barons, led by Simon de Montfort. **1265** – King Henry defeats the barons at the battle of Evesham. He gives no opportunity for capture or ransom, and orders that de Montfort has his head, hands, feet and testicles cut off, and body parts given out as presents. (Roger de Mortimer sends the head to Wigmore Castle as a gift for his wife.) The battle is said to mark the death of chivalry. It certainly marks the death of Simon de Montfort. **1266** – Manfred, king of Sicily, is killed at the battle of Benevento. **1268** Pope Clement IV dies. The Vatican can't agree on who should succeed him, and no new pope is elected for three years. **1269** – Idris II, the last Almohad Caliph, is murdered. **1269** – King Louis orders that all Jews found in public not wearing their identifying yellow badges are to be fined ten pieces of silver. *And maybe I overdid it. I leaped upon her enthusiasm too enthusiastically. I told her about the twelfth century in entirety, every bit of it, I told her about the plagues and the murders, about the persecutions of the Jews. And then I went back still further, I told her of the Norman invasion, of Danegeld, of Charlemagne. 'You'll like Charlemagne,' and I explained how he was our common ancestor. 'We're both descended from him.' And she did that gurgling thing again, and my heart just flipped over with love, she smiled, I smiled, we were both smiling (so I thought) at the relentless march of history. And still smiling she shook her head. I was a bit irritated. 'No, no, it's true, it's mathematically provable' – and then she spoke. She spoke. She spoke to me, I think for the first time, and it wasn't what I expected, it wasn't 'Daddy' or 'Dadda', she said – and this is the honest truth – she said, 'Charlemagne is descended from me.' And it was the strangest thing for a baby to say, let's be clear on that. Not petulant, but very certain. I wanted to tell her that was nonsense, Charlemagne lived twelve hundred years ago, but that certainty of hers was like a brick wall. 'You're all descended from me,' she said, and she turned away, looked around the room, looked towards her dolls and her jigsaws, looked bored. And then she yawned.* **1270** – King Louis dies besieging the city of Tunis, from dysentery caused by bad drinking water. **1273** – Thomas Aquinas abandons his masterpiece of philosophy, the 'Summa Theologiae', after having a mystical experience during mass, during which Christ appears before him and speaks to him directly. Aquinas then says of his life's work, that all he has written seems like straw to him. **1274** – The obese Henry I of Navarre dies, reputedly suffocated by his own fat. **1274** – King Edward I of England's first action on return from the Crusades is to enforce that all Jews wear yellow badges. **1275** – Eleanor of Montfort, daughter of Simon, is kidnapped by pirates under the employ of King Edward, to prevent her from marrying Llewelyn, Prince of Wales. She is imprisoned in Windsor Castle for three years, kept as a bargaining chip in Edward's attempts to take Wales under English control. When Llewelyn is forced to capitulate, Edward not only gives the bride away, he pays for the service. **1275** – The War of the Cow breaks out in modern day Belgium, all precipitated by one peasant stealing a single heifer. It lasts for three years, and claims 15,000 lives. **1276** – Popes Gregory X, Innocent V and Adrian V all die this year. They're dropping like flies. **1277** – Pope John XXI dies as well – killed when the roof of his palace caves in on him. (There is no John XX. At his election, he miscounted.) **1278** – Ottokar II of Bohemia is killed at the battle of Marchfeld, the single largest battle of knights throughout the Middle Ages. **1281** – The Mongol invasion of Japan is foiled by a large typhoon destroying their fleet of 4,000 ships. **1282** – Llewelyn attacks the English in support of his brother Dafydd ap Gruffydd, even though he is unprepared for war. He is still grieving the loss of Eleanor, who has died in childbirth. He is ambushed and beheaded. **1282** – The Sicilian Vespers rebellion takes place against the French rule of King Charles I. Thousands of Frenchmen are killed – and Charles is forced to abandon the Ninth Crusade en route to Constantinople. **1282** – Floris V, Count of Holland, defeats the Frisians at the battle of Vronen, and wins back the dead body of his father, killed and stolen away when he was a little boy. **1283** – Dafydd ap Grufydd is executed. He may well be the last independent ruler of Wales, but he is also the very first man to be put to death by being hung, drawn and quartered. **1284** – The Byzantine city Tralles falls to the Turks, and 20,000 inhabitants are enslaved. **1284** – 130 children vanish from the German town of Hamelin. **1286** – Alexander III of Scotland tries riding over the clifftops at night, and pitches himself and his horse down a precipice. He leaves behind as heirs only an unborn child and his three-year-old niece, Margaret, who lives in Norway. England are in a position to assert their influence over Scotland. **1288** – Scotland passes a law that allows women to propose to men during leap years. The men who refuse are subject to a fine. **1288** – The entire fleet of the Yuan Dynasty are destroyed by the Vietnamese, who place steel-tipped bamboo stakes in the river. **1290** – Margaret, Maid of Norway, now six, at last sets out on the journey to Scotland and the country she's ruled for the last four years. She dies of seasickness on the way. *I brooded on what Annie had said. I didn't ask her about it for a while. I thought I'd wait until she'd grown up a bit, until she'd developed the language skills necessary to provide a proper explanation. On her third birthday I took her to one side, and I said, 'What's all that shit about Charlemagne?' She said she had no idea what I was talking about. Well, she would, wouldn't she?* **1294** – Celestine V is elected pope without his permission. He quickly passes an edict giving any pope the right to abdicate – then does that very thing, expressing the desire to go back to the solitude of being a farmer. His successor, Boniface VII, finds him and imprisons him in a castle until his death. **1297** – Muslim-fighting Jew-persecuting Louis IX is canonised, the only king of France to be made a saint. *But I've been giving it a bit of thought. If my daughter were really the ancestor of Charlemagne (and all the rest of us), she must have got back to the eighth century at some point. Could Annie be a time traveller? The old argument against the future invention of time travel is that we would already have met these travellers when they journey back to see us in the past. But that assumes one thing: that the act of time travel doesn't cause amnesia. What if, I'm just speculating, there are time travellers from the future around us now, they just don't remember that they're time travellers? Of course, we're all travellers through time. We're just going forward second by second, minute by minute, in the right order. But what if, hold on. What if, yes, these amnesiac time travellers are more commonplace than we think? What if, in fact, they're the majority? What if most people in the world are actually living time backwards, and just can't recall it? Søren Kirkegaard once wrote that time could o nly be understood if experienced backwards – that it could only make sense from a retrospective position we could never adopt living through it in the present. What if he were right about the philosophy, but wrong about the direction? What if everyone is a time traveller living backwards? Then Annie could be my mother, and I could be her child, and we'd all be heading backwards towards Charlemagne, he could be the child of us all, that hourglass of the BC sands running out wasn't turned over properly, the Anno Dominis are all spilling out in the wrong direction. We're all heading back towards Charlemagne, right through history, the future is already written in textbooks and we just call it the past, it's all been done and can ever be done, and we learn it at school and think it's long dead and dry as dust but it's something we're making happen, time is imploding around us and getting smaller and smaller and more concentrated, and the only thing that keeps us sane is that we just don't know, we think that by living our lives we're creating events not just uncreating them in the process. Except for Annie. Because Annie knows. Annie's the only one who knows, and is the only one who can step outside it, she's the only one who can ever hope to achieve anything new. What a responsibility for her. And what a responsibility for her poor father, now knowing he lives with a monster capable of anything.*

PATCHES

Mother seemed cheerful about it, but then, Mother was cheerful by default. Father was wary, though. 'If it seems too good to be true,' he'd say, 'then it usually is.' He said he'd go over the house with a fine-tooth comb, although the little girl thought he was probably exaggerating. He didn't find any dry rot, or damp rot, or rot of any persuasion; the plaster wasn't crumbling, the foundations were sound. Still, Father was wary. He was a man of the world, a man of business – a *man*, at least, at any rate. He was nobody's fool.

Mother and Father would ask the little girl what she thought, but they'd never wait long enough to hear her reply. But maybe this time that didn't matter. The little girl didn't know *what* to think. Mother said she'd make new friends at the new school, and the little girl shrugged; it wasn't as if she'd made any at the old school, so what did she care? And Father promised there'd be more room in the new house for all of her toys and games and books. But the little girl couldn't help but worry a bit, when her parents packed away her things for the removal men, that somehow putting them into cardboard boxes would mean that her toys and games and books would always seem *old* to her from now on, that when she took them out of the boxes at the other end she wouldn't want them any more. And a new house would mean new creaks on the floorboards to navigate, and new places she'd have to discover when she wanted to hide.

The removal men came a little after nine o'clock, and that was very nearly punctual. Father said the family should follow on in the car an hour later: 'We don't want to overtake them,' he said, 'we don't want to get there before all our belongings, what would that be like?' Mother was cheerful in the car, and Father pretended to be cheerful too, he even let Mother sing that song that was all about the green bottles, he even joined in a bit. They stopped off at a service station along the way, and Father let them all buy travel sweets. Pretty soon it began to rain, and Father had to turn on the windscreen wipers, and the screeching noise they made against the glass acted as background accompaniment to Mother's bottle singing – 'Could you stop that now, please?' asked Father. By the time they reached their new town, and then their new street, it was pouring down, and the little girl wondered to herself why they were moving somewhere that was so wet. And there, at the bottom of a cul-de-sac, was *their* house; the little girl had been there several times before, of course, whenever Father had made one of his tooth-comb inspections, but back then it had just been a house, and now it was a home, and that felt weird. The rain fell on all the other houses, but theirs was left dry, they were lucky, overhead there wasn't a single cloud. 'It's an omen,' said Mother. 'We're all going to be so happy here!' And it meant that they could unpack the car without getting soaked to the skin.

There were so many cardboard boxes waiting for them, there seemed far more than had been taken from their old house that morning. And the little girl wondered how they would ever find the time to open them all, and yet she still marvelled that their entire lives had been crammed into such a small space. 'We'll open them tomorrow,' said Father, 'Tomorrow!' said Mother, but they nevertheless rescued from one of the bigger boxes a saucepan and some plates. Mother made them scrambled eggs on toast. By now the rain had caught up with them, it battered against the windows as if it were trying to get in, and it sounded different to the old rain the little girl was used to. 'It's a fresh start!' said Mother, with a smile. And, at Mother's suggestion, they also retrieved from one of the boxes the little girl's teddy bear. The little girl wasn't sure she wanted it, not yet; but she found, to her relief, that the teddy bear hadn't changed in transit, it was just the same bear it had been that morning. And she cuddled it in her new bed. But some time after midnight, in the pitch black, in the unusual pitch black, she realised the teddy bear now smelled a bit boxy and a bit cardboardy, and that made her feel sick. And she had to turn on the lights, and open up all the cupboards – and inside one there was an old blanket that must have been left behind by the house's previous owners. And the little girl wrapped the teddy in the blanket, and threw it right to the back of the cupboard – she knew that she was safe from the teddy now, she'd never touch it again, because to do so would mean she'd have to touch the blanket as well, and the blanket was even *worse*. And only then could she sleep – and the rain continued to fall hard all around the house, and hard on top of it.

*

The little girl's new bedroom was right at the top of the house. It was an attic, really, with a bed put in it. The very roof was her ceiling, and the walls caved in on her in an inverted V, giving the room a triangular shape. And all the shelves for her toys and games and books buckled out at her at strange angles. The little girl wasn't sure whether she liked the shelves doing that at first, and then decided she *did* like it, she liked it very much – even if she no longer liked any of the toys and games and books that sat on them. The walls were painted a pure and gleaming white. And set into the ceiling was a small skylight, and it let the sunshine in every morning, and protected her from the rain and the wind. The little girl liked this best of all, and she stared up at the skylight when she lay on her bed, she didn't need toys to play with or books to read. She was actually very happy – even if the rest of the house disturbed her, even if she couldn't get used to its new smells and colours and shapes, and the way it seemed so very very still in the middle of the night. If that still bothered her, if it woke her up, she'd just look straight upwards, through the skylight, and out at the sky beyond, and she'd be fine.

*

'It's a fresh start,' said Mother. 'Everything's going to be different from now on.' And the little girl agreed, it was already *very* different, and Father and Mother were now not talking to each other in rooms where the furniture was facing altogether new directions.

Father was still wary. The house had been too cheap, it had all been too easy, they had been taken for a ride. He wouldn't rest until he found out what was wrong with it. Mother asked, really very gently, why he'd agreed to buy the house in the first place if he wasn't satisfied – and Father just flared up, and said he'd been left really very little bloody choice, had he? But he was nobody's fool. He'd get to the bottom of it. He'd get to the bottom of everything. And it took him a few weeks, but at last, he succeeded. He called out his family into the front garden so he could show them.

'Look,' he said. 'It's obvious once you know.' He pointed straight upwards.

'I don't see anything,' said Mother, and Father clucked his tongue in irritation.

And it seemed ridiculous, but the little girl then thought she understood. 'It's the sky,' she said. The patch of sky above their house was unlike the patches of sky above the other houses. The skies were all blue, but theirs was a more muted blue, as if it had faded in the wash. And there was white creeping in to the blue, and grey. The sun was shining down on them, but not very forcefully, really rather limply, as if it couldn't quite make the effort, as if it weren't quite up to the multitasking of producing both light *and* warmth.

'We've bought ourselves a defective sky,' said Father.

It all made sense to him now. Why the house had been on the market at all. That sometimes the rain, or the wind, or the sunshine, seemed to be lagging as much as half an hour behind those of his neighbours'. That, sometimes, when he left for work, dawn had broken over the rest of the street, but not over *their* house, it made it difficult for him to find his car keys in the dark.

'What do you think is wrong with it?' asked Mother.

'Just old age,' said Father. 'It's wearing down. It's dying.'

'What are those up there?' asked the little girl. She'd seen the specks before, peeking out behind the clouds, just little brown smears in the air. She hadn't thought they were anything unusual before. Now it was clear only their sky had them, no-one else's did.

'Liver spots, I expect,' said Father. 'I don't know.'

'What can we do?' said Mother.

'We'll probably have to replace it altogether,' said Father. 'We'll have to rip it out, and start all over. God knows how much that'll cost. God. This sky's had it. It's probably years old. Probably hundreds.'

'Just think,' said Mother, cheerfully, and it was mostly addressed to the little girl, 'just think of all the things it must have seen!'

'It hasn't *seen* anything,' snapped Father. 'It doesn't have eyes. It's a sky. It breathes wind, and eats sunlight, and, and shits clouds, that's what skies do.' He glowered up at it. 'But not this one. Not well enough for my liking.'

He went indoors, got straight on to the estate agent. He shouted at him down the telephone. Father was triumphant; he'd been right all this while. And although that first conversation with the estate agent proved inconclusive, each day he'd call the estate agent back, it became like a little hobby, and he'd threaten him with lawyers and courts and things. Father seemed so much happier now. He'd smile at Mother and the little girl over breakfast and over dinner – it was a bitter sort of smile, but a smile all the same. The little girl hoped he'd stay happy for a long time.

'It's a fresh start,' Mother would say to the little girl. The little girl would nod, but nodding didn't always seem to be enough; Mother would add, so earnestly, 'I need you to believe that, I need you to believe all of this is going to work.' And then she'd cry, well, usually; but even if she cried she'd be laughing, even then she'd stay cheerful through the tears, and the little girl just didn't know what to make of that at all.

*

The little girl went to her new school. And pretty soon she was invited to the birthday party of another little girl; she hadn't been around long enough for any of her classmates to realise they didn't like her yet. The other little girl had a big house, with a big garden and swimming pool; most of the children played in the pool, but our little girl didn't like water, and stayed on the side, and on her own. And looked up at the sky. It was brighter and bluer than her sky, and had been especially polished for the occasion. There were balloons and fairy lights attached to the sky, some hanging off white puffy clouds in the shapes of elephants and sweets, and someone had rearranged the stars so that they twinkled in the daylight, and spelled out 'Happy Birthday Trudy', which just happened to be the other little girl's name. Our little girl knew this sky was nicer than her sky, but preferred her sky nonetheless. When it was time to go home, she was given a goodie bag; the other little girls had got inside it, and torn up the slice of birthday cake, and broken the toy, and had written on the napkin, 'Turdmuncher'. There was an apple, and the little girl didn't dare eat it, she thought it might have been licked, or spat on, or worse; but there was also a bar of Milky Way, and the wrapping didn't seem to have been interfered with, it had been squashed a little but the chocolate inside was untouched. So she ate that.

*

The skylight got dusty. And looking up through it on her bed, the little girl couldn't tell what was dirt on the glass and what were liver spots in the air.

The little girl was really too little to reach the skylight. Mother would have to clean it for her. But Mother would sometimes get distracted, she might sit downstairs in the kitchen all day and drink and smoke. Mother went through a lot of these distracted phases. And the little girl found she could get to the skylight – so long as she was standing on tiptoe, and standing on her bed, and standing on some of those fatter books to lend her those few extra inches she needed. She wiped away the dust. She gave the glass a push. It moved within its frame. She realised that the skylight could *open* – and she fumbled at the catch, it was stiff, she had to tug at it hard and the effort made her fall off her tower of encyclopaedias, she had to build it all up again and start over. She opened the skylight. She expected that straight away the sky would simply come flooding in. It didn't.

If she pulled herself up with all her strength, the little girl could poke her head through the skylight. If she scrunched all her limbs together, really very tight, and thought about how very small she wanted to be, she could squeeze her shoulders through too. But her stomach was too big. So she began to leave her dessert. And, when that didn't make her stomach shrink fast enough, she stopped eating her dinner as well, and her lunch, and her breakfast. She'd put the food in the bin when her parents weren't watching. And very occasionally they did take notice of her, very occasionally she *had* to eat – but she didn't keep the food inside for long, she'd go back up to her bedroom, cough it all up, wrap it in the old blanket and hide it in her cupboard forever.

One day she managed it, she was thin enough to climb up through the skylight.

She almost wasn't strong enough to do it, she felt so lightheaded and woozy, but she was a very determined little girl – she pulled herself out and into the moonlight, and the corners of the skylight cut into her sides as she did so, but she knew from now on it'd always be easier, she'd done it once and she could do it again, and it'd be easy, she'd just have to make herself a little bit thinner still. She sat on the tip of the roof, legs over both sides, and panted for breath, and tried to pretend that her body wasn't hurting so much.

The sky was above her. Very close. She lifted her hand up to it, but it was still too far away. Now she could see how livid those liver spots really were. Now she could hear the sky breathing – and it wasn't just the wind as she'd thought, that was just big puffs of breath, this was something softer and closer and private.

'Hello, sky,' she said. She didn't know what to say, really. She didn't like speaking to *anyone* very much. But the sky, of course, didn't talk back – it couldn't, because skies can't talk – and that made the little girl feel a bit less self-conscious about the whole thing.

'You're very old,' said the little girl. 'Does it hurt to get so old?'

She thought about this for a while.

'I don't want to get as old as you,' said the little girl. 'To be as old and ugly as you. I don't think that would be nice at all.'

The little girl thought about this too. And decided that maybe she'd been rude. 'Sorry,' she said. 'No offence.'

If the sky had taken offence, it seemed to forgive her. It wafted some light breezes at her, the little girl liked them, they were refreshing; she closed her eyes and opened her mouth and sucked them in, and she smiled. She stayed up there on the roof for a good hour or so.

'I'd better get back inside,' she said, at last, reluctantly. 'I've got school tomorrow. You don't have to go to school, do you? You're lucky.' She shimmied her way back to the skylight, swung her legs over the side, hoped with all those puffs of breeze she'd inhaled she hadn't put on too much weight to squeeze back through. She looked back up at the sky. She gave it a wave. 'Night night,' she said. 'I'll see you again tomorrow.'

And, each night, the sky would be there waiting for her.

Often she wouldn't talk to the sky at all. She'd sit on the roof, and pretend she was all on her own, on her own like normal – but then, once in a while, she'd look bolt upwards, and smile, as if to let the sky know that her shyness was really nothing personal. And at other times she'd chat, she'd spill her guts – that's exactly what it would *feel* like, too, that she was just letting rip, and everything in her head would just pour out; she wasn't good at expressing herself, she hadn't much practice, so it'd all be higgledy-piggeldy, her confusions, her fears – but the sky wouldn't mind. It'd just listen patiently. It never interrupted. It never tried to walk away.

She told the sky her name. Not the name her parents called her – her *real* name, the one she shared with no-one, the one that she carried secretly within her heart and never let out.

Sometimes she'd get angry at the sky. 'You're so big and powerful, but you won't do anything to help me!' She wouldn't raise her voice, she didn't want her parents to hear, but her whispered fury was sharp and cut through the clouds. Sometimes she'd simply say, 'You're my only friend.'

She realised that for all the years she'd lived in her old house, she'd never once spoken to the sky there, or thought about it, or wondered if it were all right. It made her feel very guilty.

She'd count the liver spots day by day, and see how they'd begun to outnumber the stars.

When she was bold, she tried to stand on the roof. Her feet slid upon the slates, and she knew that if she fell it'd be straight to the ground, and she'd be lost for good. But even standing, she couldn't reach the sky. And so when she was bolder still, she tried to stand on tiptoe. These were the times when she didn't mind much whether she fell to her death. But strain as she might, the sky was always out of her grasp.

'I love you,' she said one night, and she blushed hard at the admission, and felt so embarrassed that she had to crawl back through the skylight and she couldn't even wave goodbye to the sky and she didn't dare talk to it again for three whole days.

'I need you,' she said, shortly after that, and that seemed so much like a greater confession.

'Help me, please,' she said one evening. And she got to her feet – wobbled a bit, because she was nervous, perhaps, or because the roof tiles were slippery after a typically sluggish spell of rainfall. She got on to her tiptoes. She raised her arms up high above her head. If only she were taller – but then, to be that, she'd have to eat more, and then she wouldn't be able to get through the skylight, would she? 'Please,' she said again, and then she *jumped*, as high as she could – and it wasn't that high at all, it was hard to get a stable platform to leap from – she fell back again, and her feet nearly gave way, but she was all right, she steadied herself. And so she jumped again, arms still up, her hands clasping and unclasping, trying to get a purchase on *something*... And she jumped once more, and by now she was crying, and she didn't care how she landed, she didn't care if she fell, 'Please,' she said, 'I need you, didn't I say I *need* you?'

And her hand grabbed hold of the underbelly of the sky.

She was so surprised she nearly let go again.

She clung on for all she was worth. The sky had bent down for her, as far as it could go, but now it relaxed, it heaved itself back into position – and the little girl was swept up further into the air, maybe ten feet from the roof. She hung there, still crying, and she wasn't sure whether it was out of fear, or of relief, or whether they were just those tears of thwarted effort she didn't need any more but still had to come out.

The little girl dangled in the moonlit night. The moon didn't shine as brightly in this patch of sky as it did in all the others. But the little girl just thought it was the most beautiful thing she had ever seen.

She nuzzled into the sky. She was surprised to find it was furry. She began to stroke the fur with her spare hand. The sky began to purr.

She felt she could have hung like that forever. She wished she could. 'I've got school in the morning,' she told the sky. 'Double maths, and a spelling test. Bleurgh.'

So the sky lowered her back towards the roof.

And as the little girl dropped back down, oh, she couldn't help it, she fell awkwardly, maybe it was just that she didn't want to let go? In her fist she took a clump of sky with her, fur ripped from its skin. A gash was left in its belly. Just a little gash, but the sky was really so old, and very weak. And the fur in the girl's hand crumbled into flakes. And from the gash poured flakes too, raining down on her, she thought it was the sky's life blood, 'No, please no,' she said. But the flakes fell down anyway, and twisted gently in the breeze – and the sky was responsible for the breeze too, wasn't she, was she sighing? was she gasping out in pain? Like snow, but the flakes weren't cold, they were warm as breath, and they weren't white, they were the colour of twilight. 'I'm sorry,' said the little girl, and she cried, 'I didn't want to hurt you, I just wanted to touch, I'll never do it again!'

And at last the gash healed over, and the sky stopped shedding, it was over, the sky was still alive – and it gave a low rumble, maybe of relief, maybe of despair. 'I don't want you to die,' said the little girl. 'Please don't ever leave me.'

*

One day Father came home from work, and he was happy, truly happy. He'd been given a raise and a promotion. 'It'll be a lot more money,' he said. He gave Mother a piece of jewellery, and the little girl some new toy or other. 'I know things haven't been great recently,' he said, 'and I'm sorry. But this will be a fresh start. From now on, everything's going to be different. You'll see!'

He bought a better sofa for the sitting room, one made out of leather, and so deep the little girl thought she could sink in it and be lost forever. He bought a new dishwasher for the kitchen. And he looked up at the sky, and said, 'Time to put paid to you too.'

By this stage the sky really wasn't very well at all. It was shedding its flakes regularly now. Every morning Father would have to clear all the clumps of dead sky from off his car before he could go to work, he didn't like the extra effort that required one little bit. He said the neighbours were laughing at him, although Mother quietly pointed out he'd never once even said hello to the neighbours, how would he know? – and Father retorted, 'Well, now I'll be able to face them, if we get ourselves a brand new sky!' And then he smiled, because he was happy now, and this was a fresh start, sometimes he forgot about all that.

The man from the sky installations service came round at the weekend. He looked up at the sky, whistled through his teeth, and grimaced. 'Some cowboy's put that in,' he said. How long had they had it? Father said the sky had been there when they moved in. The man whistled through his teeth a bit more, and said he couldn't install a new sky until the old one had been removed. 'And you need to do it fast,' he said. 'Nothing damages property quicker than a clapped-out old sky.' Father asked him whether he could remove the sky for them, and the sky installation engineer said that was a specialist's job, he wasn't authorised to handle a sky as clapped-out as that one. Luckily, though, he had a brother in the business, and his brother had a skill with old skies that was almost crafty. He'd give his brother a call, he'd sort it out. And the brother came over the next day.

'It's dying,' said the brother, 'no doubt about that.' Father had kept some of the sky flakes to show him, but the brother didn't give them that much attention.

'It's dying, but skies are stubborn bastards, it could malinger. We'll have to give it a helping hand.' And so, twice a week, the man brought around to the house a pump, and a nozzle, and sprayed acid up into the air. 'It's my own formula,' he said, 'you can't get this in the shops.' He told the family that the acid would work its magic, it'd burn the sky inside out. He advised them to take care of the side effects, the clouds might soak it up and start dripping acid rain. After his first enthusiastic bout with the spray gun, the man looked up at the sky, put on his rubber waterproof hat, and listened with satisfaction to its squawk. 'Give it a few weeks,' he said, 'and it'll be toast.'

Every night the little girl went on to the roof. 'I'm sorry,' she said, 'I'm so very sorry.' And she cried. And sometimes the sky would cry too, and if it did, the little girl put up her umbrella to keep safe.

And every night, too, Father went out into the garden. He'd stare up at the sky, study his handiwork. It was easier to see the damage against the blackness. To see the cracks, the burnt red boils so ripe and ready to pop.

One night the little girl followed him outside. She didn't like speaking to her father. He made her nervous, and made her stammer.

'Please don't hurt her,' she said. 'Please stop hurting her.'

She said it so softly she thought at first her father hadn't heard, at first he didn't seem to react at all. But then he looked away from the sky, and looked down at his daughter, and the little girl couldn't read his expression. And perhaps that was because it was dark, but perhaps there was simply no expression to read.

'I love her,' said the little girl in a whisper.

'You think I don't?' said Father. And his jaw moved, as if for other words to come out, but they didn't, not immediately. 'You think,' he said at last, 'you think I *want* to hurt her?'

The little girl said she didn't know.

'I never wanted to hurt her,' said Father.

The little girl dared to hope. Deep inside. That maybe this meant he'd stop spraying her with acid.

'I wanted this to be a fresh start,' said Father. He wasn't looking at her now, he was looking anywhere else, he was looking up at the sky. 'I tried. You've no idea how much I tried. A new town, a new house. But you can't run away from who you are. Wherever you go, you take yourself with you. Wherever you go, you're always there. You're too young to understand.'

They both stood there silently for a while, in the garden, father and daughter.

'I could do it with you,' said Father. 'If it were just you. I'm sure I could. I know it. We could run away, just the two of us, and everything would be different. What do you say?'

'No,' said the little girl, and went back indoors.

Later that night the little girl climbed out on to the roof for the last time. The cracks in the sky's side were weeping something thick and gloopy. 'I asked you never to leave me,' she said. 'But I was wrong. I love you. I love you very much. And I need you to go while you still can.'

The next morning the sky was gone. What it left behind was nothing, really nothing at all.

Father was delighted. He called the sky installation engineer.

The man arrived, and looked upwards, and frowned. 'What's been going on here?'

'The sky's gone.'

'Dismantling a sky is a careful process, mate. This one has just been ripped out. Look at that. It's an eyesore, that is. It's just... it's just *void*.''

'So, when can my new sky be fitted?'

'You're not listening, sunshine. You can't have a new sky. Not now. There's nothing there to fasten a sky on to. The whole thing's ruined.'

Father got cross. And then began to plead. Surely there was something that could be done? And the man whistled through his teeth, and it was the most dismissive whistle of them all. 'I take patches of sky, and fix them to the heavens,' he said, 'I don't work miracles.' He jerked his thumb straight up. 'You're stuck with that, mate.'

Father raged around the house. He smashed plates. He overturned tables. The little girl and her mother had to lock themselves in the little girl's bedroom. They didn't come out, no matter how much Father demanded, no matter how much he beat upon the door with his fists and called them both bitches. And, at last, in the night, they dared to open up, they turned the key and pushed the door ajar quietly, so quietly – there seemed to be peace, the beast was sleeping.

'Come with me,' said the little girl. Mother shook her head. 'I can't just abandon him, I can't.' And she gave her daughter a big cheerful smile. 'Don't you see? I *chose* him.' 'I didn't,' said the little girl, and she took her rucksack, filled it with food, and left.

*

The little girl went looking for her sky. She didn't know in which direction it had fled, nor how fast a sky could run. She just had to hope she was going the right way, and her little girl feet could catch it up. And she walked with her head straight up, and that hurt her neck a bit, and the blood kept rushing from her brain, and she kept bumping into things.

Within a few days the food in her rucksack ran out. She got hungry. Sometimes people took pity on her, and offered her something to eat. But the little girl had read enough fairy tales to know you must never accept gifts of food, you could be trapped in the underworld forever. So she always refused. She had to steal her food instead. She got good at running. The sky, her patch of sky, that must have been good at running, she could never overtake it, but she, she got good at running too – and as she ran, as she dodged the security guards at the supermarket and *ran*, she hoped that somehow the sky was looking down on her and was proud.

She'd sleep on park benches, in shop doorways, underneath bushes. In the summer it would be warm, it'd almost be comfortable, but then other people would sleep in the same places, and she didn't like that, she didn't want to be around other people. In the winter it would be cold, sometimes freezing, sometimes she'd cry against the frost of the night. But at least she'd be alone.

Presently she came across a deep forest. She'd heard once that dying animals hide themselves away, as far from their pack as they can get. She wondered if that was true for skies as well.

The deeper into the forest she went, the darker it became, and the denser the crush of trees blocking her path. She looked above her and all she could see were thick branches and treetops, she couldn't be sure there was any sky there at all. All there was to eat was berries; but the berries here had never been picked by human hand, never been threatened by another living thing, they grew large and unchecked, they were the kings of the forest – ugly and oozing and the size of the little girl's fists – and, as she snapped their stems, and put slices of them into her mouth, she was afraid that the surviving berries would marshal their forces, that they would bite back.

And, one day, just as she thought the trees were so tightly compacted her little body wouldn't squeeze through, and that the berries were so wild that they had grown arms and legs – one day, suddenly, she found herself in a sudden clearing. And there, in the middle of it, was her sky.

It was very sick. Most of it wasn't in the air at all now. Most of it was draped listlessly across the grass. Its boils were now sunken like old tomatoes. Its liver spots now merged into one.

It gave a faint rumble, like distant thunder, when she approached.

'I just wanted to say goodbye,' said the little girl.

And she was really so very tired. So she wrapped the folds of the sky around her as a blanket. The fur was so very threadbare now she could barely feel it at all, it was as if she were hugging on to thin air. And she made the sky her pillow too, she pressed her ear right against it, and she heard its heartbeat, so thin and hesitant, and it seemed to chime with the hesitancy of her own.

It smelt wrong. The sky smelt all boxy and cardboardy. And she wondered whether this patch of sky was really her patch of sky after all. And then she decided that didn't matter. She loved it anyway, and she'd stay with it, and care for it as long as it needed her. She kissed it. And she went to sleep.

When she woke the next morning she was cold. The sky around her was dead. She cried for a little bit, and then resolved never to cry for it again.

She'd have liked to bury it, but that was silly, how can you bury the sky? So she gave it a final hug, and she walked on. She didn't know in which direction, deeper into the forest or not, she reasoned that even the deepest forest had to come to an end eventually. And so it did.

*

You're worried about the little girl. She was fine. She was fine. Don't worry.

The little girl grew up, as all little girls do. As most little girls do.

And she found happiness. Oh, she was lonely for a while – but we're all lonely, aren't we, for a while? And she softened her heart enough that she fell in love. In fact, she fell in love several times. And not all these men and women were worthy of her love, and some of the break-ups were hard and messy. But somehow the experience of every single one of these loves left her better off, and better equipped to deal with the next. She had a little girl of her own, and she loved her too, and the little girl loved her back, it was very uncomplicated, that.

She travelled. Staying in one place too long made her uncomfortable. And she'd come to rest under many different patches of sky. And she never loved any of them. Because, at the end of the day, loving the sky is a last resort. We'd all rather settle for anything else. Even if they don't smell right, or they're the wrong shape, even if they say bad things and hurt us sometimes. Even if we sometimes doubt they ever really love us at all. Still better than sky. Really, loving the sky, that smacks of desperation.

The little woman held hands with her lovers, on beaches, on bridges, on towers so tall they scraped the sky's belly. And she'd kiss them, and she'd swear undying love to them, even if she didn't believe it, and they might swear right back, even so. And, happy, or unhappy too, either way – she'd never look up, she'd never do that, she held on tight to what was in front of her. She'd never look up, and above her head the skies swam, and danced, and died.

1302 – The Ottomans win their first decisive victory over the Byzantine Empire at Bapheus. There will be others. The defeat provokes a massive migration of Christian subjects from the area, and ensures the Ottomans' expansion. **1302** – Overnight the Flemish militia massacre the French garrison in Bruges. To ensure that the people they are killing are French, the insurrectionists demand everyone says the word 'shibboleth' (shield and friend), which is notoriously difficult to do in a French accent; those who fail are struck down. **1303** – The Lighthouse of Alexandria, one of the three remaining Seven Wonders of the World, is destroyed by an earthquake (qv 262, 462). *Father phoned. We hadn't spoken in a while. 'You haven't heard from your mother, have you?' I hadn't. 'It just seems, well. That I may have lost her.' He hadn't seen her for five days. He'd woken up on Monday, and she wasn't in bed beside him, she wasn't in the entire house – and he thought maybe she'd popped out to do some shopping, some early morning shopping before the rush, but it was the weekend now, she should be back home, no matter how long the queues, where was she, when was she coming back? And he cried, just for a moment, and then he sniffed, and then I could hear him wrench his face back into its usual expressionless self. 'Well,' he said. 'Well, if you do hear from her – if she calls, if she shows up – if you find her.' He never told me what to do in that instance, he just petered out. 'Oh, God,' he said. 'Can I see you? Can you come over? Can I see you again?'* **1303** – French troops under command of King Philip IV turn up at pope Boniface VIII's private residence and demand he resign, angry at the limitation he has put upon the power of kings. When he refuses, they slap him about a bit, and take him captive. He is released after three days but never gets over the humiliation and dies later in the year – some accounts say because of kidney stones, others that he committed suicide by gnawing through his own arm. **1305** – William Wallace, rebel against English authority in Scotland, is captured. He is hung, drawn and quartered, and his remains sent to display around the country. Centuries later, as one of the nation's greatest heroes, a statue of Wallace is unveiled at Stirling – and it is immediately obvious that his likeness has been taken from Mel Gibson, who plays him in the blockbuster Hollywood movie. The statue has to be cordoned off to protect it from vandalism. **1306** – Philip IV exiles all Jews from France and confiscates their property. **1307** – Philip IV now begins his persecution of the Knights Templar, jealous of their power and wealth. **1307** – Switzerland is dominated by Austrian rule. Albrecht Gessler, newly appointed lord of Altdorf, has his hat displayed in the centre of town and demands that all the locals bow before it. One man fails to do so, and is arrested. His punishment is that he must (with a crossbow) shoot an apple off his son's head. The man succeeds – but Gessler notices that the marksman has prepared two crossbow bolts, and asks him why. 'If I had killed my son, the second would have been for you.' The man's defiance becomes a rallying cry of rebellion. His name is William Tell. **1308** – Albrecht I, duke of Austria, is murdered by his cousin. The Austrians take reprisals on the guilty men, and on their families, and on their retainers, and on their retainers' friends... It is said 1,000 people are killed. **1310** – Marguerite Porete, whose book 'The Mirror of Simple Souls' is a Christian text about Divine Love, is burned at the stake. **1313** – A German Franciscan friar named Berthold Schwarz invents gunpowder. He is not to know the Chinese already invented it a millennium earlier. **1313** – A war between Modena and Bologna is sparked by a stolen wooden bucket. The war lasts for twelve years. The bucket can be seen in Modena today, where it is displayed with all due civic pride. **1314** – Isabella, daughter of Philip IV, tells her father that all three of her sisters-in-law are guilty of adultery. The knights responsible are tortured and executed; the in-laws are imprisoned for life. The shock to Philip is terrible, and he dies some months later. Isabella is married to King Edward II of England, and her own relationship difficulties will soon come to light. **1314** – Edward II's forces are crushed by the smaller army of Robert the Bruce at Bannockburn, and Scotland regains its independence. **1315** – The Jews of Granada, Spain, are ordered to wear the yellow badge. **1315** – A great famine begins in Europe, millions of people die, peasants resort to crime, infanticide and cannibalism to stay alive. Edward II stops at St Albans on 10 August and no bread can be found for him there; it is the first time that the King of England is unable to eat on demand. **1316** – Louis X of France drinks too much cooled wine after a game of tennis and dies of pneumonia. His son John succeeds him – but John is, as yet, still unborn, still gestating within the queen's belly. The royal family wait for the birth, just so they can murder him and take the throne for themselves. At the age of five days John the Posthumous is killed by his aunt with a hatpin. **1317** – King Burger of Sweden invites his brothers to spend Christmas with him in his castle. When they get there, he leaves, shuts the drawbridge, throws the keys in the moat, and lets them starve. **1320** – Mubarak of Delhi is murdered by his favourite, Khusraw, who takes the throne. Khusraw is murdered by Ghazi Malik, who takes the throne. **1320** – Byzantine Emperor Michael IX dies of grief when he discovers that his son Andronikos has killed his other son Manuel. *We made it a little family expedition; my wife and I, and little Annie in the back. It was a three hour journey in the car, but Annie was happy, she kept herself busy by reciting out loud all the kings of England from William the Conqueror through to the present day. 'Good,' I said, 'now do Portugal.' And she did, through the houses of Aviz and Braganza, until the monarchy was overthrown in 1910. 'Good girl,' I congratulated her. 'Well done,' said my wife quietly. Father was in the front garden to greet us when we arrived, he might have been waiting out there for ages. He looked so much older than I remembered, and when we shook hands his skin felt like a wrinkled polythene bag. 'Can I make you some tea? Let me get you some tea,' he said, and he busied himself around the kitchen almost like an expert, he seemed almost proud he'd learned so much in five whole days, and my wife and I had tea, and Annie had some warm milk. 'I don't think I'm ever going to see her again,' said Father. I asked him if they'd had a fight, and he laughed, actually a little bitterly, and said they hadn't had the energy to fight since 1973. He said suddenly, 'What if she's gone off somewhere to commit suicide?' 'Was that likely?' I asked, and he shrugged. My wife tutted; did we really have to discuss death in front of little Annie, and I reassured her, I'd been teaching Annie history, she was very well versed in matters of death by now, and Annie was running around the house saying, 'Granny's dead, Granny's dead!' Oh, I could have slapped her. 'I was always prepared for the fact that she'd die at some point,' said Father. 'That's what happens when you're old, and you're together, and you realise one of you will go first, and the other will have to pick up the pieces. But this. The not knowing. If she has killed herself, how did she do it? We've lived this long story together, and now I won't get to find out the ending.'* **1320** – The Second Shepherd's Crusade (qv 1251): a teenage shepherd in Normandy is visited by the Holy Spirit with orders to fight the Moors. He leads instead his army around France and Spain, attacking churches and lepers, and – most of all, of course – Jews. **1327** – Isabella effects a divorce from her homosexual husband Edward II by deposing him, imprisoning him in a castle, and having a red hot poker shoved up his anus. This leaves him in no doubt that the relationship is over. **1327** – Petrarch sees a married woman called Laura in church one Good Friday, and relates his lifelong and unrequited passion for her in a series of poems. This day is typically used to mark the beginning of the Renaissance. **1328** – Robert the Bruce marries his four-year-old son to the daughter of Edward II and Isabella to better relations between Scotland and England. She becomes known as a result as Joan Makepeace. She's quite the older woman, nearly twice his age. They are married for thirty-four years but have no children. **1328** – The French army massacre the rebellious Flemish peasants at the battle of Cassel. **1330** – Since his father's deposition, Edward III has ruled in regency. Now he comes of age he thanks his mother and her lover who put him on the throne. He imprisons Isabella, and Roger Mortimer is charged with treason and hung at Tyburn. **1331** – The Poles and the Germans fight at the battle of Plowce, but the casualties are so high that neither side can claim a victory. **1332** – The death of Christopher II of Denmark, a name in their history synonymous with national disaster. He takes the throne only by mortgaging entire regions of the country to German businessmen. And by the time his reign comes to an end, he is allowed to retain the title of king, but has no power whatsoever: at first he's put in a small cottage, until the Germans burn it down, and then he's given a castle, but left there to die under lock and key. **1333** – William Donn de Burgh is murdered by his knights, and three members of the surviving family drag Ireland into a civil war as they fight for control of his estate. The eventual result is the loss of all Burgh lands in Ulster. **1333** – Six million die of famine in China. *He told me that Mother had spent the last few weeks going through old things. She'd been getting boxes down from the attic, picking through the contents, he didn't know why – she hadn't taken much pleasure in it, she hadn't even seemed to recognise most of the stuff. She'd unearthed something he wanted to give me. 'Do you remember that old time chart you worked on together when you were small?' And of course I remembered it, I was still proud of it, I'd kept it through childhood and into adulthood and now into middle age, I kept in it in the kitchen cupboard and fetched it down often, and on every 31 December I would make a fresh new entry for the year that was dying, I would add it neatly as a P.S. at the back. And I was going to tell him this, but he was smiling – and then he was handing me the time chart – the same exercise book – the same cover, saying 'Reporter's Notebook' – the same wide ruled pages inside – 'Here's a trip down memory lane!' he said, and chuckled, and my brain was flipping, how could this book be here, how could it be in two places at once? And I began to read it, and it was my mother's handwriting all right, so neat and round, tracing the major events from 1979 backwards. But I soon realised – this wasn't the same book – not quite – because at some point in the 1800s I'd taken over the project by myself, I'd shut my mother out – but no, here the 1800s were all written by my mother, and the 1700s too, and yes, before that, yes, all the way back to the Norman Conquest. And I was trying to make sense of it. And it could only have meant one thing: that just as I was working on my time chart, my mother was working <u>on her own</u> – and she'd never told me – she'd kept it from me – she kept it as a hobby for all that time, and when I stopped wanting to share mine with her that must have hurt so badly – she'd never told me – she'd never told – she'd never said. And I felt chilled. 'I'm sure she'd want you to have it,' said Father, blandly.* **1334** – The first recorded outbreak of the Black Death, in Hubei, in China. **1337** – The start of the Hundred Years War between England and France, which actually lasts 116 years. That inaccuracy was always of great irritation to me when I was a child. **1337** – The Muslim army sent from Delhi to conquer Tibet perishes in the Himalayas. **1341** – Civil war in the Byzantine Empire breaks out, between John VI and the regent for the child ruler John V. It lasts for seven years, and in the process the treasury is depleted, trade halts, and vast amounts of territory is lost. From this point on, it is an empire in name alone. **1341** – Margaret, Countess of Tyrol, rejects her husband to whom she has been married since she's been a child. And without formal divorce, marries into the family of the Holy Roman Emperor instead. The first civil marriage of the Middle Ages causes a scandal throughout Europe, gets Margaret excommunicated, and provokes war and invasion. When she finally dies, her lands are simply absorbed into the Habsburg Empire. **1341** – Leo IV, king of Armenia, is unpopular for his pro-Western sympathies, and murdered by his barons. **1343** – In Estonia, the St George's Night Uprising is an attempt by the natives to rid the country of all German influence. First renouncing Christianity, the rebels set upon churches and manor houses; the Estonian men spare the women and children – which sounds reasonable, except they are merely passed over to the Estonian women, who slaughter them without compunction. Four kings are elected, and at last they meet for talks with the Germans at Weissenstein castle. Where they are all hacked to death. **1344** – King Edward III repudiates the debts incurred by his French wars, and the Florentine banking house of Bardi collapses. **1346** – Blind King John of Bohemia fights the English at the battle of Crécy. He asks his faithful retainers to lead him into battle, so that he can swing about from left to right with his sword. He does not survive the conflict. **1347** – The Black Death suddenly erupts fast across Europe. In May, Genoese ships from Kaffa contaminate Constantinople. By September, it's in France. On Christmas Day, the first casualties of the plague are reported in Split, in Croatia. It will rage at its peak for several years, and by the time it is done will have killed as much as sixty percent of the world's population. However, because the plague destroys so many of the poor, landowners soon are required to pay wages to the survivors – and because there is now a surplus in basic goods, luxury crops can now be grown. We can see from this the birth of the middle class, and for the first time in history the peasants begin to have a better life... Well, those who survive bubonic plague, that is. **1348** – The Black Death reaches Italy. **1348** – The Black Death reaches France. **1348** – The Black Death reaches Spain. **1348** – The Black Death reaches England. **1348** – The French surgeon Guy de Chaulliac writes an account of the Black Death, and recommends bloodletting as a cure. **1349** – The Black Death reaches Poland. **1349** – The Black Death reaches Norway, when an English ship with all the crew dead onboard floats into Bergen. **1349** – The Black Death breaks out in Mecca. **1349** – The Jewish population of Basel are rounded up and burned alive, because they are suspected to be the cause of the Black Death. 2,000 Jews are killed in Strasbourg. **1349** – In response to the Black Death, flagellant groups spring up once more all over Europe; pope Clement VI condemns them in a papal bull. **1349** – Edward III bans football. *'Are you okay?' my wife asked me in the car on the way home. I suppose I had been a bit quiet for a while. But what could I say? And she reached out and patted my hand, just gently, on the steering wheel: 'She'll be okay, you'll see.' And I wasn't sure what my wife was talking about at first, and then I remembered my mother had disappeared. 'Oh, yes, I expect so,' I said. Annie said then, 'Granny's with Jesus.' It was so matter-of-fact, just out of the back seat, and the darkness of the night. My wife was so cross. 'Don't say that! Don't you ever say that!' And Annie sounded so surprised by her reaction, and a little disappointed. 'But I thought Granny liked Jesus?' And I told her she was quite correct, Granny had always had a soft spot for Mr Christ. 'Well, then,' said Annie, 'then everything's all right.' I could hear my wife breathing heavily, and trying to rein in her temper, and then she said, with deliberate calm, that today had been a big day for Annie, and lots of things were said about Granny that may have been shocking for her, was there anything she wanted to ask about? 'I know death seems a bit scary, but everything's all right, no-one's going to hurt you.' And I explained that death was a good thing, if we didn't have lots of death removing all the unwanted people from the world, where would all the history come from? 'We're just food for worms,' Annie said idly. My wife said it was okay, it was all going to be okay, she mustn't worry, Mummy and Daddy weren't going anywhere. And Annie said that obviously wasn't true, we clearly would die at some point. 'But not for a very long time,' said my wife. 'We'll see,' said Annie.* **1351** – Edward III introduces the Statute of Labourers, which sets a maximum wage for any peasant, commensurate with levels before the Black Death. This is an unpopular move, and precipitates later revolts. **1354** – The peculiar to-ings and fro-ings of Byzantine political struggles means that John VI is deposed and succeeded by John V. **1355** – Ines de Castro, wife of Pedro I of Portugal, is murdered. Two years later, when he becomes king, he has her body exhumed, dressed in ceremonial robes, and crowned beside him in the coronation. All the nobles are forced to swear allegiance to her, and are brought forward one by one to kiss her corpse hand. (qv 897) **1356** – The limestone casing stones of the Great Pyramid of Giza are removed to build fortresses and mosques in Cairo. **1357** – Influenza is identified as a disease. **1358** – Isabella of France dies; her will requests she be interred with the heart of Edward II, the husband she had so brutally murdered thirty years before. **1360** – John II of France has been prisoner of the English for three years. His ransom is now set at three million crowns, and John is set free to return to France to raise the money. However, in captivity John had lived a life of luxury, buying horses and clothes, and keeping an astrologer and a court band in his employ – while the France he returns to is impoverished. So John decides he'll do the honourable thing, and announces he'll go back to prison, please – and off he goes, ignoring the pleas of the monarchless countrymen he leaves behind him. On his return to England he is greeted with parades and feasts. **1360** – Muhammed VI overthrows his brother-in-law, Ismail II, to become king of Grenada – and is then promptly overthrown by his own father, Muhammed V. **1363** – Nearly a million men fight at the battle of Lake Poyang, one of the largest naval battles in history. **1367** – Otto I (the Evil) becomes duke of Gottingen. **1369** – Owain Lawgoch sets sail to reclaim the throne of Wales at Christmas, and bad weather forces him back to harbour a few days later. **1371** – Rival brothers Ivan Shishman and Ivan Stratsimir become co-emperors of Bulgaria after their father dies. Bulgaria is significantly weakened by their feuding. **1371** – Most of the Serbian nobility, including the king, are killed when they make an attack on a much smaller Ottoman army at the battle of Maritsa. **1373** – Byzantine co-emperor Andronikos IV launches a rebellion against his father John for allowing Constantinople to become a vassal of the Ottomans. He fails. And Turkish emperor Murad I commands John to blind his son as punishment. John compromises; he takes out only one eye. **1374** – The first major outbreak of dancing mania takes place at Aachen, Germany, where groups of people, sometimes in their thousands, dance and sing uncontrollably until they collapse from exhaustion. It is widely seen as a curse from the saints. **1374** – Edward III grants Geoffrey Chaucer a gallon of wine a day for the rest of his life in recognition of his services. What are you doing? He'll never finish The Canterbury Tales at that rate! *And back home I got out my exercise book from the cupboard, and compared it with Mother's. And we differed sometimes about which events we'd chosen to represent certain years – hers were generally more optimistic than mine – but it was the same world history outlined by different hands. And I noticed that the further back in time my mother traced her chronology, so, like mine, the handwriting changed too – but whereas I grew more mature and more confident, Mother just got angrier – it was neat, always neat, but the letters were spikier, and they seemed to have been pressed hard on to the page, by the thirteenth century she was writing in fury. I hoped my mother would one day come back, if only so I could ask her why. But I knew she wouldn't. 'Granny's with Jesus,' Annie had said, and she'd seemed so sure, and that was that.* **1377** – Ten-year-old Richard II is crowned king of England. The whole ceremony takes so long that the boy is exhausted, and has to be carried out from the abbey – and, in so doing, loses one of his slippers, and one of his spurs, and the crown from his head. Onlookers suggest this will mean one day he'll lose the support of his people, and the support of the army, and then finally the throne. **1378** – Muhammad Sa'im al-Dahr destroys the nose of the Sphinx, and is hanged for vandalism. **1379** – Henry II of Castile is poisoned by a monk (qv 1216). **1381** – In England, the Peasant's Revolt is led by Wat Tyler, provoked in part by the iniquities of the Statute of Labourers (qv 1351). King Richard II meets Tyler and sympathises with many of his complaints, and agrees in principle to serfdom reforms. And then the king's entourage cut Tyler's head off and stick it on a pike, and Richard changes his mind. **1382** – Joan I of Naples is infatuated with Charles of Dubrazzo, husband to her niece. Charles does not share her romantic interest. He has her imprisoned and smothered with pillows, and takes the throne as Charles III. **1383** – King Ferdinand I of Portugal dies with no male heirs, prompting civil war in the country. **1386** – Having seized the throne of Naples, Charles of Dubrazzo then ousts Mary of Hungary and seizes the throne there too. Mary's mother is irked by this, and has him assassinated. **1386** – Jagiello of Lithuania, the last pagan ruler in Europe, converts to Christianity so he can be accepted as king of Poland. It's been a long road, Jesus. **1386** – In Normandy, a sow is sentenced to death for the murder of a child. When the execution is carried out, it is dressed in human clothes. **1387** – Charles the Bad, king of Navarre, is visited by the doctor. The prescription for his aching limbs is that he is bound from head to foot in linen cloth soaked with brandy. One of the nurses, asked to sew up the cloth at his neck, can't find the scissors to cut the knot – so uses a candle instead. The king gets toasted. **1388** – The dowager queen of Aragon is accused of trying to kill her son, King John, with witchcraft. She is tortured, then put in a convent. **1388** – Richard II has secretly been attempting to negotiate peace with the French. The so-called Merciless Parliament accuses his entire court of treason, and executes or exiles the lot of them. Richard is reduced to being a puppet leader in his own kingdom. **1390** – King John I of Castile is crushed to death by his own horse while giving an equestrian performance. **1391** – Byzantine Emperor John V finally dies of humiliation, being bullied by the Turks. **1392** – Charles VI has his first of many bouts of insanity and one day, on horseback, goes berserk and kills four of his own men before his sword breaks. **1397** – Dick Whittington becomes lord mayor of London. **1400** – The deposed Richard II is starved to death in Pontefract castle. *'I'm sorry,' said Father, as we shook hands again, this time as I was leaving. 'I wish I'd loved her more. I did try. I did keep on trying.' And after I read my mother's time chart, I threw it away. I didn't want it in the house. It disturbed me.*

THE BIG BOY'S BIG BOX OF TRICKS

You'll never hear me complain about children, they're my bread and butter. And I know there are many people out there who are a lot worse off than me. Teetotal barmaids. Surgeons who are scared of blood. Bakers who are sickened by the smell and very consistency of dough. I have to work with children, there's no getting around that; it's an occupational hazard, and I shan't complain, I won't. No matter how much I personally can't stand the little creeps.

Besides, in my case, I feel that my antagonism may even be a good thing. When I go out to meet them it's usually in anger, disguised anger, and smiling so widely at them through the hatred probably gives a bit of *grit* to what I do, makes my mind clearer, my instincts sharper. 'Today I'm going to slaughter them,' I say, before I go on, 'today I'm going to knock the little shits dead,' and out comes the grin, out flows the patter, and I'm in the right mental spot for the magic to begin.

Some people tell me that children are the voice of the future. Some of these people are even in the same profession as me, they should know better, they say it's a privilege we spend so much time with them, that if we look carefully into their faces we might glimpse a prime minister-to-be, the cure-finder for AIDS or cancer. And I've tried, I've honestly tried. I let the patter take over and sometimes I go on autopilot, the words tumble out as they always do, and I give my prepubescent audience a good long hard look. In turn they just sort of stare back. It's not that they're bored, I could cope with bored, we all get bored. What I'm met by is indifference. They're listening to what I'm saying, maybe, they might even respond to some of the tricks, some of the jokes. But they really don't care whether I live or die. Yes, that's it – as I stand out there before them, struggling to raise a little bit of awe, they're thinking, I know, they're thinking that by the time they've reached my age I'll be dead, or dying, and they'll be so much more accomplished, they won't need to work so hard just to get the approval of infants, maybe they really will all be prime ministers at that.

The voice of the future, and maybe they're right, and maybe that's exactly the problem.

When you go to work, it's important to look the part. You must always be smart, and at least as smart as the smartest-dressed man in the room. If you perform at a wedding, for example, you must take care not to be outclassed by the bridegroom, you've got to find a suit that is just that little bit nattier. If the audience think you're one of them, then the first illusion is spoiled, even before you bring to the table all the illusions of your own. With children it's easy, children *never* dress well, so you're already ahead of the game – but the danger there is that if you turn up in your coat and tails you just look a little silly. So I go the whole hog. I take silly to the nth degree. My suit is velvet-trimmed, my polished shoes long and pointed. I never wear a belt but braces, there are gold cufflinks on my sleeves. And there's the top hat. I don't keep the top hat on during the show, my head would get too hot under there, and you don't want to be caught sweating in front of children, they might see it as fear, never let them think you're afraid. But I make sure I'm seen to *arrive* in one. If the children are going to take the piss, give them something to take the piss out of – and if it's extreme enough, you might catch them off-guard, they might even be a little frightened. 'You got a rabbit in there, mate?' one of them may ask, a teenager probably, probably male, and you can be nonchalant about it, you can take off your hat with genuine curiosity as if you've no idea *what* you'll find – 'so there is,' you'll say, 'I'd been wondering what had been nibbling at my ears,' and you reach inside, and you pull out a *toy* rabbit, and give it to the child. 'Would you look after him for me?' you can say. 'He gets nervous around cheeky children.' If you're lucky, the teenager in question will be too old to want a stuffed toy, but now he'll be so embarrassed he can't say no, and he'll be forced to sit there through the show with this little Bugs Bunny on his lap, a stroppy fourteen-year-old cut down to the age of six.

We're not allowed to work with real rabbits any more. Thank God. I wouldn't trust children with a real rabbit. They'd probably pull its ears off.

The top hat is also useful, then, for flushing out the enemy. The basic rule for dealing with children is to locate the troublemakers, right away, and then destroy them mercilessly, before they have a chance to corrupt any of the others. (I'm not just talking about performing to them either, I mean any social interaction with children whatsoever.) At a children's party there's always a couple of loudmouths, especially if there's been cake and fizzy drinks – usually not, in fact, the birthday child, they're usually drowning in far too much attention already and are feeling a bit exposed, and besides, their mummy is waiting next door to tell them off if things get out of control – no, nine times out of ten, the ringleader will be just some utterly ordinary random anonymous innocent-looking little tit. Destroy him, humiliate the bastard, and do it right at the start, you'll have a better time of it if you do, even the *children* will have a better time of it. And, technically, giving a good time to the kids is sort of the reason you're there. The number of kids at the party is also vital. Too many and they run riot, they think they can get lost in the crowd. Too few and they're probably with close friends and family, people who make them feel safe. Twelve is a good size, I think, just big enough and small enough to play on their insecurities. Twelve and you're laughing.

On the day it all started, on the day the children started dying, it was a group of fourteen. Fourteen is fine, fourteen's just a bit like twelve, really, if you squint. Fifteen if you count the little girl, but even at the start she didn't quite seem to belong somehow, I didn't see her as part of the gang. Everything seemed satisfactory, actually; the mother paid upfront, and she had no interest in giving any instructions beforehand – 'Just have fun!' she said, which was nice – and the birthday boy was eight, and eight's a good age, they're not too stroppy at eight. I entered the lounge, and all the children were already sitting on the floor in preparation, in ordered rows of three, and as I took my position behind the table in front of them the muttering stopped and they looked at me in polite expectation. No-one mocked the top hat, and I thought that was a good thing; I did the rabbit joke anyway, I said there was something nibbling at my ear, reached into the hat and pulled out the toy. They even seemed to enjoy the trick – there wasn't any applause, of course not, but there were smiles and satisfied nods.

This is going to be easy, I thought to myself, and I relaxed a little – just a little, I swear, I'm too experienced to relax too much – but looking back now that was a mistake and a fatal one.

*

If you want applause for your magic, don't go looking for it from a child. Children might clap, but only like trained monkeys, because that's what they've been taught to do, and usually there's some adult at the back leading them on.

But adults love magic tricks – and precisely because that's what they are, *tricks*. They're all grown up now and they've realised that life's all a big trick, really, tricks are all you get – you work all day to earn money you give away in taxes, you fall in love with people who say they love you back when they're lying through their teeth. We're taught not to trust anybody, to read the small print, that every act of generosity has an ulterior motive. All the special offers on the ads and in the shop windows, no, they're not so special at all. Everyone is trying to scam you. And what I do, I get up on stage, and I'm honest about it: 'All I have to offer you is fake,' and they *love* that, they all strain forward in their seats to see me pull off my deceptions, I look out into the audience and, really, all of them, their eyes are gleaming. And the applause at the end, the applause! 'I don't know how you did that,' they'll say. 'I don't know how you forced that playing card on to me, I don't know how you made my money vanish into thin air.' What they're really saying is, 'I don't know how you lie so well. I don't know how you lie so much better than me.'

Children, though, are fundamentally unsuited for magic. They're interested in the effect, not in the skill the effect required. You give them magic, but what do they care, they have magic in their lives every day. Miraculously there'll be food on their plates every meal time, there's a roof over their heads at night, there are always new toys to play with and new cartoons to watch on Nickelodeon. And each and every year their birthdays will roll around, they'll just roll around again, and they'll be, yes, a little bit older, but they'll be, no, not really old at all, and out of thin air there'll appear presents and cake and parties. And if they're unlucky, their parents might hire for those parties a magic act. They might get me.

I don't do many adult shows these days. For adults it's all about the patter, and my patter isn't good enough, I don't know how to talk to grown-ups, I feel all I ever see are children, where do you start with a grown-up? And I'll go on to the stage and I'm in the wrong mindset. It's as if I'm still performing to kids, and the anger and the hatred are there in my teeth-gritted grin, and the audience can *see* that, they can tell. You might be able to convince an adult that you tore up a newspaper or made a ball disappear under a cup or randomly picked a card from a pack. But you can never convince an adult you don't hold them in contempt when it's written over your bloody face for all to see.

Fundamentally, I suppose, I'm unsuited as a magician for anything other than children's parties. That's the bugger of it.

For just over two months now I've been seeing this woman called Sally. It's a bit on and off. She's a single mother, and I met her at one of the parties; she didn't see my act, she just came at the end to pick up her daughter, but she was told I was the magician, and we got talking, and her eyes started to gleam the way all adults' eyes do. I'm glad it hadn't been her daughter's party, I'd have felt awkward had the relationship started with me getting paid. We went out for dinner. 'Have you ever been on TV?' she asked over chimichangas, and I said I had. I'd once been on a spot on *Children in Need*, it was only broadcast in the Leeds region, but Sally didn't have to know that. 'Do you know anyone famous?' and I told her I'd once met Paul Daniels. 'How do you do all those tricks of yours?' and I explained that that was a magician's secret, and I winked, and I pulled a flower out from behind her ear, and she was enchanted. I did the patter. Her daughter was none too impressed, mind you. 'Say hello, Annie,' Sally would say whenever I came to pick Sally up, but Annie gave me the same sullen look I got from her at the party when she spent the majority of my act picking out threads from the carpet. 'Hello, Annie,' I'll say, I'll try, and I might flash her my most toothsome grin, pull out a flower from behind *her* ear, she doesn't give a toss. It doesn't matter, I don't see much of Annie. Sally gets in a babysitter, and by the time we come back to hers it's long past Annie's bedtime, and I make sure I never stay all night in spite of Sally's protestations, I'm never there for breakfast and the school run. We get into Sally's bed and we have sex and we try to do it ever so quietly for fear of disturbing Annie, and that's okay, that takes some skill, keeping the silence is like a conjuring act – and Sally's getting better at it too, her sleight of hand is improving. 'Do me a trick,' she'll say, and sometimes I do. 'Put on your hat,' so that's all I'll wear, naked except for the topper. And that's what she wants from me, that's all I am, she wants the tricks. She knows it's all just a lie. She'll cuddle in, 'say something magical,' she'll whisper, 'I love you, please, say something magical to me.' 'Abracadabra,' I say.

*

'Let me introduce myself,' I said. 'My name's the Great Miraculoso. But you can call me Great for short.' No laughter, not even a ripple, but that's okay, I wasn't expecting any. 'I'm a magician. I make the impossible real. It's not a bad job. My mum doesn't like it. She'd rather I was a doctor. But, eh, I told her, it's her fault, whoever heard of a doctor called the Great Miraculoso, not much else you can do with a name like that.' I hate you all.

All of the patter is misdirection, of course. As I chatter away, and I flutter one hand, with the other I'm setting up props for the first few tricks. 'How about you? Any of you want to be magicians? Which one of you is Tommy? Where's the birthday boy?' The little kids all exchanged glances, almost as if trying to decide which of them to elect, and then a boy raised his hand. Just a boy, as pointedly nondescript as any of the others, unsmiling – he looked as if he'd rather be anywhere else, doing *anything* else, and I guessed that the conjuring act aspect of his party had been entirely his parents' idea. 'What about you, Tommy, want to be a magician one day?'

Tommy said shyly, 'Yes.' I thought nothing of that. Put a kid on the spot and they'll say anything. Normally they'll say 'no', but some say 'yes', and at the end of the day a shy 'yes' has no more weight than anything else.

'That's what I like to hear,' I said. 'Come on up, and I'll show you how to do your very first trick.'

He got to his feet, stepped around his friends, and approached me warily.

'Okay, now, there's nothing to be scared of,' I said. 'You're not going to be sawing a lady in half. Not for another half hour anyway, ha! Being a magician is a great job. But you know what, the pay is awful. But that's okay, because we've got magic, we can just conjure up more money whenever we need it. All it takes is a bit of concentration. You any good at concentration, Tommy? Now, what I want you to do, is just think of some money. If you concentrate really hard it'll appear. A million pounds. No, let's not do a million pounds, that's a *lot* of concentration, you'll get a headache, let's say 20p. I want you to think of 20p, Tommy, just push out all other thoughts, just think of that coin, the shape of it, the feel of it, think what it'd be like to have an extra 20p to your name.'

Now, most kids close their eyes at this point. Even screw them up tight. Tommy didn't. He just stood there, his face as smooth and placid and sodding miserable as before.

'I really want you to concentrate,' I said.

'I am.'

I glared at him for a second, I couldn't help it. 'Fair enough. And we need a magic word, or the magic won't happen. Know any magic words, Tommy? Any magic words. Anyone, any magic words? No? Okay. We'll say "abracadabra". Say it after me, Tommy, abracadabra!'

'Abra,' said Tommy slowly, and that was my first inkling he was actually mocking me, he wasn't shy at all, he wasn't unhappy, 'cadabra.'

'Well done!' I said. 'You're a natural! Your first trick. Brilliantly done. Money out of thin air, you'll never go poor again, well done, you can sit down now!'

At this point the average child will look confused. They'll maybe point out they haven't seen their 20p. They haven't made magic at all. Tommy didn't do this, he just stood there, he wasn't going back to his seat yet, and his eyes bored into me. I looked at his friends. They had nothing to say either. I moved on. 'Oh, but silly me!' I said. 'You've magicked up the money all right. But you can't get at it. It's right there in your head. Can you feel it, Tommy, the 20p in your head? Bit cold, isn't it? How do we get it out of there? Hmm. You'll need another magician. Another, better magician. Wait a second, I'm another magician! Am I better? Let's find out, wait a second, hold still, this is pretty dangerous.' And I stretched out my hand, brushed the back of his ear. I wanted to give him a cuff right round it for playing along so badly, but I didn't, I just grinned my hate grin at him all the more ferociously. 'And 20p!' I said, and held the coin up to him, and held it up to the audience. 'That's yours to keep. Happy birthday, don't spend it all at once!'

'I wasn't thinking of twenty pence,' said Tommy. 'I was thinking of a pound.'

I didn't know what to say to that. And my brain was just starting to come up with a response, maybe tell him not to be so greedy, or make some joke about the recession, when his hand shot out – and I thought the kid's going to *hit* me, and I actually flinched – and he brushed *my* ear, and then he was holding out a pound coin to me, and then holding it out to his audience, and he was at last smiling.

'Well done,' I said.

'I had the coin concealed between my fingers,' he told me.

'Yes, I know.'

And then the smile was wider, and he made his hand into a fist, and then quickly opened it once more. 'But who knows what I did with this,' he said. And there, lying on his outstretched palm, was a five pound note.

I didn't say anything.

And nor did he for a moment. And then he stuffed the note into my shirt pocket. 'Yours to keep, don't spend it all at once.'

'Right,' I said. 'Thank you. That's quite a trick. You should have my top hat, you deserve that!' And I gave him a little clap; no-one joined in. 'And you should look after the rabbit it came with,' I added, 'he gets a little scared of cheeky young conjurors.'

Tommy's smile faded. No, not faded – it simply wasn't there any more, as if it had never been, as if it had only been an illusion, and his face was as dull and blank as before. He put the top hat on to his head. It was too big for him, he looked ridiculous, it sank down to his eyes. He took the stuffed rabbit. He made his way back to his friends.

'Now you might think,' I said, 'that I made a mistake there. Inviting Tommy up to do a trick with me. Being bested by an eight-year-old.'

'Seven-year-old,' said Tommy. 'My birthday's not till Tuesday.'

I ignored him. 'But magicians don't really make mistakes. Because we can always magic the mistakes away. Let me show you.' I took out a newspaper. 'I like reading newspapers,' I said. 'Good to see what's going on in the world. But the paper's so,' – and I ripped it – 'oops, flimsy.' I held up the newspaper, and the strip I'd torn from it. 'Now, I could still read it. I suppose. It's a bit annoying, but I can still make out what's going on. But...' And I tore the paper in half. And then into quarters. And then into eighths. 'But by now it's getting just a little more difficult. All my mistakes, they're mounting up. How am I going to get the news now? I suppose I could watch it on the telly, ha! Or...' And then, with a flourish, folding up all the pieces and then flipping them over, and displaying an entirely intact newspaper once more, 'I could just use a bit of magic. I thank you!' Yes, I thanked them, even though no-one in my audience was smiling, no-one in my audience looked impressed.

I didn't care about the audience, though. Only about Tommy. I gave him a smile. I may even have raised an eyebrow. *Well, what do you think?*

And, unsmiling as ever, he nodded. As if in acknowledgement I'd beaten him. And I felt I should say, not to worry, kid – the newspaper trick is classic sleight of hand, with a bit of practice you'll get there – but I didn't want to, I didn't like the sod. And then he looked away from me, around at his friends – he seemed to fix his eyes upon one, then gave a single, final nod. And up stood another little boy, right at the back. He had ginger hair, he wore a T-shirt, he was just a kid, he was a kid.

'What?' I said.

And the ginger kid produced a newspaper. I don't know where he'd got one from. I don't know, maybe he'd been sitting with it all the time. He tore it, he tore it again, tore it down to scraps. He didn't bother with the banter, he performed the whole act in twenty seconds. He held up the pieces for everyone to see (for *me* to see) his little child arms were full of them – and then he threw them, high up into the air, like confetti... And down to the floor fell a television remote control.

'I suppose we *could* just watch the news on the telly,' said Tommy.

Next I produced a series of eggs from my mouth. I made my eyes pop, and my cheeks bulge out, kids always love that one. Tommy nodded at three of his friends, and they performed alongside me. I made a pack of cards levitate off the table. All around the room the kids made their iPods hover, their mobile phones, their computer games – 'Are you all part of a magic group at school?' I asked, but they wouldn't reply.

I was sweating. I wish I had been wearing the hat. I could have blamed the hat. 'For my next trick,' I said, 'for my next trick,' and I wondered what my next trick might be, 'for my next trick I'm going to need an assistant.' I pointed at the little girl.

She was still sitting away from all the others. She was the only one who wasn't performing magic. When I gestured towards her, she looked startled, as if she'd been caught out – as if she were surprised I could even see her, as if she'd been practising a trick all of her own, she'd made herself invisible and now I'd ruined the whole thing. For just a moment I regretted singling her out, I wished I could have let her hide again – but, no, she was the only one who wasn't mocking me, and I felt a surge of affection for her, she was the only one who was on my side – or not on my side, maybe not, but she wasn't *against* me, was she, she wasn't against me, that was a definite plus. 'Hello, sweetheart,' I said. 'Would you mind helping me with a trick?'

'She's not part of this,' said Tommy.

'Come up here, sweetheart,' I said. 'What's your name?'

'She's not invited to my party,' said Tommy. 'She's my sister, and it's not her birthday, it's mine.'

'What's your name?' I asked her.

She looked so shy, properly shy, and I think she whispered something, and I don't know what. I imagined it was a name, but I didn't hear it, and I wasn't going to put her through that again. 'That's a nice name. Would you like to help me with a bit of magic?'

'This has nothing to do with her!' shouted Tommy. 'You leave her alone!'

'Oh, shut up. For Christ's sake, shut up. Shut up, you little bastard.' And my cheeks were burning, this was it, I'd snapped, I'd let the hate show through. He'd heard what I'd said, they'd all heard it, they'd be calling out for their parents and they'd be making complaints, and that'd be it, the grown-ups would turn on me, the grown-ups would tell all the other grown-ups, they'd be no more bookings, the magic would be over, the grown-ups would never want me now. But Tommy didn't call out. He didn't run through the door and get his mummy. He just looked stunned, as if I'd slapped him hard across the face. He'd been rising to his feet to stop me as I walked towards his sister – now he wobbled, actually wobbled, and then just slumped back to the floor. I thought he might be about to cry.

I was going to see the trick through. I smiled at the little girl. It was the sincerest smile I could muster. She tried to back away, but there was nowhere to back to.

'It's all right,' I said. 'I'm not going to hurt you. No-one's ever going to hurt you. I just want you to pick a card.' I fanned the deck to her. 'Any card you like.'

*

I don't know exactly when I saw my first magician, but I was young enough that I thought the Great Marvello was his real name.

He performed at a birthday party. It wasn't my party. My parents didn't throw me birthday parties. And if they ever had done, they wouldn't have hired a conjuring act.

'My name's the Great Marvello,' he said. 'But you can call me Great for short.' I remember that. That's the first bit I remember. It made me laugh.

For years afterwards I liked to imagine that the act had been good, but it probably hadn't been, really; I'm guessing it was the usual staple of tricks: newspaper tearing, eggs in mouth, cards. And I don't think the Great Marvello went down well, I have this memory of his performance being interrupted so that two or three of my classmates could be hauled home by their parents, they'd been playing with matches, I think. I didn't get on that well with my classmates. I probably only went to the party in the first place so they wouldn't beat me up.

I watched the show, I sat right at the front, just like I did at school, and I loved it, and behind me I smelled sulphur. For years I thought that was the smell magic made. Even now, sometimes, when I go on stage, I like to imagine that there's sulphur in the air, sometimes I almost believe it's there.

And I approached the Great Marvello at the end, as he was putting all his props away, and he recoiled from me as if I were going to stab him. And I told him that one day I was going to be a magician just like him, that it must be the best job in the world. 'Good for you, kid,' he said.

I told my parents the very same thing, and they indulged me, they bought me a magic kit for Christmas. Inside there were playing cards and rubber bands and metal hoops and a retractable wand. I studied the introduction booklet that came with them all, I studied it very hard. And in the playground I would perform my own magic shows, but it's true what I say, children aren't good audiences, they are fundamentally unsuited for magic. I did indeed get beaten up.

I clung on to my dream. I'm not saying there weren't other dreams along the way. Some days I'd want to be a train driver, or a rock star, or a superhero – but when these new passions faded, as most passions do, the magician would still be there, patiently waiting for me in the wings, hey, hey, remember me?

I went to the careers officer at school. He wasn't pleased. 'That isn't a proper job,' he said. He said that, I think, because he didn't have a leaflet for it. 'There's no such thing as magic.' And what I didn't say, because I wasn't clever enough, or because I was too shy – I *knew* there wasn't magic, even back then, I knew that life was just the same grind, and that there was nothing new in the world, all the magic tricks were just variations on a small number of routines that had been played out and honed over centuries – but that *that* was the important thing, that you were taking something that was old and familiar, and with all your practice and skill putting a fresh spin on it, you were misdirecting the audience into believing that the stale old shit you were selling them was something sparkly and crystal and new. Wasn't that a good thing, really? Wasn't that, in this day and age, a public service? But yeah, no, no, I didn't say that.

My parents weren't pleased with me either. My mother said I was selling myself short. That I could do so much better if I only put my mind to it. 'Look at me,' I said, 'really, do you think I can do anything special, you think I can make any sort of difference?' Yes, she said, firmly, quietly, yes, yes, I could. 'Then you're an idiot.'

She looked so hurt. I so wish I hadn't said that now.

Membership for the Magic Circle requires a nomination from two existing members; I didn't know any magicians, but in fact that was the easy part, I just wrote to a couple, I got their names from the Yellow Pages, they said yes, they didn't seem to care. I failed my first interview. I was told that my technical skills were competent enough, it was my patter that let me down, my patter lacked confidence. The next time I was interviewed I passed. I still wasn't confident. But I had greater confidence in pretending to be confident. I got away with it.

I asked my examiners if they knew of anyone called the Great Marvello. They said they didn't. 'Is that what you want to be called?' said one of them, doubtfully. I said no, I couldn't be a Great Marvello, Marvello just isn't me at all.

*

'Pick a card,' I said.

I like card tricks. I like the purity of them. I know that audiences can be won over by the spectacle of the newspaper trick, and that of course spectacle has its uses. But I can't help feel the more elaborate you make the con, the more superficial it really is. And there's nothing superficial about the cards; when you play with them it's just you, the magician, relying upon dexterity, and even upon the *relationship* that you have built up with them. The audience doesn't matter any more – you keep up the patter, you keep up the eye contact, but, really, the people, the stooges, they're just window dressing – all that's important is the cards and the dances they perform in your hands.

'Pick a card,' I said to the little girl. 'Any card you like. Take a look at it. Don't let me see what it is. And then put it back in the pack.'

The little girl hesitated.

'It's all right,' I assured her. 'I'll do all the actual magic. You can just relax and enjoy the ride.'

The room was silent now, and I guessed that Tommy and his cohorts were watching me keenly – but I didn't care, this wasn't for them, this was nothing to do with them. The little girl took a card gingerly, as if she were afraid it might bite.

'Have you seen it?' I asked. 'Are you happy with it?'

She nodded.

'Then put it back into the pack.'

She did so. I began to shuffle. 'Now,' I said. 'You keep that card in your head. Concentrate on it. And you think it right at me.'

'The Six of Spades,' said Tommy.

I couldn't help it. I turned around. There he was, maybe ten feet away, still sitting down where I'd left him. But he no longer looked as if he were about to cry.

'Don't be silly,' I said.

'Six of Spades,' said Tommy, slowly, deliberately. I looked back at his sister. She nodded once more.

'You don't have to go along with this,' I told her. She looked up at me, those big eyes were upon me, and it seemed as if she were begging for something, but couldn't find the words. Didn't dare speak at all.

'Six of Spades,' Tommy repeated, one last time. 'Right?'

The girl looked away from me, nodded again.

'If you say so,' I said. 'Fine. Okay. If you say so.' She must have heard the bitterness in my voice, she looked back up at me. She opened her mouth, just a little, in apology, maybe? I don't know.

'We'll try it again,' I said. 'Okay? Pick a card.' And the girl shook her head, just a little shake, I ignored it. 'Come on, pick a card, any card.' I was more brusque perhaps than I'd intended. I fanned the pack out once more, I fanned it right in front of her stupid face. She took a card.

'Three of Clubs,' said another boy.

The little girl looked shocked at this, I think, just for a moment, I think she had the decency to be shocked. Then, reluctantly, she held up her card for all to see. It was, indeed, the Three of Clubs.

This second boy was nowhere near the girl either, he was next to that ginger git who'd done the newspaper trick, he couldn't have seen the card, but he must have, that was it, that was all it could be. 'Clever,' I said. I thrust the pack back at the little girl. 'Pick another card, then,' I said. 'Go on. Pick another. Pick another!'

Unless, of course, the girl was a plant. That was it, she was telling her brother and his friends exactly what card she was holding, perhaps through predetermined gestures. No, simpler than that, they'd already agreed the cards in advance. 'Pick another card, pick another card!' She wouldn't. She wouldn't take a card, she wouldn't even look up at me, no matter how much I insisted, no matter that I think I began to shout. 'All right,' I said. 'Be on their side. That's fine. I'll do it myself.' So I fanned out the pack, I held it close, *I* picked a card, *I* didn't show it to anyone, *I* kept it hidden.

'Two of Spades,' said a third boy.

I fingered another.

'Seven of Hearts.'

And another.

'Jack of Diamonds,' said four boys, all at once.

My fingers prodded at the cards. Fast. Tapping the edges with my nail. 'Eight of Spades. Queen of Spades. Five of Hearts. Six of Hearts.' Then faster still, and angrier too, stabbing the cards now, stabbing down on them hard, 'Six of Clubs. Nine of Diamonds. Nine of Diamonds. Ace of Spades.' And now more boys were joining in, soon they all were, chanting in unison – and there was no triumph to their chanting, try to understand, it was like they were at school, it was like they were reciting their times tables, two nines are eighteen, three nines are twenty-seven, 'Nine of Hearts. Seven of Spades. King of Clubs,' and it was only Tommy who wasn't chanting along, Tommy sitting there in the middle of them, unsmiling, his face so blank, Tommy beneath that ridiculous top hat far too big for him, he ought to have looked silly but he didn't, I ought to be laughing but I wasn't, he looked like a child pretending to be a grown-up, like a child *becoming* a grown-up – everyone chanting but Tommy and the little girl, I stole a look at the little girl, and she was beginning to cry. 'How are you doing that?' I asked them, 'why are you doing that?' I screamed, and I threw the cards at them, the whole pack, and they rained down to the floor, and everyone fell quiet.

'We don't like you,' said Tommy then. It was clear and so very precise. 'And we don't respect your work.'

It was such a strange thing for a little boy to say, it sounded more like a review.

'What next?' asked Tommy. 'What are you planning to give us next?'

I said, 'Some balloon animals.'

Tommy laughed mirthlessly. He got to his feet. He walked to me, slowly.

'Don't you have anything new to show us?'

'But there isn't anything new,' I said. 'There's nothing new. This is all there is. There's nothing new under the sun.'

Tommy seemed to think about this. He put his head on one side thoughtfully, in a parody of contemplation, the top hat slid somewhat over his face, it nearly fell off altogether. 'I'll show you something new,' he said.

'Be my guest,' I said. I wanted it to come out haughty and sarcastic. I don't think it did.

'Did you mean what you said about your mother? That she'd rather you'd been a doctor?'

I was surprised. 'It's just a gag,' I said.

He nodded coolly. 'Remember what happened to Houdini.'

'What?'

But he didn't reply, the conversation was over. He took off the top hat. He handed it to me – and then, as an afterthought, he changed his mind, he took it back, he reached inside, and pulled out a stuffed rabbit toy. And another one. He pulled out seven stuffed rabbits, one after the other, gave them to me, gave me the hat.

'Very nice,' I said.

'That,' said Tommy, 'wasn't the trick.'

'Oh.'

And Tommy closed his eyes then. He stretched out his arms, wiggled his fingers. He breathed in deeply through his nose, exhaled through the mouth, in again, out again. He opened the mouth wide, rolled his tongue slowly around it.

And, at last, the other little boys were taking interest; they shuffled forwards to watch, and their eyes, I recognised the look in those eyes, the eyes were gleaming.

The little girl turned away.

Tommy opened his eyes. He was ready to begin.

He didn't say anything. He's going to have to work on his patter, I thought.

He didn't *do* anything, not for the longest few seconds. He began to gnaw on his bottom lip, and his eyes looked frightened. They were the eyes of a seven-year-old who had been caught out before his friends, who after all really had *nothing* to give, who'd shot off his mouth and been trapped in a lie. And I thought, it's over, even before it's begun. He'd lost his nerve. I'd seen it happen to performers, oh, ten times his age, and pretty soon the audience would start laughing, or, worse, feel ashamed for him.

He gnawed at his lip, and then he stopped, and he showed us what he'd done.

He smiled. The smile revealed that he'd gnawed his bottom lip clean off.

I looked for the lip, I'm sure we all did. Nowhere to be seen. It had vanished. I could only think he had swallowed it.

He continued to smile. His bottom teeth now fully exposed to the roots, you could see where they stuck deep into the gum.

'That's...' I said. That's, *what?* Remarkable? Disgusting, what?

And then Tommy held up his hand for silence. I was the only one to have broken it. I shut up.

And he bit down again. This time into his chin.

Deep into the chin too, you could see the skin yield and break under the force, you could see the teeth sink straight down like a spade through grass. He began to chew.

There was no blood.

And he chewed faster, as if he were enjoying the meal so much, as if his own flesh was the tastiest treat ever, oh, he couldn't get enough of it! And he chewed further, right to the bottom of the chin, to areas his mouth could never have reached, surely?

And there was no blood.

He paused to smile at us again, and now that smile seemed to balance upon such a thin sliver of jaw, so precariously you'd have thought there wasn't enough bone to support it, you'd have thought that the smile should have fallen off his face and straight on to the floor.

And then, the smile tightened into a little 'o' – this smile composed of just an upper lip and some exposed gum and pure white hungry teeth. He forced the 'o' upwards into a pucker, it looked as if he were trying to blow a kiss, but no-one would want to kiss that face, not now.

He puckered the mouth into a neat little funnel. He aimed it at his forehead. He breathed in deep.

I could see his forehead quiver.

It quivered as if it were trying to resist the suction. It couldn't, it couldn't resist.

And I heard, what? I thought I heard something crack. The bones, maybe? The skull as it was breaking, bending out of shape? But I might have just imagined that.

And the top half of the head suddenly tipped downwards, as if released on a pivot, as if it were a swing door blown open in the wind. The forehead was now at a right angle to the bottom half of the face, the nose pointing straight at Tommy's feet.

It was the nose the mouth was now after. It made a little snap at it, missed. Tommy laughed, as if it were part of the game, as if in trying to escape the nose was just teasing him. Another snap, and the teeth gained purchase – and a gulp, and the tip was pulled into that gaping mouth – was it still a mouth? – it seemed so much bigger now, it was a hole in the head, it was the head itself as everything caved in on it – another gulp, and the nose was in completely, the nose was lost, gone, and pulling in the forehead above it.

It looked as if Tommy were kissing his own forehead.

And still he chewed.

There was, as I say, no blood.

He chomped his way through the skin, he smacked what was left of his lips, this wasn't quiet, this was too enthusiastic, this was the sound of a starving man gobbling down his final meal, there was (I think) belching.

The tongue came out, and it was a long tongue, or maybe that's just because there was nothing to conceal it any more, we could see it in all its full red glory.

Tommy stopped munching for a moment. It was a relief, if just for the quiet – and then he let his tongue play over what remained of his cheeks. It reached an eye. It licked at the eye. Gave it a bath. Then straight in to the socket, as if it were an ice-cream cone, it scooped the ice cream out and wolfed it down.

One remaining eye winked as Tommy took a breather. He had to tip his head upwards so the eye was visible to us, he had to angle his mouth right at the ceiling to do it. So we couldn't quite see the mouth, but I'm guessing that it was smiling right along to that cheery wink.

It was nearly over now. There really wasn't much left. One final effort. Tommy took a deep breath, he breathed in hard, and the rest of the skull distorted, it thinned, and he sucked it in like spaghetti.

And all that was left was a mouth perched impossibly on top of a neck. And I think it gave me a final grin. And its teeth were gritted, and I knew what that meant from experience, I think in that grin there was hatred for its audience, for me.

The whole act had taken just over three minutes. And a part of my brain thought, that's too long, without patter or music to sustain the trick he'll lose his audience – his technique is good, but he really needs better presentation. He'll never get into the Magic Circle like that – but, really, that was only a very small part of what my brain was up to.

Tommy's body wobbled for a moment, then toppled over, crashed to the floor.

I felt the most appalling urge to laugh.

Silence. And then, the applause. Tommy's playfellows began to clap long and hard, and I thought, that's not fair, children *never* applaud.

The little girl didn't join in.

I wanted to examine the body. I thought I might find, I don't know. Hidden wires, maybe, or, or, or a secret compartment? But just as I thought to do this, all the boys got to their feet.

The clapping stopped.

They surrounded me.

'What do you want?' I asked.

They never told me. But together, as one, they began to chew on their lips.

'No,' I said. 'No.' But a part of me said yes, yes, now I can get to see the trick up close. And although I should have stopped it, I should have tried something, I didn't, I couldn't help myself, I stayed to watch as the thirteen little boys stood before me and ate their own heads.

The little girl looked ever so sad.

'I'm sure it'll all be all right,' I said to her.

And then I admit it, I ran.

I didn't stop to explain to Tommy's mother. I supposed she'd find out for herself all in good time.

*

There are many stories of the death of Houdini. One says that he drowned during an escapology act. They turned it into a movie; Tony Curtis played Houdini, looking suitably heroic and damp. Another story says he was poisoned by rival magicians jealous of his fame and skill. Houdini spent his life trading off mystery and intrigue. How appropriate, then, that the mysteries continue even as he dies – I imagine Houdini would have appreciated it!

Actually, Houdini may not have appreciated it at all. Maybe, right at the end, all he'd have wanted was some fucking clarity to his life. I don't know. How should I know? I'm not Houdini. I'll never be a Houdini. Don't compare me to Houdini, what's the use of that, don't talk to me about Houdini.

There's another story, and I think this might be the truth, because there's no glamour to it, no pizzazz. And it relates the final conversation Houdini had with his doctor. And how the great illusionist lamented that he hadn't been a doctor too. The doctor was surprised; 'But Mr Houdini,' he said, 'you have given so much pleasure to the world. You have entertained so many people.' 'That may be true,' said Houdini. 'But you're the one who is genuinely *helping* them, and making their lives better. Whereas all I do, and all I've ever done, is fake.'

And, of course, I'm aware of the irony to this, that Houdini may have been right – but, even so, history has remembered Houdini, and it's forgotten the name of this doctor.

That night I couldn't sleep. I read old magic books, lives of the great magicians. I tried to lose myself in articles giving new insight into stage techniques. I tried to recall why I'd wanted this job in the first place. And I lay in bed, mulling over all I'd seen, trying to work out how the trick had been done.

I wondered how they'd done it without spilling any blood.

*

Last Thursday I got a call from Sally. I hadn't seen her for a week or three, I needed some time to myself. She sounded nervous, and a little cross. I hate it when women get cross.

'Were you ever going to phone me again? Or, what, have you just dumped me?'

I assured her I hadn't dumped her.

'Oh,' she said. 'Well. That's all right then.'

I told her I'd had a lot on my mind recently. She apologised. She said she had had too.

'Can we go out?' she asked, and she sounded perky again, quite like her old self. 'My treat to make it up to you. A Mexican, we like Mexican, don't we?'

'Sure,' I said.

'When?' she asked.

'Oh, I don't know.'

'Tonight?'

'Tonight? I'm a bit busy tonight.'

'What are you doing tonight?' she asked, and the truth was, I couldn't think of anything.

'Let's get chimichangas,' she said.

'All right. Do you want to meet at the restaurant? We could meet at the restaurant. Let's meet there.'

'Come and pick me up,' said Sally. 'Half seven, okay?'

At half past seven I rang the doorbell and my heart was beating fast and my heart was in my mouth and I felt a little sick. I hoped Sally would be the one that answered. I hoped it was Sally's figure I could now see behind the frosted glass, the one coming ever closer, now reaching for the door knob, now pulling the door open, I hoped it was Sally, but I could see the figure was too small and too thin and I wanted to run.

'Hello,' I said to Annie. 'I've come to see your mummy. Is your mummy in?'

Annie didn't say a word. She stood back so I could come in.

'Is that you, darling?' I heard Sally call from upstairs.

'Yes,' I called back. I sounded cheery, I was surprised at how cheery I could sound.

'I'll be down in a minute,' said Sally. 'I'm just putting my face on.'

'Shall I come up?'

'I'll be down in a minute.'

I went to the kitchen. Annie followed me in. So I left the kitchen, I went into the sitting room. She was right there behind me.

I tried to be nice. 'So. Annie. How's school?'

She just stared at me.

I turned away, even hoped she'd have gone by the time I looked back. She hadn't.

'Must be summer holidays soon,' I said. Though it was May. 'You must be looking forward to that. Summer holidays!'

Nothing.

And I didn't know what to do, I reached out, I took a coin from behind Annie's ear.

'What's that doing there! That's for you. That's all yours, sweetheart. But, you know, don't spend it all at once!' And I smiled.

'I don't like you,' said Annie.

'Oh,' I said.

'I don't like you, and I don't respect your work.'

The judgement sort of hung in the air between us.

'What did you say? Why did you say that?'

And only then did Annie make to leave.

'Not so fast,' I said. 'Not so fast, I'm speaking to you, you don't... you don't get to go, not when... when a grown-up asks you a question, hey, I'm your elder and better.'

And I took her by the shoulders.

'Look at me,' I said. 'I'm talking to you!' I had her by the shoulders, and it was hard, my fingers dug in, I think it was too hard.

And she did look at me. And she smiled. And very slowly, she stuck out her tongue. Just the tip of it. And licked her bottom lip, left to right, then back again.

I released her.

'We should go,' said Sally. She was standing in the doorway. I don't know how long she'd been there. She looked very nice, all that make-up, she'd put in some effort.

'I'm sorry,' I said, and I was looking at Annie, but I was speaking to Sally, 'I didn't mean to...'

'We should go,' said Sally, 'now,' and she took my hand, and she was strong, she *pulled* me towards the door.

We left the house. We got to the car. We sat inside. 'Listen,' I said, 'I should explain...'

But she held on to me. 'Let's go and eat Mexican,' she said. 'I'm dying for Mexican. And after that, we can make love. Yeah? We can make love all night. Can I come to yours? Can I stay at yours? Let's go to yours, where we can be all on our own, and we can make love and never stop.'

'But what about your daughter?' I asked.

'What about her?'

*

Once in a while, if I was feeling nostalgic, or if I'd had too much to drink, I'd sit in the members bar of the Magic Circle and ask about the Great Marvello. And one time, just this one time, someone had heard of him.

'Oh yes,' said an old man. 'He's long retired now. Didn't have the staying power.'

A few of us had been talking about how we'd got into magic, and I'd heard a series of tales, all increasingly more elaborate and fantastical. Magicians always do this, they're liars, you can never trust any of them. So when the man spoke up, I didn't necessarily believe him.

'Real name was Arthur Travis.' Then he thought. 'Or Arthur Davenport. Definitely Arthur, though.'

I asked him whether he'd known the Great Marvello well, and the old conjuror shrugged expansively, and said, 'Who knows anybody?'

The next weekend I went down to the town I'd lived in as a boy. I hadn't returned since my mother died. It was just the same, a little smaller, maybe. I went to the library. I'd decided that Marvello had probably been local to the area, you never travel far for children's parties, the money isn't good enough. I looked through the phone directory. I photocopied the pages for Arthur Travis and A Travis and Arthur Davenport and A Davenport. There were 212 numbers in all.

It became a hobby. If I had nothing better to do, if there was nothing on the television, if I'd finished my card practice for the day, I'd phone a number from the list. And then cross it off.

One evening I got lucky. 'Hello,' I said. 'I was looking for the A Davenport who used to perform under the name The Great Marvello.'

There was a pause, and a woman said, 'What do you want with him?'

I nearly dropped the receiver. 'You mean, he's there? He's still alive?'

'Yes, he's alive. This is his daughter. Who is this, please?'

I'd never quite got far enough to think of what to say should I actually find him. 'I'm a magician,' I said. 'Just like your father. And the reason I do it, well, it's because of your father. I saw him when I was a boy, and I spoke to him, and he encouraged me, he said nice things. And he was really good, you see, gifted, that's why I wanted to become one in the first place. And I did, I'm a magician.'

'What is it you want?'

'I don't know. To tell him that he made a difference. That he changed my life.

That he was great, I mean, really great, as in the Great Marvello, ha!'

'I'm afraid he's not in right now.'

'Oh, I see.'

'But I'll tell him you called.'

'Please. And you'll tell him I became a magician because of him, won't you?'

'Do you like being a magician?' she asked, suddenly.

'Oh. Yes. Very much.'

'Good.'

'It's all I can do now, anyway! I'm not good for anything else!'

'I'll tell him.'

'Let me give you my phone number,' I said, and I did.

'Okay.'

'Have you got it?'

'Yes.'

'Because I'd love to tell him in person.'

'Okay.'

'Thank you,' I said. 'And, you know. Thank him!'

I didn't leave the house for three whole days, for fear I might miss the Great Marvello when he called back.

I should add that all this happened years ago, when I was kinder, and cared, and magic still seemed something innocent.

*

I still don't know why she visited me, and when I first saw her standing on the lawn I thought I must be dreaming; I hadn't slept well since the birthday party, it had been several nights now with no rest; and once in a while I'd get up, I'd potter around the house, put on some music, turn on the TV, look out of a window – and it was while I was looking out of the bedroom window that I saw her. And I thought, I'm not pottering, I must be asleep! – and I was so relieved I was sleeping at last I actually felt grateful, I waved down at the little girl, I wasn't frightened at all.

She didn't wave back. But she was looking at me, she was looking right up at me.

And I realised I wasn't asleep, this wasn't a dream. The little girl really was there, right in the middle of my garden, at three o'clock in the morning. I could see her face clearly, and that bothered me, because it was pitch black out there – but she was wearing a white nightie, and I thought that maybe that was what made her light up, I don't know.

We looked at each other for a long time. I recognised her, of course, and I didn't want a little girl in my garden, I didn't know how that would look to the neighbours. I wanted her to go away. And then, at long last, I got my wish, and without even the slightest gesture of acknowledgement she turned around, she started to walk – and immediately the garden grew darker and she was lost within the blackness – and I hammered on the window, I called out, 'No! Stop! Wait!'

I hurried downstairs, I opened the back door.

She was waiting for me.

251

'What are you doing out there?' I asked. 'Does your mother know you're out? Quick, come in, you'll catch cold.' And the sort of things you'd say to kids when you want to sound like a responsible adult.

Her nightie was damp, and her feet bare and wet.

'Are you all right?' I asked. 'It's okay. It's all okay. Look. I'll get dressed, okay? I'll take you back to your mum's. I'll drive you home, did you get lost?'

She shook her head at that.

'How did you find me?' I asked. But she just stared, and she looked so sad.

'Let's get you some milk. Would you like milk, or orange juice?' I opened the fridge. 'There's juice too. What's your name again, sweetheart?' And she mumbled something I couldn't catch, and I didn't like to ask again. I poured her some milk. She took it from me, and sipped at it, and when she took the glass away from her lips it had left her with a little white moustache.

'Is your brother all right?' I asked. 'Did Tommy come back?'

She nodded. She began to shake.

'You're cold,' I said. 'It's okay. You sit down. You're cold, I'll get you something, put this around you.' I gave her a tea towel, I draped it around her shoulders.

'That was quite a trick Tommy played,' I said. 'Do you know how he did it?'

She sipped at her milk again, and this time wiped away the moustache with the back of her hand.

I'd always hoped that one day a child would search me out. That, at the end of a gig, one little kid would come up to *me*, just as I had done to the Great Marvello, and say thank you, and say that I'd inspired him, and that he wanted to be a magician too. But not her brother, no, not someone like Tommy – no, someone like *me*, someone who was nice and kind and meant well (because I did once, I did). Someone like this little girl.

'Do you like magic?' I asked her. 'Do you want to be a magician some day?'

No answer to that.

'I could teach you,' I said.

Still no answer, but it wasn't a no.

'My name's not really the Great Miraculoso,' I told her. 'It's Steve.'

She was crying.

'Hey, it's okay. I'll get you home. I'll get you home safe.'

The tears were pouring down her face, but the little girl, she didn't make a sound.

'Hey. It's okay. I wouldn't lie to you. I don't lie.'

And then she began to nibble at her bottom lip, and I didn't even realise what she was doing at first – she had none of the confidence of the boys at the party, she looked so scared, and so *trapped*. 'Hey,' I said, and there appeared on her chin a tiny ribbon of blood, and downwards it trickled, and I thought, no, there shouldn't be blood, you must be doing it wrong, you're doing it all wrong. And still she cried, and it wasn't for the pain, I could see that, and still she nibbled, no, chewing now, the bites became bigger, 'Hey,' I said, 'it's okay.' And I wanted to put my arms around her, give her some little bit of comfort, but I didn't know whether that was appropriate, you have to be so careful working with children. And on she bit, and out came more tears, out came more blood, and I pulled her close to me, I felt the gleaming white nightie tickle through my pyjamas, I hugged her tight, I hugged her hard as she chewed and she bit and she swallowed.

*

The voices of the future are being silenced. That's what the prime minister said today in a statement.

He looked duly solemn, of course, but we didn't buy it, the public; we know that he still has a teenage son and a teenage daughter, and they're both intact; we know, that for all his fine words of regret, he's just relieved nothing's happened to them.

No-one took it seriously at first. It was a gag, a trick. Children in schoolrooms, playgrounds, at the dinner table, suddenly eating their own heads off. But it spread. Whatever it is, whether it's just the latest fad, like skateboarding, or the Spice Girls, or whether it's a genuine *plague*, that the young are being infected in some way, that there's a head-eating virus being passed around like verrucas and the common cold.

We asked the children, of course, but the children weren't telling. The children had nothing to say to us any more.

The sensation was confined to Britain for a little while, but then outbreaks were reported all over Europe, in America, Japan. There was news footage from Africa, showing us all the starving children there, all ribs and horseflies buzzing, and we saw how they had clearly got tired of bowls of rice and handouts from the UN, they were chewing through their own faces instead.

I'm still not convinced it *isn't* a magic trick. The little girl, the one who decapitated herself in my kitchen, she told me that her brother had come back. He'd come back. Why would she lie?

I had to dispose of her body all by myself. And this time there was a *lot* of blood.

Sally stays with me every night. In fact, recently, she's barely left my flat. Sometimes we make love, but most nights we just sit up watching movies together, most nights she sleeps on the couch. We don't talk much. I'm annoyed by it. I didn't want her moving in, I didn't want a proper girlfriend, but she's not going anywhere. Once in a while I might bring up her daughter. 'Maybe Annie isn't dead,' I say. 'Maybe you should pop around and check. She's only six, after all.' The last time I raised the subject she stormed off and locked herself in the bathroom for three hours, I'm not sure I'll bother again.

And no-one can understand it, that's what I keep hearing on the news, they talk of the tragedy, the *waste*, the voices of the future, blah blah blah, and on, and on. It's inexplicable, they say. And I think, you've just forgotten what it's like to be children.

Because *I* was a voice of the future once, and so were you. Look at us now. Go on. It's hard to credit! But we were the nation's hopes; we were presented the entire world by our parents, and told that one day it would be ours, that we would change history, that we could change everything. That that was the magic of it. But like all magic, it's just a trick. It's a trick. I think what's happened is, the kids have seen through the illusion. I think, at last, they've opted out.

The voices of the future are silenced. But maybe they simply had nothing to say.

They tell us that the epidemic is easing off. That fewer children are eating themselves each day. That no more than fifteen percent of the child population worldwide has been affected anyway, we mustn't exaggerate the problem. And maybe that's true. I see lots of kids still out there, there are tons of them. But I look in their faces and they're so bland and puddingy, I don't think I'm looking at the cure-finders for AIDS, I doubt there's a single prime minister amongst them.

Oh, yes, I still get bookings. By mothers and fathers who are desperate to prove that nothing is wrong, nothing has changed. Their little Jimmy or Jenny or John may not have spoken in weeks, but that's okay, put that aside, it's their birthday! Their birthday has rolled right round again, and there'll be presents and cake for them, there'll be parties. Let's bring the magician to the party, let's see if he can entertain the kids. And whenever I stand out front and perform, I know that the odds are at least three or four of the kids will get so bored they'll resort to eating their heads. I try not to look, it throws me off my stride.

So the government can feed me as many statistics as they like, the crisis is passing, yes, of course, if they say so, of course. But I know what I see, I'm there, I'm at the front line, I see what's going on.

And I try not to look, but I still want to know how the trick is done.

And I think of what the little girl said, that her brother came back. What did she mean by that?

I'll do the newspaper trick and the one with the eggs and I'll get out my cards and let them dance in my hands. The children look indifferent, they never applaud, but then, I'm used to that, I never expected them to. And sometimes, I can't help it. I'll stop my patter, I'll stop it dead. I'll stop talking so I can give my bottom lip a nibble, I'll bite right down hard and chew. And I can taste the blood in my mouth, the blood is flowing, and I think to myself, I must be doing it wrong.

1401 – The Archbishop of Canterbury has an act passed, outlawing as heretics anyone who owns an English translation of the Bible. **1401** – Baghdad falls to the Mongol leader, Timur. All the inhabitants are massacred. **1402** – David, heir to the throne of Scotland, is imprisoned by his uncle, and starves to death. It is said that in his hunger he gnaws at his own flesh. **1402** – Welsh rebels under Owain Glyndwr defeat the English at the battle of Bryn Glas. The Welsh women then mutilate their corpses, and the stench from the bodies left unburied is so bad that the area is avoided for months. **1402** – The English Parliament passes laws against the Welsh, in which it is a crime for them to gather together, carry arms, or live in any English town. Any Englishman who marries a Welsh woman is subject to the same penalties. **1402** – The Christian Knights of Saint John refuse to convert to Islam when Smyrna falls to Timur, and are butchered. **1403** – Bayezid I, Ottoman emperor, dies in captivity. Defeated by Timur at the battle of Ankara, he is kept enchained in a gold cage, and used as a footstool each night, while his wife is stripped and serves naked at table. After suffering eight months of the humiliation, Bayezid commits suicide by smashing his head against the bars (qv 260). His capture and death leave a power vacuum in the Ottoman empire, and Bayezid's sons embark on a ten year civil war. **1405** – Timur dies of plague. He says, 'I am not a man of blood, and God is my witness that in all my wars I have never been the aggressor.' The vast empire he has created does not long survive his death. **1405** – King Charles VI of France's delusions continue to grow. He now believes he is made of glass, and takes pains to ensure that he will not break. And for five months this year he refuses to wash or to clean his clothes – which suggests that the glass would have been particularly grimy. **1406** – King Robert III of Scotland decides to send the new heir to the throne, the twelve-year-old James, away to France for safety. But the ship is captured by pirates, and James is sold to England, where he is held in the Tower of London. Robert dies of grief, telling his wife he wants only to be buried in a dunghill, with the epitaph: 'Here lies the worst of kings and the most miserable of men.' James succeeds him, but remains imprisoned for the next eighteen years. **1407** – With Charles VI mad, there have been bitter arguments over control of the regency in France between Louis, Duke of Orleans, and John the Fearless, Duke of Burgundy. In November both swear to a formal reconciliation before the court. Three days later John has Louis brutally murdered in the streets; Louis holds on to his horse's reins so tightly that his hand is hacked off, and then, after being clubbed to death, his body is left in the gutter. This sparks a civil war between Burgundy and the royal family of France that drags on for seventy years. **1410** – King Martin of Aragon dies of uncontrollable laughter. There are worse ways to go. The resulting power vacuum that he leaves behind, however, is nothing to chuckle about, and it's two years before a successor gives the nation stability once more. How selfish are these medieval kings, exposing themselves to fatally dangerous bits of comic musing without due regard for what will happen to their entire nation should they choke as a result. **1411** – The battle of Harlaw is fought between the Highlanders and the Scottish crown. So much blood is shed that the battle becomes known as 'Red Harlaw'. At the end of the day, both sides believe they have lost, but are too feeble to retreat. The next morning, both claim a victory. **1415** – The battle of Agincourt. **1419** – Jeanne of Navarre, widow of King Henry IV of England, is accused of witchcraft and conspiring to bring about the death of her stepson Henry V through supernatural means. All her property is confiscated and she is imprisoned (qv 1388). **1419** – The first Defenestration of Prague takes place. (The lesser known defenestration, in fact.) Followers of religious reformer Jan Hus storm the town hall, and throw the council out of the window. This act precipitates the Hussite Wars (qv 1618, 1948). **1421** – The English are defeated by the French at the battle of Baugé . **1421** – 10,000 people are drowned and seventy-two villages lost in the St Elizabeth flood, as the high tide of the North Sea swamps the Dordrecht region of the Netherlands. **1421** – The first patent for a new invention is granted, in Florence, to Filippo Breuneschelli, for his barge with hoisting gear. **1422** – On 31 August, Henry V of England dies, and his nine month old son Henry succeeds him to the throne. On 21 October, Charles VI of France dies; his own son has been disinherited by the Treaty of Troyes, so English born Henry VI succeeds him to the throne. On 30 October, the dauphin defies Troyes, and has himself proclaimed king as Charles VII. War resumes once more. Henry has been king of France for nine days, and never knows it. Still, at this stage, he's unaware he's king of England either. **1422** – Constantine II dies, as last emperor of Bulgaria. His country will now be under Ottoman rule until 1878. **1424** – The ruling council for the child king Henry VI are more than keen to send the long imprisoned James I back to Scotland – but the Scottish nobility are less than enthused, having survived fairly hardily in his absence. A ransom of 60,000 marks is at last settled upon – which means that when James returns at last to his home country, setting foot there as king for the first time, it's to a disgruntled nation irritated by the tax increase. *I never expected to see the Wise Old Owl again. Once in a while, I'd take a little peek for him – but never seriously, never with any real hope, only very occasionally, only if the idea popped into my head – I might, if I had nothing to do, drop into the odd secondhand bookshop and look in the children's section – but I'd never spend longer than half an hour or so looking, and I'd never bother asking for help from a member of staff (they never understood anyway, they used to offer me birdspotting guides.) And then one evening – and I could hardly believe it – I was just running my usual check on eBay, and there it was, 'The Wise Old Owl's Book of Famous People', I almost fell off my chair. The starting price was 99p, and I offered immediately a hundred pounds, now I'd found it I wasn't going to let it go. And it was a whole week until the auction was due to end, and I kept looking back to check whether it was really still there, and I lived the time in an agony of indecision: hadn't I been a bit stingy, shouldn't I have offered £1,000, what was £1,000 worth against nostalgia? And so many times I nearly put in the bid against myself – because no-one else was bidding (not yet – I imagined them all out there, biding their time, waiting until the closing seconds of the auction when they'd swoop in and snatch the Owl from me wings and all). On the final day I took the day off work. I sat by the computer refreshing the page every minute, waiting to pounce on anyone who was waiting to pounce on me. There weren't any. Not a one. And I won the Wise Old Owl for that 99p, plus postage and packing* **1424** – Jan Zizka, the Hussite general, dies of plague. One of the few commanders in history who has never lost a battle, he orders that his corpse still be of some use to his countrymen, and that his skin be turned into a war drum so he can lead his soldiers from beyond the grave. The drum will be beaten at times of national crisis, such as the outbreak of the Thirty Years War (qv 1618). **1426** – A eunuch-dominated secret police starts to infiltrate the entire service in China, and control the palace guard. **1427** – In Switzerland, the first witch hunts begin. **1430** – Joan of Arc, a teenage peasant girl, leads the French army to victory against the English. She sees it as a point of honour to leave the battlefield last, and doing so is captured. She tries to escape custody several times, on one occasion even jumping out of a seventy foot tower into a dry moat. **1431** – Joan of Arc is tried, sentenced, and burned at the stake as a witch. Soldiers then display her charred body to the public to prove she is dead, burn the body twice more to reduce it to ashes, preventing any part of her being collected as a relic. And then pour her remains into the Seine. **1435** – In Russia, Vasili the Cross-Eyed is ousted by Vasili the Blind. **1437** – Catherine of Valois, widow to Henry V, dies. She subsequently married Owen Tudor, ancestor of the future Henry VII – and therefore is the daughter of a king, the wife of a king, the mother of a king, and the grandmother of a king, all from three different dynasties. The body remains unburied until 1793, her mummified remains on display in Westminster Abbey for a small fee. Samuel Pepys pays a shilling in 1669 to see the corpse; he takes the body in his arms and kisses her, so he can write that he had 'this day kissed a queen'. **1437** – James I of Scotland tries to escape from his assassins via the toilet pipe in his room. But he has had the drain exit sealed off to prevent tennis balls rolling into it, and James is pursued, and stabbed to death. James II, only six years old, succeeds to the throne. **1438** – King Duarte of Portugal dies, and his six-year-old son succeeds him. **1439** – King Albrecht II of Germany dies, and his as yet unborn son succeeds him. It's all getting faintly ridiculous, isn't it, all these child kings? You might even suspect that there's some flaw in basing the fortunes of an entire nation upon primogeniture. When Ladislas V (the Posthumous) is at last born, he's already ruled the country for four months from the womb. **1444** – The Treaty of Tours is signed between England and France. It lasts five years. **1444** – The Treaty of Szeged is signed between Turkey and Hungary. It lasts four weeks. **1444** – The Hungarians are crushed at the battle of Varna. King Wladyslaw is decapitated. **1450** – An Ottoman army of 100,000 men lay siege to Kruje in Albania, occupied by only 8,000 soldiers. One night Kruje sends out a herd of goats with candles attached to their horns. The Turks mistake this as an attack, and charge against the herd – and, in disarray, are picked off by the Albanians. After six months, the Ottomans have lost 20,000 men, mostly to illness – and they retreat. For the time being. **1453** – The Hundred Years War comes to an end, with the English losing Bordeaux to the French. Henry VI has a mental breakdown on hearing the news, and for over a year becomes completely unaware of anything going on around him. He even fails to respond to the birth of his own son. **1453** – Also coming to an end is the Byzantine Empire. For some time now Emperor Constantine XI has been anticipating an attack on Constantinople from the Turks. A Hungarian weapons dealer named Urban approaches him, and tries to sell him his latest invention: the most powerful giant cannon yet devised. It can fire a ball an entire mile! The Byzantines turn him down. In response, Urban takes his cannon to the Turks – who pay him four times the price tag. Mehmed II (later to be styled 'the Conqueror') has his cannon brought to the city on a cart pulled by sixty oxen. The Byzantines try to soften the impact of the balls fired by hanging leather and hay over the walls, but – unsurprisingly – this doesn't do much good. Constantine is killed, and the city is sacked. **1453** – And so comes to an end the lifespan of an empire that has lasted over a millennium, and called itself the Second Rome, as an attempt to keep going the continuity from the original empire formed in the days of Augustus. It's an example of the way that all great tyrants and despots are now so eager to historicise themselves, and to take their place in the pages of the Wise Old Owl, that the arguments over what can be called the Third Rome start here. Stefan Dusan, Tsar of Serbia, and Ivan Alexander, Tsar of Bulgaria, both claim that they are the natural successor to the original Roman Empire. As for Mehmed, he is proud to walk around his newly conquered city, and have himself called Kayser-I Rum – or, translated, 'Caesar of Rome'. Everyone just wants to pretend they're important, everyone wants to be so, so special. Killing each other and blinding each other and buying giant cannons to blow up each other, like demented little children. *The eBay listing had warned me the book wasn't in mint condition. The spine was hanging loose, and someone had drawn on the cover – they'd given the Wise Old Owl a pair of comedy fangs, so that this once imposing arbiter of all that was momentous now looked somewhat goofy and twee. But the inside was almost pristine, it was as if a child's graffiti couldn't touch history itself: I admit it, I actually stroked the book. 'Hello, old friend,' I said. I was going to wait until Christmas to give it to Annie, but I couldn't wait, I wanted to see her face light up now. She was in her bedroom. My wife had insisted that I keep my promise and cover the walls with pink paint and fairy tale animals, but I'd also hung up posters about heraldry, and a map of the world showing the spread of Greek civilisation and Roman Empire I'd got with six tokens from 'The Sunday Times'. I gave Annie 'The Wise Old Owl's Book of Famous People' and told her: 'It was my favourite when I was your age.' She didn't look overly impressed. She flicked through it briefly. 'It's very basic,' she said. And so it was, she was already three – but I sat her on my knee and I showed her the full page illustrations of Charlemagne, of Napoleon, of Sir Francis Drake. Of King Henry VIII, in a somewhat cartoonish rendering of the famous portrait by Holbein. 'Look what the Owl is trying to show you,' I said. 'Thank you,' Annie said, and climbed off my knee expertly, as if she'd spent a lifetime climbing down from people's knees. And then put her new book on the pile with all the others.* **1455** – After a hundred years off fighting the French, the English decide that they've had enough of peace, and turn their bloodletting on to home shores. The ensuing civil war is a struggle for the throne between the Houses of Lancaster and York, rather prettily named the Wars of the Roses, and its thirty years of death and confusion begin now, at the first battle of St Albans. Henry VI gets madder and madder – which, to be fair, seems somehow the sanest response. **1455** – Pope Nicholas V sanctions the conquest of non-Christian lands, and dooms all non-Christian people to 'perpetual slavery'. **1456** – A retrial acquits Joan of Arc of heresy. Too late. **1456** – Christian forces defeat the Ottomans at the Siege of Belgrade. The pope gives the order that the noon bell be tolled throughout Catholic Europe in celebration – as they are still rung today. **1456** – Vlad Tepes seizes control of the throne of Wallachia. He invites all the nobility to a banquet; after they have eaten, he has the old and infirm impaled on wooden stakes, while the younger and fitter examples of the aristocracy are enslaved and told to build him a castle. He then collects all the beggars of the region, and burns them to death in a great hall. He does this, he claims, out of charity: no-one will be poor in his realm. **1460** – James II of Scotland is killed, showing off his new cannon to his wife. **1461** – Henry VI laughs and sings during the second battle of St Albans. **1461** – Cao Qin rebels against the Ming Dynasty in China. He sets fire to the gates of the Imperial City (which are then extinguished in an unhelpful downpour), and his three brothers are killed in the struggle. Rather than face execution he rushes home and commits suicide by throwing himself down a well. **1461** – 6,000 men die at Towton, the bloodiest battle on English soil. Henry VI is deposed. **1462** – The Turks invade Wallachia, which is still under the rule of Vlad, though he's now known as 'the Impaler'. On the outskirts of the capital city they are so horrified by the sight of all the corpses – 20,000 people, men, women and children, left to rot on stakes – that they retreat. When he is finally captured, Vlad whiles his time away in his cell impaling the bodies of rats and birds. **1462** – The Jews are expelled from Mainz, Germany. **1464** – A late stab at starting a crusade, led by Anthony of Burgundy, known as the Great Bastard. He leads eighty-two volunteers towards the Holy Land – and then, at Marseilles, finding out that the pope has died, turns right round and starts back home again. **1466** – The second siege of Kruje (qv 1450). The Ottomans once more tries to take the Albanian city. This time they bring 150,000 men with them. Their leader is shot through the neck, and they retreat. *While Annie slept I took the Wise Old Owl from her bedroom and looked through the book myself. The Owl said, at the front, 'History is an adventure!' and 'Let's have fun with history!' and I don't think I'd noticed that page when I was a child. I studied the pictures, those great world leaders, and explorers, and inventors, and tyrants, and saints. And they looked all so much younger than I had remembered.* **1467** – A few months after the failure of the last one, Mehmed the Conqueror attempts the third siege of Kruje. This time he brings in forces from Bosnia, Serbia, Macedonia, Kosovo and Greece. This time they can't fail to starve out the Albanians. Except, once again, they do. **1468** – The Lancastrians surrender Harlech Castle to the Yorkists after a seven year siege of their own. **1468** – King Christian I of Denmark is strapped for cash, so when his daughter becomes betrothed to James III of Scotland, he pawns Orkney and the Shetland Islands for 58,000 guilders. The contract states that he can later redeem the islands for a fixed sum of gold; several attempts are later made to do this in the seventeenth and eighteenth centuries, but the Scots refuse to give them back. **1471** – The deposed Henry VI is murdered in the Tower of London, possibly by Richard, Duke of Gloucester (the notorious future Richard III). You can visit the exact spot where he died, you can actually stand right there and imagine it. And I'm not sure what the greater ignominy for poor Henry is, that he was stabbed during a brutal war in which he took such little interest, or that so many of the tourists who eat their ice creams where his life ended muse aloud whether he was the famous King Henry who had those six wives or not. **1473** – The Aztec army of Tenochtitlan attacks the city of Tlatelolco, and are confronted by an opposing army of naked women who squirt them with milk from their breasts. Tlatelolco is nevertheless sacked. **1478** – George, Duke of Clarence, always fond of a tipple, is executed for treason by his brother, drowned in a butt of Malmsey wine. **1478** – The Ottoman Turks once more lay siege to Kruje (qv 1450, 1466, 1467). This time they promise the citizens safe passage if they leave the city. When the Albanians come forth, however, they change their minds, and they kill the men and enslave the women and children. **1480** – Welsh poet Gwerful Mechain writes 'Ode to the Pubic Hair'. **1480** – The last remains of the long destroyed Library of Alexandria (qv 1303) finally disappear, as the Sultan of Egypt builds a fort on its site. **1483** – Torquemada is appointed the first Grand Inquisitor of Spain. **1483** – Louis XI of France becomes obsessively frightened of death, and rumours say he drinks the warm blood of infants to protect him. This year it doesn't work. **1483** – The 12-year-old King Edward V is made king, then deposed, then murdered with his younger brother in the Tower of London. Their uncle, Richard III, is usually blamed, but there is some conjecture about this – and there are societies out there centuries later seeking to clear his name. All of which is fair enough, but I do wonder – with all the atrocities committed in history, against children and family, all the murders, all the blindings, all just to seize some little bit of temporary power – why does this one in particular so grip the popular imagination? The Princes in the Tower certainly have a rough time of it, and no-one would necessarily envy them their fate – but at least they die somewhere reasonably warm. As for Richard III, if he is the man responsible, it doesn't do him much good – he'll have his head chopped off in the battle of Bosworth two years later, amidst all the carnage and the mud and wearing uncomfortable armour. As deaths go, his is the grislier. **1485** – The first epidemic of sweating sickness breaks out in England. **1487** – Ahuitzotl becomes Aztec emperor, and sacrifices 20,000 men to celebrate. **1488** – Caterina Sforza barricades herself in the fortress of Ravaldino, leaving her children as hostages. When their lives are threatened, she appears on the battlements, lifts her skirt, shows her genitals, and shouts, 'I can always make more!' **1488** – James III of Scotland is killed in battle against his own nobles. One of those responsible is his own son – who, as James IV, wears a heavy iron chain around his waist, in memory of his part in his father's death. 1491 – Alfonso, heir to the throne of Portugal, dies suspiciously from a horse accident. **1491** – Under torture, many Jews confess to the ritual murder of the Holy Child of La Guardia, in Toledo, Spain, and are executed in an auto da fe. No child's body, however, is ever discovered, and all the confessions are contradictory. The putative child is quickly made into a saint, and a cult celebrating him is still in operation in La Guardia today. *The next day I sat Annie back on my knee. I wanted her to give the book a second try. But when I opened it, the pictures were gone. And the lettering had smeared across all the pages, all the words had turned into an indecipherable smudge. 'What happened?' I asked – I almost shouted – 'What did you do to all the Famous People?' Annie said, 'Maybe the ink faded. Or just ran off the page. It's a very old book. Isn't that what happens to things that are old, they fall apart? Isn't that what all this history teaches us?' And the Wise Old Owl was still on the cover, pointing that wand out at us, but now so ineffectually – because he had nothing to teach, nothing to show us, the Owl wasn't so Wise after all. And he looked quite dumbfounded with those stupid buck teeth he had.* **1492** – Ferdinand and Isabella of Spain sign the Alhambra decree, expelling all Jews from their land unless they convert to Catholicism. **1492** – Columbus discovers the New World. On his return, he brings the first cases of syphilis to Europe. **1493** – James IV wants to discover what the true language of God might be, uncorrupted by exposure to other people. To this end he sends a deaf mute to look after two babies on a remote island, to see what they'll end up speaking without any outside influence. They apparently settle on Hebrew. **1493** – Holy Roman Emperor Frederick III dies having his leg amputated. **1494** – Columbus discovers Cuba, and threatens to cut out the tongues of any of the sailors with him who claim that it is an island. This is because he is going to tell the king it's on the mainland. **1494** – The last building blocks of the Mausoleum of Halicarnassus, one of the two remaining Seven Wonders of the World, are plundered by crusaders. Just one Wonder to go, then (qv 262, 462, 1303). **1497** – In Florence, the priest Girolamo Savonorola orders the public destruction of all sinful objects in the Bonfire of the Vanities. **1498** – Savonorola is executed for insulting the pope on the same spot his bonfire had burned. **1499** – Edward, Earl of Warwick, is put to death. He is the last male member of the House of Plantagenet

ACRONYMS

BLT

There was more to the sandwich than the acronym. This was his principle, and even if it wasn't a very profound principle, it was at least one that he could stick to wholeheartedly. Yes, people expected that in a BLT there would be the presence of b(acon) l(ettuce) and t(omato) – it was what they were paying for, of course, and he certainly didn't stint on the main ingredients. The leading players, as he liked to think of them, in his sandwich drama. The lettuce, he made sure, was crispy, the tomato was juicy. The bacon was Sainsbury's best. But it was the extra effort, the extra *love*, that made the sandwich special. After years of experimenting – *years* – he'd discovered that the best bread to highlight the charms of the bacon was a malted wheatgrain he could only get at Tesco's – that was the other side of town from Sainsbury's, so that wasn't very convenient. It soaked up the tomato nicely, it had enough grit to it to give some solid substance if the tomato leaked its flavours too wetly. And the mayonnaise was a matter of some secret pride; not a single mayonnaise at all, but three different types, from three different shops, all mixed together. The tang of a garlic mayonnaise smoothed over and thickened by the stodge of a regular brand, with a trace of a low-fat variant complementing them both nicely, full of flavour in spite of the reduced calories. He spread the mayonnaise concoction generously on to the bread, then layered it with the lettuce, layered that with the bacon, and placed quartered tomatoes on the top to complete the assembly. It was, he had decided, and he should know, the best BLT sandwich in the world.

Not that any of the customers seemed to notice. But he didn't mind that, he was used to that. Best that they didn't. Best that the artist didn't reveal himself too obviously. He'd watch them eat their sandwiches, every last bite, and be satisfied. He sometimes had complaints about his chicken tikka, and the beef and French mustard was clearly never going to please everybody. But no-one, not ever, not in the history of his little station café, not in the history of his entire catering career, had ever disliked the BLT. Or, at least, never enough to tell him so.

He wasn't a stupid man. Simple, yes, undoubtedly, with simple tastes, and simple dreams. But not stupid. He knew full well that his talent wasn't all that remarkable. That it was unlikely to be recognised, let alone celebrated. But why should that matter? He knew that his presence in the world, and the subtle little gift God had given him, made people just a bit happier. Not by much, no, not in the scheme of things. But his was still a positive influence. He was on the side of the angels. When he died – and he hoped that wasn't for a long while yet, years off, he was happy, he was in no rush – he knew he'd have left the world slightly better than he'd found it. Not everybody could say the same, could they?

Annie could; Annie didn't do anything particularly well, she worked part-time at the local library now, but hadn't much of an actual *genius* for it – but she had a nice smile, and she wasn't ashamed to use it, she smiled at everybody, and they'd usually smile back, and that couldn't be a bad thing, could it? Their daughter Joanne was on the side of the angels too, he knew. She was grumpier than either of her parents, and her face naturally relaxed into a scowl, but she was a pharmacist – she *helped* people, helped them fight off their headaches and runny noses. Mark he wasn't so sure about. Mark would find his feet, he was sure. They all loved Mark anyway.

His own was an amiable diffidence, and it always had been. Even in his youth, when all his friends and his peers found a fire in their bellies, and decided they all wanted to change the world. Truth to tell, he'd nearly lost Annie because of it on his first date. He'd asked whether she might like to share a cup of tea and a spot of lunch, and he'd been so certain she'd say no he was flummoxed when she didn't. But he believed she could do and must do better, he couldn't see why she'd give half an hour of her precious time to him – and as he sat there, shyly, barely saying a word, toying nervously with his spoon, Annie began silently to agree with him. Then he'd bitten into his sandwich. 'Oh, no, no,' he'd said. The sandwich was thin and frail, and as he lifted it to his mouth the bread all but crumbled away in his hands. 'I could do better than that,' he told Annie, 'I could.' And without even asking he'd taken a bite out of Annie's sandwich too – an act that was forward, certainly, even rude, and Annie rather thrilled to it. He was *protecting* her – he was protecting her from disappointing comestibles. 'Awful,' he said. 'Tell you what. I *will* do better.' Promptly he got up, went to the counter, and demanded another sandwich – only this time he'd put it together *himself*, thank you very much. And his effort wasn't all that much better, this was years ago, this was long before wheatgrain bread and mayonnaise experiments. But Annie let him take her out to lunch again, and after the third lunch she kissed him on the cheek, and after the fourth she agreed to be his girl.

He had maintained his amiable diffidence ever since – into marriage, into fatherhood. But he knew that Annie had seen him in a rare moment of dynamism, she'd seen him with his dander well and truly up. And even if the dander never rose again, he knew that Annie could remember it, and love him for it.

And it was with diffidence that he'd bought the café in the railway station. It was only a little café, but then, it was only a little railway station. There was only room for three tables. Once they were all filled, the shop was selling its tea and sandwiches as takeaway. He liked serving food to passengers – he liked to imagine they were all travelling somewhere exciting and romantic. He liked to fantasise about them, as he watched them enjoy their BLTs.

'A cup of tea, please,' said a man. 'And what are you having?' he said to his companion. She shrugged. 'Two cups of tea,' he said. 'And a sandwich, I suppose.'

'May I recommend the BLT? It's my specialty.'

'Uh, yeah, that'll be fine. Do you...?' – but the customer saw that his woman friend had already stomped off and sat down. 'Make that two sandwiches as well, yeah.'

He brought them two cups of tea, and two BLT sandwiches, to their table. The café was otherwise empty, they could have had their pick – and they'd chosen the table nearest the counter, and that was nice, that was his favourite table. He could see so much more easily everything that was going on there, he could share in it. Then he retreated back to his place, behind the counter, between the cash register and the muesli bars.

The man and the woman didn't speak for a while. The café owner had wondered whether they were man and wife – but he'd looked at their fingers when he put down the sandwiches, and there were no rings, so boyfriend and girlfriend, that was it. Boyfriend and girlfriend both blew on their teas. The café owner had made the teas piping hot. Best that way.

'You don't have to wait,' said the boyfriend at last.

'I'm happy here.'

'You're not happy.'

'No, of course I'm not happy. I'm not bloody happy. But if you're going to just walk away, if that's... what... if you want that, then at least I'm going to watch.'

'It's a train,' he said.

'What?'

'You said I'm walking away. But I'm catching a train.'

'Is that supposed to be funny?'

'No.'

'Because it bloody isn't.'

The café owner didn't like the swearing. It was never necessary. And sometimes, even though it was a little station, youths came into his café, youths with fire in their bellies and rude words in their mouths, and he'd be forced to fetch the station manager to ask them to leave. He wouldn't call the station manager on the woman, though. She wasn't swearing very loudly, and besides, he couldn't help but sympathise with her, especially when she said:

'You *really* don't love me any more?'

To which the man said nothing. Instead he bit into his sandwich.

She watched him eat for a while.

'Listen,' she said. Softer now. 'James. Please.'

'I'm not James any more, I'm Jay.'

'Jay then. Whatever.'

That seemed to have thrown her. She sipped at her tea. She didn't touch her sandwich.

'I just don't see how you've fallen out of love with me,' she said, at last. 'I mean, I'm not being arrogant, or... It's just that... It's sudden, that's what it is. You've *really* fallen out of love with me?'

'Yes,' he said.

'Just like that?' she asked.

'Leave it,' he said.

'No, just like that?'

'Yes,' he said.

'When?' she said, and laughed. 'Any specific time, or...?'

'Half past three,' he said. 'It just happened. There I was, in love with you, and half past three, wham, I'm not.' He chewed his BLT savagely. 'Deal with it.' Another bite, and a dollop of mayonnaise squeezed from the sandwich and on to his chin. It was a bit of garlic mixed with regular mixed with low-cal, and it slid down a little, then ground to a halt, clinging on.

'I'm a bastard,' he said, and sighed. 'You're better off without me.'

'Yes,' she said.

'It's not you, you know. It's me.'

'I know it's not me. I know it's not bloody me.'

He finished his sandwich. He checked his watch.

'I just want you to know,' she said, 'that you have made me very unhappy. Profoundly unhappy, I just want you to know,' she said, 'that that... is exactly what you have done.'

He nodded. 'Well, then,' he said.

'Well.' She nodded too, just a little nod, as if that was that. And then, 'Oh, for God's sake,' she said, and she leaned forward, and she moved her hand towards his face, and he flinched, as if she were finally going to hit him – and she wiped the mayonnaise off his chin.

'Oh,' he said. And laughed.

'You looked so stupid,' she said, laughing as well.

'I bet I did!'

The café owner smiled at them both in their merriment. He was just glad everything was all right again.

'I've got to go,' said the man suddenly, the laughter turned off like a tap, 'I'm going.'

'But the train isn't due for another...'

'I'll wait on the platform.'

'Then I'll come with you...'

'You haven't got a ticket.'

'I can buy a ticket.'

'No,' he said firmly. 'No.' And he stood over her, and for a moment the café owner thought he was going to kiss her, and the woman clearly thought so too. But they were both disappointed. And the man picked up his bags, and left.

After he'd gone, she half rose from her chair, as if to follow him – then sank back, what was the point? She looked at the blob of off-white mayonnaise on her forefinger, as if trying to remember how it had got there. Then she sucked it off. (The café owner noticed how her eyes lit up at the flavour.) Then, at last, she sighed, and got up after all.

'You haven't eaten your sandwich,' said the café owner.

She looked blankly at him, then blankly at the BLT. 'Oh. No.'

'It's very good.'

'I'm not hungry.'

'I can wrap it up for you, and you can take it away.'

'Oh. No. No, just sell it again.'

'I can't. I make each one fresh. Everyone who buys a sandwich from me, they know they're getting them fresh.' And he wanted her to see how proud he was of that. 'Look. Let me wrap it up for you. It'll only take a moment. And then you can eat it later.'

'I don't...'

'Because you're not hungry now, but you'll be hungry later. You'll be hungry again, won't you? You won't not be hungry forever. And then you'll remember your sandwich, you'll be glad of it then, won't you? Please,' he said, and he wanted to protect her, 'please.'

'Oh. Um. Yeah,' she said. 'Okay.' He thought she was about to cry.

'Lovely,' he said, 'lovely!' He almost clapped his hands. And he whisked the sandwich away, and took it behind the counter, and he wrapped it up in greaseproof paper. 'You'll like this,' he said, 'there's a bit of a special recipe to it. The mayonnaise is special. Well, you'll have tasted that.' He placed the sandwich carefully in a paper bag. He smiled at her. And she *could* have cried, but she decided to blink down the tears and smile back instead. 'I'm here every day,' he suddenly said to her, earnestly, a bit too earnest. 'I'm not going anywhere. If you want to chat about it.'

She frowned. 'Thanks.'

'Enjoy the sandwich.'

'I will.'

'I'm sorry,' he said. 'Really sorry. I'm sorry for your loss.' And she frowned again, he realised she hadn't known he'd been listening. He ploughed on anyway. 'Such a mess, such a *bloody* mess,' he said. 'Isn't it?'

She nodded. 'Yeah, it's a bloody mess.'

He smiled, and she smiled, better this time, better than before.

'I'm here,' he said. 'Remember.'

And as she left, she waved. It was an embarrassed wave, but it was meant well. He thought, looking back, it was meant well. She waved at him with the hand holding the sandwich – too tightly, he saw, the mayonnaise was squirting through the wrapping. 'Bye!'

A nice girl, he thought, in spite of the swearing. He didn't think he'd see her again, though. Why would she come back to a railway station, she hadn't even been a passenger, had she? She wasn't ever going to go anywhere. He hoped she'd enjoy her sandwich. He hoped she hadn't ruined it by wasting all the mayo.

That evening he got home, and he kissed Annie on the cheek. 'How was the library?' he asked. 'Oh, it was nice today, darling,' she said. She smiled. 'Oh, and Mark phoned.' 'Did he?' 'We've got to put our foot down with him, darling.' 'Yes, yes, I suppose we have to,' he said.

They had dinner, watched some television. 'I must have an early night,' he said. 'I've got to go to the supermarkets tomorrow, first thing. Sainsbury's *and* Tesco's.' He wondered whether Annie's love could ever just switch off like that, at half past three some day, without warning, without reason. 'I'll come to bed with you,' she said.

She cuddled up next to him. 'I love you,' he said, and he caught a note of sadness in his voice, and was surprised. 'Oh, and I love you, I love *you*,' Annie said, and she gave him a smile, and it wasn't the smile she just gave anyone, it was that *special* smile, and he knew he was safe, and happy, and very, very lucky.

MI5

When I was a kid, I had a book which taught me how to be a spy. *The Spy's Handbook*, or *Spy Dossier*, something which had 'spy' in the title. It showed me how to write messages in secret code so no-one could read them, and then how to write them in lemon juice so no-one could see them, and then how to hide them in the heel of my shoe so no-one could *find* them. I loved that book; I practised spy stuff on my school friends, it was the rage for nearly a term. I'd always thought Uncle

Michael had given it to me, but I wonder, now, whether it may have been my Dad. Probably it was my Dad.

The last time I'd visited him in the nursing home he'd slept through the whole thing. Now his eyes were bright and alert. 'Hello, Dad,' I said, 'look, I've brought you some flowers.' Flowers didn't seem quite right, but I had to bring something, and I wasn't sure chocolates were allowed. 'How is he today?' I asked the nurse, a black woman with big biceps. She sort of shrugged, and began arranging the tight little bouquet into a vase.

'Johnny,' he said, and he grabbed hold of my arm, 'Johnny, I need to tell you something.'

'It's James, Dad,' I told him. But he was having none of it, he went on gripping my arm with unusual strength, and all the more unusual because he'd never been a tactile man, he'd never hugged or put an arm around a son's shoulders the way a father's meant to do. 'Listen,' he said, 'I could never tell before, not *anyone*. Because bad things might happen, yes? But now...' And he released my arm, gestured around the room, at the blank four walls, at the little mounted TV, at the nurse pretending not to listen. And I understood. Bad things already had.

'Listen,' he said. His face wrestled with the words for a moment, and I couldn't tell whether he was hesitant to give up his secret, or had simply forgotten what he was talking about. Then, 'I'm a spy,' came out, quite simply, and he lay back on his pillow relieved.

'Has he said this before?' I asked the nurse.

'Never,' he said, before she could answer. 'Not even to your mother. The man said if I spoke to anyone, bad things might happen. It was the *might* that frightened me, Johnny, it wasn't that bad things *would* happen, it wasn't *quite* a threat. And the way he smiled, as if it were such a little thing.'

'Wait,' I said. 'What man? What are you talking about?'

And this is what he told me.

*

I'd not long been working at the Ministry. I liked it there; the staff were nice, and after work we'd usually go and have a pint at the Marquis of Granby on Romney Street, do you know it? Your mother liked me working there too, she said she was proud I was working for the government. It wasn't the Ministry of Defence, I'd tell her, nothing flash like that, it was only the Ministry of Agriculture and Fisheries. And I wasn't doing anything that special even there, I was just in admin. Itemising staff expenditure, making sure everyone had enough stationery. But your mother didn't care, she said she was proud anyway, and give me a kiss. I was working for the government, she said, I was helping my *country*. Me, I didn't care so much about that, if I'm honest. If I'm honest, I just liked those pints at the Marquis of Granby.

One evening I was finishing off one of those pints, and a man came up to me and asked if he could buy me another. I looked round for my friends, but it seemed they'd all gone. And I didn't really want a second pint, if your mother caught bitter on my breath she'd give me what for. But the man was very persuasive and bought me one anyway. I can't remember what he looked like, just sort of ordinary, maybe a little short? And he smiled a lot, that I do remember. He smiled as he told me he knew who I was, he knew all about me, he even sympathised about the staff stationery. I thought he must work for the Ministry too, but I did the payroll, I'd know, wouldn't I? And he asked if I'd like to make a little extra money.

There was nothing to it, he said. And believe me, I wouldn't have got involved if there had been, I'm no fool. All he wanted was a copy of the payroll for my department, just the names and the salaries, sent to him every month. On the first of each month, mind, never fail, even if it were New Year's Day, the very first day of each month. I said that was confidential, but he said nothing, and I asked him what he wanted it for, and he still said nothing. Then he smiled again, and said there was nothing to it, a fool could do it, and I was no fool, he could see that. And each month there'd be a little present sitting in my bank account as a thank you. An extra pound a month, he said, that's not to be sneezed at, not when there was nothing to it, just sending the information to the address he'd now give me. But it wasn't an address, not really, just a P.O. Box number. And I suppose I must have said yes, because then he was warning me not to tell anyone, not ever. Bad things might happen. And that ever growing smile.

It didn't feel like nothing, that first time I did it. I couldn't use the photocopier, it was too expensive in those days, I had to do it by hand. Going through the books, writing it all out as neatly as possible, and that was hard because my hand was shaking. At one point the head of admin came in, a nice chap called Graham, actually. And I whirled round, and told him I was just doing some housekeeping, something stupid like that, but he wasn't interested, just asked if I were coming to the pub. And I said I'd be there in a minute. And I finished up, put it all into an envelope, pushed it in the pillar box, and thought, I'm a spy. I'm a spy now. I think.

And so it went on. Most times I was copying out exactly the same thing, but once in a while someone would join or leave, someone would get a raise. And every month, that pound in my bank account. I wanted to tell your mother, of course, but I didn't dare. Bad things happening, but it wasn't just that – she was proud of me, working for my country, I didn't want those proud kisses to stop. I was still working for *some* country or other, though, and I wondered which one? Probably Russia, there was a lot of talk about Russia back then, but it might have been one of those little ones, I wouldn't know their names, I was never very good at geography. And I couldn't see that my betrayal was *hurting* anyone, I was really just a little spy, it was all right. And as the spying got easier, I began to think it couldn't be any use at all, what could Russia want with a payroll? And I had a mad moment. I changed one of the numbers in the salary, just as a whim, just to see what would happen, a three into an eight is so easy, a tick with the pen and it's done. And I popped it into the post, first of the month, same as always, went to the pub. That very evening a manila envelope was waiting for me when I got home from work. I opened it, found a copy of the payroll I'd only just sent. And in red they'd circled the little error I'd made, and written, 'No more mistakes. No more warnings.' I admit my blood ran cold, I wondered whether a Russian had written that, or that man in the pub with the smile. And I thought, if they *knew* the information already, enough to spot one tiny number, what did they need me for in the first place? And then – and this was worse still – that there hadn't been time for my information to reach them by post, by rights it should still be sitting in the pillar box. That they must be taking it from there themselves, maybe moments after I posted it. That they must be following to see when I did it, and as soon as my back was turned, they'd spring from the shadows, reach their hands down inside the slot, and make away with it. That maybe I was never really alone. After that I needed another bitter, I can tell you.

I didn't want to be a spy any more. I didn't want those pounds, there on each bank statement like an itch. But how I could stop? I began to drink more than my single pint in the Marquis of Granby. I had a fling with a girl, and your mother found out, of course, this was just after you were born, Johnny, she never guessed I was committing treason, but a bit of fun with a canteen girl and it was written all over my face. She said she forgave me, but I'm not sure she ever did, those proud kisses stopped anyhow.

And what can I tell you? It got easier. As all things do. The years went by, Graham moved on, I got his job. Now I could get my secretary to copy the payroll for me, she never asked why. And the pound payment kept coming, it never adjusted for inflation, pretty soon it wouldn't have bought me a pint. Some days I thought I was the victim of a practical joke, I'd never been a spy at all, that someone, somewhere, was getting the same useless payroll on the first day of every month and laughing themselves silly at my expense. And other days I'd sit there on the tube to Pimlico, with all the people shoving, knocking into me, and I knew what they thought of me, the same as my so-called colleagues at work, they thought I was pathetic, some sad loser who'd wasted thirty years in the civil service, that I had no hobbies, no friends, even my wife didn't kiss me any more, that had all dried up. And I'd think, you don't know it, but I'm a *spy*. And this information I'm passing on, who knows? Maybe it'll kill the lot of you. Maybe I'm killing you all, and you don't know, *none* of you know how dangerous I am.

The Berlin Wall fell; the Russians became good guys again, who'd have thought? Still I carried on with my treason, and still they paid me, even though I couldn't see who was left to do so. And on my fiftieth birthday the payments just stopped. No more pounds in my bank account. I thought maybe they'd made an error, I carried on sending payrolls. And then one month I changed all the numbers, just as I had all those years ago, just to provoke them. Nothing. Not even the hint of a threat. And I thought, who's giving you the information now? Looking round the office, one of *them*, who was the traitor, who now was getting their blood money. I'll find you out, I thought. I'll find you out. But I never did. I was a spy, but really not a very good one. When I retired I came home and took up gardening. Your mother likes the flowers. Thank you for the flowers, Johnny, thanks for bringing me flowers.

*

And after he'd finished, silence. Except for his wheezing. He looked at me as if expecting a round of applause. 'Dad,' I said to him, 'you didn't work for the Ministry of Fisheries. You worked at a post office.'

He frowned. 'That doesn't sound right, Johnny. Are you sure?' Then he shook his head. 'No. Your mother knows, ask your mother.'

'Mum's dead,' I said. 'Remember? And I'm not Johnny, I'm James, I'm bloody James.' I looked at the nurse, but she didn't react, she was still working on the flowers, for God's sake, how long does sticking flowers into a pot take? I wanted to tell Dad Mum was dead and it was unfair, because she'd always been alert, she'd been the strong one, she'd never have needed a nursing home. The wrong parent had died. And if Dad was going to have a fantasy about being a spy, couldn't he have been James Bond, something just a little *heroic*? 'I've got to go, Dad,' I said, saying none of these things, thank God, 'I'll be back next week.'

In fact, I didn't find the time for nearly three. Nothing special, the usual distractions. I brought Dad some fresh flowers. I asked for him at reception. 'I'm sorry, sir, there's no-one here by that name.' I asked again. And then for the nurse, the one who'd looked after him, I described her as black with big biceps. I may have got a bit angry. They called security, and I left.

And I wanted to tell my other half all about it. Because, obviously, it's all madness – but what if it isn't? 'How's your dad?' she asked. 'Fine,' I said. She'll never ask for details, she didn't like him. And I won't give her any. Just in case, who knows, bad things might happen. It's why I can't tell *anyone*. And why I've written this down. Only in secret code, mind, and in lemon juice. And folded tight and small, in the heel of my shoe.

GPS

At the funeral Joanne took Mark to one side, and told him to pull himself together. 'What do you mean?' said Mark. 'I'm not an idiot,' Joanne seethed, 'I can smell it all over you. This is a *funeral*, Mark. Just look at yourself. Just look.' Mark did, he looked; he was wearing his suit, and a tie. 'What do you mean?' he said again.

'It's about time you pulled your weight,' said Joanne. 'You need to start looking after Mum.' 'Why me?' asked Mark. Innocently enough, he thought, but it still made Joanne flare up, Christ, he couldn't say anything. 'Because I was the one, while Dad was dying, I was the one who visited every weekend. Most weekends, and it's your turn now, you have to make sure Mum is all right. And besides, Mark, *I've* got a *job*.' Mark was a little frightened of his younger sister, so he agreed he'd do what he could.

It was hard to get Mum on her own that day. She was always busy, doing funeral stuff. But he cornered her at last. 'All right then?' he said. Mum said, 'Thanks for coming, Mark,' and gave him a hug. She buried her face into his suit for a few seconds. 'I could come over some time,' said Mark, 'you know, see how you are.' 'Oh, yes. Yes.' 'I mean, not for a bit, right? I imagine you'll be too busy mourning.' 'How about Thursday?' Mum said.

So on Thursday, a bit before noon, Mark sat in the car opposite his parents' house. The house he'd grown up in, he felt comfortable there. But still, it took a bit of courage for him to go in, he had to have a toke first, just a little one. 'All right,' he said to himself, 'all right, we're doing it, we're getting out of the car, we're doing it.' And a few minutes later he sighed and did.

'You look nice,' said Mum. 'Come in!' He *did* look nice; he was wearing his suit, the same one he'd worn to the funeral. (Though he hadn't bothered with the tie.) She made him a cup of tea. 'You all right then?' he asked. 'I'm fine, how about you?' 'Yeah, I'm good.' They sat down in the lounge; Mum on the sofa, Mark on the visitor's chair, opposite her. He hoped they weren't going to talk about death.

'How's work?' he asked her.

'Oh, you know,' she said. 'It's only part-time.'

'What is it you do again?'

'I work in the local library.'

'Doing what?'

'Oh, you're not interested.'

'No,' he said, 'I am.'

'I'm on the issue desk, mostly. Stamping the books.'

'Is that fun?'

'It's nice,' she said. 'Yes.'

'I could pop in one day,' he said. 'See you, if you like.'

'It's not very interesting.'

'You know, see you in action.'

'It's not interesting. I'm sure you have better things to do!' Mark supposed that libraries hadn't changed much since he'd last been in one, he supposed there wasn't much talking allowed. That would be good. 'I miss Jack,' said Mum, suddenly. Oh God, he thought, here we go.

'Do you?' said Mark.

'I mean, it wasn't as if it were out of the blue. And Jack had always said it'd be his heart that'd get him. He used to joke about it, actually. You know, because his dad had died of heart problems too. Do you remember Grandad?' Mark said he did, but what he really remembered were old photographs, and getting the day off school when they buried him, he'd liked that. 'So Jack used to joke about that.' Mum frowned. 'I can't remember actually what the joke was.'

'Right,' said Mark.

'I mean, it was British Rail who killed him in the end,' said Mum. 'When they closed down the local station. They said no-one needed it any more. But Jack needed it. He said he'd move the café somewhere else, but he never did. And look, within a year, dead. Makes you think, doesn't it?'

'Right,' said Mark. 'Still.' He looked at his watch. He'd been in the house for only seven minutes. Jesus Christ. 'Still, I wondered if there was anything you'd like to *do?*' Besides talk. About death.

'Do?'

'Yeah, I mean, I've got the car. So if there's anywhere you want me to take you...'

Mark had been thinking of a supermarket. Instead Mum said, 'Hever Castle.'

'What?'

'Hever Castle.'

'What's at Hever Castle?'

'I don't know. I've never been.'

'Why Hever Castle?' Mum shrugged. 'I don't know where Hever Castle is,' said Mark.

'That doesn't matter,' said Mum. 'I'm sure I've got a map somewhere. Hang on.' And she went off, and Mark sat in the lounge unhappily for a few minutes – and was just about to go looking for her, maybe the old lady had forgotten what she was doing, he didn't know – when she all but came bounding back with a road atlas. 'Here we are!' she said, gaily.

So, they set off for Hever Castle. Mark had no real expectations that they'd ever *reach* there. 'You're going to have to navigate,' he said to his mum, 'are you all right with that?' 'Oh, I think so,' said Mum amiably, and laid out the atlas on her lap, and traced a route with her finger. 'Now, we're going to have to end up on the B2023,' she said, 'and the best way to reach *that* is...' Mark waited while she pondered the problem, none too patiently, but his mum was too busy to notice. 'Right,' she said, 'right. All right. You can start the car now. And at the end of the road, turn right.'

The journey took about an hour and a half, which was good timing, all told. But the castle closed at five o'clock, and it was already gone three when they got there. There wasn't much time to do more than scurry around, looking at where Anne Boleyn had slept, peer at the gardens, peer at the maze. 'I enjoyed that,' said Mum. And Mark realised he had too. They'd talked on the way there in the car, but it was always about road directions – which junction to take off which motorway, whether there was a roundabout coming up. 'Can I navigate us home again?' asked Mum, 'please?' and Mark said he'd have it no other way. When they got back to base camp, it was getting dark. 'Thank you for a lovely day, darling,' said Mum, and kissed Mark on the cheek. 'Can we do it again soon?' 'What, Hever Castle?' asked Mark. And Mum laughed, 'No, no, silly! Somewhere else! Somewhere else, wherever you like.' 'Okay,' said Mark, 'but it's wherever *you* like. I do the driving. You do the choosing.' 'And the map reading,' said Mum. 'And the map reading,' said Mark, 'yeah!'

Pretty soon, though, he began to pick some of the Thursday outings as well; Mum liked that, she liked the odd surprise. But she always got to navigate. And there was an unspoken rule that they'd never go anywhere that wasn't within a hundred-mile radius of Mum's home (or so – they broke it a few times, without knowing) – just so they could comfortably do the whole trip there and back in a single day. And he'd get to her house first thing every Thursday morning, bright and early, to make the best of it – sometimes in a suit, sometimes not, but always clean. Sometimes she'd pick art galleries and museums, and Mark didn't like those much; he didn't want to *learn*; but it was okay, Mum wasn't the sort to gawp at every painting or broken pot, it was just another destination to tick off the list. And indeed, the destination wasn't the important part, it was the journey, and they began to choose places that were as obscure as could be. 'There's a doll museum in Newark,' she'd say, and he'd say, 'just tell me how to get there!'

In the Woburn Abbey toilets Mark got caught smoking a spliff, and it was only because it was the end of the day and the guy from security wanted to go home that he didn't get into any trouble. After that, though, Mark was a little more careful. He'd hide deep in the gardens of stately homes, when his mum was in the gift shop or the café , where no-one could see. Sometimes he didn't even smoke at all!

And Mum would start to pick routes that were more of a challenge to her. 'No motorways today,' she'd say, as she thumbed through the atlas to find the right page, sitting in the passenger seat in her best clothes, looking so proud and happy. 'Motorways make this one too easy.' And Mark would laugh, and off they'd drive.

They learned to drive in silence, without awkwardness, without a need to fill the void – because it wasn't a void, was it, it was just two people not wanting to talk for a bit, what could be more normal than that? One day Mark began to sing under his breath, and it was a pop song he knew, and Mum asked him to sing louder – and he did so, and he taught it to her, and she sang along to the chorus. And she taught him a pop song of her own. A really old one. And he'd never much liked being taught, but it was lovely, actually, it was lovely.

'Your dad always loved you,' she said to Mark one day, on the way to Chislehurst Caves.

'Oh, okay,' said Mark.

'I want you to know that. He was always proud of you, no matter what.'

'Okay.'

'It was always me,' she said. 'It was me... I'm sorry. I'm sorry.'

'It doesn't matter, Mum,' said Mark. 'It really doesn't.'

One day he told his mum he was seeing this girl he knew. That they'd been going out for nearly a month now, that made it pretty serious. 'How did you meet?' said Mum. 'Don't worry about that,' said Mark; that part wasn't so great, they'd both been off their faces, and they'd gone back to hers for sex. And in the morning when they woke up they decided, with surprise, that they liked each other. Mark felt proud of that. Mark felt that was a sign he was ready to commit. 'What's her name?' 'Nita.' 'Nita? What's that?' 'Short for Anita. She prefers Nita. And she's got a son called Lewis, he's three.' 'Oh dear,' said Mum, 'she's got a baby!' 'He's not a baby. He's a nice kid, Mum.' 'Oh, I'm sure,' said Mum. 'But being with a child that's yours is hard enough.'

Mark remembered that first morning, waking up to find Nita in bed, not knowing quite how he'd got there. And there was this little kid bouncing about, and he *hadn't* freaked, he'd actually rather liked it. He wanted to say to his mum that he thought his new-found maturity was all because of these trips he took with her, it was all because of her. He didn't. 'I'd love you to meet them, Mum,' he said. 'I'd love you to like them.'

'You said what?' Nita was livid. 'What do I want to meet your mum for?' 'I thought we could go out on a trip,' said Mark, 'all four of us. It'd be nice for Lewis. I'll drive.' 'No fucking way am I going to spend the day with some old lady,' said Nita, but Mark insisted, he put his foot down, it was their first argument and he won it. The night before, Mum phoned Mark up. 'Darling, do we *have* to go in a group?' she said. 'These Thursdays, they're just about us, aren't they?' 'You don't want to meet them.' 'I do. I do. But not right now.' 'Okay,' said Mark, and he was a bit relieved really, 'but you will meet them some day.' He let Nita think she'd won the argument after all, and she was so pleased she gave him a blowjob that night without his even having to ask. And Lewis was pleased too, probably, he wasn't an expressive kid, it was always hard to tell.

Christmas didn't fall on a Thursday, but Mark went to see his mum anyway. He wanted to be there when she opened her present. She was all fingers and thumbs, or maybe he'd put too much sellotape on, he wasn't very good at wrapping. It was the best present ever. And expensive too, he hadn't been able to afford anything for Nita or Lewis at all. 'What is it?' asked Mum, holding the box away from her. 'It's a satellite thing,' said Mark. 'It means that next time we're in the car, we can go *anywhere*.' 'But I don't have a car, I can't drive,' said Mum. Mark laughed. 'It's *yours*, Mum, and I'll keep it in *my* car, and I promise you, I'll only ever use it on our trips together, that's what it's for.' His eyes were tearing up. Mum put the box down, she didn't look very impressed – couldn't she see this was the most generous thing he'd ever done? In his whole life? And it was actually *all* his own money, he'd *really* paid for it, it was all from him. He actually began to cry a bit, he was *good*, he was a good man at last, he was good, he was so good. And this is what good felt like, a heart soaring with pride, and runny eyes. 'We'll try it out on Thursday,' he said, 'wherever you want to go.' 'It's your turn to choose,' she said quietly. 'No, no, wherever *you* want, whatever *you* want to do.' That soaring heart. That pride. 'I love you, Mum. Mum?' 'Yes. Yes, I love you too.'

On Thursday she picked Whipsnade Zoo. 'Zoos are a bit cold this time of year, Mum,' said Mark. Mum shrugged. She got out her atlas. He turned on the satnav. 'Turn left at the end of the road,' she told Mark. 'At the end of the road turn right,' the satnav said. 'There seems to be a difference of opinion!' laughed Mark, and turned right.

Mum didn't speak much on the trip to Whipsnade Zoo. Or on the trip to Portchester Castle the week after, or Cobham Bus Museum the week after that. She tried a few times, but the satnav would honk at a speed camera suddenly, and she'd fall silent again. But silence was good, that wasn't an awkward thing any more. And sometimes Mark would sing. He didn't know any more pop songs, he'd lost touch with so much these last few years. But he'd picked up some songs Lewis had learned at nursery. He'd sing those. Sometimes Mum would sing along.

And each trip Mum would bring the atlas. 'You don't need to, Mum,' laughed Mark. 'In case the Machine breaks down,' said Mum. She always referred to it as 'the Machine'. 'It won't break down, I charge the battery every night before coming,' said Mark. 'Oh,' said Mum. But she brought along the atlas anyway.

One Tuesday Mark came to the house bright and early. Mum fairly gawped at him there on the doorstep. 'But it's Tuesday,' she said. 'I know,' said Mark, 'but I thought a surprise trip would be fun.' He couldn't keep still, she noticed. He wasn't wearing his suit either. 'But I work at the library on Tuesdays,' said Mum. 'But it'll be fun, though, and the library won't care,' said Mark, 'come on, let's get a move on.' 'I haven't even chosen a place to go,' said Mum, 'let me have a look in the AA handbook.' 'Okay,' said Mark, 'but quick.' Mum chose the Tring Natural History Museum, in Tring. 'Sounds good,' said Mark, 'let's go.' She went to fetch the atlas.

The satnav took them to Tring in a little under two hours. The Natural History Museum there was stuffed full of stuffed animals. The free leaflet at the info desk said that it offered a unique experience for all the family. Both Mark and his mum agreed that was probably true. As they walked around, looking at stuffed zebras, and stuffed goats, Mark kept fiddling with his mobile phone. When it finally rang, Mark jumped, as if he hadn't been expecting it to ring in the first place. He walked a little way from his mother, hid behind a stuffed crocodile. She could still hear every word he said.

'It's borrowed. I've borrowed it, that's all. Because I. Because. Because I say so. Yeah. Well, fuck you. Baby. Baby, listen. No, can't you. Fuck. No, listen. I said

I borrowed it, I'll give it back, I just need. Well, fuck you. Baby. Well, fuck you. Fuck.'

'Is there a problem?' Mum asked.

'No,' he said. 'Do you want to see any more stuffed animals, or...?'

'I think we can go,' said Mum.

When they got back to the car, Mark just sat there for a while.

'Mark?'

'I've got an idea,' said Mark. And he turned to his mum, and smiled. 'Let's not go home just yet.'

'Oh,' said Mum. 'Well, where would you like to go?' She thought he might be hungry. She was thinking he might say a supermarket.

'Let's go to Land's End.'

'What?'

'I love you, Mum.'

'I know you do.'

'I love you.'

'Why Land's End?'

'Or the other one,' he said. 'John o'Groats. What's the one at the top, Land's End, or John o'Groats?'

'I don't know,' said Mum.

'I'll have a look on the satnav. It doesn't matter. Let's just drive on. Let's just drive on as far as we can get.'

'Won't that take rather a long time?' asked Mum.

'Right,' said Mark to himself. 'All right. Let's go for it. We're going for it. All right.' He started the engine. He left the car park. 'At the end of the road, turn right,' said the satnav.

They drove on in silence for a while. Even the satnav didn't dare speak. Then Mark turned to his mum, and beamed at her, and said, 'All right then?'

'I want to go home,' she said.

'It's early yet,' said Mark. 'And we've done everything around here, every castle, every museum, every single bloody art gallery. Haven't we?' Still beaming. 'We need to be braver. Let's find somewhere new to explore.'

'I want to go home, darling, really...'

The mobile phone rang.

'Hold that thought,' said Mark cheerfully. He answered the phone. 'Fuck you,' he said. 'No, fuck *you*.' And he hung up, flung the phone angrily on to the back seat. 'I'll bet there's a great museum at Land's End,' said Mark. 'If I were in Land's End, I'd put a museum there. Or a castle. Or some nice gardens, I'll bet.'

They drove on. At length Mark began singing one of the nursery songs. Mum joined in on the chorus when he asked her to.

It began to get dark. 'Here's the plan,' said Mark. 'I've got money, okay. Not a lot of money, but it'll keep us going for a while. So long as we use it on the essentials, okay? Food. Petrol. Admission fees for the tourist attractions.'

'Where did you get the money?'

'Shut up. I borrowed it. It's okay. That's not the important bit, shut up. But, you see, we don't need hotels. You don't need hotels, do you? Because hotels would eat up the money really fast. I think we should just sleep in the car. You can sleep in the car, can't you, Mum?'

'It's very cold,' said Mum. The roads were beginning to freeze over, as the satnav directed them down ever more narrow and remote country lanes. 'Bear right,' said the satnav, and Mark did, into the darkness.

An hour or so later Mark found a field. He drove on to it. 'Turn around when possible,' said the satnav. 'We can sleep here,' said Mark. 'We'll be all right. And tomorrow we'll drive on, tomorrow another museum, okay?'

He went outside. He peed, paced about, lit up. Mum watched him through the window. She couldn't tell whether the smoke coming from his mouth was cold night air or dope. She wound down the window. 'Come back into the car, Mark,' she said. 'You'll catch your death.' He looked ashamed that she'd seen him smoking. 'It's all right,' she said, 'it's all right, you can smoke in here if you have to.'

So he did.

'Can I have a puff?' she asked eventually. He looked at her in surprise. And then, without a word, passed her the joint. She took a quick hit. 'Does nothing for me,' she said, a little sadly, and handed it back.

'Good night,' said Mark. 'I'll lower down your seat. And you can use my coat as a blanket.'

'You need your coat. You'll be cold.'

'I'll be okay. I'll be okay. I want you warm, Mum. I love you, Mum.'

'Yes, I love you too.'

She slept for a while. Sometimes when she surfaced she thought Mark was sleeping, but he hadn't bothered to lower his seat, it was hard to tell. At other times he was smoking, and filling the car with something sweet and sickly, and crying.

They were both woken by the sound of the mobile phone. It had gone dawn, there was sunlight peering in through the windows, and cows. Mark scrabbled in the back seat to find it.

'Hello? No. No, I'm not coming back. Do not get the police. Do not get the police, if you get the police, it's over between us. Because I don't want to. Because I don't love you. It just stopped. Yes. Yeah. You have no idea what I'm going through, you have no fucking idea.' He hung up. He beat at the steering wheel angrily. He began crying again.

'Mark?'

'She's calling the police.'

'How much money did you take?'

'Not enough. Christ. The police won't care. Bet you, the police will just laugh. I'll protect you, Mum. I'll protect you from the police. Where shall we go today? You just keep an eye out for anywhere you fancy, you know, any museums and shit, and we'll stop, okay?'

They reversed through the cows, back on to the lane.

He began smoking again. She wasn't sure that was a very good idea. She even said so. He didn't reply.

The phone kept ringing. 'Ignore it,' said Mark.

She wondered why he didn't just turn it off. She wondered too where the Machine was taking them. All these narrow roads, not even roads, farm tracks sometimes. This couldn't be the best route to Land's End, that made no sense. Or John o'Groats, whichever one they were heading to. She wondered whether Mark simply hadn't put in the destination properly, and the Machine was now just giving them ever more random instructions. Turn left, turn right, keep going, keep going, keep going. She wondered whether the Machine simply wasn't as good at the navigation as she was.

Mark suddenly defied the Machine, and pulled over to the side of the road.

'What is it?' she asked.

Mark didn't move. He sat there, rigid. He gripped the steering wheel so tightly his knuckles blanched.

'Mark?'

'I'm dying,' he whispered.

'What?'

'I'm having a heart attack,' he said. 'Oh God. Oh God.'

'You're not dying.'

'There's a pain in my chest. It's so bad. I can't move, it's so bad, Mum.' He began to cry. 'I'm going to die like Dad.'

'Let go of the steering wheel.'

'I can't. If I let go, my heart will pop.'

'That's nonsense.'

'Holding on is the only thing I can do, if I hold on, it won't pop, I know it.'

'At least give me your little cigarette thing. That'll do you no good at all.' She reached between his fingers, pulled from them a spliff that had nearly burned down to his skin. His left hand relaxed as she did so. She unwound the window, threw the spliff away. 'Now then, let go,' she said. He did.

'Oh, Mum,' he said.

'It's all right.'

'Oh, Mum. You made me good. You taught me, you made me really good.'

'Shut up,' she said. 'Shut up and listen. I want you to relax a moment. Good...'

'I can't...'

'You *are*, good. And move over.'

'You can't drive.'

'I've been watching you. I've been watching you for months. How hard can it be?' She gave him a smile. One of those special smiles his father had known and loved, one of those smiles she'd never quite found it in her heart to give Mark since he was a baby. 'Do you really think that in all this time we've had together you weren't teaching me too?'

And very gently Mark slid over to the passenger seat. Clutching his chest all the while, as if doing so would keep his heart intact. And Annie got out of the car, walked around, and sat behind the wheel.

'Now,' she said. 'Listen to me. I love you. And I'm not going to let you die too.' Mark, now just sniffing back his tears, nodded. 'Now,' she said, this time to the car. 'Where do we go?'

'The satnav,' he said. 'It'll direct us to a hospital. Oh God, hurry.'

'We don't need that,' she said. She unclipped the satnav from the ventilator, unwound the window, threw that too away. Mark gave a little cry of despair as she did so.

She reached across, grabbed the atlas from the floor where it had fallen as she'd slept. There was such a sweet fug to the air that her head swam as she bent down – she thought she might pass out, even, but she got a grip on herself. She was okay to drive, she was okay to do anything. 'I'll protect you,' she said to her son. And she leafed through the atlas, and began looking on the maps for any symbols marked 'H'.

AKA

You don't deserve a name any longer. That's what they're telling you. Maybe, if you behave yourself, you'll get your name back one day. Maybe, if you behave, you'll get *another* name, a better name, maybe. But for the time being you'll be JBW. This is how you must refer to yourself. This is now who you are. Any attempt to pretend you have more than an acronym, to use a name to which you no longer have a right, will only delay any future restoration of that name in the first place. Pretend not to be JBW if you want to risk it, they say – but that'll only keep you as JBW all the longer. JBW. You think it makes you sound inhuman. You think it sounds like a car registration plate.

Oh, it wasn't acronyms at the beginning. They take you out to dinner, all smiles and politeness, tell you to order from the menu whatever you want. It's first names when they're being friendly, and surnames for respect. 'We have a job offer for you,' they say.

'I already have a job.' And you like your job, too, it's a nice job, and the people who work there seem to like you; they remember you on your birthdays, they ask you to take part in Secret Santa at Christmas.

'This is only part-time, you can do your other job around it,' they say. 'And it'll help your country. You want to help your country, don't you?' Truth is, you're not bothered. I mean, as countries go it's all right, but it's just an accident of birth, isn't it? You look at their earnest faces, their hopeful faces, and you realise they're mixing you up with somebody who gives a toss.

But of course, you knew they'd come for you in the end. One of them is a black woman with big biceps, and you've been looking out for her for *years*. She doesn't say anything, she lets her colleagues do all the chat, but it's nevertheless to her you direct all your answers.

'I know what you want me to do,' you say. And you tell some fantastical story of how your father was a spy, how he sent payroll information to a P.O. box address. They look bemused by this. Well, the man in the smart suit, and the other man in the smart suit, and the woman in the smart suit, they all look bemused. The black woman with the big biceps doesn't seem to react at all.

'That sounds like a paranoid delusion,' says the man in the smart suit.

'Maybe we've got the wrong man for the job,' says the man in the smart suit – the *other* man in the smart suit, not that first man in the smart suit.

You begin to protest. You're sure you're the *perfect* man for the job! Whatever it turns out to be.

'You want to help your country?'

You do, you do, whatever it takes. The woman in the suit smiles reassuringly at you. And you know you're going to be all right.

They want you in surveillance. They want you surveilling things. You like the sound of the word 'surveillance'. 'What would you want surveilled?' People. Mostly. Entirely. 'What people?' It's very easy. They want you to get on a bus, preferably at rush hour, when it's nice and busy. And *choose* someone. You can surveille them. See where they go, see what they do. 'What, just anyone?' Yes. 'No-one in particular?' No, it's up to you. 'And what, write a report on them? What am I looking for?' No report, no writing necessary, you just surveille them. Follow them around for as long as it takes. For as long as it takes.

They offer you a pound a week for the regular service you'll provide. You talk them up to one pound fifty, and all bus expenses. You love your country, but you drive a hard bargain. They talk amongst themselves, and then the black woman with the big biceps nods. You feel quite proud of your negotiation skills.

They suggest you get to work right away. There are a lot of people out there! Your first stab at the job should be seen as a dummy run, just something to show you the ropes. They think this first time that you should be accompanied. You choose the woman in the smart suit with the smile, and she smiles at that, and pulls down her suit flaps straight to look even smarter. The black woman with the big biceps has the gall to look disappointed she wasn't picked.

You both go to the nearest bus stop. 'Normally we'd want you to work on the 59 bus route,' says the woman, 'but this is only practice, it doesn't matter.' You like the 59 bus route, that's right by your house, that makes it nice and easy. 'That's why we chose it,' says the woman. A bus comes; it's not full, but full enough; you both get on; she pays for you. 'Who do I pick?' you say. 'Who do I follow?' There are children going home from school, mothers with shopping, some old man with a stick. It's up to you, it's your choice, it's *up to you*. So you choose the man sitting right in front, nodding his bald spot at you as he reads a book. 'Yes, he'll do,' confirms the woman.

You watch that bald spot intently for a while. 'You don't need to stare,' says the woman. 'You won't want to draw attention to yourself. Just glance at him every now and then. And see when he gets off.' And, eventually, he does; he rings the bell, puts away his book, stands up. You both stand up too, you follow him from the bus. He sets off down the pavement. You make after him in pursuit, but the woman grabs your arm. 'Give him a bit of space,' she says. 'Bend down to tie your shoelaces, that always works.' You tell her you wear slip-ons. 'Get shoelaced shoes,' she advises you.

You follow him at last, down the street, around the corner, and into the town centre. You hold back as he looks in the window of a greengrocer's, and he clearly decides not to buy any fruit. 'Eyes on him all the time, but not staring, keep it subtle.' Your mark goes into the supermarket, you do too. He takes a shopping basket – not a trolley, he doesn't need much today, or maybe he's just shopping for one, maybe he's single? 'Doesn't pay to be curious, you might form an attachment,' the woman warns you. She suggests you pick up a basket of your own, and load it with groceries every once in a while – 'You don't have to buy them, it's just for cover.' You end up with a basket full of dog food, even though you don't have a dog. 'Keep your eyes on him,' she reminds you, and you *do*, that's what you *are* doing – but it's getting harder because the man seems to be growing paler somehow, his clothes are losing their colour, and the very outline of his body is thinning and merging with the stacks of toilet paper rolls through which he's now sifting. And then, suddenly, he's gone altogether, he's just vanished into thin air.

'There you are,' says the woman. 'You're a natural.'

'What the hell happened?'

'I'm not really meant to tell you,' says the woman, and she bites her bottom lip a little coyly. 'No, come on,' you say. 'All right, let's go and get a coffee, you can buy me a coffee. Leave the shopping basket.' You go to a café just by the supermarket. The coffee you buy her costs more than the bus ticket she bought you.

'A man may be judged by the company he keeps,' she says.

You nod at that, and then admit you have no idea what she's talking about.

'Geniuses,' she says, 'will congregate around geniuses. Behind every great man is a great woman. And in these enlightened times, every great woman has a great man nipping at her heels too.'

'Okay,' you say. Then you shrug. You bought her a coffee for this? 'So. Tell me what happened to the man with the bald spot.'

'I'm getting to that,' she says.

And she explains that the reverse, then, is also true. That a great man can be brought down by an *inconsequential* woman. That a genius who surrounds himself with fools is tainted by their foolishness. That mediocrity is a weapon. That the mediocrity of one can sap the potential brilliance of another. 'And in extreme cases, even cause that person to disappear altogether.'

You don't quite like where this is going.

'You,' she says, 'are just such an extreme case. You are quite *astonishingly* mediocre. If you even *look* at someone for long enough, they're in danger.'

You don't think you're quite *that* bad.

'Oh, you are,' she says, and laughs, a little nervously. 'I've been through training, but let me tell you, hanging around with you this long is making me feel quite faint.' And you realise she is looking a little faint too. A bit off-colour, and tired. And you can see the outline of the table behind getting ever sharper through her head.

'A couple of hundred years ago,' the woman says, 'millions of people lived, and died, and there was no record kept, and they made no impact upon the world, and no-one remembered their names. They might as well have never existed. And that was fine, because that's the way it's *meant* to be. You want no more than one brilliant person in, what, a thousand? A true genius in maybe a million?'

The people at work remember your birthday, but you know you're not one in a million.

'But nowadays, everyone's told they're important. That they matter. They have votes, rights to opinions, their names catalogued forever on census reports. Everyone's just so, so special, and it means that "special" itself is being undervalued. "Special" means nothing any more. So. We have to use your mediocrity to make others more mediocre too. We need you to make the special people stand out.'

'And what happened to the man who disappeared? Is he dead? Did I kill him? Am I some sort of assassin?'

She smiles. 'If that makes you feel a bit more exciting,' she says, 'you go with that. Knock yourself out. Now forgive me, I have to go.' And she hurries out of the shop while she still has legs to carry her.

That night you go back home, eat dinner with your girlfriend. It occurs to you that she isn't remotely special. She's been hinting vaguely at the idea of marriage, and you were actually giving it a bit of thought, but you know now you never will. You wonder why she hasn't vanished yet. Perhaps she has. Perhaps she went ages ago, and you're just wasting your home life with an afterimage.

You wonder about all the people you work with at the office. Come to think of it, there is quite a high staff turnover.

And no-one ever wants to sit next to you at lunch.

'Are you all right?' says your girlfriend, and she takes your hand in hers. You love her. You love her in your own pathetic little way. It makes you sad. 'Penny for your thoughts?'

'Oh,' you say. 'They're not worth that much.'

*

It's easy to follow people. No-one bothers to look behind them. No-one thinks they're important enough to be followed, and they're right, of course, that's the point, isn't that the point? They're all stupid, even before you set to work on them. But after a little exposure to you, you see them get even stupider – they start frowning at long words in the newspaper, on the pavement they begin to forget which direction they were walking in. Most people vanish within the hour. Some take as little as five minutes. You feel guilty for the five-minute jobs, you don't think you've put in a good day's work, and so you vanish a second person straight after to give your money's worth.

You buy shoes that have laces.

You begin to enjoy the job. You do it impartially. At first you feel like taking out anyone you don't like the look of – the teenagers on the bus playing their iPods too loudly, the selfish women taking up extra seats with their shopping bags. But soon you realise that your victims just pick themselves. You can just *tell* who's ripe – and they aren't the unkind ones, or the boorish ones, they're too often just the ones sitting on their own, minding their own little businesses, not doing anyone any harm. They seem like nice people sometimes. Most of the time, they seem nice. Even nice people have to die, especially the nice people. You think of yourself as a grim reaper, but you're not reaping, are you? And you're not all that grim either. A bit *grey*, yes, nondescript and grey – but cheerful, cheerful.

You worry, sometimes, about the power you have. To murder with your mediocrity. You worry that it might make you too interesting, or too important – even, perhaps, just a little bit special – and that as a consequence your power will be blunted. That you might not make anyone vanish any more, or only make them *half* vanish, leave them a bit transparent – that'd be awful, that'd be like *maiming* them, you always want to be humane. And maiming with mediocrity doesn't sound half so good.

You worry, sometimes. And it's always about the wrong things.

Your girlfriend notices that you're happy, and for a while she's happy too, she thinks that it might have something to do with her. Then she stops being happy, because she suspects it's something to do with another woman. She snaps at you over dinner, and sulks, and you begin to wish you didn't have to come home at all, that you could spend your life just riding the 59 bus over and over, back and forth. You wonder whether you could vanish her out of spite.

And then, one day, it does become something to do with another woman.

You feel no connection to her at first. She's pretty, but not *especially* pretty, she seems like one of your nicer targets, but so what? She's easy to spot on the bus, she's wearing a red bow in her hair, and that's a bit odd, and it draws the eye – you'd probably have picked the man in front of you, look, he's already labouring over his crossword, he's getting stupider already and you've only just sat down. But the red bow is what you keep seeing, the splash of colour in the commuter grey, bobbing about as the bus bumps down the road. And you think, I'll follow that. The man with the crossword is safe for another day. You get off when she gets off.

She goes to the cinema. You like it when they go to the cinema, that's a treat. All you need do is sit behind them, and enjoy the movie, and they'll have disappeared by the time the end credits roll. It hardly requires any effort at all, just the occasional glance thrown to the back of the head during the boring talky bits, concentrating into that glance all the dullness of your personality you can muster. It's not a movie you'd have picked, but never mind. She buys popcorn. You don't; after all, once she's gone, you can eat hers.

She's still there at the end of the trailers, and that's okay. She's still there at the end of the feature, and that's a surprise.

She stays until the very last credit, she's one of those. And then she's outside, and blinking in the sunlight – and you're blinking too, but with bemusement, because by now you'd expect her outline to be a little wobbly at least, she should surely by now be a little see-through. She sets off and has a coffee. You follow. You sit opposite her, directly, and that's a bit daring, she might see – but by now you want to speed things along; eye-to-eye contact is fast and sure, if she looks into those vacant eyes of yours there's no way she'll stay intact for long. She catches your eye, but it doesn't leave an impression. She finishes her coffee, and then has a croissant too, just for good measure – just to rub in your failure, it seems – and as she eats it she stays so stubbornly solid you can't see any of the flakes of pastry falling down her throat and into her stomach the way you ought to.

Four hours later, after she's done some shopping – clothes, mainly, but essential groceries too – and you've stared balefully at her as she's made a phone call (she laughs a lot. Her husband? Boyfriend? You're surprised how jealous you feel) – and she's caught *another* bus, she's at last walking home. And you're almost racing after her now, because you've been thwarted, and it's against all the rules of stalking, but maybe if you actually *touched* her it would work, nothing much, just brushed her arm or something, nothing weird, nothing pervy, you want to kill her, not freak her out. And before you get a chance, she's suddenly turning into a driveway, up a path, and putting a key into the front door. She closes it behind her, shutting you out, shutting you out completely.

It shakes you. It would, wouldn't it? Your ego's fragile at the best of times.

You don't sleep well that night. At two in the morning you get up. Your girlfriend grunts, but doesn't wake. You had a fight over dinner, so she's been sleeping the other side of the bed, as far from you as she can get. You leave the house. Go for a walk. There's a service station down the road, you head towards it. There's a twenty-four-hour kiosk there, a man will serve customers through glass shutters. 'What'll it be?' he asks. 'I'll have a Kit Kat,' you say. He's vanished into thin air before he has a chance to take your money. You don't get the Kit Kat, but you don't need it now, you feel much better.

The next morning you feel re-energised. And happy again, you apologise to your girlfriend, you've been a bit out of sorts lately. Maybe the two of you could have an evening out, she suggests. You've not done anything for ages, not together, what about the cinema? You agree. You all but sprint to the bus stop for the 59, today's going to be good, you'll take out your target today, no problem – hell, why stop at one, let's take out a whole busload of the bastards! You select your victim, and you think, very deliberately, I'm going to *enjoy* this. And then you see the red bow is back, waving at you, on the other side of the bus.

She goes to the cinema again. This time you buy your own popcorn. (You're wise to do so, you'll be getting none from her.) Why does she keep going to the cinema, doesn't she have a *job* to go to? You prefer this movie. It's funny. She laughs, and you laugh, and you think, we're laughing *together*, there's a connection. You're glad that her taste in films has changed since you first met her, you're proving to be a positive influence in her life. After the movie she goes for a walk in the park. She sits on a bench and reads a book. It's a thick novel, and it looks a serious one, the author's surname has *lots* of syllables – and try as you might, you can't make her lose her place in it, you can't make her stumble over the difficult words.

She breaks off and makes a phone call. She laughs again. You glare at the phone. You wish you could make the person she's talking to so easily and with so much obvious *pleasure* just disappear. Maybe you can – at one point she takes the phone away from her ear and looks at it in frustration, she's been cut off.

You go up to her. Blushing furiously, you ask her anything. You ask her what time it is. 'Half past three,' she says. 'Half past three, thank you, thank you,' you say.

Your girlfriend was expecting to go to the cinema, but the red-bowed woman doesn't get home until gone eight o'clock. Your girlfriend is all dressed and made up. 'Where were you?' she asks. *Forgot.* 'We can go to the cinema tomorrow,' she says. *Don't want to go to the cinema. Not with you.'*

There's a message on the answering machine, asking why you've not been into the office for two days. And after you've listened to it, the phone rings, and you pick up the receiver.

'Is there a problem, James?' asks a voice.

'Who is this?' you ask.

'Don't waste time on the special ones,' says the voice. 'Get back to work on the mediocrities, and forget all about her.' You wonder if it's the black woman, it's not a voice you've heard before, and as she speaks you can imagine her biceps rippling.

But you refuse to listen. You *can't* listen. And at half past five the next morning you're standing outside the house of the red-bowed woman. Waiting for her. She doesn't come out till gone nine, but it was time well spent, you love looking at her house and imagining her inside it. And then you have the day together. She doesn't wear a red bow today, instead her hair is down, and long over her shoulders, it is beautiful, it's beautiful.

On the fourth day you're outside her house at half past five again. And before six a car pulls up beside you, and tells you to get in. You think it may be the police. But it's much worse.

They surround you on the back seat. The man in the smart suit says, 'You've done a lot of good work for us, but frankly, you're beginning to piss us off.' The other man in the smart suit agrees. The woman in the smart suit won't smile, she just looks so disappointed. Biceps won't even look at you. 'I love her,' you say, and it's only then, absurdly, that you realise it. They tell you they find this very funny, and they laugh, but there's no joy in the sound of it, you think they're faking. 'She's special, she's not for you. You mustn't see her again. You mustn't even think of her.' You tell them they can't stop you from thinking, and they tell you they *can* – and they know precisely what you're thinking all the time, they know what you're thinking *right now*, and they tell you, and they get it right.

They can't make you vanish, not in the usual way. That's your talent, not theirs, they're just not mediocre enough. But they can remove your identity. They tell you they've taken away your name. You're no longer James Brian Wilson, you're now just JBW. All they've left you is the acronym.

Even after that you show defiance, and they tell you they can hurt the people close to you. To prove it they get out a file of your cousin Donald – and with a stroke of the pen he's been scaled down to a D. Do what they say, or they'll keep going through your whole family, and your friends. Everyone you've ever loved, reduced to a series of capital letters. 'And the worst of it is, *we won't even tell them.*'

You go back home, go straight to bed. 'I'm not feeling well,' you tell your girlfriend. 'And you should know I've not been at work this week, I've been stalking a woman with a red bow, and no matter what I do she just won't go away.' In bed you try to stop thinking about her, but it's impossible! You treasure the afternoons you've spent together, the laughter you've shared, that conversation you had in the park! 'Half past three,' she said, and you thrill at the memory of it. And then there's the other woman, that girlfriend of yours, the one who's banging on the locked door (just as well you're not trying to sleep, just as well you're thinking about not thinking). You loved her once, you know you did. And now she's in danger too. You'll have to escape. It's the only way to protect her.

Within an hour you've packed your bags, and you're at the train station, ready to leave forever. The girlfriend came with you. She's sulky again, it gets right on your wick. Doesn't she realise that this is the most selfless thing you've ever done? It's all for her sake, you're a good man, you're good. You tell her you fell out of love with her yesterday. She gets angry. At half past three, you explain. You can't say more, there are spies everywhere: look, even the old man who served you the tea and the sandwiches is eavesdropping. 'Listen, James, please,' she says. 'I'm not James any more,' you remind her. 'I'm J.'

*

You have money. But most of it is in a bank account protected by plastic cards which carry a name that's no longer your own. You don't feel they belong to you any more, and you snap them all in half. You live to regret that. You later wonder whether they might have still worked after all. When you attempt to sign on the dole, they ask you for your name. You tell them you don't have one. 'If you haven't got a name, we can't give you any benefits,' you're told. So you're forced to whisper the name you once had, that man who so recently killed all those poor mediocre people. You get your money, but the shame of using that name makes you cry.

You get little jobs here and there. You want to warn everyone of your condition; that whatever work you're given, you'll probably end up murdering most of your fellow employees. But you keep it to yourself, and just try hard not to look at anyone very much. You work on a building site for a while, and then one day run when your foreman disappears. You work as a gardener. You work in a fish and chip shop. You work as a security guard at some abbey somewhere; busloads of tourists come in every day, and by five o'clock they've all vanished, and you're not sure whether that's your fault or not. No-one at the abbey wants you mixing with the public. Your job is to check that the toilets are safe.

One day you kill a man there.

'Hello,' he says. And there's smoke coming out of his mouth, and the smoke is sweet. 'I'm sorry, I'm just having a spliff, I'm sorry, I'll get rid of it.'

You're feeling very mediocre that day. You can feel the warning signs, you can feel the waves of failure and dullness coming off you, they could vanish a man at a hundred paces. 'You shouldn't be here,' you say to the man in the toilet.

'Please don't arrest me,' says the man. 'Please. I'm trying so hard. And I'm getting better. Please. My Mum's outside. Think of what it'll do to my Mum!'

And then the man vanished anyway, so very quickly, he must have been *very* mediocre to vanish so soon. And you feel so sorry, because he seemed like such a nice man, and you didn't want to hurt him, and you bet that the two of you would have had so much in common.

That's why you give up work for a while. You decide not to bother with work again. You'll have a very long holiday.

And you think of her, of course you do. She's the best of you. She's your soul. You know it's wrong to think of her, but how can it be so wrong? When she makes you feel as if you're worth something, even when you know you're not?

One day you see her again.

Your heart nearly stops. And then, it just keeps on beating.

You follow her. You haven't followed anyone for a while, and you fear you might be a bit rusty – but it all comes back to you, and you were once so good at this, you were *good*. She walks with her friends, and you hold back, you don't want any of them vanishing by mistake, that might draw attention to you. And then she stops off in the newsagent's, and buys herself a chocolate bar, and you hold back, you do the shoelace trick – you're glad you kept the shoes with laces, that works out well. You follow the red bow all the way home.

It's a different house. But that's okay. It looks like a nice house. So long as she's happy there.

You do what you should have done a long time ago. You walk up the path, and ring the doorbell.

You wonder whether she'll be nostalgic about those movies you saw together, or about that half past three joke you shared!

She answers the door. Standing right there in front of you, you realise she's a lot shorter than you remember. And you understand – it's all right – this *is* her, but back in time. This is her, but as a little girl.

'Hello,' you say. 'I just want you to know you're very special. One day you're going to be very special. And I'm never going to be able to hurt you, because of that.'

She says nothing, just gives a little girl frown. You're not saying the right words. Come on, find them. Find them, find them. You nameless idiot. You mediocrity. You piece of grey.

'Can I come in?' you ask.

PS

And the woman *did* return to the café, after all.

It was a few days later, and Jack had all but forgotten her, and the incident with the BLT sandwich. But when she came in she waved from the far side of the shop, a little warily, with a quizzical smile. And his face lit up at the sight of her.

She'd cried all she could, she'd thought, and she really wasn't going to cry any more.

'Hello!' he said to her.

'Hello,' she said back. 'I don't suppose you remember me, but…?'

'I do, I do!' said Jack.

'But I loved that sandwich of yours. Can I have another?'

'Of course,' he said. 'Please, sit down. Any table you want. I'll be a few minutes, I make each one fresh. They're my specialty.'

And he gave her his warmest and proudest smile, and it was infectious, she couldn't help smiling back. And he got out his best bacon, his lettuce, his tomato. And he set to work.

1505 – A young man studying to be a lawyer rides to his university during a thunderstorm. A lightning bolt nearly strikes him, and in his terror he calls out to the heavens that he will change his calling and become a monk. He keeps his vow. His name is Martin Luther, and his new interest in religion will inspire Protestantism, irrevocably change the face of the Christian world – and lead to an incalculable amount of bloodshed. **1506** – The death of Alexander, king of Lithuania – and the last monarch who is able to speak his country's language. **1506** – King Philip of Castile dies from typhoid fever, and his wife Joanna cannot bear the loss. She refuses to be parted from his dead body, and when she flees the plague takes her husband's coffin with her, opening it to ensure he is still inside, then kissing and cuddling his rotted corpse. She is pregnant at the time she is widowed; when her daughter Caterina is born she sees her as a final reminder of her beloved Philip, and jealously keeps her away from the world in a locked room in a castle. **1507** – Italian alchemist John Damian de Falcuis promises James IV of Scotland he can fly, and strapping wings made from wood and chicken feathers to his arms, leaps from the battlements of Stirling Castle (qv 1010). **1507** – Leonardo da Vinci finishes his masterpiece painting, the Mona Lisa. Francis I of France hangs it in his toilet. **1509** – An earthquake destroys Constantinople, just laying on thick what the Turks had done to it fifty years before. **1509** – Accession to the English throne of Henry VIII. *Charles Dickens once described Henry VIII as a 'spot of blood and grease', and it's certainly the image of him I prefer, this sociopathic despot with a mania for killing his own wives. I studied Henry VIII at school, and was soon surprised to find out that all the books I'd been reading about him for fun when I was a child were 'out of date'; yes, scholars were once very happy with the old blood 'n' grease theory, but if I were to write such stuff in my exams I would get a failing grade. I had no idea that perceptions of history can fall in and out of fashion: that the accepted facts could stay exactly the same, but the interpretations of what they meant were all so easily put up for grabs. And to discover moreover that 'history' is all about that grabbing – it's an academic exercise in which opinions and hypotheses are advanced then discredited, a strange little dance of the centuries. It's not as if there's any new archaeological evidence to discover about Henry VIII – it's simply that nowadays it's a little more cool to admire him than it used to be. And I remember going to a historical conference in the 1980s, and watching two Henry VIII experts, one G R Elton and one J J Scarisbrick, sneering at each other's biographies of the exact same man behind the exact same lectern. Apologies to Messrs Elton or Scarisbrick in the unlikely event that they're reading this (in the unlikely event that Annie has left them still alive): I wasn't at the conference through choice, it was a school trip; and this wasn't how I wanted history to be, I wanted it to be a simple long list of dates written down in an exercise book, not a matter of foggy academic rivalry; and besides, my future wife had arrived on the scene by this point, and she'd started being so much more blatant about kissing in public, and I was less concerned about the discrepancies of Henrician research and more about how to breathe and snog at the same time.* **1511** – King Henry VIII and his wife Catherine have a baby son. He is named Henry, like his father and grandfather before him, made Duke of Cornwall, and as Heir Apparent seems to ensure the healthy continuation of the Tudor line. Born on 1 January, he is known as 'the New Year's Boy'; there are extravagant celebrations at his birth, and Henry carries the favour of his beloved wife in a tournament, riding under the banner of 'Sir Loyal Heart'. Little Prince Hal dies at less than two months old. Had he survived, the entire history of Britain would have been very different. **1513** – Scotland suffers its worst military defeat at the battle of Flodden; about 10,000 soldiers are killed, including King James IV. His one-year-old son succeeds him as James V. **1514** – Henry and Catherine give birth to another son. Again, they call him Henry. Again, they name him Duke of Cornwall. Again, he dies in infancy. *Of course, Henry VIII was never intended to be king of England in the first place. He was only the second son of Henry VII; the eldest was Arthur. And so named, quite deliberately, to instil in the minds of the English people beleaguered by long civil war the promise of a new golden age, reminiscent of the mythical King Arthur a millennium before. He died too young to succeed his father (as, presumably, King Arthur the Second). What did we miss out on? Who knows? Personally, I bet he'd have been something of a disappointment. Everyone would have expected so much from his new Arthurian age. I bet all his courtiers would have nagged him to get a big round table. 'Go on, your majesty,' they'd have said, 'you know, like the proper King Arthur had.' And if he'd given in, if he'd gone out and bought a round table, that would just have been the start of it: next, they'd have been urging him to name his sword Excalibur and to go out on quests. And when he finally had to buckle down to the affairs of state of any normal monarch, and focus on laws about taxes and tithes, it would have seemed such an anticlimax. A second King Arthur would have seemed unoriginal at best, a call to a false nostalgia that could never have succeeded; at least, with his brother, we get a brand new myth altogether, the* _Six Wives of Henry VIII_*. (It's worth noting that any attempt to get someone on to the English throne called Arthur always ends badly, qv* _1203_*). I feel sorry for the young Henry, suddenly required to fill his brother's shoes, satisfy all those hopes that his brother inspired. He had to pretend to be Arthur. They even made him marry Arthur's wife, Catherine of Aragon. There's a marriage with problems right there.* **1517** – Martin Luther nails to a church door in Wittenburg his list of abuses practised by the papacy, provoking the Reformation. He later admits that a lot of the ideas came to him on the toilet, while suffering his regular bouts of constipation. **1518** – Holy Roman Emperor Charles V gives the first royal seal of approval to the slave trade. **1519** – Monteczuma, emperor of the Mexica, greets the Spanish conquistadors with gifts of gold and jewels. Though he could easily have the expeditionary force slaughtered, he mistakes Hernando Cortes for a reincarnation of the god Quetzalcoatl. Effectively he gives up his entire civilisation without a struggle; within three days he is a prisoner in his own palace, within two months he accepts vassalage to Charles V. **1519** – Leonardo da Vinci dies. His last words: 'I have offended God and mankind because my work did not reach the quality it should have.' **1519** – A widespread epidemic in the New World, a consequence of Europeans bringing new diseases to the continent, kills off much of the indigenous population in Central America. **1520** – The Stockholm Bloodbath: Danes murder the nobility and the clergy after they have invaded Sweden, despite a promise of general amnesty. **1521** – Ferdinand Magellan is killed halfway through his attempt to circumnavigate the globe. Juan Sebastian Elcano assumes command, and finishes the expedition in his stead. No-one ever refers to the Elcano line. **1523** – Martin Luther smuggles twelve nuns out of the Nimbschen Cistercian convent in herring barrels. He falls in love with one of them. 'Suddenly, and while I was occupied with far different thoughts, the Lord has plunged me into marriage.' **1524** – The world is predicted to end with a flood on 1 February. The Prior of St Bartholemew's in London builds himself a fortress, with enough food for two months. The skies remain obstinately clear. **1525** – The Ming Dynasty in China gives orders that all ships bearing more than one mast are to be seized and destroyed, to deter piracy and international trade. **1527** – Felix Manx, co-founder of the Swiss Anabaptists, is executed by drowning for being rebaptised as an adult. He is the first to be martyred by fellow Protestants. **1527** – Sixty Anabaptists meet in Augsburg to discuss the various differences between Swiss and German Protestant teachings. So many shortly afterwards are killed for their beliefs that it becomes known as the Martyrs' Synod. **1529** – The battle of Shimbra Kure (literally, 'chickpea swamp') is fought between the Adal sultanate and the kingdom of Ethiopia. Although outnumbered, the Adals have acquired the new hand-held firearms, and win the day. **1530** – St Felix's Flood washes away large parts of Flanders and Zeeland; some 400,000 Dutchmen are drowned. **1530** – The battle of Gavinano is fought between the Holy Roman Empire and Florence. The imperial commander, the Prince of Orange, is killed when shot in the chest twice with a musket. The Florentine leader, Francesco Ferruccio, too, is killed. He is captured by Fabrizio Maramaldo, and executed. Ferruccio's last words of defiance – 'You are killing a dead man' – make him a folk hero, and an icon as Italy battles for unification in the nineteenth century. In Italian, 'maramaldo' now means 'cowardly murderer'. **1531** – Thousands die in an earthquake in Lisbon. **1531** – Juan Diego Cuauhtlatoatzin has a vision of the Virgin Mary, and becomes the first indigenous American to witness a miracle. He is canonised by the Catholic Church in 2002. **1532** – Under Francisco Pizarro the Spanish conquistadors fight the Incas of Peru. Facing 3,000 natives at the battle of Puna with less than 200 men, Pizarro defeats them thanks to his modern weaponry. 400 Incas die, compared to three Spaniards. **1532** – A heavy drought in the Henan province of China coincides with a gigantic swarm of locusts. The population resorts to cannibalism. **1532** – The Paris Parlement has the city's beggars forced to work in the sewers, chained together in pairs. **1532** – A Viennese bishop with the delightful name of Federico Nausea proclaims that the world will end this year. **1533** – In his quest to find a legitimate male heir for his throne, Henry VIII divorces Catherine of Aragon and marries Anne Boleyn instead. He is excommunicated by the pope, and this leads to the English Reformation, and a whole new splinter religion outside the Catholic Church. *When I was a kid, I would remember the fate of Henry VIII's six wives with the saying: 'divorced, beheaded, died; divorced, beheaded, survived.' It's almost tempting to think Henry was despatching them in deliberate symmetry. I used to think of Catherine Parr as the 'winner' queen, but now I'm not so impressed. 'Survived' – if she were still surviving centuries later, then, yes, I'd take my hat off to her, but she's now wormfood just like all the other wives, so what difference does it make? Anyone can survive, if we're going to celebrate temporary survival as an achievement; good God, survival is what you and I are doing at the moment, that's nothing. My favourite wife is Jane Seymour. She died, but at least she did it doing her job, as it were – her exit from the royal stage, if not exactly of her own volition, was at least productive. (And she also gave her name to an actress who would one day go on to star in the popular TV series, 'Dr Quinn, Medicine Woman'. That was one of my own wife's favourites. She used to watch it every Sunday. And every time Jane Seymour's name popped up in the opening credits, I'd think of the original model, and give her a salute.)* **1533** – To avoid being burned to death by Pizarro, the last Inca Emperor Atahuallpa converts to Christianity. And is garrotted instead. **1534** – Jan Matthys leads a group of Anabaptists to seize Munster. Declaring it 'the new Jerusalem', he proclaims that on Easter Sunday Christ will return, and only Munster will be spared the apocalypse. As it turns out, on that very day he himself is killed in a siege; the rest of the world just goes on spinning. **1535** – Fray Tomas de Berlanga accidentally discovers the Galapagos Islands when he is blown off course in a storm. **1536** – The Pilgrimage of Grace, a rising in the North in protest against England's break with Rome, is resolved peacefully when its leader, Robert Aske, is pardoned by the king. Aske is later hanged in chains from the walls of York Castle. **1536** – Catherine of Aragon, wife to Henry VIII, dies of cancer. **1536** – Anne Boleyn, wife to Henry VIII, dies of decapitation. **1537** – James V of Scotland marries Princess Madeleine of France, and brings her home. Madeleine cannot suffer the Scottish climate and promptly dies of consumption. **1537** – Pope Paul III publishes the Sublimis Deus, declaring that all natives of the New World must be recognised as rational beings with souls and must not be enslaved. No-one seems to take much notice, and the pope rescinds it the following year. **1537** – Jane Seymour, third wife of Henry VIII, dies giving birth to the future Edward VI. **1539** – The first pigs are introduced to America. **1540** – The first muskets are introduced to Japan. **1540** – Henry VIII marries Anne of Cleves as his fourth wife, based upon flattering portraits painted by Holbein. When he meets her he is disappointed and tries to get out of the marriage, but can't do so without breaking a new German alliance. He can, however, have Thomas Cromwell, the man who recommended Holbein in the first place, arrested. He divorces Anne of Cleves on grounds the marriage has never been consummated, and promptly marries again – this time, Catherine Howard, and on the very day Cromwell is beheaded for treason. **1542** – James V of Scotland dies, feverish and humiliated, after his forces are defeated by the English at the battle of Solway Moss. It is the news that his wife has given birth to an heir – and that she's only a girl – that finally does for him. Mary becomes Queen of Scots at the age of one week. **1542** – Catherine Howard is beheaded for adultery. **1543** – Henry VIII marries his sixth wife, Catherine Parr. **1544** – Rats are introduced to America. **1545** – The future Ivan IV of Russia (the Terrible), at the age of eleven commits his very first rape. **1547** – Henry VIII dies at last. His last words: 'All is lost. Monks, monks, monks!' *I record all this because Henry VIII has gone. He's disappeared off the page. He's been lost forever. Unless I can find some way of keeping his history intact – his, yes, and all of his poor six wives. I phone the school secretaries again, 'Have you heard of King Henry VIII?' But they're weak on me, they just hang up on me, and before they do so I'm sure I can hear a lack of recognition in their irritated grunts. I ask my wife, 'Have you heard of King Henry VIII?', but she doesn't know any history any more. I ask Annie. But Annie just gives me that smile.* **1548** – At Uedehara, firearms are used for the first time on a battlefield in Japan. **1550** – Julius III is elected pope, and makes one of his servants a cardinal as thanks for looking after his pet monkey. **1551** – Taverns are licensed to sell alcohol in England and Wales for the first time. **1551** – Barbary pirates invade the Mediterranean island of Gozo, capture all the inhabitants, and sell them into slavery in Libya. **1553** – King Edward VI dies at fifteen. If he wasn't going to live very long, was it really worth his father beheading so many people and changing the entire country's religion so he could be born? **1553** – To avoid England falling back under Catholic rule under his sister Mary, Edward VI has named his cousin Lady Jane Grey to succeed him in his will. She reigns technically for nine days before she willingly hands over the throne to Mary. She is imprisoned in the Tower of London and never leaves it again. Ironically, she has spent her entire reign within the Tower of London, too, so this does not make much of a difference. **1553** – On Christmas Day, Spanish conquistador forces led by Pedro de Valdivia are entirely massacred by Mapuche Indians in Chile. The captured Valdivia offers in exchange for his life that the Spanish will leave their lands entirely, but as he is pleading the Mapuche cut off his forearms, roast them, and eat them in front of him. Which constitutes a no. **1554** – Queen Mary understands that Lady Jane Grey is merely a pawn in other men's politics. But has her executed regardless. **1554** – Mary sees a full length portrait of Philip II of Spain by Titian, and immediately declares herself in love with him. The Tudors have little luck with marriages based on Renaissance art (qv 1540). Philip marries Mary, but only as a political move, openly admitting he feels 'no carnal love for her'. And the union with the hated Catholic Spain causes great resentment in England. Mary, though, is happy. Until after a couple of phantom pregnancies Philip tires of her and takes off to lead armies in Flanders, and the abandoned wife sinks into a depression. **1555** – Ivan the Terrible has St Basil's Cathedral built. On completion he has the architects blinded, so they can never design a more beautiful building. **1555** – The Esperanza and the Bona Confidentia, two English ships under the command of Sir Hugh Willoughby, are recovered. They went missing a year before in the Arctic Circle, searching for the Northeast Passage. The dead are frozen into positions of working, eating or resting, like statues. **1555** – Queen Mary relieves her depression somewhat by burning Protestants for heresy. Over the few years of her reign, she gets through 284 of them. **1555** – The Spanish term for a black person, 'negro', is first used. **1556** – The Shaanxi earthquake kills 830,000 people in China. **1557** – Anne of Cleves, Henry VIII's 'ugly' wife, dies, having survived much longer than all the others. **1558** – Jean Nicot sends tobacco to France, lending his name to the word 'nicotine'. This single act leads to widespread addiction to a drug that has killed more people than the Shaanxi earthquake. But will, admittedly, make the addicts look really cool and rebellious. **1559** – King Henry II of France takes part in a jousting tournament to celebrate a peace treaty. He is killed. **1559** – Francis II succeeds his father to the French throne. At his coronation the teenage stammerer finds that the crown is too heavy for him, and needs it to be held in place by the nobles. He dies within the year. **1561** – St Paul's Cathedral is struck by lightning, and burns (qv 962, 1087, 1136). **1562** – The Earl of Tyrone ends hostilities against Elizabeth I of England, and swears homage to her in London. Five months later, back in Ireland, he launches a fresh rebellion against her. **1562** – Sir John Hawkins leaves Plymouth to begin a slave trade between Africa and Haiti. **1564** – Naples bans kissing in public, on penalty of death. **1566** – Lord Darnley, jealous husband to Mary Queen of Scots, has her secretary Rizzio stabbed fifty-six times. **1567** – Darnley is strangled, and then his house blown up. Mary is strongly implicated – and matters aren't helped when she marries the Earl of Bothwell, who is accused of the murder. She is deposed and imprisoned, and her one-year-old baby James becomes king instead – making this a hat trick of Scottish monarchs who have taken the throne as infants. Bothwell escapes to Denmark, where he is captured, chained to a pillar for ten years, and becomes a spectacle for paying tourists. **1567** – The Spanish invade the Netherlands, and establish the Council of Blood to weed out Protestantism. **1568** – Erik XIV of Sweden starts to believe he is his own brother John, and is deposed by his army. **1568** – The mentally unstable Don Carlos, heir to the throne of Spain, is left to die in solitary confinement by his own father. **1569** – The first recorded lottery is played outside St Paul's Cathedral; tickets cost ten shillings each. **1570** – Ivan the Terrible massacres the 60,000 inhabitants of Novgorod. **1572** – Catherine de Medici, queen mother of France, orders the extermination of all Huguenots (Protestants) within Paris. 3,000 people are slaughtered. Pope Gregory XIII sends a message of congratulations to the royal family. **1573** – The Inquisition condemns Paolo Veronese's painting of the Last Supper because it introduces secular and indecorous images into the scene. So he simply changes the name to The Feast in the House of Levi, and makes it another supper altogether. **1574** – Juan Fernandez discovers islands off the coast of Chile quite by chance. **1575** – Edward de Vere, Earl of Oxford, bows before Queen Elizabeth and loudly breaks wind. So mortified is he by this that he goes into voluntary exile for seven years, on a long journey around Europe. On his return Elizabeth greets him, and reassures him with the words: 'My lord, I had forgot the fart.' **1577** – Eric XIV is poisoned by pea soup laced with arsenic, administered by John – the very brother, now himself king, he imagines himself to be. **1578** – The king of Portugal dies at the battle of Ksar El Kebir. King Sebastian's body is never recovered, and many pretenders over the next forty years pop up claiming to be the missing king; by the nineteenth century a cult known as Sebastianism is in full swing, saying that the young and bold monarch will return to save the nation. **1578** – Sebastano Venier, the doge of Venice, dies of a broken heart after a fire damages his palace. Get over it. **1581** – The English Parliament outlaws Roman Catholicism. **1581** – Ivan the Terrible stabs his son and heir in a rage during an argument. **1583** – The world's oldest surviving amusement park is founded, in Denmark. **1584** – Reginald Scot argues, in his book 'The Discovery of Witchcraft', that those accused of being witches are suffering from mental illness. His book is burned. **1584** – William the Silent, prince of Orange, is assassinated. The man who does the deed had just been given a sum of money by William to help him out of his poverty – and with that money the assassin bought the guns used to shoot him. **1586** – Walter Raleigh founds a colony in Virginia, and takes with him the English language. It's the first time that English is established outside Britain. At this point, only seven million people speak it (about 1.5 percent of the world's population); by the twenty-first century it'll be the most widely spoken language in the world, with 760 million speakers. **1587** – The Spanish attempt to plunder Penryn, in Cornwall – but are frightened back to their ship when they overhear the sound of coarse acting during the annual mystery play performance and assume they are discovered and under attack. **1588** – The Spanish Armada, sailing with 130 warships and 30,000 men, is no more successful than the attempt on Penryn the year before. **1589** – James VI of Scotland brings to trial a coven of witches, who confess they have thrown cats into the sea to cause storms while the king was en route to Norway for his wedding. **1589** – In Japan, Hiroshima is founded. **1595** – Ottoman succession law has long allowed new sultans to murder their brothers to ensure the stability of their reign. His father has had such great sexual prowess that when Mahomet III succeeds him he is obliged to murder no fewer than nineteen pre-teen brothers, and throw seven pregnant concubines into the Bosporus river tied in sacks. **1596** – In response to a famine, Queen Elizabeth orders all Africans should be expelled from Britain so there will be more food to go round. **1598** – In Russia, the Time of Troubles begins; a period of interregnum where a series of usurpers and impostors take the throne, and a famine kills off one third of the population. **1600** – The astronomer Giordano Bruno is burned at the stake for asserting that the stars in the sky are other suns like our own. He becomes the first martyr for science.

THIS FAR, AND NO FURTHER

Polly hadn't loved Nigel for years, so she supposed it was unfair of her to mind so much when over breakfast he told her he was leaving her for another woman. But she did mind. It irked her.

He told her as he was fiddling with his toast. He never fiddled with his toast, he never fiddled with any of his food, he was the sort of man who just put things straight in his mouth without preamble and gave them a good simple chew. That was the first indication she had that something untoward was happening. 'I don't think we're compatible any more,' he said. Fiddle, fiddle.

Polly privately agreed, but then, they'd *never* been compatible. And she'd really rather have had more respect for him had he decided to leave her at any other point during their twelve-year-long marriage when they'd been just as incompatible as they were now. But she knew he was only telling her because of that other woman. Really, he wasn't leaving Polly because of Polly at all. That was the irksome thing, she decided, that was the point of her irk. Even in the moment she was being abandoned by her husband, it really didn't have an awful lot to do with her.

Nigel began to tell Polly that she mustn't blame herself, that none of this was Polly's fault, and that a part of him would always care for Polly, and Polly very quietly asked him to hush up, and Nigel did, and both of them were relieved.

Polly asked Nigel whether he intended to move out straight away, and Nigel said he thought that was best, it'd be a little awkward otherwise. And the other woman was quite keen that he move in ASAP – he actually used that word, 'ASAP' – they had the rest of their lives together and she didn't want to delay a moment longer. 'Do you want me to pack your things?' asked Polly. 'I can get down that old suitcase from the spare room.' Nigel told her that was very thoughtful, but she mustn't worry – after all, he might not agree with her on what was his and what was hers, it'd be best if he came round and packed for himself. He'd be very fair, only take what was his, and divvy up the rest of the stuff fifty-fifty. 'I could make a start, though,' said Polly. 'I could pack what is *definitely* yours. Like all your clothes, I'm not going to want your tracksuit bottoms, am I?' And Nigel said that was very kind, if that really wouldn't put Polly out, then that *would* save him a bit of time; what a nice woman she was, what a fine wife. He'd come over and take the rest of his belongings at some point when she was out, that'd mean they wouldn't have to see each other again. 'And if I don't agree with what you've taken,' asked Polly, 'I can give you a call, and we can discuss it?' Nigel agreed, of *course* she could do that, but he was going to be very fair, when was he ever not fair? But if she insisted, yes, she could do that, of course. And he looked a bit irritated, and Polly felt petty, and wondered whether it was that pettiness of hers deep down that had always made them so incompatible, that had so doomed their marriage right from the start.

Soon after that Nigel stopped fiddling with his toast, put it in his mouth, and left.

For the longest while Polly sat in the kitchen and didn't do anything. She prodded at her feelings, just gingerly, just a prod, and she concluded that she was depressed. She wondered if she should talk to someone. She thought of calling her mother. But she knew what her mother would say, her mother had never wanted her marrying Nigel in the first place, she'd tell Polly she'd been right all this time, she'd say it was probably Polly's fault it had all gone wrong. Mother wouldn't be sympathetic at all, and Polly supposed that was fair, Polly hadn't been particularly sympathetic when her mother had phoned to say that she'd been abandoned either. Polly could pop round to her neighbour's; she didn't know her neighbour well, but she was bound to be sympathetic, she always smiled at Polly in the street, and Polly was pretty certain she was kind and churchy, she was always knocking at the door asking for charity donations. Polly wasn't sure she could cope with the sheer fount of sympathy that would come welling out of her. What Polly wanted, Polly reasoned, was something between sympathy and no sympathy, and then she realised that the best way to get that reaction was by telling nobody at all. And that's exactly what she had been doing! – she hadn't told a soul! – and Polly was so pleased that quite by chance she'd been doing everything right that she perked up for a few minutes, and even made herself a cup of coffee to celebrate.

Then Polly realised with a start that there was someone she really ought to tell. Her seven-year-old daughter Samantha, it was bound to be of interest to her. She wondered where Samantha might be, and then thought she'd most likely be in the place Polly had last left her. Polly went upstairs, opened Samantha's bedroom door – and Polly was quite right, there Samantha was, fast asleep under the duvet.

'Hey,' said Polly. 'Hey, Sammy. Rise and shine.' And, 'Your father's left us.'

Samantha yawned, stirred. 'Why?' she asked.

'A combination of reasons,' said Polly. 'Another woman, and incompatibility.' She wanted to see whether Samantha would give her sympathy or no sympathy at all, and she got neither; she supposed that had been what she'd wanted, but she couldn't help but feel a little hurt all the same. 'Shouldn't you be at school?' asked Polly.

'It's the school holidays,' said Samantha. 'Remember?'

Polly could barely remember her own school holidays, she couldn't see why she should be expected to remember her daughter's. Oh yes – weeks of sunshine and freedom, they seemed to stretch on forever, they had no ending to them. Polly had been happy then. She'd had boyfriends, and sometimes they dumped her, and sometimes she dumped them, and it never mattered because they were only kids, and they never gave compatibility issues a single thought. She realised she resented Samantha, a white-hot hate that flickered only for a moment and took her quite by surprise – Samantha didn't know how lucky she was, she hadn't a care in the world. She wondered briefly whether Samantha had boyfriends, and then decided she didn't care, and asking her now would only start a conversation in which she'd have no interest whatsoever.

On the way back to the kitchen Polly stopped short. She'd forgotten all about Samantha. So had Nigel. Who was to get custody? This was an unwanted complication to the divorce. She'd better phone him and remind him.

Nigel worked in a big office in town. The receptionist took Polly's call, and said she'd put her through to Nigel's secretary, and then Nigel's secretary said she'd put Polly through to Nigel. Both the receptionist and the secretary sounded as if they'd been laughing. Polly wondered whether Nigel had told them about the break-up, and thought that he probably had. He'd probably told all of the office by now, they were probably all guffawing away.

'What is it?' said Nigel.

'We forgot we have a daughter,' Polly told him. 'Do you get her, or do I?'

'Oh, for God's sake,' said Nigel, and he seemed most put out. 'I told you, I'd divvy up all the stuff fifty-fifty. Now, please. I'm trying to work.'

*

And it turned out that Nigel didn't want his daughter anyway. One day Polly came back from her shopping, and found Nigel had visited, and he'd taken his half of their belongings – and he *had* been fair, just as he'd promised, he'd left her so many things, he'd left her her collection of Tom Jones CDs, he'd left hanging in the hall that painting of a matador she'd bought from a market in Spain. And he'd left her Samantha. Polly found her, upstairs in her bedroom, playing with her Xbox.

'Daddy's been then?' asked Polly, rather pointlessly really, and Samantha just sort of shrugged.

Over the next few weeks Polly spent a lot of time sitting in the kitchen on her own and drinking coffee, and then going to the supermarket when the coffee ran out. Sometimes, when she remembered, she took Samantha to the supermarket with her. 'Why do I have to come?' Samantha would complain, and Polly really didn't know; she just felt somehow that she should make some effort with her daughter, now that she was the last bit of family she'd got. They should have fun together. But Samantha never seemed to have much fun. Polly had a vague memory that when Samantha had been a little girl she'd loved pushing the supermarket trolley, 'can I push the trolley, Mummy?' she'd ask, and she was really too small, but Polly would let her, she'd give her a hand steering it around the corners but basically it was all Samantha's work, it was Samantha in charge basically, and Samantha felt like *such* a grown-up. And now she didn't want to push the trolley, even though she was still nowhere near being a grown-up, she was still just a little girl; Samantha would stand around the breakfast cereals and the tinned soup and the sugar and sulk. Polly couldn't work it out. And over the weeks she remembered to take Samantha with her less and less often.

One day she forgot about Samantha altogether. She'd been to the supermarket, and was now at home unpacking the shopping. She put the coffee in the cupboard, and the milk in the fridge, and then pulled out from the carrier bag a box of Rice Krispies. She stared at the cereal in astonishment; she didn't eat Rice Krispies, something about that snap, crackle, pop was just a little too *childish* for her – and then she remembered, oh! but I have a child, don't I? Samantha must have put the box in the trolley. This must have been one of those instances when she'd remembered to take her daughter shopping with her – but she hadn't remembered her for long enough, had she, she'd forgotten to bring her home. She couldn't be sure. She went to Samantha's bedroom, rummaged around for her. She looked under the duvet, and behind the Xbox, but there was no sign; she even looked behind the Xbox twice, just in case she'd overlooked her somehow. No, Samantha had clearly been abandoned at the supermarket. Polly looked at her watch. The supermarket was closed; or, at the very least, it'd be closing soon, they'd be busy, wouldn't they? There'd be no point calling them. Samantha would find her own way home. Samantha wasn't a fool, she knew where she lived. And the crisis over,

Polly breathed a sigh of relief, and made herself a fresh cup of coffee from the fresh jar she'd bought from Asda, and put Samantha out of her mind. Indeed, she had quite a pleasant evening, she watched a nice movie on the telly. It was only as she was getting into bed and turning off the light that she remembered – 'oh my God,' she said, out loud, 'I forgot her again!' And she had to put on her nightie, and go downstairs, and leave a Post-it note on the fridge door. 'Things-To-Do. Find Samantha.' And she underlined it for good measure. 'That'll do the trick,' she said, with satisfaction.

She went to the police station. 'I want to report a missing child,' she said. The policeman huffed a little at that, then sighed, and wearily opened up a ledger to take down her particulars. 'When did you lose her?' he asked. 'Four days ago,' admitted Polly. And then said, although it did nothing to help the investigation, 'I don't use the fridge very often, I prefer my coffee black.'

The policeman showed all due diligence, if not much interest. He asked Polly all the right questions. 'What's the child's name?' 'Samantha.' 'Sam-an-tha,' said the policeman slowly, writing down each painstaking syllable. 'And how old is she?' Polly counted on her fingers. 'I think she's seven, or thereabouts,' said Polly. 'Seven.' 'Or thereabouts.' 'And does she have any distinguishing features?' Polly had a think. 'I don't know,' she said at last. 'She's a bit nondescript, really. I think she has freckles. Do freckles count?'

At this the policeman laid down his pen and looked at her gravely.

'I don't mean physically. Has she done anything distinguished? Any achievements you can list?' Polly looked at him blankly, and the policeman huffed again. 'Let me put it this way,' he said. 'Has she ever won any awards, or been on the telly?'

Polly tried to remember. 'I don't think so,' she said. 'She's only seven,' she added.

'You see, that's the problem with missing children,' said the policeman, not unkindly. 'They haven't yet done anything with their lives. So it's hard to justify the expense of finding them. I mean, if Stephen Hawking was missing, then, yes, we'd put all our muscle behind it. He cracked the secrets of space/time, after all. Or Sir Andrew Lloyd Webber, if Sir Andrew's mum popped in and told us Sir Andrew was nowhere to be found. He hasn't written a decent musical since *Phantom*, it's true, but all credit to him, he still packs in the tourists.'

'Samantha hasn't done anything like that,' said Polly.

'There are sixty million people in Britain,' said the policeman. 'And they're all lost. All of us, we're all lost. Every single one of us.' For a moment he looked as if he were about to cry. 'I don't suppose you've got a photo of her?'

'I never thought I'd need one.'

The policeman nodded. 'Well, I'll keep her name on record, and we may stumble across her. In the mean time, I'd suggest you speak to your neighbours, get them to check their sheds, that sort of thing. Don't lose hope, I can't pretend we'll prioritise this, but, you know, she may show up.' And Polly smiled, and felt a little reassured.

During the day Polly might forget, but her dreams were haunted by her missing daughter. She'd be trapped at the bottom of darkened supermarket aisles, she'd be fending off strange customers and shelf-stackers alike with whatever discount groceries came to hand. Polly went back to the supermarket, of course, just in case the manager had seen her (just in case the manager had her hidden in his office) but she was coolly informed that the safeguarding of personal items was not the store's responsibility. When she remembered to, she'd ring the doorbells of random houses in the area and make enquiries. When she remembered to, she'd stick handwritten posters to lampposts and telegraph poles, asking for any information about a lost girl of no discernible talent or features. She even offered a reward – just a small one, she didn't want to attract time-wasters.

The first thing Polly lost was any sense of what Samantha had looked like. And that didn't surprise Polly, she'd have had a hard time describing her even when she'd been living upstairs. But now she'd watch movies on TV, and they boasted *lots* of seven-year-old children, and she soon believed they all looked like Samantha – Samantha would be a watered down version of them all, of course, not as polished, not as shiny, the teeth not as straight, the nose not as aquiline; she'd be a synthesis of all these child stars, all their blandest features but stars' features nonetheless, put them all together in the melting pot and stir, Samantha is what would pour out. And in the movies all the kids had their special skills, they *were* special – they were beautiful, they were witty, they traded quips while solving crimes with Bruce Willis, they were experts in judo or horse jumping or deflecting meteor showers. Polly liked to imagine that Samantha had all these skills too. She'd drowse in front of the television and get angry that the police hadn't found her little genius yet, the country *needed* her, for God's sake! – and then she'd remember her kid was just dull and ordinary, and she'd feel really disappointed.

And she'd look at the post-it note on the fridge. 'Find Samantha', it said, and she didn't have a hope of finding Samantha, after a while she crossed out the 'find' part, the distraction of it annoyed her, it wasn't relevant. 'Samantha' said the note now, and that was good, that was useful. Because Polly didn't like to admit it, but she was finding it increasingly hard to remember her lost daughter's name; she'd known there had *been* a daughter, somehow, somewhen, but God knows what she'd been called. And that was shameful, really, wasn't it, so shameful? She'd wake in the morning with a start of guilt, the name just beyond the reach of her mind – and then she'd come downstairs, she'd go straight to the fridge, she'd read the post-it note there, and back the memory would come, *Samantha*, yes, of course it was. Samantha, how could she forget? Well, she wouldn't forget again. She wouldn't.

In September the holiday break ended, but of course Samantha couldn't go back to school. No-one phoned Polly to find out why her daughter hadn't shown up, and for a while Polly was glad about that, she really didn't need the extra hassle – she was much happier sitting in the kitchen drinking her coffee without having to speak to anyone. But at last she decided she ought to call the school secretary to explain. 'I'm sorry,' Polly said, and she was shaking with nerves, she didn't know why, and she drank some more coffee to calm herself down, 'Samantha's not been to school lately. She's been sick. Actually, she's been missing. I lost her.' The school secretary was a kindly-sounding old woman, and she assured Polly there was nothing to worry about – they had no record of a Samantha anyway, so there was no harm done – was she really *sure* she'd had a daughter in the first place? And Polly thanked her, and put down the receiver.

She began to lace her coffee with just a smidgen of rum.

She got through a lot of coffee and a lot of rum, so she had to go to the supermarket more often. She didn't like going to the supermarket much, but she couldn't quite recall why. She at last worked out that if on each visit she bought twice as much coffee and twice as much rum she could go to the supermarket half as often. She liked this new system. She delighted in its implementation.

November was easy, and she didn't think of Samantha much at all. Only when she opened the fridge, and sometimes not even then – sometimes she couldn't quite work out what a post-it note was doing stuck there in the first place. She watched a lot of movies that featured only grown-ups doing grown-up things.

December was bad. In December the shops were full of toys, and she was quite sure that had she had a little child then that child would have liked toys. Children just did, didn't they? The memory she'd had a child blindsided her one morning, and she almost threw up at the thought of what she'd once had and what she'd once lost. She could imagine buying her daughter a doll, or a jigsaw puzzle, or an iPhone, and watching her unwrap it on Christmas morning, the joy stealing across her thin/fat clear/spotty white/black face.

And it was in December that she lost the post-it note. One morning she went to the fridge for her daily reminder, and her daughter's name wasn't there any more. After so long the gum had loosened, the note had fallen off. Polly looked all over the floor, she looked under the table, she looked in all the corners, but it wasn't to be found. On Christmas morning she was watching a movie on the television, and today *all* the movies featured small children, and all the children were remarkable, and all of them had names that might have been her daughter's own. She'd got Nigel's home number, he told her to use it only in emergencies. But this was an emergency, surely. She put down her rum laced with a smidgen of coffee, she reached for the phone.

It wasn't Nigel who answered. 'Hello, I want Nigel, please,' said Polly. 'Who is this?' said a woman. 'I want Nigel,' said Polly. Nigel came to the phone. 'Hello?' he said. 'Nigel!' said Polly, 'Nigel, it's you!' Nigel said, 'Polly, this is Christmas, this is a bad time.' 'Nigel, I've lost our daughter. I lost her *months* ago, Nigel. I'm sorry. And I've forgotten her name.' 'Our daughter?' said Nigel. Polly said, 'I don't know her name, Nigel, please, please tell me her name. I think,' and Polly's eyes flicked back to the television, 'that it might have been Heidi.' 'We never had a daughter,' said Nigel. He sounded awkward, and Polly could imagine he was fiddling with something, fiddle fiddle. 'Are you sure?' asked Polly, and Nigel said he was pretty sure, he was sure he'd remember one – besides, he *had* a daughter now, and she was very pretty and very skilled, and utterly *descript*, she wasn't nondescript in the slightest. 'That was quick work,' said Polly. 'She's Amanda's daughter, but she's *like* a daughter to me, she's even started calling me Daddy, well, she's called me Daddy once.' 'I'm so happy for you, Nigel,' said Polly, and she began to cry, 'you deserve the best, you're such a nice man.' 'I have to get back to my family now, Polly,' said Nigel, 'it's Christmas, for God's sake, this is a bad time, for God's sake, Pol.' 'Merry Christmas,' said Polly. 'Yes,' said Nigel, and he hung up.

Polly renewed her hunt for the post-it note. She'd never been able to get under the fridge, it was such a thin gap, and no matter how much she forced her fingers her knuckles always got in the way. So she pulled the fridge towards her – she grasped its sides, and began rocking it, as if it were a dance partner (*as if it were a little baby girl*) – it was very heavy, she thought she wasn't strong enough, but then,

then it began to tip over, and her muscles were screaming with the strain – and then it was falling, straight towards her, and she could hear inside the splashing of forgotten food, and she tried to scrabble out of the way – but it was no good, the fridge fell fast now, it fell on to her foot, she thought it might have *crushed* her foot, she thought she heard bones snap (though it may just have been all those mildewed tomatoes popping in the vegetable drawer) and there was a shriek of agony, and she realised she was the one making it. But then – but then! – the shriek became a cry of joy, she forgot the pain, she *saw* the post-it note, a grubby bit of paper amidst all the grime she'd uncovered – she had to heave the fridge off her foot to reach it, but she didn't spare more than a glimpse to see the damage she'd done herself (there was blood, and was that a bone now sticking out through the skin, no, she wouldn't look) all she wanted was the note. 'Samantha', the note said, of course it was, of course that was it. She'd write out that name over and over, she'd post-it up all over the house, she'd never lose it again. And she cradled the little square of yellow paper in her arms, 'I've found you,' she said, 'I've found you,' and she hobbled out of the kitchen, bleeding all the while. 'I'll never let you go, not again,' she told the note, and she even stroked it, and for a while she really thought the ordeal was over, that her daughter was safe, that she'd got her daughter back, not just the memory of her name.

She spent the next few days on a lot of painkillers. She'd tried washing the blood off her foot, but it hurt too much – so she decided she'd let it harden, it'd flake off when it was ready. On New Year's Eve, the post-it note beside her, she watched the television. She watched the crowds gather by the Thames to hear Big Ben chime in midnight, to sing and cheer and celebrate. She watched all the famous people, the celebrities, the ones who were special.

During the minute's countdown, Polly realised where Samantha was. It made her feel so stupid she hadn't thought of it before.

'Twenty, nineteen, eighteen,' chanted the crowds on the screen.

Samantha was in *this* year. In the year that was now passing. Polly had definitely seen her there. And she knew that if she let the world shuffle into a new one, she'd have lost her for good.

'Ten, nine, eight!'

Everyone prepared for fireworks. Big Ben began to whirr.

'No,' said Polly. 'Enough. *Enough.*'

*

It took a long while for the police to find her. It was impossible to say quite how long, of course; time just didn't work that way any more. Eventually Polly had got bored waiting and hobbled to the phone, and called to confess she was the one responsible. The first two times she told them no-one believed her, they thought it was a hoax. So she had to call and pretend to be a neighbour who wanted to shop her – and that seemed to do the trick.

The police broke the door down. They trained guns at her, panting, scared, in their bulletproof vests. 'Get on the ground *now*!' screamed their leader.

'No.'

'You're going to come with us!'

'I'm not,' said Polly. 'My foot hurts. I want to speak to someone in authority, and they can come *here*.'

The police guarded her while she waited for this figure of authority to show up. She continued to watch the television. It was still showing its live broadcast of Big Ben, and the crowds waiting for the clock to strike. Cold, impatient, and a little frightened.

Authority came in the figure of a thin middle-aged man wearing spectacles. 'Are you really the highest authority?' asked Polly.

'I am.'

'Well then,' said Polly.

'Do you understand the full implications of what you've done?' asked the man sternly.

'Probably not,' admitted Polly.

'Right, this is classified,' said the man. 'We don't want the public getting hold of this. If they realised the extent of the disaster there'd be mass panic.'

'All right,' said Polly.

'In the rest of the world, it's now *March*.'

'Oh.'

'The British people are confused. They can tell that time's got a bit stuck somehow. Not by much, they'd think, just a little glitch, a few minutes out here or there. If they knew the New Year was now nearly three months late... As it is, just imagine the stock market. Can you do that for a moment, Polly?'

'I'll try,' said Polly.

'It's a fiscal *disaster*,' said the man. 'The dollar is *killing* the pound. It's slaughtering us. For God's sake, even the Swedish krona is slaughtering us, Sweden are basking in next year's economic spurt while we're still stuck in last year's recession. What you've done, you're bankrupting millions, you're putting merchant bankers out on to the streets. Or you would be, if the merchant bankers actually realised what was going on. Most of the merchant bankers are still celebrating at New Year's Eve parties. Most of the merchant bankers will be too drunk to understand anything.'

'I see,' said Polly.

'That little stunt of yours hasn't just affected Great Britain, you know. You've frozen time in about a hundred and fifty square miles of Northern France as well. The French aren't taking this lightly. They say if we don't resolve this soon, they'll be forced to consider military action against us. Polly, we haven't been at war with the French since the nineteenth century! The nineteenth century, Polly, that's olden times!'

'I hear you,' said Polly.

'You can't want that.'

'I don't want that,' said Polly. 'No.'

'Then do the right thing. Send time merrily back on its way again. Can you do that?'

'I think so,' nodded Polly.

'Good.'

'But I'm not going to.'

'Oh,' said the man. 'From the sound of it, this last year hasn't been too good to you. Your marriage broke up, didn't it? And there's that child you claim you've lost. Surely you'd rather see the back of this year altogether.'

'This year's been ghastly,' agreed Polly. 'But I haven't finished with it yet.' She gave the man her demands. He had nothing to say to them. 'I don't believe you're the highest authority at all. I'll only speak to the highest authority.'

'You mean the prime minister?' squeaked the man.

Polly hadn't meant the prime minister necessarily, she didn't expect to get someone so very special. She nodded. 'Fetch the prime minister, yes.'

On the television there was a forlorn attempt to start another round of *Auld Lang Syne*. It soon stuttered to a halt.

The prime minister arrived. He was shorter than he looked on the telly. 'Well,' said the prime minister. 'This is a bad business.'

'It is,' agreed Polly.

'This is an act of terrorism.'

'No,' said Polly.

'It is, it's exactly what it is. You're holding the nation to ransom. And for what?'

'I want my daughter,' said Polly.

'Exactly,' said the PM. 'A single, ordinary, little girl. Look at those people on the television screen. They have daughters too. Some of those daughters have spent three months standing by the Thames waiting for the New Year to begin. By now they'll be getting hungry and fractious. You're endangering their lives, making them that hungry, that fractious. How can you put your daughter before theirs?'

'Because she *is* my daughter,' said Polly. 'Samantha. Her name's Samantha.'

'Samantha, yes, we know.'

'Samantha. I want you to remember that.'

'Yes.'

'I want you *all* to remember that.'

The prime minister's aide suggested, softly, that maybe the hostile would be satisfied with some other daughter; did it have to be the exact same one? The PM turned to Polly hopefully, but Polly shook her head.

'I don't negotiate with terrorists,' said the PM. 'It sends a message around the world. Pretty soon everybody will be stopping time, just so they can get *their* daughters.'

'I can't help that,' said Polly. 'I'm not going into another year without her.'

'All right,' sighed the PM. 'We'll begin a nationwide hunt. You've not given us a description, there's not much to go on. But if she's there to be found, we'll find her. You do realise,' he added, 'that she might very well be dead?'

'That's fine,' said Polly amiably. 'Then in that case, I want you to bring me her fucking corpse. I want to see her fucking corpse for myself, I want to hold her fucking corpse, I want to say goodbye to it.'

'All right,' said the PM shortly. He walked to the door, and Polly thought he was just going to leave, just like that, without another word. And then he turned to her. 'I want you to know,' he said. 'I have three children. They're all special children. Monica can play the violin at grade two level. Louis is studying Greek. And James, he's going to be like me, one day James will be prime minister too, you'll see. They're special. These kids, they'll make a *difference*.' His stiff upper lip quivered with pride. 'And yet, at the end of the day, they're still only kids. And I'd sacrifice them all if I had to.'

Polly nodded. 'I believe you would.'

At that the prime minister gave a half smile, and he didn't look entirely sure what he was smiling at. He fiddled with his briefcase, fiddle fiddle, and then he was gone.

And they tried to fob her off with fake Samanthas, of course they did. They'd parade a series of little girls in front of Polly, 'here she is, your darling daughter!' they'd say. 'Go on,' they'd say to the girls, 'go to Mummy,' go to the terrorist, and they'd give the girls a little shove, the girls would take a few terrified steps forward – all of them a bit average, a bit nondescript, but of different sizes, different shapes and colours, Polly had never realised that nondescript had such rich variety to it. 'This isn't Samantha,' Polly would say each time, 'I don't recognise her.' But secretly Polly was scared – what if she *couldn't* recognise her? What if she'd already been presented with her daughter, and rejected her? If she saw her face to face would she really ever know? And sometimes they brought her bones. One time they brought her a complete skeleton. They came dressed in black, they had hats they could hold respectfully just for the occasion. 'We're so sorry for your loss,' they said, and they looked very serious. 'Not Samantha,' Polly would say. 'You *can't* be sure,' she was told, 'you wouldn't be able to recognise her *bones!*' 'I have to,' said Polly, 'I have to, I have to. I'm her mother.'

Europe was reporting the hottest summer in years. France was beginning to mobilise. Nigel came to visit. He looked like a pirate; he'd clearly spent New Year's Eve at a fancy dress party. 'What have you done to your foot?' he asked Polly. 'You do realise there's a bone sticking out of it, right? It won't heal unless you let time run on.'

'I know,' said Polly. 'But I prefer it the way it is.'

Nigel told Polly he had a proposition for her. And it was all his own idea, nothing to do with the government at all. 'I'll leave Amanda,' he said. 'I'll come back to you. And we can have another daughter. Call her Samantha, even, if you like. What do you say? We could get to it right now. I could impregnate you ASAP.'

'Do you remember our first Samantha?' Polly asked him.

Nigel licked his lips. 'Oh yes,' he said. 'You bet. Nice kid.'

'I don't think we're compatible,' said Polly. 'Please go away. I don't want to see you again.'

And eventually a seven-year-old girl was brought to Polly. Her hair was splotched with pink and green dye, and a safety pin had been driven inexpertly into the side of her nose.

'You stupid cow,' she said to Polly. 'My name's *Sandra*, not Samantha. It was always bloody *Sandra*.' And, ferocious as she looked, she burst into tears.

'Yes,' said Polly. 'This'll be the one.'

And without any hesitation, she nudged time forward into a glorious new year.

*

It took a few months for Greenwich Mean Time to catch up with the rest of the world. But when Polly pushed time onwards, she put a bit of a fast spin on it –

and some time around October the 'then' and the 'now' collided. Most people felt a not-alarming jolt, just a moment when the ground jumped beneath their feet. The only place that really felt the force was Greenwich itself; the Cutty Sark reverberated, then collapsed, and nobody really cared.

There was some attempt to bring Polly to justice. A number of people around the country called for the death penalty. But the powers that be concluded, somewhat reluctantly, that Polly could compromise them all were she put in the dock. She was charged with causing a breach of the peace, and let off with a caution.

Sandra's hair was dyed back to a colour more suitable for a seven-year-old; Polly couldn't remember what colour it was supposed to be, and Sandra wasn't telling, so Polly opted for a bland brown. The safety pin was extracted from Sandra's nose. And she was sent back to school, to teachers and classmates who had once forgotten she had ever existed. She was a celebrity now, of course. They wouldn't forget her again. For a few days Sandra basked in the attention, but she quickly tired of it. 'They all know who I am,' Sandra told her mother. 'That's good,' said Polly. 'But they all know me for the wrong reasons,' said Sandra. 'Sorry about that,' said Polly.

Some of the girls at school began to beat Sandra up. Sandra had to learn how to defend herself. She could soon win all her fights. She began to beat up all of those who had bullied her. And then she began to beat up everyone else too. Sandra got herself quite a reputation; she put one girl in hospital; she became famous at the school for a new reason of her very own. 'I'm much happier now,' she told her Mum.

Sandra began to bring school friends home. They'd go and play with Sandra in her bedroom, they'd play loud music, and swear, and smoke. Polly thought all of the friends looked very frightened of Sandra. Polly tried not to have much to do with them; it hurt to go upstairs, her foot had never properly set – and if she wanted to go to Sandra's room to tell her to keep the noise down, she'd be forced to hop her way from step to step while clinging to the stair rail. The girls would all laugh as they heard her approach, they'd mimic her, clump, clump, clump. And as they clumped about, Polly would hear them call her Pegleg, and Footloose, and Cripple.

Polly would sleep on the sofa, and she'd drink coffee, and she'd drink rum.

Sandra wanted to get her ears pierced. All the other girls had their ears pierced. Sandra wanted to wear nail varnish to school. All the other girls did. Sandra wanted to stay out late, go to parties with boys. Just like all the other girls, just like all the others. 'Don't you want to stand out from the crowd?' her mother asked her. 'Don't you want to be special?'

Don't you want to find just one thing in yourself that might make you worthwhile?

One night Sandra went out to a party without her mother's permission. Polly stayed up, drinking black coffee to keep her awake, yes, that's what the coffee was for. At two in the morning Sandra rolled in, drunk, wearing a skirt so short Polly could see her knickers, wearing too much make-up, her eyes ringed with mascara so she looked like a panda bear. 'What are you doing up?' Sandra asked her mother.

'Samantha,' said Polly. 'Sammy, Sam. You can't do this. You mustn't do this.

You're only seven. You're seven years old.'

'I'm fifteen, Mum,' said Sandra. 'I'm grown-up now. Christ.' She sniffed at Polly's coffee mug. 'You're pissed again, aren't you?'

'Fifteen? Really? Have the years gone by that fast?'

'Christ.'

Polly hugged Sandra, and Sandra was pissed enough herself to hug her back. They both hugged there on the sofa for a while, they rocked back and forth, and neither could be sure whether they were doing the rocking or the whole room was rocking around them.

'I'm sorry,' said Polly. 'I'm so sorry.'

'Yeah, it doesn't matter.'

'I'm sorry, it all went wrong.'

'Yeah, never mind.'

'Oh, Sammy. I'm sorry.'

'Sandra. Christ.'

'I love you,' Polly told Sandra. 'You believe me, don't you? You believe me when I say I'd do anything for you, don't you? I did once. I did. I did.'

'Yeah. I don't feel well, Mum, actually. I'm off to have a puke.'

'No, listen. Listen. Do you trust me?'

'Yeah. Okay.'

'You really trust me?'

Sandra frowned. 'If you like.'

'Then enough of this,' said Polly. 'Enough.'

And time stopped. And she stood up. And she reached for her daughter's hand. And, in spite of herself, the daughter took it.

And Polly pushed time going again, she gave it another nudge. But now she nudged it in the other direction. And again she put a little spin on it, it sped away from them, fast. 'Quick!' said Polly. 'Let's catch up!' And still holding Sandra's hand she began to chase it, she began to run. And at first she couldn't run very well, but soon the pain in her foot was gone, she felt free, and she could *sprint*. And she looked at her daughter, running alongside her, and she laughed. And Sandra laughed too, because already all the wrinkles on her face were beginning to smooth, all the harshness and spite and rancour that was written there was peeling away. 'Run!' laughed Polly, and pretty soon she had to pick Sandra up, Sandra was too small to run any more, she cradled her in her arms, 'I'm never going to let you go again,' Polly promised. And then Sandra *was* gone, she was an infant, and then she was a baby, and then she just winked away – but Polly hadn't lost her, Polly could feel her daughter inside her, she'd always be there. And Polly felt she should slow down soon, she should stop, but she couldn't stop running, not now her body was younger and her heart was so strong, not now she had her whole life ahead of her, nothing had gone wrong yet, nothing now ever would. And the smaller Polly got the faster she raced, running on and on and on and laughing all the while, laughing like a little girl.

My wife is trying to turn me into a cannibal. I wouldn't mind, but she's hardly being subtle about it. I was picking through my ravioli one night – and there it was, all the evidence I needed, speared on to the end of my fork. 'What's this?' I asked, though it was pretty bloody obvious what it was – and she sort of shrugged, 'I don't know, it just came out of the tin like that.' 'It's a human finger,' I said. 'Are you sure?' she asked. 'Sometimes the pasta can come in funny shapes. They're always doing that, making pasta in different shapes, then giving them funny names.' So I didn't press the subject. It was easier that way. But it had a knuckle, a definite knuckle, and a fingernail too, it looked as if it had been chewed at already, maybe chewed at by its original owner. And so I ate it down. It wasn't too bad, I just had to think of something else during the actual swallowing, but there was so much history I could think of, that wasn't hard really. I ate it down, and I ate down all the other fingers and toes and folds of human skin she'd feed me. My wife and my daughter were both vegetarian and they looked across at me as they both made me prehistorical, they watched me in judgement over their tofu. **1601** – Robert Devereux, Earl of Essex, long-time favourite of Queen Elizabeth I, is beheaded for treason. **1601** – Famine in Estonia kills half the population. **1602** – The Chinese philosopher Li Zhi is imprisoned for fomenting dangerous ideas: he has taught that women are the intellectual equals of men and should be educated accordingly. He commits suicide in his cell. **1603** – On her deathbed, Elizabeth I offers all of her possessions for just one more moment of time. She is succeeded by James VI of Scotland – and, after hundreds of years of warfare, the two nations are united almost accidentally. **1605** – On the death of Boris Godunov, his son Feodor is proclaimed Tsar of Russia. But a runaway monk called Grigory Otropyev emerges, claiming to be Ivan the Terrible's long-ago murdered son Dmitriy. Within weeks Feodor and his mother are imprisoned and strangled. **1605** – English Catholics led by Sir Robert Catesby attempt to kill King James by blowing up the Houses of Parliament with gunpowder. Guy Fawkes is the luckless lackey given the job of lighting the fuse, and he's the man who gets caught and ruins the whole operation. Unlike his co-conspirators, Fawkes is never executed, but jumps to his death from the scaffold to save himself the agony of further torture. But he is tortured in effigy for hundreds of years to come, burned on bonfires for entertainment on 5 November, with a backdrop of Catherine Wheels and sparklers and firecrackers all about. Back when I was a child, it was standard practice to drag a scarecrow around the shopping precincts asking for a 'penny for the guy' – and one year I remember attending no less than seven bonfire celebrations, a different Guy Fawkes burned on a pyre on each one. Nowadays the idea of torturing even a scarecrow to death for fun is frowned upon, and all the displays I go to dispense with the grislier side of the evening altogether – they sell weak mulled wine and charcoal burned hot dogs, they set off fireworks that go 'phub' – history has gone soft. **1606** – Ten months into the False Dmitriy's reign, conspirators storm the Kremlin, in part antagonised by his marriage to Marina Mniszech, 'the Polish witch'. Dmitriy breaks his leg escaping through a window, and is shot on the spot. His body is put on display, then cremated; his ashes are contemptuously shot from a cannon towards Poland. **1606** – Bernard Bluet d'Arbres, fool to the Duke of Mantua, starves himself to death in the belief that this would bring to an end the plague in Paris. **1607** – A tsunami sweeps along the Bristol Channel, killing 2,000 people. **1607** – The Flight of the Earls: Gaelic chieftains defeated by the English in their battle for independence run to Rome and live out their lives there as papal pensioners. **1607** – The second False Dmitriy appears on the Russian stage – this time pretending not only to be Ivan the Terrible's son, but the False Dmitriy whose dead body was displayed the previous year. He is miraculously 'reunited' with his own widow, Marina, who announces it is the same man, even though they share no physical similarities at all. He gathers the support of those who had backed the first pretender, and with an army of 100,000 men advances on Moscow. He is eventually killed, while drunk, by a Tatar prince he had humiliated. **1610** – King Henry IV, the most liberal French king in years, whose policy of religious tolerance has brought to an end the Wars of Religion that have ravaged the country for decades, is stabbed to death by a Catholic fanatic. **1610** – The Hungarian countess Elizabeth Bathory is put on trial for murder. She has come to believe that the blood of virgins can stave off old age, and has for years been hunting down peasant girls and slitting their throats. Eventually she establishes a finishing school, believing that girls from noble families might have better quality blood, and this at last draws the attention of the authorities. For the remaining four years of life she is walled up in a tiny room in her castle, fed through a small slot in the surrounding stone. **1612** – The Cossacks proclaim a third False Dmitriy as Tsar of Russia. You can have too many False Dmitriys. He is captured and executed privately in Moscow. **1614** – Christianity is banned in Japan. **1616** – Father Christmas is the main character of a masque written by Ben Jonson. This version carries a truncheon. **1618** – Osman II, Ottoman Emperor, practises his archery only if the targets are live prisoners of war, or, failing that, page boys. **1618** – The Second Defenestration of Prague. Protestant noblemen throw representatives of the German Catholics out of a window in Prague Castle. The lucky defenestrees survive the experience; the Catholics claim this is due to the mercy of angels, the Protestants, rather more practically, pointing out that a large mound of horse shit broke their fall. **1618** – The defenestration triggers the Thirty Years War. Jan Huska's skin is beaten in response (qv 1424). **1620** – Taichang becomes emperor of the Ming Dynasty; his reign lasts less than a month, curbed by a lethal bout of diarrhoea. **1620** – The Mayflower brings the Pilgrim Fathers from England to Massachusetts. Except for Dorothy Bradford, who falls overboard on the way. **1621** – Popularly the first British victim of tobacco poisoning is Sir Thomas Harriot, friend of Walter Raleigh, whose excessive pipe smoking gives him a nose tumour. **1621** – George Abbott, Archbishop of Canterbury, accidentally shoots his gamekeeper with a stray arrow. The verdict is 'death by misadventure and his own fault'. **1621** – The Dutch East India Company send 2,000 soldiers to the Banda Islands to enforce the trade monopoly on nutmeg. Most of the 15,000 inhabitants are massacred. **1622** – Osman II has kept his uncle Mustafa imprisoned in a small cage for the four years of his reign. On Osman's death, Mustafa is made caliph; he refuses to leave his cage at first, and has to be dragged out on the end of a rope. Mustafa executes those responsible for removing him from his incarceration, then spends his reign running around the palace searching for his dead nephew and begging him to release him from the pressures of government. At length he's simply put back in his cage again, where he dies sixteen years later. **1623** – The first breach of promise lawsuit – in Virginia, the Reverend Gerville Pooley files a suit against Cicely Jordan. He loses. **1623** – Prince Charles of England travels to Madrid and asks for the hand of the Spanish Infanta. When he is rejected, he calls for war against Spain. **1623** – On 5 November, ninety-five people are killed in a Catholic service in London when the floor beams break. The Fatal Vespers is seen by Protestants as God's judgement on the Gunpowder Plot. **1623** – Procopius' long lost 'Secret History' is discovered by chance in the Vatican Library (qv 553). **1626** – Charles I is crowned king of England – but his wife, Henrietta Maria, chooses not to attend. She doesn't want to be present at a non-Catholic ceremony. **1626** – Witch trials begin in Wurzburg, Germany. Over the next five years 900 people will be burned alive at the stake – for crimes ranging from murder, to singing with the Devil, from vagrancy, to merely passing through the town. Men, women and children are executed in the hysteria. **1626** – Queen Maria of Sweden bears a child for her husband, King Gustavus Adolphus. It has such thick black hair and such a huge nose that at first the baby is mistaken for a boy – and the mother is in such a fragile state that it's days before anyone confesses the truth. While her husband is out playing soldiers, Maria is left to care for her unwanted daughter Christina; she drops her on to stone floors, throws heavy objects into her crib, and pushes her down stairs. **1626** – In exchange for pots and pans, some cloth, and a few fish hooks, the Dutch buy the island of Manhattan from the indigenous population (qv 1667). **1627** – Thomas Herbert makes the first recorded use of the word 'dodo', to describe a peculiar flightless bird discovered in the Mauritius (qv 1662). **1628** – Shah Jahan kills all his male relatives, and imprisons his stepmother. And becomes the Mughal emperor of India. **1629** – On its journey to the Indies, the Dutch East India Company ship the Batavia is shipwrecked off the coast of Western Australia. There is mutiny amongst the survivors, and from that two exiled murderers become the first European settlers in Australia. **1630** – The Native American Quadequine introduces popcorn to English colonists. **1630** – In France, the Day of the Dupes: the Queen Mother begs Louis XIII to dismiss Cardinal Richelieu as his political advisor. He must choose, she tells him, between him or her. He chooses him. **1632** – Gustavus Adolphus is killed at the battle of Lutzen. Queen Maria brings home the embalmed body, and locks herself, Christina, and the corpse in a darkened room; Christina is forced to sleep in a bed above which swings the heart of her father encased in a golden casket. Christina finds herself queen of Sweden at the age of six. **1633** – Galileo Galilei is tried before the Inquisition at Rome, and made to recant his view of the universe. *My wife is trying to turn me into a caveman. It was simple things at first – she'd hide my razor so I couldn't shave, and my stubble would grow long and hairy. She'd grunt at me over the dinner table, just grunt, and in time I began to grunt back. But it's the drawings on the wall that convinced me there's some plot going on. I thought it might have been Annie at first, playing on the walls with crayon the way small children might do (the way <u>normal</u> small children might do) – and then the squiggles began to take shape, they weren't random at all, they took on the forms of woolly mammoths, of sabre toothed tigers, of men (like me) hunting them with spears. My wife does it when I sleep. When I wake, they're on the ceiling above my head, these lurid murals red with berry juice. I don't know how she gets up there, I try to catch her in the act, I pretend to be asleep so I can turn on the light suddenly and surprise her – but every time I do she's lying beside me, she's pretending to be asleep too, we both lie there faking it. And it's working, I can feel – oh God – it's working, she's trying to take me back in time, to the days of cannibals and cavemen, before recorded history began.* **1634** – The supreme commander of the imperial army in the Thirty Years War, Albrecht von Wallenstein, is first declared a traitor by the emperor, and then assassinated. **1635** – Old Tom Parr dies at the alleged age of 152, and is buried in Westminster Abbey. King Charles has met him, and asked what is the secret of his long life. Parr tells him that it's down to vegetarianism, and to moral temperance – at the age of 100 he had an affair and fathered a child out of wedlock, but he's done penance for that since. **1636** – King Christian of Denmark orders all able-bodied beggars must either build ships for his navy, or be employed as galley rowers. **1637** – Louis XIII has placed his wife Anne under close watch, suspected of treason; she has allied herself with elements caught in correspondence with the enemy Spanish. In spite of this, and owing to bad weather detaining him, Louis spends the night with Anne. The future Louis XIV is conceived amidst doubt, guilt, and naked lust. **1640** – Turkish Emperor Murad IV dies at last. He has been a homicidal maniac, known for his habit of walking the streets accompanied by his executioner and murdering passers-by on a whim. Anyone caught with tobacco or liquor is executed, even though he himself is a chainsmoking alcoholic. His favourite sensation, he finds, is the physical thrill of decapitating men with thick necks. He dies of terror while watching a solar eclipse. **1642** – Civil war in England between the Royalists and Parliament, who are outraged by the way Charles I tries to establish himself as an absolute monarch. Pssch. Frankly, they should try living in Turkey. **1642** – The first execution of a juvenile in the American colonies, for the crime of bestiality with a horse and a cow. It is not reported what happens to the horse or the cow. **1644** – The best soldier amongst the Royalists in England is Prince Rupert. Some Parliamentarians blame his military prowess upon Satanic help – and that help, they claim, comes from his pet white poodle, Boy. It is claimed that Boy is dagger-proof, and can catch musket balls in its teeth, and talks to Prince Rupert in a Hebrew dialect. (There are suggestions of carnal relations between man and Boy.) Boy is one of the casualties at the battle of Marston Moor – after which, it must be admitted, the war does start to swing in Parliament's favour. **1644** – The Ming Dynasty which has ruled China for over 300 years comes to an abrupt end. Emperor Chongzhen, under attack from the rebel Li Zicheng, decides to spare his family the humiliation of capture and execution. He gathers them all to a feast, then kills them all with his sword – all, with the exception of his daughter, Changpin, whose arm he severs accidentally instead. He then goes outside and hangs himself from a tree. Li Zicheng is now free to declare himself emperor, of the new and glorious Shun Dynasty. **1645** – Li Zicheng is defeated in battle. The Shun Dynasty that has ruled China for fifteen months comes to an abrupt end. **1646** – Massachusetts enforces the death penalty for having a rebellious child. **1647** – Christmas is banned by English Puritans. **1648** – Ibrahim I, successor to his mad psychopathic brother Murad, is strangled. Ibrahim has had an obsession with obese women, employing agents to find the fattest possible for his harem; once, whom he names Sugarbit, weighs in at 330 pounds. On hearing that one of his concubines has been unfaithful, he has all 280 of them tortured to find out which one; when they cannot give him an answer, he drowns them all in the Bosporus. **1649** – King Charles I is executed, and Britain becomes a republic. **1649** – Drogheda is besieged by Cromwell's forces; the governor, Sir Arthur Aston, is beaten to death with his own wooden leg. **1650** – Rene Descartes dies. He no longer thinks, therefore he isn't. **1654** – The British attempt to capture Jamaica from the Spanish is thwarted by the sound of fiddler crabs scuttling about the island, the soldiers mistaking them for the enemy lying in ambush. **1654** – John Casor becomes the first man in the future United States to be declared a slave for life. **1657** – Miles Sindercombe commits suicide in the Tower of London, after his fifth attempt to assassinate Oliver Cromwell, Lord Protector of England, ends in failure. He first rents a house from which he can shoot Cromwell as he rides past in his coach – but then changes his mind realising it would be hard to escape afterwards. Then he rents another house, but at the moment of truth gets unnerved by the large crowds. He then plans to shoot Cromwell as he travels through a narrow passage on his way to Hampton Court, the route he follows every Friday – but on the day Cromwell changes his itinerary. The fourth attempt is foiled when Cromwell amiably stops the would-be assassin to talk about horses. His most elaborate attempt, to blow up Whitehall Palace with gunpowder, is what finally gets him caught. But then, gunpowder plots so rarely work. **1658** – Oliver Cromwell dies anyway; really, Miles Sindercombe should have saved his efforts. Cromwell appoints his son Richard as his successor. Richard – or, as he becomes known, 'Tumble Down Dick' – does not have the personality of his father. He resigns in 1659; the monarchy is restored in 1660. **1658** – The Bishop of Armagh uses his study of the Bible to pinpoint the exact date of creation at 4004 BC. **1660** – The restoration of a monarchy to the British throne under Charles II causes John Bigg, scholar and clerk, to fall into a depression. His remaining thirty-one years are spent as the Dinton Hermit, living in a cave on the charity of locals. Meanwhile, the Royalist exile Sir Thomas Urquhart dies of apoplexy following an uncontrollable fit of laughter. **1661** – Superintendent of Finances under Louis XIV, Nicolas Fouquet, puts on a spectacular fireworks display for the newly crowned king of France. And is arrested for his extravagant ostentation. **1661** – Oliver Cromwell's body is exhumed so his corpse can be put on trial for treason. He is hanged and then beheaded; his head is displayed on a pole at Westminster Hall until 1684. **1662** – The last sighting of the dodo, rendering Thomas Herbert's inventive bird-naming skills somewhat redundant. *My wife is trying to turn me into a seventeenth century peasant. Into someone that history has never touched. Someone that was born, and lived, and died, and was forgotten. 'You're nothing,' she said to me one day. 'I thought you were somebody once, but you're nothing, and you do nothing, and Annie deserves better, don't you think Annie deserves better?' And I tell my wife of the seventeenth century peasants, that they're the last humans who died leaving no trace whatsoever, that from this point on we heave ourselves awkwardly into the Modern World where everybody is required to have an identity and to be registered by the state, that these are the last days when a man can just vanish completely. 'I sometimes wish you'd vanish,' she says softly. But she's the one who vanishes.* **1666** – The Great Fire of London. St Paul's Cathedral burns (qv 962, 1087, 1136, 1561). **1666** – In Sweden, the city of Pitea is destroyed by a great fire too. But, hey, it's Sweden, who cares? **1667** – The blind and poor poet John Milton sells the copyright of his masterpiece 'Paradise Lost' for ten pounds. **1667** – The Dutch give the island of Manhattan to the English in exchange for the island of Pulau Run; it's a disastrous deal. **1668** – Sir Francis Drake's head is finally buried, fifty years after his execution; his widow has spent the intervening time carrying it around everywhere in a small red bag and showing it to friends. **1669** – The Venetians surrender Crete to the Turks after a twenty-one year siege. **1675** – King Philip's War breaks out in Massachusetts, between the Native Americans and the English colonists. It's the bloodiest and costliest war in US history. The war is named after the leader of the Wampanoag tribe; his name is Metacom, but the colonists find Philip easier to say. **1678** – The Popish Plot, a conspiracy of leading Catholics to assassinate Charles II, and utterly fictitious to boot, is concocted by Titus Oates to generate anti-Catholic sentiment in Britain. At least fifteen people are executed in the hysteria – the House of Commons is searched in the expectation of a second Gunpowder Plot, Catholics are driven out of London – before Oates' lies start to unravel. Oates is arrested for perjury, fined, and imprisoned. On the accession of the very Protestant William of Orange, he is released, pardoned, and awarded a pension. *Annie and I come back home from the pub. She's been very well-behaved, toying with her lemonade and the beer coasters. 'But where's Mummy?' I ask, 'where's Mummy got to?' And I don't bother to turn off the burglar alarm, beeping away at me, mocking me, it knows where she's gone, it knows and won't tell me – and I hold Annie close, and she whispers up to me over the sirens, 'She's gone to a better place.'* **1681** – A woman in London is publicly flogged for 'involving herself in politics'. **1683** – The Turks lay siege to Vienna. They are beaten back by an army of Poles, Austrians and Germans – and defeated in part too thanks to the diligence of the local bakers, who, working at night time, hear the enemy tunnelling into the city and raise the alarm. To celebrate their pride in the affair, the bakers produce a pastry in the shape of a crescent, mocking the Turkish flag – it's later called a croissant. As for the Ottoman Empire, this is traditionally seen as the point at which its fortunes begin to fail; no Muslim army will ever again venture so far into Europe. **1684** – Oliver Cromwell's severed head is blown down from its pole in a gale. One of the sentinels finds it, hides it under a cloak, and takes it home to his family. His daughter sells it to a family in Cambridge, and later it's passed to an actor named Samuel Russell. In the eighteenth century it's bought by James Cox for his museum, and it eventually ends up in the possession of Sidney Sussex College, Cromwell's own college in Cambridge. **1685** – The Duke of Monmouth lands in the West Country and tries to take the throne from the new king, James II. He fails, and is beheaded. It's only after sentence has been carried out that it's discovered the Duke has no official portrait – and so Monmouth's head is taken, stitched back on to the body, and committed to canvas. **1687** – To celebrate Louis XIV's recent recovery from illness, the composer Lully conducts a Te Deum in his honour. He stabs his foot with the staff he uses to keep time, and dies from gangrene. **1688** – The Glorious Revolution, in which British nobles beg the Dutch William of Orange to invade their country and rid them of James II. **1689** – Sir Isaac Newton serves a year's office as member of Parliament. His only recorded statement in the House of Commons is a request to shut a window to keep the draught out. **1692** – The Salem witch trials begin in Massachusetts; in the mass hysteria, and accusations and counter-accusations, 150 people will be imprisoned, and 20 executed. **1694** – The English slaver ship, 'The Hannibal', purchases 692 people in Africa for transportation to the New World. Only 372 make it to the destination – the others have died or been dumped overboard en route. **1695** – A window tax is introduced in England. Many shopkeepers simply brick up their windows to dodge it. **1696** – Dutch undertakers revolt after funeral reforms are imposed in Amsterdam. **1696** – Famine kills a fifth of the population of Estonia (qv 1601) and a third of the population of Finland. **1698** – In an attempt to westernise Russia, Peter the Great imposes a tax on beards. **1700** – The dying Charles II of Spain, at thirty-eight years old bald, toothless and riddled with ulcers, orders the bodies of his wife and relatives to be exhumed so he can look upon their faces one last time before joining them.

I know that I've never said what my wife's name is. I'm not being coy. I can't remember it. I can't remember. It's not there in my head any more. If I knew it, be sure, I'd tell you.

DEAD ROMANS

Trudging around the Roman Forum, Trevor had begun to liken its second century ruins to the ruins of his own marriage. It was just a silly thought that popped into his head, but he liked it, it seemed quite witty. Look at Rome – once so majestic and, and *imperious* – it could have taken on the world – well, it *had*, hadn't it, wasn't that the point, wasn't that the reason people bothered with the ruins in the first place? And now it was old, and crumbling, and something to be gawped at by tourists in their sunglasses and baseball caps and their manga T-shirts... Fair enough, Trevor thought, the analogy wasn't *perfect*, no-one was gawping at his marriage, not even he and Eileen had wanted to look at it full on for quite a while. But, you know, witty. The conceit kept Trevor amused, it kept him smiling for ten whole minutes, until Eileen had glared at him, and he stopped.

She hadn't spoken to him for an hour. Indeed, it was probably well over an hour now. He'd only thought to time it when he'd begun to notice the silence, and that was only because it had been so long since she'd last bothered to open her mouth – and that had been at twenty past three, and, look, it was gone four now, so, yes, an hour, easily, surely. He wiped the sweat off his brow. It was so hot. There were patches of shade behind some of the larger columns, but that was where the Japanese had congregated, they were smart like that – and though she seemed to be baking in the heat just as much as he was, her face was just one big puff of redness, Eileen showed no interest in trying to barge her way through them and take some of that shade for herself. It was as if she were sleepwalking through the whole tour, punch drunk in the sun. Other couples strolled about, and they were silent too, but they were hand in hand, they were smiling, they were *sharing* their silence. Whereas Trevor had his hands in his jacket pockets; and Eileen, she was clinging on to her handbag with grim tenacity, he'd read to her from the guidebook one too many warnings about Italian pickpockets.

And Trevor read to her yet another titbit from that very same book. 'That bit there was built in AD 193,' he said. 'Makes you think, doesn't it?' He pointed. She didn't look. 'Been here all this time. Survived this long. Makes you think.' He didn't expect her to say anything, of course not, she hadn't at the remains of the Roman market, or the exact spot at which Julius Caesar had been cremated – but now she sighed, and it was a sigh so heavy it was almost verbal. And Eileen seemed to recognise this as well, that the sigh had broken the silence, that if she'd never again intended to communicate with her husband she'd now *lost* – so she added, 'Can we do something else soon, please?'

She stared up at a broken column, as if in new-found fascination. And then, 'I want to do something else,' she said, as if it were a new observation altogether, and Trevor knew that by something else Eileen meant shoe shopping.

Because, clearly, yes, it had now been *ages* since she'd been inside a shoe shop. Because, yes, she must by now be having withdrawal symptoms. The ruins were a bit dull. All right. But they were famous, the guidebook said so, you couldn't get to see them at home. They were obviously more worthy of attention than the Gucci off the Via Condotti. 'They look just the same as the shoes you could get in London!' Trevor had said last night, when she'd brought back to the hotel yet another pair. Trying to sound amused, trying not to lose the holiday spirit. 'There's nothing even to say they're from Rome, who would know?' 'I'll know,' said Eileen, and she'd cradled the shoes to her chest, and that had been that.

She pushed her way through the gaggle of Italian schoolchildren hanging so listlessly about the Arch of Septimius Severus: 'Oh, for God's sake,' she muttered. A few of the kids actually flinched. Trevor felt rather sorry for them. They were as bored by the ruins as Trevor and Eileen were, it was true. But Trevor felt they had a *right* to be bored. It was their history, after all, they'd been the ones who'd lived through it, them and their ancestors. Trevor and Eileen, though – they should put in more effort, this wasn't their past, they were strangers here. At the exit to the Forum a Roman centurion waggled his sword at them, coaxing tourists to pose for photographs with him. He pointed the weapon straight at Eileen – 'Come on, come on!' he urged, somehow divining she was British, somehow, even though Eileen hadn't uttered a word, even though the silence was back.

The guidebook had recommended that they allow three and a half hours to explore the Forum and the neighbouring Palatine area. They'd given it forty minutes. And ten of those had been spent trying to find the way out.

And only ten minutes later they were inside a shoe shop. And privately Trevor had to admit it was nice in there – the shop was cool, and wasn't crowded, and was posh enough that the sales staff spoke their excellent English with beautiful accents. As Eileen prised her feet into shoe after shoe after shoe, Trevor took out the guidebook, and mentally crossed off what they had already seen. The Pantheon, check. The Trevi Fountain, check. Castel Sant'Angelo, the Colosseum, the patch of barren grass that had once been the Circus Maximus, check check check. In spite of Eileen's lack of enthusiasm, in spite of the way she seemed determined to look on the best the Roman Empire could offer her with hostile bemusement, they'd achieved a lot. Good progress. Good. Especially considering they'd only been here a day and a half. Keep up this pace, they might get the whole city finished by Wednesday. Then that would give them two days of the holiday left to mop up the best bits again. He put the book away. Eileen held up a pair of shoes to him, as if asking his opinion. And he shrugged, and then smiled, as if to show there'd been nothing dismissive in that shrug – no, he couldn't care less what she spent her money on, but whatever made her happy made him happy, and they were on holiday, they were happy, weren't they? And he smiled just a little wider to emphasise the point.

'I think,' Trevor said, 'we should do the Vatican next.'

'All right,' said Eileen.

'That's a bit of a biggie. We can't not do the Vatican.'

'Then let's do the Vatican.'

'Unless, I don't know. You want to try on some more shoes.'

'Let's do the Vatican.'

'Because you could. But, you know. We only have so much time here.'

'Let's,' said Eileen, 'do the Vatican. If I can just pay for these first? Can I just pay for these first? Can you wait just a minute while I pay?'

'Of course,' said Trevor. 'We're on holiday. We can do whatever you like.'

She paid for the shoes. Then Trevor watched as she slid her credit card back into the purse with all the others. He deliberately waited until the purse was back in the handbag too before he spoke, he didn't want to seem impatient. 'All right,' he said, 'all right, *andiamo*, let's go.'

The Vatican was big. 'It imposes itself upon the landscape,' said Trevor, as they walked down the Via della Concilazione towards it. 'Don't you think? That's what the book says. We're nearly there.' Half an hour later they still hadn't reached it. 'We're not there yet,' Trevor told Eileen, rather unnecessarily, 'but that's because distance is deceptive, because it imposes itself upon the, because, you know, it's big.' The Vatican was big, and the queues to get in were long; they snaked around the countless signs warning tourists they wouldn't be admitted wearing disrespectful clothing, and that they mustn't smoke, or eat, or wantonly use flick knives. 'Do we really have to go in?' asked Eileen, 'the queue is *huge*.' 'Only going to get huger!' laughed Trevor, as they took their positions. He entertained her en route with more statistics from the guidebook; the basilica was 452 feet high, and 500 feet wide, and 730 feet long, and had 20,000 people visiting it each day. 'I feel sick,' said Eileen, and Trevor didn't seem to notice, he was describing the quality of the frescos they were soon to witness, and then she was heaving, long dry heaves that creased her body in two. 'I feel sick, I've got to get out of here!' And Trevor put down his guidebook. And his first thought was how embarrassing it would be if Eileen proceeded to throw up in front of all these people, 20,000 of them (the Vatican was so *big!*) and the second thought: if they left the queue now they'd only have to go back to the start again, could someone hold his place while he dealt with his wife? – was that something he could quickly find in the phrase book? – could he find it in time before Eileen threw up in front of 20,000 people? And then Eileen was pushing her way free, still doubled up – 'I need you to hold my place,' Trevor said, loud and slow, to the blank-eyed couple behind him, 'we are coming back, comprende?' – and then he was following her, he put his hands on her shoulders, and she shook him off, not unkindly, and she sat down under one of the archways ringing Saint Peter's Square, and Trevor put his arms around her again, and this time she accepted them. 'I'm sorry,' said Trevor, 'I'm sorry,' although he wasn't quite sure what he was apologising for, 'are you okay?' And Eileen didn't throw up after all; instead she raised her head to him, and her face was pale, but her eyes were bright, and she was smiling, she was actually smiling. 'I believe in God,' she said. 'I believe. And I'm going to become a Catholic.'

*

Eileen had a secret. She didn't like shoes.

Sometimes she'd bring as many as a dozen pairs back with her from a holiday. Sometimes they wouldn't all fit in the suitcase, and she'd have to leave a few behind in the hotel, stuffed into drawers so that Trevor wouldn't see.

She didn't like shoes. Shoes were for walking. Why did she want to walk anywhere?

She quite liked *buying* shoes, though. She enjoyed the politeness of the customer assistants, the way they called her 'madam'. No matter which country Trevor had dragged her to this time, no matter how rainy or humid or sandy, the sophistication of their shoe shops was one thing each destination had in common. 'Good day, madam,' they'd say, and then they'd fetch her as many shoes as she could stand. They'd fuss around her as much as she liked, and she could pretend that for all their peculiar accents she was back in London, that she could run out of the shop at any moment and catch the bus home.

She only wished she could go shoe shopping without having to bother with all the shoes. But it was a small price to pay for her sanity.

Eileen didn't like shoes, and she didn't like holidays either. She couldn't work out why Trevor hadn't realised that yet. She had rather hoped he'd have taken the hint by now.

She hadn't minded holidays at the beginning. She'd enjoyed their honeymoon (Paris) and a couple of the holidays following (Tenerife, Crete). And then, one day, she'd just stopped being happy. She hadn't even known why, and it made her feel somewhat churlish and ungrateful. She felt despondent exploring the great vineyards of the South of France, she'd not been charmed by the Niagara Falls, no more so by the Grand Canyon. She'd positively sulked the length and breadth of the Orient Express. 'We should broaden our horizons,' Trevor would say, and, 'travel broadens the mind,' and she didn't want anything broadening, thank you, neither mind nor horizons, leave them as they were, they weren't bits of elastic, were they? They weren't elastic, they might snap. And there had been the ennui, and some years later it had grown into resentment, real resentment that left a taste in the mouth, and, after that, there'd been the panic attacks. Because everywhere they went, there were always new people, new strangers. And everywhere they went, there was always Trevor.

Eileen could cope with Trevor on home territory. She knew in which rooms he belonged, in which *parts* of which rooms he belonged. He had his very own dinner plate, his own armchair, his own side of the bed. He wouldn't talk to her much, or he *would*, but he didn't really say anything worth listening to – but that was fine, he didn't need to, that was safe. He'd leave for work in the morning, he'd come back in the evening. Dinner plate, armchair, bed (right-hand side, nearest the door) then the same again tomorrow.

She loved the Trevor she got at home. In the same way she loved the tiles they'd chosen for the bathroom, the lamp fittings in the lounge. She loved Trevor. She knew that. If anything ever happened to him, she was almost positive, it would quite throw her into chaos, it would seriously put her out.

Quite why shoes she didn't know. She couldn't even remember which holiday it had been on that she had discovered this security blanket. Probably one of the European ones, the language had been funny but the crowds had been *white*, there'd been that reassurance at least. She'd suddenly felt very hot, and very frightened, and the streets of whichever-city-it-had-been seemed to be folding up and closing tight around her – which was stupid, because at the exact same time they were stretching out in front of her endlessly, there would never be a way out of this strange country, it'd go on and on and on into the distance forever. And she'd backed into a shop, and the girl there had been so charming, and sold her three pairs of Manolo Blahniks.

She took an extra suitcase with her now, every time they went abroad. It was empty for the journey out. Came back full of things she'd never wear and couldn't like. Trevor never said anything. Oh, he'd mention the shoes. He'd laugh at the shoes. But he'd never mention that empty suitcase.

She was fine. She was coping. All she feared was that, sooner or later, she'd start to buy shoes back at home too. She sometimes felt the pricklings of that impulse, the itching of the urge, as she went to the supermarket, as she went into town to get her hair done or her legs waxed or her teeth cleaned. She'd fought it so far. She always beat it back. But one day she'd fail, she'd start to need the shoes, and that was when the walls would come crashing down, and she'd be lost, utterly, irretrievably. But, on the bright side! It hadn't happened yet!

Trevor had said to her over dinner one night, eating his favourite meal off the usual plate, 'I think it's time we had another break soon, don't you?'

'Can we afford it?' she asked. Though she knew they could.

'Oh, it's only money!' he laughed. 'Might as well enjoy it!' They were still paying for Annie's university course, and that curbed his holiday spending a bit. Thank God for Annie. She'd graduate soon. Then there'd be more money. Eileen was trying hard to persuade her to do a PhD.

'I thought Rome,' he said. 'The Eternal City!' Eileen said that would be very nice. 'You could say it with a bit more enthusiasm!' he laughed, ever so amiably. So she did, she gave enthusiasm a really good shot. And he took her to the computer, he wanted to show her pictures he'd bookmarked on the internet. And she listened to all his plans, and then washed up his dinner plate, and then very politely went into the toilet to vomit.

Eileen took the window seat on the plane, and Trevor took the aisle seat. Eileen liked the window, and Trevor liked the aisle, so that, at least, was all right. Eileen liked to look out at the clouds. She liked to make little shapes out of them. She liked to imagine that if the aeroplane ran out of fuel, or the engines stopped dead, or the wings just dropped off – that they could simply park on one of those clouds, that the fluffy islands were strong enough to support them. Not a wispy cloud. One of the *thicker* ones. She wasn't daft. She liked to pretend that if she had enough of the flight, if she felt claustrophobic, suddenly had enough of all those stewardesses offering her coffee and talking to her as if they knew her, when they didn't, they really didn't – then she could just open the window, and jump out, and lie down on one of those clouds for ever more. And she could wave goodbye to the aeroplane, and to Trevor, 'Don't worry,' she'd cry out, as they sped away from her, 'I'll be perfectly happy here!', and she'd be free, she'd be *free*.

And Trevor liked the aisle seat in case he needed to get up and use the toilet.

The hotel wasn't as nice as it had looked on the website. The wardrobe wouldn't shut properly, and the wallpaper was peeling off in big dirty clumps. 'Never mind!' said Trevor, though she could see he was disappointed. 'We won't be here much anyway. This is Base Camp. And we're just ten minutes away from the Spanish Steps, so, you know, so... Location, location, location!' And then he was trying out the bed, and pulling the double into two singles – 'It's two singles stuck together, it'll be better this way,' and fussing about the pillows, and she wished he'd just stop and leave everything alone. All she cared about was whether there was sufficient drawer space for any unwanted shoes. There was, yes, good. She rather suspected she'd be getting through a lot of shoes this week.

She didn't want to spoil Trevor's fun, she tried to keep smiling, just for his sake. He'd stride a few paces in front of her, reading out from that guide, so proud, as if because he owned it he'd written the thing. '*Andiamo*, let's go,' he'd say each time they set off, '*andiamo*' was a phrase he'd read there, and he always added the translation right afterwards, as if that made it funnier. She didn't dare say anything, she kept her mouth shut as they went around the tourist sites, because she was afraid of what might come out if she didn't: 'Shut up', or 'I want to go home' or 'I don't love you, not here, I don't love you here.' And, by God, he was still wittering on – what was the man talking about now? – 'This dates back two and a half thousand years, makes you think!' – shut up. Shut Up. And with an effort she'd grind her teeth and clamp her lips together tight.

It wasn't that Eileen disliked Rome. If anything, she just felt a bit sorry for it. Trevor would talk on and on about its beauty, as if beauty were a factual thing bestowed by a guidebook – but she couldn't see that beauty, no matter how much it told her to look. The Colosseum had once been a vast amphitheatre, and now it looked like a collapsed cake, half of the outer wall missing, the inside overgrown with grass and rubble. One good shove and it'd fall over. What good was a theatre, she thought, if it didn't put on any shows? Stick on a decent Lloyd Webber, and she might begin to care. The guidebook told her (via Trevor) how Mussolini had built a road through the ruins leading to the Colosseum, and how that was a travesty, an act of vandalism against history – and she couldn't see why. For the last few thousand years the Romans had been taking the stone and the marble from dead buildings to make new ones – wasn't that an honourable thing, really, wanting to create something new? Not to rely on past glories, but to embrace some sort of *change*? – broadening their horizons, that's what they'd been doing, wasn't that *good*? Exactly when did history become so bloody important that the world around had to sidestep it and give it a wide berth? She wasn't saying they should do away with history altogether – she was sure (she was told) there was a lot archaeologists could learn from all these columns dotted about the place. So why not keep the *best* one (they could choose which, whatever they thought was nicest) and get rid of the rest? Then there'd be so much more *room*. There was precious little space here for the living, not now it was congested with so many tourists with their cameras and their ice creams, so how about just pushing all the dead to one side so they could all breathe – all these ruins, they didn't tell her anything, except that the city was in thrall to something bigger than itself, that it would always be defined by what it used to be and not what it could become. Clear away all the headless statues, the pillars that no longer had anything to support. For God's sake, get over it!

'I think,' Trevor said, 'we should do the Vatican next.' Oh yes. Let's do that very thing. Gird your loins, screw your courage to the sticking place, and clasp your new shoes to yourself as tightly as you can.

And the queue *was* long. And Trevor had started emphasising just *how* long, that there were 20,000 people inside, 20,000 different faces and different voices, saying things in different languages she'd never understand, and she'd never know who they were, she'd never affect their lives and they'd never affect hers, these people would be at the same point of space at the exact same time as her, against all sense and probability 20,000 different life stories would converge with hers and it *wouldn't matter a jot* – all the extraordinary coincidences of those 20,000 encounters would count for nothing. And she looked above her, and the Vatican was so *vast* – and yesterday there'd been another 20,000 people in there, and if she and Trevor hadn't gone to the Colosseum they'd have gone to the Vatican and they would have crossed paths with those people instead – and just as purposelessly, the whole thing was just random, it was all random chance...

... and yet this was the house of God, such a big house, so did that mean that one God equalled 20,000 people, is that how it worked? And then she began to feel sick. And she went hot, and then cold, and the world seemed to spin, and she had to get away, away from the 20,000. Away from them all watching her (although they weren't watching her at all, and they never would, that was the problem) away from God (and he wasn't watching either, was he? Was he?) – she thought the shoes might help, get out the shoes, give them a sniff, take yourself back to the smell of the shop where everything was safe and polite, and there was no God there, God doesn't live in shoe shops – but no, there were too many people about (20,000) and she could smell them instead. And she rushed away, and she felt Trevor's arms around her shoulders, but he was one of the 20,000, she didn't want him...

... and God...

... and the ruins were just bits of rubble, there was nothing in them, nothing to say to her, but here was God...

... and the Vatican wasn't so big after all, was it, was it? The House of God was laughably small, how did they expect God to be squeezed inside? Was this palace of marble and stone the best they could do? Yes. Yes, it was the best they could do.

... and 20,000 suddenly seemed such a very small number.

... and she knew she wouldn't be frightened again.

... and she didn't throw up. (This last, in particular, that was a relief.)

'I believe in God,' she told Trevor. And she didn't know it until she said it. So *that's* what would have come tumbling out of her mouth had she only opened it earlier! Who would have thought.

And all the panic attacks, they hadn't been attacks at all – that had just been God knocking on the door, asking to be let in – they'd all just been a means of getting her to this exact point, hadn't they? Hadn't they? Little moments of truth, no, of *self-revelation*, that she'd chucked away on shoe shops. (And brandy. And Prozac.) It had all been building up to this. To the biggest 'attack' of all, when she'd finally crack open, her brain would split right down the middle, and her new self would come flooding out.

Trevor seemed surprised.

'Are you all right?' he asked.

'I can't even begin to tell you,' she said, 'just how all right I am.'

'Right,' he said. 'Good. Good, that's good.'

'I'm going to be a Catholic,' she told him.

'Yes. You said.'

'Everything's going to be different from this moment on.'

'Shall we go back to the hotel?' asked Trevor. 'You're looking a bit pale. We can do the Vatican some other day. Maybe.'

'All right,' she said. 'Something I need to do first.' And she went to the nearest litter bin, and dropped her new bag of shoes inside.

'Oh,' said Trevor.

'I didn't want them any more.'

'No,' said Trevor. 'I can see that.'

'Is there a problem?' asked Eileen.

'I just thought... you know... you could have taken them back. Got a refund.'

'Yes,' mused Eileen. 'But then, that would have meant my having to go back into the shoe shop. And I am never entering another shoe shop for the rest of my life.' She smiled at him. She hoped he'd understood. He could see, surely, how very reasonable she was being.

They both walked back down the Via della Concilazione together. For a while, Trevor kept his mouth shut. This time, mercifully, the silence was mutual.

But Trevor couldn't help it. The guidebook seemed to itch in his fingers. Soon he was passing ruins, looking them up on maps. Looking then at Eileen, considering saying something – and then she'd give him that smile, and he'd decide not to.

'Cats,' he said, at last.

'What?'

'Look down there,' said Trevor. 'Amongst the ruins.'

They'd reached a crossroads. And in the middle of all the interconnecting streets, a large square protected by railings. And he was leaning over, gazing deep down at the ruins beneath.

'I don't want to look at any more ruins.'

'No, sure. But look. Cats! There's another one. And another... Look, it's full of them...'

'I don't need ruins or shoe shops.'

'There are *dozens* of them. Where do they all come from?'

And then Eileen told Trevor how much she hated the ruins of Rome. How they were relics of a bygone age, a time of paganism, of false gods, of heresy. 'They're useless,' she said. 'It's all just about... dead Romans. Dead Romans, that's all. Who cares? Let them rot. Because there's something more important, something that's *alive*, and *true*, and before which all of this is just... dust, you know, in the wind.'

'Dead Romans?' repeated Trevor.

'That's all they are.'

'At least,' suggested Trevor, 'the Romans actually existed.'

Eileen glared at him with such fury. 'Then you stay with the dead,' she said. 'You stay here.' And she marched away.

'Dead Romans,' she heard him call after her, 'and *cats*.' But she didn't so much as turn her head around in response.

*

It wasn't originally going to be Rome. Trevor had set his mind upon Paris.

Going back to Paris played against all of Trevor's instincts. The world was a very large thing. There was more to see in it than he could ever possibly manage. So why would you want to see anywhere *twice*? Take Desmond, in the office, technically his superior (though, in practice, they were just about equal, weren't they?) – every year Desmond and his wife would go on holiday to the Algarve. They had a cottage there. Trevor thought Desmond was an idiot. What new sights could the Algarve offer him now? Trevor had got hold of a guidebook for the Algarve; he was pretty sure, with a bit of forward planning, he could cover all the sights in two days *tops*. That would barely be a holiday, that'd be a *weekend break*.

And he had no need to see Paris again. He knew Paris. He'd seen the Eiffel Tower, the Champs Élysées, the Louvre, the Arc de Triomphe. Three and a half days. And that had been doing it leisurely. That had been doing it with lots of sex in between, that had slowed him down.

But Trevor had seen that Eileen had been out of sorts for a while. He wasn't quite sure why. (Though he had an awful suspicion. But he wasn't going to bring that up. That would ruin any chance of recovery, that would only make the niggling little problem a really big crisis, what would be the sense in that?) And he knew she'd liked Paris. It had been where they'd been on honeymoon. They'd laughed in Paris. Eaten croissants. Walked along the Seine. Had sex. Quite a few times, the sex, no really, it *had* slowed them down, but it had been nice.

To go back to Paris would be senseless in any *real* terms, if he wanted to broaden his horizons. But... if he could make Eileen happy. If she could be reminded of where she had been happy, very obviously happy, at least the once. God, how she'd laughed, she'd laughed so much back then.

He told Alice that he was thinking of taking another holiday. Alice was his secretary. (Not in name, but she did secretarial things for him, and she was very definitely his inferior.) Alice was loud and plump and funny. He liked Alice.

'You do go away a lot!' she cooed.

'It's a big world,' said Trevor.

'My favourite place to visit,' said Alice, and she sucked at the knob of her pen, 'is Rome. I love Rome.'

'Ah, the Eternal City!' said Trevor.

'Neil and I went on our honeymoon there. Lots to do.'

Alice was not only loud and plump and funny, but had a habit of making cow eyes at Trevor across the office floor – it seemed very flirtatious. Trevor had for a while assumed that Alice had something wrong with her contact lenses. But then he'd checked, he'd kept watch, and if that were true, the contact lenses only played up for him.

'I have always wanted to go to Rome,' Trevor admitted.

'I'd love,' said Alice, 'to know what you make of it.'

'Would you?'

'It's beautiful. Only word for it, beautiful. And old, too.'

And Alice stood over his computer, and showed him some tourist websites – all the fountains and statues, and Trevor agreed, they did look pretty. 'I think Rome's a very good idea,' said Trevor, and Alice stayed for another half hour helping him book the flights and the hotel. She stood over him as he gave his credit card details, he could smell her deodorant, and if he looked up at her face it'd be partly obscured by her breasts. It was a good afternoon.

The truth was, Trevor didn't much like going on holiday any more. But needs must.

In the beginning it had been different. It didn't matter where they'd go, to which strange art gallery, to which strange church. They'd stand shoulder to shoulder, amidst all these foreigners, they would stand their ground in the face of overseas indifference, Trevor and Eileen Stafford united, the Staffords forever! No matter whether it was Athens or Lisbon or Disneyland, the Staffords were a *team* – and that had only been strengthened when they'd had Annie, when they went around the holiday attractions of the world as a threesome, two adult tickets, please, and an infant getting in free. That's what Trevor now wanted, all he ever could want – to stand in the Roman Forum, at the Colosseum, in the gardens of the Villa Borghese, and all the different accents of tourists from a dozen different nations could buffet them on all sides and they'd not care, they'd rise above it all, they could safely despise everyone with their better countries with better histories, because they had each other. But then Annie had become a teenager, and then Annie had wanted holidays of her own, and with a strange succession of boyfriends (Trevor couldn't keep up, he didn't think it polite to try) – and he thought he and Eileen would go back to the way it had been before. But you couldn't go back, you never go back, you should never go back – and what they had now were the silences.

Trevor was scared of Eileen. It was okay, it didn't matter, nothing to be ashamed of – though now, every day, he'd come home from work, and he'd pause before putting the key in the lock, he'd take a deep breath, he'd cross his fingers, he'd even mutter a little prayer. And that was silly, because God didn't exist. Eileen always looked so sad, and he didn't know why, or how to stop it, and so he'd talk, he'd talk a lot to drive the fear away, he'd read her bits from the newspaper, anything...

And they hadn't had sex. For a long while now. And it was his fault. Entirely his. He knew *logically* that this was the same woman he'd slept with before – that he'd gone knocking on that little space between her legs many a time. But now the very thought of paying a friendly visit down there made his extremities shrivel. She wasn't ugly. She looked different, though. She was bony, when did she get bony, he hadn't knowingly married a bony woman. And all her body parts were present and well and functioning, but it was as if they'd all been slightly misplaced somehow, how and why had his wife's organs swapped about, what was the idea? She was so *close* to looking like Eileen, that was the worst of it. It was like sleeping next to a parody. Hoping he wouldn't touch her, even accidentally, brushing alongside, ugh. If she'd been completely different – like, I don't know, Alice! for example! – then it would have been okay. He could have had sex with her quite cheerfully. Perhaps. Almost certainly, probably.

He couldn't remember the last time they'd made love. He hadn't thought to check the date. And when he finally did, that was only because it had been so long, it must have already been a few months since sex by then, and that was four years eight months ago. So that would mean five years now, yes, five years, easily, surely.

On his pub quiz team there had been a doctor. He didn't know him well. But he'd asked if he could bend his ear. And over a pint he explained the problem.

'I'm not sure I can be of much help,' said the doctor. 'I sort of specialise in feet.'

'You must know something, though,' said Trevor.

And the doctor said, after another pint, that he'd heard that changing location could sometimes work. That might make things seem fresh again. Was there any other room in which Trevor could initiate congress? And Trevor thanked him very much, and bought him another pint, and didn't stay to watch him drink it, and never quite dared go back to that pub again.

The only other possible bed in the house was in Annie's old room. She still slept in it when she came to visit. She'd kept all her old toys and school books there. The bed had a teddy bear on it that she didn't want anywhere even *near* her university digs, but absolutely refused to have thrown away.

'Why do you want us to sleep in Annie's room?' asked Eileen. She didn't smile. And Trevor still felt so, so scared.

Because maybe in there your vagina won't eat me. 'I don't know. Fancied a change!'

'I think Annie would mind. Don't you think Annie would mind?'

'I don't think she'd mind,' said Trevor. 'I could give her a call, see if she minds,' and why was he talking, bail out, bail out *now*, because he suddenly *knew* it'd be no better in Annie's room, the vagina would eat him there just as easily. Worse, this was where his daughter belonged, and she was the *product* of that vagina, the vagina's power would be *strengthened*. No, worse, worse still! There'd be *two* vaginas in there now, mother and daughter, each taking turns, gobbling away at him, gobbling him up, it'd be the lair of the hungry fannies, 'Tell you what, I'll leave it,' he said.

So. If nowhere in the house, then maybe in hotel rooms. Somewhere anonymous. Some city they'd never been to before. On some holiday.

While the vagina was disorientated. Then he'd make his move.

Alice had stood over him as he'd made his hotel booking to Rome, and Trevor could sense those breasts bobbing right above his head, if he stood up suddenly there'd be the most awful wonderful collision. On the registration form he was asked whether he wanted a double room or a twin, and he suddenly wished Alice wasn't there – he wanted to explain to her, might as well go for a twin, I don't sleep with my wife any more, I'm practically free and single. But the whole point of the holiday was that double bed, wasn't it, hadn't that been the point? And maybe Alice would prefer to think of him as still sexually active, pity was such a turn-off. So he clicked on the double bed option, and looked up at Alice, neatly avoiding the boobs as he did so, and she was nodding appreciatively, so he thought he'd done the right thing.

That night he told Eileen he was taking her to Rome, and she barely even smiled, and he wanted to say, look, I don't even want to go to bloody Rome, this is all for you, don't you understand it's all for you.

One day Alice brought a book into work.

'This is for you,' she said. 'I had a bit of a dig around, and I found it!' It was a guidebook for Rome.

'Oh, thank you,' said Trevor. 'I'll take good care of it, bring it back safe.'

'No, no, keep it. You may as well.'

'So, this is a present?'

'Well, yes. Sort of.'

'That's very kind!'

'No, it's nothing.'

'I must get you a present too. What would you like?'

'Oh, there's no need for that.'

'Seems only fair. If you got me a present!'

'It's just an old guidebook! Years old. Out of date, it still thinks everything is in lire. But I don't know, the ruins will still be the same, won't they? They won't have gone anywhere!'

And Alice laughed. Trevor laughed too. Come with me, Alice. Come with me to Rome.

'That's true! They're pretty old!'

'They're unlikely to have been updated!'

'No, I imagine not!' Alice laughed at this as well, and Trevor laughed a bit more too. Lots of laughter, holidays should be about laughter, shouldn't they? Come with me, Alice. Rescue me. Maybe I can rescue you too. Maybe you're frightened Neil's penis will eat you. Maybe your husband's got a hungry dick. You never know. 'Well, I'll have to buy you a drink some time. If that's okay.'

'And you can tell me all about Rome.'

'I can! I will! I'll tell you, ha, if it's been updated!' And they smiled at each other. Oh, he'd have to get her a present, you know, just a little one, it'd only be fair.

On arrival at the hotel in Rome, the first thing Trevor did was to check out the quality of the bed. He spreadeagled himself across it. It was hard. Too hard for sex? Possibly. He inspected the pillows. They were good sleeping pillows, but he wasn't certain they were good shagging pillows. 'I'm not sure about the pillows,' he said, but Eileen wasn't even listening, she was opening drawers. Trevor felt beneath his back, frowned. There was a crack, a decided crack, running down the centre of the bed. He looked under the blanket. 'It's not a double bed,' he said. 'It's two singles pushed together. I asked for a double bed.' He thought about this for a moment. The crack put him off. He didn't want to be in the throes of ecstasy (well, any throes he could get) and fall down a crack in consequence. He could have stomached the pillow, but this was too much. Better separate the beds altogether, better they were two singles, let's have no pretence. He pushed them apart. The far bed now jutted across the doorway, it'd make it a little harder to get in or get out of the room, but that couldn't be helped.

'Does it matter?' asked Eileen.

'No, no, it doesn't matter,' said Trevor. And nor did it. This could be Base Camp, couldn't it, a perfect place from which to explore Rome. There'd be no sex in Rome, that was now clear, and that was a shame, obviously, although actually a wave of relief swept over him and he couldn't stop smiling. He was sure there was more to Rome than sex, and now the sex was out of the way, they could relax and enjoy themselves. And the sex would be okay, he'd simply have to try sex on some other holiday soon instead. Yes. He'd ask Alice for recommendations.

He bought Alice's present within the first hour of the holiday. The first thing Eileen wanted to do after she'd unpacked was to visit a shoe shop – and normally Trevor might have minded, it'd put them behind schedule from the get-go, but it gave him ample opportunity to pop into the jeweller's next door. He didn't want to get Alice anything too flashy. Possibly the necklace was a bit too flashy. It's all right, he thought, as he hid it in his jacket pocket, he could always buy her something more suitable later. Maybe he'd never have the courage to give her the necklace, he'd find a back-up in case his nerve failed him. Why not? He's on holiday, he can do as he likes. And off he sets around Rome, brandishing Alice's guidebook ahead of him – and it's ridiculous of course to think that that means he's holding a little piece of Alice, so he refuses to think that, not even once. But he does imagine, as he reads aloud all the facts and figures, that he's reading them to her. And that she'd find them interesting. And maybe smile every now and then.

The incident at the Vatican didn't alarm Trevor too much. If anything, it rather put his mind at rest. He didn't have to try so hard to be jolly, now he could luxuriate in a nice sulk. The sulk felt good. The fact he could stop smiling, that felt good. And he was more truly happy than he had been all holiday – and, look at her, Eileen was grinning away too, in her newly found beatitude, the pair of them were probably enjoying themselves more than they had in living memory.

'Cats,' he said.

He looked down into the courtyard of ruins. And there was a black cat sunning itself on a marble slab, there was a tabby asleep in the shadow of a broken archway. There was a fat ginger tom draped over the sides of a stunted pillar – careful, you might fall off! – but the cat seemed to know what it was doing. At first Trevor thought there was only the handful there, but as he looked over the tableau of shattered history, he could see cats everywhere, hidden and dwarfed by the thousands-year-old monuments.

Something living amongst the dead. These cats didn't give a toss about Augustus Caesar, or Trajan, or Nero, or the decline and fall of the Roman Empire. And Trevor realised this was the best thing yet he'd seen on his holiday.

'Cats,' he said to Eileen again. 'Look.' And Eileen made it very clear that she wasn't interested, and stormed off. And that was the second best thing he'd seen on holiday.

There were steps leading down into the square. These were the only ruins he'd yet seen not pored over by tourists, so Trevor supposed they weren't open to the public. But there was nothing to stop him taking a closer look. He went down the ancient stairs, half expecting at any moment some Italian policeman would pop out and arrest him. He picked his way over the wild bracken covering the remains of the Empire's finest, reached for the nearest cat, stroked its head. The fur was warm, so warm it bit at his fingers.

'I'd be careful,' said a voice. And Trevor looked around for that Italian policeman. Instead he saw a blonde girl, twenties, wearing a baggy T-shirt and shorts.

'Sorry,' said Trevor automatically. 'Is this private? I didn't see any signs.'

'The cats aren't feral,' the girl went on, and now Trevor could hear that her accent was American. 'But they've had pretty rough treatment from humans, one way and the other. They're friendly, mostly. But they might change their minds, give you a nasty scratch.'

'I was wondering,' said Trevor, 'what they were all doing here.' What are *you* doing here, baggy T-shirt girl?

'The Romans don't have a good track record with cats,' she said. 'If they get fed up with them, they abandon them. The number of abandoned cats is growing every year. And the government doesn't help. Any strays, they're subjects for animal experimentation.'

'God,' said Trevor politely.

'Would you like to read a leaflet?'

'I would.'

'Okay.' And she turned away, presumably to fetch one. She then turned back. She tilted her head as she regarded him, considered him. She put her tongue out, pressed it on her top lip, really *pressed* it, you could see the indent. Then smiled. 'You can come too, if you like.'

So Trevor did.

Only now he was in the square could he see it wasn't a square at all; the ruins continued on into darkened caves under the roads. And Trevor realised just how much was covered up by all the hotels and restaurants and shoe shops, that only a scratch beneath the surface would reveal ancient Rome in its broken glory. It was into one of these caves that the girl led Trevor; he was surprised that there were light bulbs hanging off the walls, carpets. Cages.

'A group of volunteers set up this place a few years ago,' said the girl. 'A sanctuary for these poor cats. The healthy ones we let roam outside, but most aren't so lucky. We feed them, we vaccinate them, we neuter them. Though not,' she suddenly laughed, as if going off script, 'necessarily in that order. We survive on private sponsorship. Would you like to give a donation?'

'Yes,' said Trevor.

'Great!' said the girl. 'Let me show you around.'

There were maybe a hundred cages, and each of them was occupied by a cat. Most were sleeping in boxes, on rugs – a few lucky ones even had cushions. Some were awake. Most of them stared at Trevor without interest, but a few felt curious enough at his arrival to offer a tentative mew.

'Ideally, we'd want to find homes for them all,' she said. 'They were domesticated originally. But no-one wants them, no-one wants to give house room to a damaged cat. Just because something's damaged, it doesn't mean it's useless, does it?'

'I wish I could take a cat,' said Trevor, 'but, you know, I'm allergic, and...'

'Quarantine laws won't permit you to take a cat to Britain,' said the girl, waving her hand dismissively, 'I know.' She sighed. And then looked him straight in the eyes. Her face was shadowed somewhat by an ineffective light bulb; she stood close. 'It's such a waste,' she said softly. 'They have such love to give.'

'I can see that,' said Trevor quietly.

'But they've had that love thrown back in their faces.'

'That's cruel.'

'And not all of them have the courage to try again.'

'You're American, aren't you?'

'Yes,' she said. She frowned.

'Thought so,' he said. Then added, 'I like Americans.'

'We have volunteers here from all over the world,' said the girl. 'Americans, Australians, British. You know.'

'Italians?'

The girl wrinkled her nose. 'A few. The Italians don't much care. They prefer their ruins. Some Italians want to force us out of here. Can you imagine? Because, do you know, right where we're standing, Julius Caesar was murdered? Or, no, not Julius Caesar. Another Caesar. There were a lot of Caesars.'

'If only the cats knew!' joked Trevor. 'They'd be honoured!'

The girl smiled politely. 'This is Maria, she's blind in one eye. And this is Santa Maria, she's blind in both eyes. Luigi, he was abandoned with two broken front paws, aren't people shits? Sorry. Romulo, he can't walk straight, he has a neurological disorder.' Though somehow the girl managed to say the word with at least two syllables missing. 'And this is Emilia, cancer, and this is Amore, cancer of the ear, we had to cut off his ear to save him. And here's my favourite! Yes, you are! Ciaobella, he hits on all the girls. Ladies' man! We neutered him, he hasn't realised yet, have you, he's still jumping on them, yeah, yeah, cancer.'

Her American accent suddenly seemed so exotic after the blathering of Italians. She stopped talking now, though, frowned, did that tongue thing again on the top of her lip, just a sliver of red, red on red, as he watched her, as she watched him. 'Erm,' he said. He wanted her to talk again. He liked her talking. 'Erm. And what's wrong with this one?'

'I told you,' said the girl. 'Noologcal disorder. I think you should know, I never sleep with married men.'

And it came out so matter of fact, cheerfully even, that for a moment Trevor thought he must have misheard. Or that this was a particularly peculiar name for some damaged or dying feline. 'What?' he said, at last. And then, 'Of course not. I hope you don't... That I...' And then, 'I mean, I'm old enough to be your father.'

'Oh, I like older men,' said the girl. 'You're exactly my type. Shame.' And she smiled at him, a little apologetically, Trevor thought. 'Are you going to give us a donation?'

Trevor gave her a hundred euros.

*

One day Annie had come home from school. 'I'm a Christian,' she told her mum, as she hung up her coat and her satchel. 'I converted.'

'And when did this happen?' said Eileen.

'In RE class. We were learning about Jesus, and all the things he did. And Mr Fox said, if we wanted, we could convert. So we did. We all did. We said the right prayer, the one that makes you a Christian, and we're all Christians now.'

'We'll have to see what your father says.'

But Trevor wasn't sure what to say. As ever. 'Well, I don't know,' he said privately to Eileen. 'It *is* a Christian school. I went to a Christian school. Prayers at assembly, that sort of thing.'

'So did I,' said Eileen. 'But I was never asked to believe in anything.'

Trevor spoke to his daughter over dinner. 'Are you all right, Bunny?' Annie said she was. 'I'm concerned you might have joined a cult.'

Annie rolled her eyes. 'It's the Church of England.'

'Oh, okay,' said Trevor.

He told Eileen that night, in bed, 'I bet it'll blow over. You wait. I'd give it a few weeks.'

'I don't like it.'

'It'll blow over, you'll see,' said Trevor, and then he climbed on top of her, and they made love.

And Eileen watched with suspicion, and yes, a little jealousy, as her daughter

313

took down her posters of Madonna from her bedroom wall and stuck Jesus up instead; stayed late after school to go to Christian Club; asked her parents to say grace before each evening meal. Eileen didn't like that bit in particular, it made the food taste funny.

But Trevor had been right. Three weeks later, Annie had moved on to something else. She'd been hanging around with the sixth-form boys, and she and her friends were put in detention after school for wearing make-up, and wearing jewellery, and smoking to look cool. 'Told you so,' said Trevor smugly, and Eileen breathed a sigh of relief, tinged with a little irritation that Trevor took his daughter's fall from grace as his own personal triumph.

Now, as Eileen walked back to the Vatican, she felt a stab of guilt that she'd so discouraged her daughter's faith. And then she thought, no – if Annie were going to give in *that* easily, her faith wasn't worth having. Everyone needs to be tested. Eileen didn't know the Bible well (yet) but it was chockablock full of tests, wasn't it? Eileen had been tested. She'd been tested by a weak husband, a bad daughter. By shoe shops and cold sweats and panic. She'd come through. The tests had made her stronger. By the time she reached Saint Peter's Square she'd convinced herself that she'd been God's instrument in Annie's conversion, and Annie had been found wanting.

Annie had made her bed, and now she must lie in it.

Eileen settled down in the archways surrounding the Vatican.

The queues to enter were just as long. Eileen had no need to join them. She was full of the Holy Spirit already, full to the brim, she didn't require a top-up. She watched as the tourists filed past her. Those people with their cameras and their backpacks, laughing and chatting and treating it all as such fun. How many of the 20,000 really were true believers? Not many. Most of them were just popping inside to ogle Christ. She hoped He'd burn their eyes out.

She wasn't saying she was the *best* Christian at the Vatican. After all, she wasn't very experienced yet. You couldn't expect miracles. But look how good she was already, and she'd only been a Catholic for an hour and a half!

She kept careful watch. Hundreds of people went into the Vatican. But no-one ever seemed to come out. She wondered whether the church was hungry, whether it swallowed them whole. Or maybe there was an exit at the back.

Now she was hungry too. Around the corner there was a gelateria. She bought herself a pistachio ice cream. It was nice.

There were a lot of nuns about. They were all so old, and so small, they bumbled about the square like wind-up toys. Behaving like tourists too, taking out their cameras and posing with grins in front of the Basilica. Eileen wondered whether being old and small was part of the job requirement. Whether, when you filled in the nun application form, putting down you were old and small got you a big smiley tick. Or whether, yes, becoming a nun *did* that to you; you'd put on your habit, you'd put on your wimple, and Eileen didn't know how it'd work, but right away they'd start feeding on you, they'd suck out your youth and suck out your girth. Maybe you were better equipped to serve as a bride of Christ looking like a dry hard prune. Maybe Christ just preferred his women that way.

Eileen licked out the last gobbet of pistachio hiding at the bottom of her cone.

Eileen decided she'd become a nun.

Eileen decided she wanted another pistachio ice cream. The old man who served her in the gelateria was very nice. She tried speaking Italian, said '*grazie*' when he topped her cone with whipped cream – and he smiled, and said '*prego*'.

She bought herself some good Christian things from the shops surrounding the square. She bought a postcard of Jesus, and a postcard of the Pope. And a set of rosary beads. She wasn't sure what she was meant to do with the rosary beads, they didn't come with instructions. She'd learn.

She sat back down, and played with her rosary beads. She played with them for hours.

It began to get dark. The crowds began to thin out.

By the time she went back for her third ice cream, it was nearly midnight. The gelateria was shutting up shop. The nice old man looked concerned. 'Aren't you cold?' he asked her. She was still dressed for the heat of the day. 'I'm warm in my love for Jesus,' she assured him. Her pistachio cone with whipped cream was his last sale of the day.

Eileen supposed there were a lot of tombs in the Vatican. That's what churches did, isn't it, keep the poor dead Christians sealed in tight? She supposed the Vatican had a lot of dead Romans, buried underneath slabs of stone, and now that the tourists had gone home, and the nuns had taken their last photographs, at last she was left with the dead, the dead of the Catholic Church now outnumbered the living. She shivered, and it may have been the cold, it may have been the ice cream running over her hands, but it was a delicious shiver. How easy it must be, to be one of those dead Christians. They were all from the olden days, and everyone was a Christian in the olden days – you were born one, pretty much, you went to church, no-one questioned a thing. You knew God existed, you just *knew*, and everyone else you'd meet knew the same thing. You'd never be sitting at some strange office party of Trevor's, and feeling embarrassed as the conversation turned to religion, too much wine and everyone was bored of discussing politics and football – and the arguments would start, and some atheist would get into a squabble with someone who had faith, and you'd just sit there awkward because you didn't know *what* to think, you sat on the fence and wished you believed one way or the other, even if what you ended up believing in was not believing in anything at all. But in the olden days *everyone* believed, and *everyone* was going to Heaven, no problem, and just as a consequence of turning up! You were a good Christian, that was what you started the game with, that was safe, no-one could take that away from you. And if you really put your back into it, and maybe got just a little bit martyred, you could even upgrade to a saint.

But it required effort to be a Christian these days. She knew, back home, they'd laugh at her. Her neighbours. The Book Club. That lady in the newsagent's she knew whose name she kept forgetting. Oh yes. She knew what they'd say. About poor Eileen, who went off on holiday and 'found religion', in the same muttered tones as if she'd 'been mugged' or 'caught cancer'. All those sympathetic smiles they'd give her, the ones you gave the handicapped, people who were no longer quite all there – and if she ever went to Trevor's office parties, and the conversation ever turned again to religion, she'd be obliged to speak up, to tell the marketing managers and those who worked in recruitment all about her true faith, she wouldn't be allowed to sit on the fence any more, oh God. It was *hard* to be a Christian these days. Even here, even at the Vatican, in the most Christian place she could think of, here too there were sceptics. The policeman who asked her if she was all right, he was one.

'Madam, do you have a home to go to?'

'The Catholic Church is my home.'

'It is four in the morning. Maybe you should go to your hotel?'

Persecution on all sides. But she'd rise above it. That was what made her better than all the dead Romans buried so comfortably in their Vatican graves, who'd never struggled for their beliefs. That was what made her special. 'I'm special,' she told the policeman.

By the time she got back to the hotel dawn was breaking. But Trevor was still awake. Lying on the right-hand-side bed, staring at the ceiling. 'Where were you?' he asked gently.

'I'm sorry. Were you worried?'

'Yes.'

'You don't need to worry about me ever again.'

'Where were you?' he asked again, just as gently.

'The Vatican,' she said.

'Was it nice?'

No, it wasn't *nice*, it was *terrifying*. That was its purpose, it was designed to intimidate. And Eileen realised she'd got it wrong before. It wasn't the House of God, it didn't exist to glorify God at all. It was there to subjugate Man. 'Yes, it was nice.'

'All right.' He turned on to his side, facing her. 'Now, listen. I think we can say we've done the Vatican now, yes? We can cross it off the list. What I thought, tomorrow, looking at the guidebook, we could do the Baths of Caracalla. What do you say?'

'What,' asked Eileen, 'are the baths of Caracalla?'

'Ah, interesting things,' said Trevor. 'Third century AD, Roman baths. For Caracalla. He was an emperor.'

'I'm not seeing any more ruins.'

'Right. Okay. I suppose they are a bit ruin-ish.'

'I'm going back to the Vatican.'

'Oh.'

'That's where I want to be.'

'Oh.'

Trevor turned on his back again, once more to stare at the ceiling. Scratched at his balls. 'Look,' he said, 'I've been thinking. If you really want to give this Christian thing a shot. You know. It's fine with me. Whatever you want, darling, I... I just want you to be happy. And if there's anything I can do to help...'

'What could you do to help?'

'I don't know. I mean. Do you want me to convert as well?'

Eileen honestly hadn't thought. She supposed it would be better if Trevor were a Catholic too. Or, better for Trevor. But this was hers. She wasn't sure she wanted to share it. She hadn't wanted him at the Book Club either.

'I mean, I don't know.' He was still talking. 'I don't know whether I can believe in God. I mean, everything in science speaks against it. And, well, common sense. Don't they have the Big Bang nowadays? And all those dinosaurs. But, you know, if it'll help. If it'll help you, I'll give it a go.'

'Hmmm.'

'Just be patient with me, okay?'

'Hm.'

'I just might not believe in God as much as you!'

He grinned at her. Then, seeing the grin wasn't making an impact, modified it into a cautious smile.

'If you can't believe,' she said, 'you'll be going to Hell. I can't help you.'

Trevor had nothing to say to this.

'I must get some sleep,' said Eileen. 'I'm going to the Vatican in the morning.'

'Yes,' said Trevor. 'And I'm going to the Baths of Caracalla.'

She turned out the lights. 'I'm going to become a nun!' she told the darkness, brightly.

The next morning she went back to Saint Peter's. She took with her her rosary beads, her postcards of Jesus and of the Pope. She sat down in her favourite archway, by her favourite column. There were tourists there already, but she shooed them away. It was going to be another hot day.

At length, she went to get herself some breakfast. She knew just what she wanted. The old man in the gelateria recognised her with a wave. '*La donna del pistachio!*' he laughed. '*E crema!*' '*Sì*,' said Eileen, '*grazie*.' 'Coming right up,' said the man, as he scooped the gelato into a cone. And that's when, at last, Eileen recognised him.

She had to double check. She studied her postcard. There was no doubt.

'You're the Pope!' she said.

The old man frowned at her. 'I don't think so, *signora*.'

'What are you doing working here?'

'Please, *signora*, it's ridiculous.'

'No, it's you, it *is* you, look!' – and she held out her postcard for him, and he snatched it away.

'Listen to yourself,' he said. 'It is madness.'

And then Eileen did something she hadn't done for many years – in spite of all temptations, in spite of her husband, her slutty daughter, whatever they'd both done to her, the way they'd broken her inside. 'I'm sorry,' she said, 'I'm sorry,' but she couldn't help it, the tears poured down her cheeks, and there were so many, the muscles on her face ached with effort and disuse.

'Okay, okay,' said the old man. And he took off his apron. 'Come with me. We'll have espresso. Do you like espresso?'

'Yes,' sobbed Eileen.

'But not here. They know me here.'

*

One evening, just a few weeks ago, Annie had phoned. Trevor answered. Eileen had her hands in the washing-up.

'Hello, Bunny,' said Trevor. 'I'll get your mum.'

'No, Dad,' said Annie. 'I was hoping to speak to you.'

'Oh,' said Trevor.

'Can you go somewhere private? Where Mum can't hear?'

'Oh,' said Trevor. 'Well. I suppose. All right. What is it?' And, 'What's wrong?' because he could hear that Annie had been trying to be so brave, but had now let go, there was crying down the phone, frankly there was *honking*. 'Wouldn't you rather have your mum?'

'I'm pregnant.'

'Oh,' said Trevor. 'So, that means, well. That you've had sex, then?'

'Yes, Dad. I've had sex.'

'Right. Do you. Um. Know who the father is?'

'Yes, I know who the father is! I'm not a virgin, but I'm not a slut!'

'Okay.'

'Somewhere between the two.'

'What do you want to do?'

'Martin says it'll ruin his life.'

'Who's Martin, the...?'

'The father, yes.'

'Right, I thought you might mean the baby was called Martin...'

'There isn't a baby, is there? I wouldn't have named it yet...'

'No, sorry...'

'... Even if I were having it...'

'... Wasn't thinking, look...'

'... Which I'm probably not.'

'... Look, this is a bit of a shock.' He breathed in deeply. 'What do you say? Do you think it'll ruin your life?'

Annie said, in a very small voice, 'Yes.'

'All right then. Then we'll deal with it.'

'You don't hate me, do you, Dad?'

'Bunny, I could never hate you. The important thing is that we get you back on your feet. That's what matters. You'll soon be as right as rain.'

'I'm not ill.'

'Now, how much will it all cost? Do you want me to send you money? I have plenty of money.'

'That won't be a problem, Dad.'

'We're going to have to tell your mother, though.'

'NO!'

'But she'll want to know.'

'I don't want her to feel ashamed of me. I don't want her to hate me. Oh God, Dad, she wants me to do a PhD! She's always on at me, do a PhD...'

'No, okay...'

'I may not even *pass* my degree. I don't know. I've been busy. She doesn't even know what a PhD is! Could you ask her,' and Annie gulped back more tears, 'to get off my fucking back about the fucking PhD?'

'Are you sure you want to go through with all this?' asked Trevor. 'Because, you know, if you want the baby. We'll stick with you. Whatever you decide.'

'Okay.'

'Whatever you decide. Your mother and I are going on holiday soon, maybe we can all sit down and talk about it when we get back.'

Silence. He cleared his throat.

'We're going to Rome!' he said. 'The Eternal City!'

Still silence. He cleared his throat again.

'Maybe this abortion will bring us closer together.'

'Thanks, Dad,' she said, and hung up.

And he went and told Eileen anyway.

She pulled off her rubber gloves, and went and sat down on the sofa. 'Oh God,' she said.

'Do you want to cry?'

'No,' she said. 'I'm not going to cry. Why didn't she tell *me*? Why tell *you*?'

'She asked me not to tell you. She wanted it kept a secret. You won't tell her I did, will you?'

'Of course I will.'

'But she'll hate me.'

'Why *did* you tell me?' shouted Eileen suddenly. 'Why didn't you just keep it to yourself? Couldn't you just do that?'

'I'm sorry,' said Trevor, miserably. 'But we don't keep secrets from each other. Do we?'

Trevor had intended to go to the Baths of Caracalla. He honestly had. But he somehow found himself back at the cat sanctuary. 'Hello,' said a chirpy Australian. 'Would you like a leaflet? Would you like to sponsor us?' 'I wonder if you could help,' said Trevor. 'I wonder if I could volunteer.' He hadn't noticed before how badly the cave smelt, ripe cat food and stale piss. 'Do you know if the blonde American girl is in, uh...?'

'She doesn't come often,' said the Australian flatly. 'Just when she feels like it. Maybe she'll never come back. You can clean out the cages if you want. Those ones over there, that can be your patch.'

For the next hour, hour and a half, Trevor scrubbed away at the cages. Wiping away dregs of wet food, and biscuit, and blood. One more cage, he'd think, and then he'd throw in the towel, he'd go and see what Caracalla had been getting up to. But still he'd stay, always one more cage. All the other volunteers were so *young*, and decidedly female, they must be Annie's age, they chattered away to themselves as they fed the cats, and stroked them, and stuck needles in their paws. Trevor began to feel very out of place. Even the cats stared at him, asking him what he thought he was doing there. With each new cage he'd reach inside and scoop out a cat, and it'd be a dead weight in his arms, utterly unresisting, but utterly uninterested. He'd plop the cat down on the floor, and there it'd curl up around his feet, and he'd clean out its muck. He wouldn't mind if just one of them deigned to give him a purr.

'You'll never get them to purr,' said a voice over his shoulder. And it was her, it was her, she was back! He nearly dropped the latest cat in the sheer gratitude of the moment.

'Hello again,' he said.

'There's precious little to purr about,' she said. 'Poor things.'

'The girl said you weren't coming back,' said Trevor.

'Which girl?'

'The Australian. Over there.'

'Oh yeah? Well, she's a bitch. I wouldn't believe anything she says. So, what are you doing back here? Did you fall in love? I thought you had.'

'What?'

'All of them, little heartbreakers.' She bent down and stroked the cat that Trevor had plonked, now forgotten, down by his feet. 'I thought you said you were allergic.'

'I am, but I just thought, I...'

'Just don't expect them to purr,' she said.

Trevor cleaned out some more cages. In fact, he wanted to clean every single cage. It'd take all day, but he'd do it. The cat sanctuary was very pleased with him.

'You should stay on,' said the Australian, admiringly. 'Good job!'

'You're welcome,' said Trevor, a little frostily. He didn't like the Australian, she was a bitch. And he'd sneak the odd glance at the American blonde, *his* American, his friend. A different baggy T-shirt. Same shorts. No make-up. She looked so young. She might even be as young as Annie. Annie was twenty-one. Could this girl be twenty-one? Oh God, please, don't let her be twenty-one, a bit older than that, surely. Her breasts jiggled up and down as she worked on the cages next to him. Trevor didn't think she was wearing a bra.

'That thing you said yesterday,' said Trevor, and he studiously set about the cage of one Frank Sinatra – rather ineffectually, because he'd already cleaned Frank Sinatra's cage half an hour before. Trevor thought he might leave the half-sentence there hanging, something for her to pick up on – but when he dared turn to her he could see she was just smiling, expectant. 'That thing you said yesterday, about not sleeping with married men. You know. Well. How do you know I'm married? I might not be married. I mean. I might be divorced. Or widowed. Or something.'

'But,' said the girl, still smiling, and she put her tongue to her lip, and Trevor's entire groin flipped, 'you are married, aren't you?'

Trevor had to admit it.

'I can always tell. It's like a sixth sense. I'm always falling for married men, having sex with married men. In fact,' she said, and thought, tongue, lip, perfect precision, 'I'm not sure I've ever slept with a man who *wasn't* married.'

'Aha,' said Trevor, 'right.' No good, groin still flipping. 'But you said... I'm pretty sure... that you *never* sleep with married men.'

'Absolutely,' nodded the girl. 'From this point on.'

'Okay,' said Trevor.

'If you *can* get one to purr,' she said, and winked, 'I'll give you a present.' And she walked away.

Trevor looked for a cat that had a happy expression. But the closest he could get was Frank Sinatra who looked a bit quizzical, quizzical would have to do. Trevor stroked Frank's head. Trevor stroked Frank's tummy. Trevor tickled his chin, even though Frank wanted none of that, and Trevor had to pull his head back by the scruff so he could get his fingers under there. 'Come on, purr, you bastard, muttered Trevor; Frank raised a paw at one point to swipe away, and then looked Trevor in the eyes, and just seemed to *give up* − what was the point, this man would just keep coming back, this man would keep forcing his love on him, there was nothing he could do. And Trevor didn't give up, he wouldn't − and eventually, his persistence was rewarded with a little buzz from Frank's throat, he put his ear closer to check, and yes, the engine was now running. He waved at the American girl. She was too busy to see. He had to go and fetch her.

'Oh,' said Trevor, when they got back. 'He *was* purring.'

'He isn't now.'

'It was just a little one, but you know, definitely a purr.'

'I believe you.'

'Come on,' Trevor said, 'do it again, how much love do you need?' And Frank Sinatra was trying to sleep, that purr had worn him out. He'd had quite enough of the man's fat hand now, and sank his teeth into it.

The girl laughed. 'Okay, okay,' she said. 'You'll get your present.'

'I will?'

'I was going to give it to you anyway,' she said. 'Because, I don't know, I like you.' And she took one of her leaflets, and scribbled an address on the back.

'Is this where you live?'

'It's a night club. Best in the city. See you there eight-ish, yeah?'

'I really don't do night clubs, I'm not really built for...'

The girl looked at him seriously, no hint of a smile, and Trevor thought it might have been the first time she *had* taken him seriously. 'Don't you think it's time to broaden your horizons? Yeah?'

'Yeah,' said Trevor. 'Yes.' And she was right, it was time to stop just looking at the sights, it was time to explore them properly. 'Wait,' he said, because she was walking away again, leaving him with a bored and biting cat, 'I need to know. How old are you?'

'How old am I?'

'Yes.'

'You don't ask my name. Just how old I am.'

'Well. Yes.'

'Okay.' She wrinkled her nose. 'I'm twenty-three. Is that all right?'

And Trevor nodded, happily, very happily.

Trevor went back to the hotel. Eileen wasn't there. He had a shower. He lathered the soap all over. He cut his toenails and fingernails, they seemed to have grown in the heat. He wished there was something he could do about his hair. He was excited. He was scared.

He didn't know what he'd say to Eileen if she got back before he went out. But she didn't. It was a sign.

He left, wearing his best clothes. He was so glad he'd packed them.

The night club was the other side of Rome, down in Trastevere. He followed the map in his guidebook to get there. The guidebook reassured him, Alice's presence reassured him. His heart sank as he reached the club. Loud music blared out, the very cobbles on the street seemed to thrum with it. It was packed full of young people, shouting, laughing, smoking, dancing.

He didn't even recognise her at first. She'd dressed up as well. There was no bagginess to be seen, she'd been squeezed into those clothes. She'd streaked the blonde. She was wearing make-up. She looked like a child pretending to be an adult – and in a way Trevor was pleased, he'd rather pretend she was an adult, really, that'd make it all so much easier. But he felt a little sad for her too, she hadn't realised quite what she'd obliterated from her face with all that mascara and rouge.

'Hello!' she shouted. 'Come and meet my friends!'

'Hello,' said Trevor.

'This is Marco! This is Paolo! And this is another Marco!'

'Hello,' said Trevor. Marco I raised his hand idly in greeting. Said something to Paolo in Italian, they both laughed. The girl laughed too, just a little. 'Want to sit down?' she said. 'Sure,' said Trevor. And she said something to Paolo, who raised his eyebrows, laughed again, and moved chairs so that Trevor could sit next to her. 'Want a beer?' she said. 'Sure,' said Trevor. 'The bar's over there,' she pointed – and so he got up from the chair again, fought his way through the crowd, shouted at an expressionless barman that he wanted an overpriced bottle of Heineken. When he returned to his new friends, Paolo was back sitting next to the girl; this time he didn't bother to get up.

'Having fun?' she said to him.

'Yes.' They all looked so cool. He wished he hadn't worn a jacket. He wished he hadn't worn the tie. His sweaty balls twitched irritably in his too too smart black trousers. 'Why no Roman music?' It was hard to hear the lyrics at that volume, but every word he managed to catch was definitely demonstrably unapologetically English.

'Roman music is dead,' she said.

'I thought,' he said, and she frowned, because she couldn't hear – he leaned forward, so did she – 'I thought you liked *older* men.' He gestured at Marco I and Marco II and Paolo, chain-smoking in their leather jackets; they couldn't be any older than she was.

She shrugged. 'I don't like them,' she said. 'They're just guys I know.' She bummed a cigarette off Marco II, Marco II said something to her in Italian, and all the table laughed. 'Want a dance?' she said.

'To this?'

'Yeah.' And there was no way he was dancing, he hadn't danced for years, and that had been at his sister's wedding, and that had been with his aunt. But he got up anyway, helplessly. 'Take off your jacket!' she shouted at him. 'I don't want it stolen!' he shouted back. 'It won't get stolen,' shouted the girl, 'the guys will guard it!' And Paolo and Marco II smiled, and Marco I once again raised his hand idly in acknowledgement.

They gyrated for a while. Never touching. The girl closed her eyes, swaying about on her little spot of floor space, as if the only way she could enjoy herself was to pretend she wasn't really there. Trevor bobbed about a little. His balls were still sweaty, they were literally gushing water, he'd take off his trousers later and a bucketload would come pouring out.

There was a break in the song, and Trevor took that as his cue. 'That was great!' he shouted, and began to walk back to the table. And it wasn't the end of the song after all, the refrain was starting over, but he wasn't bobbing any more now. Trevor rescued his jacket. The wallet was still there. So was the necklace (he'd forgotten about that). But not the guidebook.

'Where's my book gone?' he asked. Then, louder to the guys – one of them had finished his beer – 'Hey! Where's my book?'

'What's the problem?' asked the girl. She'd made it back from the dance floor. Evidently, at some point, she'd noticed Trevor wasn't there any more. Evidently, at some point, she'd opened her eyes.

'I had a guidebook in here,' said Trevor, 'right here,' showing her the jacket pocket, as if she could magically find it somewhere at the bottom. 'And I think,' and he knew it to be true, 'that one of *them* took it.'

They openly laughed at him.

'Don't be silly,' she said. 'What would they want with your guidebook? They *live* here!'

'Give it back,' said Trevor, gently enough. Paolo openly ignored him, so Trevor was forced to grab his arm. And Paolo grabbed his arm with *his* arm, there were arms everywhere. And no-one said anything, but there was hardly silence, not with that awful pop music, blaring out something to do with love in the background.

And then Trevor gave up, and grabbed his jacket, and his remaining belongings, and went outside.

The girl followed him out.

'Hey,' she said, 'hey. Wait up.'

He did.

'You embarrassed me in there,' she said.

'I thought we were going to be alone,' he said.

'It's just a guidebook.'

'It was a present. It meant a lot to me.'

'A present from your wife?'

Trevor considered. 'Yes,' he then said.

'Perhaps,' said the girl, with a forgiving smile, 'you should go back to her?'

Yes. Yes, thought Trevor. And thank you. You are wise beyond your years. Thank you. You've saved me from making a fool of myself. I'm still decent. I'm still intact. I'm still...

'And then,' she said, 'you can come back to me tomorrow. Yeah?'

No. No, no. No. 'Yes,' he said.

She kissed Trevor on the nose. 'There,' she said. And then, once again, just a little peck. As if he were an infant or something, or, or a pet cat. 'There,' she said, 'all better.'

Trevor tried to say something, but was breathing too heavily.

'And thank you,' she whispered. 'I saw what else you have in your pocket.' And he struggled to work out what she meant, and thought it sounded a bit rude, and he went on, 'It's a beautiful necklace. Thank you. Give it to me tomorrow, though, yeah? Don't want any more jealousy. Tomorrow, we'll be on our own.'

And then, very slowly, she opened up that mouth of hers, and it was such a big mouth, it was Vatican-sized, you could get 20,000 people in there – and she zoomed in – and Trevor thought, this is it, and he puckered his own mouth in expectation, this is *it*, the first time he'd been kissed (properly) in so many years, the first moment of his adultery. Sorry, Eileen, sorry, Alice – and her lips looked so very thick, and his weren't at all, but he'd take them on, he'd send them into battle and they'd just have to do their best – but – but, hang on – but her lips didn't close around his, they instead closed around his *nose* again. And Trevor shut his mouth with a frustrated snap. His teeth clicked together. And she was sucking at his nose, what was she doing? – she was eating away at it, her eyes were shut tight, in full concentration, as her lips rubbed themselves up and down the whole length and breadth of it. Exploring little crevasses, he hadn't known his nose had so many crevasses. Gnawing away at the bridge, her tongue flicking lightly at the edge of his nostrils. 'Mmm,' she went, '*mmmm*.' And he smelt beer and cigarettes, yes, but mostly he smelt the hot air of her breath as she panted all over him – and those lips were still so thick, but they were just in the *wrong place*. And then, one last lick, and she was done.

'There,' she said softly. 'And there'll be more of that tomorrow.' More of *what*? 'See you at the sanctuary, yeah?' And she turned and went back inside the club.

And she would see him, that was the shame of it. He'd go to the cat sanctuary. He'd give her the necklace that was never meant to be hers, she'd squeal, she'd put it on, it'd look weird against the baggy T-shirt. And he'd let her suck his nose. Because, what else? What else, really, was he to do? Nobody wanted him, but at least some girl who looked like his daughter would pretend. Oh God. Oh God. He even prayed, and that was silly, because God didn't exist. Oh God, please, God, do something to *stop me*.

As he hurried back to his hotel along the bank of the Tiber, he suddenly sneezed. And then another, he couldn't help it. His nose still felt a bit damp after its ordeal – or maybe it was the cat allergy, who could tell? And a man walking past with his girlfriend broke off from his Italian jabber to say, in respectful English, 'Bless you.' – Bloody hell, thought Trevor, I even sneeze like a tourist.

*

The Pope carried over the two wooden espressos on a wooden tray, and took a seat opposite Eileen. 'You must know, *signora*, I am not the Pope.'

'You might be.'

'No.'

'Maybe you serve ice cream once in a while. Just as a change of scenery.'

'I don't think so.'

'Maybe you get bored in the Vatican all day, that close to God.'

'I'd be recognised. *Signora*, wouldn't I? Think. With the postcards. The postcards are everywhere. The Pope, he's a very famous man.'

'Yes,' said Eileen. She sipped at her espresso. It was too hot, and too strong, too everything, really. 'All right. But can you pretend to be the Pope? For me?'

'*Signora*...'

'Or can I. At least. Pretend?'

The old man sighed.

'Do you believe in God?' asked Eileen.

'Am I being the Pope now, or me, or...?'

Eileen waved her hand irritably. 'Yes,' said the Pope. 'I believe in God.'

'No doubts?'

'No doubts.'

'What's that like?' asked Eileen. 'To have no doubts?'

The Pope frowned. 'Well,' he said. 'It's a life.'

'What does it feel like? I'm just worried. That I'm not feeling the right thing. That other Christians are feeling it differently. That I'm just pretending to feel.'

'Please, *Signora*...'

'That, really, I just feel nothing inside at all, that there is nothing inside. Yes, sorry, what?'

'*Signora*. I expect these are the wrong questions.'

'I'm going to become a nun.'

'Oh yes?' asked the Pope, politely.

'My daughter won't talk to me. My husband won't *touch* me, even. I'm going to be a nun. Might as well. I just want. To be. A good person. Yes? I want to be a good person, very much.'

'Aren't you a good person?'

'I don't think,' said Eileen, 'I make anyone very happy.'

The Pope nodded sadly at this. Then drained his espresso in one gulp. Eileen decided to do the same. It tasted better that way.

'I just need a sign,' said Eileen. 'That I'm doing the right thing. Do you think I could ask for a miracle?'

'You want a miracle from God, to tell you to become a nun?'

'No. I want a miracle from God, to tell me to stop.'

The Pope played idly with his empty espresso cup. 'I've asked for miracles. I've never received one.'

'No. Still. Maybe if I asked nicely.'

He smiled, and reached inside his pocket, and pulled out a small book. He gave it to her.

'What is it?'

'A present. All the answers are in here. Think of it as a sort of guidebook.'

'I can't read Italian...'

'It's in English.'

'You just carry English Bibles around? What sort of ice-cream man are you?'

The old man smiled.

'I've asked for miracles,' he said. 'Many times. I've never seen one. I don't know why. I think I probably don't deserve one.'

Eileen stared at him.

He went on. 'Sometimes I get bored in the Vatican, it's true. Sometimes I want a break from it. To be around ordinary people again. So I take a job selling ice cream, people like ice cream, it makes them happy.'

'But, no. What about the postcards? You'd be recognised...'

'Oh, *signora*,' said the old man, a little sadly. 'No-one expects the Supreme Pontiff to be selling ice cream. No-one looks. At what's right in front of their noses.'

'I don't believe you're the Pope,' said Eileen.

'You did before.'

'And now I don't.'

'Would you like another espresso?' he asked. And Eileen said she would. He brought over another tray.

'I have this recurring dream,' said the man who may or may not have been the Pope. 'That I'm dying. I'm on my deathbed, and no matter how much medicine they pump into me, and how much the faithful pray, I'm on my way out. There's no pain. Or, if there is, I don't notice, it's not the pain I fear. What I fear is that the doubt will creep in. I know God exists. I *know*. But as I die, with eternity staring me in the face, or perhaps the prospect of simple oblivion – I stop believing. I know God, I *know* Him, but in the terror of the moment, I choose not to know. Do you understand?'

'Yes,' said Eileen. Though she didn't.

'And it's all right,' said the Pope. He took out a handkerchief and blew his nose. 'God forgives me. God forgives the lapse of faith. I go to Heaven. The angels know me when I get there. Of course they do, I'm the Pope. "Good to have you here, Father", says one of them, wings all a-quiver with respect, and I thank him. I don't have to queue, I bypass the tens of thousands, the millions, all lined up before the pearly gates waiting for Paradise, but I'm all right, I'm taken straight to the front. Saint Peter is there waiting for me, the very first Pope, my predecessor. "So, you're the latest," he says. And he takes me to God. God sits with Jesus, and with the Holy Ghost, and they look like all the statues, and the paintings, and the monuments, they look like every single one of them. "Who's this?" says God. And Saint Peter whispers in His ear, and I hear Jesus mutter, "Not another Pope, we get through such a lot of them!" And God turns to me, and smiles, and says, "Well done, my good and faithful servant" and I bask in that for a moment, I *have* been a good man, I wanted to be a good man, I was a good man after all. And then God says to Saint Peter, "Take him to the Pope Room, put him with all the others." And we go to the Pope Room. It's all right, the Pope Room. It's a big room. Very comfortable. Stained glass windows. Comfy chairs. A buffet. But there's not much space, it's crammed full of Popes, all 250 odd of them. They're all talking in groups, they seem to get on so well, but they don't know me, they say hello, they're polite, but you know, just *polite*. There are the top Popes, you know, there's Gregory the Great, there's Innocent XII, there's Boniface V, he's one of my heroes. I've nothing to say to them, I'm nothing to them. I'm shy. I stammer. I'm the Pope, but I'm out of my league, I'm not a *bad* Pope, but I'm not a good Pope, I'm middling. I'm a middling Pope. And I have to queue for the buffet. It takes me two hours just to get a cheese sandwich.'

Eileen had nothing to say to this.

'I ask for miracles. I've never seen one. But maybe you'll do better. Maybe you're a better woman than I am a Pope.'

'I just want a sign,' said Eileen, 'that it's worth staying with my family. Because I think it's dead. I think it's dead. I'm dead.'

'Hmm,' said the Pope. 'Do you want to see inside the Vatican?'

'The queues are so long.'

'I know,' said the Pope. 'Don't worry. I know a secret way in. I use it all the time.'

Eileen considered. 'No,' she said, at last.

'No?'

'Then I'd *know* you're the Pope. And I'd much rather just believe you could be.'

The Pope smiled. He got out his wallet, and Eileen said, 'No, no, I'll get this, my treat.' And she paid for their espressos. 'Thank you,' said the Pope.

'Thank you,' said Eileen.

*

He'd practised so many ways of broaching the subject, smart, subtle ways. But when Eileen at last came into the hotel room, what Trevor said was, 'I want to have sex with you.'

All right, thought Eileen. At least he hadn't asked her where she'd been. Because she'd been walking around Rome for hours, waiting for her miracle. She'd looked everywhere. And now she even wondered whether *this* could be the miracle, Trevor wanting to make love, to touch her – but then she thought, no, that would've meant that the 1990s had been nothing but an endless stream of miracles, and she couldn't believe that; she was trying so hard to believe, but there had to be a limit. But all right, she decided, if this was going to be the last time she'd ever see Trevor – her poor, silly, shadow of a husband – after this, she'd become a nun, or a saint, or go mad – all right, if this is the last time, let's give him what he wants.

But she didn't say anything at all, for fear that the words would come out, words of this and other truths, words that would ruin everything. She stripped, and as she did so, Trevor felt a stab of such anger and such hurt – she wasn't going to *say* anything, it was just the old silence, back to the silence. He should leave now, he should go back to the night club, he should get his nose sucked clean off...

And then she was naked – no, not a word, not a smile, but willingly enough – and she was shivering with, what? the cold? nerves? excitement? And he stripped too. And he too was shivering. With nerves, really. Yeah, nerves.

'You're beautiful,' he said. She nodded at this. And he took her to the bed...

... Which was still separated into two singles. 'Give me a hand,' Trevor said, and the two of them pushed them back together. 'Heave,' he said, and they lifted the bed off the ground, saggy breasts, saggy cock, all bouncing about.

Oh God, a miracle, now, she thought. He could speak in tongues. A beacon of light issuing from his head. Anything. No. 'Are you ready?' is what he said, and she nodded, and he lay down, and she lay down beside him. He kissed at her face, and she kissed at his, and she thought his lips were thin and dry, and she thought hers must be too, oh God, a miracle now, how about it?

... But not kissing at the nose, he thought; that, at least, is a relief.

And that was the foreplay done with. It hadn't lasted long, but she had had enough, it made her feel like a *liar*, somehow – and she couldn't open her mouth properly to kiss, because of all the truths that'd tumble out, all those words she mustn't say. So she gently pushed him off, opened her legs...

... Right, then, he said, *andiamo*, let's go! Let's go, let's go. And he wished his penis would behave, but it was retreating – it was saying, no, don't send me in there, please, the vagina will eat me...

As he bustled about on top, she began to think about whether this was what Annie had done, whether Annie had simply lain underneath some man she didn't really know, whether Annie was good at this, whether Annie could open her mouth during sex, why Annie couldn't tell her.

Oh God, a miracle, he prayed, let's *go*... And he pushed himself inside. Oh God, please don't let the vagina eat my cock, please. Or rather, yes – let it chew it up, every last scrap – because he didn't want to be unfaithful, he didn't want to see the blonde girl again, he wanted to be a good man. Sacrifice my privates if need be, Lord, it's entirely up to you.

And she thought, actually, this isn't too bad – better than she'd remembered – and she'd have told him so, encouraged him (except for the whole mouth opening thing) – and it would have improved with a bit of practice. Except there wouldn't be any more practice, because she was about to become a nun.

And the vagina didn't bite off his cock, but the cock didn't celebrate, the cock didn't take advantage of this unexpected victory the way any good cock should. It just waggled inside, rather ineffectually. I'm not feeling anything, thought Trevor in a panic, shouldn't I be feeling more than this? Maybe everybody else feels it differently. Maybe they just pretend to feel.

Oh God, she thought, last chance, one miracle, one little sodding miracle, give me back my life!

Oh God, he thought, put a bit of life down there, or I'll be forced to visit the nose-sucker tomorrow. 'Oh God!' he cried, out loud, as if to pretend he were happy, as if to usher on his errant orgasm.

Oh God!

And then, for both of them, the earth moved.

*

The earthquake that so devastated Rome only measured six point three on the Richter scale. There had been many worse earthquakes, even in recent history – but perhaps not one whose effect upon world landmarks had been more calamitous. The Pantheon was no more. The Colosseum was laid as flat as a pancake. All the various little ancient ruins scattered about were now lost beneath a sea of modern ruins, concrete and plaster and fibreglass.

Only the Vatican was left standing entirely intact. Unspoiled amongst the debris. Saint Peter's dome poking jauntily up at Heaven, saying, 'Look, we're still here!' Staring down at the Earth, saying, 'Don't you think, now, you'd better start believing?'

Trevor and Eileen were only aware there had been an earthquake when they got up to go to breakfast that next morning. When Trevor opened the door, he almost stepped out into space – the hotel around them had gone. All that remained was their room, perched perilously on the top of a long thin column of rubble jutting out high into the sky.

It took four days for them to be rescued. It seemed they were at the very epicentre of the disaster, it took two days for any aid workers to realise there were any survivors there – and another two to get the means to bring them down to safety.

During those four days they made love a few more times, and got a little better at it.

And throughout, Eileen didn't speak. Trevor couldn't tell whether this was simply because she didn't want to, or because she no longer could as some traumatic reaction to the catastrophe. After all, she wasn't offering any explanations. He worried that she'd bit her tongue during the quake, maybe she'd bit it clean off; she refused to open his mouth so he could see. Once they were rescued, the emergency doctors had no greater luck in finding out what was wrong. They were able to force open the mouth, and they discovered the tongue was unharmed – but Eileen screamed with such anger and such *fear* that no-one tried to get her to open it again. They let her keep her lips tightly sealed from that point on.

But maybe it didn't matter. Trevor and Eileen still made love, and sometimes she'd smile.

Trevor wondered whether the American girl was alive. He'd have asked someone, but he'd never known her name. He wondered too whether the cats were all right. He hoped so. He hoped the quake had burst open their cages, set them free. He hoped they were now sunning themselves, draped across the top of all those new ruins. He'd have gone to look – but the area had been cordoned off.

The city was officially designated a disaster zone. And it took over a week before all the British holidaymakers could be flown home. The planes were crammed. But Eileen and Trevor secured a row for two – Eileen got the window seat, and Trevor the aisle seat next to her. So that, at least, was all right.

As they sped down the runway, Trevor reached for Eileen's hand. Both held on to the other. They didn't look at each other, Eileen stared out of the window, Trevor at the safety instruction card. And once they were in the air, Trevor gave Eileen's hand a little squeeze. And he thought that maybe she gave a little squeeze back. Yes, she did, he was pretty sure she did.

And for the longest while, neither let go.

Eileen didn't like the clouds this time. They were too thin. She knew that if she jumped out of the window, she'd fall straight through. Her Bible was in her hand luggage, and she considered giving it a read. But somehow, up here in the air, so high up and yet still so far from Heaven, the Bible just seemed too thin as well to bother with. So she closed her eyes and went to sleep. And dreamed, as ever, of all the Romans she'd killed.

And at last Trevor dared to look at her. And dared to let go of her hand, and he *looked* at her, full on, studied her, he gazed deeply into the face of the woman he'd once loved. And searched his heart to find out whether anything was still there. There might be, there might. He wished he hadn't let go of her hand. But he now thought that if he were to take it again, if he touched her in the slightest, he might wake her up. He might ruin everything. 'I love you,' he said. Just to try it out, really – but he thought she answered him with the ghost of a smile.

He wondered if he'd dare give the necklace to Alice. It was a bit flashy. He wondered if he'd dare give it to Eileen. Perhaps he'd just throw it away.

He put away the safety card. For want of anything better to read, he fished the Bible out of Eileen's bag, and turned to the first chapter, and lost himself within the story.

1701 – The deposed James II of Great Britain dies in exile in France. He suffers cerebral thrombosis, and vomits blood from his mouth. Staunch in the Catholic beliefs – which cost him his throne – to the very end, his last words to his queen, as he fades away on his deathbed, are, 'Think of it, madam, I am going to be happy.' **1702** – James' usurper, King William III, dies soon after his horse stumbles over a molehill. The Stuart supporters for years after raise their glasses to the mole as 'the little gentleman in black velvet'. *There is a part of William Shakespeare's 'Julius Caesar' that I've always found rather curious. Before the battle of Philippi, Gaius Cassius Longinus, murderer of Caesar and famed for his 'lean and hungry look', confides to a soldier that he's frightened he will die in the forthcoming conflict; it's his birthday, and there's something horribly apt about a man leaving the world on the very day he came into it. Cassius does, indeed, die. And yet it's clearly an invention of Shakespeare's, because we have no accurate record of even in which year Cassius was born. It's silly to accuse Shakespeare of historical inaccuracy – there are so many anachronisms in 'Julius Caesar', from nightcaps to chiming clocks, that it's clearly deliberate. What's peculiar is that dying on his own birthday will be something that will happen to Shakespeare himself – born on 23 April 1564, dying on 23 April 1616 – and so a bit of personal foreknowledge is inserted into the drama about which Shakespeare could not possibly have been aware. History of course is littered with coincidences; there is so much history, really, and so many people living through it, that the oddity is that there aren't more people out there who die on their birthday. But I find it interesting inasmuch as we all know, logically, that each year we limp over the anniversary of our future death – and that we never seem to sense it, really such an important event should echo back to us somehow, really it should chill our very hearts. But King Harold of the Saxons wouldn't have felt any special qualms on 14 October 1065, on 21 October 1804 Horatio Nelson would have had no urge either to kiss or be kissed by anyone called Hardy, 11 September would have been confronted with complacent equanimity by all the movers and shakers moving and shaking at the World Trade Center on every date since its construction in 1971 right up to 2000 – they'd have read the same memos, taken the same coffee breaks, enjoyed the same conversations about the ball game over the office watercoolers, the bland combination of the numbers '9' and '11' wouldn't have haunted them in the same way they would haunt their grieving families forever after, haunt an entire nation humiliated and scared and bent on revenge. The context of history is lost on us, and laughs at us. I know now that my mother died on 7 April, my father on 18 May, my wife on 3 February, my daughter Annie on 6 March. A perfectly ordinary 6 March at that, 6 March is a date I have no doubt enjoyed with thoughtless ease for the whole of my life, and yet one I will never be able to live through again without feeling such great pain and such great guilt.* **1702** – The French grammarian Dominique Bouhours dies. His last words are, 'I am about to, or I am going to, die – either expression is correct.' **1703** – The Man in the Iron Mask dies in the Bastille after five years imprisonment. His face always concealed, his identity remains forever a mystery, and has been the subject of many a novel and movie. He is the most famous anonymous man of the century. **1705** – On Christmas Day, an army of over 1,000 peasants march on Munich and are massacred. **1706** – In London, Thomas Twining opens the first known tea room. **1706** – During a military campaign, Iyasu I, emperor of Ethiopia, learns that his favourite concubine has died. In his grief he leaves the war and retires to a monastery. The empress has their son Tekle Haymanot declared emperor in his place; Iyasu protests, but when he emerges from his hermitage is assassinated. **1707** – Mughal monarch in India, Aurangzeb, dies. His empire collapses. **1707** – Faulty navigation causes four British Royal Navy ships to run aground off the Isles of Scilly. Thousands drown. **1708** – In Ethiopia, Tekle Haymanot is stabbed to death by some of his late father's courtiers. His uncle Tewoflos is brought out of captivity to succeed him. Tewoflos takes revenge on those who had murdered his brother Iyasu – he has the empress publicly hanged, and her two brothers speared. **1709** – Peter the Great crushes Charles XII's army at the battle of Poltava, in one fell swoop destroying the Swedish Empire. **1709** – Scottish sailor Alexander Selkirk is rescued after having spent four years marooned on the Juan Fernandez Islands (qv 1574). His adventures inspire 'Robinson Crusoe'. *I went to fetch my time chart from the cupboard.* **1710** – The English South Sea Company is founded to trade slaves with South America. *One day in March I went to fetch my time chart from the cupboard, but it had gone. And I thought, Annie* – **1712** – England taxes soap, as a 'frivolous luxury of the aristocracy'. *On 6 March I went to fetch my time chart from the cupboard, but it had gone. And I thought, Annie – no, oh God, Annie – and I ran up the stairs, two at a time, and pushed open her bedroom door, but it was too late...* **1713** – The French Canadian inhabitants of Acadia are given one year to swear allegiance to their British invaders, or leave. **1713** – Peter the Great dreams of bringing his nation up to date, in line with the splendour of the rest of Europe. To this end he decides to found a new city, named St Petersburg after him. He forces thousands of families to leave Moscow on pain of death to populate it – it's estimated that 100,000 people die on the journey. And in defiance of nature he builds the city on a swamp, forcing his labourers to work without proper tools, often waist deep in water, as he canters amongst them and beats them with cudgels to work faster. Thus the Age of Enlightenment reaches Russia. **1714** – Queen Anne of Great Britain dismisses her most senior minister from office. Four days later she is dead. George, the Elector of Hanover, succeeds her. He cannot speak a word of English. **1715** – The first Jacobite rebellion, an attempt to restore the Catholic Stuarts to the throne. The Old Pretender is defeated at the battle of Preston. **1716** – The Yamasee War, between the British settlers of Carolina and the indigenous Cherokee tribe, reaches its bloody peak at the Tugaloo massacre. **1716** – The death of Martha Apraksina, wife to the childless former tsar of Russia, Fyodor III (who had died in 1682). Peter the Great personally dissects his brother's widow to satisfy his curiosity about whether she'd died a virgin or not. **1717** – The first Druid revival ceremony is conducted at Primrose Hill, London; this will later become established as the Ancient Order of Druids. **1718** – Peter the Great despairs of his irritatingly timid son Alexis, and sees his unsuitability to be a power crazed tsar as an attack upon the state. He accuses him of treason and has him tortured to death. **1718** – While inspecting trenches during his invasion of Norway, Charles XII is shot dead at close range. The Swedish carry his body back, losing nearly 6,000 men in the harsh winter storms. **1719** – Peter the Great executes his mistress Mary Hamilton for infidelity. He picks up her severed head from the basket, gives a lecture about its anatomy, kisses it, then tosses it into the dirt. Fifty years later it is recorded as still being displayed, preserved in alcohol, in the Royal Gallery (qv 1746). **1719** – In the Swedish copper mines of Falun a petrified body is found. The hardened corpse is one Fet-Mats Israelsson, who had disappeared over forty years ago; he is identified by his fiancée, now somewhat past her prime after years of waiting for him to show up. Israelsson is adopted as a totem by the romanticism movement in Germany, inspiring stories and philosophical texts, ballads and operas. Exhibited in a display case in all his ossified glory, he is only laid to rest in 1930. **1720** – The South Sea Bubble: the English stock market crashes. **1722** – Pennsylvania introduces a fine of £5 on any person who has imported a sodomite to the colony. **1723** – Philip, Duke of Orleans, the debauched and obese regent of France, has a stroke after sex with a mistress thirty years younger than him. During his post mortem, Philip's favourite dog jumps up, makes off with his master's heart, and eats it. **1724** – Philip V of Spain abdicates in favour of his teenage son Louis, probably because he realises his mental health is in decline. He retires to a monastery. **1724** – Louis of Spain dies of smallpox. Reluctantly, Philip V resumes the throne. **1725** – In New Hampshire, the first case is reported of white men scalping Native Americans. **1725** – Louis XV of France rejects his intended bride, the Spanish Infanta. Relations between France and Spain get strained. **1726** – Mary Toft of Godalming so fools the surgeons into believing she has given birth to sixteen stillborn rabbits that the rabbit trade in Britain slumps overnight. **1727** – Philip V becomes ever madder. He now refuses to change his clothes – he believes that personal filthiness is his road to salvation, and that if he washes, he'll die. He stays king until his death in 1746, and spends much of the intervening time biting chunks out of his arms, and lying stock still in his own shit. **1728** – A fire rages for four days in Copenhagen, Denmark, destroying over a quarter of the city. **1729** – Istanbul is ravaged by fire too. 7,000 of its citizens are killed. **1729** – Natchez Indians rise up against the colonists in Mississippi at Fort Rosalie; over 200 French men, women and children are slaughtered. **1730** – Tsar Peter II dies of smallpox on his own wedding day. His bride jumps into his deathbed in a futile attempt to make herself pregnant. **1730** – Ottoman Sultan Ahmed III is deposed in favour of his nephew Mahmud I. **1730** – Frederick William I of Prussia sees his son Frederick's interest in culture as a sign of homosexuality. When Frederick attempts to flee to England with his best friend, he is arrested and imprisoned, and forced to watch his companion being decapitated. **1731** – Robert Jenkins gets his ear cut off by a Spaniard. Eight years later it will be used as an excuse to declare war on Spain. **1733** – Quebec upholds the right for all Canadians to keep Indian slaves. **1736** – Riots break out in Edinburgh after Captain John Porteus orders his men to open fire at the angry mob attending a public hanging. Porteus is arrested, and condemned to death for murder; but the Scottish people spring him from his cell, and hang him themselves. Tour guides in the city still invite their customers to spit on his memorial plate where he died. **1739** – The highwayman Dick Turpin is hanged for being a horse thief, and promptly becomes a popular folk hero. **1740** – On his deathbed, Frederick William asks his physician how long he has to live. The doctor solemnly tells the king to expect the worst, because he no longer has a pulse. This makes the king lose his temper, and he proves he must have a pulse by the fact he can so wave his hand about in rage. He has a point. But the effort kills him. **1740** – The cultured Frederick succeeds his father as king of Prussia. During the first war of Silesia, he gives instructions that all his soldiers must keep darkness in their tents overnight. He personally inspects his men himself – and discovers one Captain Zietert, hastily snuffing out a candle, having just composed a long letter to his beloved wife. Frederick tells the captain to open the letter. And to add a final sentence, that the king will dictate: 'I shall die tomorrow on the scaffold.' The hapless Zietert is indeed executed. But what's frightening is the way this brutal anecdote has been adopted by US Christian groups as a parable, exhorting their children to obey their parents in all things or to suffer the consequences. (It's true. Google it and see.) **1740** – The Dutch East India Company massacres some 5,000 to 10,000 Chinese inhabitants of Batavia. **1741** – The one-year-old infant sar Ivan VI is overthrown, and imprisoned under guard in a fortress. He spends the remaining years of his life in a small damp cell; he never sees the sunlight again, he is forbidden to have conversations with others. On the accession of Peter III in 1762, Ivan is visited by the new Tsar, who takes pity on him – but a few weeks later Peter too is overthrown. Catherine the Great refers to him as the 'nameless one', and has him murdered in 1764. **1744** – The last words of poet Alexander Pope: 'Here am I, dying of a hundred good symptoms.' **1746** – Philip V succeeds his mad stinking father to the throne of Spain. For his entire marriage he is obsessed by sex, and demands that his wife sleep with him at least three times a day – yelling for his confessor each time he comes, just in case he dies in the act and is damned for his lust. **1746** – The second Jacobite rebellion, this time in support of the Young Pretender (qv 1715), ends in disaster at the battle of Culloden. **1747** – Consequently, the Jacobite supporter Lord Lovat is captured, and becomes the last man in Britain executed by beheading. Spectators crowd to watch his death; fifty of them are killed when the wooden viewing platform gives way under their weight. **1747** – The wearing of a kilt is banned in Scotland under orders of the Dress Act. **1749** – A British soldier is wounded in the groin at the battle of Devicotta. Medical treatment is so bad that it's another year before she's exposed as a woman, Hannah Snell, who has dressed up as a man and gone to war. She sells her story to the papers, and makes a living on the theatre circuit, singing songs and presenting military drills. **1750** – King John V of Portugal dies. His obsession with building religious establishments means that one in every ten of his subjects has to become either a monk or a nun just to fill them. **1751** – The Prince of Wales is killed by a cricket ball. **1752** – In adjustment to the new Gregorian calendar, and conforming to the rest of Europe, Britain loses eleven days from the calendar, and jumps straight from 2 to 14 September. You'd have thought these missing dates from history would have been the most peaceful ever, since there was no human in them to screw anything up. But the riots that break out from the populace demanding they get their missing time back more than makes up for that. **1754** – Ottoman Sultan Mahmud I dies; he has spent his reign chiefly avoiding the business of government in exchange for writing bad poetry. His brother Osman III succeeds him. As Turkish law dictates, Osman has spent his life incarcerated, and does not adjust well to his new-found freedom and power. He decides he hates women, and takes to wearing iron shoes, so that his heavy footfall will give the fairer sex a chance to hear his approach and run away from him accordingly. *But it was too late, she was waiting for me, 'Hello, Daddy,' she said, and she was holding my time chart out for me, the one I had laboured on for so many years, and I could see that the years were left intact, but all the events I'd chronicled beside them, they had all gone. 'We can create a* <u>*new*</u> *history, Daddy,' she told me, 'we can start all over again.' And I said to her, 'But you like history, I thought you liked history, why destroy it?' And she smiled. 'I* <u>*love*</u> *history,' she said, 'and I want to eat it. I want to eat it all up, every last scrap.' And she smiled wider, and I could see now that her teeth were stained black – and I thought at first it was just the ink, but now I believe it was the very detritus of ages past, all the lives of famous men (and not so famous women) reduced to little specks of spit. 'I want to eat,' she said, and she licked her lips, and when she smiled again, even those specks had gone forever – she opened up the time chart, she held it up to her mouth, and she sucked at it, desperate, as if trying to find one last crumb. I took the chart from her – and she didn't fight it, she let me take it from her hand – I looked through it – so much history was lost, entire centuries were blank, the empty whites of the pages were vast and gaping and hurt my eyes. And just two dates were left intact – no, they weren't my handwriting, the lettering was big and clumsy and childish, Annie had put them there – 463 had just one phrase beside it, and it said 'Granny died here today'; and in 1801 just a single word, just one – 'Mummy'. That was all. That was all. That was all my wife got. And Annie asks me the question – that crass question – that crass question I get asked at parties – 'What period of history would* <u>*you*</u> *have been happiest to have lived through?' And she grins, and that grin now shows teeth that are so white and pure. She says, 'I love you, Daddy, I'm giving you a* <u>*choice*</u>*.' And I held on to the time chart, I wasn't letting it go, not ever again, and I pushed Annie to the back of the room, and I ran for the door, and I slammed it behind me, and I locked it, I trapped my own child – just as Augusta had her daughter (qv 31), just as the Russians had Ivan VI (qv 1741), just as the Ottoman sultans had their own brothers (qv 1595, 1622, 1754 etc). She wasn't going to feed again, I'd sooner she starved first.* **1755** – The British attempts to capture Fort Duquesne from the French in the American colonies are foiled, and the leading commander is killed. One Colonel George Washington survives. **1756** – The Nawab of Bengal takes Fort William, and imprisons 146 British soldiers and civilians in cramped conditions. Only twenty-three people emerge from the Black Hole of Calcutta alive. **1757** – Robert-Francois Damiens stabs Louis XV with a pen knife. Louis survives. Damiens is informed that before his execution he will have his right hand cut off and the wound cauterised with boiling pitch. 'It's going to be a hard day,' he says. **1757** – Minorca falls to the French during the Seven Years War. The British admiral, John Byng, is court-martialled for 'failing to do his utmost', and is executed by firing squad. **1758** – Suffering from a fear of being buried alive, a Miss Beswick of Manchester leaves her doctor £25,000 on condition that he visits her regularly after her death. To this end the newly moneyed physician has her corpse embalmed and stuck inside a grandfather clock case at the top of his house. **1760** – King George II of Britain dies of an aneurysm while straining on the toilet. **1762** – The Great Holocaust of the Sikhs is carried out in Punjab by Ahmed Shah Abdali. Over half a million are killed. **1762** – The new Tsar Peter III of Russia delights in his army, but has no-one to fight. He creates the illusion of war by ordering constant cannon fire in St Petersburg from dawn to dusk. He is deposed and murdered by his wife, Catherine the Great. **1763** – The Chippewas divert the garrison at Fort Michilimackinac by playing a game of lacrosse; they manage to invade the fort by chasing their ball into it. **1765** – The British Parliament passes the Stamp Tax, the first direct tax levied on the American colonies. **1766** – In France, Chevalier de la Barre is tortured and executed for blasphemy, after refusing to take his hat off during a religious procession. **1768** – Jeanne Baret becomes the first woman to circumnavigate the world. She does so disguised as a man, male valet to a naturalist on an expedition. **1769** – Nicolas Cugnot becomes the world's first motorist after inventing the steam car. He also becomes the world's first car crash victim when he drives the car into a wall. And the world's first man jailed for dangerous driving. **1769** – The city of Brescia, Italy, is devastated when its church is struck by lightning; the church stores some 200,000 pounds of gunpowder, and the resultant explosion kills 3,000 people. As a result, the Catholic Church revises its stance against the use of lightning rods. **1770** – Five American civilians are killed by British troops in the Boston Massacre. **1770** – In Paris, the fireworks set off to celebrate the wedding of the crown prince cause a fire that kills 132 people. **1773** – America opens its first insane asylum. **1775** – The American Revolution begins. **1775** – An earnest French schoolboy is chosen to deliver an address to the new king Louis XVI. He waits two hours in the pouring rain for the king's coach to arrive; he then kneels and reads his speech; the king then drives on without a word. The schoolboy's name is Robespierre, and he will meet the king just one more time. **1780** – In Italy, pioneering experiments are conducted on the artificial insemination of dogs. *My task is clear. I have to recreate all of history. It's all still there inside my head. While I remember it. While, oh God, I can still remember it. I have to set it down on paper again before it's too late.* **1780** – A peculiar darkness settles over New England on 19 May, which many take to be Judgement Day. **1780** – In Ireland, Lady Berry, sentenced to death for the murder of her son, has her punishment commuted when she agrees to become an executioner. **1781** – The slave ship Zong jettisons its human cargo into the sea to claim on the insurance. **1785** – Louis XIV passes a law that all handkerchiefs must be square. *The fear of celebrating birthdays is called fragapane phobia. I have no particular fear of dying on my birthday more than any other – if anything, I think I'd rather prefer it were my birthday, at least there'd be cake. I am forty years old now. I have at least forty times lived through the date on which I'm going to die; the roulette wheel continues to spin, and now I feel it's slowing, and each day I survive feels like a day that won't be reached again, there's just not enough power for the wheel to make another revolution – and I feel oddly relieved each night I go to sleep – so it* <u>*wasn't*</u> *11 June, it* <u>*wasn't*</u> *12 June... And on my death dates the sun will have shone and my mother will have baked cakes and prayed her thanks to God and my very own daughter will have burbled and smiled and been happy. It's my birthday soon. Let's see. Let's see if I get through it. Let's see.* **1785** – A hot air balloon crashes in Tullamore, Australia, and the fire burns down a hundred houses. It's the world's first aviation disaster. **1786** – The Constitutional Convention of the newly independent United States writes to Prince Henry of Prussia, inviting him to be their king. Henry is non-commital, so the Americans decide on an elected presidency instead. **1788** – Arthur Phillip lands in Sydney, and establishes a penal colony there, the first permanent European settlement in Australia. **1789** – William Bligh, captain of The Bounty, is cast adrift by his mutinous crew in a small boat (qv 1808). **1789** – Dr Joseph Guillotin proposes to the National Assembly in Paris a wonderful new invention of his, that will inflict capital punishment in the most humane way devised. **1789** – The Bastille prison falls, heralding the start of the French Revolution. In his diary that evening, Louis XVI writes: 'Nothing.' **1793** – Deposed and renamed Citizen Capet, Louis XVI is guillotined. 'I pray to God,' he says, 'that the blood you are about to shed is never visited on France.' Mrs Capet, former queen Marie Antoinette, is also guillotined. Her last words? 'Monsieur, I beg your pardon,' as she accidentally steps on the executioner's foot. **1794** – Robespierre, whose reign of terror brought down the French monarchy, is also guillotined. He has no famous last words; the mob shoot him in the jaw to stop him from talking. **1794** – At the battle of Fallen Timbers, Captain Asa Hartshorn is separated from his men and surrounded by Indians. After they kill him, they cut an incision in his chest, and insert two leather hearts to honour his bravery. **1797** – Rising star on the French scene, General Napoleon Bonaparte invades Venice and brings to an end its independence which has lasted over 1,000 years. **1797** – London milliner James Hetherington wears his new invention – the top hat – and is arrested for disturbing the peace.

THE RUNT

It was Annie who first saw something was wrong with her dog, that as it walked its undercarriage was dragging along the carpet. 'Fifi's got fat,' she said. Her parents both asserted that she couldn't be pregnant, because Fifi had been fixed; it then transpired that Mummy thought Daddy had taken Fifi to the vet's, and Daddy thought Mummy had, and they both got cross at each other, and it seemed that Fifi had had her way with the dachshund next door.

'Can I keep a puppy?' asked Annie, and Mummy said no, she already had a pet, and Daddy said yes, she could choose just *one*, but the rest would have to be sold. It took two hours for Fifi to produce her litter, and as each new scrap of doghood plopped out Annie stood over to size them up. The final puppy that emerged, nearly half an hour after its brothers and sisters, had no fur at all. It was pink and covered in taut stretched skin that let the bones show, and it had fingers and toes growing from its paws. It wailed noisily for attention the moment it hit the floor. The other puppies seemed embarrassed by the noise it made, they didn't know where to look.

Annie loved this last puppy the most of all. 'It's just the runt,' said her parents, but Annie was stubborn, this was the puppy she wanted to keep. Even Fifi kept her distance from it, and wouldn't let it suck at her teats like all the other newborns. And the runt looked confused at that, and not a little hungry, and Annie fed it milk from the fridge with a spoon. 'I'm going to name him Furball,' she said. Mummy and Daddy pointed out this was hardly apt, the thing was completely bald, but Annie put her finger to her lips: 'Ssh,' she said, 'I'm trying to make him feel better about that.'

Daddy took Furball to the vet for vaccinations. Annie held him. The vet took Daddy to one side, and said it wasn't worth the money – this was a *runt*, it wasn't going to live long – and Daddy shrugged, what's a Daddy to do? A few months later Furball was taken back to the vet, and the vet said he was surprised the runt was still alive. And then he cut off Furball's testicles, snip snap.

Furball liked to play in the garden; sometimes he caught squirrels, he brought them to the doorstep with such pride, the dying creatures quivering in his jaws. Annie thought it was funny to see the little fellow chasing them around the lawn, yapping away for all he was worth, his fleshy paws balling up in tight fists of frustration. He got good at catching things – he soon learned to use those fists, he learned he could jump up on hind legs and grab hold of the squirrels and pluck them out of the trees, he could dig his long fingers in deep and break their necks, he could swing them hard against the bark and knock the life out of them. He'd bark for his supper, he couldn't get enough of the dog food put in his bowl, and he'd bark for Annie, he'd get so excited when she came home from school, he liked nothing better than when she stroked his belly. Fifi felt neglected. Fifi died. She was getting old anyway. If Furball were bothered his mother was gone, he never showed it; he pranced around the house on all fours just as merrily, giving the same little yips and growls of pleasure, swishing his bare anus from side to side as if it were a tail. 'Furball's growing fur at last!' said Annie one day. But only on the top of his head, and decorating the groin. 'That's one ugly dog,' muttered Daddy.

Before long it was Furball's first birthday. 'They age quicker than we do,' said Mummy, 'he's seven in dog years.' Indeed, very soon Furball looked older than Annie; by the time Furball was three he was six foot two, had spots, and wispy facial fur. He was too heavy for Mummy's lap any more – 'Get off, Furball,' she'd say, 'you're a lump!' But he'd still sleep on Annie's bed, as pink and shiny as ever, lying spreadeagled across her body with his remaining floppy bits dangling. It quite disconcerted Annie's schoolfriends the time she invited them over for a slumber party; one girl cried; one girl threw up. And while Annie was at school Furball would annoy Mummy, he'd get under her feet as she did the housework – he'd just laze about on the sofa with the television on, he'd find his way into the fridge with those paws of his and steal human food, steal Daddy's beer. 'He's getting too big to stay indoors,' said Daddy, 'we'll have to get him a kennel.' Annie sulked at that, but Daddy cheered her up – 'We can build one for him ourselves, it'll be fun!' So over the weekend Daddy set to work at all the scraps of wood he could find, and Annie helped, she'd hand Daddy his hammer and his nails, and Furball raced around the garden, and Annie had to laugh, Furball had *no* idea what was going on! 'This is going to be your new house, Furball, this is all for you!' The finished kennel may not have been as smart as one you could buy in the shops, but Annie had helped build it, it was made with love. Furball refused even to poke his nose inside it at first, let alone to spend the night there – but Mummy fetched a blanket off Annie's bed to line the floor, it had Annie's smell all over it. And that made Furball feel a little better.

And at night they'd tie Furball to the kennel, and once they were in bed Furball would undo the leash. He was very good with knots. And he'd prowl the streets, sometimes on two feet, sometimes on all four – he'd pad up and down the pavements and explore his territory. The police might mistake him for a naked tramp until they got up close. 'Oh, it's okay,' they'd laugh, 'it's just that dog from number sixty-five.'

One such night Furball didn't come home. Annie was distraught. She put up posters asking for information about her missing pet. She had lots of photos of Furball, she loved him so much, she'd taken so many of him as he dozed on the carpet, as he dug holes in the lawn, as he licked at where his balls had once been – and she quite used all these photos up, sellotaping the whole collection to the lamp posts in town. She cried for a week. Each morning she'd eagerly race downstairs to the kennel in the hope that Furball had returned; each night she'd hug her duvet tight and mould it into a runt-shaped ball. One day she came home from school to discover her parents had bought her a new dog – a pretty one, one with fur, one with a tail; the coat was glossy, the eyes bright, nose wet, and when it said 'woof' it didn't sound like a sulking teenager. Annie didn't want this new dog. Annie hated it. But she took it to bed with her anyway. She stroked its belly nonetheless.

A neighbour one morning brought Furball to the door. He'd found him inside his shed, he must have got locked in there. Furball had survived eating bugs and spiders. He looked wretched. And there were patches of dried blood everywhere, he must have got into a fight. 'Oh dear,' said Mummy. 'But my daughter's got a new dog now, she's moved on. What am I to do?' Furball slumped to the kitchen floor. Furball II growled at the newcomer suspiciously.

Annie was still at school, she'd be there for hours. Mummy phoned Daddy, and

Daddy came right home from work. They discussed what would be best for Annie, and as they talked so seriously Furball wolfed down a second tin of dog food, he lapped at the saucerful of his favourite lager they'd given him as a treat. 'Walkies!' said Daddy suddenly. 'Time for walkies!' And in spite of how tired Furball felt, in spite of the gashes in his side, he got excited and started to bark. Daddy opened the car door for Furball, but Furball was resistant – and it was only when Mummy thought to fetch the Annie-scented blanket from the kennel that Furball calmed and got in.

They drove Furball a long way, out of the town, into the very countryside. Furball looked out of the window as all the fields whipped by. The air was cleaner here, there was grass, and squirrels to chase, and barbed-wire fences, and it was all so *green*. Mummy and Daddy found a field that looked just perfect, it seemed so big and friendly; they opened the car door and pushed Furball out. 'You're free now, boy!' said Daddy. 'Free! You can do whatever you want!' 'You'll be happy here,' Mummy said. And off they drove, waving goodbye to Furball till he could see them no more.

And Furball pulled himself up on to his hind legs. He'd normally do this only if he wanted to play, or was keening for a biscuit, or for a cuddle, it had always delighted Annie, she'd thought it was cute – but he'd long ago learned he could totter about on those hind legs quite easily. He stared down the road where the car had gone. He panted with tongue out, he scratched at where his balls had been, he waited. He flapped one of his paws in imitation of the wave his owners had given him. It didn't bring them back. He was sure they'd be back soon. Of course they'd be back soon. He gave his tailless bottom one last waggle, he yawned, he stretched out his furless arms as far as they could go until he heard his ribs crack. And then, beneath a grazing cow, he settled down to sleep.

1801 – Mummy. **1801** – Tsar Paul I is suffocated with a malachite paperweight. **1802** – Napoleon Bonaparte reinstates slavery, overturning its abolition during the French Revolution. **1804** – Napoleon has himself crowned Emperor of France, in direct imitation of Charlemagne (qv 800). Beethoven has just composed his third symphony in Napoleon's honour, naming it 'The Bonaparte'; he is so outraged by the news that Napoleon is just another petty tyrant after all that he rips out the front page and retitles it 'The Eroica' instead. *And I want to chronicle all the great events, all the acts of courage and honour and selflessness. But they're not what history remembers, and nor do I – as I write down each and every date on this new time chart, what strikes me is all the greed and all the waste, and yes, the very banal evil that is present, year after year, century after century – that as we progress through time so we always regress a little as well, so we crawl out of caves and discover fire but only so we can move into high rise tower blocks and discover reality TV – that every small advance we make is always cancelled out by something else. We discover a new continent, we start the slave trade. We form the League of Nations, we declare world wars. As the medicine improves, so do the weapons; the growth of education gives people a greater vocabulary to describe their suffering. We dress up invasion as peacekeeping, cultural rape as missionary work; we live longer than our medieval forebears, but most of our extra time is spent on Facebook.* **1805** – Admiral Horatio Nelson defeats Napoleon at the battle of Trafalgar, but at the cost of his own life. He exhorts Captain Thomas Hardy to take care of his great love, Lady Hamilton, and then asks for a kiss before he expires. There has been much embarrassment about this, no doubt because it implies a homoerotic relationship quite inappropriate for a sailor, let alone one standing in effigy at the top of an enormous phallic column by Charing Cross – and there has been some attempt therefore to suggest that Nelson's dying words were instead 'Kismet, Hardy', as some dry comment upon fate. This seems rather unlikely, especially considering that that definition of 'kismet' isn't recorded before 1830. Besides, if Nelson had meant 'kismet', Hardy himself apparently misunderstood, because he kissed the admiral anyway. *And I'm creating all this history anew, and I know I could change it. I could, say, rewrite the battle of Hastings so that Harold won, I could prevent the Black Death. But I'd only be swapping one loser for another – if the Saxons aren't defeated by the Normans, then the Normans are defeated by the Saxons, if sixty percent of Europe isn't wiped out by the rats, then the rats look like such idiots, don't they? And that's what history is, then: however I choose to list it, no matter what I alter, it still remains a litany of bungling, a study of mediocrity on an epic scale, a parade of non-entities whose only life achievements were that when the chips were down and everything was in the balance they failed.* **1806** – Future US president Andrew Jackson kills a man in a duel, in retaliation for his accusing Jackson's wife of bigamy. **1806** – Francis II dissolves the Holy Roman Empire, established by Charlemagne (again, qv 800) after his army is crushed by Napoleon at the battle of Austerlitz. **1806** – Jean-Jacques Dessalines, the first emperor of the newly independent state of Haiti, is assassinated. **1807** – Brother and sister, Charles and Mary Lamb, publish 'Tales from Shakespeare', one of the most popular books ever written for children. Mary has killed their mother some eleven years previously and composes her share of the book mostly from an insane asylum. **1807** – Henry Stuart dies, serving as a cardinal at the Vatican. He is the last possible claimant from the Stuart line for the British throne. **1807** – The Royal Navy bombard Copenhagen in an attempt to protect it from invasion by Napoleon. 2,000 Danes are killed, and thirty percent of the city is destroyed. **1807 –** Ottoman Emperor Selim III is imprisoned, and deposed in favour of his nephew Mustafa IV. **1808 –** Mustafa then consolidates his position by having Selim put to death. Of all the ways Ottoman emperors have been murdered over the years, Selim is the only one to be despatched with a sword. Mustafa also tries to kill his brother Mahmud, but Mahmud survives by hiding in his bath – and takes the throne when Mustafa is overthrown a few months later. **1808** – Twenty years after he suffered the ignominy of mutiny on 'The Bounty' (qv 1788), William Bligh is governor of New South Wales in Australia. And once again he is the victim of mutiny, as his soldiers tire of him, lock him up, and take control of his colony. It must be something in his manner. **1809** – King Gustav IV of Sweden is deposed in favour of his uncle. **1809** – In Boston, it is declared that the wearing of masks at balls is illegal. **1811** – A slave revolt in Louisiana is brutally put down; the heads of executed rebels are displayed by the roadsides. **1812** – British prime minister, Spencer Perceval, is shot dead by a businessman when leaving the Houses of Parliament. His last words are, 'I'll have one of Bellamy's veal pies!' **1812** – Napoleon's conquest of Europe is, it seems, unstoppable. He marches on Moscow, but his army is all but annihilated by the savage winter cold; the Russians burn their own city to deny Napoleon's forces any food or shelter. A monument on one side of the road there reads: 'Napoleon Bonaparte passed this way in 1812 with 400,000 men.' And on the other side of the road, leading out of the city, another monument reads: 'Napoleon Bonaparte passed this way in 1812 with 9,000 men.' **1813** – A workman removes a fingerbone from the body of Henry VIII in Windsor Castle (qv 1547) and uses it to make a knife handle. *Sometimes I think that all these events I'm recording are just a fiction, that I really have created them out of my own head.* **1814** – Joanna Southcott, a farmer's daughter in Devon, and sixty-four years old, proclaims that in October she will give a virgin birth to the second Messiah. She attracts some 100,000 followers. On the day in question the new Christ fails to present itself, and Southcott falls into a coma from which she never awakes. Her more assiduous pilgrims insist that she's in a trance, and only give up her body for burial when it begins to rot in front of them. **1814** – Nine people drown in the London Beer Flood, when vats containing some 323,000 gallons of ale are ruptured. **1815** – American forces defeat the British at the battle of New Orleans, in the War of 1812. The peace treaty has been signed some two weeks before, however, on Christmas Eve, and the news hasn't yet reached the armies. Nearly 1,000 men lose their lives. **1815** – Napoleon decides to skimp on his troop inspections before the battle of Waterloo, because he's suffering an acute attack of haemorrhoids. He is defeated in a battle so fierce that, though it's fought in Belgium, the sound of the guns can be heard as far away as Sussex. Napoleon is forced to abdicate, and is exiled to the island of St Helena. His four-year-old son, Napoleon II, reigns as emperor for two weeks. **1815** – The Amiston, transporting British troops home from Ceylon, is wrecked off South Africa. Only six people of the 378 on board survive. **1816** – The Medusa sinks off the coast of West Africa. A large raft carries 149 survivors – over a hundred of them die before rescue, many eaten by their crewmates. **1820** – Louise, Queen of Prussia dies. 'I am a queen, but I haven't the power to move my arms.' **1820** – French King Charles X's son Ferdinand is assassinated. He is a notorious philanderer, and his widow Caroline is visited by a score of women from Nantes, each one claiming they are expecting his child. Caroline refuses to believe it's true, and then finds out her husband visited Nantes for an entire week. 'Oh well, then,' says Caroline, 'it is entirely possible.' **1823** – The British Admiralty are presented with the newly invented electric telegraph system, and reject it. **1825** – Simon Bolivar gives up the title, 'dictator' of Peru – he prefers the word 'liberator'. **1825 –** The Decembrist revolt, against the accession of Nicholas I to the Russian throne, fails. One of the leaders, Kondraty Fyodorovich Rylelev, is led out to execution by hanging. The noose breaks, and Rylelev mutters that in Russia they cannot even make a rope properly. Tsar Nicholas I's response: 'Let us prove him wrong.' The second noose holds firm. **1826** – Cayetano Ripoll, a village schoolmaster convicted of heresy, is garrotted in Valencia. He will be the last victim of the Spanish Inquisition. **1827** – The Shrigley abduction causes a scandal in Britain. Edward Wakefield forcibly marries a wealthy heiress of fifteen years old, Ellen Turner; Wakefield is caught, and sentenced to three years in prison. Wakefield later becomes an early leader in the colonisation of New Zealand. Ms Turner marries again, and dies in childbirth at nineteen. **1828** – Driven mad by grief at the death of his mother, Shaka, first king of the Zulus, orders random mass executions. His brothers kill him and take his throne. **1828** – The enigma of Kasper Hauser. **1829** – Lord William Bentinck finds the traditions of India horrifying and barbaric, and passes a law that anyone aiding the practice of suttee (in which a widow will throw herself on her husband's funeral pyre) is guilty of homicide. It's the beginning of a process in which the British attempt to 'civilise' their colonies (qv 1857). **1830** – Charles X attempts to compensate the nobles for the events of the French Revolution. This prompts another French Revolution. **1832** – William Howley, new Archbishop of Canterbury, is attacked by an angry mob on his first official visit to his diocese. **1832** – The Supreme Court rules that the Government of the United States has exclusive control over all Native Americans and any land they might happen to own. **1833** – The English Factory Act improves the lives of children everywhere, by requiring they must be at least nine years old to work. **1833** – Britain takes the Falkland Islands from the United Provinces of South America (now known as Argentina). **1835** – For the only time in its history, the US reduces its public debt to zero. **1836** – Americans are slaughtered by the Mexicans at the battle of the Alamo in the Texas Revolution. **1836** – Native Americans attack Fort Parker; they capture a nine-year-old girl, Cynthia Ann Parker, who will spend her life with the Comanche, and give birth to their future final leader. **1839** – Prince Milan II rules Serbia for twenty-six days in a coma; it is doubtful he ever even knew. **1840** – Frederick William IV becomes king of Prussia. His favourite family pastime is to take his wife and children to hospital to watch surgical operations. **1840** – The Greek Orthodox community on Rhodes accuse the Jews there of the ritual murder of a young Christian boy (qv 1144, 1255, 1491). **1841** – William Henry Harrison is elected president of the United States. His inaugural speech is the longest ever, running at one hour forty minutes, and delivered by Harrison on a freezing day in March without wearing a coat, hat, or gloves. Within a month he is dead from pneumonia. **1842** – Visiting America, Charles Dickens is irritated by first time writer Edgar Allan Poe who wants help in getting published. **1845** – Sir John Franklin sets out to the Arctic to find the Northwest Passage, and is never seen again. Notebooks found after his death record that his entire crew will die of hypothermia, starvation, tuberculosis, scurvy, exposure or lead poisoning. **1847** – The invention of nitroglycerine. **1847** – The invention of ring doughnuts. **1848** – Revolutions in France, Italy, Germany, Denmark, Brazil, Belgium, Wallachia,

Hungary, Slovakia, Switzerland and Poland. **1849** – David Rice Atchison becomes acting president of the United States for a full day when the elected representative Zachary Taylor refuses to be sworn into office on a Sunday. **1849** – Ranavalona I, queen of Madagascar, starts a campaign of Christian persecution, executing anyone found owning a Bible. **1851** – Jacques Leroy de Saint Arnaud leads the gendarmerie in Paris, and they stand, facing a mob. Arnaud has a bad head cold, and is given to exclaim, 'Ma sacree toux! (My damned cough!)' It is misheard as 'Massacrez tous!' 800 people die as his soldiers fire into the crowd, and it is a pivotal moment in Napoleon III's ascent to become emperor of France. **1852** – The publication of 'Uncle Tom's Cabin', exposing the iniquities of slavery. It is countered with the publication of 'Aunt Phillis' Cabin', which shows just how great slavery really can be, and how much happier black people are without their freedom. **1854** – The Charge of the Light Brigade. Noble 600. **1854** – In London, a cholera epidemic kills 10,000 people. The cause is traced back to a single well's water pump. **1857** – The Indian Mutiny is provoked by British officers ordering their sepoys to load their new Enfield rifles. In order to do so, the cartridge has to be bitten open, and it is sealed with pork fat which is regarded as unclean by Muslims. 11,000 British people are killed; in reprisals, countless thousands of Indians are killed too. **1857** – In the case of Dred Scott vs Sanford, the Supreme Court of the United States rules that black men are not citizens and cannot sue for freedom. **1857** – The Xhosa tribe of South Africa destroy their cattle and burn all their crops as an act of faith that the spirits will restore fertility to their land and drive out the hated British colonists – proof given when the sun reverses direction on 18 February. It doesn't. Most starve; the others abase themselves before the British and their food. **1858** – The 'Great Stink' of raw sewage on the streets of London causes the House of Commons to soak their curtains in chloride of lime to drive the smell away. *And I suppose the question you'll be asking (if you've made it this far) is – how much of this stuff is true? I don't know. All of it? Some of it? As I write it all down, as I excavate from my memories all the history I thought I ever knew, I realise there's no end to it, one event leads to another event, and I can't be sure where Real History stops and my own invention begins. If I'm frank, looking back at all these words, most of it seems pretty unlikely. I don't know where I'd got the idea that someone called Charlemagne ever existed, for God's sake. Or Joan of Arc (was I thinking of Noah's Ark?), or Diocletian (who sounds to me now less like a Roman Emperor and more like a type of detergent) – was there ever really a King Henry VIII? Doesn't that sound like a more sensationalist sequel to King Henry VII? And taken as an ongoing story, then the history of the world seems to be a novel written by someone with no sense of pace or of structure – the same events seem to happen over and over again with monotonous regularity. How many times do monarchs have to be overthrown and blinded in castles, how many times (for Christ's sake!) does St Paul's Cathedral have to be burned down for the reader to get the point? And as for the characterisations: there's no identifiable hero here at all, no-one lives a span of more than two chapters, it's as if the author drunkenly lurches from bit part to bit part and keeps forgetting to give the reader anyone to care about. I don't know whether the thudding inadequacy of the History of the World as a piece of fiction makes it more likely to be true or not, or whether God is simply a bloody poor storyteller who wouldn't understand basic simple plotting if it jumped up and bit him on the arse. (Or whether I'm God, since I'm the one writing all this, and just because this is what I think I find in my head as memories, just because I no longer have control over my delusions, just because I am demented, why should I be any judge of this work's authenticity?) When you look at it, all history ultimately is just a collection of memories, and then interpretations and reinterpretations of memories by people who weren't alive to remember the events in the first place – and that seems a remarkably flimsy and unreliable method on which to found civilisations and form cultural identities – what if, let's be honest, all of this is just guff? So, believe what you will. My advice – is if at any stage reading this list of historical events you recognise even one of them, then you may as well trust it, and take all the others on trust too. I'll have done my job. If Charles of Dubrazzo seems real (qv 1386), or Phocas (qv 602), then maybe, against all the odds, Jesus Christ was real as well.* **1859** – On the boundary between the United States and British North America, an American farmer shoots a large pig that is eating the vegetables in his garden. The pig is owned by an Irishman, and there is a row about compensation. This soon escalates to the military – the Americans send infantry soldiers, the British retaliate by sending warships. When news about the crisis reaches Washington and London, both governments are shocked, and put an end to the Pig War – a war in which no-one is killed. Unless, of course, you count the pig. **1859** – Thomas Austin decides to have a Christmas hunt on his property in Melbourne, Australia, and has shipped over twenty-four rabbits. The rabbits breed. By 1866, more than 14,000 are shot on Austin's estate alone; by the end of the century, they have successfully migrated in their millions across the continent. Millions of acres of Australian land are destroyed by the infestation, and seventy percent of indigenous domestic species are wiped out. **1861** – The American Civil War begins. **1863** – Stonewall Jackson, the Confederate general, defeats the Union army at the battle of Chancellorsville. And then is shot by his own troops while returning to camp. **1863** – Abraham Lincoln delivers his Gettysburg Address – only a two minute addendum to the main two hour long speech given by Edward Everett before it. **1863** – World famous midgets Tom Thumb and Lavinia Warner are married in New York; PT Barnum charges an entrance fee. **1864** – 'They couldn't hit an elephant at this distance' – the last words of Union army general John Sedgwick at the battle of Spotsylvania Court House. **1864** – In his Syllabus Errorum, pope Pius IX claims for the authority of the Catholic Church over civil society, and roundly denounces liberalism and rationalism. **1864** – The first condom is made by the International Condom Company. **1865** – Hundreds of theatregoers have their evening ruined when one of the actors goes all improv and assassinates the president of the United States. No refunds. *And on that basis – just a thought – maybe the whole thing is made up! Maybe I never had a daughter at all! Maybe there never was an Annie. (And it does seem unlikely now – after all, if I had made a whole human being, shouldn't that feel like the greatest act of creation? If that were true, how could I ever stop loving her, how could I ever have hurt her, how could I not have made her the very centre of my universe – dear God, I'd have killed any fucking man who'd ever dare lay a single fucking finger on my poor darling Annie.) Maybe I never had a daughter. Maybe I never had a wife. Maybe I never had a mother.* **1865** – The summit of the Matterhorn is reached for the first time; four of the seven mountain climbers die in the descent. **1867** – William Bullock dies, his leg caught in the printing press he's invented. **1867** – The Reverend Thomas Baker is cooked and eaten by the Navatusila tribe on Fiji, the last missionary to die from cannibalism. **1870** – So many Paraguayan soldiers have been killed in the War of Triple Alliance that the country legalises polygamy, to boost population growth. **1870** – Juan Prim, prime minister of Spain, is assassinated. **1872** – Susan B Anthony is the first woman to vote in the US elections; she is arrested and fined. **1875** – The King of Fiji returns home from a state visit to Australia with measles, and wipes out a quarter of the population. **1876** – Ottoman sultan Abdulaziz is deposed and imprisoned. A few days later it's thought a really good idea if the sultan were to commit suicide, and indeed his dead body is found next to a pair of scissors, both wrists cut through. It isn't clear how he might have got the scissors in the first place, nor how it would be medically possible for him to sever two wrists at the same time – but it's pronounced a suicide anyway. **1876** – General Custer is defeated at the battle of Little Big Horn by the Sioux led by Sitting Bull. His arrogance and impatience cost him his life and the lives of his entire regiment. And seals the fate of the Native Americans who defeat him, who are quickly destroyed in retaliation; Sitting Bull spends the rest of his life as a circus act in Buffalo Bill's Wild West Show. **1879** – The first publication of 'The Watchtower' by the Jehovah's Witnesses. **1880** – The first British telephone directory is published. It has 255 names. **1881** – James Garfield, president of the United States, is shot. Alexander Graham Bell, inventor of the telephone, invents a metal detector specifically to find the bullets in Garfield's body, but all it can locate is the bed springs beneath him. Garfield is the second US president to be assassinated. **1882** – Roderick Maclean fails to assassinate Queen Victoria with a pistol. This is the last of some eight attempts on Victoria's life spanning some forty years, provoked by a curt response to some poetry he'd written and sent her. **1885** – King Leopold II of Belgium establishes the Congo Free State as a personal possession, and in a regime unparalleled in its cruelty subjects the natives to slavery and humiliation. The population halves. *It takes two weeks for me to complete the chart. I barely sleep, I just keep dredging my mind for all the history it's got. The banging on Annie's bedroom door gets fainter and fainter. And I set her down in history too. I give her a long life. I do, I want her to be happy. I assign her three dates in the chart, centuries apart, I fix her in time, I fix her name in bold, I give her all that history as a gift. And the banging at last stops.* **1886** – Mad King Ludwig II of Bavaria murders his own psychiatrist. **1887** – The artificial language Esperanto is devised. **1889** – The Eiffel Tower opens in Paris to bad reviews. **1890** – Wilhemina becomes queen of the Netherlands; Luxembourg refuses to be ruled by a woman, and primly declare independence. **1896** – Britain declares war on Zanzibar; the Royal Navy destroy the palace; Zanzibar capitulates. Lasting thirty-eight minutes, it's the shortest war in history. **1897** – Heroin is created as a cough remedy. **1899** – The US patent office declares, 'Everything that can be invented has been invented.' **1899 – ANNIE.** *And now, as I come out of the nineteenth century, and prepare the last chapter and its scrappy epilogue, I get the urge to build up to some sort of climax. I don't trust that. It makes the whole thing smack of fictional plot contrivance. After all the wars we've been through already, why do I now want to write about bigger wars – wars between every nation on Earth! – let's call them, World Wars! It's just too neat and pat. And other bits of overkill – I have this idea for a story about aeroplanes being hijacked and flown into a large building – no, not even a building, an entire two-pronged double-phallic metaphor for Western civilisation! Dear God, in its final spurt I'm taking world history and giving it the flavour of a mass market thriller. Believe none of it.* **1899** – On New Year's Eve, just hours before the 1900s begin, one of the huge standing stones at Stonehenge, in position for over four thousand years, suddenly lists forward and topples over. At any other time in history this would be seized upon as something prophetic, something dread, about the century to come. But we're all far too sophisticated for such things now. **1900** – The British put 120,000 Boer women and children in concentration camps.

GRANNY'S GRINNING

Sarah didn't want the zombie, and she didn't know anyone else who did. Apart from Graham, of course, but he was only four, he wanted *everything*; his Christmas list to Santa had run to so many sheets of paper that Daddy had said that Santa would need to take out a second mortgage on his igloo to get that lot, and everyone had laughed, even though Graham didn't know what an igloo was, and Sarah was pretty sure that Santa didn't live in an igloo anyway. Sarah had tried to point out to her little brother why the zombies were rubbish. 'Look,' she said, showing him the picture in the catalogue, 'there's nothing to a zombie. They're just the same as us. Except the skin is a bit greener, maybe. And the eyes have whitened a bit.' But Graham said that zombies were cool because zombies ate people when they were hungry, and when Sarah scoffed Graham burst into tears like always, and Mummy told Sarah to leave Graham alone, he was allowed to like zombies if he wanted to. Sarah thought that if it was all about eating people, she'd rather have a vampire: they sucked your blood for a start, which was so much neater somehow than just chomping down on someone's flesh – and Sharon Weekes said that she'd tried out a friend's vampire, and it was great, it wasn't just the obvious stuff like the teeth growing, but your lips swelled up, they got redder and richer and plump, and if you closed your eyes and rubbed them together it felt just the same as if a boy were kissing you. As if Sharon Weekes would know, Sharon Weekes was covered in spots, and no boy had ever kissed her, if you even so much as touched Sharon her face would explode – but you know, whatever, the rubbing lips thing still sounded great. Sarah hadn't written it down on her Christmas list like Graham had done, she'd simply told Santa that she'd like the vampire, please. Just the vampire, not the mummy, or the werewolf, or the demon. And definitely not the zombie.

Even before Granny had decided to stay, Sarah knew that this Christmas was going to be different. Mummy and Daddy said that if she and Graham wanted such expensive toys, then they'd have to put up with just one present this year. Once upon a time they'd have had tons of presents, and the carpet beneath the Christmas tree would have been strewn with brightly wrapped parcels of different shapes and sizes, it'd have taken hours to open the lot. But that was before Daddy left his job because he wanted to 'go it alone', before the credit crunch, before those late night arguments in the kitchen that Sarah wasn't supposed to hear. Graham groused a little about only getting one present, but Daddy said something about a second mortgage, and this time he didn't mention igloos, and this time nobody laughed. Usually the kitchen arguments were about money, but one night they were about Granny, and Sarah actually bothered to listen. 'I thought she was staying with Sonia!' said Mummy. Sonia was Daddy's sister, and she had a sad smile, and ever since Uncle Jim had left her for someone less ugly she had lived alone. 'She says she's fallen out with Sonia,' said Daddy, 'she's coming to spend Christmas with us instead.' 'Oh, for Christ's sake, *for Christ's sake*,' said Mummy, and there was a banging of drawers. 'Come on,' said Daddy, 'she's my Mummy, what was I supposed to say?' And then he added, 'It might even work in our favour,' and Mummy had said it better bloody well had, and then Sarah couldn't hear any more, perhaps because they'd shut the kitchen door, perhaps because Mummy was crying again.

Most Christmases they'd spend on their own, just Sarah with Mummy and Daddy and Graham. And on Boxing Day they'd get into the car and drive down the motorway to see Granny and Granddad. Granny looked a little like Daddy, but older and slightly more feminine. And Granddad smelled of cigarettes even though he'd given up before Sarah was born. Granny and Granddad would give out presents, and Sarah and Graham would say thank you no matter what they got. And they'd have another Christmas meal, just like the day before, except this time the turkey would be drier, and there'd be Brussels sprouts rather than sausages. There wouldn't be a Boxing Day like that again. Partly because on the way home last year Mummy had said she could never spend another Christmas like that, and it had taken all of Daddy's best efforts to calm her down in the Little Chef – but mostly, Sarah supposed, because Granddad was dead. That was bound to make a difference. They'd all been to the funeral, Sarah hadn't even missed school because it was during the summer holidays, and Graham had made a nuisance of himself during the service asking if Granddad was a ghost now and going to come back from the grave. And during the whole thing Granny had sat there on the pew, all by herself, she didn't want anyone sitting next to her, not even Aunt Sonia, and Aunt Sonia was her favourite. And she'd cried, tears were streaming down her face, and Sarah had never seen Granny like that before, her face was always set fast like granite, and now with all the tears it had become soft and fat and pulpy and just a little frightening.

Four days before Christmas Daddy brought home a tree. 'One of Santa's elves coming through!' he laughed, as he lugged it into the sitting room. It was enormous, and Graham and Sarah loved it, its upper branches scraped against the ceiling, they couldn't have put the fairy on the top like usual, she'd have broken her spine. Graham and Sarah began to cover it with balls and tinsel and electric lights, and Mummy said, 'How much did that cost? I thought the point was to be a bit more economical this year,' and Daddy said he knew what he was doing, he knew how to play the situation. They were going to give Granny the best Christmas she'd ever had! And he asked everyone to listen carefully, and then told them that this was a very important Christmas, it was the first Granny would have without Granddad. And she was likely to be a bit sad, and maybe a bit grumpy, but they'd all have to make allowances. It was to be *her* Christmas this year, whatever she wanted, it was all about making Granny happy, Granny would get the biggest slice of turkey, Granny would choose which James Bond film to watch in the afternoon, the one on BBC1 or the one on ITV. Could he count on Graham and Sarah for that? Could he count on them to play along? And they both said yes, and Daddy was so pleased, they were so good he'd put their presents under the tree right away. He fetched two parcels, the same size, the same shape, flat boxes, one wrapped in blue paper and the other in pink. 'Now, no peeking until the big day!' he laughed, but Graham couldn't help it, he kept turning his present over and over, and shaking it, and wondering what was inside, was it a demon, was it a zombie? And Sarah had to get on with decorating the tree all by herself, but that was all right, Graham hadn't been much use, she did a better job with him out of the way.

And that was just the start of the work! The next few days were frantic! Mummy insisted that Granny come into a house as spotless and tidy as could be, that this time she wouldn't be able to find a thing wrong with it. And she made Sarah and Graham clean even the rooms that Granny wouldn't be seeing in the first place! It was all for Granny, that's what they were told, all for Granny – and if Graham sulked about that (and he did a little) Daddy said that one day someone close to *him* would die, and then *he* could have a special Christmas where everyone would run around after *him*, and Graham cheered up at that. On Christmas Eve Daddy said he was very proud of his children, and that he had a treat for them both. Early the next morning he'd be picking Granny up from her home in the country – it was a four and a half hour journey there and back, and that they'd been *so* good they were allowed to come along for the trip! Graham got very excited, and shouted a lot. And Mummy said that it was okay to take Graham, but she needed Sarah at home, there was still work for Sarah to do. And Sarah wasn't stupid, the idea of a long drive to Granny's didn't sound much like fun to her, but it had been offered as a treat, and it hurt her to be denied a treat. Daddy glared at Mummy, and Mummy glared right back, and for a thrilling moment Sarah thought they might have an argument – but they only *ever* did that in the kitchen, they still believed the kids didn't know – and then Daddy relaxed, and then laughed, and ruffled Graham's hair, and said it'd be a treat for the boys then, just the boys, and laughed once more. So that was all right.

First thing Christmas morning, still hours before sunrise, Daddy and Graham set off to fetch Granny. Graham was so sleepy he forgot to be excited. 'Goodbye then!' said Daddy cheerily; 'Goodbye,' said Mummy, and then suddenly pulled him into a tight hug. 'It'll all be all right,' said Daddy. 'Of course it will,' said Mummy, 'off you go!' She waved them off, and then turned to Sarah, who was waving along beside her. Mummy said, 'We've only got a few hours to make everything perfect,' and Sarah nodded, and went to the cupboard for the vacuum cleaner. 'No, no,' said Mummy, 'to make *you* perfect. My perfect little girl.' And Mummy took Sarah by the hand, and smiled at her kindly, and led her to her own bedroom. 'We're going to make you such a pretty girl,' said Mummy, 'they'll all see how pretty you can be. You'll like that, won't you? You can wear your nice dress. You'll like your new dress. Won't you?' Sarah didn't like her new dress, it was hard to romp about playing a vampire in it, it was hard to play at *anything* in it, but Mummy was insistent. 'And we'll give you some nice jewellery,' she said. 'This is a necklace of mine. It's pretty. It's gold. Do you like it? My Mummy gave it to me. Just as I'm now giving it to you. Do you remember my Mummy? Do you remember the Other Granny?' Sarah didn't, but said that she did, and Mummy smiled. 'She had some earrings too, shall we try you out with those? Shall we see what that's like?' And the earrings were much heavier than the plain studs Sarah was used to, they stretched her lobes out like chewing gum, they seemed to Sarah to stretch out her entire face. 'Isn't that pretty?' said Mummy, and when Sarah said they hurt a bit, Mummy said she'd get used to it. Then Mummy took Sarah by the chin, and gave her a dab of lipstick – and Sarah never wore make-up, not like the girls who sat on the back row of the school bus, not even like Sharon Weekes, Mummy had always said it made them cheap. Sarah reminded her of this, and Mummy didn't reply, and so Sarah then asked if this was all for Granny, and Mummy said, 'Yes, it's all for Granny,' and then corrected herself, 'it's for *all* of them, let's remind them what a pretty girl you are, what a pretty woman you could grow up to be. Always remember that you could have been a pretty woman.' And then she wanted to give Sarah some nail varnish, nothing too much, nothing too red, just something clear and sparkling. But Sarah had had enough, she looked in the mirror and she didn't recognise the person looking back at her, she looked so much older, and greasy, and plastic, she looked just like Mummy. And tears were in her eyes, and she looked behind her reflection at Mummy's reflection, and there were tears in Mummy's eyes too – and Mummy said she was sorry, and took off the earrings, and wiped away the lipstick with a tissue. 'I'm sorry,' she said again, and said that Sarah needn't dress up if she didn't want to, it was her Christmas too, not just Granny's. And Sarah felt bad, and although she didn't much like the necklace she asked if she could keep it on, she lied and said it made her look pretty – and Mummy beamed a smile so wide, and gave her a hug, and said of course she could wear the necklace, anything for her darling, anything she wanted.

*

The first thing Granny said was, 'I haven't brought you any presents, so don't expect any.' 'Come on in,' said Daddy, laughing, 'and make yourself at home!' and Granny sniffed as if she found that prospect particularly unappealing. 'Hello, Mrs Forbes,' said Mummy. 'Hello, Granny,' said Sarah, and she felt the most extraordinary urge to curtsey. Graham trailed behind, unusually quiet, obviously quelled by a greater force than his own. 'Can I get you some tea, Mrs Forbes?' said Mummy. 'We've got you all sorts, Earl Grey, Lapsang souchong, Ceylon...' 'I'd like some tea, not an interrogation,' said Granny. She went into the lounge, and when she sat down in Daddy's armchair she sent all the scatter cushions tumbling, she didn't notice how carefully they'd been arranged and plumped. 'Do you like the tree, Mummy?' Daddy asked, and Granny studied it briefly, and said it was too big, and she hoped he'd bought it on discount. Daddy started to say something about how the tree was just to keep the children happy, as if it were really their fault, but then Mummy arrived with the tea; Granny took her cup, sipped at it, and winced. 'Would you like your presents, Mummy? We've got you presents.' And at the mention of presents, Graham perked up: 'Presents!' he said, 'presents!' 'Not your presents yet, old chap,' laughed Daddy amiably, 'Granny first, remember?' And Granny sighed and said she had no interest in presents, she could see nothing to celebrate – but she didn't want to spoil anyone else's fun, obviously, and so if they had presents to give her now would be as good a time to put up with them as any. Daddy had bought a few gifts, and labelled a couple from Sarah and Graham. It turned out that they'd bought Granny some perfume, 'your favourite, isn't it?' asked Daddy, and 'with their very own pocket money too!' 'What use have I got in perfume now that Arthur's dead?' said Granny curtly. And tilted her face forwards so that Sarah and Graham could kiss it, by way of a thank you.

Graham was delighted with his werewolf suit. 'Werewolf!' he shouted, and waving the box above his head tore around the sitting room in excitement. 'And if you settle down, old chap,' laughed Daddy, 'you can try it on for size!' They took the cellophane off the box, removed the lid, and took out the instructions for use. The recommended age was ten and above, but as Daddy said, it was just a recommendation, and besides, there were plenty of adults there to supervise. There was a furry werewolf mask, furry werewolf slippers, and an entire furry werewolf body suit. Granny looked disapproving. 'In my day, little boys didn't want to be werewolves,' she said. 'They wanted to be soldiers and train drivers.' Graham put the mask over his face, and almost immediately they could all see how the fur seemed to grow in response – not only outwards, what would be the fun in that? but inwards too, each tiny hair follicle burying itself deep within Graham's face, so you could really believe that all this fur had naturally come out of a little boy. With a crack the jaw elongated too, into something like a snout – it wasn't a full wolf's snout, of course not, this was only a toy, and you could see that the red raw gums inside that slavering mouth were a bit too rubbery to be real, but it was still effective enough for Granny to be impressed. 'Goodness,' she said. But that was nothing. When Daddy fastened the buckle around the suit, straight away Graham's entire body contorted in a manner that could only be described as feral. The spine snapped and popped as Graham grew bigger, and then it twisted and curved over, as if in protest that a creature on four legs should be supporting itself on two – the now warped spine bulged angrily under the fur. Graham gave a yelp. 'Doesn't that hurt?' said Mummy, and Daddy said no, these toys were all the rage, all the kids loved them. Graham tried out his new body. He threw himself around the room, snarling in almost pantomime fashion, he got so carried away whipping his tail about he nearly knocked over the coffee table – and it didn't matter, everyone was laughing at the fun, even Sarah, even Granny. 'He's a proper little beast, isn't he!' Granny said. 'And you see, it's also educational,' Daddy leapt in, 'because Graham will learn so much more about animals this way, I bet this sends him straight to the library.' Mummy said, 'I wonder if he'll howl at the moon!' and Daddy said, 'well, of course he'll howl at the moon,' and Granny said, 'all wolves howl at the moon, even I know that,' and Mummy looked crestfallen. 'Silly Mummy,' growled Graham.

From the first rip of the pink wrapping paper Sarah could see that she hadn't been given a vampire suit. But she hoped it wasn't a zombie, even when she could see the sickly green of the mask, the bloated liver spots, the word 'Zombie!' far too proudly emblazoned upon the box. She thought it must be a mistake. And was about to say something, but when she looked up at her parents she saw they were beaming at her, encouraging, urging her on, urging her to open the lid, urging her to become one of the undead. So she smiled back, and she remembered not to make a fuss, that it was Granny's day – and hoped they'd kept the receipt so she could swap it for a vampire later. Daddy asked if he could give her a hand, and Sarah said she could manage, but he was helping her already, he'd already got out the zombie mask, he was already enveloping her whole face in it. He helped her with the zombie slippers, thick slabs of feet with overgrown toenails and peeling skin. He helped her with the suit, snapped the buckle. Sarah felt cold all around her, as if she'd just been dipped into a swimming pool – but it was dry inside this pool, as dry as dust, and the cold dry dust was inside her. And the surprise of it made her want to retch, but she caught herself, she swallowed it down, though there was no saliva in that swallow. Her face slumped, and bulged out a bit, like a huge spot just ready to be burst – and she felt heavier, like a sack, sodden – but sodden with what, there was no water, was there, no wetness at all, so what could she be sodden with? 'Turn around!' said Daddy, and laughed, and she heard him with dead ears, and so she turned around, she lurched, the feet wouldn't let her walk properly, the body felt weighed down in all the wrong areas. Daddy laughed again, they all laughed at that, and Sarah tried to laugh too. She stuck out her arms in comic zombie fashion. 'Grr,' she said. Daddy's face was shining, Mummy looked just a little afraid. Granny was staring, she couldn't take her eyes off her. 'Incredible,' she breathed. And then she smiled, no, it wasn't a smile, she *grinned*. 'Incredible.' Graham had got bored watching, and had gone back to doing whatever it was that werewolves do around Christmas trees.

'And after all that excitement, roast turkey, with all the trimmings!' said Mummy. Sarah's stomach growled, though she hadn't known she was hungry. 'Come on, children, toys away.' 'I think Sarah should wear her suit to dinner,' said Granny. 'I agree,' said Daddy, 'she's only just put it on.' 'All right,' said Mummy. 'Have it your own way. But not you, Graham. I don't want a werewolf at the dining table. I want my little boy.' 'That's not fair!' screamed Graham. 'But werewolves don't have good table manners, darling,' said Mummy. 'You'll get turkey everywhere.' So Graham began to cry, and it came out as a particularly plaintive howl, and he wouldn't take his werewolf off, he *wouldn't*, he wanted to live in his werewolf forever, and Mummy gave him a slap, just a little one, and it only made him howl all the more. 'For God's sake, does it matter?' said Daddy, 'let him be a werewolf if he wants to.' 'Fine,' said Mummy, 'they can be monsters then, let's *all* be monsters!' And then she smiled to show everyone she was happy really, she only sounded angry, really she was happy. Mummy scraped Graham's Christmas dinner into a bowl, and set it on to the floor. 'Try and be careful, darling,' she said, 'remember how hard we worked to get this carpet clean? You'll sit at the table, won't you, Sarah? I don't know much about zombies, do zombies eat at the table?' 'Sarah's sitting next to me,' said Granny, and she grinned again, and her whole face lit up, she really had quite a nice face after all. And everyone cheered up at that, and it was a happy dinner, even though Granny didn't think the turkey was the best cut, and that the vegetables had been overcooked. Sarah coated her turkey with gravy, and with cranberry sauce, she even crushed then smeared peas into it just to give the meat a bit more juice – it was light and buttery, she knew, it looked so good on the fork, but no sooner had it passed her lips than the food seemed stale and ashen. 'Would you pull my cracker, Sarah?' asked Granny brightly, and Sarah didn't want to, it was hard enough to grip the cutlery with those flaking hands. 'Come on, Sarah,' laughed Daddy, and so Sarah put down her knife and fork, and fumbled for the end of Granny's cracker, and hoped that when she pulled nothing terrible would happen – she'd got it into her head that her arm was hanging by a thread, just one firm yank and it'd come off. But it didn't – bang! went the cracker, Granny had won, she liked that, and she read out the joke, and everyone said they found it funny, and she even put on her paper hat. 'I feel like the belle of the ball!' she said. 'Dear me, I *am* enjoying myself!'

After dinner Granny and Sarah settled down on the sofa to watch the Bond movie. Mummy said she'd do the washing up, and she needed to clean the carpet too, she might be quite a while. And Daddy volunteered to help her, he said he'd seen this Bond already. Graham wanted to pee, so they'd let him out into the garden. So it was just Granny and Sarah sitting there, just the two of them, together. 'I miss Arthur,' Granny said during the title sequence. 'Sonia tells me I need to get over it, but what does Sonia know about love?' Sarah had nothing to say to that. Sitting on the sofa was hard for her, she was top heavy and lolled to one side. She found though that she was able to reach for the buckle on her suit. She played with it, but her fingers were too thick, she couldn't get purchase. The first time Bond snogged a woman Granny reached for Sarah's hand. Sarah couldn't be sure whether it was Granny's hand or her own that felt so leathery. 'Do you know how I met Arthur?' asked Granny. Sitting in her slumped position, Sarah could feel something metal jab into her, and realised it must be the necklace that Mummy had given her. It was buried somewhere underneath all this dead male flesh. 'Arthur was already married. Did you know that? Does it shock you? But I just looked at him, and said to myself, I'm having that.' And there was a funny smell too, thought Sarah, and she supposed that probably *was* her. James Bond got himself into some scrapes, and then got out of them again using quips and extreme violence. Granny hadn't let go of Sarah's hand. 'You know what love is? It's being prepared to let go of who you are. To change yourself entirely. Just for someone else's pleasure.' The necklace was really rather sharp, but Sarah didn't mind, it felt *real*, and she tried to shift her body so it would cut into her all the more. Perhaps it would cut through the layers of skin on top of it, perhaps it would come poking out, and show that Sarah was hiding underneath! 'Before I met him, Arthur was a husband. And a father. For me, he became a nothing. A nothing.' With her free hand Sarah tried at the buckle again, this time there was a panic to it, she dug in her nails but only succeeded in tearing a couple off altogether. And she knew what that smell was, Sarah had thought it had been rotting, but it wasn't, it was old cigarette smoke. Daddy came in from the kitchen. 'You two lovebirds getting along?' he said. And maybe even winked. James Bond made a joke about re-entry, and at that Granny gripped Sarah's hand so tightly that she thought it'd leave an imprint for sure. 'I usually get what I want,' Granny breathed. Sarah stole a look out of the window. In the frosted garden Graham had clubbed down a bird, and was now playing with its body. He'd throw it up into the air and catch it between his teeth. But he looked undecided too, as if he were wondering whether eating it might be taking things too far.

Graham had tired of the werewolf suit before his bedtime. He'd undone the belt all by himself, and left the suit in a pile on the floor. 'I want a vampire!' he said. 'Or a zombie!' Mummy and Daddy told him that maybe he could have another monster next Christmas, or on his birthday maybe. That wasn't good enough, and it wasn't until they suggested there might be discounted monsters in the January sales that he cheered up. He could be patient, he was a big boy. After he'd gone to bed, Granny said she wanted to turn in as well – it had been such a long day. 'And thank you,' she said, and looked at Sarah. 'It's remarkable.' Daddy said that she'd now understand why he'd asked for all those photographs; to get the resemblance just right there had been lots of special modifications, it hadn't been cheap, but he hoped it was a nice present? 'The best I've ever had,' said Granny. 'And here's a little something for both of you.' And she took out a cheque, scribbled a few zeroes on to it, and handed it over. She hoped this might see them through the recession. 'And Merry Christmas!' she said gaily.

Granny stripped naked, and got into her nightie – but not so fast that Sarah wasn't able to take a good look at the full reality of her. She didn't think Granny's skin was very much different to the one she was wearing, the same lumps and bumps and peculiar crevasses, the same scratch marks and mottled specks. Hers was just slightly fresher. And as if Granny could read Sarah's mind, she told her to be a good boy and sit at the dressing table. 'Just a little touch up,' she said. 'Nothing effeminate about it. Just to make you a little more alive. A little more you.' She smeared a little rouge on to the cheeks, a dash of lipstick, mascara. 'Can't do much with the eyeballs,' Granny mused, 'but I'll never know in the dark.' And the preparations weren't just for Sarah. Granny sprayed behind both her ears from her new perfume bottle. 'Just for you, darling,' she said. 'Your beautiful little gift.' Sarah gestured towards the door, and Granny looked puzzled, then brightened. 'Yes, you go and take a tinkle. I'll be waiting, my sweet.' But Sarah had nothing to tinkle, had she, didn't Granny realise there was no liquid inside her, didn't she realise she was composed of dust? Sarah lurched past the toilet, and downstairs to the sitting room where her parents were watching the repeat of the Queen's speech. They started when she came in. Both looked a little guilty. Sarah tried to find the words she wanted, and then how to say them at all, her tongue lay cold in her mouth. 'Why me?' she managed finally.

Daddy said, 'I loved him. He was a good man, he was a kind man.' Mummy looked away altogether. Daddy went on, 'You do see why it couldn't have been Graham, don't you? Why it had to be you?' And had Sarah been a werewolf like her brother, she might at that moment have torn out their throats, or clubbed them down with her paws. But she was a dead man, and a dead man who'd been good and kind. So she nodded briefly, then shuffled her way slowly back upstairs.

'Hold me,' said Granny. Sarah didn't know how to, didn't know where to put her arms or her legs. She tried her best, but it was all such a tangle. Granny and Sarah lay side by side for a long time in the dark. Sarah tried to feel the necklace under her skin, but she couldn't, it had gone. That little symbol of whatever femininity she'd had was gone. She wondered if Granny was asleep. But then Granny said, 'If only it were real. But it's not real. You're not real.' She stroked Sarah's face. 'Oh, my love,' she whispered. 'Oh, my poor dead love.'

And something between Sarah's legs twitched. Something that had long rotted came to life, and slowly, weakly, struggled to attention. You're not real, Granny was still saying, and now she was crying, and Sarah thought of how Granny had looked that day at the funeral, her face all soggy and out of shape, and she felt a stab of pity for her – and that was *it*, the pity was the jolt it needed, there was something liquid in this body after all. 'You're not real,' Granny said. 'I am real,' he said, and he lent across, and kissed her on the lips. And the lips beneath his weren't dry, they were plump, they were moist, and now he was chewing at her face, and she was chewing right back, like they wanted to eat each other, like they were so hungry they could just eat each other alive. Sharon Weekes was wrong, it was a stray thought that flashed through his mind, Sharon Weekes didn't know the half of it. This is what it's like, this is like kissing, this is like kissing a boy.

1901 – Alzheimer's disease is identified for the first time, by German psychiatrist Alois Alzheimer. He doesn't cure it, though. Note that. He doesn't cure it. Well done on finding it, Doc, but you know, isn't there something you've forgotten? Don't you think you left the job half done? And for this he gets his name on the lips of every fearful patient waiting for test results back in every hospital waiting room: 'But what if it's... might I have... oh no, God, no, please, God, don't let it be...' Sitting in your brain like a parasite and eating up all your history. When someone cures it, when someone rids the world of it, then, then, they should rename the disease, give the one who saved us a bit of fame instead. But by then, of course, no-one will care. *If the entire history of the universe could be squeezed into a single year, measuring 365 days, then the Earth wouldn't even be formed until some time mid-September, and the first human wouldn't have walked the planet until the afternoon of New Year's Eve. Jesus Christ would have been crucified ten seconds before midnight. These last 2,000 years, the entire length of this time chart, all the disasters and treacheries and violence herein, take place within that ten second blip. All those ADs. So don't thank me all at once. Don't thank me for recreating the last two millennia, because it's really such a little thing, a tiny thing All those ADs. My Annie, all those Annie Dominis.* **1901** – William McKinley is the third US president to be assassinated. He is shot twice; the first bullet is easily removed, but the doctors can't find the second bullet and leave it where it is, fearing the harm invasive surgery might do. Ironically, the hospital has access to a new x-ray machine, one that might save McKinley's life – but the staff are afraid to use it, still uncertain what side effects it might cause. **1903** – Cuba leases Guantanamo Bay to the USA in perpetuity. **1904** – The Dogger Bank Incident: the Russian fleet sink a British trawler in the North Sea, mistaking it for a Japanese torpedo boat. **1905** – Albert Einstein publishes his paper on the special theory of relativity. Einstein will campaign in his later life for nuclear disarmament, but it is the equation $e = mc^2$ that is a crucial step in the development of nuclear weapons. **1905** – Wolves become extinct in Japan. **1907** – The Romanian Peasants' Revolt is suppressed; 11,000 men are killed. **1908** – Nearly 1,000 square miles of forest in the Siberian region of Tunguska is destroyed in a massive explosion, probably caused by an asteroid or comet. **1908** – King Carlos I of Portugal is shot dead travelling through Lisbon in an open carriage. He is with his two sons; the heir, Luis Filipe, automatically succeeds him, but dies of injuries twenty minutes later. The younger son, Manuel, is shot only in the arm. He will be Portugal's final monarch. *What, then, is this book? A bunch of disparate short stories, connected by a loose and baggy theme? A thousand and one sick jokes, all in want of a decent punchline? Because now it's spread out all before me, and don't let this be History, please don't call this History. History cannot be as trivial as this, please, no, History has to be about the ascent of Man, about the triumph of reason, about civilisation, progress, redemption – not this, this, a collection of failures beating their pathetic fists against the certain knowledge that their lives will be so very brief and they will accomplish so very little.* **1908** – The Young Turk Revolution forces Sultan Abdul Hamid II to restore a more constitutional government within the Ottoman Empire. A year later he is deposed in favour of his brother. **1908** – Abdelaziz, sultan of Morocco, is deposed in a rebellion, in favour of his brother. **1909** – Mohammed Ali Shah, shah of Persia, is deposed in a revolution, in favour of his son. *Do you know what – I think it's family. That's what this book is about. If you accept the hypothesis that we all share ancestry with Charlemagne, then the whole array of world history is really just a series of family squabbles. And even if you don't – it's still a story of betrayal – of parents betraying their children (Ivan the Terrible, qv 1581, Empress Irene, qv 797, Don Carlos, qv 1560, Peter the Great, qv 1718, Frederick William, qv 1730, 'I can always make more!', qv 1488), of children in turn betraying their parents (qv 509, qv 547, qv 604, qv 810, qv 944, qv 1330, qv 1373, qv 1488, qv 1706). And it makes perfect sense, of course history does that, because parents are the past, and children are the future, the two are incompatible, one would always destroy the other. The past arrogantly vast and unchanging, the future just as arrogant in its belief that everything is up for grabs. And I have betrayed my child too, and she betrayed me. I betrayed the future while she betrayed the past, but what choice did either of us have? Tell me. When it came to it, I had either to embrace her future, a future I could never be a part of, a future that by definition would go on past my ceasing to be – or defend a past that she was erasing, and I am part of that past, and so are you, we can't help it, the past is within us, I only exist in the past, as every second ticks by I am just so stuffed to bursting with it.* **1909** – Joan of Arc is beatified in Rome (qv 1431). **1910** – The Portuguese monarchy is overthrown. **1910** – Boutros Ghali, the first native Egyptian to be prime minister, is assassinated. **1910** – In a heavyweight boxing match, James L Jeffries is defeated by his African American opponent, Jack Johnson; race riots break out across the country. **1910** – A craze for marmot hunting, to satisfy the demands of Parisian fashion, causes an outbreak of bubonic plague in China that kills more than 50,000 people. **1912** – Lawrence Oates steps from his tent and tells his companions on Scott's expedition to the South Pole that he may be some time. Liar. Do you know, I don't think he intended to return at all. **1912** – The Titanic sinks. **1912** – The prime minister of Spain, Jose Canalejas, is assassinated. **1913** – Emperor Menelik II of Ethiopia becomes convinced he can stave off death by eating the Bible. He dies of a stroke while chewing over the Book of Kings. **1913** – The president of Mexico, Francisco Madero, is assassinated. **1913** – The president of El Salvador, Manuel Enrique Araujo, is assassinated. **1913** – The King of Greece, George I, is assassinated. **1914** – The Archduke of Austria-Hungary, Franz Ferdinand, is assassinated. At last, finally, this is one that causes a world war. *My time chart suggests that the world is ugly, that man is shallow, that everything decays into dust. And yet. And yet. Every day I see husbands who delight in their wives, and wives who cling on tight to their husbands– in spite of all the historical precedents otherwise (qv 963, 1034, 1193, 1327, 1536) – I see them, they walk arm in arm, they talk, they laugh, they even kiss in public with no ceremony and no shame. They love each other, and the evidence of that love is there for all to see. And they have parents too, and they love them, they have children, and love them – I look out of the bloody window and see nothing but love everywhere, and then I look back down at my time chart and it's nowhere to be seen! – what's happened to it, history, that's what – history sweeps lovers aside and judges them an irrelevance. You'd barely believe people are capable of love at all. They wouldn't have time for it, not amidst all the assassinations and excommunications, all the savagery. So, what are they, all these people, all of these people – are they just anomalies? Billions upon billions of footnotes, not worthy of being featured in the main text? How can we take any part of history seriously if it doesn't reflect them, if it insists upon looking in the wrong direction so cynically? – Because – I can say it now – I loved my mother – who was always kind, who loved me regardless – I loved my wife – who knew me as a child, and then knew me as a man, and somehow reconciled the two – I loved my daughter – oh God – oh God – I loved my daughter – I loved her – and when I think of her my heart burns, and I know who I am I've discovered myself the historian is gone the man stands in his place – I am son, and husband, and Dearly Devoted Daddy – oh God – oh God* **1914** – And the assassination of Franz Ferdinand should really never have happened, it's botched from the start. The plan to blow his car up as he makes for a reception in the town hall is foiled; one of the students is too scared to throw a bomb, a second misjudges his aim and blows up the car behind instead. Franz Ferdinand goes on to attend his meeting as planned. It is only as he is being driven away hours later, and by a new route, that he passes Gavrilo Princip, another of the students, who is consoling himself for the failure of his friends' mission with a sandwich. He is amazed to see the Archduke there so suddenly, seizes his chance, runs forward, and shoots him and his wife dead. **1915** – The Turks launch a campaign of genocide against the Armenians, and kill one and a half million of them over the course of the First World War. **1916** – More than one million soldiers die in the battle of the Somme, which includes 60,000 British casualties on the first day alone. After four months of fighting, the Allies have only driven Germany back seven miles. **1916** – In New York, Emma Goldman is arrested for lecturing about birth control. **1916** – Iyasu V, emperor of Ethiopia, is deposed in a palace coup, in favour of his aunt. **1916** – Yuan Shikai, emperor of China, is deposed in a revolution, and replaced with a republic. **1917** – As the First World War wears on, the royal family of Great Britain change their surname to Windsor to disguise their German origins. **1917** – Nicholas II, tsar of Russia, is deposed in a revolution, and replaced with a republic. **1918** – Germany signs an armistice with the Allies; the First World War is over. The Austro-Hungarian empire collapses. **1918** – A Spanish flu epidemic breaks out in China, and quickly spreads through Asia, Europe, and the Americas. Within a few months over twenty million people are killed, making the casualty figures for the entire First World War look like some bagatelle. **1919** – The Treaty of Versailles is signed, and calls for such harsh reparations against the Germans that in retrospect a second world war seems inevitable. **1919** – In Milan, Benito Mussolini founds his Fascist movement. **1920** – Adolf Hitler presents his theories of National Socialism in Munich. **1920** – In France, Georges Clemenceau, the prime minister, is defeated in election because it is thought the Treaty of Versailles was too lenient. **1920** – King Alexander II of Greece is killed by his two pet monkeys. **1922** – The Ottoman Empire is abolished. **1923** – France and Belgium demand their reparation payments from Germany, and occupy the Ruhr area to force the issue. **1926** – The escapologist Harry Houdini dies from a punch in the gut. **1926** – Revolutionaries in Portugal establish a National Dictatorship. **1929** – The economy of the Western world is devastated in the Wall Street Crash; over $8.5 million dollars is out on loan, which is a higher sum than all the money in circulation in America at the time. The Great Depression of poverty and joblessness that follows dominates the US and Europe for the next decade. **1929** – Josef Stalin, the General Secretary of the Communist Party of the Soviet Union, unveils his Five Year Plan of economic development, designed to surpass the ailing West in a single jump. **1930** – One of the victims of the new Stalinist repression is the poet Vladimir Mayakovsky, who shoots himself. His suicide note advises, 'I do not recommend it for others.' **1931** – The Huang He floods in China are the deadliest natural disaster in history, killing anywhere between one and four million people, and leaving countless more millions homeless. **1932** – Adolf Hitler at last obtains German citizenship, which allows him to run for president. **1933** – Hitler is appointed Chancellor of Germany in February. A few weeks later he burns down the Reichstag – and, the very next day, passes laws in response which nullify civil liberties. The Jews are blamed (qv 64). **1933** – In March, the very first Nazi concentration camp at Dachau opens, brand spanking new and ready for business. **1935** – Italy invades Ethiopia. Emperor Haile Selassie mobilises his entire population on pain of death, excusing only the blind, the lame, and the infants. They are all beaten into submission regardless. **1935** – Elvis Presley is born; the board game Monopoly is released by Parker Brothers; Porky Pig makes his Looney Tunes debut in 'I Haven't Got a Hat'; Hitler begins the rearmament of Germany in defiance of the Treaty of Versailles. **1936** – Stalin intensifies his campaign of repression and persecution of political opponents and undesirables in the Soviet Union. The Great Purge is directed against peasants and intelligentsia, those instrumental in the early days of Communism and those suspected of any capitalist sympathies. Men are arrested for being the first to sit down and stop clapping in audiences giving the mention of Stalin's name a ten minute standing ovation. Over 700,000 people are executed or sent to the gulags. And he begins a procedure of mass deportation and population restructuring to change the ethnic make-up of the Soviet Union, with over three million expelled from their homes. **1938** – Nazi SS leader Heinrich Himmler sends an expedition to Tibet to find evidence of a species of subterranean supermen from which the Aryans are descended; in America, Superman makes his first comic book appearance. **1938** – Ronald Reagan's application to the Communist Party is turned down because he's thought to be too dim. **1939** – King Ghazi of Iraq is killed in a car accident. Conspiracy theorists spread the rumour that the British Government is responsible for his death (qv 1997). **1939** – The creation of Rudolph the Red Nosed Reindeer, in a poem given out to children in department stores. The story tells of a Germanic beast ostracised by others of his kind, who yet becomes their hero when he demonstrates that with special powers in a single night he can take on the entire world. And Hitler invades Poland. World War II breaks out. *The old man comes back to me – in a dream, or not, I don't know. With his cardigan and his flat cap. And he still smells so stale, and there are still worms where his fingers should be – but I see now his smile is worms too, it was always worms, he doesn't speak to me through leering lips but through worms. 'Any regrets?' he says.* **1945** – Karl Donitz succeeds Adolf Hitler as the president of the Third Reich. As job promotions go, it's something of a poisoned chalice. **1945** – The US Secretary of War vetoes the choice of Kyoto as the target for the first atomic bomb, as he's spent his honeymoon there. So the bomb is dropped on Hiroshima and Nagasaki instead. Japan sues for peace. **1946** – World War II is over. The Chinese return to a state of civil war, King Rama of Siam is assassinated, there's a civil war outbreak in Greece, and the bombardment of Haiphong signals the start of the French Indochina War. Business as usual, then. **1947** – India at last wins its independence. A year later, Gandhi is assassinated. **1948** – The foreign minister of Czechoslovakia, Jan Masaryk, is found dead on the pavement underneath his bathroom window. It is generally believed he was the victim of a Third Defenestration of Prague (qv 1419, 1618). **1952** – In Kenya, the Mau Mau try to expel British settlers with acts of terrorism. Their insurgency will last four years, and claim some 13,000 lives. **1952** – In London, 4,000 people die from a strange poisonous smog in the winter air. **1953** – Robert Oppenheimer, who directed the atomic bomb project against Japan, falls victim to the Communist witch trials instigated by Joseph McCarthy. His opposition to the construction of a hydrogen bomb is seen as evidence that he is a Communist sympathiser, and he has his security clearance revoked. **1954** – The fifteen megaton hydrogen bomb Castle Bravo causes one of the worst ever radioactive contaminations ever when tested in the Pacific Ocean. It is set off at Bikini Atoll; the name is appealing, and is used to describe the new range of women's swimwear launched later that year. **1955** – Albert Einstein dies; his last words are in German, and are lost to us, because the nurse in attendance can't understand the language. **1956** – Stalin has been dead three years; only now does his successor, Nikita Kruschev, feel safe enough to denounce the tyrant to the Soviet Communist Party congress. The shock is nevertheless too much for his audience – some suffer heart attacks on the spot, others go home to commit suicide. **1956** – Francois Duvalier is elected president of Haiti. Known affectionately as 'Papa Doc', for his background in medical science, he declares the state religion to be voodoo, and tyrannises his country through using the machine gun activities of a police force he claims are living skeletons raised from the dead. **1957** – Mao Tse Tung, chairman of the Communist Party in China, admits that some 800,000 'class enemies' have been murdered so far during his rule. **1958** – Pope Pius XII declares Saint Clare the patron saint of television. This is on the basis that when she was unable to attend mass because of illness, at the mid-point of the thirteenth century, she was still able to watch it on the wall of her room. **1958** – The United States Air Force loses a 7600 pound hydrogen bomb in the waters off Tybee Island in Georgia. Attempts to recover it fail. It's still there, you know. **1958** – The first of several Cod Wars break out between Britain and Iceland over fishing territories in the North Atlantic. **1958** – The Iraqi monarchy is overthrown and executed in a revolution. **1961** – The USA attempt to overthrow the Communist government of Fidel Castro in Cuba by invading at the Bay of Pigs. They are beaten back within two days. **1961** – Gene Deitch revives the Tom and Jerry cartoon franchise, and, quite frankly, makes it rubbish. If you ever catch a Tom and Jerry episode on television, and the colours look cheap and nasty, and the characters have no charm, that's a Deitch. **1963** – President John F Kennedy is assassinated. **1965** – Pope Paul VI decrees that the Jews are, after all, not collectively responsible for the killing of Jesus Christ. **1969** – War breaks out between El Salvador and Honduras when the former beats the latter at football in a World Cup qualifying round. During the opening ceremony before the game, the Honduran flag is replaced with a dirty dish rag; in the growing hostility between the two countries Honduras is invaded, and 6,000 people are killed or wounded before a ceasefire is declared a week later. **1970** – Apollo 13 fails to land on the Moon. It does bring its astronauts safely home, mind you. NASA declare the mission a 'successful failure'. **1971** – Following a military coup, Idi Amin becomes president of Uganda. During his eight years of rule he will be responsible for the systematic murder of half a million of his people. **1972** – The Oxford English Dictionary adds the word 'fuck' to its new edition. **1974** – Ned Maddrell, last native speaker of the Manx Gaelic language, dies. **1975** – Pol Pot becomes prime minister of Democratic Kampuchea. As leader of the Communist Khmer Rouge party, his regime is responsible for the extermination of three million of his people. **1975** – King Faisal of Saudi Arabia is shot dead by his own nephew. Though the murderer is a prince, and declared officially insane, he is publicly beheaded. **1975** – The Vietnam War, which has been raging for nearly twenty years finally ends as the Communist forces take Saigon. It is one of the most humiliating defeats in American history. **1977** – Jean-Bedel Bokassa, president of the Central African Republic, declares himself emperor instead, and throws himself a coronation designed to emulate Napoleon's (qv 1804, and by extension, 800). It costs $20 million, a whole third of the country's budget. **1977** – Hamida Djandoubi is the last person to be executed by guillotine in France. **1981** – The president of Egypt, Anwar Sadat, is assassinated by his own troops as he watches them on parade. **1981** – The president of Bangladesh, Ziaur Rahman, is assassinated by his own army officers. **1981** – The president of the United States, Ronald Reagan, survives his assassination attempt. **1981** – A new disease to the West, already common in Africa, is named AIDS. It is mistakenly believed that it only targets gays, and religious groups see it as God's punishment against homosexuality. All about there is prejudice, and there is ignorance, and there is on harsh display the dehumanising effect of mortal fear. **1982** – During the Falklands War against Argentina, the British sink the cruiser 'General Belgrano'. It causes controversy, as all footage clearly shows that the ship was retreating at the time. The loss of 323 lives amount to over half of the Argentinian fatalities during the entire war. **1983** – Reagan describes the USSR as an 'evil empire'. The Soviets believe that this gung-ho actor with his movie rhetoric may well be preparing for war. And the world gets just that bit more paranoid, and the prospect of nuclear armageddon seems that bit more likely. **1986** – Challenger. **1986** – Chernobyl. **1986** – Chris de Burgh. **1986** – Emperor Bokassa is arrested by the Central African authorities, and tried for treason, murder, cannibalism and embezzlement. He is acquitted of the cannibalism. **1987** – Robert Mugabe declares himself president of Zimbabwe, abolishing his former position of prime minister and giving himself new powers in the process. **1987** – The US frigate Stark is destroyed by Iraqi missiles. Saddam Hussein, Iraq's president, apologises for the mistake. **1987** – Prozac is released on the market. **1988** – In Romania, Ceausescu's urban housing reforms destroy 8,000 villages. **1990** – McDonalds builds a restaurant in Moscow's Red Square. **1991** – Furious at the concessions made to the West by president Mikhail Gorbachev, a group of Soviet hardliners stage a coup in a last ditch attempt to save communism and save Russia. It fails. **1992** – Pope John Paul II issues an apology to Galileo Galilei for his treatment at the hands of the Inquisition (qv 1633). **1995** – Mississippi is the last US state to approve the abolition of slavery. **1996** – An army of Islamic fundamentalist students called the Taliban depose and execute the Communist president of Afghanistan. **1997** – Diana, Princess of Wales, is killed in a car crash. Conspiracy theorists spread the rumour that the British Government is responsible for her death (qv 1939). **1999** – The United Nations designates 1999 as the International Year of Older Persons. They just want to honour all those people who have lived through history, who have got right up close and personal, who have rubbed their noses hard against it and survived the experience. Isn't that sweet? *I have saved the past. I can still save the future. I'll set her free. I'll unlock her bedroom door. I'll even leave the door ajar, so she can see it's been opened, so she can come out in her own good time. I'll give my daughter the means of escape, I'll give the whole of future time the same means of escape. And then I'll go. I'll take nothing with me. I'll leave behind this time chart, it's for you, because I've lived it now, and what's past is past, right? I feel time passing all around me. History, the old dry bastard, it doesn't stop, it won't stop. I'll go upstairs. I'll unlock the door. I'm coming, Annie, I'm coming. Hear me, hear my footsteps on the stairs, can't you hear how eager they are, and how sorry? Hear me come to rescue you.*

A HISTORY OF BROKEN THINGS

All right, true story. Except for the bits that aren't.

*

Once upon a time, long ago and far away, there lived a king. This king was very powerful, and very ferocious, and all his subjects were very scared of him. The subjects only existed to perform his slightest bidding. The king would say, 'Do this!' and, right away, it was done; 'I want this!' he'd cry, and snap his fingers – snap! – and before the snap had finished echoing around the palace, what he wanted would be there at his feet. He really was a very lucky king.

And what the king wanted most was to fight with all the other kings. The country he ruled was big already – so big that it would have taken weeks to walk from one side to the other, so big, in fact, that the king had never even done this. But, still, he wanted it to be bigger. And what he wanted, he got. He went to war, and that was fun for a while. And the other kings thought he was powerful and ferocious too, and quite a few of them were as scared of him as were his own subjects.

But still the king wasn't happy. So one day he summoned to his palace the two best shipwrights he could find. They were brothers. 'I want you to build me a ship,' said the king. 'Yes, sire,' said the shipwrights, not much surprised because, after all, building ships was what they did. 'But this will be no ordinary ship,' said the king. 'I want my ship to be the biggest ship the world has ever seen. I want it to have lots of guns, all over it, so I can shoot at the ships of other kings! And I want it covered with sculptures, a hundred sculptures, of mermaids, and lions, and sea monsters, so that when all the other kings see me coming they'll be even more scared of me than they were to begin with.' The two shipwrights exchanged glances. 'Very well,' they said. The king snapped his fingers. 'Well, get to it, then!' he said. 'Chop chop!'

The two brothers set to work. The country didn't have enough cloth for the sails, so they had to order cloth from France, from Germany, from the Netherlands. It didn't have enough hemp for the rigging, so they had to order hemp from Latvia. They set armourers to work on the great cannons, and teams of artists to start sculpting. Once in a while the king would send a letter. 'Where's my ship?' he would ask. But it was such a *big* ship, this new ship of his, it'd take time to build.

And as time went on, and the king grew more impatient, he kept demanding that the ship be made ever bigger. 'I need the keel to be larger!' he decided one day. The brothers pointed out that the timber had already been cut for the keel, to change that would delay them further, but the king was adamant. 'There's only one gun deck, now I want two!' The brothers realised this would make the ship top heavy, but they knew the king wouldn't care. 'I want more sculptures, a hundred's not enough, I want *five* hundred, come on, some really *huge* ones!' The sculptures weighed so much the brothers thought they'd make the ship sink.

But the king was the king. And what the king wanted, he got.

One of the brothers died. The king told the other brother he now had to work all the faster. 'I want to put my ship to sea!' he said. 'A ship's no good sitting in a shipyard. I want it out on the waves, and fighting!' The ship looked *odd* – it bulged every which way with all the king's improvements, it listed to the side. But the king insisted, and so, one day, the ship was readied for departure. The day was calm. There was only a light breeze. The ship was towed into position at the harbour, its sails were raised, its gun ports opened to fire a triumphant salute. Thousands of the king's subjects stood to watch as the big new toy began its maiden voyage across the seas. And not just the king's subjects were there, but spies for the other kings; they'd all heard tell about the ship, and they wanted to see it for themselves in jealous awe. And the ship was away! Everybody cheered! Even the spies!

And it rode the waves, the waves had never known anything like it, they'd never carried anything this heavy before, the ship crushed the waves beneath it, the ship was massive, it wasn't just a plaything of a king, it was a king in its own right! The ship rode the waves for *minutes*. And then there was a gust of wind – oh, hardly even a gust, a puff. And the ship tipped suddenly to port. The crew struggled to cast the sheets off, they all had to rush starboard to steady it. The ship righted itself. All was not lost. Until there came a second puff of wind, no greater than the first puff, and the ship tipped to port again – and this time there was no stopping it, not for the weight of the cannons, not for the weight of its sculptures of mermaids and lions and sea monsters. The water flooded in through the lower gun ports, and the ship fell over, plop! on to its side, and then sank, sank to the bottom of the sea.

The king was very angry. This wasn't what he wanted at all! He looked around for someone to blame. But the surviving members of the crew said they weren't to blame, they'd only been following orders. And the surviving shipwright said he wasn't to blame, he'd been following orders too. (Following *whose* orders? Can *you* tell who was to blame?) And so the king harrumphed, and said it was clear to him who was to blame. No-one was to blame, it couldn't be helped, it was an act of God. No more need be said about it, everyone was pardoned – except for those who'd drowned, of course. And the king stayed ferocious for the rest of his days, he continued to fight the other kings and to snap his fingers – but he'd learned his lesson, and he never again tried to build the biggest ship the world had ever seen.

*

What is the moral of this fairy tale?

There's an explicit criticism of the king, of course, and his spoiled brat arrogance, and his insistence that he can rule the waves (and defy the laws of physics into the bargain). So maybe the moral is, when you're king, don't act like a prick. But not many of us get to be kings. It's not, then, a very useful moral. But is there not also a criticism of his subjects here? That *really* at fault were those who knew what they were doing was wrong, but never found the courage to say no. 'We were just following orders,' – it's not much of an excuse. And doesn't it especially leave a bad taste in the mouth with that phrase's modern day connotations, in the wake of the holocaust and ethnic cleansing?

Maybe the king was just teaching his subjects a lesson. He was playing devil's advocate, and showing them the dangers of blind obedience. And we're reminded, aren't we, of the story of King Canute? And how he exposed the sycophancy of his courtiers who believed that as an all-powerful monarch he could stop the waves by will alone. He plonked his throne in the sand, ordered the waves to stop dead, and instead got his feet wet – all to demonstrate that he was just a man after all. And, ironically, in wanting to humble himself, our fairy tale then reinstates The King as authority figure, and the one dispensing moral judgements. We must respect our leaders, but never put them on pedestals so high that we don't take responsibility for our actions.

Or maybe not. I don't know. Maybe the king is just a prick, after all. I'm confused.

Sometimes it's hard to discern what moral we're supposed to take from a fairy tale. It's even harder with history. History has no morals. History is just a bunch of people with complex and contradictory agendas colliding with a bunch of other people of similarly complex but just as frustratingly contradictory agendas. It's just chaos out there. Turn on the news, read the papers – shit, just look out of the window. Really, chaos. That's what I think, anyway. That's what I think sometimes.

Because what happened to the ship isn't a fairy tale. It's a piece of Swedish history. In 1625 King Gustavus Adolphus commissioned from brother shipwrights Henrik Hybertsson and Arendt Hybertsson de Groote the construction of the *Vasa*, intended to be the largest warship ever built. It sank less than one nautical mile out on its maiden voyage, felled by a light breeze. The constant adjustments that King Gustavus made to the design, to make it ever bigger and more opulent, were almost certainly what made it so unseaworthy.

It strikes me how similar the story of the *Vasa* is to the story of the *Titanic*. Two ships that were built as acts of hubris, invincible, unsinkable. And yet I find the fate of the *Vasa* rather comic, and the *Titanic*'s not. Maybe it's because I can picture my own grandfather aboard the *Titanic*, alongside all those noble passengers with stiff upper lips, drowning so stoically with British Empire reserve. (My grandfather wasn't on board the *Titanic*, actually, but he was old enough, he'd have been five.) Maybe it's because they made a movie out of the *Titanic*, and they never made one out of *Vasa*. Maybe I just find seventeenth century Swedes too alien to sympathise with. I can't speak Swedish. And even if I could, what would we have in common to talk about anyway?

And if I choose to see history as a fairy tale, if that's the way I want to see it in my head – then who are you to stop me? What's your problem?

*

Not that I've anything against the Swedes. I've only been to Sweden the once, but the people there seemed very nice. They perhaps charged a little too much in restaurants, but the exchange rate was against us, so. Not remotely warlike, I thought, and no more incompetent, either in ship construction or in anything else, than any other nationality.

My now-ex-wife had a friend who was getting married in Sweden, and we were invited, so we flew all the way there. I'd never met this friend of hers. I didn't see why we had to go. My now-ex-wife told me that it'd be exciting to visit Sweden, that it'd be fun.

On the day of the wedding, as my now-ex-wife got changed into her new dress in the hotel bedroom, and I watched her as she fixed her make-up and did her hair and attached all the matching jewellery, and it was so *bloody prim*, I told her I wasn't going to go. 'What?' she said. 'I want to look around Sweden. I don't know Sweden. I don't know your friend. I think, of the two, I'd rather know Sweden, I think, of the two, I'd rather see what Sweden looks like.' She told me it'd be humiliating for her to go to the wedding without me, and I assured her that no-one knew me either, it'd be okay, no-one would care. And I got out of my best suit and back into smart casual, and I set off to explore Stockholm.

In 1961 the *Vasa* was raised from the seabed. And in 1990 an entire museum was opened to house the ship. I went along to see it. It was hugely impressive. You could look at the wreck from viewing galleries at different levels, and boggle at the size of it, and at the audacity of its construction. And its folly too; I mean, I don't know much about ships, but it seemed pretty obvious to me that the thing would fall over the moment you dunked it in water. That's what looks so ridiculous to me about that inquest into the ship's sinking, when it was ruled that no-one was to blame: you take a look at it, so thin and narrow at the bottom, so sprawling and bulky at the top, and you want to cry out to them, 300 years ago, no, don't risk anyone's lives with this! There's no *way* this is ever going to work! Everyone at the harbour that day, all those people cheering and waving the *Vasa* on as it set sail, *everyone* was to blame.

As you approach the museum, you can see how the top of the mast sticks out high through the roof. It's probably deliberate. It was probably designed just that way. But it looks a little like another accident, as if someone built the museum without bothering to measure the ship that was to sit inside it.

That night my now-ex-wife refused to share the room with me, and I was obliged to go down to reception and ask for another. It became an expensive holiday.

*

In 1628, had you asked the average Swede in the street about the sinking of the *Vasa*, they'd have said it was a Bad Thing. The construction of the ship had crippled Sweden's budget, and its loss under the waves – before firing a single cannon, before getting out of sight of shore! – crippled its self-esteem too.

But now the *Vasa* Museum is one of the most successful tourist attractions in the country, and over a million people visit it each year. (The tickets to get in are *very* pricey.) So, one is tempted to say that ultimately the *Vasa* disaster was actually rather good for both Swedish economy and Swedish heritage full stop.

In much the same way, back in 1912, the sinking of the *Titanic* was seen as another Bad Thing. But it spawned the 1997 movie of the same name, and that's grossed nearly two billion dollars at the box office, and has been seen by hundreds of millions of people worldwide. A hundred million people having a good night out in the cinema, versus only the fifteen hundred people who perished when the ship hit the iceberg. That's one drowned frozen casualty to 66,000 happy moviegoers, there's no contest, really, is there? There's no clearer demonstration of dying for the greater good. Surely, one can argue, at last, long term – that the *Titanic* disaster must be seen as something of a triumph?

Surely, with history, it all ends up being a matter of perspective. And every disaster comes good in the end, if you can just wait long enough.

I loved *Titanic*. I knew it wasn't historically accurate, but so what? I rented *Titanic* from the video store thirty-six times. (I counted.) I loved the bit where DiCaprio dies in the Atlantic Ocean, and Kate Winslet watches him sink beneath the surface for the last time, and Celine Dion sings about how her heart will just have to jolly well keep going on. After a while, whenever I rented the movie, it was that bit, and that bit alone, that I'd watch. I'd play the sequence over and over again, and tears would stream down my face. My now-ex-wife refused to watch it with me. 'I can't believe you're putting on that piece of crap again,' she'd say. 'It's not as if you don't know what happens.'

*

The doctor told me that history is what we remember. That we shouldn't struggle too much against the memory loss, that what we lose is simply no longer part of our history, that we don't need it any more.

It's an attractive idea. To take history, the vast unfeeling mass of it, that rolls over us all and crushes us so casually, and somehow get the better of it, somehow be its boss. To tame it, even. But I'm not convinced. 'So, what,' I asked, 'are you saying every single person just has a different history? That there's no such thing as a single history, just six billion little histories all over the place?'

I may have been shouting. I think I was. If I was, the doctor mistook my anger for academic enthusiasm. That happens to me every once in a while.

'Yes,' she cried. 'You've got the idea exactly!'

Hmm.

So I decided, then and there, that if my memory was going to go, then I'd stuff my brain with as much history as could fit. So that there'd be a chance. So that some of it might survive. Not my history, of course. I don't have a history. I don't have a past. You won't hear me talk about my past. That's already gone. Gone the way of the dodo, ha! No, I'd rather hang on to the *Vasa* warship sinking into the Baltic Sea. And Leonardo DiCaprio there, poking his head out of the waves.

*

When I was a little boy, history was easy. It was just a series of fairy tales, with beginnings, middles and ends. English history was a wonderful pageant of princes in the tower, kings with six wives, wars with the French, and Alfred burning the cakes.

Then you grow up, and they start expecting you to put ambiguities in. No, I say. I don't want ambiguities. I can see that if you were living through the events at the time it must have all been a bit complex and confusing, but surely the whole point of history is that from a calm and collected future perspective we can iron all of the bumps out. There should be, I don't know, some sort of moratorium on historical events. Let's call it fifty years, say. And so, fifty years after some bit of history or other, we can look back, say what clearly happened was *this*, and this bit was good, and this bit was bad. We can look back and reach one conclusive consensus. Napoleon, bad. Garibaldi, good. The French Revolution, bad. The American Revolution, good.

I want the fairy tales back. Nice and simple. They're so much easier to remember.

And that's why I go for the wars. Not because I'm especially bloodthirsty (I'm not) but because these are periods in which history sort of settles down a bit and takes clearly differentiated opposing sides. Ambiguity cast away for the time being. And there are goodies and baddies! Goodies (usually) are on the side that wins, baddies (usually) are on the side that loses. History has a very optimistic view of warfare, actually. The heroes of the piece pretty much always come out on top.

And wars are simplest at their beginnings. Whatever the root causes for the conflict, however political and complicated, the spark – the little event that gets both sides to mobilise – is wonderfully and charmingly simple. For example:

(i) 1415 – Henry V revives the Hundred Years' War against the French because he doesn't like a gift of tennis balls;

(ii) 1739 – England fights Spain in the War of Jenkins' Ear because a Spaniard cuts off the ear of some chap called Jenkins;

(iii) 2001 – the Americans declare war on Iraq, because a group of non-Iraqis crash a couple of aeroplanes into the World Trade Center.

As I say, charmingly simple. These are the bits of history that seem small enough so that I can grasp hold of them, squeeze them into my brain, and make them my own. These are the bits of history I can feel some sympathy for.

*

There's a fairy tale version of the story of Henry V, and it's the one I read as a child. It was in a Ladybird book, I think, and I seem to remember it was accompanied by a full-page colour illustration. Rising from the throne there's a king, fresh-faced and handsome. And around him there are courtiers reeling in shock. The king is pointing down the steps to the throne at an ambassador – a swarthy fellow, very tanned, very *foreign*, and the ambassador is backing away from the king's righteous fury, but there's a smirk on his face too, he knows the trouble he's caused. Swarthy and smirky, that's the man in a nutshell. And by the king's feet lies an overturned box, a gift box – and rolling and bouncing down the steps are tennis balls.

So the story goes: once upon a time there was a young and wise king. He was England's finest. You could have carved him up, and you'd have found the word 'England' running through him like a stick of rock. And one day the king of France sent him a present. The king of England opened it. It was a box of tennis balls. It was a surprising present to receive, really, the king of England was a *king*, after all, if he wanted tennis balls, he could get some closer to home – but inside the box there was a message to explain it all. The message said, don't even *think* about invading our country, boy king; you'd be better off staying at home and playing tennis, you'd be better off practising your backhand and lob. And the king was angry – this was an insult to him, and an insult to England too! – and at once he rallied some troops. He didn't rally all that many, because England was such a small country, and France is *so* big, like a playground bully. And when he and his soldiers got to France, it was to discover that they were heavily outnumbered. The English soldiers were sore afraid, but the night before battle the king visited his army in disguise and reassured them all one by one. He gave them courage. The next day the English met the French upon the fields of Agincourt, and though they were outnumbered – oh, ten to one – they absolutely crushed them. (They crushed them very mercifully, naturally, because they were English.) And the French learned their lesson, and vowed never again to send the king such cheap birthday gifts.

It is, of course – and appropriately enough, given the nature of that gift – balls. The insulting present from the French court (if it ever happened) was just another little jibe eighty years through a protracted war that set off in fits and starts according to the energy or sanity of the kings in power at the time. The Tennis Ball Incident, as I personally like to call it, was one of the V-signs being flicked back and forth across the Channel.[1] The English army for the invasion of France (and we don't like that word 'invasion', do we?) was the largest assembled at that stage of English history, and many historians now believe it was likely only to have been only matched in number by the French forces they faced. And Henry V's treatment of French prisoners – soldiers, women and children alike – was savage butchery, barbaric even for the standards of the time.

But it's a good story, and it's the story that prevails. It's pure David and Goliath. We always love the underdog – especially when the underdog is *us*, and very especially, when the underdog *wins*. Right from the moment of victory the English are keen to exaggerate the size of the French army they faced, and pooh-pooh the size of their own. When a victorious King Henry returns to England in triumph, he is greeted in London by a couple of giants, just to emphasise the point. Propaganda, of course. But not *just* propaganda. We all love a good fairy tale, we always have done – and our ancestors were no different. They had to mythologise their kings, if only just to make more sense of them. For example: when Henry V was crowned in April 1413, the coronation was hit by a freak snowstorm. It was clearly an omen of some sort. Something mythic. But no-one could agree what sort of omen it might be. And that's because they were only at the beginning of the fairy tale, and didn't yet know whether their new king would turn out to be a goodie or a baddie. It's altogether unhelpful to know that something historical is happening, but because you're in the thick of it you can't yet interpret it; it's a pain in the neck to be living through history when you can't tell what's going to happen in the final reel.

As it turned out, the snowstorm was a *good* omen, clearly. And the people of England could celebrate the freak weather retrospectively.

In fact, the V-sign originated at Agincourt. The two finger salute was waved at the French soldiers by the English longbowmen. The French had claimed that, in victory, they would cut off the arrow-shooting fingers of all the English archers, and after the French were duly trounced, the English were cheekily able to demonstrate that their fingers were all still intact and in tip-top V-sign flicking condition. So, that's the real legacy from Agincourt the English gave the world.

And King Henry V was a goodie, and Agincourt was a battle that showcased us all at our most splendid. Cry God for Harry, England, and Saint George!

*

And the myths endure, because they're better for us. You can see why Laurence Olivier in 1944 made a movie out of Shakespeare's *Henry V* to aid the war effort. And why it was so pertinent, with its message about English resilience, and the underdog triumphing against all odds over a large and implacable foe. So what if it wasn't strictly speaking true?

And I wonder, somehow, whether being part of that myth would have been of any comfort to those men facing death on Agincourt field. Henry V's rallying cry, 'Come on, lads! This is going to be one of the "Big" Battles. One of the very few every single schoolboy will know about, this'll be up there with Hastings (1066) and Trafalgar (1805) I'd definitely put it in the Top Three! Cry God for Harry, England and the History Books!' To have faced death, certain you'd be remembered? Do you know, it might have been.

Agincourt didn't do much to change the course of English history. We were back invading the French again a couple of years later. Pretty soon we were fighting Joan of Arc. (And she was a goodie, don't you see how suddenly we swap sides?) England never held on to the parts of France it seized, and our expansionist ambitions were soon lost within the murk of interminable civil war.

In 1421, King Henry's troops faced the French at the battle of Baugé. And this time, it really *was* David and Goliath; the English army was twice the size! And it was literally decimated. A thousand casualties on the English side, only negligible losses on the other. But no-one talks about Baugé. It's not a good enough story.

Pity the poor sods who died at Baugé. They're barely in the bloody history books. Because this time they were the Goliaths. And no-one wants to be an ugly giant with an attitude problem.

*

David and Goliath again. Maybe that's why I find the *Vasa* funny, big ship felled by little gust of wind, and the *Titanic* tragic, big ship felled by even bigger iceberg.

But sometimes I feel sorry for the Goliaths. The number of cells in the human brain, that's maybe 100 billion of them, that's a huge army, there's a Goliath for you! And felled by a little shadow growing in the cerebellum, such a little shadow eating away at those cells, and all the memories they hold, and all that defines us and makes us who we are.

*

I told my now-ex-wife about the battle of Baugé. I was crying quite a lot back then, and she asked why, and out spilled this story about Baugé, and how all those men there died in ignominy, and she supposed that was the reason I was upset. I dare say it wasn't an unreasonable conclusion to draw. She tried her best. She asked whether maybe going to Baugé would help. She asked whether we should go there on holiday, and pay our respects to the forgotten dead. She asked where Baugé was. I said it was somewhere in the Loire valley. 'Do you want to go, then?' she asked. 'Not really,' I said.

*

My grandfather was too young to have died in the First World War. Indeed, by a coincidence that is mildly interesting but not very relevant, he reached only his seventh birthday on the very same day that Gavrilo Princip shot the Archduke Franz Ferdinand in Sarajevo, thus providing the spark for the war in the first place. (Every war has a little spark.)

At school we studied the First World War for O-level, and one day I told the whole class that my grandfather had been killed in it. I don't quite know why. I suppose I must have been wanting attention, but that really wasn't my nature at all; I was the sort who was bullied rather easily, and I'd learned after years of rib-punchings and head-flushings that the best way to avoid getting hurt was never to put your head above the parapet. Unlike my grandfather, in this instance: 'He put his head above the parapet,' I said, 'and it was shot clean off.'

I like to think now that it was my way of lending a little purpose to those lessons. We'd been studying the bloody war for *weeks* now, and it had been nothing but dates and names and maps of the various alliances drawn in our exercise books (goodies in red, baddies in black). And it was all, frankly, a bit bloodless. So by introducing a sense of real loss to the story, a casualty who wasn't just a statistic, maybe I wanted to make the First World War seem a bit more urgent and admonitory. Or, more likely, I just wanted attention. Yes, it was probably just attention, after all.

I was asked which battle he'd died in, and I didn't want to say the Somme or Passchendaele, because they were too obvious somehow – it'd be like saying Hastings or Agincourt. So I said Ypres. There were lots of battles at Ypres, it just made my grandfather's death that much more mathematically probable.

From that point on, in O-level class, it seemed somehow that the First World War story was *my* story. So, when the teacher pointed out the harsh conditions of trench living, it'd be in reference to my grandfather's suffering; when he alluded to the phrase 'lions led by donkeys', Lord Kitchener would be the donkey, but my grandfather, *my* granddad, that brave and faithful tommy who shared my name and my blood, he, he would be a *lion*. And the teacher would point at me as he said this, with such respect, as if his sacrifice had been my sacrifice. I did very well in all my essays, I think I always got marked up a grade.

I liked my grandfather being picked off by a sniper bullet. So much more fun than the Huntington's that got him.

What I hadn't thought through was that, in order for the timing to work out, my father would have had to have been conceived some time before 1918. And that would have put him in his late sixties, as opposed to the very middle of his middle age, in which he genuinely and comfortably sat. For Open Evening that term, when my parents would visit the school and meet my teachers, I asked my father whether he wouldn't mind greying his hair a bit. My father refused. He said he didn't understand. My mother didn't understand either, but my mother thought it was funny, my mother laughed, and to make my mother laugh was the best thing of all, I was always trying to make Mum laugh. My mother was the one with the sense of humour.

*

If my grandfather was too young to have died in the First World War, then my great-grandfather was a bit too old. I resented him a bit for that. I never met him – he died before I was born – and so I never got the chance to explain my disappointment to him personally.

In fact, as far as I could tell, no-one in my family had ever died in armed conflict – and as a child I often wondered whether I would be the first. I thought it might be quite exciting, really. I liked the idea of being a pioneer. Indeed, I was fairly sure I *would* die in war, but that it wouldn't be on a battlefield somewhere, on green grass, standing shoulder to shoulder with Henry V – this time the war would be nuclear, there'd be a dispute over something small, tennis balls, maybe, and someone in America or Russia would press the button, and that would be *it*. And we'd all get turned to dust, and we'd all be dead, and I'd achieve something my grandfather and my great-grandfather couldn't, I'd be a casualty of war – but it wouldn't be all that impressive, really, would it, if we were *all* casualties of war? What would make *me* special?

And we'd sit in history class, and we'd study the First World War, and it was a little hard to see the point, really, what use would O-levels be if we were all about to get nuked? And one boy (it wasn't me, unfortunately) he said to the teacher, Mr Cramp, he said, there was no use doing his history homework, because history was dead. History was dead. We were all dead, really, all of us, but history was even more dead, the deadest thing there was. And Mr Cramp, he used to turn bright red whenever he got angry or embarrassed, and he turned bright red then because he was one or the other, and he told the boy that nuked or not he'd do his homework or he'd do detention. And the boy, he never raised his voice, he wasn't being a troublemaker – he just said that he'd do the detention then. I wish I remembered that boy's name.

Come to think of it, that was why I made up that story about my grandfather. It was to impress that boy. Yes, yes. Yes, I really think so.

*

I hadn't visited my parents for a while, so I was surprised by how shrunken my father looked when he met me in the hospital reception. And for one silly moment I thought that my memory was playing tricks on me, that he'd never been the fat man I remembered from my childhood at all, he'd always been this strangely sad creature with arms like sticks. 'You've lost weight,' I said, and he smiled wanly. I wasn't sure whether to hug him or shake his hand, and so in the end I did neither.

'I want to prepare you,' he told me. 'Your mum's not the way she was.' And indeed she wasn't – if my father looked shrunken, my mother's entire body seemed to have caved in on itself – thinner, yes, obviously, but shorter too, smaller all over, her head was *tiny* – that's what struck me, seeing her head on the pillow, that huge pillow too big for that tiny head. And her hair was white and the face just wrinkled, really.

'Does she know me?' I asked, and at my voice her eyes lit up, so I thought that yes, she did. Her hands made little grabby motions, like a baby wanting its bottle. I reached out for her, and she clasped hold, surprisingly tight, she put my hand to her lips, she held it to her cheek. 'Hello, Mum, how are you feeling?' I asked, and that was a silly question. 'Do you know who I am?' I asked, and that wasn't; 'Do you know me?'

And I wanted to tell her how sorry I was I hadn't seen her for such a long time, and that I'd be a better son from this point on, I'd be there every week. But I knew I wouldn't, because she scared me.

My father didn't have much to say. It was Mum who'd been the clever one. The one with words, the one with a sense of humour. So all three of us were silent for the longest time, my father, awkward, me, awkward, my mother beaming from ear to ear.

And then she let go of my hand. Her eyes were flinty now. And she glared at me with something like hatred.

*

In 1989 another movie was made of Shakespeare's *Henry V*, this time by actor/director Kenneth Branagh. We weren't at war with anyone at the time, but he made it anyway. It was nominated for two Oscars. And Branagh tells the story of how, during the awards ceremony, he left to go to the bathroom. And as he was doing his business, as even Oscar nominees must do, he turned around and there, pissing next to him, was Jack Nicholson! Dressed in shades, probably, and in a swanky suit, and grinning that trademark Jack Nicholson grin. 'Hello, I'm Jack,' said Jack, and Branagh laughs, of *course* he's Jack, everyone knows Jack! And here's this twenty-nine-year-old actor from Belfast, and he's at the Oscars, and he's meeting Jack Nicholson, and Jack Nicholson is introducing himself to *him*!

It's a nice story. And there are several ways we can interpret it. Firstly, from Nicholson's perspective – we either have to believe

(a) that Jack Nicholson honestly thought he might not be famous enough for Branagh to know who he was, or

(b) that Jack Nicholson knew full well Branagh should know who he was, and so was

(bi) making a joke about celebrity, to a fellow celebrity, about the vanity of Hollywood, viz. King Canute on the beach, viz. Gustavus Adolphus and the *Vasa*, or

(bii) deferring to Branagh, as if implying Branagh was more famous than he was, or *should* be more famous than he was, or *would* be more famous than he was, some day soon, or

(biii) patronising Branagh, and thinking that this low budget Shakespeare-sucking British art-house flick merchant was so off the Hollywood scale he really *might* not who he was.

And that Kenneth Branagh tells the story because

(a) it's a joke against himself, that here he is with a man who is the very metaphor for Hollywood, and therefore the metaphor for America itself (carve him up, you'd find the word 'America' running through like a stick of rock) and therefore the symbol of all America's power and wealth and history-shaping self-conviction, and that symbol is treating him – him! – as an equal, or

(b) it's a joke against himself, but the joke in itself is a symbol – because this is the moment when everything will change for Branagh, he's only twenty-nine, his whole career is ahead of him, and his first meeting with Nicholson in a bathroom is a turning point, from now on Branagh's rise will be meteoric, his movies will get bigger and ever more acclaimed, he'll be part of the Hollywood royalty, he and Nicholson will forever more be pissing in the same trough.

And I've no idea which of these interpretations is correct, but I rather like the last one, if only because it chimes so neatly with that image of King Henry V himself, standing on the fields of Agincourt and rallying his troops, 'Cry God for Harry!' and believing – because every man *does* – that the moment is epic and that history will remember it, and for once actually being *right*; but not knowing that he'll be dead in a few years, that Agincourt will leave behind nothing more sophisticated than the V-sign insult, that the Hundred Years will just drag on for decades, that this battle will be the one bright spot in the whole smudge of fifteenth century English history. 'Cry God for Ken!' – and Branagh standing there on his own field of history, or the toilets at the Shrine Auditorium, take your pick, enjoying the moment of triumph for all that it's worth, but it is *only* a moment, not knowing that triumph is but short-lived, that history is a capricious arsehole. Not knowing that the next movie he'll direct will be *Dead Again*, and that it'll be shit.

I like Kenneth Branagh. I hope he gets another Oscar nomination one of these days. Everyone deserves their second chance in the sun. Everyone deserves their second Agincourt. He deserves a second Agincourt rather more than Henry V, let's be fair, who left nothing behind him but thousands dead in a pointless war. At least Branagh leaves behind him a *Henry V* that's fun to watch, has in it both Richard Briers *and* Brian Blessed, and comes on DVD.

*

I read Kenneth Branagh's autobiography on a flight to Los Angeles. Or, to be accurate, I skimmed it. I was going to Los Angeles to attend a wedding. I found the book in the seat pocket in front of me, along with the plane safety instructions and the sick bag. I thought that between flights the air crew were supposed to clean the plane, and they'd throw away all the rubbish and keep anything worth having for themselves. No-one had thrown away Branagh's book, which suggested it couldn't be that bad, but none of the stewardesses had wanted to hang on to it, which suggested it probably wasn't all that good either. I had brought a book for the flight, but I'd left it in the hand luggage now stowed over my head, and to have fetched it down would have meant climbing over my now-ex-wife in the aisle seat, and my wife was asleep and gets very testy when she's woken up. So I made do with the Branagh.

I'd love to pretend that I read the bathroom anecdote in the autobiography, but I'm not sure I did. As I say, I skimmed. I looked out of the window a lot. I looked at my sleeping wife next to me, I didn't often get the chance to do that in the light, and I remember thinking how alien she seemed like that. I don't, at that point, also remember reading Branagh's account of meeting Nicholson at the Oscars.

I'm pretty sure I must have heard the story somehow. Maybe I saw Branagh tell it on a chat show once? But I don't like chat shows. Since writing the paragraph above, I've tried to do some research. I fired up the computer, got on to the World Wide Web, and typed into the search engine: 'Kenneth Branagh' 'Jack Nicholson' 'toilet anecdote'. Nothing. Or, at least, nothing useful. Which makes me wonder whether I've made up the whole story, and rather maligned both actors in the process.

Branagh was nominated for an Oscar at the age of twenty-nine. Fair play to him, I've never been nominated for anything, and at twenty-nine I was getting married to my now-ex-wife. The one who'd later accompany me on flights to Stockholm and to Los Angeles, the one who'd keep dragging me to her friends' weddings. Our own wedding was quite a lavish affair, her family insisted. A church ceremony, even though I'm not religious, and I don't think my wife was either, in all the years we put up with each other I don't think I ever heard her allude to a God or supernatural being in any manner that wasn't either ironic or expletive. My parents were both there. My father, I remember, looked very smart in his suit, and his hair had greyed, he could have passed off as a sixty-something at an Open Evening. And my mother, my mother laughed a lot, and she wore a hat.

At one point I had to wake my wife up. I had to go to the toilet. She didn't like, as I say, being woken up. I asked her why all her friends had to go and get married in expensive places overseas. She told me that I hadn't had to come. Like I'd have heard the end of that, I told her. 'Like I'm hearing the end of it now,' she said, and closed her eyes, and went back to sleep.

*

I didn't like the way my mother looked at me with hatred. It disturbed me. So I had a word with her doctor.

'You're upset,' she said.

'Of course I'm upset,' I said. 'How can this happen to a person?'

'It's a shock for you,' she said.

'Of course it's a shock. Does she even know who I am any more?'

'I'm sure she knows.'

'Can she talk?'

'She can talk. She may not easily remember the words with which to express herself.'

'Does it hurt?' I asked. And the doctor frowned. 'Does it hurt to lose yourself like that?'

'You can't think of it that way,' she said. 'She's the same person, just with fewer memories.' I told her that it was as if I were watching her entire life being erased. Her entire history, erased.

'You know what I think history is?' said the doctor. And she smiled very sweetly. 'And I think this may help you. History is just the things we remember.'

'What do you mean?'

'What I'm saying is. She's got a whole world in her head. Of experiences and knowledge. And that world, yes, it's getting smaller. But she won't *know* her world's getting smaller, because it's outside the world, isn't it?'

'I don't think that does help, actually,' I said. But I thought how appealing that would be, if history could be tamed like that. If history weren't this vast unfeeling mass crushing us all, but something we could control. But I wasn't convinced. 'So, what, are you saying every single person has a different history? That there's no such thing as a single history, just six billion little histories all over the place?'

She said I had the idea exactly.

'And what happens to me,' I asked, 'when I'm no longer a part of her history?'

She told me she was sure I wouldn't be forgotten. I was her son, and she must love me very much. I would always be a part of her history.

I wondered whether, when she forgot me, when my very own mother couldn't remember who I was any more... I'd just vanish.

'I need to know something,' I said. 'Of course,' she said, and gave me an encouraging smile. 'Please,' I said. 'Yes,' she said, and smiled a bit wider.

'What's happening to my mother. How do I know one day it won't happen to me?'

And the doctor's smile wobbled a bit.

*

So I decided, right then and there, that if my memory was going to go, then I'd stuff my brain with as much history as could fit. So then there'd be a chance. So that some of it might survive.

I told my now-ex-wife I wasn't going to work any more.

'What? Why?'

'No time,' I said. 'No time for anything but history.' And I laughed at that, because somewhere in what I'd just said there seemed to be a clever joke.

I read books. I went to museums. I watched movies. I cried at *Titanic*. I went to a couple of weddings abroad, but I didn't actually attend the services.

One day my wife told me she couldn't take it any more. 'I don't think I even know you,' she said. 'I'm sorry for you. But I don't think I *ever* knew you.'

I stuffed my brain with history. Not my history, of course. I don't have a history. I don't have a past.

*

Branagh's movie of *Henry V* uses a whole ton of familiar faces from British stage and screen. It doesn't feature Kate Winslet, who wasn't familiar at all at this time, and at this point hadn't even played that small part in *Casualty*. But seven years later she was a bit more famous; and Branagh's movie of *Hamlet*, this time using a whole ton of familiar Hollywood faces (Jack Lemmon, Robin Williams, Charlton Heston - but not, let's note, Jack Nicholson) finds room for Kate Winslet as Ophelia.

The very next movie Winslet was to make after *Hamlet* was *Titanic*. And I like to think that Kate Winslet may have asked Branagh's advice about that, about taking on the big-budget Hollywood movie that would turn her into a star. And that maybe, in response, Branagh might have smiled, and told her his anecdote about his Oscar nomination for *Henry V*, and how he met Jack Nicholson in the bathroom. Told this time perhaps with a hint of weary sadness, from a man who knows he's peaked, to an actress on the rise with Oscar nominations of her own to look forward to.

I don't think I read that story in Branagh's autobiography at all. Maybe, if he *did* tell it to Kate Winslet, I read it in her autobiography? Could that be possible? I don't know, I don't remember ever reading Winslet's autobiography, but there are so many books I've forgotten (is that the first thing to go?). I don't know, actually, if Kate Winslet has even written an autobiography.

I wish that Kenneth Branagh had been in *Titanic*. Not in the Leonardo DiCaprio part, DiCaprio was perfect. But maybe as that nasty aristocrat Kate Winslet was supposed to marry? Branagh is very good at playing nasty aristocratic parts, he got that down pat from Shakespeare. He'd have been great at that, I bet.

*

Every few days I'd go to the video rental store on the high street, to get myself *Titanic*, to get myself another fix of that iceberg goodness. The man behind the counter began to get used to me. The thirty-sixth time I rented it, he gave me a rueful grin that was meant, I think, to be sympathetic.

'*Titanic* again, eh?' he said. 'Your wife must really love it!' And I explained that no, on the contrary, my wife didn't like *Titanic* at all, she found it overlong and schmaltzy. I was the one who really loved *Titanic*, and correspondingly, that was why I kept renting it.

He was surprised. 'It's a chick flick, though, isn't it?' he said. 'I mean, women go for all that weepy stuff. Men don't, not real men. It just seems a bit gay.'

And I wanted to protest, to tell him that there were icebergs in it, and drownings, what was gay about that? And I was especially drawn to the way that though this was a fictional representation of history, it had somehow already supplanted the truth in the mass consciousness, and this only fuelled further my suspicions that soon – not now, but in a hundred years, say, when all the *Titanic* survivors were long dead, and all the survivors' children – *soon*, though, this filmic record of the disaster would be more *real* than what actually happened, that it'd be the only version of events that was of any use any more, that to all intents and purposes Kate Winslet and Leonardo DiCaprio would *become* history.

But I didn't, because I had a feeling he'd think that was gay too.

And he was still waiting, wanting some justification why I wanted to rent the same movie so often, I knew otherwise I'd never dare return to the video store again. So I told him that my grandfather had been on the *Titanic*. Yes, when he had just been a little boy. And yes, that he'd drowned there, actually, lost in those frozen wastes. That renting *Titanic* was my way of reaching out to him, and perhaps, if in only a small way, of keeping him alive.

The clerk went white. 'Oh man,' he said. 'I'm sorry. I'm really sorry.'

'That's all right,' I sniffed.

'No, but... I mean. I'm sorry for your loss.'

I assured him it had happened a long time ago.

'Please,' the clerk said, 'I don't want your money. This rental's on me.' And I thanked him. 'See you again soon!' he called out to me as I left. Though, funnily enough, I didn't ever go back. Seeing the clerk again, I thought, might be a little awkward, and besides, I didn't want to watch the movie now, not if I could picture my grandfather dying in it so tragically, it must have been awful for him. Come to think of it, I never returned the tape. It must still be in the sitting room somewhere. Hang on, wait. Yes, here it is.

*

My now-ex-wife and I weren't talking at all by the time our plane touched down in Los Angeles.

I didn't like Los Angeles. It was immediately so bright and shiny, everything laid out bare for all to see, 'Here we are!' There were no shadows. And that's where history takes place, within the shadows, in the cracks, the gaps, there were no cracks or gaps here, there was no history here, I didn't want to stay here.

'Well, that's a shame,' said my now-ex-wife. 'Because here's where we are.'

We got a cab to the hotel. The driver was very polite. The hotel was bright and shiny too. 'Now, listen to me,' said my wife, once we were checked in, 'I know you've been going through a bad time. But we need to put an end to that now, okay? We're here together. And this wedding of Lynne's is very important to me. Promise me there won't be a repeat of what happened in Sweden.' And I promised, and she seemed satisfied.

The next morning she got into her best dress, I got into my best suit. And then I decided I wasn't going to the wedding after all. She could go without me. I don't know Lynne, and I didn't want to know Lynne. And though I was sure this would be a momentous day in Lynne's life it wasn't going to be in mine, and if one day my memory failed and all the important stuff disappeared and what was left was Lynne's wedding I'd be so pissed off. I'd rather go somewhere historical instead. And my wife said I'd promised not to do what I'd done in Sweden, and I said there was no question of my doing what I'd done in Sweden, Los Angeles didn't even *have* a warship museum! And she threw her shoe at me. And she was angry. And she called me an emotional cripple. And I knew I should probably have been hurt by that, but frankly, it was hard to disagree.

I went out and hailed a cab. The driver was very polite. 'Where to, buddy?' he asked. I told him to take me somewhere historical.

He took me to Disneyland, which didn't seem particularly historical, but I gave it a try. It was September, and still holiday season, and so the queues for the rides were long. I joined a few of the queues, but didn't bother with the rides once I reached the front, the queues were much more fun. I didn't stay at Disney for long. Everybody kept staring at me in my wedding suit, and I admit I did stand out a bit, but I thought the staring was a bit rich considering how many of them were dressed up as pirates and chipmunks and mice.

I asked one of the pirates whether Disneyland really was the most historical place in Los Angeles, and he went to consult with a chipmunk, then said that it was. So I thanked him, and I left the park, and I decided I might as well go to the wedding after all. I hailed a cab. The driver was very polite.

'What are you dressed like that for?' he asked.

'I'm going to a wedding,' I said. And then, because I'd heard it in a movie, I said, 'Step on the gas!'

He said, 'You're English, aren't you?'

I told him that absolutely I was.

We drove for a very long time. The driver made a couple of calls on his phone, but I couldn't understand what he was saying, he was muttering and, besides, it was Spanish. I began to suspect I'd miss the wedding. I didn't much mind. I closed my eyes and went to sleep.

I woke up when the car came to a halt. And I'd been wrong about Los Angeles, the area was full of shadows and cracks and gaps. I was about to tell the driver that this had been just what I was looking for, and to thank him profusely, even offer him a little tip – when the back door opened, and another man got into the cab beside me.

'Hello,' I said.

'Shut up,' he said. 'Now, listen. You're going to give me all your money. And all your credit cards.'

I handed over the dollars I had, and there weren't very many, and that seemed to make both the driver and his friend angry. 'And now,' said the man, 'get out of the cab. I'm going to beat you up, you piece of English shit.'

'Why?'

'Because the Spanish hate the English.'

And yes, I supposed that it hadn't just been the French we'd had all these historical squabbles with. We'd been at war with the Dutch, and the Scots, and the Turks, and the Portuguese, and the Italians – and the Spanish too, yes, of course!

The men kicked me to the ground. 'This is for the War of the Quadruple Alliance!' they said. 'And this, for the War of Austrian Succession! And this, for the War of Jenkins' Ear!'

And I began to tell them I hadn't even *heard* of the War of Jenkins' Ear, for all that it had a peculiar name. And how it was odd, really, when you care to think about it – our history was a series of endless conflicts, it was violence, it was always violence, century after century. But so few of them are taught in schools. We so carefully edit our past. We try to tell the story of our nation, and to make that story coherent we cut out all the extraneous detail – but who's to say what's extraneous? Certainly not the people who fight in these wars, it's like Baugé all over again! The only war with the Spanish I could even remember was that one with the Armada in, and the men now kicking me in the stomach hadn't even *mentioned* that one, wasn't that funny? It was all just a matter of perspective – we'd opted for our history being a straight line from Hastings (1066) to Agincourt (1415) to Trafalgar (1805) and sod the rest. The War of Jenkins' Ear sounded fascinating, I'd be sure to look it up.

But I think they kicked me unconscious.

*

The War of Jenkins' Ear was fought between England and Spain from 1739 to 1741. It's a war without any heroism, or even any interesting battles, just a few indecisive skirmishes now and then. But it does have a great name, and it does indeed involve a man called Jenkins and an ear. All in all, if I was going to be beaten up because of an eighteenth century war, there are worse I could have ended up with.

The story goes like this: Robert Jenkins was an English sea captain. One day (once upon a time) his ship was boarded by Spanish customs officials. When they found he was carrying contraband, they took Jenkins, they tied him against the mast, and then they sliced his ear off. And the officer in charge whispered to him in parting that he'd do the same to the king of England himself if he could. (Presumably he whispered it into the other ear.)

Imagine the scene. Jenkins goes to the House of Commons. He tells them what has happened. How the Spanish have defiled him, and have mocked his country. And then, at the climax to his tale, he produces the very ear that has been cut off! Because he's had the forethought to pickle his ear and stick it in a jar. I can imagine the sunlight pouring in through the windows, and glancing off that glass jar, all England's great and good staring at it in horror, and Jenkins holding it high in injured triumph. The House of Commons is in uproar! They must teach Spain a lesson! They can't just go around lopping off English ears... And they've been looking for an excuse to declare war on Spain, actually; this pickled ear can be their tennis ball.

I like the story. Even though parts of it bother me.

The first problem I have is that the demonstration to the House of Commons takes place in 1738, but the whole ear-slicing outrage was in 1731. And so I'm left with the irresistible impression of Jenkins as the sort of bore who for seven years carries the pickled remains of his own ear everywhere he goes. I can picture him in a pub, after just one pint, 'Did I ever tell you about my ear?' he'd ask, and everyone would groan, and roll their eyes, 'Oh God, Jenkins is banging on about his ear again,' and 'Watch out, he'll get it out in a minute.' And he has, Jenkins has put it up on the bar, he's pointing at it, he's showing it to everyone, 'There you are, that was sliced off by a Spaniard!' Who in their right minds has the urge to pickle their own body parts, just in case they might one day years later be useful as a means of swaying foreign policy?

Seven years is a long time, Jenkins. Stop living in the past. Get over it. It's only an ear. It's not as if you've lost your memory, is it? It's not as if it's within the ear your memories are stored, your sense of self, your whole identity. You bastard. You stupid selfish bastard. Stop whining. It's not as if you're my mother. It's not as if you're lost, like my mother. Bastard.

Seven years. I'm surprised the English weren't embarrassed to bring it up before the Spanish in the first place. My now-ex-wife could be like this. When we were fighting, she'd dredge up all sorts of ammunition from the past to use against me – nothing was too old – birthdays and anniversaries forgotten years ago, snubs and slurs she'd resented for so long I couldn't even remember making them. My abandoning her at a wedding once in Stockholm. Anything. It seemed petty, and, I might add, rather ungentlemanly.

And it sounds like a wonderful *coup de théâtre*, the sensation of displaying a severed ear to the heads of government. You can imagine the anticipation beforehand, all these MPs bored by the daily grind of land taxes and social reform and South Sea Bubbles – 'There's a man outside who's bringing in one of his own organs in a jar!' What organ might it be? The MPs would have taken bets! And then, in walks Jenkins, and he's a thoroughly earless chap, it's a bit of a bloody giveaway, the moment is lost. Some might still be hopeful, maybe the earlessness is a red herring, maybe there's a twist, he'll produce his jar and there, bobbing about in formaldehyde, there'll be a heart, or an eyeball, or a buttock. But no.

One MP turned to the other as Jenkins began his story, the jar still hidden from view so as not to spoil its grisly denouement, and everyone focused upon the very flat side of Jenkins' head, and the MP yawned, and he said, 'Well, I can see how this is going to end.'

*

My now-ex-wife used to complain when I kept renting *Titanic*. (I rented it thirty-six times, I counted.) 'But you know how it's going to end!' And one time I got angry. I said, of *course* I know how it's going to end, it's the bloody *Titanic*! I knew how it was going to end the *first* time I saw it! What do you think, that it's a fucking *whodunnit*? That the iceberg at the end is supposed to be a *twist*? That you're meant to be watching this trying to guess whether the ship's going to suddenly snap back together and be as good as new and sail off into the fucking sunset? You cunt, you stupid *cunt*, history isn't a suspense story, we know how it's *always* going to end, in pain, and death, and being forgotten, no-one is ever going to remember us or anything we've done, and our brains will just shrink smaller and smaller and eat up our past until we no longer have a past, and our past and our future will be as one, they'll be gone, there'll be nothing left. And history will be dead.

She let me show her the movie once. And she huffed all the way through the first couple of hours. She was just waiting for the bit where the ship sank. The rest of it didn't interest her at all. What was the point, if people were doomed to die, you don't want to see them living, she said – let's just get straight on to the deaths.

*

I woke up in a Los Angeles hospital. My nurse was attentive and, I thought, pretty. She told me I'd got five broken ribs, I could easily have punctured a lung,

I'd been very lucky. I told her that didn't *sound* very lucky, and she laughed, and told me I was cute, and that she loved my English accent. I asked her where she was from. She said she was from Connecticut. I told her I assumed then there were no historical enmities specific to the peoples of England and the peoples of Connecticut, and she agreed, she didn't know of any.

My now-ex-wife came to see me. I asked her how the wedding had gone.

'I was so angry with you,' she said. 'I'm so sorry.'

I told her I'd been trying to get to the wedding, I really had.

'I know,' she said. 'You poor brave thing. You poor brave baby.' And she kissed me on the forehead. 'I love you,' she said. And she kissed me on the lips.

*

It is not recorded what Robert Jenkins' wife thought about her husband's ear starting an entire war. But she must have been proud of him, don't you think? Surely she'd have been proud.

History never remembers things like that.

*

I had to stay in the hospital for one more night. The next day, on the television, all that was playing was the World Trade Center collapsing. Two planes flying into the building, over and over again. It was visually spectacular, I admit, but I began to tire of the repeats.

I could see why, of course, the American media was making so much of it. They didn't have much history to celebrate. Here they were being given a big chunk of it, unexpectedly, quite gratis, and they were seizing it with both hands. But there is such a thing as overkill, and I'd had quite enough. I asked my nurse to turn the television off.

She wasn't her usual happy self that morning. I asked her what was wrong.

'I feel so useless,' she said.

I told her she wasn't useless.

'I'd rather be looking after wounded American heroes,' she added, 'than some strange Brit who got mugged. No offence.'

I told her there was no offence taken.

'It's a dark day,' she said, and I corrected her, it was an *historic* day.

'There is no more history,' she said, dully. 'History's finished.' And she reminded me of that kid in my O-level class studying the First World War, and the way we all felt we were going to be nuked, so what was the point? And I told her there was point. Don't worry, I said, history will go on regardless. Or, rather, worry: history will go on regardless.

'We'll kill those bastards for this,' said my nurse from Connecticut. 'America won't take this lying down.'

I had really nothing to say to that, but I told her that history could be a great comfort. She looked at me, and she stopped her sabre-rattling, she softened. And she asked me by name. 'Then, please,' she said, 'comfort me.'

So I told her, as I've told you. That history is all a matter of perspective. The terrorist act that day against New York might seem a bit depressing now. But give it time. Hollywood would make a billion dollar grossing movie out of it. Someone would build a nice museum. We'd all turn it into a wonderful fairy tale. Sooner rather than later, we'd come to see 9/11 as being a happy thing. Those people who died in the Towers, and on the planes, they'll have died for the greater good.

The nurse didn't say anything.

And I told the nurse that I wanted to protect her. That I loved her. That I had my history, and she had her history, and we could bring them together into some sort of alliance. Our histories could merge and tell the same story. And she left the room, and I never saw her again.

*

When my now-ex-wife came to pick me up, I told her I'd fallen in love with my nurse. 'What, this nurse?' she said, and I said, no, not *that* nurse, the other nurse, the one who was there earlier. 'What's her name?', and I said I didn't know, she was the nurse, that was all, I loved her, and I didn't love my wife.

'I don't think I even know you,' sighed my wife. 'I'm sorry for you. But I don't think I *ever* knew you.' And my wife went off and became my now-ex.

*

Sometimes I tell people I was in America the day the World Trade Center fell, and that I was first-hand witness to a nation roaring like a wounded beast. And they say, were you in New York? And I reply that no, it was Los Angeles – and then they lose some interest, because that was thousands of miles away. So I say, yes, I was in New York. Did you see it happen? they ask, and I say yes, I was standing there watching, I saw first one plane hit and then the other, I saw the whole thing. And what did it feel like? they ask, and I tell them that I knew I was in the presence of history. Someone might then tell me how they'd watched it live on television, and that they had felt the significance too, and I'd say yes, it was pretty impressive on television, but to really grasp the historical enormity of it you really had to have been there. Sometimes I tell them I was inside the World Trade Center, and that gets even more interest, too much interest, actually, I don't want to be seen as a survivor, just as a witness to history, it's the historical importance I'm getting at. So I don't say I was inside too often. Those conversations get confusing so quickly. And sometimes I say that my grandfather was inside, that my grandfather died inside. I had him shot at Ypres, I drowned him on the *Titanic*, why not kill the poor bastard in 9/11 too? And sometimes I kill my wife there instead.

*

One day my father phones. I haven't visited my parents in ages. He sounds awkward. I think the worst. I think funerals, and getting out my best suit, will it still fit, I've put on weight? 'I've met someone,' he says.

Her name is Maggie. He met her at the hospital. 'A nurse?' I say, because I could understand that. 'No, she's another patient. Just a few rooms down from your mother's. When I'd visit your mother, sometimes Maggie's door would be open, and sometimes I'd say hello if it was, and we became friends, and there we are.'

'There you are,' I say.

'I'm in love,' my father says.

'How is Mum?' I ask.

'Oh, much the same.'

We don't say anything for a bit. 'Don't hate me,' he says, at last, and so I don't.

'I've a right to a bit of happiness, haven't I?' he asks me.

'Of course.'

'I'm going to marry Maggie.'

'Oh.'

'Not a *real* marriage, obviously. Not with your mother still alive. But just like the real thing. A proper ceremony and everything. As near as damn it.'

'Oh.'

'Here in the hospital. With all our friends.'

'What about Mum?'

'I don't think she should be there. I don't think that would be right.'

'No, I mean. What will you do about Mum? Are you going to divorce her? Can't you just wait until she dies? I mean...'

'I can't divorce your mother. It wouldn't be kind. Besides, I don't think she'd even know what was going on. And dying, well, she's not well mentally, of course, but physically, she could be around for years. She could outlive me! She'll outlive Maggie. Maggie's got cancer.'

I say, 'Oh.'

'Maggie and I don't have much time left. I want to give her everything I can.' I ask whether he really loves this woman. 'I do.' I ask him whether he loves her more than my Mum. He thinks for a long time. 'No,' he says.

'I see.'

'But she's gone. Hasn't she? There's nothing of your mum left. Nothing inside. Mummy's gone.' And I thought, she's not *your* Mummy; and I thought, why can't you use her name, are you so ashamed?

'It would mean the world to me,' he says, 'if you'd be my best man.' And it's only then I realise I'll have to fetch out my best suit after all.

I set off to the hospital, but I know I won't get there. I never make it to weddings. Sooner or later I'm bound to take a detour, to a museum, probably, or a castle, or old church. So I'm shocked when my taxi pulls up at A&E, so much so that when the driver asks me for the fare I very nearly tell him to turn right round again.

I find my father waiting for me at reception. Like me, he is wearing a suit. He has a white flower in his buttonhole. He offers me one, but I decline, I tell him I don't have that sort of buttonhole. 'Thank you for coming,' he says. I think he's going to shake my hand, but then he folds me in a hug, and slaps me on the back.

Maggie isn't in a wedding dress, she's in a nightie, and she's propped up on pillows. There aren't many people in her room. Maggie and my father clearly don't have many friends. There's my Uncle Ray. And some strange old woman in a blue floral dress who doesn't speak, not even when I say hello to her. Maggie smiles at me when I come in, and it's a nice smile.

'I'm so pleased to meet you,' she says.

'Thank you,' I say. 'And congratulations.'

'Thank you.'

'So. You've got cancer?'

'Yes.'

'What sort of cancer?'

'Pancreatic.'

'Tch,' I say, and nod. 'Bad luck.'

'Thank you.'

She smells of milk, somehow. I don't like it. My father takes me to one side. 'Isn't she wonderful?' he beams. 'And so lucid!'

My father addresses the room. 'Now, we're going to have to be a bit hush-hush,' he says. 'Because my getting married, it's not strictly legal. So, keep schtum!' And he puts his finger to his lips and laughs, and pours everyone sparkling wine in paper cups. He gives me a little jewellery box, and inside there's a ring. It's big. It's sparkly. 'You're really taking this seriously,' I tell him. 'Of course,' he replies.

'You're going to have to be the vicar,' he adds.

'I thought I was the best man.'

'You'll have to be both.' And he hands me a printout of the things vicars say at weddings, he's got it from a website.

He takes Maggie's hand as I begin to read, and they both look at each other adoringly.

During the service I leave space for my father to say his vows.

'I thought everything was over. I thought my life was behind me, all in the past. But then I found you, Maggie, and you're the dearest and sweetest woman in the world, and I realised that nothing is ever over. And this, now, is the happiest day of my life, this is the peak, the absolute best. And I promise to love you completely for the rest of our days.'

Maggie has some vows too, but I don't pay attention to them, she's not family.

It's around this point that I remember I'm wearing the suit I was beaten up in, and my ribs seem to throb at the memory.

I pronounce them man and wife, there's applause and a little laughter, and my father and the stranger snog.

*

Things to Remember about My Mother
A) Personal Things.
(Things I Might Forget. Things She Has Already Forgotten.)

I remember:

(i) how she'd put on the television for company, always, even if you were there.

(ii) the way she used to cup her hand behind an ear so she could hear you better, but only if you said something interesting. And how hard I'd try to say things good enough to make her want to cup her ear!

(iii) how one day my father came back from a business trip with a moustache, and she took one look at it, and just said, gently but firmly, 'I don't think so, Harry.'

(iv) the sulk she'd have in rainy weather, the little pout she'd pull.

(v) the way she used to protect me from spiders when I was small, I never liked spiders, and if I saw one in the bedroom I'd call for her and she'd run to rescue me. And only years later I realised she was scared of spiders too. Just as scared as I was! And I remember when I was twelve or thirteen, around then, and she found a spider in the kitchen – and she called *me* to get rid of it, it was too big for her to handle, she needed me. And how proud I felt then, I hated touching that spider, but I felt so very grown-up.

(vi) that she'd rather squint than be seen in public wearing spectacles.

(vii) how at Christmas she'd treat herself after cooking dinner to a port and lemon.

(viii) the little fat lump on the side of her nose, and how she was always so self-conscious about it, and tried to cover it with make-up. It's gone now. It disappeared when her body shrank. It went with the shrinking. My mother wouldn't have missed it. I do.

(ix) the sulk she'd have in hot weather.

(x) that time she sat me down, just before I went on my first date, and told me very seriously how I had to be nice to girls. 'Be better than the other boys,' she told me. It wasn't a proper date. I was only twelve.

(xi) that she was the only one who could make a Marmite sandwich I'd enjoy.

(xii) her laugh.

(xiii) the day she caught me taking money from her purse.

(xiv) the way she'd hold on to the steering wheel so tightly when she picked me up in the car after school.

(xv) that she never trusted the dishwasher, and would always rather do the dishes by hand. That my father bought her a dishwasher once as a surprise gift. That he led her into the kitchen, had her keep her eyes closed until he was ready to present it to her. That she wrinkled her nose at it, sort of sneered at the thing. As if to say, 'what do I want with that?'

(xvi) that she never trusted the microwave either.

(xvii) but was on perfectly cordial terms with the toaster.

(xviii) her other laugh, the one she used only for me.

(xix) how she looked at her mother's funeral. I was fourteen years old, I got the day off school. And we all had to get up very early, and drive down to Sussex. My mother wore black. She didn't cry. But she seemed so very sad. And I so much wanted to help her. I so much wanted her to be happy again. So afterwards, as we stood in the cemetery, I took her hand. 'Not now, darling,' she said, very nicely.

(xx) her collection of cardigans.

(xxi) the day she got her ears pierced. She was nearly forty. I was shocked. So was my father. 'Everyone's doing it now,' she said.

(xxii) the hat she wore to my wedding. She never wore hats. It made her head look square.

(xxiii) her smell.

(xxiv) that she kept up the pretence of the tooth fairy, long after I knew that she knew that I knew no such thing existed.

(xxv) that she kept my first tooth.

(xxvi) the shopping lists she'd give me of groceries to pick up at the supermarket. The butter underlined twice, because she liked butter.

(xxvii) her hair.

(xxviii) the first thing she said to me when I told her I was engaged.

(xxix) her laugh, her smell, her hair.

(xxx) her touch.

(xxxi) the way she'd watch the news so avidly. And after I left home, if something important happened in the world, the way I'd come home from work to find her on the answering machine wanting to discuss it.

(xxxii) the way she wasn't on the answering machine after 9/11. Oh, she'd have loved that one.

(xxxiii) her inability to pronounce the word 'chrysanthemum'.

(xxxiv) ...

(xxxv)

Things to Remember about My Mother
B) Practical Things.

Maiden name:	Stott
First name:	Joanne[2]
Middle name:	Mary
Date of birth:	4th April 1931
Sister's name:	Auntie Eileen
Brother's name:	Uncle George (deceased)
Nationality:	British
Ethnicity:	Caucasian
Religion:	Undetermined
Allergies:	Pollen, pencillin
Blood type:	O
Funeral request:	Simple service, 'Onward Christians Soldiers', flowers, cake, ashes round the garden.

*

And now my father's married, I walk down the corridor to see my mother.

She's dead. That's what I think at first. And I don't mind, actually. I think it's rather apt. And then I see her breathing, the breaths are very shallow. And I realise I'm pleased she's alive, I really would have minded after all.

Oh, the breaths are so, so shallow. And her face is smooth, and strangely young, as if it's had all the past wiped from it. The whole jumble, all its irrelevances and contradictions, gone.

I kiss her on the forehead. The forehead is cool. She doesn't stir.

'I'm sorry,' I tell her.

And I kiss her, again, on the forehead. I kiss her right above the brain. And I think how it might be, if through my open mouth all my thoughts could pour out now and flood that brain, if I give her all the memories I have – not medieval wars necessarily, or Swedish ships, though she's welcome to them if she wants – I'd give my mother back to my mother, I'd give her back the history of her self. Please. Please. And I press down my lips, hard, hard, and I don't ever go away.

---

[2] Her given name was Joanne, but she liked her friends to call her Annie.

2001 – On 11 September, two commercial aeroplanes are hijacked by Islamic terrorists, and are flown into the twin towers of the World Trade Center, in New York, USA.

And so, now what? What history shall we write now?

HISTORY BECOMES YOU

And, one day, the Towers came back.

Later there were those keen to tell the world how they had witnessed the miracle first-hand. How they'd been right on the spot when the 500,000 ton structures of concrete and glass had so impossibly popped back into existence. How they felt blessed they'd been there to see it, how they'd felt *chosen*, how it had brought to their eyes tears of patriotic fervour. But they were lying. Some of them didn't even know they were, they wanted so much to take their part in history. But no-one had seen the Towers appear. They came back at the exact moment when everybody in the vicinity just happened to be looking in the wrong direction at the same time.

In the instant of their arrival the Towers blotted out the sunlight, and the sudden shadows that they cast caused passers-by to shiver.

The police cordoned off the area. The yellow tape around the buildings' perimeter said 'Crime Scene' – although there wasn't a crime, not really, or there *was*, but the crime that had been committed there had happened such a long time ago and on such a scale that 'crime' seemed too paltry a word to describe it. But 'Crime Scene' was the best they could come up with, the police just didn't have an appropriate yellow tape.

And into the buildings were sent doctors, firemen, the police. They soon reported that the structural integrity of the Towers was sound. The ninety-third floor was intact, as if it had never been cleaved through with aeroplane fuselage. And it was clean; the window panes were polished and fair sparkled in the New York sun, the toilets smelled of pine bleach, the carpets seemed newly shampooed.

There was no-one to be found. Not a trace of a single body. Not a trace, moreover, that any body had ever worked there. The desks were empty, the memo boards were blank. The windows were fastened shut tight, as if indeed they'd never been opened at all, as if indeed no persons had ever felt the urge to climb through them and jump to their deaths. Even the soft swivel chairs were pristine and plump, there was not the merest indentation from any bottom to be found.

As good as new.

The media weren't sure at first how to play the story. The default stance was one of panic; this was the signal for another attack; another Godless foe had designs upon America. But no-one could quite see how bringing the Towers *back* could be construed as a terrorist act. And so, broadly, it was reported as a Good Thing. One expert pundit said that he could explain the phenomenon. That sometimes events take place that are so important that they shatter the world stage and change the course of history. That the destruction of the Towers was one such event. That the impact it had made was so great, its legacy so incalculable, the Towers would be a part of everyone's lives forever; so, therefore, the very *absence* of the Towers was at once weird and contradictory, how could something that so defined the mood of the twenty-first century *simply not be there*? History itself had brought the Towers back into existence. History could not let them go.

It wasn't a very scientific theory, and no-one necessarily understood it. But it quite caught the public imagination. For a good few hours, at least. For as long as the Towers stood intact.

Because, at a little before half past ten the next morning, the Towers vanished once more.

The same expert claimed on breakfast television that this in no way contradicted his earlier theory. Rather, it was an extension of it; that the Towers' fall had been so momentous an event of history that what they were now seeing was its echo. Why hadn't such things happened before? Well, maybe no event before had been important enough. Maybe this was the most significant historical event there had ever been. This was a reminder. God was reminding them not to take the tragedy for granted. God was reminding them never to forget.

But the news was less interested in the whys. It would rather focus upon the human drama. Because the Towers had not been empty at the time they had vanished. They had taken eleven souls with them: seven firemen, and four police officers. No trace of them could be found. They were described as fresh victims of the 9/11 attacks, as new American heroes. Journalists were dispatched to interview the bereaved, the wives, the lovers, the children. One wife declared, with tears in her eyes, but they were angry tears of determination, there was no *weakness* to those tears, that she was proud her Brad had struck a blow in the war on terror. That she would love him forever, and that she knew Brad was looking down on her from Heaven. That their son was still too young to understand, but she'd *make* him understand, one day, just how lucky he had been to have had a father who had died so nobly and so selflessly to ensure that he could live in a better and purer world. The newspapers loved it. They wrote up long features on Brad, and on all his companions. Fallen heroes, all; all of them sacrifices in the crusade for democracy, liberty and truth.

Expressions of sympathy poured in from all over the world. They spoke of deep regrets, of common bonds, of alliances never to be broken. They were accepted with cool politeness. As a whole, the American people saw them for what they were. These other nations, they were just jealous *they* hadn't had a miracle. They were trying to muscle in on the act.

Nine days after they had vanished, late in the afternoon, the Towers came back again. It was rush hour, and quite a few people were looking in the right direction at the right time. But the Towers appeared at the exact split second when everybody blinked.

The police cordoned off the area once again with their yellow tape. And the military stood by for a full hour and a half to see whether or not the Towers would simply wink back out of existence. At last a major said that he was prepared to inspect the buildings, but that he would do so alone, he refused to risk any of his soldiers' lives in there. He would go in with a walkie-talkie, he'd be in constant communication, he'd be able to give the world a second-by-second commentary of his impressions and insights. Before he made his entrance, he found time to acknowledge his bravery exclusively to Channel Eight News. He said that he was 'taking one for Uncle Sam', and spoke directly to his wife: 'I love you, Moira, and I love the kids, and if I die today, this is how you should remember me forever, as a hero, as a patriot.' America watched collectively, hearts in mouths, as the major embarked on his mission – it went out live on all stations; families held hands and prayed, mothers cuddled up close to children, men drank bottled beers and wept openly together in downtown bars. The major was soon able to tell the viewers that there was no-one to be found, neither the original victims of the attack nor those so haplessly taken in the aftermath. The major spent a good two hours inside the Towers, establishing just how immaculate those carpets were. Two hours, that was longer than an average movie, and yet the live broadcast stuck with him for the whole thing. He was ordered out; he claimed there was still so much more he could investigate; he was ordered out again, very strictly; he emerged, somewhat reluctantly, to the cheering of crowds. 'It's nothing, I would have taken one for Uncle Sam,' he said, 'it's all I wanted, to take one for Uncle Sam.' And then went home to Moira, and to the kids, and to a new contract as a TV anchorman.

The expert said that night that he hadn't meant an echo, not as such; but *ripples* – if you imagined History as one big pond, and the Twin Towers as one big rock; two big rocks, technically, but let's for the sake of argument call them one; if you were to drop your one big rock right into the centre of your pond, then there'd be a ripple effect; this is the situation they had here, rock, pond, and America was blessed, it was seeing the ripples, getting ripples on all sides, God was buffeting them with ripples. He'd go into further detail, he said, but it was better examined in his new book which would be available next week. The interviewer complimented him on the speed at which he must have written it. 'We must all do our bit for our country in these dark and difficult days.' Would the Towers now be safe? 'It's in the book,' said the expert. But when pressed, 'I think by taking away the Towers God gave us a reminder of a tragedy past, and by restoring them, a beacon of hope for the future. Those Towers right now are the safest places in America.'

The next morning, again a little before half ten, the Towers vanished. This time they took fourteen firemen, six police officers, and a tramp who hadn't been deterred by yellow tape. The expert was not available for comment. Luckily for him, the press left him alone – they had the families of the new fallen heroes to interview.

One night the NYPD received a call from a woman. She said the crisis wasn't over. She knew the Towers would come back, and take more lives; she knew that she was responsible. The NYPD had been plagued with hoax calls ever since the first reappearance. The woman sounded a bit drunk, and very distressed, and no-one on duty was inclined to take her seriously – but they were obliged to bring her in. What she said when they did convinced them all.

She explained that she had once worked at the Towers. And how the day that they fell she ought to have been inside, she ought to have fallen with them. But on September the tenth she'd been out to a bar, she'd met a man, she'd had a few drinks, and one thing had led to another – she'd taken him back to her apartment, they'd fucked all night, and in the hangover and satiated exhaustion that followed she'd slept through her alarm clock the next morning. By the time she'd thought to ring her office and pretend that she was sick, her office didn't exist any more. At first she'd taken this as a sign from God. He'd *spared* her, He had other plans for her; rather than die in fear and fire she was supposed to be with this man she'd picked up. But that soon turned out to be wrong. The man was a liar, and used drugs, and was married – and, worse still, was bad in bed; he wasn't someone on whom she could pin any salvation at all. And ever since it had haunted her, how close she had come to dying, how she had been *meant* to be there with all her colleagues, with the office managers, with the girls on reception and the boys in the post room. She'd tried to live her life, she got a new job, she found a boyfriend who wasn't married and only got high at weekends – but it always seemed so wrong to her, that all about her was a lie. She had been destined to be a victim of America's greatest tragedy, she'd been destined to be special.

When the Towers had come back, she'd known they'd come back for her. They were calling her. And they'd appear, and then disappear, appear and disappear again, over and over, until they got what they wanted – until they took her – until they gobbled her down and swallowed her whole. As was meant to be. And only then would it all stop. 9/11. It was about her, it had always been about her, and her alone, that's all it had ever been for.

She wasn't the only one to come forward.

A man in New Jersey petitioned for the right to die in the Twin Towers. His story touched the nation. He told how his wife had died in the attack, and they'd never even said goodbye. So many farewell phone calls sent out that morning, but never one to him – he didn't know whether she'd died quickly, or in pain, all he knew was she hadn't come home again. He'd have to live through it – so said his friends, his doctors, the therapist – he'd live through it, one day things would get better. But they hadn't got better. No day was ever better. Because they were days without *her* in them. He'd flirted with suicide – but he'd never taken quite the right number of pills, never cut quite deeply enough. He'd always supposed Heaven was a big place, it must be *huge*, just to house the sudden influx of new American heroes – what if he were sent to the wrong bit of it, the bit reserved for pill-poppers or wrist-slicers, what then, how would he ever find her then? Now he knew he could find her. He wanted to be at her work desk. He wanted to be on her swivel chair. He wanted to know that when he vanished, he'd vanish right to where she'd be waiting for him, this woman who'd make him forever happy, they'd be reunited at last in an open-plan office of their very own. He wanted to die the way she had died. He wanted to die *right*... And he was pretty sure his sister-in-law would take care of the kids.

And there was the elderly couple that lived in Arkansas, no-one dreamed of sending suicide bombers to Arkansas – it wasn't fair, they too wanted the honour of dying for America. And there was the man who'd had tattooed '9/11' on his left arm, and on his right a picture of an aeroplane in flames – across his chest it said 'never forget', and he never would, he wouldn't. And there was the old man who believed in God so much. And there was the young girl who just wanted to believe. And there were the lost. And there were the lonely. And there were the ones who were so happy and so safe and were living the American dream, and the guilt that it had come too easy and they'd never been called upon to make a sacrifice for it gave them nightmares. And those who'd tried to enlist for the army, for the right to serve and fight, but their country had turned them down, they weren't good enough to fight, they were too old, or too diabetic, or too gay. All of them, all of them, they claimed that when they saw the Towers on their TV screens, unbowed, undefeated, and so majestic now, and so *clean* – they'd felt pulled towards the Towers, they knew it was their God-given right to become part of them. 'I want to be a hero,' said an unparticular someone. 'And I don't know any other way of doing it.'

And, one day, the Towers came back.

Cameras had been set up to record the possibility, but all of them glitched at the very same moment. And the police cordoned off the area, and this time they had new tape already prepared, it was *red*, and it said 'Crime Scene!!!' with three exclamation marks, and the exclamation marks were an even brighter red! the whole thing was really very red indeed!!! And once the authorities had done their checks to make sure it was safe, they didn't want anyone to slip on those shampooed carpets, they didn't want anyone to *sue*, they let in all those who'd queued up for days, ready to take their places in the Twin Towers. All of the chairs filled quickly. Soon there was standing room only in the lobby and in the corridors and in the rest rooms. Everyone admired how the windows sparkled, and the pleasing scent of bleach. 'We're going to Heaven!' said one delighted six-year-old child, to a Mummy and Daddy who were laughing along with him, 'we're all going to Heaven, and we'll be there in the morning!'

Indeed they would be. And none of us really want to die, of course we don't. But we all know we will, it's like a ticking bomb inside all of us, and we never know when that bomb is going to go off, and doesn't that spoil everything, just a little? And we know too that our deaths won't be *grand* deaths, most likely they'll be lung cancer, or cancer of the oesophagus, or cancer of the brain – we'll die, and it'll be *pathetic*, we'll maybe not even remember our own names as we stare into the abyss, the moment when we could have been special will have passed long ago and we'll never even have realised when, and we'll end as we began, confused, infant-like, and just the same as everybody else. But what if you could be more? What if your death could become history? Ensure that in your final seconds you'd be part of something bigger than you would ever be on your own, what if you too could be part of the 9/11 Experience? Just like Our Fallen Heroes, but no, better – cleaner, simpler, no pain, no doubt, just erased away, no need for burning flesh, no need for tears as people scream out desperately for families they'll never see again, certainly no need to jump out of any windows! (The windows sparkle in the New York sun, and are fastened tightly shut.) Better than Our Fallen Heroes too because they died in ignorance, they never knew what their martyrdoms would represent and how they would change the world, if they could only have seen the news reports the next day imagine how thrilled they would have been! – but *you* will know, you'll *know*, how can you resist? Be a part of history, let history consume you, and your death can never now be a trivial one, you too can be a hero, you too can be like Superman (or Wonder Woman, if that's your preference) – and if your *death* isn't trivial, maybe, just maybe, it'll mean your life wasn't either, maybe, maybe. And you'll look just so dandy, history will become you, and after you're gone friends will tell of how important you were, and they'll feel important by association – 'I knew a guy who died in the Towers!' – really, it's a win-win scenario, the 9/11 Experience is a gift not only to you but to *them*, to your family, doesn't Junior deserve a Daddy who's a hero? a mummy who bled out stars and stripes? Come to New York, take in a Broadway show, a meal at Sardi's, enjoy the best New York has to offer! Safe in the certainty that the very next day you're making a stand for something noble we can all believe in.

The world has changed, and we all now stand in the shadow of the Twin Towers. But who wouldn't choose to be part of what casts that shadow?

By the time the Towers next returned, there was a box office service all ready and waiting.

*

One day, in Baghdad, the twelve-metre high statue of Saddam Hussein popped back into existence. American troops pulled it down immediately, and razed the ground with fire. It never returned.

*

And, one day, the Towers stayed right where they were.

The Towers were packed. Of course, they were always packed. But this was the height of summer, and the waiting list for summer reservations was especially long. You could get such a lovely view from the top when the weather was nice!

The complaints started only minutes after the scheduled half past ten departure time. Families who were taking hands and composing themselves for the rapture kept on having to let go and recompose themselves all over again. They were so determined to keep their minds pure for the moment of deliverance: 'For Christ's sake,' they asked, 'what the hell's going on?' By noon customers were being advised to vacate the Towers. The buildings were cordoned off with tape saying 'Technical Difficulties,' and 'Your Patience is Appreciated.'

There was no system in operation to cope with dissatisfied customers, nobody had ever complained before. It was chaos. Overseas passengers wanted reimbursement not only for the 9/11 tickets, but also for their plane fares. Others demanded compensation for all the earthly possessions they had given away. One woman sued the Towers for mental distress – now she'd have to find some other way to kill herself. Her claim for three million dollars was rejected, but it only provoked a spate of claims for smaller sums that were more successful. Within three weeks the Towers were bankrupted. No-one could now have afforded to let people die in there. Not even if the Towers had been working properly again, not even if they started winking on and off like the lights of a Christmas tree.

But the Towers implacably, resolutely, refused to leave. They weren't going anywhere.

Nobody was quite sure now what to do with them.

It was suggested that they take on the job for which they had originally been intended. They could be rented out for office space. That didn't sound unreasonable. And so, in preparation, a crew of maintenance workers were sent inside. The windows no longer sparkled, but were grey, and blotchy, and spattered with the bodies of bugs and birds. The water in the rest rooms had gone stale. The carpets were matted stiff.

No matter how much the carpets were shampooed, they could never have restored that scent everyone had enjoyed before. The windows might be made clean one day, but the next they'd be smeared, whorls of dirt caught in the sunlight and distorting it, making each pane look as if it had been prodded hard with enormous stained fingerprints. And there was dust everywhere. You could never get rid of all that dust. The dust, it got into everything.

No businesses wanted to move into the Towers. The desks stayed bare, the memo boards empty. There was a strange film clinging to them all, and it may have been mould, and it may have been something else. It became too expensive to clean the Towers. From the outside the windows grew blacker with dirt, until no-one could see in, until the Towers seemed somehow to suck all light into them.

The Twin Towers squatted lugubriously in position and dominated the New York skyline.

Someone suggested they be pulled down. But while many privately agreed that would be the best thing, no-one dared give the order. It would be an insult to all those who had lost their lives there – a casualty list that now nearly numbered a cool two million worldwide. What was needed, everyone thought, was some outside force to take down the Twin Towers for them. Some outrage that would leave America blameless. But this time no suicide bombers were forthcoming.

The decision to conceal the Towers wasn't undertaken lightly. The cost alone was staggering. But, it was reasoned, they had built two gigantic towers before – so now they could build *dozens* of them, all over the city – and taller, too, so they'd dwarf the originals! And a whole *ring* of towers could now surround them, they'd be completely encircled, and these new ring towers would be the very tallest of all, you'd have to climb to the very top of them, right into the very clouds, and peer down from the roof to get so much as a glimpse at what was hidden beneath.

And the inner windows to these towers would be made of jet-black glass, so no-one could see through to the Twin Towers behind. And workers could sit at their desks quite happily, and do their accountancy, their share-brokering, their telemarketing calls. And only the smell might remind them what was nearby – no matter how high the air conditioning was turned, no matter how strong the scent of domestic shampoos or bleach, there was always that smell. Rotting history, just a few feet away.

*

One morning one of those new towers disappeared, taking with it 4,000 souls. But there were so many towers, no-one even noticed.

Ladies and gentlemen –
We hope that you have taken pleasure in this   Flight from
                    That you have enjoyed the in-flight entertainment
system, that you have enjoyed our specially prepared meals and

We now need to inform you that we will soon be beginning our descent into
        And we ask you to pay attention to the following information and act upon
it accordingly.

                                                                there's a
chill to the evening.

We hope that may be possible. The captain says he'll do his best.

        that's all the time we have. I'm sorry.

        fasten   seatbelts   fasten
    seatbelt,
                                                        seatbelts
                                                        seatbelts

And, ladies and gentlemen, be advised. It is all a matter of faith.